TOUCH

THE COMPLETE SERIES

CARA DEE

TOUCH

THE LITTLE BLACK BOOK OF KINK

Aware Consensual Kink, and PRICK; Personal Responsibility, Informed, Consensual Kink.

Edited by Silently Correcting Your Grammar, LLC.
Formatting by Eliza Rae Services.
Proofreading by Rachel Lawrence.

ACKNOWLEDGMENTS

Lisa, Stephanie, Rachel, Deb, Adèle, the Sadists in my life, Eliza, my friends, my dirty crew, my readers.

Stay kinky!

THE TOUCH SERIES

LOOK BUT DON'T TOUCH

CHAPTER 1

NICHOLAS FORD

Goddammit. Amanda launches into her next tantrum as soon as I exit the bathroom.

"I really don't understand why you have to show your face at Switch so often." The distaste is clear in her voice. "Thank goodness you're not into that BDSM lifestyle. It's disgusting."

Indeed, thank goodness...

Safe to say, telling her I'm very much involved in that lifestyle—or used to be—wouldn't go over well. To her, I'm merely an entrepreneur, a club owner. I have five of them here in the Bay Area, in one of which I met Amanda four months ago, but Switch is most definitely my baby. At this stage of my life, it's the only place I can breathe.

"And I really don't understand why I would have to explain how this works *again*," I tell her pointedly. "It's my job, for chrissakes."

Reentering my bedroom after my shower, I walk into my closet and pick out what to wear. I can hear Amanda; she's fled to the kitchen where she's slamming cupboards and pulling out pans with way too much force. She has no reason to be upset, in my opinion. I told her countless times I would be unable to spend time with her family tonight, yet when today arrived, she thought I was "tactless" if I didn't go with her.

I don't see the issue. I will meet her family tomorrow at her sister's wedding; she can go to the rehearsal dinner by herself. I'd go with her, obviously, if I hadn't had this event planned for months.

Whatever she is doing in the kitchen is just an attempt to gain attention, seeing as the rehearsal *dinner* is only an hour away. Less than that, even.

It's what I get for letting my family's incessant talk of leaving bachelorhood behind get to me. That, and loneliness. *"You're thirty-six years old, dear. You're not getting any younger."* After one particularly gruesome chat with my mother, I surrendered and went out. I went *vanilla*. I met Amanda.

I became miserable too, but that's my own fault.

You know what you should do.

I suppress a sigh.

I'm not blind. We're heading in that direction, regardless. This won't last. I don't have enough willpower, and Amanda wasn't lying when she implied I'm at Switch often. Perhaps a bit more than my job requires.

After tucking in my button-down, I hesitate upon inspecting my ties. In the end, I decide to skip it. On a night like this, I need to be comfortable, which is kind of ironic. Since abandoning D/s, tonight's event will most definitely leave me *uncomfortable*.

I suppose I'm a glutton for punishment, but I'm aching to at least watch. Sure, making an appearance is important; however, I can't deny that I *want* to be there. It's the only aspect of my old life I have left, and I find myself clinging to it desperately.

My phone dings on my nightstand, so I walk over and check to find a message from Cade. I assume he's already at the club.

Who's the new boy? Southern accent, complete goofball.

I smirk and respond.

You sniffed him out fast, my friend. His name is Dylan. Recently moved here.

By the time I've put on socks and shoes, he's replied.

Is he a relationship guy? I wouldn't mind some casual playtime.

"Good grief," I mutter to myself. I'm not the only Top in my circle of friends a bit too jaded and settling for the wrong things. Cade's right there with me, a fellow Daddy Dom who recently got out of a toxic relationship.

I don't know him well yet. I'd be careful.

After texting him once more, telling him I'll be around tonight, I pocket my phone and return to the bathroom.

A while later, I'm back in my bathroom. Leaning closer to the mirror, I inspect my freshly shaved face, and I can't help but grimace. To my dismay, my age is beginning to show. A bit of gray stands out against the brown. The corners of my eyes crinkle more than before when I smile. Though, I frown more than smile nowadays. My body may be in great condition, but that matters little when I'm barely content. I stand tall at six-two, yet I feel hunched.

Hopefully, I will be in good spirits after tonight. I just need a dose of what my past used to offer. That's what I keep telling myself, anyway.

"Nick!" Amanda calls. "Are you ready to go?" She appears in the doorway, her blond hair bouncing lightly with her movements. "You're handsome." There's a small smile on her lips, but I can see she's still upset.

"And you look pretty," I reply automatically as I fasten my watch.

She's already tall at five-ten, so the high heels are unnecessary if you ask me. Then again, I'm more into delicate ballet flats when it comes to girls—*women*. In my past, I've been involved in what my Littles wear, and now it feels odd to only offer an opinion. Not only that, but it has to be complimentary.

In an extremely revealing blue dress, Amanda does look attractive; it's just not something I would've chosen for her. Or the blood-red nail polish. Because I don't go for bold colors when there are pastels.

I want soft cotton, coy smiles, adorable giggles, a round little bottom, baby smooth skin, pigtails, pert tits, and pleas for Daddy's thick cock.

I almost have to close my eyes and take calming breaths to rein it in.

"So, are you ready to go?" she asks again, tapping her foot. "We could share a cab."

I shake my head and roll up the sleeves on my shirt. "I'm not drinking tonight, so I'm driving. If you want, I can drop you off at the hotel."

"Sounds good," she agrees, and we leave the bathroom. "By the way, we still need to talk more about my moving in here."

This again.

"I've already told you it's way too soon." I clench my jaw and pocket my keys, phone, and wallet. She is here all the time, and I don't mind it—much. The ad agency she runs is just a five-minute walk from here, so I see the convenience.

"Too soon," she scoffs. "Be serious, Nick. It's time. We're not getting any younger."

I cringe, disappointed I fell for that line when it was my mother who said it. Now it only grates on my nerves. We're hardly *old*.

"That's not a reason to rush into things. Especially not if we argue as often as we do." I shake my head, refusing to get sucked into this now. "I don't have time for this. Let's go."

"Fine," she grits out. "But we're talking about it soon. We need to move forward, not take steps backward."

I pretend I don't hear that and walk toward the hallway, wondering how long I can take this—the faking, the pretending everything is okay.

It worked swimmingly for about two months, and I foolishly

believed I loved her. We even exchanged the dreadful words, something I regret. It's not fair to either of us.

I've cared for her; I've enjoyed spending time with her, she's good in bed—albeit a little too demanding for my tastes—and I've agreed to meet her family, but the good hasn't outweighed the bad in over a month. We're destined to crash and burn, yet she talks of moving forward—together.

About fifteen minutes later, we're on our way in my car, and while the silence is fine by me, it's not for Amanda. I'm still irritated beyond words.

She, on the other hand, starts yapping about her family as if we didn't just have an argument.

Perhaps it's the excitement of seeing her family again. Only her sister and she live here in San Francisco; the rest reside in Oregon. But everyone is down for Amber's wedding tomorrow. It will be the first time I meet any of them.

And last. You can't deny that anymore.

"...but we call her Drifter." Amanda chuckles wryly about another cousin of hers. "I swear, that girl is always on the move. Last I heard, she lived in Florida." She sighs and looks out the window. "We can only hope she won't make another spectacle. Last time we all got together, she caused a scene and stormed out, just because we didn't agree on something. So immature."

I hum in acknowledgment, pretending to listen, and stop at a red light. I can't help it, really, but my mind is occupied with thoughts about tonight—and *not* Amanda's night. We have themed events at Switch every month, and it's been a long time since that theme was for Daddy Doms and Littles. The closest we've come recently was a few months ago when Fetish Night was about spanking, and many Daddies showed up with their little ones.

CHAPTER 2

When I enter my club, it's buzzing with anticipation. I'm relieved, being in a place where I can finally let go and be myself. I greet several friends and acquaintances on the way, and I try to keep my eyes off the submissives, many of them wearing frilly dresses or just skimpy underthings. Looking is obviously allowed, but merely being here is tempting enough. If I were smart, I'd stay out here in the lobby, or maybe even hide out upstairs in my office. *If* I were smart...

The club area, square-shaped with high ceilings and kept deliberately dark, is simply furnished, the only decoration being erotic photos on the walls. The main seating area is to the left when I enter; I nod hello to Cade and a couple others before heading right to the bar.

Contraptions such as a St. Andrew's Cross, benches, a leather sling, and suspension bars take up most of the space beyond the dance floor, which bothers me lately. We're getting more and more members, and it's not uncommon for kinksters to complain about the lack of space for scening.

"Evening, my friend." I greet Mark, one of my bartenders and a close friend, and order a tonic water with lime. We talk a little while I survey the club, and he mentions that his divorce has been finalized. "That's a relief," I note. "You settling into your new place all right?"

"It's a damn haven," he chuckles wryly.

I can imagine.

The rock music playing is loud, though not so loud that I have to shout to be heard, and I smile, satisfied with the large crowd. The dance floor may be pretty empty, but this isn't a night for dancing. The booths are full, and a few groups of people have already gathered near the demo platform by the eastern wall.

"Um, hi! May I have a Sprite, please?" a happy voice asks Mark. Tilting my head, I see a young woman, definitely a Little, standing there. Her lush, auburn hair is gathered in two low pigtails, long enough to reach past her ample cleavage. Her baby-doll dress is both innocent and provocative as hell. In light yellow with white lace, it's cute. But the way it pushes her tits together shoves "innocent" out the window. It's also short, ending right below her ass, and exposes her sexy legs. *Fuck.* White cotton kneesocks. Flat Mary Jane shoes that match her dress.

She's fair-skinned, delicate-looking, but her *eyes...* I chuckle quietly to myself and take a sip from my tonic. Her pale blue eyes have a spark of mischievousness in them.

"Here you go, hon," Mark says, and he's about to tell her the price when I wave it off. He smirks and nods once. "Never mind, then."

The girl turns in my direction, smiles shyly, and gives me a small curtsy. "Thank you for the drink, Sir."

"You're very welcome." I incline my head and smile. Happy and bubbly have been replaced by demure and coy, and I'd be a liar if I said I wasn't attracted to her. As long as I'm only looking...

"Um." She fidgets with her glass. "Are you here alone?"

"I am." It's technically true.

"Oh." Her head bobs in a small nod, eyes focused on her drink. "I see."

Leaning closer, I ask, "Hasn't Daddy told you not to speak to strangers, little one?"

"I'm here alone, too. I have no rules." She meets my gaze and juts out her chin. *How cute.* I think this one has a stubborn streak in her. That makes me yearn even more. "There aren't only couples here, you know."

"I'm aware," I concede with a laugh. Of course unattached people come here. "You're a sassy one, aren't you?" And she doesn't have a Daddy to take care of her or keep her in line? *Christ.*

"Shit, sorry." In the faint glow of the spotlights behind the bar, her cheeks flush scarlet. She looks down again and shuffles her feet. "The Daddy I had in Texas told me I was a brat sometimes. I'm really sorry, Sir."

When she once again meets my gaze, it feels like she could make Bambi look evil. Because this girl's doe eyes have to be the most beautiful ones I've ever seen. I also realize she has to be very young. Age difference has never bothered me, but I've never had a Little Girl more than five or six years younger than I.

"No reason to apologize, sweet girl. I happen to enjoy brats." Taking a step closer, I set down my drink and silently ask for her hand. She offers it straightaway, and I hold it in both of mine. "I'm Nicholas Ford."

Her eyes grow wide. "K-Kayla Brandon," she stutters. "Did you —I mean...Nicholas Ford, as in—this is your c-club?"

I nod, a bit amused to see her so flustered. "That's correct."

"Oh," she exhales. "Chelsea—a friend of mine in New York, she told me I had to come here. She said this is the best BDSM club in San Francisco. Crap, sorry, I'm rambling." She cringes. "I blame jet lag."

I laugh through my nose and give her hand a squeeze. "Well, it's nice to meet you, Kayla. I take it you're new in town?"

"Yes, Sir. I just got back from visiting a friend in Spain. Before that, I was in Florida, and now I'm here." She blows out a breath before taking a big gulp of her Sprite. "I'm thinking about moving here. I don't know. I have some family here, but they hardly count —" She grimaces. "And now you know a bunch of stuff you never asked for." I grin as she rolls her eyes at herself. "Rewind. Yes, Sir. I'm new in town."

"Too cute." I chuckle and tap her on the nose. She flushes again. "If you're here for the scenes later, I hope you enjoy." I take a step back. "I'll be around, so if you need me, don't hesitate. Okay?" I dip down a little to come face-to-face with her. She's a short one, with a small frame, yet she's curvy, plump, and gorgeous.

"Thank you," she responds shyly.

With a light touch to her cheek, I leave her to socialize, as is my job here tonight. My club manager is obviously here too, but for events such as this one, I like to show my face as well.

Two hours later, I disappear upstairs into my office to calm down for a while. A couple from Los Angeles just finished a scene involving the whipping bench, and when I saw Kayla in the crowd, watching intently, it was almost too difficult for me to remain where I was.

Studying her from afar, I could see what she liked and didn't during the scene. I saw how her pouty lips pursed when the Daddy Dom pushed his Little onto the rather hard whipping bench and paddled her bottom. I saw how her eyes softened when the Daddy hugged his little one close and whispered in her ear. And I saw how Kayla's chest heaved when the Daddy flipped his girl over onto her back and proceeded to ram his cock into her.

Up here, in my office, I find Kayla easily down on the floor. She's at the bar again, ordering another soda, and it seems like she's looking for someone. Seeing as she's new in town, I can only hope it's me she's in search of, which causes something feral inside of me to flare and come back to life. But I'm already balancing on the proverbial line, one that cannot be crossed. *Look, but don't touch.* That's my rule.

Always...one or two steps from caving. Goddammit.

Sighing heavily, I walk away from the large window and end up pacing the hardwood floor in front of my desk. I try to minimize everything that's happened so far this evening. My reason for being drawn to Kayla stems from the desires we share, and of course, physical attraction. She's indescribably beautiful.

In the grand scheme of things, though, mere attraction isn't much to go on. Far from it. I know virtually nothing about her, so my wish to possess and claim must have something to do with the fact that I haven't been in a D/s relationship in a long time. Vanilla sex, while pleasurable, isn't enough. That's why I come here—to get my fill.

It's... It's not enough anymore, is it?

I slump down in my desk chair. Elbows on the desktop, I run my hands through my hair and tug at the ends. I'm about to begin a new internal rant when a knock on the door interrupts.

"Mr. Ford, it's Kevin," my club manager says, and I tell him to enter. However, it's not only Kevin. Jesus Christ, it's Kayla, too. "Sorry to bother you, but Ms. Brandon insisted on seeing you."

Of course she did, I think wryly. How else will she plague my thoughts? "That's quite all right," I half-lie and wave her in. "You're excused, Kevin." Again, if I were smart, I would've told him to remain. Alas, he's already gone. "Kayla. What can I do for you?"

She shifts her weight from foot to foot, either uncomfortable or nervous. Maybe a combination of both. "Um, I was wondering if you had any painkillers or something," she mumbles, chewing on her lip. I frown, now concerned. "I have a headache, and..." She lets out a nervous chuckle. "Sorry, I shouldn't have bothered you—"

I cut her off with a firm yet gentle tone. "Have a seat, honey." I point to the couches by the window. In the mini fridge under my desk, I grab a bottle of water, and in my top drawer, I locate a bottle of Tylenol.

"I'm sorry." She needs to stop apologizing. "I guess I should've slept more than two hours after my flight." Her smile is rueful.

"You need your eight hours, Kayla," I chastise and sit down next to her on the couch. "Here, take two." I hand her the pills and the water. "So, let me get this straight. After countless hours on flights, you come to San Francisco, check in to a hotel…?" She nods. "And then you only sleep two hours before coming to my club." I give her a disapproving look.

"Yeah," she says sheepishly. "But my friend told me about the event tonight. I wanted to be here."

"Have you at least eaten?" I arch a brow, annoyed and more than a little bit worried. Thankfully, she nods and tells me about going to a restaurant before coming here. She really does appear to be in pain, so I urge her to lean back and close her eyes for a bit. I bet the music downstairs hasn't been much of a help to her. I'm glad she came up here, to be honest. "Is there anything else I can get you?"

Eyes still closed, she smiles softly and shakes her head. "No, thank you." She hums as I drape a blanket over her. "I just need a moment for the Tylenol to kick in. Then I'll be on my way."

I frown at that, wanting her to stick around but knowing that'd be stupid. Too tempting. I'm already thinking thoughts I should be ashamed of. For instance, I know very well what could release some tension and help with her headache—something much more pleasurable than painkillers.

"Mr. Ford?"

"Hmm?" I look down at her, only to be met by another shy expression. "What is it, sweet girl?" I brush a piece of hair away from her face.

"Do you, um…" She pulls the blanket up to hide her face, only her eyes visible. "Do you have a Little Girl of your own?"

I chuckle. "Do you really think I'd be up here with you if I did?" Then I sober, knowing that while I don't have a sub, I certainly have a girlfriend, and I'm still here with Kayla. I clear my throat and slide away from her. At the same time, the blanket slips down to her chest. "There *is* someone else," I admit and scrub a hand over my face. "I'm in a vanilla relationship."

"Oh." Fuck me if she doesn't pout. "Lucky woman." She offers a small smile. "I should probably go." I don't think; I just do. When she makes a move to get up, I gently push her back. I will kick my ass tomorrow, but now...I can't resist any longer. "What?" She looks to me, confused.

I swallow, my mouth too dry. *Look, but don't touch.* "Stay," I command quietly. I can feel myself slipping into a role I've suppressed for so long. "How's your head?"

She shrugs and sucks her bottom lip into her mouth.

"I can't touch you," I murmur. "But I can help."

My mind begins to spin, and the first thing I do is look inside of myself for guilt. It's there, I suppose, but not enough to stop me.

"How?" Her pupils dilate.

The smirk on my face tells her all she needs to know, and my cock hardens at the sight of her expression. Judging by her face, her breathing, and her posture, I'd say she's more than a little aroused.

"Will you let me help you?" I ask softly and place an arm on the back of the couch. With my free hand, I pull away the blanket and drop it on the floor.

Kayla doesn't reply verbally, but she does nod—quite furiously.

"That's a response from a needy little girl." I smile and inch closer. "Are you in such desperate need of an orgasm that cat got your tongue?" Looking down, I have the perfect view of her tits, all pushed together in her light yellow dress. Her pigtails linger down her chest in loose curls, and I can't stop myself from twirling a lock between my fingers, which causes them to brush against her cleavage. "Tell me—" I notice her shiver when I exhale into her neck "—when you're alone and needy, do you fantasize about a big cock destroying your pretty little pussy?" Her breathing hitches, a flush spreading over her lovely cheeks. "Or maybe pushing inside your tight bottom?"

Dropping my hand, I wrap my fingers around her wrists and keep them in her lap.

"Yes," she whimpers and rubs her thighs together. "Yes, yes, *yes*." She licks her lips, another word on the tip of her tongue. I can feel it in my gut.

I want her to scream for me, call me Daddy—if only to let me have this one moment—beg for more when I fuck her silly. I want her to be desperate. I want her to suck on my cock like it's her pacifier.

She represents the life I'm caving to.

"What kind of panties are you wearing?"

She lets out a breathy moan. "White cotton."

I hum and release her hands. "Don't move." Bunching up her dress, I finally get a look between her thighs. I tsk her. "Look at that wet spot. Your little kitty has ruined those pretty panties." I shake my head at her, to which she squirms and whimpers again.

"Please," she begs. "I-I need..."

Oh, I need too. I need her pussy riding my hard cock.

"You little baby slut." Slipping off the couch, I kneel before her on the floor and push her legs apart. Fuck, she's so wet. When her eyes widen, I know she's seen my cock straining in my pants. I chuckle. "You're easy to read, little one."

"I want you," she whines.

I want her too, but we can't have everything in the world. Lines have already been crossed, and there's no going back for me, *but*...I won't touch her anymore. I won't touch her intimately while I'm officially unavailable.

"Slide your panties down for me," I order her softly. I wet my bottom lip, watching as she obeys without a moment of hesitation, and then I'm granted the sight of her flawless pussy. Bare and so smooth. Her folds glisten with her arousal in the dim light; her fingers twitch, itching to touch. "How is it that you don't have a

Daddy to take care of you, Kayla?" This girl needs someone—someone to make sure she gets her eight hours of sleep, proper meals, plenty of attention, a firm hand when she misbehaves, affection, and a thick cock to fuck her into oblivion.

"I haven't found anyone in a long time." She pouts.

I know how she feels. "And now your kitty's all needy and achy?" I trace a finger up her thigh, stopping before I want to.

"Yes." Her eyes shine with emotion.

"Oh, sweet girl." I wish I could tell her I'll be the one to look after her from now on. "Do you want us to stop?"

"No! Please, please, please." Her bottom lip trembles. "I need this—*please*."

I nod, both resigned and elated. It's become abundantly clear to me that I can't leave this lifestyle behind. I surrender. And it feels so fucking good. Though, it will feel better once I've ended things with Amanda.

"Touch yourself." There's no masking the lust in my voice. "Rub that little clit and let me watch."

"Oh God," she moans and slips a hand between her legs. "I'm so wet."

"I can see that," I grunt and palm my erection outside my pants. Two of her fingers slide between her slippery lips, gathering arousal which she brings to her clit. I groan under my breath, staring hungrily as she touches, rubs, and circles. "Push two fingers inside. Right now. And spread your lips."

She does as I've said, and it's all I can take. When I see her two fingers slip inside her slick pussy, I undo my belt and push down my pants. My black boxers, too. My grip on my cock is hard, rough, and Kayla cries out at the sight and starts to fuck herself with her fingers.

"You're a filthy fucking girl," I accuse huskily. "There's only one type of person who can fix that, isn't there?"

"*Yes*," she pleads, watching as I stroke myself. "A Daddy. His cock—I'd be a good girl. I just need—" She stops abruptly and squeezes her eyes shut; it looks like she's close already.

"You can't come yet." I forbid it. I want to savor this. "Tell me, where do you want Daddy's cock?"

"In my kitty," she whines and rubs her clit furiously. "Or in my bottom. Or in my mouth, *mmm*... Lots and lots, all the time."

I chuckle darkly. "Cock slut." Using the pad of my thumb, I spread out the bead of arousal on the tip of my cock. I moan and tighten my grip, imagining how it would be to bury myself in her pussy, ass, and mouth. "You must be a good girl to get that much cock."

"I am," she vows. "I'm a really good girl."

"Then show Daddy your tits." I nod at her dress, realizing a second too late that I referred myself as the Daddy. That's not good, and I curse myself. It's not a title I throw around casually. So why won't I take it back? "Push it down."

"Okay." She quickly shoves down the front of her dress, exposing her two perfect breasts. They're more than a handful, yet still perky. "Do you like them?"

I doubt she knows how much her innocence is turning me on. "You have no idea," I mutter, a bit out of breath. "You're gorgeous, Kayla. Now, lick off your fingers before touching your kitty again."

My abs tense and the muscles in my neck strain as I watch her suck on her fingers. She lets out a small giggle, causing my cock to grow impossibly harder. Then she settles back against the couch again, feet up, legs spread wide, and returns to circling her clit. Every now and then, some of her juices trickle out of her tight entrance. Since I'm so close, I can also see how her opening contracts, as if it needs something to squeeze—like my cock, fingers, or tongue.

"*Fuck,*" I spit out and jerk my cock faster.

"Are you close? I wanna come so bad." She throws her head back, pushes out her tits, and moans. "If you want—" she pants "—if you want, you can come on me. I swear, my kitty likes it."

"Oh, Jesus Christ," I groan and close my eyes. It's easy to tell she's deep into her role—a role she can't deny, a role I'm already craving, a role that brings out my inner beast. A role that isn't really a role at all. The pleasure builds quickly, almost too quickly. I won't last much longer. Reaching down, I use my free hand to cup and massage my balls.

Her whimper sets me off, shaking me to my core. "*Daddy...*"

"I'm there—close." My eyes flash open as "close" becomes "now," and I start coming. I pump my cock roughly, stream after stream landing over her hand, pussy, and thighs. It feels like my entire being uncoils, months of stifling and suppressing finally unleashing.

Kayla moans and writhes, spreading my release all over her pussy, and she's close too, fucking herself deeper and faster. "Daddy," she cries out. "May I—may I please come?"

I tell her she may. Through heavy breathing and husky murmurs, I tell her to be a good girl and come for Daddy. I tell her how perfect her pussy looks with my come on it, and I whisper, as she climaxes with a silent scream, that I want nothing more than to feel her orgasming around my cock.

"Oh, yes!" she wails. "So good, so good, so good..."

Coming back down from her high, she pants and gasps and chants how good it felt. She truly is like a little girl, and had I been in my teens, I probably would've been ready for another round by now.

"You know how we feel about wasting come, don't you?" I can only hope she does, really. Every Daddy Dom has his own set of rules, and I have no idea what kinds Kayla has been with.

With me, though, she would lick that up.

"Of course, Daddy," she giggles in delight. "That's a silly question."

She shouldn't be calling me that.

I shouldn't have taken things this far. A rock settles in my stomach, yet it doesn't stop me from smiling at her.

She runs a finger over her pussy and brings it to her mouth. Jesus, she's one alluring little girl.

Now that we've both been temporarily satisfied, I'm disappointed it's over. Had she been mine, this would've been only the beginning. Perhaps we would have showered together. I'd wash her; I'd allow my hands to wander freely and make sure her pretty pussy and cute bottom were very clean. I'd own my little one. I'd fall asleep with her in my bed.

She would suckle my soft cock, because little girls always need something in their mouths.

"Good girl," I whisper, tucking myself back into my boxers and pants.

Kayla grins around her finger and hums.

It's an image I will never forget.

"Kayla," I start quietly, "may I ask how old you are?"

"Twenty-two," she sings, sticking another finger in her mouth.

Truth be told, her youth turns me on like nothing else.

"Mmm, this is so good." Her smile is sweeter than sugar as she offers me a come-coated finger. "Wanna taste?"

I do. I really *fucking* do want to taste the combination of us, but I can't. I'm already guilt-ridden because of what I've done. Not only have I betrayed Amanda, but I haven't been fair to Kayla; she deserves someone who can commit fully to her.

There may still be a few lines left uncrossed, though I've done enough. I caved—plain and simple.

"Hopefully another time," I murmur and sit down next to her on the couch. "I mean that, honey." Once I've ended what I never should've started.

"You do?" She's back to being shy, but I can see the hope in her eyes.

I nod and help adjust her dress, for once being a gentleman. "If you decide to stick around San Francisco—"

She cuts me off, beaming like the sun. "I've already decided!" She nods furiously. "I'm going to stay; I promise. But—" she bites down on her lip, her face falling "—what about your relationship? The last thing I want is to cause problems..." She averts her eyes and lowers her voice to a whisper. "I feel bad. I'm sorry, Mr. Ford." In fact, she looks crestfallen. "Oh, God. I'm awful—"

I shake my head, and I don't want another word from her—not if she's going to say such things. "This is on me. I've made some mistakes that I need to handle, but I want to see you again."

Because maybe, just maybe, this wasn't a one-time thing.

Perhaps she could be more than the face and body of a lifestyle I've denied for too long.

Perhaps this indescribable chemistry between us means something.

CHAPTER 3

The next day when I arrive at the church where Amber is getting married, I'm met by a frosty Amanda. Not only does she know I want to talk to her, but I'm fairly certain she knows what it's about, too.

When I got home last night, she'd already gone to bed. So, I approached her this morning instead, though as soon as the clichéd "We need to talk" escaped my mouth, she insistently bit out that it could wait until after tonight. She was already being testy, having found me asleep in the guest room instead of next to her in bed, and that's another reason I'm sure she knows what I want to say.

I'm not trying to be insensitive by ending things with her on her sister's wedding day; it's just the opposite. Why go through an entire day where I'm introduced to her family as the boyfriend when it's over? Yet, after several tries to get her to listen to me, I didn't get far. She shot me down each time, and then she left.

"Hello." I stick my hands into the pockets of my black dress pants. It's a warm June day, so I left my suit jacket in the car. "You look nice." As the maid of honor, she's wearing a deep green dress, a few inches longer than the four bridesmaids' dresses. Her hair is up in an elaborate do, and she's holding a small bouquet of white roses.

"Thanks," she mutters as I adjust my black tie. "I take it you can find your seat? You're in the second row."

I nod and take the hint. She's obviously still mad at me, but now that we're here, I'd rather not ruin the day more for her. "I'll see you inside." That said, I walk in, and I'm a stranger so far, which explains why I can walk down the aisle without anyone stopping me. Some smile and nod in greeting, but that's it.

I suppose a few wonder who I'm here with, and I can't help but think how easy it would be to crash a wedding, especially one this big. I recall Amanda telling me approximately three hundred people were attending.

By the time it's three o'clock, the pews have been filled with guests, and the bells ring before the traditional wedding march begins. The four bridesmaids and then Amanda walk down the aisle to take their places at the front. Brian, Amber's fiancé, is a man I think Amanda wishes I were more like. He wants the white picket fence, the dog, the minivan, and the 2.5 children. Amanda never shies away from talking about all the things Brian does for Amber.

The ceremony is over pretty quickly, and then we all pile into our cars and drive over to the hotel where the reception is. The wedding party will arrive separately in two limos, so I wait outside the hotel for Amanda to show up. In the meantime, a few guests approach me and ask if I'm the man Amanda has spoken so highly of. That makes me cringe inwardly; I had no idea Amanda's been talking about me to her extended family. Parents and siblings—I get that, but aunts and grandparents? I sigh to myself and struggle to keep the polite smile on my face.

More guests trickle in. I remain outside, standing a little to the side with all the smokers.

"Mr. Ford?"

Shocked to hear *that* voice, my head snaps to the left so fast that it almost hurts. *Fucking hell.* It's Kayla. Kayla, whose number I now have in my phone. I wasn't supposed to see her again until I was officially unattached. Now, not only is she here, but she's dressed to the nines—as if she's a guest at a certain wedding. Her dress reminds me of the white one Marilyn Monroe wore, though this one is silky and dark blue.

I don't know whether to be disappointed or relieved, though she's incredibly gorgeous as always. Her auburn hair is down, pigtails only a memory. The wispy curls tease me by resting on her chest. Meeting her gaze again, I see that she's equally shocked to see me here.

"Kayla," I say quietly, taking a step closer. I definitely don't want people to hear us. "What are you doing here? Are you a guest? I didn't see you at the church." Then again, I arrived early and I was sitting in the front. She could've gotten there later, and amongst hundreds of people... Never mind.

"Wait..." Her eyes widen like she's figured something out. "Your girlfriend... Are you the Nick my cousin's been bragging about? Amanda Stevens?" She looks at me in disbelief; meanwhile, I pinch the bridge of my nose and curse internally at this turn of events. They're *related*, for fuck's sake. "Oh, my God," she whispers shakily, "your girlfriend is my cousin. I can't believe this."

Neither can I, but when I see two limos pulling up to the curb, I know this isn't the time to dwell on that.

"We'll talk about this later, all right?" I look over Kayla's shoulder as the wedding party exits the cars.

"Hang on." She grasps my arm and gives me a pleading look. "You haven't spoken to her yet, have you?" My brows furrow. "You can't. Don't—" She shakes her head quickly and purses her lips. "Don't break up with her."

I nearly choke on saliva. "Excuse me?"

She blows out a frustrated breath and looks behind her before facing me again. "She hates me. If you end things with her, and I'm the reason..." A dark, shaky chuckle escapes her. "I'm already the black sheep of the family." At my confused expression, she goes on. "Long story short: my mom and dad died when I was thirteen; Amanda and Amber's parents took me in. From the start, those two loathed me. I-I can't get into all that now, but let's just say I wasn't the perfect little girl—I didn't fit into their family."

I arch a brow, finding the irony a bit entertaining, no matter how ill-timed it is. *Perfect little girl.* To me, that's exactly what she is.

"I only see them a couple times a year, at reunions." She actually looks close to panic. "I didn't even want to be here today, but Aunt Mary insisted." She's referring to Amanda's mother. "I'm lucky I got out of the rehearsal dinner, really." Now she's rambling like she did yesterday, something I find incredibly endearing. Though, it's time to cut her off. Amanda has already spotted us.

"Quiet, sweet girl," I urge her softly. "Amanda's coming over." And she doesn't look happy.

Kayla stiffens but manages to plaster a smile on her face as that almost ex-girlfriend of mine reaches us.

"I see you've already met my Nick," Amanda drawls and slips her arm around my waist. Her other hand slides up my chest, which I can't say I appreciate. "Long time no see, Drifter." She smirks condescendingly, causing me to frown. I have never seen an ounce of maliciousness in her before today. "I'm surprised you made it."

Next to Amanda, Kayla suddenly appears to be tiny—so much shorter than she already is. This isn't the type of vulnerability I like. Kayla is honestly intimidated by her cousin.

"Hello, Amanda," she mumbles, wringing her hands awkwardly. "It was a beautiful wedding."

"I know," Amanda sighs. Then she faces me with a bright smile. "How about we go inside, handsome? I want to have a drink with you before we split up again." Right. We're not at the same table. She's seated with the wedding party, and I will be a couple tables away with the other bridesmaids' and groomsmen's spouses. "Oh, and I must introduce you to my parents. They're dying to meet you."

Before I can get a word in edgewise, she's already dragging me along. I do manage to send Kayla a pointed look that says this isn't over, and then I pull away from Amanda a little and follow her into what can only be described as a ballroom. It's straight out of an overblown fairy tale with billowy fabrics, chandeliers, and a pompous interior in gold, beige, and white. Round tables are scattered around the dance floor, the finest china and silverware practically sparkling on expensive-looking cloths.

"Why do you insist on this?" I grit out quietly as we walk across the floor. Straight ahead, I can see an older couple, and judging by the way Amanda looks at them, I'd say they're her parents. "You know exactly what I want to talk to you about."

"Stop it," she hisses. "Don't make me look like a fool tonight." She glares at me, our pace slowing until we come to a complete stop in the middle of the dance floor. "My entire family is here, Nick. I don't see them very often. Now my sister's married; she's successful, and—"

"You think by coming here alone...it would paint you as a failure? You're unbelievable." I'm fucking shocked, truth be told. While I've noticed that Amanda is a competitive woman, this goes beyond that. I'm merely here so she can look good in front of her family. "This is why you've pushed, isn't it? Why you've been so insistent that we move in together. More for you to tell your parents."

"Oh, please." She scoffs. "You're going too far. We love each oth—"

"Don't finish that sentence," I seethe.

It feels entirely wrong to speak about love when it comes to us. The past four months don't just disappear; we definitely shared something good in the beginning. She even made me feel better than I did before her. But I'm finally able to see that's the extent of it. We've both been so into this for the wrong reasons; we've used each other. I can't deny what I really want, and Amanda...well, I actually don't have a fucking clue. Maybe she's only after success—more milestones to tick off. Me, on the other hand? I want to see if there can be more with Kayla.

"Introduce me as whatever you want," I tell her, shaking my head, "but once this night is over, so are we."

"Don't overreact," she beseeches and grasps my forearms. "We're good together, Nick."

At this point, I don't think it matters what I say. Luckily—or unluckily, depending on how you look at it—we're interrupted. By her parents.

"Mom! Dad!" Amanda's bright smile is back, and she proceeds to introduce me as her boyfriend. In turn, Mr. and Mrs. Stevens say it's a pleasure to meet me after hearing so many stories. I'd be freaked out about how animated Amanda gets when she speaks—how terrific of an actress she is—had I not been too disappointed in us both. Because I find it a bit disheartening how easy it is to let her go.

Shouldn't it be harder? Or does the possibility of returning to the lifestyle I've craved—perhaps with Kayla—mean that much, when it hasn't even been twenty-four hours since we met? That puts things into a new perspective, and we, Amanda and I, obviously haven't been worth much as a couple.

The dinner is in full swing when I leave my seat and walk over to Table Nine across the room. It's where Kayla is sitting, and for the past half hour, she's looked positively miserable. I've tried to catch her gaze, but she hasn't looked my way even once, and I want to reassure her—*protect* her.

Reaching her table, I dip down and murmur in her ear. "Come with me." I've startled her, and when she finally looks up, she appears nervous and unsure.

Wedding guests all around us are busy being cheery in their festive mood; no one turns their head as I take the lead. Yet, I can practically feel someone staring a hole in the back of my neck, and it's not Kayla. But I don't look back.

"Where are we going?" Kayla asks behind me, following at my quick pace. "She's going to notice you're gone, Nicholas." That's the first time I've heard her say my name. I like it. Correction: I love it. However, I want something else right now. "Are you gonna answer me?"

I smile and round a corner; she keeps up. "Someplace private."

I hear the breath she releases.

Doubting we can find privacy on the first floor, I head toward the elevators in the lobby. It's when I press the button that I realize how tightly wound I am. My back feels rigid, my shoulders are stiff, my neck is strained, my jaw is clenched, and my hands are balled into fists. I'm all over the place, overwhelmed by thoughts that have been swimming in my head since yesterday.

The elevator to my right dings, followed by the doors sliding open, and I quickly usher Kayla inside.

Classical music plays in the car, though it does nothing to calm the storm raging in me.

Kayla looks up at me, apprehension clouding her features. I take a step toward her after pushing the button for the top floor. She bites down on her lip. I swallow hard. Another step. My eyes drink her in. She backs into a corner. I stalk her like she's my prey. Christ, I fucking want her.

"Nicholas?" she whispers, eyes wide.

I shake my head slowly. *No.* Not this time. There's another name I need right now.

She gulps as I reach her. "D-Daddy?" Her voice is so small, so vulnerable, so fucking *sweet*.

"That's the one," I murmur and dip down to nuzzle her soft cheek. While one hand slides back to cup her ass, my other ghosts across her stomach, up her tits, over her chest, until I hold her jaw in a firm grip. "Fuck, you smell good." I breathe her in, and her sweet scent works to calm me down, if only marginally. "I've been aching to touch you."

She whimpers and fists my shirt.

"Do you want Daddy to touch you?" I ask softly, nipping at her earlobe. "So much to get lost in." My voice has lowered to a whisper. "This ass," I hiss and palm her ass roughly.

She moans.

"Daddy wants to fuck you." For emphasis, I pull her closer so she can feel my cock against her stomach.

"But," she breathes out.

I shake my head just as the elevator comes to a stop. "No buts." Taking a step back, I regard her face. "Unless you don't want—"

"You know I do." Her chest heaves, lust evident in her eyes. "But what about...?"

"It's being handled." Grabbing her hand, I guide her out of the elevator, and then we walk briskly down the hall. Anybody could be leaving their rooms at any point, and I don't give a flying fuck. There's a small nook between two rooms where an ice machine is, and that's where I press Kayla up against a wall. There's no waiting. No hesitation. I crash my mouth to hers and swallow her gasp.

Tilting my head, I kiss her deeply as I reach down and grab on to the backs of her thighs. I groan as she hitches both legs around my hips instinctively. In response, I grind my cock against her pussy.

She giggles breathlessly, a sound that makes me shudder in pleasure. I notice it in her movements, in her expression, and in her sounds; she's slipping into character, though that particular word rings wrong. It's not a damn character. It's who she is. And I'm...

"*Daddy.*" That giggle will be the death of me. "There's something hard poking me in my tummy."

I freeze.

Breathing heavily, I stare into her eyes, my own eyes hooded and ready to devour, and it's like my mind resets.

No, definitely not a character—for either of us. We're letting go, that's all.

We have so much to talk about.

"I want to try..." I whisper. "This—you and me. See if there's more."

She smiles. "So do I."

I nod, thinking about the things we need to discuss before we take this any further. "Then, let's do it right."

She's confused, I can tell, but she won't be for long. I need her to know she can trust me, that I will take care of her properly, and that she can depend on me. All of that will take time, and I can't even begin to be that person right here. Not in a hotel corridor, and not with a wedding reception going on fifteen floors below.

Reluctantly, I lower her to her feet. "Come home with me," I request and kiss her softly. "I want to play with you. Start getting to know you."

Her smile is tender. "I want that. *But*—" that smile morphs into something salacious and mischievous "—I want to take care of you, too." Deft little fingers work my belt and pants. I'm once again frozen in place. "Pretty please, Daddy?" She bats her lashes and sinks to the floor, at the same time pushing down my pants and boxers.

Fuck me. I groan internally and scrub my hands over my face. "Right here? Now?" Public sex is a major turn-on, but a bit more is at stake here. We haven't established anything yet; everything is up in the air.

"I want it." Ah, the pout.

With a shake of my head, I chuckle and tap her jaw. "Fine. Open up." She does, and I grip my cock, smearing the bead of arousal over her upper lip. "Lick that off." And she does it slowly, my naughty little baby. Placing one hand on the wall right behind her, I brace myself and swiftly push my cock deep. She gags a few times, to which I murmur sweet nothings about how good it feels.

In the end, she relaxes completely and swallows. "Just. Like. That." Good fucking God.

My free hand goes to the back of her head before I begin to thrust in and out of her hot little mouth. She soaks me in saliva and makes cute yummy noises, and I discover she's a suckler. When I slowly pull out, she suckles the head of my cock as if she's desperate for my come to reach her taste buds.

"Greedy," I moan, letting my head loll back. My hips push forward, and she swallows repeatedly before I pull back again.

Threading my fingers through her silky hair, I control our movements and focus solely on my own pleasure. I savor, revel... feel how her tongue flicks, luscious lips tighten, throat constricts, and teeth graze. She's so eager to please. One hand cups my balls, altering between caressing and massaging. The other slides up and down the backside of my thigh, nails scraping gently, teasingly, against my skin.

"You like to suck cock, don't you?" I ask quietly, my chin almost dropping to my chest. My brows are furrowed in concentration; there's no movement, expression, or sound I want to miss. I grit out a moan when she bobs her head in an eager little nod. A whisper of a smile plays on her mouth, but Daddy's cock is in the way. "God... look at you." I move my hand from the back of her head to her face. As I give a particularly hard push into her mouth, my thumb ghosts over her wet bottom lip. She hollows out her cheeks and sucks me perfectly, and I trace the indentations with another finger. "Such a beautiful little cocksucker."

In the background, I hear the ding of an elevator arriving.

I don't stop fucking Kayla's mouth.

She doesn't stop sucking me.

"Good girl," I whisper down to her.

As someone passes the nook we're in, I keep my gaze locked with Kayla's. It's an unbreakable bond. Eyes smoldering as my glistening cock keeps moving in and out of her. The gasp followed by the rapid clicking of heels we hear doesn't faze us, either. We know it's not a wedding guest; fifteen floors take longer to search through than this. And we don't give a shit about the rest.

"I'll give you my come soon, baby." I keep whispering and caressing her face. My strokes slow down, yet I go deeper. The ridges of my erection look like shiny trails, and when her teeth graze over me, it feels too fucking good.

Too fucking good, too fucking good.

I close my eyes and clench my teeth together; my jaw tightens. "Now, Kayla." Speeding up, I fuck her perfect mouth faster and faster as the orgasm takes over. Down her throat, my cock throbs with each stream of come. One, two, three...and a fourth slides down, each sucked out by the sensation of her throat muscles contracting around me. Shudders rip through my body—another moan here and there. And Kayla, the good girl that she is, licks me clean like a cute little kitten.

The club... I can't wait to go back there with her by my side.

"Thank you, Daddy," she says sweetly as I try to regain my breath. I don't move, still bracing myself against the wall, when she tucks me back into my boxers, my pants, and lastly fastens my leather belt again. "I really needed that." She finishes with that giggle of hers, and I help her off the floor, a small grin on my face.

"Adorable," I murmur and kiss her softly on the lips. "Ready to go back to my place now?"

"Mmm, yes." She hums and snuggles into my chest.

CHAPTER 4

Not wanting any distractions around, such as hair products and blow-dryers that don't belong to me, I take Kayla to my guest bathroom instead of the master bath. The Jacuzzi is slightly smaller in here, but that works just fine.

On the way to my apartment, we discussed safety, limits, and immediate plans, no longer caring about what we left behind. Our meeting has been...less than ordinary, and there will be ramifications with her family if she and I end up dating—which I find myself hoping for—but we don't want to rush. What we want is to give this an honest chance, and we'll enter our little relationship with eyes and minds open.

I can no longer believe she's nothing but a representation of a fetish. The chemistry between us is undeniable; she can floor me with a look, and drawing out my need to care and dominate so strongly takes more than mere desire.

"Are you ready, darling?"

We'll begin with the sweetest introduction, in my opinion—one where we'll get to know more about each other. It's my way of letting my Little Girl know what kind of Daddy I am, and when I told Kayla about it earlier in the car, she was definitely turned on.

She's regressing, going back to the innocence she once possessed—back when she was a virgin and BDSM didn't have a name; they were just naughty fantasies that she couldn't help but get wet from.

"Yes, but..." Her brows knit together. "Why do you want to take a bath with me?"

After checking the water, I approach her, the anticipation building up inside of me. The tension crackles. "It's so I can make sure you get clean enough." I chuckle softly and slip a finger under the shoulder strap of her dress. "I think this needs to come off, don't you?" In the dim lighting of a few lit candles, there's a sparkle in her eyes. "I mean, we can't very well bathe with our clothes on."

"So—" she scrunches her nose "—we're gonna be naked together?"

I incline my head and gently push down her dress. "That's correct."

Other than the small "o" shaping her lips, she doesn't respond. She lets me undress her, giggling when I accidentally touch a ticklish spot, and she stands still when I kneel before her and slide down her white satin panties.

"You're so beautiful, baby." I touch her soft skin, her flesh giving way when I apply pressure. There's not a single unwanted hair on her flawless body. "And such a pretty little pussy." I run the pad of my thumb over her wet slit.

"Oh, Daddy." She looks away, embarrassed, and that giggle comes out as a squeak. "Why are you touching my no-no place?"

"Did it feel good?" I stand up and look down at her in question. "Did you like it when Daddy touched you down there?"

She swallows. "Um...I-I don't know," she whispers. "No one's ever done that to me before."

"That's good." I smile and step close to unclasp her bra behind her back. "You don't want to let boys do that. It's better you come to someone who knows what he's doing."

Completely naked, she shifts nervously from foot to foot. She's magnificent, and she knows what she's doing, too. This comes as naturally to her as it does to me. "I don't understand," she mumbles, flushing.

"It's all right, honey. I'll explain everything. Now—" I step back "—since I helped you with your dress, perhaps you should help me, too. You can start with my shirt." I get rid of my tie myself.

Shoes and socks, too.

"Okay." With shaky fingers, she unbuttons my shirt. I watch her, and I can sense my hungry gaze is the cause for her squirming. "And now?" she squeaks, letting my shirt fall to the floor. I simply point to my pants. "Um..." I'd say she's noticed my erection now. "What's that?"

A shiver runs through me. "Unzip and find out. It's best if you get down on your knees."

I have to swallow a moan as she sinks to her knees before me.

What a sight.

As she slowly loosens the belt, unbuttons the single button, and unzips me, I weave my fingers through her long hair and draw humming noises from her. She pushes down my pants, and that leaves my black boxers. With a quick glance my way, she asks if they're coming off, too, and I nod firmly. So, she hooks her fingers beneath the waistband and tugs them down.

"Oh!" she gasps as my cock slaps against my lower abdomen. I momentarily close my eyes and groan under my breath. "Is that..."

"Daddy's cock," I finish and extend my hand. "Up you go. It's time for our bath."

There are no bubbles in the water to obscure my view, and the jets aren't on. All there is—that makes us shiver and moan in contentment—is hot water. The tub is big enough for four people, but we don't need that much space. Evidently, I need to let my baby girl know that, because she sits down across from me.

"Closer, Kayla," I coax. "Sit with Daddy."

Sucking her bottom lip into her mouth, she scoots over to sit next to me. The water comes to her collarbone, but without bubbles, I see the rest of her perfectly.

"This is nice, isn't it?" I drape an arm around her shoulders. "Just you and me, relaxing together." She gives me a shy smile in return, and I brush the knuckles of my free hand down her arm, not-so-accidentally touching her right breast under the water. "You really do have a fantastic body, sweet girl." In a more deliberate move, I touch her breast and cup it in my hand.

"Daddy," she gasps and clenches her thighs together, "I feel— um, in my tummy..." She widens her eyes. "It's tingly."

I hum, nodding slowly, and caress her farther down. "Do you know why that is?" Fingers spread, my large hand nearly covers her smooth stomach. She shakes her head no. I smile down at my girl. "It's because you like Daddy's touch." I level her with a more serious expression. "*Only* Daddy's touch, Kayla. Am I making myself clear?"

"Yes, of course. I understand," she whispers in a rush.

"Good." I smile. "Now, can I have a kiss?"

She giggles and reaches up to give my cheek a quick peck.

"My sweet little baby," I chuckle. "Come here. Sit on my lap instead." I open my arms. "I'd like to try a new thing now." She looks nervous again and confused as to why on earth she would sit on her Daddy's lap, but she obeys nonetheless. "There—perfect," I murmur and pull her a bit closer. Since she's straddling me, she can certainly feel my cock wedged between us, though she makes no mention of it. She only sucks on her bottom lip again and peers down at us. "Are you looking at Daddy's cock?" If possible, her cheeks turn even redder, and she ducks her head. "Uh-uh." I grip her chin, forcing her to look me in the eye. "There'll be none of that. No hiding."

"Okay." She gulps. "So, what, um...what was it you wanted to try?"

"Kissing on the lips." I caress her thighs, each pass going higher and higher, but I keep it slow. "Will you give Daddy a kiss on the lips?"

"Sure," she says, sounding anything but. Cautiously, she leans forward; I place my hands on her hips instead. Our noses brush together and then our lips. Softly and gently at first. Merely ghosting over. Then I take the next step and swipe the tip of my tongue across her bottom lip. She gasps. "Oh! I-I liked that."

Fuck, she's killing me. With a low groan rumbling in my chest, I kiss her firmly and cup her cheek with one hand. The other one slowly moves to her pert ass. With her legs parted enough, her back entrance taunts me until I can't take it anymore and allow myself to caress her there, too.

"*Daddy!*" She backs away, her face actually flashing with anger and shock. I doubt she has any clue how turned on I am, even with my erection reminding her. "You can't touch me—*there.*"

"Of course I can, honey." I draw her close again. "If you only give it enough time, you'll see that you *want* it."

She looks dubious. "Really?"

"Really," I confirm, claiming her mouth again in a possessive kiss. She lets out another gasp, though this time quieter, and I take the opportunity to slip my tongue into her mouth. She tastes like the sweetest sin, one I can't wait to corrupt and defile. Kayla will be my naughty little slut in no time. "You make Daddy so happy." I moan into the kiss and carefully begin to move her over my cock.

"I'm tingling again," she whimpers as I kiss my way to her neck. "You're so...your, um..."

"Say it," I whisper in her ear. I resume stimulating her ass, teasing her with barely-there strokes of my fingers. I can't fucking wait until it's my cock pushing in there. "I'm so...what?"

Her breathing hitches. "Your thing," she squeaks, "it's hard."

"It's because you're so gorgeous," I explain gently. "And it's okay that you want it. You can't help that."

"Oh," she mouths. "How do I know I want it?"

I purse my lips, pretending to ponder that for a moment. In the meantime, I slide both my hands to her tits. Since she's on my lap, her luscious tits are above the surface, so when my fingers aren't enough, I lean in and capture a nipple between my lips. One light suck has her squirming. *She loves this.* It's the perfect time for me to get to know her body.

"I'm going to show you something, and I need to touch your no-no place. Is that okay?" I brush some hair away from her face. "Remember, I only want what's best for you."

"Um, all right," she answers hesitantly.

"Good girl." I kiss her nose. As we both look down between us, I gently cup her pussy in my hand. "God, you're perfect," I mutter to myself.

My middle finger slips between her smooth lips, and when I come in contact with her clit, she cries out softly and buries her face in the crook of my neck. I feel her eyelashes fluttering against my skin. Her breath, hot and humid like the room, makes me shiver.

"You like that, don't you?" I add a little pressure to her clit.

"Oh, yes," she breathes. "I like it lots."

"I knew you would," I chuckle huskily. Fingers skimming over her bare lips, I soon reach the first hole I can't wait to fuck. Even in the water, I sense her arousal—slightly thicker and slicker than water. I coat the pad of my middle finger in her wetness. "You're so tight, my little girl." Eyes still downcast, I watch as my finger slowly pushes into her. In response, Kayla groans and digs her short fingernails into my shoulders. At the same time, she constricts around my finger. "That little squeeze your kitty just made around Daddy's finger? That means it wants more."

"Another finger?" she guesses breathily.

I shake my head no and start to finger-fuck her deeply. "No. Because you're a greedy girl. You want something much bigger." Gripping her chin with my available hand, I study her flushed face. I sigh and shake my head at her. "I don't think you're going to be satisfied until you have Daddy's cock."

Her eyes grow wide. "In my k-kitty?" I nod solemnly and slam a second finger into her. "Fuck!" she cries out, throwing her head back.

"Kayla!" I scold. "Since when do you curse? Another bad word out of that mouth...I will turn your ass red. Understand?"

"I'm sorry, I'm sorry," she gasps just as I add a third finger. "Oh, my God! Please, Daddy!"

"Such a dirty little slut," I hiss. I work her pussy firmly, fingering her hard and deep while I stimulate her clit with my thumb. "You already need more, don't you?"

"I can't help it." She buries her face against my neck again, clinging to me. "I can't help that I like it."

"Like I said—" I abruptly push her off me and stand up in the middle of the Jacuzzi "—you're a greedy girl."

Her face flashes with shock and despair at my sudden movements, but she has nothing to fear. She wants more; I will give it to her.

"My fingers aren't enough." I stare at her accusingly as I advance on her. Step by little step, I back her into the edge of the tub. I tower over her, water cascading down our naked bodies. They glisten in the candlelight. "Place your arms along the top of the tub."

I help her get into position, feeling my muscles tense as I stare down at her exposed body. Her breathing catches in her throat; her eyes are still wide, but I pay her no mind. With her arms in place, holding her up, I bend over to lift her lower body to the surface. I grab at the back of her thighs and pick her up; she's all but weightless in the water.

"This is what you want, Kayla." Her legs are firmly wrapped around my hips, and she can see my cock sliding against her pussy. "You want Daddy's cock in your greedy little cunt."

"But it's so big," she whimpers. "I don't—I'm not sure..."

I tsk her and drag my erection along her slit. "Now you want to change your mind?" I chuckle darkly, pushing the head of my cock inside of her. I stifle a groan at the sensations. "I'm afraid that's not how it works." Another inch. She grits out a moan. "You've teased Daddy, and now he wants this."

I slam my cock inside of her, causing water to splash around us. Kayla cries out.

I groan and let my head loll back.

Holding onto her ass, I fuck her pretty little pussy deeply. "Fuck—amazing." I close my eyes. My hips buck into her repeatedly. I pull out slowly. I push in again—fast—and my little slut's moans and cries spur me on like nothing else. Opening my eyes once more, I stare down at her—as I fuck her, use her body for my pleasure...as I give and take. We come alive. "You love this." It's a statement. "I bet you've even dreamed of it. Haven't you? Lying in bed at night, you wish Daddy would come in and fuck your needy pussy."

"Yes!" she admits breathlessly. "God—oh, please! Daddy, fuck me harder..."

"Dirty fucking mouth on you." I pinch her left nipple. Hard. "I told you. No cursing." I make a mental note to spank her before bed. She spasms around my cock. I start panting. "Get out of the tub." I point to the sink, the marble counter there, where I want to fuck her even harder. Without water slowing down my movements. "It's time you take a look at what a naughty girl you've turned into."

Her expression tells me she's both aroused and ashamed; she quickly scrambles out of the Jacuzzi, anything to obey me. Quickly.

"I can't help it," she repeats weakly.

Adrenaline and adoration—a weird combination—surge through me.

"I know you can't, baby girl," I murmur and leave the tub myself. Ushering her to the mirror, I kiss her softly on her neck and say, "It's a good thing you have Daddy to help you with all those dirty fantasies."

"I'm very lucky," she agrees as I place her hands on the counter.

My cock skims her ass, and I catch her lusty gaze in the mirror. "Thank you for teaching me, Daddy."

I smile and slowly drag two fingers down her spine. "Bend over." She does, and I grasp her left hip. "Spread your legs." Since I'm so much taller than she, I'm glad to see she immediately stands up on her toes, which makes it easier for me to reach. She also pushes her ass out, and that...yeah, that makes me laugh under my breath. My Kayla really is a cock-slut, isn't she? "Now, keep your eyes focused on the mirror. Daddy's going to fuck you from behind."

She giggles nervously. "You use so many bad words."

"I'm allowed." I give her a pointed look in the mirror, and with our gazes completely locked, I ram my cock deep into her pussy. "Jesus Christ," I spit out. She almost feels too good—a hot little pussy that just sucks me in. I breathe heavily, dropping my forehead to her shoulder.

"Too big, too big, too big," she whimpers and squirms.

I hadn't realized my eyes were closed again; I open them to read Kayla's expression, to see if she truly is in pain. Discomfort, for certain. Her pussy slicks me up further, squeezing me in fluttering little contractions.

"Shhh, baby." I soothe her with caresses and soft words. "You will like it soon, I promise. Just let Daddy fuck you." Taking a deep breath, both hands gripping her hips, I slip out before pushing in again. "Oh, that's it," I groan. I set a steady pace, keeping my strokes long, deep, and hard. "From now on—" I pant "—I'll want you in my bed." My hooded eyes meet hers once again. "As often as possible. Naked. Your kitty's going to need a lot of touching." I kiss her neck, my tongue peeking out to taste, my lips latching on to suck.

"I like to cuddle," she moans as I cup her tits. I squeeze them firmly, rolling her nipples between my fingers. "Can we cuddle lots, Daddy?" I grind into her, my hips meeting her ass, and I nod against her neck. "Can I, um, cuddle your—" she lowers her voice to a whisper "—penis, too?"

Thrusting shallowly and impatiently into her tight pussy, I feel my climax take over, shooting through my entire being at lightning speed. A strained groan slips out. My fingers dig into her flesh; I go rigid. Streams of come soak her inner walls which creates a sloppy sound as I fuck my way through one of the most spectacular orgasms of my life. The sheer euphoria only intensifies when I hear my little girl screaming out her own climax, her sweet pussy sucking on my cock.

"Oh, fucking hell," I pant. My knees nearly buckle. I feel spent, drained, milked.

It takes several minutes for us to calm down, but in the end, I manage to submerge us into the hot water of the Jacuzzi again. This time, I put on the jet streams, and Kayla sleepily snuggles up against my chest, her legs straddling me.

She's all humming, cuddling, stretching, purring like my little kitten, and giggling in delight as I kiss her, wash her, and caress her in the water.

"You've really turned this day around for me," she whispers after a moment of comfortable silence. By her voice, I notice she's slipping out of her regression, slowly but surely returning as the beautiful young woman I wish to take on dates. Lifting her head, she gives me a soft smile. "You're amazing, Nicholas."

"So are you," I murmur and cup her cheek. I kiss her because I want to, our tongues meeting almost lazily. "I want this, you...us."

"I do, too." She hugs me tightly. "I know we have a lot to talk about..."

That's certainly true. There are no rules or relationship boundaries established. We haven't discussed her family yet, and with my phone vibrating on the floor, that can't be postponed. There's no living arrangement, and given that Kayla's new in San Francisco and has no place to stay, it would be so very easy to give her the same offer I've given my previous Littles: a guest room, only...different. Because I want more this time. More than kinky weekends and lonely weeks. I want her in my bed, I want the dates, the vanilla side of things, too.

Patience.

I kiss her on the forehead and squeeze her to me. "This is just the beginning."

TOUCHING TRUTH

A BEHIND THE SCENES NOVELLA

PART I

GREG COOPER

I have more money than they do. Greater success. A bigger home, a nicer car, the latest technology... Yet, they're the ones who are smiling, goofing around, and living life to the fullest.

I see it every time I come here, and I always have to pause before I enter their bar. A hole-in-the-wall kind of place I normally wouldn't set a foot inside. Hell, I shouldn't even be in this neighborhood, which happens to be San Francisco's gay district.

Ryan Quinn runs his bar with the familiar ease of a man who's always on top of things. He's friendly though constantly assessing, comes off as lethal and intimidating, and can flash the kindest grins as well as the most wolfish smirks. His chiseled body is battered and full of tattoos and scars, the latter serving as reminders of his years in the Marines.

He's got an easy two decades on his impish wife. Angel works alongside him in the bar, and she can't be more than twenty-two or twenty-three. She's short, soft, and curvy where he's imposing, hard, and immense. Her green eyes meet his steel gray eyes, and they quirk smirks at each other. They *worship* one another. He

47

throws a wineglass her way, which she catches before opening a bottle for a patron.

When he passes her, he catches a wisp of blond hair that's escaped her cheeky pigtails and drops a kiss to her neck. She's dyed the tips of her hair pink.

The envy burns hotly within me.

The envy is new.

Straightening my tie, I clear my throat and square my shoulders. Let's at least pretend I have some composure before they take it away from me—again. Twice a month, like clockwork. I always come back for more, because I am a weak fucking excuse for a man.

I take a deep breath, then open the door and enter the establishment. Memorabilia from the Marines, a sports team or two, and political messages fill the walls. *Fucking liberals.* Breathe a word of anything conservative around them, and they'll string you up by the balls. I would know.

Considering it's early, only a handful of customers are here, and they're gathered along the bar. The five tables and the dart area stand empty until people get off work.

Ryan sees me first and greets me with a lazy grin.

Angel, the little girl with the most deceptive name known to man, smirks deviously. "Hello, pet."

I suppress a shiver and choose a mild scowl instead. I absolutely loathe being called that in front of others, and she damn well knows it. Not that she gives a rat's ass. The only thing she respects are my hard limits.

"Miss Angel," I greet quietly, far more polite than I would've preferred. She grates on my nerves purposely, to push my buttons, and I won't do anything about it. Because I don't know what's scariest, facing her wrath or Ryan's.

They're both Dominants in a small, private BDSM community. Although, technically, Angel would be a switch. However, she submits to one man and one man only—her husband. She's his angel, princess, baby, wife, treasure, the list goes on. He's her Sir, Master, Daddy, husband... And I'm...none of those things.

"How about a drink before Tory and TJ get here?" Ryan strolls over and pours me a beer, speaking of their two employees. While Angel busies herself with refilling bowls of peanuts, Ryan leans close as I sit down on a stool at the end of the bar. "A heads-up. She's extra punchy today."

Marvelous.

Of course, Ryan loves that.

I swallow hard and reach for my beer. If I were smart, I would hightail it out of here, but I know I won't. Ryan and Angel know it, too.

"You okay?" Ryan bends over slightly, resting his forearms on the bartop.

I incline my head. "Yes."

He cocks a brow.

Fuck. "Sir. Yes, Sir." I struggle with those goddamn titles.

"That's my boy." He winks and returns to work for a minute.

I gulp down my beer. *My boy.* I truly am not his boy. He needs to stop calling me that. I'm thirty-eight, for chrissakes. I run a successful law firm with two of my brothers.

Along with the envy toward their evident adoration for each other, a couple other things are new developments. For about six months now, I've been their degradee, punching bag, and... I feel irritatingly embarrassed to even continue that thought. Nevertheless, what I'm *not* is anything sweet. Yet, the past three or four scenes they've done with me, aftercare has evolved into something deeper, and they've been a bit more affectionate with me.

It's awoken a yearning I have to squash down every time I leave.

I won't allow it.

I'm hardly special, regardless. Given that they're both Dominants, they take in male subs and bottoms regularly for their own amusement. I'm just one of them. I've heard mentions of three other guys, though I suspect one is no longer in service to them.

It's a trade-off. I get to be pushed down twice a month, and they get to let their sadistic streaks run wild. Nothing to yearn for.

Nothing.

An hour later, I'm the one who's *nothing*. In the Quinn couple's apartment upstairs, they roughly push me into their second bedroom, which is more like a playroom. I swim in shame and naked desire as Angel beats the shit out of me.

While I'm restrained on the bed, Ryan's sitting in a chair nearby, lazily stroking himself and enjoying the show. I can't see him too clearly for the tears blurring my vision. Whenever I do catch his heated gaze, the humiliation sears through me with as much force as Angel's lashes. The strands of her floggers patter my exposed body, until she switches to her favorite paddle.

"Kiss it, you meaningless waste of space." She holds the thick paddle in front of my face, and I screw my eyes shut and turn away. *Meaningless waste of space.* A hot tear trickles down the side of my face, and I have to bite my lip to withhold a pathetic whimper.

This is who you are, Cooper. Face it. Fucking meaningless.

"Daddy, he won't kiss the paddle." She stomps her foot.

"I guess he doesn't respect you." Ryan hums gravely. "Is that's how it is, boy? Don't you respect my princess?"

I nearly crush my molars with how hard I bite down. "I'm sorry, Sir," I manage to grit out.

In a heartbeat, Ryan is out of his chair and looming over me, a painfully tight grip on my jaw. "Are you really that fucking stupid? I'm not the one who deserves the apology." With that said, he grabs my balls and squeezes them.

"F-fuck," I choke out, eyes bulging. "I'm s-sorry!" The pain shoots through my body, threatening to cripple me. "Miss Angel, I'm *so fucking sorry.*"

"Satisfied, my love?" he murmurs to Angel.

"Not yet, but I will be," she replies sweetly.

"Please," I rasp.

Take it. You deserve it.

I weep like a baby. By now, I'm on my stomach. Hands and feet restrained again. Thighs, chest, and arms burning from Angel's sadism. My cock and balls... I have no words to describe the pain. My skin is on fire, blood rushing, adrenaline pumping, shame suffocating.

Take it. You deserve it.

"Ten more," Ryan directs.

It's a thin cane this time. Angel strikes me across my buttocks and growls, "Count, garbage!"

"One, M-Miss Angel," I gasp hoarsely. Oh fuck, I can't. I can't. The pain is too much. "Two, Miss Angel." With each strike, it feels like she cracks my skin. I half expect to see my ass a bloody mess later. "Ow—motherfu—three, Miss Angel."

I bite into the pillow I've soaked with tears, snot, saliva, and sweat.

"Beautiful welts, baby." The lust is clear in Ryan's voice, drawing a shudder from me. "His back might need some claw marks, though."

"Ooh, can I, Sir? Pretty please?" Angel's giddy.

"Go ahead." This is one of Ryan's ways to spoil her rotten. He gets off on seeing her torturing me. "Then it's my turn."

Fuck.

"Yay!" Angel claps her hands and then straddles my ass. I flinch, her cotton panties feeling more like sandpaper. "Color, boy?"

"Gr-green," I cough, and she doesn't waste time. "Oww!" The agony shocks me when I feel the trail of fire Angel's nails leave behind. All across my spine and shoulder blades, she digs her manicured fingers into my flesh. Downstairs in the bar, I spotted the pastel pink nail polish and white polka dots. Now they might as well be rusty knives.

Piercing through the haze of hurt, the sound of foil being ripped reaches my ears. *This is it.* More shame. My cock gives a weak twitch, proof of how fucking pathetic I am. Whether it's Angel who uses a toy or a strap-on, or it's Ryan who fucks me, it's the highlight of every scene.

This isn't why you're here. You can't fucking do anything right.

Ryan unties my hands and ankles, not that I budge an inch. I can't. *Breathing* hurts. Moving my arms would send me into hysterics. My thighs are even worse.

He climbs onto the bed, the mattress dipping with his weight. Angel, on the other hand, is as light as a feather and skips off with grace. I tense up as Ryan plants his big hands on my buttocks and kneads the flesh. I whimper, unable to hold it in.

He makes an appreciative sound. Then he's leaning over me, ghosting a kiss to my neck. "You take my little wife's beatings perfectly, pet."

I shiver to the point of shaking, and his thick cock presses against me, exactly where I'm not supposed to want it. *So fucking badly.*

He chuckles, clearly noticing when I involuntarily push my ass against him.

Rotten. Rotten through and through, Cooper. You don't deserve to enjoy anything.

Hauling me farther down the bed, Ryan makes space for Angel, who returns with her favorite vibrator and finds a seat on the pillow I've smothered my sobs in. I cringe at the pain and drag a sore hand down my face, the stubble on my jaw creating a soft rasp. Opening my eyes again, I suck in a breath when I see she's removed her underwear. She spreads her legs, giving me an exquisite view of her baby-smooth pussy.

The words escape me, unbidden. "M-May I serve you, Miss Angel?"

She scrunches her nose. "Um, no. You probably wouldn't do it right. No offense, but you're kind of useless."

Ouch. I lower my gaze and dip my chin in acknowledgment. Fresh tears well up, and *this* is why I'm here. To feel awful. To embrace the shame. To get what I deserve.

"I don't know, princess..." Ryan leans over me again, this time pushing the head of his cock inside me. Slowly. Just an inch at first. "He's been good today, hasn't he?" Another inch. One more. I gnash my teeth together, eyes closed, and accept the burn. I push back, the way he's taught me. My cock fills with blood and arousal, something I hate but can't stop. "Maybe he can earn a taste?"

Angel pretends to think about it as the vibrator buzzes to life. I doubt she'll want me too close. Fucking her is off-limits, and that's okay with me, but I do get to please her with my mouth and fingers sometimes.

It makes me feel like I can at least do something good on this earth.

I hiss, Ryan's cock pushing deeper. He groans under his breath, and next I feel his large form covering my body. He's warm and oddly comforting. He's the thuddy hurt. Angel is the sharp, stingy pain. More bite in her.

"Such a sweet bottom." He grips my hip with one hand and drives all the way in, and we curse in unison. "Lovely little cock whore, aren't you?"

"Fuck," I breathe out. "Thank you, Sir."

"You're welcome." He rumbles a husky chuckle and begins to fuck me slowly. Deeply. "What do you say, my angel—should we let him come today?"

I don't deserve to come.

Angel lifts my chin and forces me to look her in the eye. Her gaze is almost as calculating as Ryan's. Sharp, knowing, severe.

Not knowing why, I turn my head and brush a kiss to the inside of Angel's thigh. *Don't give me pleasure, please.* Her gaze softens, which wasn't my intention. Maybe I should call her a stupid bitch? I wonder what they'd do to me then.

No. This is the one place I won't step out of line and act like a complete asshole.

"Yes." She nods decidedly and turns off the vibrator. I find myself holding my breath, resigned by the affirmative I don't deserve but frozen with anticipation because she's scooting farther down. "Kiss my special place, sub."

I'm not a sub, but I'll definitely kiss her special place. Letting her sweet scent invade my senses, I drop a gentle kiss over her clit.

"Know what a fucking privilege that is." Ryan's lust-filled warning is emphasized by a harsh thrust of his cock. "Treat her like a queen, or you'll be breathing through a tube for a month."

"Yes, Sir." I bite back a moan and slide my tongue between the soft, glistening lips of her beautiful pussy. She smiles glowingly in approval, the sight filling me with warmth and contentment. It shouldn't, but I'm helpless. I ache for them to be pleased with me. So I give her all the attention I can muster. I lick her greedily, slowly, quickly, tenderly, and lavish every inch of her with touches. They allow me to use my hands too, and I finger her lightly while I wrap my lips around her clit and suck gently.

"Oh..." She exhales and lets her head fall back. "Maybe he's not completely useless, Daddy."

No, I am.

Ryan grunts and picks up the pace, fucking my ass like he owns it. I suppose, in a way, he does. Without my permission, he has me meeting his thrusts, and my cock is painfully hard. The sensitive skin around it stretches in a way that I feel phantom zings from Angel's beating earlier.

"What would you say, boy?" Ryan dips down and nips sharply

at my neck. Then his tongue follows in an openmouthed kiss that elicits an embarrassingly loud groan from me. "Are you completely useless or not?"

"I am," I pant. "Useless, can't do anything right, cock whore, waste of space—" I cut myself off.

Ryan and Angel are good people. If they knew exactly why I was here, they'd stop seeing me.

Angel snickers and snorts softly. "Spell all those words out with your tongue. Right here." She taps her clit.

I shudder and push my erection against the mattress, needing the friction. Even though it hurts like nothing else.

Ryan keeps fucking me, laughing breathlessly. "She's wicked, isn't she?"

"Yes, Sir."

I get lost in them. The pleasure can't fucking be stopped. Unbeknownst to them, he's the first man I've gone all the way with, and Angel... I swallow a trickle of her sweet juices and tongue-fuck her carefully. She's the first woman for whom my desire runs much deeper than I've ever experienced.

They can never know.

It becomes too all-consuming in the new position. My sore legs wrapped around Ryan's hips and Angel sitting on my face, they fuck me expertly into bliss I haven't earned for shit. Angel's moans whenever she bucks against my mouth and fingers create a surge of pride and joy within me. She's facing her husband, and I hear when they kiss hungrily above me, the sound only getting hotter with Ryan's groans and growls.

They whisper dirty promises and I-love-yous to each other, using me as the toy I am. I'm a mouth that gets Angel off. I'm a hole Ryan fucks his release into. And then...the goddamn bastards, they fist my cock and stroke it firmly, slickly, too damn seductively. I nearly jump at the initial touch, but then I'm just begging, pushing my hips upward, and getting too greedy. Not by their standards, maybe. Definitely mine, though.

I'm sorry, I'm sorry, I'm sorry.

I'm not suffering enough.

Aiming to get Angel off again, I push two fingers deep inside her and kiss whatever wet spot I can reach. She curls against her Master and moans while he murmurs things in her ear. His breathing is labored, a sound I'm growing too fond of.

The lust explodes inside me. I groan against Angel's pussy. Ryan's filthy talk gets to me, and I can't hold back. My entire being stiffens. *No, please, stop. Don't.* But the second he growls, "Come," there's a shock to my system. The command scares me enough to stop fighting. I let go too eagerly and give in to the orgasm.

Spurts of my release splash against my stomach and chest.

Angel crashes, too. With a gasp and a plea, she falls apart in Ryan's arms.

The self-loathing strikes harder than ever during their aftercare.

In the beginning of our arrangement, I didn't even know it was a thing. My little brother is involved in another BDSM community here in the city, and he's open about it, but I can't say I've listened to any stories he's shared of the lifestyle. And when Ryan and Angel explained it to me, I admit I balked at it. I was firm in my decision. I do not want aftercare. I don't want *care*, period.

Lately, they insist.

"It's for us, too." Ryan gathers me close, and I screw my eyes shut. "We don't go easy on you, Greg."

I clear my throat, unable to speak. My eyelashes are thick with useless tears, and I'm sick of my own weaknesses. For some reason, I can let them see me sobbing like a loser while they take turns degrading and beating me, but once the scene is over and the

vulnerability hits me, I can't stand it. So I hide. In the protectiveness of Ryan's arms, I hide my face and try and fail to reject his
comfort.

Angel kneels behind me and rubs cooling lotion into my skin.
The room smells of sex and aloe vera, and it's time for me to go.
The sex, I can handle. The lotion symbolizes care. Same with her
soft kisses. I feel them whenever she reaches a particularly
nasty mark.

"I should go," I croak.

"Not yet," Angel sings. "You're our responsibility until you feel
better."

I shake my head, about to protest, because I'm sure as hell *not*
their goddamn responsibility. Except, Ryan shushes me before I
can open my mouth.

He presses his lips to my forehead. "We didn't feel good about
letting you go home before. Not without knowing how you'd fare.
That shit's over now." He strokes the shell of my ear, down to my
jaw and chin. "If you want us to hurt you, you better accept the
patching up, too. End of story, you hear?"

There's no point in arguing. I can't go without their harsh treatment. I suppose I'll have to suck it up and suffer through this aftercare crap in order to get it.

"Fine," I mutter.

He pats my ass. "Fine, what?"

"Fine, Sir."

———

I'm back in my suit, showered and ready to go home, when Ryan
tells me he'll walk me downstairs.

"I hardly need a chaperone."

"There's something I want to discuss with you," is his answer.

My crisp button-down scrapes my damaged skin on the way
down the stairs, and I loosen my tie, wishing I lived a life where I

could be naked more often. But that's not who I am. It's a slippery slope between indulgences and a life that will fuck you up, so I'll stay rigid. Twice a month. Nothing more. Outside of their building, I'm someone else. Someone who definitely isn't naked because two Sadists have bruised me.

The bar has filled up, and Tory and TJ are busy enough that they don't notice us when we walk through the establishment. Mostly gay men frequent the bar, with the addition of groups of girlfriends and a few straight couples.

Stepping outside, I take a deep breath and wait for Ryan.

I check my watch. It's dark by now, and I contemplate returning to my office. I have a court date next week and wouldn't mind distracting myself with an all-nighter of reviewing a case I'm already familiar with.

Ryan lights up a cigarette, looking like my opposite. Jeans and wife-beater, all those tattoos, scruff, that lazy smile...

"Hotshot." He's amused by my suit.

"What did you want to discuss?"

His mouth twitches. "So impatient." He exhales some smoke. "It's about our D/s relationship."

"I'm listening." Though, I dislike the term *relationship*.

Ryan doesn't beat around the bush. "Angel and I have released our other two boys. We don't want to release you, but things are changing, so if you want to stay with us, you'll have to agree to new terms."

Unease trickles down my spine, and my forehead creases. What changed? Did something happen? Is everything all right? Oh, for chrissakes. I'm losing it. Focus. I clear my throat.

"What would the new terms be?"

Something dims in his assessing stare. "Perhaps it won't matter. Your *interest* would be required, Greg." He takes a drag, the tip of the cigarette glowing brighter. "Angel and I are trying for a baby."

Trying for a baby.

I flick my gaze up to the second floor where their apartment is.

They're starting a family above a noisy bar? While being *kinky*. My jaw tenses. Children and alternative lifestyles don't mix.

"Congratulations," I manage stiffly. "As for the new terms...?"

Ryan smiles thinly and takes a final puff before stubbing it out on the pavement. "You don't really care about us as people, do you? You see two Tops." There's no malice or accusation in his voice. It's a frank statement, an observation. Mostly false, however. Nothing of which I can admit. "It's okay, pet." He's already retreating. "We would've liked to get to know you. Create something more meaningful and meet up more often. We want stability for our children, so we're done with casual lovers who come and go."

The unease grows. I can't give more. Despite what I might want, I give everything I can, and I know it isn't much. We can discuss current events and engage in insignificant chitchat, but that's it. All they know of me is that I'm a lawyer and I live outside the city. They've seen results from an STD screening, they know my name, and they know what beer I like.

They know my limits.

"I..." Fuck, this hurts more than it should. Perhaps it's best to call this off now. "I don't have room in my life for more."

He nods tightly, though his gaze flashes with something I can relate to. A bit of hurt. "I figured."

I swallow hard, and a gust of wind gets caught in the Pride flag that hangs alongside the American flag by the door. *I don't belong here.* In an attempt to punish myself, I've gotten nothing but satisfaction from Ryan and Angel—and a taste for something I can't have. I've discovered what gives me bone-deep pleasure, even though I sought it out for reasons of which they wouldn't approve.

"I should go." Before I make a bigger fool of myself. I wouldn't be able to blame physical pain on the emotions now.

Ryan doesn't object.

I toss a final glance at the second floor, then the Pride flag... I shake my head, mournful, and start toward my car. My feet feel heavier than lead. *There you go. You got what you deserved.* No more secrets to keep, I suppose. Not from Ryan and Angel, not from my family.

Enough with the indulging. I have strong beliefs where family and children are concerned, and I wouldn't be able to witness it— much less be part of it—when Ryan and Angel have their child anyway. Enough with the emotional releases, too. I don't need the Quinns. It was only their pain I sought out, and it was wrong of me. Time to pull my shit together. I certainly don't cry and show myself as weak.

I'm Greg Cooper, ruthless lawyer, traditional—a family man. My daughter is my number one priority.

Getting in my car, I reach over to open the glove compartment and slip on my wedding band again.

No more secrets.

TWICE THE TOUCH

CHAPTER 1

MARK COOPER

Throwing the rag over my shoulder, I survey the bartop, making sure it's clean and spotless. In my periphery, more and more people trickle in for a night at the club, and I grin when I see Nicholas and Kayla, back from Venice. That means Kevin is around, too, since he's itching to give Nick the latest figures.

Expanding the club was a wise decision; now we have people flying in from all over the state to visit Switch, and Nick has Kayla to thank for it. It'd been her idea, and since she has Nick wrapped around her little finger, there was no hesitation. Granted, Nicholas Ford is one badass businessman, so I doubt he would've gone through with the remodeling if his financial projections hadn't agreed with her vision.

"Welcome back, you two." I shake Nick's hand over the bar and tip an imaginary hat in greeting to Kayla. "How was your vacation?" Before the last word is out, my eyes have already strayed to her left ring finger.

Someone said yes. *Of course he went with yellow.* It's Kayla's favorite color. A fairly big, yellow diamond surrounded by small, clear ones on a white gold band. Or...knowing Nick, it's platinum.

"Magical," Kayla sings as she scoots onto a barstool. "We're engaged!" A big smile stretches across her lips. I congratulate them both, happy for them. "Thank you, Sir," she says sweetly. She's looking very pretty in another one of her baby-doll dresses. "It was the best vacation *ever*." Nick is content to let her do the talking, and he sits there, watching his little fiancée as if she's the center of the universe. Of course to him, she is. "I can bring photos tomorrow. If you want to see?"

I nod and pour her a Sprite. "I'd like that, honey." With a wink, I turn to Nick and ask him if he wants a drink, but he declines. *All right, then.* "Have you spoken to Kev yet?"

"He ambushed us in the lobby," he chuckles. "I'm happy it's going so well." He tugs on one of Kayla's pigtails. "This one's more business-savvy than I thought."

"Daddy." She giggles and squirms. "Always pulling my hair."

"You love it." He moves closer to her and lifts her chin, their noses nearly touching. With his free hand, he cups one of her tits and pinches a nipple through the fabric. "I can do whatever I want, can't I?"

"Yes, Daddy."

I smirk at Kayla's blush. She is too adorable for words. Not really my cup of tea, but I can still see the appeal—obviously. She's experienced despite her young age, beautiful, naturally submissive, with a mischievous streak that'll keep Nicholas on his toes. She's also a sweetheart, so I wasn't surprised when Nick told me he was going to propose to her. Now, only six months after they met in the beginning of June, they have a lot going on. To some it might seem rushed—expanding the club, getting engaged, buying a house...but I guess they know what they want.

I can't say I'm envious. I used to have what he has now—sans the clubs—and I barely escaped unscathed. Admittedly, it's left me a little jaded.

"Are you on the floor tonight?" Nick asks me.

"Yeah." I nod.

He tilts his head in my direction as Kayla snuggles against his chest. Even seated on a barstool, he can have her on his lap. "Playing or working?"

"Work, I'm afraid." I jerk my chin at Dante a few feet away who asks for a beer. Now that Nick has created a big scening area for Switch, more regulations have been instituted for the guests. If you want to scene, there's a drink limit, and anyone who plans to partake in any type of play wears a blue rubber wristband. After giving Dante his first drink for the night, I scan his ID into the system so he's on the list for tonight. Then I return to Nick, who knows I'm usually all for participating in these events. "Liam called in, and he can't make it because his daughter's sick."

"Ah. So, you're manning the bar in the Cave?"

"Yep." Unfortunately.

When Nick bought the restaurant next door, he decided to keep the bar in the center of the new space. Four bartenders were hired as soon as the area was ready to be used, and Liam was supposed to work tonight.

Seeing as Nicholas has left me in charge of the bartending staff, it means I have to pick up the shifts that no one else can cover. Luckily, it doesn't happen often.

"Are you and Kayla playing?" I ask and grab a soda for myself.

"We are," he chuckles as Kayla grins widely. "I promised my baby girl."

I have a feeling she's going to give him a run for his money. The new part of the club is fairly big, and when the lights go out, it's only going to make things more difficult for the Doms. But worth it in the end. So fucking worth it.

I scan the area, noticing the growing crowd. Some are playing before the main event, and some are socializing.

Half the wall on the other side of the club has been removed, so I can see straight into the Cave. Tearing down that wall was basically the only thing that needed to be done—aside from a paint job and refinishing the floor. Exactly like the original Club, the new section is perfectly square. The only difference is that the ceiling isn't as high in there as it is here; it creates a more intimate atmosphere, which is why we refer to it as the Cave.

Instead of another dance floor or seating area, dividers are lined up with the walls, each one making up a scene room. And in the middle of the floor, there's the bar, the one I'll be working in a couple hours.

There's still the kitchen and the private dining room behind the Cave to be dealt with, and I'm not sure what Nicholas is planning there. Those areas have been sealed off for now.

"Speaking of, we should probably put on our wristbands, little one," Nicholas murmurs, handing Kayla a white one. Everyone who's participating in tonight's Hide & Seek has to wear one, and they glow in the dark. "I should go tell Cade to turn on the floor lights, too."

No one wants anyone to walk into a wall or something and hurt themselves. This game is all about thrill—predators hunting down their coveted prey, Daddies chasing their Littles—and so the tiny lights embedded in the floor help the participants stay on their side of the makeshift playground. The dance floor in the Club and most of the Cave are free to play in, marking the scening stalls and seating areas as off-limits.

"Cooper!" Simon, one of the dungeon monitors, runs over. I jerk my chin in *what's up?* and get started on a drink order from a waitress. *Miranda.* Pretty sub. I've topped her before. "Is there any way you can help with a scene?"

I give the vodka bottle in my hand a pointed look before I meet his questioning gaze again. "A little busy here, man." This early into the night, there's only one bartender in each bar. I'm here, and Max is in the Cave. Facing Miranda, I ask, "Are there any IDs I need to check in?"

"No, Sir." She flutters her eyelashes at me. "They're not here to play."

I smirk at the redhead but say nothing and turn back to Simon again.

"What's the problem?" Nick inquires.

Simon huffs a breath; he looks as winded as the guys who are pushing big EVA foam blocks onto the dance floor. Hiding spots for the subs later. A few are big enough for two or three to fit inside.

"A new couple," he replies a bit sullenly. Simon has been with his sub for over fifteen years, so patience doesn't come easily for him. "The Dom—and I use that term loosely—has his sub restrained to the St. Andrew's, and he's actually asking her what to do next."

I let out a laugh. "So, tell them to observe before they play."

It's not an uncommon occurrence that we have guests who *think* they're into the lifestyle, when all they really want is a little extra spice in their vanilla sex life.

"Is the sub topping from the bottom?" Nick asks.

Kayla, still in his lap, snuggles deeper into his embrace and starts sucking her thumb, her free hand playing idly with Nick's tie.

Simon shakes his head. "She doesn't want to. I paused the scene to come here. Thing is, I don't trust either of them to continue." He eyes me. "That's why I don't want to send them home."

I frown and pour a glass of red, the last drink before Miranda's order is complete.

Nick frowns, too. "You don't believe the sub will safeword?" An educated guess. If this couple is already in a committed relationship, sometimes the trust comes *too* easily.

"Basically." Simon nods.

"Well—" Nicholas faces me "—you like a challenge. Go with Simon; I'll tell Kevin to man the bar for a while."

I grin. Kevin, Nick's right-hand man, is a Suit with a capital "S," and it's difficult to picture him behind a bar. However, he's the only option at this point.

"Lead the way." I wave a hand for Simon and round the bar to follow.

We cross the dance floor and enter the Cave, the smell of lemon from cleaning supplies coming on a bit stronger. I wink at a sub who is sterilizing the straps on a bondage chair.

There are a total of twelve stalls in the Cave, each one approximately twelve by twelve feet. The three by the eastern wall are as temporary as the wall itself and will be removed once Nick's figured out what to do with the extra space behind. Turning a big dining room into a dungeon was easy enough. Tearing up a restaurant kitchen is another matter.

"I'll be by the cross." Simon points toward a scening stall on the other side of the Cave, and I see that the stall in question has its curtains closed. Not safe for newbies.

I incline my head and duck into a cleaning station to wash up. My reflection in the mirror shows me I could use a vacation, but that will have to wait 'til January. That's when I'll drive down to the beach house in La Jolla I inherited from my grandparents.

Thank fuck my ex-wife never cared for the place. Otherwise, she would've fought for it in the divorce.

I shake my head just thinking of Alexa. I spent seven years married to her, and that was six years too many. Damn woman was a skilled manipulator.

As the years passed, I heard more whines and complaints than "Yes, Master." Not to mention how she abused her safeword.

She changed so gradually that it took time for me to notice. I didn't notice how she wore me down, either—not until much, much later. I wouldn't go so far as to say I lost myself, but I did end up ignoring what I wanted in order to please her. And I guess I clung to the image and impression of how she was when we first met.

Good riddance.

Taking a closer peek at the mirror, I try to see if I can spot another gray hair in my dark mess, but nothing yet. I'm due for another buzz soon, though. An inch is a bit too long. My brother's wife cut it for me last time, and I remember my niece saying, "So, you wanna go halfsies on the inch, Uncle Mark? Mommy, cut half-sies." I grin to myself and step back, wiping my hands on my jeans.

Time to be the Dom, not the jaded, maybe even bitter, divorced guy.

Just as I reach the stall, Simon pushes the curtain aside to exit. "Ah, there you are. I've already told them you're going to offer assistance." He holds open the curtain. "Do you want me to be here, too?"

I shake my head no and let the fabric close off the outside world.

CHAPTER 2

Fastened to the X-shaped cross, a lovely little brunette gazes at me with big brown eyes. I'd say she's in her early twenties. A heart-shaped face, soft-looking lips, and a slightly upturned nose. *Gorgeous.* She gulps and shoots an almost panicked look to the man beside me, but I'm not focusing on him yet. My main priority is the naked beauty who's restrained.

Full, round tits, rosy nipples, a slender waist, and nice, curvy hips. A bare little pussy. Exquisite legs, dainty feet—not a scar in sight. Also not in sight: any trace of arousal or excitement.

I approach her with slow, measured steps, and the first things I check are her bindings. With her arms raised so high, it's not good to have her restrained for too long, but it's looking good here. Simon has undoubtedly checked already.

"Not too tight?" I gently wrap my fingers around her left wrist, noticing the different wristbands she's wearing. Green for being approachable by other Doms, blue for partaking in scenes—which means the drink limit is in effect, and yellow for being new.

"N-no," she stammers in a soft voice, "they're good."

I raise a brow at her and clasp my hands behind my back.

"Sir," she adds hastily.

"There's a good girl," I murmur. "What's your name, kitten?"

She swallows before exhaling shakily. "Evangeline, Sir."

With a slight nod in acknowledgment, I turn to her Dom and see a man who certainly doesn't strike me as a Dom, and it has nothing to do with physical appearance. He's a handsome young man—in his mid-twenties, I'd say—though he doesn't carry himself confidently. He's not as broad-shouldered or muscular as I am, but he's definitely built. Instead of lifting weights, I imagine him doing laps in a pool. He's fairly tall, too—perhaps a few inches shorter than my six one. Narrow hips. Dark hair, wavy and untamed, styled to belong to a surfer or skateboarder. Sharp jaw, straight nose, and pale green eyes. It's the vulnerability in those eyes...

Biting his thumbnail doesn't help him project confidence, either.

"Name?" I cock my head at him and note the clothes he's wearing: brand new leather pants and a dark red T-shirt. Doc Martens, also brand new. He doesn't look comfortable.

"Brayden, S—" His *Sir* is on the tip of his tongue, but he doesn't verbalize it. He managed to cut off the sentence just before.

"How long have you been with Evangeline?" I ask, giving the girl a smile.

"Um, three years."

So, the trust is already there. Angling myself toward Evangeline again, I brush my knuckles down her ribs, enjoying the way her skin pebbles under my touch. "Am I allowed to touch her intimately, Brayden?" I keep my eyes on the girl.

"Yes. We t-talked about it." He's nervous. And flustered. "We, uh, we need help...I guess. I mean, we're new."

I withhold my smile. "I've noticed." Studying Evangeline's face, I reach up and twirl a strand of her shoulder-length hair around my finger, ending with a little tug. Her pupils dilate as she stares up at me. "Such a pretty little kitten." I brush the pad of my thumb over her bottom lip. The tip of her tongue darts out, and I chuckle lowly.

"Oh, you want this, don't you?" I don't wait for an answer. "Do you know your safewords?"

"Red to stop, Sir. Yellow if it's becoming too much, and green if it's...all good."

All good. That's one way of putting it. I grin. "Good girl. Don't be afraid to use them." Taking a step back, I motion for Brayden to join me. He does, and I position him so he's right in front of me. "Now. The DM told me dominating isn't easy for you, Brayden—that you asked little Evangeline here what to do next."

"I'm not really a Dom," he mumbles.

I squeeze his shoulder. "I know. But I'm glad you told me."

My guess is that they want to pursue this lifestyle but can't agree on who to be top and bottom. The most confident man on earth may want to be bossed around behind closed doors; it's fairly common. A CEO, for example, has to carry a lot of responsibility by day, so when he comes home, perhaps he wants someone else to take over.

"Tell me more about your arrangement." I presume they have one. Brayden tries to turn, but I stop him by holding his shoulders in place, and I keep my hands there. "No. Watch Evangeline instead."

"Okay." He releases a breath. "Uh, we've talked about this for about a year. We want to try it, but we're both pretty, um..."

"Submissive," I finish. I see the tips of his ears tinting red, and I don't like that at all. "Don't be embarrassed." To loosen him up, make him relax, I rub his shoulders. It's mainly to get a better read on him—to see how he reacts to my touch—but also to reassure. "Just because you're a man doesn't mean you have to be in charge. Understand?"

"Yes..." Another breath. "Sir."

I smile, seeing Evangeline's reaction to her boyfriend's final word—or title, rather. Excitement is building up in her eyes, slowly but surely, and Brayden's not the only one letting go. She is, too.

"Go on," I coax.

"Right." He clears his throat. "We eventually agreed to switch every once in a while. So, I'm the dominant one sometimes..."

"And you're both comfortable with this decision?" I ask.

They hesitate to respond, and I'm not surprised. They've compromised. They love each other—that's clear from their expressions—and any sensible human being in a relationship knows that you have to compromise at times. But these two don't *have* to...so long as they're willing to let someone else dominate them both. There are several Doms and Dommes here who have more than one sub.

I never shared when I was with Alexa, and the occasion hasn't arisen since our separation, but I'd done it a few times before I met her. It's challenging but twice as rewarding.

"No need to answer," I say and change tactics. This isn't about teaching Brayden the first steps on how to touch his sub anymore, because they're both submissives. "First rule: I want honesty and complete answers unless yes or no is enough." With a small nudge, I shift Brayden to the side so we're both in front of Evangeline. "Is this your first time in a BDSM club?"

"Yes, Sir," they reply.

I barely manage to withhold my wince. Their first time at a fetish club and they head straight for the cross? *Jesus Christ.* "Have you played at home?"

"Yes, Sir."

"With restraints?" I arch a brow at Brayden. "Bondage?"

It takes longer to answer this time, and when they do, they say no, though Evangeline seems to remember something and quickly mentions that she's tied Brayden down once.

Once.

No wonder Simon didn't want them to leave. They're both fucking hazards.

"I see. And what was the plan here?" I wave a hand at the cross. "You must've had a scene in mind." Caressing Evangeline's soft cheek, I tell her to answer.

She shivers. "We..." She trails off, distracted as I let my hand slowly slide down her neck. "We—we wanted to try flogging."

My fingers curl themselves loosely around her throat. "Is this something you've done before?"

"No, Sir," they mumble, both sounding nervous.

"Well." I push down my urge to paddle their asses for being irresponsible and surge forward. "Brayden, tell me what you *have* done."

"We've used toys." His voice nearly cracks. "Um—"

"Stop with the 'um's," I command softly. "Take a deep breath and relax."

As he obeys and inhales deeply, I take a step forward and place my hands below Evangeline's breasts. Her breathing hitches, and then again when I ghost my thumbs along the undersides.

"Vibrators, beads, dildos..." Brayden's voice is huskier now. Quieter, too. "Plugs, blindfolds—she gagged me once, the time she tied me to the bed. And she likes it when I spank her."

I tense my jaw and let my hands fall to my sides. "Did you ever use a safeword at home?"

"We trust each other—"

"Not what I asked, Brayden." Under my glare, he shrinks visibly and lowers his gaze as he whispers a no. *Deep breaths.* I return to Evangeline, ready to teach them something important. "Will you allow me to do a scene with you?" I ask. "I will only use a flogger."

"*Yes*, Sir." She's almost pleading.

Turning to Brayden, I wait for his response. He's part of this, too.

"Yes, Sir." He nods quickly. "Please."

Well, then.

"I want you to sit down over there." I point to the leather ottoman in the corner near the curtain. Next, I walk behind the cross and pick one of the softer floggers. "And, Brayden?" I speak over my shoulder. "Clothes off." He won't be treated any differently than Evangeline.

"All of them?" he blurts out.

I turn to him and stare.

He gulps. "I mean...yes, Sir."

"Good pet." With the flogger's handle stuck down into the back pocket of my jeans, I step in front of Evangeline once more. She has her eyes on her undressing boyfriend, and when I snap my fingers, her wide-eyed gaze meets mine. "So beautiful." I touch her cheek. "Are you comfortable?"

She replies that she is, and I push the tip of my thumb into her mouth.

"Suck." I clench my teeth together, my pants feeling tighter, as she swirls her tongue around my thumb and starts to suck. Seductive little subbie. "Now..." I force myself to create some distance. "You can of course play however you want at home, but something we take very seriously at Switch is 'Safe, Sane, and Consensual'— same goes for honesty. If we're not honest with each other, there won't be any trust. Understand?"

"Yes, Sir," Evangeline answers, and I look to my side and hear Brayden say the same words, also confirming that they've read about that. As instructed, he's sitting naked on the ottoman, hands gripping the edge of the leather cushion, and a semi-hard cock between his thighs.

Okay, maybe he's more than "handsome."

I'm attracted to him, too.

"There's more." I go on and face Evangeline as I pull out the flogger. "A lot more." I run the black ends of the flogger over my hand, between my fingers, pleased at the little kitten's reaction. Definitely aroused. "For instance, a safeword is always recommended—even if you've been in a relationship for years." That said, I flick my wrist and let the leather strands make impact on Evangeline's left thigh.

"Fuck!" she cries out.

Brayden's breathing picks up.

Evangeline's chest heaves with each breath, a blush creeping forward, pupils dilating again, and hands balling into fists in her restraints. She's more than all right. It's written all over her gorgeous body.

"Another rule: don't cut off any senses when restrained." I flog her again, this time her other thigh, and she cries out once more. "Not when you're new," I amend. "You might not think that gagging is anything serious, but it is if you can't move and you suddenly have a panic attack."

There are hand signals, squeeze toys, bells...anything to substitute a safeword. The next time the flogger's strands whip through the air, they come down on her hip, a couple stray ones landing over the bare mound of her pussy.

Evangeline chokes on a moan; Brayden groans under his breath. One glance at him tells me he's struggling to keep his hands off his straining cock. *Good boy.* He obviously knows he needs my permission to touch himself.

Several lashes later, they're both panting. Evangeline's skin has reddened. By the look of her wet pussy and constricted nipples, I'd venture a guess to say she might be into some pain. She keeps trying to rub her thighs together, but with her restrained ankles, that's impossible.

"Mark?" Damn. *Simon.* On the other side of the curtain.

"*What?*" I wipe my brow, hoping he'll disappear quickly.

"Kevin wonders when you'll be done."

I put down the flogger. "Not yet," I say flatly, closing the distance between Evangeline and me. She's riding on some wave of euphoria, though it's way too soon to talk of subspace. "It's going to be a while. Talk to Nicholas."

He'll understand. I know he will. To distract the girl in front of me, I cup her luscious tits and pluck at her nipples. She squirms, eyes closed, and lolls her head from side to side. Damn, she's really sexy.

"Brayden, come here." He's with me in a flash, his green eyes darker than before. His muscles are taut, his jaw tense. One might think it's anger—perhaps at having another man touching his girl-friend—but that's not it. He's beyond turned on. "Release her hands, pet."

"Yes, Sir." He gets started right away, and I keep playing with Evangeline's tits, this time letting my mouth get some action, too. The moan that slips through her lips when I suck a nipple between my teeth is enough to turn my already-hard cock into steel. Except, this isn't about me.

"Do you like it when I suck on her breasts, Brayden?" I squeeze them and let my teeth sink into her flesh deep enough for her to whimper. Then I let my tongue soothe the sting.

"I—" He hesitates. *Conflicted.* "It's complicated, Sir," he whispers.

I don't think it is. "Come." I pull him in front of me and reach under his arms to massage Evangeline's wrists, now resting idle at her sides. "You love her," I murmur in his ear. Getting a whiff of his musky scent—soap, man, arousal—I nearly groan. "You want to see her this way—out of control, needy, ready to beg for a good, hard fuck—because it's what *she* wants."

"Please," Evangeline whimpers.

Ignoring her pleas, I let go of her wrists and place my hands on Brayden's shoulders. "You see how badly she wants it, don't you?" Slowly, I slide my hands down his arms. "And just because you're not the one dominating her doesn't mean you're not giving it to her. Think about it." Covering his hands with mine, I bring them to her hips. "Most boyfriends would refuse." I guide our right hands down to her pussy, eliciting a gasp from her and a sharp exhale from him. "But you don't, and this is the reward. You feel how wet she is for us?"

"Yes, Sir," he groans as I coax our middle fingers inside her. "Oh, fuck."

Evangeline keeps begging, and we keep ignoring her. When

she lifts her hands, I give her a stern look that has her lowering them again. I knew she was going to go for that, anyway. It's time to restrain her again, but this time I'll use something a bit more intimate—a bit more personal.

"Don't stop, pet," I tell Brayden before I slip out my finger. With Evangeline watching, I suck that finger into my mouth and moan quietly at the taste. The taste of pussy and whatever body wash she uses. "Feel free to talk to her. I bet she likes dirty words whispered in her ear."

"She does," he admits and leans in. Meanwhile, I pull my shirt over my head and twist it until it's a firm, thick rope. Then I walk around the cross and gather her hands behind the smooth wood and tie her wrists together.

We both whisper in her ear as I tie the knot.

"You're so wet."

"Imagine it's my hands holding yours together."

"You like it when Sir uses you, *ma belle*."

"Dirty fucking girl."

"You like Brayden's fingers, kitten? I know you do, but you want more."

In the end, she's panting again, testing her bindings. I'm willing to bet our whispers make her head spin, not quite sure who is whispering what. But it doesn't matter; all she needs to know is we're both toying with her. And I'm in charge of them as a couple...

It's a heady feeling.

Returning to Evangeline's front, I order Brayden to kneel before his girl's pussy, and satisfaction courses through me when he doesn't even hesitate. He just drops. "I want you to use your mouth and tongue like you do when you're kissing her. Make out with her pussy."

I watch as his tongue delves deeply between her smooth folds, his mouth closing over the entrance. More tongue. Some sucking on her lips. Nibbling. Circling her clit. Nuzzling it.

"I want to come," Evangeline begs breathlessly. "Please, Sir!"

"Silence." The sight is intoxicating, but I find myself wanting more. "Enough." I thread my fingers through Brayden's hair and tug. "Stand up." He does, while his chest heaves. Both subs are covered in a light sheen of sweat, and they're equally desperate for a release. The fact that only I can grant it to them makes me feel ten feet tall. "Brayden, release Evangeline's hands again."

While he gets busy, I walk over to the ottoman and sit down. I'd push down my pants if I was sure they wouldn't freak out. As it is, we haven't discussed anything at length, and I doubt sex is on the table for me tonight.

Interrupting a scene for negotiating isn't my style.

Once Evangeline is freed, I motion for her to come to me.

"I want you in my lap, kitten." I pat my thigh. "Your back to my chest."

She takes a few, quick, tiptoed steps over, excitement in her eyes, and plops down on my lap, her pert ass pressing enticingly against my hard cock.

"No more restraints?" I'm pretty sure there's a pout in her soft voice.

Sweet, unassuming little sub.

Leaning forward and wrapping my fingers around her ankles, I move her feet to anchor them behind my calves; then I spread my legs, forcing her legs to spread, too. Next, I gather her wrists behind her back and hold them in place with my left hand. My right hand snakes around her narrow waist, ending up splayed over her soft stomach.

"Try to move your arms." I keep my voice low as I breathe in her sweet scent. My lips brush over her slightly damp neck. "Give me a struggle." When she realizes there's no escaping my hold on her, she starts to breathe heavily, shallowly, rapidly. "That's right." With an openmouthed kiss to her shoulder, I let my teeth scrape over her skin. "And with Brayden's face between your thighs, you won't be able to move your legs, either." I give him a pointed look, one that tells him to come here and kneel down before Evangeline.

"*Oh, putain, ce que j'en ai envie,*" she moans in...French, evidently. Her entire body melts into mine, her head lolling back to my shoulder. It's a surrender I can taste in the air.

"Fuck, I love this," Brayden mumbles and slides his hands up his girlfriend's smooth thighs. His eyes are trained solely on her pussy; he licks his lips, then looks up at me for further instruction.

Good boy. I give him a firm nod. *Lick her up.*

The first stroke of Brayden's tongue along Evangeline's pussy causes her to jump in my arms, and I hold her steady. She's completely at my mercy. They both are. They do as I say. Their pleasure belongs to me. And my mind wanders to Brayden's pleasure.

Would he take it from me?

Submission turns me on; it doesn't matter if it's a man or a woman. When I had my first sexual encounter with a man, who happened to be the Dom who trained me years ago, it wasn't a startling discovery to find out I was attracted to him. I think my childhood has something to do with that. My parents lead their own little lifestyle, hence the laidback attitude with which we were brought up.

As for Brayden...I find him attractive as fuck. His sharp jaw and taut body give him a sexy edge, and I'm even more drawn to the softness in his pale green eyes.

Reading him on that particular subject isn't the easiest though, I reluctantly admit, and I wouldn't want to ruin the scene for him by grasping his cock if that's not his thing. But he does deserve to come—just like Evangeline does—so I only see one solution at this moment.

"That's enough for now, Brayden," I murmur. He doesn't look happy about backing away, but he does it. He also manages to mask his disappointment quickly, and that pleases me.

Ignoring Evangeline's moan of protest, I lower her slightly between my legs, my forearms hooked where her knees bend—literally playing the part of stirrups—and expose her further for Brayden. My erection strains in my jeans against her lower back, and fuck me if she doesn't squirm against it.

Again, she tests her leg restraints, but it's futile. She's not going anywhere. In this position, her knees nearly touch her shoulders; she's deliciously spread open.

"What color are we, pets?" I ask.

"Green, Sir!" Evangeline mewls.

Brayden bobs his head, breathing heavily. "Green, Sir."

"Do you want to get fucked, kitten?" I whisper in her ear, though I keep my eyes locked on Brayden.

While she whimpers and nods furiously, her boyfriend visibly shudders. His cock throbs. With Brayden kneeling and Evangeline restrained by me between my legs, they're at the perfect level for each other. She will have to take whatever I tell Brayden to give her.

"There are condoms here." I jerk my chin to the bowl on the floor. Even if they're protected and clean, we always use condoms in the club.

Undeterred, Brayden swipes a foil packet, tears it open, and rolls the rubber down his length. He doesn't waste time as soon as I've given him permission. Closing the distance, he places his hands on Evangeline's waist and guides his cock inside her.

"Fuck," he grits out, setting a fast pace. Uninhibited and needy, he uses his girl's body for his pleasure. "So good, Lina." His mumbled nickname for Evangeline fits her. It's the first time I've heard it, but I can see it. She's definitely his Lina.

My kitten—for now.

Chin tucked to her chest, she cries out as Brayden hammers into her. Each and every thrust is like torture on my cock, seeing as I can fucking feel them.

"Rub her clit," I tell Brayden. He obeys and circles the pad of his thumb around and over Evangeline's swollen clit. She's wet beyond words, and it won't be long before both climax. "Pinch it."

"Please!" Evangeline starts to spasm, her body tensing in my hold. Through moans and wails, she begs to come. "Oh, God —*please*, Sir! I need to come so bad!" She thrashes—well, tries—and locks her right arm around my neck. "I need..." With a tilt of her head, she reaches up and kisses my throat.

My chest rumbles with a low groan; without thinking, I lean down and crash my mouth to hers. It's pure fucking need that surges through me, and I think it's the first time in years—if not ever —that I'm actually not a hundred percent in control of myself. I kiss her fiercely, pushing my tongue into her mouth, eager to taste her. *Mint. Cherry.* Soft lips moving with mine. I moan when she tangles her fingers in my hair.

Meanwhile, Brayden speeds up and cries out.

"Come," I rasp into the kiss. "Both of you. Come now."

Evangeline gasps and throws her head back to my shoulder, immediately sobbing out hoarse screams as she comes. My jaw ticks with tension; her body is just too fucking delectable to watch. At the same time, I can't look away. Her entire being convulses and trembles. When I look down to where she's joined with Brayden, I see how she's drenching him in arousal. *Jesus fucking Christ.* And Brayden's next. With clenched teeth and eyes squeezed shut, he delivers a few more jerky thrusts before he stills.

A few moments pass in silence, the outside world slowly making itself known again. The heavy beat of some metal band, more screams, a lot of begging, Mistress Judy's taunting chuckle, a sub pleading for a Master's whip, and low murmurs of spectators watching various scenes.

"You all right?" I caress Evangeline's cheek, and she nods sleepily in response. Glancing at Brayden, I ask the same question, and he breathes out a yes. "Good." Not that we're done here. "You can both get dressed, and then we'll get a drink together."

CHAPTER 3

Brayden stands first, and then I help Evangeline up. Studying her, it's easy to tell she's a bit detached from time and space, so I help her with her clothes, too. Like many other subs, she isn't wearing much. A purple latex skirt that ends right below her ass, a matching tube top that only covers her breasts, and black gladiator sandals.

Before I pull open the curtain, I put on my T-shirt again. "Here we go." I pick up Evangeline in my arms. I carry her much like I would a child, securing her on my hip; that way, I have one hand free.

"Are you okay, Lina?" Brayden asks softly as I usher them to the bar in the middle of the Cave. Max is there, working his ass off, but he gives me his attention quickly when he notices I'm here with subs. "Is she okay, Sir?"

"Oh yeah, she's fine." I smile and brush away some hair from Evangeline's face. "It's just endorphins."

Evangeline hums in contentment and buries her face in the crook of my neck. She's fucking adorable. "I'm more than okay, *mon ange."* She yawns. With a little squirming, she tightens her legs around my hips. "Mmm..."

"Aftercare kit?" Max asks.

I nod. "Couple blankets, too. And sodas." I raise a brow at Brayden, and he tells me Coke for both him and Evangeline. "Add two waters, as well. Thanks, man."

Max acknowledges the request. "One or two kits?"

"One's fine," I answer. "Can you tell one of the waitresses to have Stall Nine cleaned?"

"Will do, buddy."

Within a few seconds, he hands over two sodas, two bottles of water, and one aftercare kit on a tray. I grab the blankets, and Brayden offers to carry the tray. Then we set off toward the original club space where I know I can find some privacy in Nick's reserved booth.

We cross the big dance floor, which is now filled with foam blocks, and reach the wall that was once the only scening area at Switch. The platform is still there, taking up a generous amount of the floor for public demos, but the spot in the corner between said platform and the main bar has been roped off for Nick and his closest friends.

It's a large corner booth, seating six or seven people, with soft leather seats and a black table in the middle. Not only that, but it's the BDSM version of a fucking cabana. Since the ceiling is so high in the Club, he specially ordered the booth to have three posts draping fabric over it to make it more intimate. If someone wants seclusion, there's also the option to close the curtain of thick velvet that goes around the booth.

Nicholas always goes all out, and I have a feeling Kayla had something to do with this, because it's one of her favorite spots in the club.

I'm not surprised when I see that she and Nick are there now. He's seated with an arm casually draped at the back of the booth, and his Little is lying down with her head resting on Nick's thigh.

"Got room for three more?" I ask over the music. There's no hiding my smirk when I realize *why* Kayla has her head in Nick's lap. Neither is naked, but his slacks are unzipped and his leather belt is on the table.

He inclines his head. "Of course. Shut the drapes too, will you?"

"Sure thing." After telling Brayden to enter first, I fasten the rope again and follow inside, letting the heavy fabrics close us off from the world once more. The music is still loud, but the small confinement offers the privacy I was after. Sliding into the corner of the booth, I position Evangeline sideways on my lap. Brayden scoots in next and picks up his girlfriend's legs to rest them on his own lap. Then he makes a move to use both blankets on her, but I stop him.

"One's for you, sweet boy." The last thing I want is for him to think the aftercare is all about Evangeline.

He looks both curious and wary, and that's why I'm here. To offer comfort, to answer any questions he may have, and to make sure he's fine emotionally before he leaves.

"What happens now?" he whispers, very aware of Nick and Kayla a few feet away.

"Now we take it easy for a bit." I motion for him to start with his water; meanwhile, I bring a glass of Coke and ice to Evangeline's mouth. "Take a sip, kitten."

In the aftercare kit, there's also an energy bar and some chocolate, mainly preserved for heavier scenes. Evangeline hums and takes small sips through the straw, licking her lips every now and then.

I find it difficult to believe our playtime on its own caused her near-subspace like behavior. What's more likely is that she's craved dominance for so long, and now she finally got to experience it. It can be overwhelming.

"Good girl." Wanting to slowly but surely bring her back to the present, I tell her to hold her glass herself. "Are you cold?" I pull the blanket over her shoulders.

"S'all good." She peeks at me with a sleepy little smile.

I chuckle and place my arm behind Brayden on the back of the booth, making sure his blanket's drawn up, too. And since I'm seated in the corner, I have a clear view of Nick's side.

I smirk again. A shake of my head in amusement comes next. Someone's being punished by using Nicholas's cock as a pacifier. At first glance, she looks content to lie there and suckle his soft cock, but a second look shows the shame in her eyes.

"What did she do this time?" I ask. While Kayla's one of the sweetest girls I've ever met, she has the tendency to mouth off if she sees extreme pain. One time she told a Sadist who was tending to his sub after a harsh caning that he was a "bad, bad man." It didn't seem to matter to her that the sub was a masochist and totally blissed out.

Safe to say, Nick was livid at Kayla.

Nicholas smiles wryly and reaches for his tonic water on the table. "She asked if Dante—during a scene, mind you—would like a beating himself."

Oh, shit. I wince. Interrupting scenes is a big offense.

"Yeah, he didn't appreciate it." Nick strokes Kayla's hair, the two exchanging a look. "So, I decided to put your mouth to better use, didn't I, baby girl?" She nods sullenly and keeps suckling. When he slides a hand down to cup Kayla's ass under her dress, she flinches and her eyes well up. I assume Nick's put his leather belt to use, too.

"Is that really a punishment, Sir?" Brayden whispers and leans into me.

I grin and nod for Nicholas to answer that one.

"It is if I don't allow her to swallow," he says, amusement in his eyes.

Brayden's wide eyes meet mine, and I let out a laugh at his expression before elaborating.

"Kayla's bratty mouth is full of more than cock."

If possible, his eyes grow even wider. "So, he has...?"

"Come?" I raise a brow. "Oh, definitely." And I'm sure Nick will come again before he lets Kayla off the hook. Before then, she will simply keep what he's given her in her mouth.

"Oh." Brayden shudders and scoots even closer to me.

I withhold my smile and refocus on my subs. Evangeline's returning to us in her own time, and she's still taking small sips of her Coke. With her free hand, she idly plays with the hem of Brayden's T-shirt. "You should drink some of your soda, too," I murmur to him. He nods dutifully and grabs his glass. "Do you have any questions about the scene? Or maybe tonight in general?"

"I don't know." He gulps down some Coke and licks his lips. "I'm kind of blank." Yet, his expression shows curiosity; he takes in his surroundings with wonder in his eyes. "I feel like I have a million questions, but I can't think of any right now."

"That's okay," I answer. "What do you think about the club? Do you reckon you and Evangeline will return?"

I know they will, but I want him talking for a while so I can gauge his headspace. Some subs feel emotional and vulnerable to the point where they need a lot of reassurance after a scene—it can happen right after the scene or hours after; sometimes days later. They begin to question themselves, and if left alone, there's a possibility that they start looking down on themselves. After all, no one "normal" can really enjoy being tied up and beaten, right? The shit we grow up hearing, about what's appropriate and not, tends to leave some sort of mark.

"I like Switch." Brayden nods. "I want to come back. But I think we need to learn more..." He trails off, brows knitting together. "I suppose we'll look online."

I purse my lips.

"If only you had someone experienced to ask, huh?" My mouth quirks up.

He's confused for a second before realization hits. "Oh! I—I didn't think of that." His cheeks heat up; it's a sight I find too fucking appealing. "Can you help us? Sir." He swallows, nervousness flashing across his features.

"I can. And never hesitate to ask." I wait for his nod before I go on. "First of all, I recommend you speak to Kayla when she's done being a brat." I send Nicholas a grin that he returns. "Next week, she's going to start organizing munches—you know what those are?"

"Yes, Sir. A social gathering for people in the lifestyle that's held in a vanilla setting." That sounded like a recitation of something he's read online.

But it's correct. "Exactly. If you don't get the chance to speak with Kayla tonight, you can find her on the club's website." Which reminds me... "There's also a forum and a chat room on the site. Could be a good way to meet people who come here on a regular basis." Since this is their first time at Switch, I'm willing to bet they've only paid a single entrance fee instead of buying a membership. Once they get more involved, though, I'll make sure to recommend at least the month pass.

We fall silent for a while, and I spend some time checking Evangeline's wrists and ankles. Aside from the energy bar and the chocolate, the aftercare kit contains a packet with two aloe wipes, a small jar of soothing lotion, and some other stuff—like the little booklet of aftercare tips and two mild painkillers. But it doesn't look like she'll need any of it. I suppose I want them to see it, though. For comfort and reassurance, maybe.

"Um, Sir?"

"Yes?" I turn to Brayden and move my arm from the back of the booth to his shoulders. He hesitates to speak, so I rub my fingers over his neck, letting him know he has my attention. "Take your time, but remember that no question is stupid."

He looks down. Under the blankets, Evangeline reaches out to grasp his hand. The evidence of their solid bond comforts me. These two won't face this alone; they'll do it together.

Eventually, Brayden stops fidgeting and asks his question. "Have you played with male subs before?"

Oh. Not the question I expected, but all right. "Yeah, sure." I dip my chin. Is this bothering him? Perhaps playing with a man is new to him, but it wouldn't make him any less straight to do so. "Would you prefer to scene with a Mistress instead?" I do a mental count of the Dommes who are regulars at the club. Judy sometimes invites a man to play with her and her little Elysia. Mistress Meredith loves taking on newbies; she also works here as a DM. But...I'm not sure where that would leave Evangeline.

"No. No," he says softly, shaking his head while keeping his eyes downcast. "I liked it—I mean, I didn't mind when you—" He gulps and his cheeks turn a shade darker. I will my cock to stay down. Not that it's easy. With his vulnerability and Evangeline literally sitting on my cock...fuck. "When Lina and I discussed all this and talked about asking someone for help, it was kind of implied that we'd turn to a male Dom." He shrugs with one shoulder.

"What else have you discussed?" I'm curious. Something about this submissive couple pulls me in. There's a challenge, and I haven't had one in a long time.

While Brayden's shy and struggling to open up, his girlfriend is subtly tilting her head toward Nicholas and Kayla. She can hear them—hear that Kayla's got her Daddy hard again, that she's sucking him off for all she's worth—and Evangeline wants to see. I feel it in her body, too. The way she shifts, the way her breathing has picked up slightly, and the way she presses her thighs together. Perhaps there's a voyeur in my kitten.

"Focus right here, subbie," I murmur to her; then I nod for Brayden to answer.

"We've talked about limits and stuff," he replies and bites his lip. I can tell he's aware of my hand cupping his neck. "We don't like edgeplay, and—"

"Subjective definition," I comment with a little smirk.

There are gray areas within the entire lifestyle. What's considered edgeplay for one couple might be tame for another. Rules and limits apply to the couple who agrees on them, no one else.

Even more difficult to categorize are specific implements. Little Kayla would scream "Danger, danger!" and run for her life at the sight of a cane. Dante's sub would kneel down and propose.

"Can you tell me what edgeplay means for you?"

"Too much pain," Evangeline chimes in, and Brayden agrees. "We don't like that. We're not masochists."

"Ah." I nod. "But edgeplay and masochism are two different things. One describes something you might be, and one is a category of acts involving greater risks." I pause. "For example, have you heard of fire flogging?"

Brayden gulps; Evangeline shudders.

"*Fire?*" she squeaks out.

I smile and give her hair a tug, forcing her to face me. "Yes. Fire." The thought of using a fire flogger on these two makes my cock harden again. "Imagine me flogging you." Turning to Brayden, I tighten my hold on his neck and bring him a few inches closer. "Or you." His pupils dilate. "Imagine being surrounded by darkness. Tiny flickers of fire coming down on your skin so fast you hardly register the feeling." Facing Evangeline, I continue. My voice lowers. "Imagine seeing the ends whipping through the air, the fire creating shadows that dance over your naked body." She exhales shakily, eyes widening. "Imagine that as soon as the heat smatters your skin, the slight chill of the air follows right away."

She shivers, much like she would if I used my flogger with Kevlar lashes on her. Fire play might be edgeplay, but it has nothing to do with pain. Like any act, there *can* be pain—a lot of it. But *I* use it to heighten the sub's senses. He or she will be extremely aware of my every move.

"Have you ever swiped your finger through the flame of a candle?" I ask Brayden. He nods hesitantly and licks his lips. "It didn't hurt, did it?"

With fire play, the impact varies depending on the implement you use, but there's no talk of real heat when I play. No one's getting *burned*. It doesn't mark the skin.

"Well, when you put it that way..." Brayden chuckles, though the wariness and unease remain.

"You have nothing to worry about," I assure him. "It takes trust and a lot of work before I would even think about it. My reason for bringing this up is to make you see. There are acts you know too little about to push away and set as hard limits. The only thing I ask of you is to keep an open mind."

Outside our bubble of privacy, the music changes into something more ominous, and Cade begins to welcome tonight's participants to the game of Hide & Seek. It's Nicholas's signal to end Kayla's punishment since they're going to play, and it's my cue to get my ass back to work. Well, I should've returned a long time ago, but now I really need to. Max's shift is ending in the Cave, leaving me to take over.

I wait to speak while Nicholas and Kayla get up to leave; she looks like she wants to say something to Brayden and Evangeline—having probably heard me earlier about the munches—but Nick shakes his head no.

Once we're alone, I hand over my contact information to Brayden. I make it clear that they have to call me if they experience their moods dropping or anything like that. It's not optional. It's easier to release them, though, since they're two. They will be each other's support, and that certainly helps.

A few minutes later, we're all standing in the pretty empty lobby of the club and I'm helping Evangeline with her trench coat. Tonight's main event has just started, so this is hardly a time to leave. But these two do look like they could use some time alone to share their thoughts about our scene and to simply be together.

"Sir?" Evangeline's big, brown eyes peer up at me. "What about you? We haven't given you any pleasure."

My mouth quirks up and I touch her cheek. "On the contrary,

kitten." I may not have gotten a release, but I will. At some point. For our scene, I didn't care. I suppose I was too wrapped up in wanting them to get a proper introduction to my lifestyle. "I enjoyed myself very much." I give Brayden a glance because he's just as included. "If we scene together again, expect me to crank it up." I smirk as two sets of cheeks flame with heat.

"You—you're willing to do another scene with us?" Brayden asks hesitantly.

"Of course." There's no denying that. "But if we do, we will sit down and talk beforehand—about limits and so on." The thought of maybe having them in a bed where they're both restrained...or perhaps strapping Brayden to a sawhorse...or maybe fucking Evangeline into oblivion in a swing...*fuck.*

Too many possibilities.

CHAPTER 4

"You owe me, my man." Kevin walks up to the bar in the Cave and sits down on a stool. "I'm all sweaty and drenched in beer."

I chuckle as I prepare a Jack and Coke for one of the guests. Switch in all its entirety is dark and foggy, subs and Doms running around playing Hide & Seek, so it's not easy to see what I'm doing. "Tell your wife to go easy on you tonight. Or...maybe extra hard?" Kevin's wife is one scary Mistress. Sadist, hard-core, and unforgiving. "But you're right." I set the drink down in front of the Dom who ordered it and return to Kevin. "I do owe you. Thanks for covering for me."

One naked sub runs into the Cave, quickly finding a hiding spot in one of the hollow foam blocks, and Kevin and I watch in amusement as her Dom—or Daddy Dom, actually—is hot on her tail. John, I note, when I squint my eyes to see in the dark. That means the subbie's Gabriella, his Little. Also Nicholas and Kayla's friends.

The fog the DMs keep releasing makes it near impossible to recognize faces unless you're close enough.

"I'm surprised you're not playing tonight." Kevin turns in his seat to face me again. "There's always a line of subs around you, so it can't be that you haven't found anyone."

"Liam's daughter is sick. I'm covering for him," I answer, but my focus is on a sub who might be skirting the rules soon. Because she's standing near a scening stall, fiddling with the curtain. Considering. Looking around. And when she lifts the curtain to slip inside, I let out a sharp whistle to get her attention. Oh, I get it, all right. *Caught with her hand in the cookie jar.* Folding my arms over my chest, I stare her down as she dutifully walks over. "You know the stalls are off-limits."

"Yes, Sir. This one is sorry, Sir." She gulps, her eyes flicking around, presumably to see if her Dom is near. "May this one go now?"

Speaking about herself in the third person is a sure giveaway to the fact that she's probably a slave.

"What's your color, slave?"

"Oh, green." She nods furiously, and I give her body a once-over. She's only wearing a thong and her collar. Flushed cheeks, eyes wide with excitement, constricted nipples, and thighs pressed together for friction. *Fair enough.*

I snicker and quickly jot down two lines on a notepad. Next I tear off the top sheet and fold it together. "I want you to give this to your Master." I tuck it into her white glow-in-the-dark wristband. "Off you go."

"Yes, Sir. Thank you, Sir." She runs.

Kevin and I share a laugh and then someone orders a beer, so I get to it.

"What did you write on the note?" he asks.

"That she tried to hide in one of the stalls." I slide the beer over the bar to the patron, as always checking for wristbands, but this man isn't wearing any. "That's seven dollars, sir."

"What if I know the owner?" The man lifts his head and smirks.

I'll be damned. "Rio!" I laugh in disbelief and shake his hand. "When the hell did you get back?" This guy is always in some remote corner of the world. Doctors Without Borders—an honorable man for sure. "Damn, it's good to see ya, buddy."

"You too." He grins and takes a sip of his draft. "It's good to be home." When he pulls out his wallet, I wave it off. "Cheers, mate." A geographical cocktail, that's what he is—with looks to match. With a half-Brazilian mother, an Australian father, and one grandparent who is Irish, he's inherited a bit of everything. Black hair, alabaster skin, striking green eyes, and his own little accent. It's mostly American since he actually grew up in the States, but there are definitely a few quirks. "I just got back yesterday." He answers my previous question. "For good."

My eyebrows rise. "For good?"

As far as I knew, those two words didn't exist in his vocabulary. Unless it's saying that he'll be a vagabond for good. He used to work at a private hospital here. Then his fiancée died in a car accident five years ago, he left it all behind and joined Doctors Without Borders. I don't think he's mourning her, but there's been a definite change in his behavior. A bit more subdued. Quiet. Detached. Maybe he can return to kink now, too. He's been absent for too long.

He shrugs and eyes a laughing sub being chased by his Domme. "I'm getting old." His gaze travels back to mine. "My last stint made me miss home."

I scoff. "Old. You're what, thirty-five, thirty-six?"

He smirks and tips his glass at me. "Cheers—but it's forty in a couple months."

Eh. Still not fucking old. Christ, people are too obsessed with numbers these days. If my mother's not complaining I haven't settled down yet, it's my sister-in-law who wants cousins for my niece. It's like every time I see them, they remind me I'm thirty-four. As if I've forgotten.

"So, you're going to look for a job here, then?" I assume. Despite being a trust-fund baby, he's a hard worker.

"I'm in no rush, but...yeah, eventually." He gives the club an appreciative glance. "Nick's really done well with this place. I've missed it." He points to a few stalls. "Good idea—this expansion."

No arguments from me, and we keep talking a little about this and that; I also introduce him to Kevin, who started working here a right after Rio took off for...Cambodia, I think.

We fill Rio in on what's new, mainly Nicholas meeting Kayla, and I chuckle my way through the story of how they met. Nick told me earlier this evening that they're flying up to Oregon this Christmas to see Kayla's family, which will be the first time since his ex's sister's wedding when he came with one woman and left with Kayla.

"Sounds like drama to me." Rio shakes his head in amusement. "Is he around? I couldn't find him earlier."

"He's playing." I jerk my chin toward the Club.

At this point, several subs have been found by their Doms, and the laughter of those who are running mixes with the sound of owners staking claim. Some scream out in pleasure as they get fucked publicly, some beg for mercy, some plead for more.

CHAPTER 5

The day after, I make my way toward my big brother's house in Sausalito and park outside, seeing all the cars I expected to see. My younger brothers—Ted and Seth—are here, as are my parents. An unconventional family. Only our immediate family is invited because my siblings hate the others.

Walking up the path littered with Abby's outdoor toys, I steel myself for another dinner with the family. God knows I love them, but sometimes I don't know how I put up with their shit. I'm talking about my conservative brothers, not my parents. Mom and Dad are the opposite. Here at my brother's place, we get white picket fences, the suburban feel, and the all-American dream sprinkled with a few extra zeroes in the bank account. All my brothers are the same.

Greg followed in Dad's footsteps first and became a lawyer. Only, instead of having half a load of pro bono cases and working for the environment like our father, Greg prefers Corporate America.

When Dad retired early and left the firm his own father started, Greg changed things around. Seth joined a few years ago.

Cooper Law II is all about billable hours now, and I know it's only a matter of time before Ted makes partner too and turns that II into III. Three money-hungry Coopers owning a law firm.

I ring the doorbell, and my seven-year-old niece rips the door open, a gap-toothed grin on her face. "Uncle Mark!"

I chuckle and ruffle her hair. "Hey, pumpkin. Pretty sure you're not allowed to open the door by yourself." And as the words leave my mouth, I hear Tess calling Abby's name from inside. I grin and cock a brow, eager to get out of the cold, harsh winds. "Uh-oh. Sounds like Abby's in trouble." She's fucking cute, this one. Had Alexa and I been good together, maybe we would've been parents now, too.

"You come save me." She giggles and pulls me into the hallway. "My new friend also saves me from Mommy lots and lots." Ah, that means she's got a new babysitter. Again. Greg rarely approves of the people watching Abby after school, so he fires them. It's up to Tess to find a new sitter. Ideally for Greg, Tess would stay home with Abby, but she doesn't want to give up her job. "She's here for dinner, 'cause Daddy wans'ta talk to her a bit more."

"I see." My brother—much like me, I suppose—needs to be in total control. Only, he's obnoxious about it. Even Tess rolls her eyes when he gets going, both affectionate and annoyed. She gets him, loves him, which makes Greg a lucky bastard. Removing my jacket and shoes, I follow Abby toward the noise; as always, there's a choice to make. In the kitchen I will find my mother, Tess, and probably Ted's fiancée. In the living room I will find Dad, Greg, Ted, and Seth. It's a no-brainer. "Kitchen, pumpkin."

"I know," she replies frankly. "You gotta meet my new friend. Her name is *not* easy to say."

I smile down at the little whirlwind and roll up the sleeves of my gray button-down.

We reach the kitchen, and it's a familiar sight. Mom and Tess by the stove, and Ted's fiancée—Jessica—pulling something from the fridge.

The scents permeating the air are enough to make any man's stomach growl.

"Darling!" Mom's the first one to spot me, and she gives me a bright smile as she walks over to me, her reddish-brown curls bouncing. While my brothers have inherited her Irish features, I look just like my dad. Darker hair, blue eyes, and a skin tone that doesn't turn lobster red in the sun. Dutifully, I dip down so she can peck my cheek; then I return with a kiss to her forehead. "You're almost late, I'll have you know."

I wink. "Emphasis on almost."

"Abby, what have I told you about opening the door without asking us first?" Tess is busy fussing over my niece, but she gives me a quick smile in greeting.

Just as I'm about to ask what's for dinner, the fridge door closes, and I see that it's sure as hell not my brother's fiancée standing there. *What in the...?* Not another blonde with the perfect Stepford appearance. No, this one's a petite, curvy brunette. One I distinctly remember flogging last night. One I restrained while her boyfriend fucked her.

My eyes grow wide, and I note that hers don't. She doesn't look shocked one goddamn bit. There's guilt instead. Written all over her too-fucking-beautiful face. Which can only mean she somehow knew.

Knew what?

Knew I was coming. That I'm me. That the favorite uncle Abby always raves about is *me*.

"Oh, that's right," Tess mutters with an apologetic smile. "You two have met." My eyebrows rise. Next she cups Mom's elbow and says, "Let's leave Mark and Evangeline for a moment. They need to catch up."

"Evangel..." Mom trails off, confused. "You know each other?" Her question goes unanswered as she disappears from the kitchen with Tess and Abby.

I tense up, despising being left in the dark, and shoot Evangeline a stare that's hard enough to make her fidget and shrink. No longer wearing fetish clothes in latex, but dressed modestly in black pants and a form-fitting soft pink cardigan. Submissive and lovely as ever. Apparently also dishonest. Hard limit of mine.

"Speak, Evangeline," I grit out quietly.

Her eyes well up rapidly. "I'm *so* sorry." Voice almost breaking, she takes a breath and bites down on her quivering lip. "I really am, Sir—um, Mark." My name on her lips sounds weird but not unwelcome. "I wish I, or we, had an excuse, but there isn't one. I was gonna tell you last night, but I chickened out."

I raise a brow, hands on my hips. "You were going to tell me what, exactly?" Anger continues to boil up inside me.

"That I knew who you were before..." *Before last night, Sir. Before you flogged me. Before you restrained my legs and spread them for Brayden's cock.*

My jaw ticks and I fight the urge to growl like some savage animal. The sounds of Abby's laughter and family members talking about whatever filters through, reminding me that this isn't the time or place for...*for what?* Shouting at Evangeline for omitting the truth? For taking her over my knees and turning her ass red? For having a sub at my brother's house?

All of the above.

"Tess," I say flatly, nodding once to myself, and look down for a moment. Evangeline must've heard of me through Tess. I've never made my lifestyle a secret because I have no reason to hide it.

My brothers find it degrading, whereas my parents find it fascinating. Tess stands close to them on that matter.

"Yeah. Tess, um, she recommended the club." Evangeline sounds closer now, so I look up and there she is. Right in front of me, looking vulnerable, remorseful, and guilt-ridden. "I accidentally let it slip one day that my boyfriend and I were looking for, ah..." A blush spreads over her cheeks. "Something different, something else—that's more for us." I assume Tess and Evangeline know each other from before a simple babysitting gig, then. Though, at first glance, I have to wonder what they could possibly have in common. "We met at our book club." Book club. Got it. One might wonder how they go from discussing books to BDSM, though. But what the hell do I know? "And she told me about you—that you work at Switch, and that you're a Dom."

I find that hard to believe. "If you're telling me Tess sent you and Brayden to me, I'm not buying it." Tess can be casual and free-spirited, but not to the point where she'd send an acquaintance or whatever to be topped by her brother-in-law.

"Oh! No. No, no." She shakes her head. "Tess just recommended the club. She said that since you work there, it had to be good. A trustworthy place. So, Brayden and I went last night—as you know," she chuckles nervously and wrings her hands awkwardly. "But, I mean, we didn't seek you out." I can tell that my even thinking that would cause Evangeline stress. There's a tremor of need in her voice. Need to be believed. "After we filled out the form—the one for first-timers?"

I nod in acknowledgment.

"Yeah, so, after that, we looked around for a bit and..." A small shrug and a scrunch of her nose. *Cute.* "We decided to try the St. Andrew's Cross." And look how that turned out. "That DM, Master Hill?" *Simon.* "He interrupted—paused the scene to get someone who could guide us through it properly." That someone turned out to be me. "When he came back, he mentioned a few things about what we were doing wrong, and then he said, 'Master Cooper will assist you. You'll refer to him as Sir.' Then he checked my bindings and left right before you entered." She swallows, her words coming slower, as if the urgency has left her. "There was barely any time for me to react." Her eyes turn beseeching, tugging at me uncomfortably. "He said Cooper—Tess's last name, *your* last name—and I nearly freaked."

Averting my gaze, brows knitting together, I do recall the almost panicked look in Evangeline's eyes when I entered their stall.

"You came in right after," she adds quietly. "I didn't know what to do, and...to be honest, I was selfish." Her shoulders slump. In defeat, perhaps. "I wanted this so badly—Brayden did, too."

Well, I appreciate her honesty. I just wish it'd come sooner. A *lot* sooner. With an absent nod from me, I acknowledge what she's said, and I don't really know what to say in return. Again, this isn't the time or place. Plus, we all fuck up at times, right? The anger drains out of me, though I still detest dishonesty.

One glance at the timer above the stove tells me we only have another three minutes and thirty-four seconds before dinner is ready.

"I'm so, so sorry, Mark," she whispers. "What you gave us exceeded our wildest dreams, and then I just chickened out. I should've told you. I'm sorry—"

"Enough, Evangeline," I say with a tired chuckle. "I believe you." That's the truth. And while I have a question or ten, I don't want to ask them at my brother's house. "You can stop apologizing now." I reach out and squeeze her shoulder gently, lingering. The relief rolls off her, causing the wryness in my smile to vanish. More genuine. "You little troublemaker."

Her dark eyes brighten. "I want you to know that Brayden and I are willing to take your punishment. Anything to make you forgive us."

Oh, is that a fact? That amuses me for sure. It also intrigues me, lures me in, and turns my thoughts into something far less than proper.

I'm pretty fucking creative.

"You're very naïve, kitten—you know that?" I murmur and pull her close to my body. Her breathing hitches, eyes widening in wonder and excitement. A pinch of fear, too. Perfect. "So eager to throw yourself into the lion's den. Some would call that stupid."

She gulps.

I lean down and slide my nose along her jaw. "Do you even have the slightest idea how I punish my subs?" I whisper in her ear.

My fingers curl around her wrists, tightening swiftly. *Like cuffs.* Some think that just because I'm a boisterous and carefree bartender, I'm one of the nicer Doms. Big mistake. "Remember when we talked about edgeplay last night?" Like she'd ever forget. A shallow breath, a quick nod—yeah, she remembers. "That's my game, kitten." Fire play, erotic asphyxiation…intense scenes that last for days, humiliation, pushing limits fearlessly. "It's what I do. But you don't like pain, do you?" Now I'm taunting her.

"I—" She's all breathless. I fucking love it. "I d-don't know enough about it."

Good girl. She was listening to what I said last night. With her reply, she's also saying that she's open to try.

"So, you'd let me punish you?" Gripping her hips forcefully, I push my hardening cock into her soft stomach. The timer says I have one minute left. That's enough to envision two willing bodies at my mercy—much like I dreamed about last night. Fuck, I woke up panting this morning, sweaty and tangled in my sheets.

"Yes, Sir," she whimpers.

She'll discover that I have a low tolerance for disobedience. My rewards for good behavior are generous; I never hesitate to spoil a sub. But my punishments are as generous in the opposite direction.

I swallow a groan and nip at her jaw. The urge to kiss her is goddamn insane, but I don't have the rules yet. I don't know what's okay for me to do. If I'm going to scene with these two again, I need to find out as much as I can—in order to maximize the pleasure.

Thirty-four seconds.

When Evangeline tilts her head toward my mouth, I straighten a couple inches and stare down at her in question.

"It's okay—you're on our list," she blurts out. Fidgeting, fierce blushing, and stuttering follow. "All right, not so much a l-list as it's a Post-it note with y-your name on it, but…" A little squeak ends it all, and she buries her face in her hands.

Master Cooper on a Post-it, huh?

My shoulders begin to shake with silent laughter and I hug her to me, finding this young girl too fucking endearing for words. *A damn Post-it.* I snort a laugh.

"Adorable," I murmur, giving in to chuckles. *Eleven seconds.* I sigh and drop a kiss on the top of her head. "You will have to tell me more about this, ah, list of yours later." I tilt her chin up and kiss her nose, too, enjoying the blush still gracing her cheeks. "Our time is up for now. Did Tess warn you about Greg?"

She responds to my abrupt question with a swift nod. "Yes, Sir." The timer beeps, so I walk over to shut it off while Evangeline continues. "Tess told me he's pretty strict."

"Understatement." I smile wryly and hear Tess announcing from the living room that dinner's ready. Which means everyone will move into the dining room now. "Whatever you do, don't let him find out about your interest in BDSM." My brother would fire her—simple as that. Now, I don't know how important a babysitting job is to Evangeline, but I figure it's best to lay it out there.

"Yeah, Tess told me that, too." She grimaces a little. "Is he really that bad, though? I mean, I've only watched Abby for a few weeks, so I can't say I've run into Greg a lot, but still...he hasn't seemed that straitlaced. And Tess is so different."

"That's probably why you were invited here today," I answer. "If Greg doesn't know you very well yet, prepare to be questioned." My brother trusts Tess's judgment enough for her to hire babysitters, tutors, and nannies, but he will still have the chance to veto. "Paint yourself as a churchgoer and he'll love you."

Being around my brothers sometimes makes me want to shock them out of their Armani suits. They pull off polite conversation about current events, the best school districts, and sports flawlessly, and...all I can think about is walking over to them and telling them what I did last night while they enjoyed a bottle of wine and a foreign film.

Evangeline giggles. "Actually, aside from being a submissive, I can't say I have anything inappropriate to dish out."

Good. That means dinner will probably be enlightening for me, too—in a way that I'll learn things about her that are true, as opposed to stories to appease Greg.

As it turns out, countless questions are thrown Evangeline's way throughout dinner. Had it not been for Tess and my parents occasionally telling Greg to slow down, I would've stepped in. Alas, Evangeline has found support in my family, and she shoulders the questions like a champ.

Having her age confirmed is the one thing that shocks me a little; I find out she's only twenty-three. I had expected her to be in her early twenties, but I somehow leaned more toward twenty-five for some reason. She's so young. Other than that, I'm only intrigued by what she tells us. She carries herself well; she's mature for her age, and my image of her becomes clearer as the dinner goes on.

Her love for children is evident, and I watch how her eyes light up at the mention of working with kids. Just this past spring, she graduated with a degree in Early Childhood Education. Before her four years here, she also studied art in Paris for two years, and I'm pretty sure there's more to that story. Her name sounds French, and I recall hearing her and Brayden speak French at the club.

Anyway, since it's not the easiest to find a job in this day and age, especially for someone fresh out of college, she takes on smaller assignments here and there. Tutoring, babysitting, a few temp gigs, and so on.

Once we're done eating, I manage to catch Tess alone for a minute, and I'm thankful she doesn't know just how well I already know Evangeline—only that we met briefly at the club last night.

Briefly. Sure, we'll go with that.

Mom corners me in the kitchen, too, and asks me the question that no one answered when she was ushered out of here earlier. But I only give her a smirk and shake my head.

"Oh, tell me." She playfully slaps me on my bicep. "From—"

she lowers her voice "—from Switch? Is that how you know Evangeline? Is she a sub?"

I can't help but chuckle. "Don't ask questions you don't want answers to, Mom. Let it go." My parents may be very...different...in their viewpoints on relationships and marriage, but nobody wants to hear about their child's bedroom activities, so to speak. "Now, how about that dessert, huh?" I point to the two pies on the counter.

"Nice try at changing the topic." She huffs. "Too bad it's not going to work. Evangeline has a boyfriend, so color me intrigued. She can't be *your* sub...can she?"

Fuck that—I'm not falling into her trap. Being married to Dad doesn't stop Mom from having fun with Ben and Hank. And Dad with Annie and Marie. So, I merely raise a brow and ask, "Are you saying I can't know a woman without sleeping with her?"

She scrunches her nose. "Sounds good in theory." Then a shrug. "Just didn't go so well for us."

"You don't say." I snort in amusement, too aware of how that never worked out for Mom and Dad. Their attractions caused for an interesting upbringing, that's for sure.

Three couples with nothing but friendship between them, then things changed after a few years. I'm sure alcohol was involved when it was time to confess desires, after which they were all suddenly living together in a huge house outside San Francisco. It's how I grew up—three families living as one. My brothers and I were disciplined by any adult, not only our parents. Same went for Ben and Annie's daughters, as well as Hank and Marie's son.

Biologically, I have three brothers, but my mother would say we're seven siblings altogether.

I agree with her.

Greg, the oldest kid of all of us, started to resent Mom and Dad's lifestyle when a high school girlfriend dumped him because of it. And I understand him to an extent; we did put up with a lot of shit in school. Even so, I've stood my ground from day one, and so have the rest of us—well, except for Greg, Ted, and Seth. Nowadays they only drive out to our parents' for Thanksgiving, which is coming up soon. Otherwise they'll stick to our biological family.

My younger brothers and Jessica have already left when Evangeline announces that it's time for her to go home, and I follow her lead. It'll give me the chance to talk to her about our next scene that I'm too fucking eager to plan.

After having watched her all night, it's all I can do not to bend her over Greg and Tess's couch and fuck her into next week.

"Thank you for joining us tonight, Evangeline," Greg says politely while I'm putting on my shoes. "Perhaps you'd like to join us next week, too? You could bring that boyfriend of yours."

Racking my brain, I try to remember the few things Evangeline mentioned about Brayden, and I come up empty, almost. I've found out he's a software engineer, and that he was born and raised here in San Francisco like the rest of us.

"Honey," Tess says with an eye-roll, "I think that's enough with the questioning. Evangeline is perfectly able to take care of Abby— no need to bring in Brayden, too."

"Nonsense." Greg waves her off dismissively. "I'm simply being polite. I'd like to meet Evangeline's boyfriend." Well, speaking as if Evangeline isn't even here can't really be considered as polite, can it? "And you can't possibly blame me for wanting only respectable people around our daughter."

"You're always so fucking pleasant," I say dryly and slip on my jacket. Since Abby has gone to bed already, I don't bother with the language filter. "Respectable people." I scoff and shake my head. "God help him if he's ever received a speeding ticket."

"That's enough, little brother," Greg responds with a sneer.

I flip him off.

"Boys," Mom warns.

Evangeline looks torn, and I can't blame her. She won't like Greg—I know that—but she already feels for Tess and Abby.

"We should get going," Dad says and gives Tess a kiss on her cheek. "If you wouldn't mind, perhaps you could work on removing the stick up my son's ass." That earns him a glare from Greg.

After thanking them for dinner once more and saying a few more goodbyes, we trickle out from my brother's house, though not before he makes Evangeline promise to ask Brayden about next Sunday. But by the time my parents have driven off, I have a solution—something that will keep my two subs from coming here next week. It will keep me from it, too, which is a big, fat bonus.

"Next weekend..." I pause by Evangeline's car farther down the street as she unlocks it. "If you don't have plans already, I'd like to scene with you and Brayden."

She looks up surprised and leans back against the car door. "All weekend?"

Stepping closer, I nod slowly and tug on one end of her knitted scarf. "If you think you can handle it, yes." I'm supposed to work Saturday, and I have no qualms about letting Liam cover for me. "It would be at my place—not at Switch."

Since my divorce, I haven't scened outside the club, and I'm itching to create memories in my new condo. Cade, a friend from the club, designs fetish furniture, and I blew a substantial amount of money on that after the separation.

"What do you say, kitten? You'd arrive on Friday night and leave on Sunday after dinner."

She nibbles on her lip. "You'll punish us for that long?"

"Oh, sweetheart." I laugh. "No, definitely not." I'll do that on Saturday after devoting Friday to making them comfortable around me. "You haven't been *that* bad of a girl." I wink.

Even in the darkness, her blush is visible. "Okay. I want that. I mean, I'll talk to Brayden, but..." She nods. "Okay."

I grin, then let it fade as my eyes flick between hers and her mouth. At her shy smile and subtle nod, I dip down and kiss her.

CHAPTER 6

Evangeline calls me the next day to confirm our weekend plans, and I try to tamp down at least a little of my excitement, because it seems I'm served with an extra thrill around her and Brayden. Excitement is good; attachment is not. For the past several months, I've enjoyed my newfound freedom, and I'm not sure I'm ready to seek out commitment. Or accept it even if it smacks me upside the head.

Except, as the week continues, a niggling thought at the back of my mind gets louder.

On Wednesday, it's S/M Night at Switch, and that thought in my head gets a voice in the form of Kayla Brandon. She and Nicholas are only here because there's a demonstration in the Cave, and Nick always supervises when there's a higher-risk demo.

"You could get married and have a bunch of babies together!" Kayla exclaims happily. I give her a look and slide over her Sprite with crushed ice and lime. "Two men—" she nods "—that could make an awful lot of babies."

"A woman can still only get through one pregnancy at a time, hon." Not to mention that I'm not ready for a new relationship. Or babies. I think. No, I'm not. No.

"Of course." She pouts and smooths out the frilly hem of her light purple baby-doll dress. "Now I feel dumb."

Not dumb. She's just excited at the prospect of gaining more friends.

"You're turning out to be our little matchmaker here at Switch." I grin and lean my elbows on the bar top. "Nicholas told me that you helped a sub flirt with Max."

She giggles. "Well, Natalie is like super shy, and Mr. Giles is always busy behind the bar. But he sure noticed her!" Kayla looks nothing but triumphant at her success. "My next goal is to help Chelsea—she's a friend of mine from New York." She nods and purses her lips. "She's moving here after Christmas."

Hopefully, that will keep Nick's little one busy, then.

"Speaking of Christmas..." I raise a brow, amused.

And Kayla scowls. "I don't wanna talk about it." She does so anyway. "I don't get why we have to fly up there. I almost never see my family—maybe once or twice a year..." She huffs a breath. "But Daddy says it's the right thing to do. Plus—" a mischievous smile creeps into place "—if I'm good, maybe he'll give me a kitten for Christmas."

I know he will. She's been pleading for a pet since they moved into their new house, and Nicholas loves spoiling her. She will definitely like her Christmas present.

The only kitten *I* want would be a curvy little brunette whose name my niece can't quite pronounce.

"Well, right now you can be a good girl and bring your Daddy his drink." I prepare Nick's tonic water and slide it over the bar. "Off you go now."

"Yes, Sir," she says in a singsong voice and hops off the stool. "Thank you for the Sprite."

I smile. "Any time, hon."

Back to work, I'm left with thoughts about commitment and settling down.

Then on Friday morning, I've managed to push down all those thoughts. Or rather, I've replaced them with a compromise. I may not be ready for anything resembling romance, but a D/s arrangement sounds fucking appealing. Even more so if it's with *two* subs. It would certainly provide me with a challenge, and I've missed that.

If it's something Evangeline and Brayden are interested in, I'm ready to negotiate terms.

As I'm about to leave my car for a lunch meeting at a wharfside restaurant, my phone starts ringing, and I see that it's Evangeline calling.

"What's up, kitten?" I answer the phone, placing it between my shoulder and cheek, then exit the car. "You two better not cancel on me tonight."

"Fat chance!" she laughs. "Nope, not happening." Good. I smile to myself and lock the car. "But I wonder if you have a free minute?"

Looking up, I spot my accountant as she steps into the restaurant. Free minute. I'll be damned if I don't make a free minute. Important. "Sure thing. Is something wrong?" I fiddle with my keys and walk slowly toward the restaurant, suppressing a shudder at a particularly punishing gust of wind.

"Not wrong, per se." She hesitates. "Just something about Brayden I wanted to mention."

"All right? I'm listening."

"You said when we talked on Monday that you plan to bring up our limits—stuff like that. And..." She blows out a breath. "Okay, the thing is, I can't really go into detail, because it would betray his trust in me, and he doesn't want me to say anything. So, all I'm going to ask is that you go easy on him when it comes to his sexuality."

My eyebrows rise; meanwhile, I look down at the ground, thinking. "His sexuality," I state.

"Yes. It has to do with his childhood, and—I really can't say any more on that—"

"Evangeline." I interrupt her, worried and tense. "If something happened to Brayden, someone who's qualified to help needs to know."

I'm not that person, as much as I want to be. There are people who've suffered everything from emotional abuse to brutal rape and then turn to BDSM, using it as either therapy or, much worse, a way to punish themselves.

"Oh! It's nothing like that. Fuck. Um." She's hesitating again. "Let's just say...he's struggling to come to terms...? There's no trauma, just a stupid-ass father."

I exhale heavily, both relieved he isn't a victim of abuse and...a little aggravated because Evangeline's speaking in riddles. But appreciation makes itself known; she's protective of her boyfriend, and that's admirable.

Though, if I were to venture a guess—given the earlier mention of his sexuality—I'd say Brayden grew up hearing his father's no doubt conservative thoughts on masculinity—possibly even homosexuality and bisexuality. It makes sense, especially if Brayden, a sub, wants a Dom who is a man.

"I don't even know if I'm making any sense," she says softly. "But if you could give him some time..."

I cut her off again, though gentler this time. "You do make sense. And I promise I'll take all of this into consideration."

"Thank you so much." Her relief is evident. "So, we'll see you tonight? Seven o'clock?"

"Sharp."

"Sharp," she echoes with a smile in her voice. "Bye."

"See you soon." I end the call.

Making my way inside the restaurant, I greet my accountant and Brent, my gym manager, the two people whom I trust with my company. It's a small chain of gyms around the city, and it affords me the luxury of not needing to worry about my bank statements or whether to buy a cheap brand of cereal or the one I like. I won't say the company runs itself, but it does run without me. The only thing I need to do is meet up with Tara and Brent once a month to make sure it's all good.

With that steady paycheck, I can work as much or as little at Switch as I want, and it's a job I enjoy. That's why I accepted the responsibility when Nicholas needed someone to be in charge of the bartenders. It also provides free membership—a definite perk.

I'm no chef, so by the time our evening is about to begin, the takeout I've ordered arrives.

After paying the delivery guy, I spread out the containers on the kitchen table, hoping Evangeline and Brayden like Spanish food. Beers and sodas follow.

Being hungry as fuck, I grab one of the tapas servings and eat as I absentmindedly walk through my condo to adjust the lighting. Dimmed low is good for tonight. It'll create a comfortable atmosphere in my already homey place. A three-bedroom apartment. Old wooden floors, walls in warm colors, furniture made of sturdy, dark wood. It's a bachelor pad with a touch of "my mother interfered."

I got lucky with this place. A friend of my dad's wanted to get out of the city, so I headed straight to the bank to sign papers. 'Cause even as financially independent as I am, you'd have to be a millionaire to own a condo with a rooftop terrace.

When the doorbell rings again, it's seven PM on the dot, and I nod to myself, pleased, and walk straight for the hallway to get the door.

I'm greeted with the sight of two unbelievably attractive people on their knees. Eyes downcast. *Motherfucking hell.* We didn't discuss this—for them to greet me this way. I haven't told them what to wear, either, which means...they're only out to please me. *Fuck me.* Warmth courses through my body as I let my eyes drink them in.

The black lingerie set, stockings included, that Evangeline's wearing makes my mouth water. The push-up bra and panties, both in the same see-through material, are lined with black fur, matching the pointy kitty ears on her head. *My little kitten.*

The only thing missing, I note as I step out into the hall, is a tail.

I'm more than happy to provide one for her. It shouldn't be too difficult to find a butt plug with fur for a tail similar to the kind lining her lingerie.

A voice in the back of my head whispers that she's missing another item, too: a kitty collar. One that says "Master Cooper's kitten," I decide right then and there.

I'm just as satisfied with what I see when I glance over at Brayden. He's only in black silk boxers—not as elaborate an outfit as Evangeline's, yet equally sexy.

Before I walk back into my condo, I pick up two discarded jackets, pairs of jeans, shoes, and one overnight bag. All of it is dropped on the floor inside the door; focusing on my two subs is more important. *Understatement.*

Squatting down to their level, I inspect them for traces of arousal, and I'm happy to find several. Brayden is semi-hard beneath the silk, and his chest heaves with shallow breaths. A few locks of dark hair have fallen down his forehead, so I can't see his eyes, but that's all right. For now. And Evangeline...oh, she's too horny for words. My mouth quirks up. I see how her nipples strain against the sheer fabric, how goose bumps appear on her skin, and how a pink flush spreads over her chest and cheeks.

"Very beautiful." I reach out to cup her left blushy cheek. Knowing that my neighbor could walk out in the hall at any moment only makes things hotter. "So..." My free hand goes to

Brayden's jaw, and I brush my thumb over the slight stubble. "If Evangeline is my kitten, does that make you my puppy?"

He shudders, and when I look down, I see the bulge growing slightly in his boxers.

This is a perfect opportunity to learn what they like, because I don't think they're into the same things. They're two individuals, even if they come as a pair.

"You may stand," I say and stand up myself. Unlike their incredibly appealing getups, I'm in black leathers and a T-shirt. Bare feet. Nothing special. But what I have planned is. And I'm ready to get started. So, I usher them both inside, close the door behind me, and then position myself in front of them. "First of all, thank you for this." I kiss Evangeline on the forehead and gather Brayden close, draping an arm around his shoulders. "I'm definitely pleased." In fact, I might make these outfits their standard ones when we play in public. *When.* Not if. "Secondly, I'm Mark until I say so. Not Sir. Understood?"

They nod. I crack a grin.

"I won't punish you if you do call me that, but it's not necessary. We're just going to have dinner now—get to know each other a little better. I want you comfortable, and I want you to feel that you can talk about anything without asking. All right?"

"Okay." Evangeline smiles. Brayden nods, and I detect a hint of nervousness, more now than before. I bet this is what Evangeline was talking about earlier. Opening up might be more difficult for him than simply following an order to do something.

We'll work on that.

"Good. I don't cook well, so I ordered in a bunch of stuff." I extend an arm, motioning them to the kitchen. "We'll do the grand tour thing later, 'cause I'm fucking starving."

No lie.

"Oh, I love your kitchen," Evangeline gushes. "My kind of place—old building with character. And this..." She reverently runs a hand over the solid wood kitchen island. Her finger ghosts over the surface, the age-old traces of knives cutting in, and the few darker rings left behind from damp glasses. I wonder if she's forgotten her state of dress...or undress, as it is. Or maybe she's simply comfortable that way. "Not easy to hose down—" she flashes a grin "—but it gives..."

I chuckle silently and swipe a beer from the table. "Character?"

"Right." She giggles and ducks her head. "Sorry—I have a thing for furniture that's not mass-produced and brand new. I love some modern accents." She points to my fridge and freezer, all in stainless steel. "It blends in, but there are limits." The image of Evangeline keeps getting clearer and clearer. Little bits of information give greater peeks into her mind. "I'll shut up now."

"Don't," I reply and pull out her chair. "Now I know never to take you to IKEA." I wink at her and she sits down, smiling happily. "You too, Brayden—sit down." The round table seats four, and after some deliberation, I pick the seat next to Evangeline. I don't want to crowd Brayden, though I hope he won't think I'll ask him any fewer questions. I'll just...give him a slightly slower beginning. A bit more distance. "Dig in, guys. There should be something you like." For myself, I grab a container with paella, glad it's still hot.

Throughout dinner, I study Brayden and notice several things. For one, Evangeline is his world. If she speaks, he listens. And I find that I do the same, only I can still keep an eye on my surroundings. Not that Brayden isn't aware of my presence, because he sure as fuck is, but it's clear that he could live to make her happy and die to make sure she stays that way.

Another thing I notice is that he's on guard. His walls are up, and if I asked him something now—something off-limits—he would either bolt or...or...yeah, that's it: Evangeline would swoop in. I'm willing to bet he banks on her saving him. Perhaps she has in the past.

I wouldn't call Evangeline's protectiveness anything negative— far from it. She's not enabling him. But...it might be time for him to let someone else in, too. And if he grows to trust more and more people, it could eventually help him to relax fully.

All in due time.

"You know what I realized?" I ask Evangeline and grab a Styrofoam box with grilled fish. "I don't know your last name." I've learned her occupation, her hobbies, her age, and more about who she is. "I don't know yours, either." I face Brayden. I've learned a lot less from him. I know he works with computers—software and animation—I know he's twenty-six years old, and that he likes metal and punk.

"Oh. My name's Lacroix," Evangeline says.

"Doesn't get much more French than that, does it?" I grin. I've already guessed there's something French in her, so I'm not surprised.

"My father is French." She smiles. "But he was born here."

"Are you fluent?" I'm not good at languages. In school, I was all about sports, math, and, my favorite subject: free period.

"Somewhat." Her smile turns modest. "Brayden says I sometimes mutter to myself in French—and, like, I use terms of endearment, curses... Brayden's my angel—*mon ange*. Oh, and—" she laughs "—I tried to teach him a few things, but he stopped after finding a pet name for me."

"Which is?" I glance between the two, ignoring the slight twinge of envy.

In a perfect world, I'd have what they have. Instead, I got an Alexa.

Evangeline blushes. "*Ma belle.*"

I can guess that one. "Very fitting." I smile at Brayden. "No French last name for you?"

He fidgets in his seat a little and clears his throat, looking away. "No. Um, Zeagler. Brayden Zeagler."

Unusual. And... I frown. *Oddly familiar.* I'm pretty sure I've heard that name before, though I can't pinpoint it.

"Brayden's father ran for mayor a couple years ago," Evangeline says with a tight-lipped smile. And that's all I needed. Zeagler. Clark Zeagler. He didn't win. He's not the mayor—much to my brothers' disappointment—but he's an influential man. He's also a strict Catholic, the most conservative of Republicans, and can wrap up a "fuck you" and an "I hate gays" in five-dollar words and a political smile.

Greg donated generously to his campaign.

"My condolences," I mutter, tipping my beer bottle at him. With just his name, it's easier to understand him. Not only is Brayden a submissive, but I'm fairly positive he's bisexual, too. Couldn't have been easy to grow up with his dad.

"*Je te l'avais bien dit, mon ange*—I said he'd understand." Evangeline gives Brayden a teasing little smirk. "You should tell him more—"

"Lina." Brayden's voice is soft and his gaze isn't harder, yet the warning's clear. He's not ready.

"It's okay." I nod to him. "I won't pressure you." *Yet.* Limits are meant to be pushed, though I know when to be patient. "In fact, let's drop this subject and move on." While Brayden looks relieved, Evangeline appears remorseful for pushing her boyfriend. I want none of that right now. "If you're finished eating, I think we should take this into the living room." Ironically, *I'm* not done eating, so I shovel some grilled fish into my mouth and then chase it down with my beer.

As much as I want to tell them to just march into my bedroom and wait for my orders, it's too soon.

CHAPTER 7

I find out that the right way to mellow out Brayden is to let Evangeline take the lead. The setting might appear romantic— lit candles, music on in the background, and wine on the table—but the mood is light thanks to Evangeline's babysitting stories. Not the sexiest topic, though it certainly helps Brayden lower his guard.

We're seated on my big couch, and I even have my kitten on my lap. Brayden's next to me, and much like we did after our scene at Switch, he has Evangeline's legs in his own lap.

"I remember you came home one day and told me about that couple who wanted more from you." Brayden grins cheekily at her. "You were so flustered."

"I was shocked!" she argues, giggling. "They were like sixty years old." She makes a face.

I chuckle and aimlessly caress her thigh. Hard not to. "And they had young kids you babysat?"

"Well—foster kids." She smiles. "The couple was really sweet; they'd always wanted kids of their own, but they never could. So, they helped out with children who were waiting for permanent families."

I raise a brow. "And they came on to you?" Oh yeah, I'm amused as fuck.

"Yes." She blushes so hard that she covers her face with her hands. "I was so embarrassed—you have no idea!" Next she ducks her head and buries it in the crook of my neck. I chuckle and give her upper thigh a squeeze. "I was about to leave one night when they told me to wait." Her voice is partly muffled by my skin. "At first I thought they were gonna talk about next time I babysat. But instead they told me I was beautiful—then they asked if I ever wanted to stop by when the kids weren't home."

I laugh.

"I was so confused, 'cause..." She groans. "They were this strict couple. Sweet but strict. Kind of like your brother, actually." She pokes my ribcage, and she obviously doesn't know Greg very well yet. "The kids could only drink the most vitamin-rich OJ, eat the best meals, wear the fanciest clothes, and they all came home with straight As and weren't allowed to watch TV until after dinner."

"But what if they'd been a sexy, younger couple?" Brayden waggles his eyebrows.

Evangeline lifts her head and sticks out her tongue. "You know chicks don't do it for me, *mon ange*."

"No." I snort a chuckle. "You need *two men*, apparently." I pinch her hip, causing her to squirm over my semi. "Greedy little girl, aren't you?"

"Mmm." She hums and nuzzles my jaw. "I guess I'm guilty there."

Tease. "Hey, come here," I murmur, cupping her cheek. Looking into her eyes, I try to see if she's had too much alcohol, but I see none of that. Two glasses of wine should be safe anyway. What I do see is arousal. With a faint smile, I close the distance and kiss her softly. Once, twice, three times. By the third, I linger. "I think that's enough talking for now. What do you say?"

Before they can even reply, I claim Evangeline's mouth again and blindly reach for Brayden's hand. He says he's not ready for me to be intimate with him, but there's no forgetting the moment at the club when we both finger-fucked the young woman on my lap.

Slowly, I slide our hands up Evangeline's thigh. Breathing grows labored for all of us, stories about babysitting long over and forgotten. Eventually, I need air, so I break from the kiss and urge Brayden closer. Closer and closer—until their heads tilt together and I'm four or five inches away from a deep kiss between two people who love each other. I watch as their tongues meet; it's sensual and beyond passionate.

Only a few seconds after, Evangeline whimpers as Brayden and I reach her damp pussy, and she tries to part her legs for us. Leaning in, I start to kiss her neck. Openmouthed. I taste her, nip at her skin, and breathe her in.

"I want your panties off." My voice is rougher, huskier. The hand I've had on Evangeline's back trails toward the clasp of her bra. I flick it off. "Help her, Brayden." And while he does, I remove her bra and toss it aside. I also pull my T-shirt over my head. "You've got beautiful breasts." I capture her mouth in a kiss, at the same time cupping her tits in my hands, feeling the roundness, the heaviness, and two tight nipples that I pinch between my fingers.

"Damn." She breathes heavily. "I want more—" she hesitates "—is it Mark or Sir?"

I smile against her cheek. "Still Mark. Don't worry, I'll let you know." And right now I want her mouth on me. "Will you kneel for me?"

As a response, she stands up long enough for Brayden to slide down her panties, and then she drops to her knees between my legs. Fucking gorgeous. So willing to submit.

Keeping our gazes locked, I unzip my leather pants and push them down my thighs, my cock slapping against my lower abdomen. I'm acutely aware of the need in Evangeline's eyes, but what turns me on even more is Brayden in my periphery, licking his lips. The battle he has within himself will make for the sweetest motherfucking surrender one day. Surrender to *me*.

"Suck me off, kitten."

She takes a breath and leans forward, placing her hands on my thighs. A wet kiss to start with, then cute little laps and licks. Fuck. Kitten is correct. Her noises fit, too.

Dizzy with lust, my head lolls back as her hot mouth slides down my cock, soaking me in saliva. I groan under my breath and buck my hips. In turn, she hums around me and takes me deeper.

"Jesus." I hiss and grind my teeth together. "Brayden—" I swallow a moan, pointing to behind Evangeline "—fuck her. Right now." This wasn't exactly my plan for tonight, but as I watch Brayden tugging down his boxers and getting behind his girlfriend on the floor, his cock hard as rock, I don't give two shits about my plans. "Do you need a condom?" I think I have one in the back pocket of my discarded leathers.

"No, we're clean and covered," he says quickly, aligning his dick with Evangeline's pussy. "You ready, Lina?" With my cock in her mouth, she manages a small nod, and that's all Brayden needs before he pushes inside. "Oh fuck, yeah..."

My mind spins, registering that this is getting out of control—or rather, out of *my* control—so I decide to keep this up until they can't take it anymore. After that, we'll go to my bedroom. Before, though, I will grant myself a fucking release. I've earned it.

"Fuck, that feels amazing, sweetheart," I groan. Fisting her hair, I guide her over me and thrust, coating the roof of her mouth in pre-come. Long, deep strokes that make the head of my cock touch the back of her throat. The irony of our positions causes my mouth to edge upward slightly, because I have something similar in mind for my bedroom.

The sound of Brayden's hips slapping against Evangeline's ass reminds me of later, so I say, "You're not allowed to come." Mark, Sir, Master—they can see this as a transition. They can call me what they want at this point.

"I'm already close," he grits out. His eyes plead with me, a surge of possessiveness settling in my gut at the sight. They come to me for permission—nobody else.

"You better hold back, pup." I return my attention to Evangeline. The wet noises she makes, combined with Brayden slamming into her from behind, are enough to push me close to the brink. My balls grow firmer, and Evangeline cups them in her hand. She massages them like a fucking expert, all while tightening her soft lips around my erection. "Almost there." I throw my head back again, feeling the familiar tingling sensation surge down my spine.

It's only a couple passes of her mouth later that my climax takes over. Pleasure builds up and explodes; every fucking nerve ending is a live wire. "*Fuck.*" I spit out a curse. Cock throbbing, I release in three streams down her contracting throat.

I slump deeper into the plush couch, barely able to think straight.

"You can stop now, Brayden."

He won't be able to fight back his own orgasm if he keeps going.

He complies with an expression of despair.

"Was that good?" A smug smirk tugs at the corner of Evangeline's mouth as she crawls up my body. She's breathing heavily, cheeks and chest flushed, and she's evidently cocky enough to be proud. "Thank you for letting me taste you." She kisses my chin.

I grin lazily and scrub a hand over my face. "You won't be smirking for much longer, kitten. But yeah, that was good. Or un-fucking-believable is more like it." She's not taking my promise seriously; her satisfied smile is proof of that. Her mistake. "I think I'm ready to continue this in the bedroom."

Sitting up straighter, with Evangeline still on my lap, I gather Brayden close as well and zip up my pants. He definitely needs to come. And if I go by the wetness on his glistening cock, Evangeline is desperate for a release, too. Hell, I can feel it as she shifts. She's soaking wet.

"The second we step foot into the bedroom, you will refer to me as Sir or Master." The latter is only because I intend to pursue an arrangement with them. Otherwise, I'm always Master *Cooper* when I play while being unattached. "What I demand is honesty, quick answers to my questions, and that you're vocal. In other words, I want you to speak freely—as long as you remain respectful. Got it?" They nod, eyes telling me I have their undivided attention. "Good. Brayden, as I understand, you're not ready for me to touch you sexually. Am I correct?"

His cheeks darken, possibly at my straightforwardness. "Yes, Sir—um, yes."

"And that's fine," I implore quietly. "Really. Though, there will be *some* touching. You didn't mind how close I was at the club, right?" He shakes his head no, blushing harder. His nipples tighten, too. "I won't go much further than that, I promise. What about toys? Am I allowed to use a plug on you? Dildos, beads, blindfolds, cuffs?"

"That's—" he coughs and lowers his gaze "—that's fine. All of that."

Fucking splendid. "You're going to make this hard for me, pup." The corners of my mouth tug upward slightly at the pun.

I'm serious; I want him to know that I find him attractive as hell —that I desire him, too. And judging by the way he's shifting in his seat and the smile he's trying to hide, I'd say my comment sits well with him.

"And you, kitten..." I tilt my head in her direction. "How can I use you for my pleasure?" Her pupils dilate as I ghost my thumb over her jaw. "I've already had my cock here." I slowly push my thumb into her mouth. "But..." My hand trails down her exposed front 'til it rests between her luscious tits. "What about here?" She nods, seemingly dazed. Then farther down, I cup her crotch—her wet pussy. She parts her legs more. I feel her heat. "What about here, subbie?"

"Yes," she breathes out. "Please. I-I want it."

I suppress a groan and lean in to whisper in her ear. "There's your sexy ass, too. One day—" I leave an openmouthed kiss below her ear "—will you let me take you there?"

"Yes." She whimpers when I apply pressure to my thumb that's pushing against her slit. "I like that." The confession turns her a little shy. "I know Brayden does, too. We've—we've done it."

"That sounds like something I'd love to watch." I smile against her skin, noticing how a shiver courses through her. "You're good with me restraining you?"

There's a final nod, and then I'm satisfied for now.

Leaving the living room, I usher them into my bedroom where I stand behind them in the doorway. As they take in the large room, I remind them of their safewords and that I want them to speak up. I also ask if they have any joint issues or if they cramp easily. They shake their heads no.

My room looks like any normal bedroom, though a few touches tell people in the lifestyle that so much more can go on in here. Warm and inviting in browns, whites, and greens—and intimidating to a knowing eye.

Brayden stares wide-eyed at the big four-poster bed straight ahead, or more correctly: the metal rings screwed into the wood. Meanwhile, Evangeline peers over to a bench in the western corner, right now only decorative, and I wonder if she knows it's a spanking bench as soon as one side is lowered. The flat surface of polished wood is as large as a torso, and I wouldn't mind bending either of my subs over it for a spanking. Even the large window to our right can be used in a scene. Stretching eight feet up from the floor, the window frame is the perfect spot to scare—or thrill—a submissive with the thought of onlookers. Especially if that sub is shackled—one metal ring in each corner would see to that.

In the eastern corner, near the bed, there's an armoire full of toys and other implements. Both my little ones have noticed it. They've also noticed the hook in the ceiling in the right corner closest to us. The floor is empty around that space, and the sex swing I've bought for that hook is in the armoire.

Lastly, in the corner to our left, obscured by the open door, there's a table housing fresh towels, a fully-stocked mini fridge, the docking station to my iPod, my camera equipment, and a few boxes with lotions, condoms, lube, painkillers, wipes, antibacterial gel, and a first aid kit.

For months, I've had this room—hell, this whole apartment— designed and prepared for playtime. To say I'm ready to christen the place would be the understatement of the year.

When I speak, I startle them, perhaps because they're so busy staring into my room. "Brayden, I want you in the middle of the bed. On your back. Evangeline, you can open that armoire over there."

As they scurry to obey, I walk over to the table and push play on my Goth metal list, keeping the volume low. The heavy beat will add to the atmosphere, as will the dim lighting and lit candles. Quickly leaving the room, I duck out to the kitchen to fill up a bowl with hot water for later. When I'm back, I leave it next to a few washcloths. Walking over to the armoire next, I drop our clothes near the window. All that's left are my leathers. And one sub's kitty ears.

Evangeline's waiting for me, and Brayden's gaze follows us from the bed. Both naked. Ready to be used and pleasured.

"These will suffice for tonight." My chest presses against Evan- geline's back when I reach closer and pull out four black silk ties from the armoire. I'm saving cuffs and shackles for another night. Evangeline has undoubtedly seen them.

All of it. Dildos, beads, rope, plugs, bullets, spreader bars, feath- ers, crops, floggers, switches, tawses, a cane, my bullwhip, BDSM tape, wax candles, clamps, blindfolds, gags, paddles... All on display in the compartments.

"Hmm, what else?" I pretend to ponder while I leave a trail of kisses along her neck and shoulder. "I have plans for your mouth and pussy, so that's covered. But what...about..." I lean over her and pick out a new plug and a J-shaped vibrator. That small anchor will make any man go insane, vibrating against the spot between balls and ass, while the longer end is inside and applying pressure on the prostate. "And this." I unwrap a small flexi crop hanging on the inside wall of the armoire, because I want to test my theory on giving Evangeline some pain with her pleasure. "Hold it, please." I give her the crop, letting her get acquainted with it.

Then I leave her there and put down the toys on one of the nightstands, not saying a word as I begin to tie up Brayden. The black silk wraps around his wrists and ankles. Arms and legs spread. Tied to the rings in the wood. Not too tightly; silk is deceptive with how quickly it can cut off the circulation. Satisfied with my work, I stand at the foot of the bed, admiring Brayden's naked body as I rub a palm over my cock that's slowly waking up after that blow job.

He tests the bindings, pulling and twisting, and when he understands he's not going anywhere, he groans and stops struggling. His cock juts up toward his lower abs, looking painfully hard. And it gets me thinking... He's naked, vulnerable, exposed, and I've never seen him so aroused. It could be one of his kinks—being scrutinized, preyed upon... For many, that's humiliating. Which turns some subs on like nothing else. Could that be it? We'll see.

After retrieving lube, wipes, and condoms from the table, I tell Evangeline, "Kneel next to Brayden on the bed."

I walk to the opposite side and kneel on Brayden's other side. With him between us, I pull Evangeline close and slam my lips to hers. I swallow her moan, thrusting my tongue into her mouth. The crop in her hand lands on Brayden's chest with a muted slap, and then I have Evangeline's arms around my neck. The skin around my cock tightens, blood rushing and surging.

The preparations and everything leading up to this moment fades at the crackling tension. The fire sizzling around us makes everything else appear technical and mechanical.

I groan, my kiss going from hungry to downright bruising. Evangeline takes it. She cries out, as if saying she wants more. She even clings to me, seemingly forgetting that her boyfriend is still tied to the mattress between us.

"Master..." Brayden's voice snaps me back to reality, and I grab Evangeline's jaw and break away from the kiss, panting. The first thing I see is the effect our kiss had on my boy. Arousal has beaded at the head of his cock, and it's slowly trickling down his shaft. *Fuck me.* My mouth waters, and I swallow.

Reaching for the J-shaped vibrator and the lube, I get between Brayden's parted legs and look him in the eye. "Growing desperate, pup?" Testing his limits, I lube up two fingers and press the pad of my middle finger against his hole. He tenses up, but at the same time, he nods furiously. Either in response to my question or as in my touch is okay. This was what I meant earlier when I said there would be some touching. Because I won't have a sub doing my job. That's a line I won't cross.

I look down and watch as my finger disappears into him, past the ring of muscle, until I can't get deeper. He's tight, but he's not a stranger to anal play.

"Evangeline has fucked you with dildos before, hasn't she?" I add a second finger, and a part of me wants to pleasure him just like this.

"Yes," he grits out, breathing heavily. "Yes, Master." *Fuck*, it feels good to hear that title coming from his mouth. "I—I can't help it. Can't help that I like it." He groans when I press in a third. "Oh, *God.*"

"I'm glad you like it, Brayden," I murmur huskily. "You have no fucking idea how much that pleases me. I'm grateful you're willing to share this with me." He shudders and relaxes. Slowly withdrawing my fingers, I prepare the vibrator for him and then use a wipe for my fingers. "It'll feel a bit cold in the beginning." Gently cupping his balls, I start to push in the slicked-up vibrator. He squirms and moans, eyes closed. "Such a good boy." Much like Evangeline, Brayden is bare for me. She waxes; he shaves. "That's right—relax for your Master." When the vibrator is in place, I switch it on.

"Fuck!" A spasm rolls through him. His firm muscles contract. Defined abs and pecs. "Oh, fuck, fuck, fuck."

"You're not allowed to come until I say so." I position myself across from Evangeline once more and pick up the crop. With Brayden between us, I plan to explore her tolerance for pain. "You know what this is, kitten?"

"A riding crop, Master," she whispers fearfully. "I know I said that I don't know enough, but..." Misery flashes across her features as she eyes the implement. "I don't like pain, Sir." Yet, she loved it when I flogged her.

It gives me a deep sense of satisfaction to figure them out, and this isn't a journey of discovery only for me. It's for them, too, and there's a lot to unravel.

"And I think you're wrong, beautiful," I whisper back. "We'll start with just one, okay? You know your safewords."

She nods jerkily and sucks in a breath. In her eyes, I can see that she's expecting the worst. She's preparing herself for pain—severe pain. And I could stun her; I could let the crop snap against her skin without a warning, except I want to prove a point. So, I draw out the anticipation and slide the patch of leather over her skin, down her neck, over her exquisite tits, circling her nipples, and allow her eyes to follow each movement. She wonders where I will strike. Fully aware of the tool, waiting, she steels herself for impact.

"Ready?" I lower the crop to her stomach, then even farther down until it settles on the mound of her pussy. She grits her teeth and gives me another jerky nod. At her sides, her hands are balled into tight little fists. I smile. And with a quick flick of my wrist, the crop comes down with a *snap!* on her slit.

"Ouch! That fucking hurt!" She lets out a cute snarl. "*Master.*"

My smile turns wry. "Did it really?"

Brayden grits out a moan.

She glares. "Yes. It did. *Sir.* It hurt—a lot." Liar, liar. Flogging did it for her at Switch. This isn't worse.

Her eyes betray the surprise of the impact—the fact that it hurt less than she feared. Probably also that the pain it did inflict gave her a thrill of pleasure. Now she's only holding on to her pride. Being proved wrong is never fun.

I keep staring at her, giving her a chance to retract the claws. It takes a moment, and I turn my focus on Brayden while I wait, but then she's evidently done.

She huffs. "Fine. Maybe it didn't hurt *that* much. But it still hurt!"

This time I don't warn her. Before she can react, I flick down the crop three times in quick succession right over her clit. Just as she's about to cry out, I grab her jaw and pull her close.

"Explain this, then," I hiss and show her the leather of the crop's end. It's fucking *drenched.* With a dark grin on my face, I smear the wetness of the leather across her pouty lips. "Are you going to tell me it's juices from being turned on earlier?" I lower my voice. "Or are you going to tell me the *truth.*"

She whimpers. "It did hurt a little—"

"It's supposed to."

"Okay, okay." Her eyes well up slightly. "I liked it."

I nod and release her. "Because you don't hate pain, Evangeline." I point to Brayden's dripping cock. "Suck him." Jumping off the bed, I unzip my leathers and walk over to the armoire. In there, I locate another four silk ties, and then I return to the bed. "I want you between Brayden's legs. But don't stop sucking him. He's needy and fucking desperate."

Brayden groans and digs the back of his head deeper into the pillows.

While Evangeline positions herself, I push down my pants and grab one of the condoms. Making a quick decision, I take the lube and the plug, too. Then I get behind her on the bed and tie her left leg to Brayden's right. The right with his left follows.

"Hands behind your back, subbie." She obeys immediately, her head still bobbing up and down on Brayden's cock. I gather her wrists with the third silk tie and secure it with a knot. For her, my goal now is both pain and discomfort. "Not too tight?"

"No, Master," she breathes out.

"Good." The last tie goes under Brayden's lower back, then over Evangeline's neck, where I secure the ends. As a result, she's locked in her position. The only room she has is a few inches to move over her boyfriend's dick. "Comfortable?"

It's a pitiful whimper this time. "No, Master."

Excellent. Next is the plug. Fingers slicked with lube, I slowly push one into her ass. Aside from tensing up, she takes it perfectly. By the second finger, she relaxes and redoubles her efforts to pleasure Brayden. I praise her with words and caresses, letting her get used to every intrusion. The plug I prepare isn't a large one, so after warming her up with three fingers, I press the piece inside her and encourage her to push back. It helps her accept it with less resistance.

"Color?"

"Green," she croaks.

"Good girl." I finger her pussy for a beat, my fingers coming out wet and fucking delicious. "Take a deep breath." Reaching for the condom, I tear the foil and roll the rubber down my length. Then I grip her hips and tease her pussy only for a second, slapping the head of me across her clit, before I slam inside her.

Oh, Jesus fucking Christ.

I grind my teeth together. So hot, so wet, goddamn tight.

"Oh, my God," Evangeline chokes out.

"Color?" I ask them through clenched teeth.

"Green, Master—I need to come," Brayden spits out in a rush.

"Not yet, pup." I laugh, out of breath, and rub Evangeline's soft ass. "You, kitten?"

"Yell—" She pauses and sucks in air.

I'm proud of her. I know I'm pushing her; not only is she

completely restrained with an anal plug in her ass, but I drove into her mercilessly at the same time as she was forced to keep her mouth on Brayden's cock.

"It's never wrong to safeword," I murmur. "Is it your neck?" I know it's straining. And I can feel how tense her thighs are. She nods as much as she can. "Try to breathe. Breathe and accept me deeper." I pause for a moment, letting her center herself. Meanwhile, I caress her skin and reach under her to cup her tits. Not all women have sensitive nipples. Evangeline definitely does. "Your color?"

"...Green, Master." She nods for emphasis. "I'm sure."

"I'm proud of you, gorgeous girl." I kiss her spine, then straighten and pull out slowly. "Tell me if it gets to be too much, all right?"

She promises, and I push inside of her again.

It doesn't take long for me to lose myself in control—an oxymoron if there ever was one. In quick, shallow thrusts, I fill Evangeline's pussy with my cock over and over.

Her muffled whimpers, Brayden's gritty pleas, each push, every pull, muscles clenching, silk ties restraining, the vibrator, a plug, the sound of wetness, skin slapping, tremors...I find focus in all of it. I let it sink in; I feel everything.

Swiveling my hips, I grind deeper into my kitten. She pants and moans around the cock in her mouth. Brayden keeps begging Master for a release. I fuck Evangeline harder, hammering into her softness. Sweat beads on my body, biceps throbbing, thighs tensing, and abs contracting. My breathing goes harsh and shallow. Power pummels through me like a *fucking* hurricane.

Deeming Evangeline's suffering enough for now, I snake a hand under her stomach and begin to rub her clit. Fast, hard. She chokes on a gasp, her entire body quivering. I had a feeling this would happen. A certain amount of pain will intensify any kind of relief I offer her.

If you give a parched man a glass of water, won't he enjoy it more than a man who has unlimited access to it? That glass of water might even *taste* better, be more *gratifying*.

"Please, Master!" she sobs. "I—I, oh God!"

"Hold it, pet," I growl. I know she's close. I also know she can't believe it. The pain mingling with the pleasure confuses her. But she can't control the way her pussy clenches down on me.

My hand on her hip slides up the damp skin of her spine. I keep stroking and pinching her clit with my other hand. Finding her neck, I rub her gently, loosening the tension in her muscles.

"Breathe, Evangeline. Focus on your breathing."

"Master, please..." At Brayden's despaired moan, I look up the bed to see him fighting against his approaching orgasm. His face is contorted in pain—a need to please me.

"Fuck," I breathe out, squeezing my eyes shut. Mouth dry, I swallow a couple times, then open my eyes again. Only to find Brayden's hooded gaze on me. I shudder and ram my cock as far as I can into Evangeline's pussy, knowing Brayden can feel it as she sucks him off. Just like I felt his thrusts earlier when I had Evangeline's mouth on me.

"I can't stop—" He presses his lips together and shakes his head. Eyes screwed shut, too. Yet, despite his words, he keeps struggling.

"Come, Brayden." I allow it only fractions of a second before he'd lose the battle. "Come." With a guttural groan, everything unleashes in him. His back arches, his hips buck, his head is thrown back, and the ties strain between the bed frame and his wrists. "Swallow him down, kitten. Make it good for him." I slow down only to let her focus on Brayden.

As soon as his muscles unclench, making it look like he collapses down on the mattress, I order Evangeline to come, too. I twist the plug in her ass, press my middle finger down onto her swollen clit, and grind my cock as deep as possible. Nothing but a breathless wail escapes her throat, and while she rides out her violent orgasm, I chase my own.

It comes crashing down on me when Evangeline's pussy

tightens fiercely around the base of my cock. Through jerky thrusts, I spill into the condom and feel all the tension draining out of me.

A low groan rumbles in my chest; all I want is to lie down and catch my breath.

That will have to wait a little. Reluctantly withdrawing my softening cock, the first thing I do is remove Evangeline's plug. My breathing is still too choppy, and I have to blink for clarity. After pulling out Brayden's vibrator, I quickly get off the bed and place the toys, crop too, on a towel. Then I dispose of the condom, grab the wipes and two more towels, and return to the bed.

"Scene's over, subbies," I whisper.

CHAPTER 8

Evangeline breathes out in relief when I untie her from Brayden.

"Lie down and relax, beautiful." I kiss her on the forehead. Moving on, I untie Brayden and then return the ties to the armoire. If my weekend goes as planned, he and Evangeline will be the only ones I will ever use those ties on. "Is there anything that hurts?" I check them over as I join them on the bed and swiftly clean them up with a warm washcloth. That seems to embarrass Brayden, but I go on as if I don't notice.

"I'm sore all over," Evangeline mumbles sleepily into a pillow. She hums as I draw the soft fabric over her pussy and ass; *she* clearly doesn't care. Which makes me grin to myself. "My butt hurts a little, but not much." With another humming sound, she snuggles close to Brayden. "G'night."

I chuckle under my breath. "Not so fast." Buck naked and armed with soothing lotion, I slide in behind Evangeline and pull the covers over us. "I have eleven years on you—if anyone should be tired, it's me." Facing Brayden, I ask, "Any discomfort, pup?"

He shakes his head no and draws the covers up to his nose. "A little sore, that's all." His cheeks redden. "The scene was great—um, perfect."

"Oh, yes." Evangeline stretches between us, purring like a cat, and peers up at first Brayden, then me. A sleepy smile on her face. "Perfect scene, perfect Master." She giggles at my amused expression. "It helps that you're super sexy."

"You have no fucking shame." I laugh through my nose, wrapping my fingers around her wrists. They're a little red, but that's nothing. Hooking a hand under her knee, I pull up her leg enough to check her ankle, too. "And the other one." I have to push down the covers to see, and when I do, I see it's all good. "How about you, Brayden?" He shows me his wrists, the same light red shade flashing—nothing bad. That's what you get after yanking at your restraints. "You both feel all right?"

"Better than all right." Evangeline smiles. "What about you?" A crease forms between her brows. "You look worried."

I'm not. Well, not really. They might still be high on endorphins, which would explain their carefree behavior. At Switch, Evangeline dropped quickly. I suppose I half-expected something similar to happen now. But every scene is different. Usually, there's no drop whatsoever to speak about. I'll just have to keep an eye on her—both of them—in case it happens.

After assuring them nothing is wrong, we talk about the scene in detail; I make them voice their thoughts about everything we did —from arrival to now—and, in turn, I explain my own agenda. Specifically about Evangeline and pain.

She frowns, wonders if she's weird, and then tries to backtrack —that, no, she doesn't enjoy pain. Not believing her own lie.

Brayden kisses her temple and murmurs, "Would it be bad if you did? And, for the record, we've only just started this weekend. It was one riding crop. We don't know yet where you'll end up on, um—" he chuckles "—the pain scale."

"Still..." She grumbles. "Is it normal to like some pain?"

I withhold my smile and brush some hair away from her forehead. "Think about it, kitten. At Switch, didn't you see a lot of ways to inflict pain?"

Maybe it will take some time for Evangeline to let this settle, but I have no concerns regarding how she'll handle it. She's an open-minded woman. This is just a small bump in the road, her own road, and that's common. No matter how strong you are as a person, you will sometimes be taken off guard and learn something new about yourself. And I tell her this, or remind her, because she's a smart girl; she knows it already.

"I'm glad you're the one who walked into our stall," she admits. "You seem very understanding. And it's like you have answers to everything."

"Afraid that's not true—but thank you." I kiss her shoulder, smiling against her skin. Under the covers, my arm reaches across her to include Brayden, too. I let my hand rest on his back. "I have experience, though I learn new things all the time."

"No, I get that. But I think you're perfect for us." Her own smile is uncharacteristically shy. To mask it, she turns to teasing. "Is there any way we can keep you?"

Little does she know that's exactly my hope. Only, I will do the keeping.

I will own their bodies.

Their hearts, their souls?

Fuck that. Annoying goddamn voice. Which, disturbingly enough, still sounds like Kayla. Meddling little brat.

"If you feel like keeping me after this weekend is over, come talk to me." I smirk.

———

Maybe my years with Alexa and all that misery granted me some fucking luck, because it turned out that Brayden and Evangeline were more than a little excited to have me as their Master.

Now, three weeks later, I arrive at the club for another shift behind the bar, and Kayla immediately runs up to me asking me if I have the collars.

"Yep, they arrived today." I wink at her, bump fists with Liam, exchange a grin with Nicholas, and jerk my chin in hello at Rio and Cade. "Maybe Daddy should put a leash on you, honey." I tug on one of her pigtails, seeing as she's actually followed me behind the bar. "Only Liam and I are allowed back here."

"I just wanted to hug you and say congrats." She pulls off a playful scowl before wrapping her arms around my middle. I chuckle, give her a squeeze, and kiss the top of her head. "Now all you gotta do is fall in love with your subs." She finishes that off in her singsong voice and then skips around the bar again to sit on Nicholas's lap. "Doesn't he, Daddy? Doesn't he?"

Nicholas, amused as hell, is about to say yes—I know because he's already nodding—but my glare stops him. He's all about humoring his girl, who is bubblier than freaking champagne.

"Ahem." He clears his throat. "That's enough, baby girl." Yeah, see, if he'd said that without grinning like a fucking schmuck, maybe I would've believed him. "So—" he faces me with a smirk "—anything special planned?"

"Still fine tuning the details," I say, resting my forearms on the bar top. Liam doesn't end his shift until ten, so I have a few minutes. "No elaborate ceremony for me."

Some Doms plan grand ceremonies for when they collar their subs. That's not really my thing. It's not Evangeline and Brayden's thing, either. Though, that doesn't mean I'm not eager to have my name on them.

Over the past three weeks, we've met at the club a few times, and we've had long weekends together at my place. I'm exploring their limits, I've grown comfortable having them with me, and I enjoy teaching them new things. Whether we scene in public or at my place, we click very well.

I also admit to myself that I enjoy not waking up alone.

Brayden is still wary about having a man touch him, so we haven't progressed much there. I can use toys on him, fuck him with a dildo, put on condoms and cock rings, hug him, and guide him into positions, though that's it. If he wakes up in my arms, he stiffly moves away while hiding his haunted expression and erection.

I wouldn't mind putting my boot up his dad's ass or shoving my fist down his throat.

I've become particularly protective of my Brayden.

Evangeline, too, but she's not as vulnerable. She throws caution to the wind; she's carefree, has a huge heart, and a strong spirit. She's also one the most selfless people I've ever met. It'd be too fucking easy to fall for her. Effortless. The way she responds to my touch is exhilarating, and it only serves to make things more difficult for me when it comes to drawing the line between an arrangement and a complete relationship. I may be in charge, but she's got her hooks into me—there's no denying that.

"When will your subs be here?" Cade asks, bringing me back to the present. He grins. "Thought they were always attached to your hip now."

"You jealous?" I laugh. Don't think for a second I haven't caught him eyeing Brayden like he's on the menu. Hell, Evangeline too. Especially last week when I had them both walk around naked. "They're mine, buddy."

"Oh, Cooper's getting territorial." Rio smirks.

"Nuh-uh." Kayla huffs and folds her arms across her chest. "Mr. Kingsley is *not* jealous." She's referring to Cade, who smiles at Kayla. "'Cause he's going out with my friend Dylan tomorrow. So, there."

I shake my head in amusement and tilt my head at Nicholas. "Your little matchmaker's at it again, huh?"

"Damn straight." He nuzzles Kayla's neck. "But no more of that now. We need to go home, baby." That's right. They're taking a quick vacation to Mexico before flying up to Oregon in a week. I think I heard Nick saying that his parents will be in Mexico, too. "Time to pack."

"So, anyway..." Rio twirls a finger. "Back to Evangeline and Brayden. When are you collaring them?"

"Tomorrow, I think," I answer and grab a soda for myself. "I have something in mind for them tonight—" checking my watch, I see that they should be here in a couple minutes "—and that will sorta decide what we'll do for tomorrow." It depends on Brayden's reaction to tonight.

Only Nicholas in our group knows what's going on, and that's because I need his office.

"Speak of the devils." Cade jerks his chin toward the entrance, and I see Evangeline and Brayden walking over.

I doubt it's a sight I'll ever get tired of. They're dressed in the same outfits they wore for our first weekend together—a standard now. Too fucking sexy, both of them. Now I just need to focus on the fact that this is a D/s relationship, nothing more.

Which has become increasingly difficult.

Getting to know them has started to make me feel an...attachment. Whether it's during a scene where I push their limits, shove them out of their comfort zones, only to haul them back in, make them beg, make them come, then take care of them...or if it's before and after playtime when we talk about everyday things and hobbies and music and what-the-fuck-ever...this wasn't the plan.

You and your fucking plans.

That voice didn't sound like Kayla. For once.

"Hi, guys!" *That's* Kayla. She's quick to wave Evangeline and Brayden over to us.

Now that my subs are attending munches with her once a week, they've formed a friendship, too. Evangeline, especially, has grown close to Kayla. A few days ago, for instance, I scened with Brayden alone; Evangeline and Kayla ran around the club, thick as thieves, and served drinks for kicks.

"Actually, you two can come over here." I point to where I'm standing. That earns me a *look* from Kayla, and when I wink at her, she smiles, ducks her head, and burrows into Nick's chest. "Hello, you two," I murmur and gather Evangeline and Brayden close to me. At Switch, they're a lot more demure and shy than they are at my apartment; it takes a while for them to relax. Most often they can't until I have my arms around them. "You smell nice, kitten." I dip down and breathe her in, smelling her floral shampoo and body wash. For some reason, I like that she has shower products at my place, too. "Can you give me a kiss?" She tilts up her face immediately, and I claim her mouth with mine.

A bone-deep ache in me reminds me I haven't seen them in a few days.

Now they're mine for the next three days.

Her greeting words are drowned out by the music, but I read them on her pouty lips. "I missed you, Master."

I swallow that fucking ache, nod, and kiss her some more. "I missed you, too." Hugging her impossibly closer, I turn to Brayden; he's resting his cheek against my collarbone, one hand on my stomach. It's a light touch, yet it sears through my T-shirt. "That goes for you as well, pup." I kiss him on the forehead, hoping like hell tonight will change things. A small push in the right direction is all I need. It doesn't even have to be physical—he can open up to me and I'll consider it a triumph. Because denying himself won't work forever. Unless he wants to be miserable.

"I reckon I really need to find a plaything," Rio mutters as whatever song changes into another. "How fair is it that he gets two?"

"I can help you, Master Rio," Kayla says sweetly.

Nicholas laughs. "I'm sure you can, baby girl—but not now. We're going home to pack."

And I need to start my shift. Get that shit over with. So, we can go upstairs later. For the scene we're going to watch.

I need it to work.

TOUCH TO SURRENDER

CHAPTER 1

BRAYDEN ZEAGLER

"What are you doing?" I chuckle and bat away Lina's hands. A Dom walks past our booth with his sub on a leash, and my cheeks heat up as my girlfriend tries to be funny, not caring that people are watching us. "Christ, stop it!" Though, she doesn't; she keeps giggling and trying to pinch my nipples. "You annoy me." I growl playfully against her cheek and squeeze her to me. That way, she has no access to my chest. "My little shit."

"Aww, so affectionate." She grins impishly at me and pops a kiss on my chin. "But hey, I got you to smile."

I Eskimo her. "You always do." That couldn't be more true. Whenever I'm down, Lina's there for me. Sometimes I feel like I don't deserve her—the way she loves with all her heart, takes care of her loved ones, stays loyal... She's fucking amazing. "I love you." Giving her another squeeze, I lower my head and kiss her deeply.

She melts into me, the furry trim of her sexy bra tickling my skin. "I love you too, *mon ange*." She gets this tender look in her eye, one that maybe seems at odds with a BDSM club, but it never fails to make my day. "We're lucky, aren't we?" She brushes some hair away from my forehead. "I've never felt this happy. Have you?"

I shake my head, agreeing with her.

Our relationship has been smooth sailing all the way through. The day I met Evangeline Lacroix, I asked her out on a whim, knowing if I didn't I would regret it for the rest of my life. She said yes; we dated, we fell in love, we moved in together, and everything was perfect. Too perfect. We're eager to please, both so compliant, and both incredibly alike. It's been easy—a straight and narrow path.

It got to the point where we frustrated each other because we both hate making decisions. Sex wasn't the issue—far from it. It's our everyday lives; we want someone there to guide us, tell us what to do, and make sure we don't lose ourselves. Thankfully, Lina and I are both honest, too, so we confessed our desires pretty quickly.

Researching, exploring, and eventually venturing to Switch... led us to Mark Cooper.

The only problem is that Lina and I have gotten attached to him to the point where deeper feelings are now involved. While our love for each other has strengthened, a new bond has tied us to Mark in a way where we want more and more and fucking more. More of him, more of us together, and most importantly, more of us all together as *partners*.

We want it all, domination and submission along with a real relationship.

That's where my past comes in to fuck me up...

Having feelings for another man?

Wrong, disgusting, twisted, immoral, sinful.

Being a submissive was a hard pill to swallow, but I did ultimately choke it down and accept it. Being bisexual...I've accepted that, too, but it doesn't mean I can act on it. It's a line that's too "revolting" to cross.

"No. Dammit, the frown is back." Lina hands me my Coke, first taking out the straw, knowing I prefer to drink without one. "Here. Drink. And stop—*please* stop beating yourself up with whatever it is you're thinking right now." Her eyes turn pleading. "You *know* nothing is wrong with what you feel, Brayden."

My smile is small and forced. Taking a sip of my Coke, I try to compose my face, but it's impossible to hide around Lina. She reads me too well. We clicked so fast and perfectly when we got together that there was never a question about whether or not I should divulge my past. She pulled it out of me without effort.

She's also the only one who has managed to do so.

"I know." I really do. "But it's easier said than done." A part of me wishes I was still confused or lived in denial.

It would be so much easier. But now...I know exactly what I want—*who* I want—but I'm struggling to accept it. Setting the glass back on the table, I wrap my arms around Lina again and bury my face in her hair.

"Do you think we're setting ourselves up for..." My mumbling trails off as I can't find the right word. Misery? Heartbreak? Failure?

"With Mark, you mean?" she asks softly, the pounding Goth music nearly drowning out her voice. I nod and hum, feeling her fingers in my hair. "I hope not. But we knew the risk from our first weekend at his place."

True. Maybe it's because we're so in tune with each other that we know how the other feels. My attraction for Mark—hell, Lina knew before I did. It was during our first stay at Mark's; I could see how Lina just melted into his arms, a sign of trust, comfort, and...*more*. More, as in she feels more. Perhaps I saw it because I felt it, too. It's just that I couldn't show it like she did—still can't, and it's eating me up inside.

After that weekend, we went home to our run-down apartment, already knowing this was becoming much more than we ever dreamed. What was once simply attraction for *what* he is grew into affection and care for *who* he is.

"We'll have to stay positive and hope for the best," Lina says firmly, bringing me back to the present. "We should work on getting that man to fall for us." Mischief lights up her eyes, and I can't help but chuckle at her. She's always so optimistic. "I bet he'd love it if you walked over to the bar—" she points in Mark's direction; he's currently busy mixing a drink or something "—and kissed him."

I roll my eyes, though I can't hide my grin. "You forget that I know you, *belle*. You have more voyeuristic tendencies than Tom."

She scrunches her nose. "Tom, who?"

"Peeping Tom," I laugh.

"Oh, my God!" She cracks up, too. "That was so bad!"

I shrug, a smirk on my face.

CHAPTER 2

As soon as Mark's shift is over a couple hours later, he disappears quickly to freshen up in Mr. Ford's personal bathroom upstairs, and then Master returns. *Master*...because now he's in his snug leather pants, a black T-shirt that clings to his body like a second skin, and his boots. *Fuck me.* While he's not some bodybuilder—far from it, really—he's still muscular. You can tell he lifts weights judging by his arms. He has a defined torso, too, and strong, firm thighs.

I swallow hard, feeling my cock stir in my loose boxers. In my fantasies, I've had my hands and mouth all over his hard body, much like Lina has. As for reality...it's a lot bleaker.

"You ready to play, pets?" He smirks and extends his hand to us. By now, Lina and I have found seclusion in Mr. Ford's private booth near the bar—the booth with a ceiling and drapes and privacy. "We won't be in the Cave tonight."

Huh. Where else would we go? Maybe to his place...except, that doesn't make sense. He specifically told us to be ready to scene at Switch the minute his shift ended.

Instead of reading more into it, I brush all my questions aside, content to let my Master take the lead. It's so fucking relaxing not having to worry about anything.

Lina slides out of the booth first, and Master kisses her knuckles before pulling out the collars he uses when we scene. Aside from those, we always wear our red rubber wristbands at Switch now. They tell others we're attached, unavailable—that we belong to someone, Master in this case. He's got one, too, as does everyone who's in a relationship or arrangement. And if you do wear a red wristband, you don't also have to wear a yellow one for being new even if you are, because you're someone else's responsibility.

"Will you please repeat the rules for playtime, kitten?" he asks and holds out the two-inch-wide leather collar with a soft inner lining.

"Yes, Master. My safewords are green for safe, yellow for caution, and red for stop," Lina recites dutifully. "I will only answer direct questions unless you say otherwise, and the only other sounds you allow are, um, when I moan and stuff." Even in the darkness of the club, I see the blush gracing her cheeks.

"That's correct," Master chuckles. "When you moan and stuff." With a kiss to Lina's lips, he positions her next to him instead, then reaches for my hand. I follow obediently and stand up in front of him. Eyes on his. "Your turn, pup." He holds up my play collar, identical to the one Lina has. "The rules, please."

"Yes, Master." I nod as a shiver rips down my spine. "My safewords are green for safe, yellow for caution, and red for stop. I will only answer direct questions unless you say otherwise, and the only other sounds you allow are sounds of pleasure."

"Good pet." He fastens the leather around my neck. "Additionally, you will both keep your eyes on the floor until I say it's okay for you to look up. Understand?"

"Yes, Master," we answer.

"Good. Let's play."

Doing as we're told, Lina and I follow Master through the club area, a few feet behind him, eyes downcast, and then we end up in the lobby, much to our confusion. Master doesn't stop; he continues past the bathrooms and then leads us up the stairs that are off-limits to regular guests. As far as I know, only Mr. Ford's office and a few supply closets are up here. Oh, and Kevin's office.

"Here we are," Master murmurs to himself and stops in front of Mr. Ford's office. Producing a key, he unlocks the door and ushers us inside, and I take subtle glances around me while keeping my gaze lowered. "You may look up, and then you can sit down on the couch closest to Nicholas's desk."

I obey and look up, taking in the large office, its honey-colored hardwood floor, erotic art on the dark red walls—black and white photos of Kayla in various states of undress—Mr. Ford's desk, filing cabinets, and small seating area. For such a vast space, he's really not doing much with it. It's very classy and sexy, though.

Grabbing Lina's hand, we walk over to the two gray couches by a massive window, and we're both kind of awestruck when we see the view of the entire club. Just a floor down, everyone is having a blast: scening, dancing, drinking, socializing, and I get an odd thrill watching them. I already know it's one-way mirrored glass—I can see them, but they can't see me—because I know exactly what they see. I mean, I knew Mr. Ford's office was up here, but when you're down in the club, all you see is a blackened mirror. It's so private up here; not even the music penetrates the walls, except for a muted beat that is easy to ignore.

Lina gives my hand a tug, so we quickly move on and take our seats on the couch Master told us to go to. In front of us, there's a low table and another couch.

"We're waiting for a friend of mine to get here," Master says and puts down some drinks on the table. Two bottles of water and two sodas. "And his sub."

He can definitely see the questions written on our faces.

Just a few seconds later, there's a firm knock on the door, and Master grins and says, "That would be Donovan and his Rory."

He walks over to the door, and I try not to ogle his ass in those leather pants, but I fail and Lina totally catches me, causing me to flush bright red. She giggles behind her hand but says nothing, and then we refocus on Master, who is now ushering in two people.

Oh.

I'd immediately assumed Rory was a woman, but that's no woman—unless she's got no breasts and likes boxer briefs, 'cause that's all he's wearing. Master greets the taller one, Donovan, warmly with a firm handshake, and the two exchange words that are too quiet for me to hear.

Both newcomers are handsome, in very different ways. Donovan reminds me a little of Mr. Ford with his CEO-like manner and expensive suit. Strict, polished. Rory, on the other hand, appears shy and fidgety, yet still eager to be here. He hasn't been told to look down, so I can take in his appearance without any problem. A slightly crooked nose, hazel eyes, fair skin...and he's pretty short and slight in stature. But cute. Very cute. I'm guessing there's an at least ten-year difference between the two, Donovan looking like he's in his late thirties or early forties.

I wince internally, Dad's disapproving face flashing before my eyes. I've appraised the two men for too long.

Lowering my gaze, I wring my hands in my lap, just waiting for Master to tell us what to do.

Soon enough, I hear them moving closer, and I look up as Master introduces his friends. "This is Donovan Moore—that's Sir or Mr. Moore to you, pets, although I doubt there'll be much talking —" he smirks "—and his sub, also husband, Rory."

Husband. There's a sharp pang of envy hitting me in the chest, and not because of their marital status, but because they're obviously embracing their sexual orientation. With Master seemingly studying me, I try to keep my face composed, but he can read me almost as well as Lina can.

"Evangeline and Brayden," Master goes on, making sure he's got our attention, "Donovan and Rory have flown up all the way from San Diego to scene for us." I swallow thickly, willing my dick to stay calm in my boxers. The black silk gives me away too fucking easily. "Thank them."

"Thank you, Sir, Rory," Lina says, flushing, while I say, "Thank you both for taking the time, Sir and Rory."

"It'll be my pleasure," Mr. Moore responds in a smooth voice. With a quick snap of his fingers, Rory is there to remove his Master's suit jacket.

Lina and I watch how fluidly Rory moves around, now the opposite of fidgety, and I know myself the calming effect a command has. Our eyes follow as he kneels to slip off Mr. Moore's shoes, unbuckle his belt, unzip his pants, and slide them down. Meanwhile, Mr. Moore takes care of his tie and dress shirt, and our own Master walks over and sits down between Lina and me. By the time Mr. Moore sits down across from us, clad in only boxer briefs, Rory is tenting his own briefs, and I try not to stare.

"Get my bag outside the door, too," Mr. Moore tells his boy, and Rory speeds off without a word, retrieving a brown leather duffle.

Behind me, I feel Master's arms settle on the back of the couch, his fingers softly caressing my neck and shoulders. "Unbutton my pants, pup," he murmurs in my ear, "and pull out my cock."

I exhale shakily, feeling my dick stir under the silk, and shift closer to Master to carry out his command. I've done this much in the past, and it never fails to turn me on as if it's the first time I've ever been near him. Struggling with the button, I finally get control of my trembling fingers, and I work the zipper carefully before gently grasping his semi-hard cock and tugging down at the leather. He lets out a breath and lifts up, making it easier for me to pull his pants down past his thighs.

His cock is the last thing I let go of, and I hate that I want so much more.

"Good boy." He gives the back of my neck an affectionate squeeze, then turns to Lina. "Get me hard, kitten. With your mouth." His hand, still grasping my neck, applies pressure in a way that makes me tilt my head toward Mr. Moore and Rory—a silent order of where I should keep my eyes. Still, I see Lina in my periphery as she leans over and starts to suck Master's cock.

Lucky her.

Eventually, I refocus and pay full attention to Rory, who's been commanded to lie across Mr. Moore's lap. Naked. His pretty fucking sexy ass in the air.

I squirm in my seat, surrounded by things I want more of.

"My little Rory is an anal slut," Mr. Moore chuckles huskily as he roughly kneads Rory's ass cheeks. "He'll beg shamelessly for a spanking, for a hard fuck...for me to mark him." My eyes are glued to them as Mr. Moore pulls out a small paddle and slides the smooth wood over Rory's skin. I can imagine the pleasurable feeling caused by the cool surface of it, and it makes my own ass clench. "You're ready to beg right now, aren't you? Answer."

"Yes, my Sire," Rory groans and pushes his ass upward. *"Please."*

Fantasy images of Master hauling me over his lap cause me to break out in a sweat. Mr. Moore's face gets replaced by Master's, and I'm suddenly Rory. Lina would make it all ten times better, too. The perfect trio. Hot, sweaty, sexy. Limbs tangled...*fuck, fuck, fuck.* I've done so much fantasizing that I've rubbed my dick sore in my morning showers every day. Well, unless Master's told us not to masturbate.

Ignoring Lina devouring Master's cock next to me, I watch hungrily as Mr. Moore lubes up a couple fingers and spreads Rory's ass cheeks. A drawn-out moan slips through Rory's lips while Mr. Moore's fingers slowly disappear into his ass. With those fingers buried deep inside, he uses his other hand to rub the narrow paddle up and down Rory's thighs and ass. There's no warning; he strikes with precision, and I'm willing to bet Rory clenches down around Mr. Moore's fingers so hard it's gotta hurt.

"Let's leave Donovan and Rory to their warm-up for a bit." Master decides quietly. "Evangeline, I want you to sit on my cock. Your back to my chest." My mouth waters, and I wonder what he'll have me do. "Brayden, you're gonna eat our little girl's pussy." Oh, I can *definitely* do that. "Kneel between my legs, pup," he grunts as Lina sinks down on him with a needy whimper.

Once she's lowered onto him, I take my position on the floor, licking my lips at the sexy sight. Not just the way Master stretches my girlfriend's pussy, but also how she coats him in her arousal. Now that we're all in a committed relationship and have all been tested, we don't have to bother with condoms, for which I'm grateful. And technically, Mr. Ford's office is not *in* the club, where condoms are a must.

To the sounds of Rory getting finger-fucked and paddled behind me, I place my hands on Master's knees and lean forward, dropping an openmouthed kiss on Lina's swollen clit. Master grips her hips, moving her over him in slow strokes, and it's goddamn mesmerizing to watch. I'm so close, and I see every ridge of Master's cock as it fucks Lina. Once again, I lean in, this time licking her instead of kissing, and I'm not going anywhere.

I lap at her soft, smooth flesh, easily getting into their beat. To make Lina moan and cry out, I suck hard on her clit. To make her squirm and gasp, I lick farther down and nibble on her spread lips. *So close.* Just a couple inches away from Master's glistening cock. In a moment of surrender—my mind is completely blank, or perhaps overcome with lust—I lick them exactly where they're joined.

"Fuck yeah, Brayden," Master moans.

I groan, suddenly frantic with need. My tongue laps around Lina's hole, snaking around Master's thick cock. At the same time, my fingers dig into his knees and I move my face even closer, effectively burying myself in their arousal. I ravish both of them and notice how Master slams Lina down on him faster and harder.

With each slap of Mr. Moore's paddle, Lina whimpers and tenses her pussy.

I think that's where her mind is, because she does get a thrill from a little pain.

Unlike me, she fully embraces the world Master introduced us to.

Then there's a hand at the back of my head, pushing me against their crotches, and Master not giving me a choice makes it so much easier for me. I pretend I'm only doing it because he wants it, because he silently commands it, which triggers me to go further. For a moment, I leave Lina's sweet pussy for Master's cock, and I close my lips over the base of him, sucking on his tight skin. I taste him. I taste my lovely girl. I suck, I lick, I kiss...I go even farther down and tongue his balls.

My own balls are aching, tight and drawn up, and my dick is leaking, causing the silk of my boxers to stick to it.

"Jesus Christ, pup." Master starts panting, and I redouble my efforts, desperate to give him the same gratifying satisfaction he always gives me. "That's enough." He stills all of us, heavy breathing the only sound in the office. Even Mr. Moore's paddle is quiet. "It's time to switch positions," he says, pulling off his T-shirt. All that remains are his leather pants pooling around his ankles. "Evangeline, I want you on your knees, and Brayden, take off your boxers and sit on my lap."

There's no room to be embarrassed, so I unceremoniously drop my boxers and let my cock slap mutedly against my lower abdomen.

While I've been on his lap before, this still feels a lot more intimate and sexual. Not only 'cause we're naked, but because we're in the middle of a scene and there're two men in front of us about to have sex. As I position myself on Master's thighs and Lina kneels before us, Mr. Moore is kneeling behind Rory who's on all fours on the other couch. Rory's dick juts out, glistening with pre-come, and the way he pushes his ass toward his Dominant makes it so fucking clear that he's more than willing. He's not afraid to beg for a cock up his ass.

The hard cock wedged between Master and me won't be begged for, because I'm too chickenshit.

"Suck Brayden's cock, kitten," Master murmurs, encouraging me to lean back and rest my head against his shoulder. He's only a couple inches taller than me, but since I'm straddling his thighs and not his groin, it's easy enough to sit back and relax. Okay, relax isn't exactly the right word. I'm turned on and wound-up, nervous and full of anticipation.

Soon, Lina tortures me with her hot, wet mouth. She licks me much like I licked her earlier, suckles the tip, and then engulfs me in slow strokes, her lips tightening around me.

"Perfect little subbie. Keep that up." Master praises her. "Brayden, listen to me closely now." He's lowered his voice, husky and seductive, and his hands grip my hips firmly. "Tell me what you see when you look at Donovan and Rory." He nips lightly at my shoulder, and a shudder bolts through me.

"I—I see Mr. Moore preparing Rory," I say, groaning when Lina sucks one of my shaved balls into her mouth. "Fuck. Um—" I clear my throat "—I see Mr. Moore fingering him."

"Is what they're doing wrong?" Master asks softly.

My breath catches, my instinctual "no" on the tip of my tongue, and I have to watch myself here. How can I admit the truth when I won't embrace it for myself? I know what's right and wrong, but... There's that *but*.

"You know it's not wrong, pup." He kisses my shoulder. "Look at them now."

I do, and Mr. Moore is leaning over Rory's slender body, kissing up his spine and whispering something to him. Rory shivers and nods. For coming off as so strict and almost cold earlier, there's something very tender in Mr. Moore's actions right now.

"You see it, don't you?" Master runs his fingertips down my arms; the lust in his voice and the way his touch affects me almost steal focus from Lina's mouth on my cock. Actually, it divides it—the attention. I'm so aware of both of them yet still able to watch what's going on across the low table. Thankfully, my girl has slowed down. She sucks to tease me, to keep me hard, to wet my dick, but she's making it last longer. *A lot longer.* Maybe I missed it; maybe Master ordered her to suck me this way. Either way, it's perfect.

"Are you looking at Donovan's hand?"

I am. His fingers wrap around Rory's hard cock, firmly stroking him while dropping kisses along his back. Rory keeps begging, his Master, Sire, whatever, reducing him to a pleading addict.

"Watch, Brayden."

I bite back a groan, feeling Master's fingers caressing my hipbones. My eyes shift to Mr. Moore's dick, so close to Rory's ass, sliding between spread cheeks, all lubed up and wet.

"You know I want to do that to you, too," he whispers in my ear.

"Fuck," I whimper, instinctively bucking my hips. My cock slides deeper into Lina's mouth, and that sweet little cocksucker is so experienced by now that she just keeps sucking me down. "*Master...*" I'm dizzy with lust, burrowing myself deeper into his arms. I squirm against his own erection, and I don't think I've ever wanted it so much.

"That's right, baby." Master keeps whispering, his fingers seductively stroking my skin closer to my crotch. "I'm your Master, aren't I? And there's nothing I want more than to keep you, to own you, to use your body, to make you come..."

The next thing I hear is Rory's cry as Mr. Moore rams his cock up his ass. Tenderness gets replaced by raw, animalistic desire. It's hard fucking. Both loving it. Both in their zones. One receiving, one delivering.

Lina starts sucking me harder, faster.

I hold my breath, all of it becoming overwhelming.

"You want to come, little puppy?" Master scrapes his teeth along my shoulder, and I nod frantically. *Please, please, please.* "Then beg me. Beg Master to let you come."

"Please!" I beg shamelessly, feeling the beginning of an orgasm tingling down my spine. "Please, please, Master. I want to come—I *need* to come." Completely out of control, I start to fuck Lina's mouth roughly, chasing a climax I haven't been granted yet. "M-Master—" I tilt my head, gasping, and press my nose in the crook of his neck. He smells delicious—soap, his aftershave, invisible beads of perspiration that make his skin slightly damp. "*God.*" I groan.

Shame washes over me because he turns me into a begging slave, but it's the kind of shame that, for unknown reasons, turns me on. I'm embarrassed, too, and I feel two feet high. I can only hope Master accepts it. Accepts *me*.

"Come, baby." It's the same whisper: intimate, soft, raspy, and it's my undoing. "Fill Evangeline's mouth."

The heat of the orgasm burns through me, the rolling waves of ecstasy causing me to go rigid in Master's arms. As my cock pulses out streams of come into my girlfriend's mouth, I flush all over and feel a sheen of sweat being pressed out through my skin. With my surrender to the climax, I also grow clingy. I don't even notice holding on to Master until he's slowly loosening my grip on him. He's whispering stuff to me, but I can't hear it, still not down from my high.

"...that's a good boy," I eventually hear him uttering as my muscles unclench. I melt into his body and try to get my rapid breathing under control. "Just relax, pup. I've got you." I shudder violently, a vulnerable mess, but manage to take comfort from his words. A big part of me urges myself to back the fuck off and run away, though this time I won't escape so quickly.

As the last little shiver from the release makes its way through me, an unsettling sense of displeasure sets up camp in my gut like a fucking boulder. A rock is too small. This is bigger. More hurtful. But for once—*for-fucking-once*—it's not because I'm greedily taking the pleasure Master, a man, is giving me.

It's because I'm not sure I've really earned it.

"How about I take care of Evangeline now, huh?" He places a

final lingering kiss on my shoulder, then quietly tells me to sit down next to him. Shifting off his lap, I accidentally brush against his thick erection, which reminds me of the fact that he feels he can't come to me for help with it. *I've* made sure he feels that way. "As much as I love having you watch me—" Master grabs my jaw and looks me deep in the eye "—you're going to watch Donovan and Rory while I fuck Evangeline's tight ass." I gulp. "Watch them closely. Am I making myself clear, sub?"

I nod slowly, trapped in his piercing gaze. "Y-yes, Master."

He nods back, just once, then ushers Lina off the floor and a few feet away from the seating area. Allowing myself just one more look at them, I see that there's a camera set up on a tripod in the corner, and Master walks over to it to switch it on. *For Lina.* At least I think so. Because she loves to watch like the little voyeur she is, and she's requested videos.

As I was instructed earlier, I drag my eyes back to the couple on the couch across from me.

Truth be told, I'm not really feeling it anymore. Yeah, it's hot as hell to watch the two men fucking—or rather, one man fucking the other—and I already know why Master wants me to watch: to understand that there's nothing wrong. Which I already know.

It hasn't been about understanding for a long time. Understanding, if anything, was the first thing that came to me. Then came acceptance. I *know* there's nothing wrong with bisexuality and homosexuality. It's actually not about others at all. It's entirely a personal issue. In my twenty-six years, my father's ways and lessons have been so ingrained in me that it's close to impossible to let them go.

I want to, though. I feel like I'm close to exploding with how badly I want to go my own way.

Even an idiot would see I'm not happy. After all, I'm sitting on a couch, sexually satisfied for the moment, with two hot couples screwing like animals. I should be like a pig in shit, right? I should soak it all up, enjoy the sex show, and think I'm pretty fucking blessed. Instead I'm wallowing in self-pity, ashamed I can't be the submissive Master deserves, and it's all because of my goddamn daddy issues.

I shake my head, disgusted with my own internal whining, and refocus on Mr. Moore fucking Rory from behind.

CHAPTER 3

When we come home—er, I mean, when we get to Mark's apartment—it's the middle of the night, and we're all tired and hungry.

One of my favorite things about Mark's place—though it applies generally to our relationship—is that we fairly easy go from Master and subs to...well, I'd call us more than friends. For lack of a fitting term, I'll go with that. Maybe it's not a minute switch, but it does happen smoothly through Mark's aftercare. For which we can probably thank Lina. She's so easygoing that any spell we're under fades away when she cracks a joke or something.

Right now, it's not Evangeline or "kitten," our Master's sub, who's flitting about in the kitchen while Mark and I sit at the kitchen table; it's just...Lina. Following Mark's gaze and seeing him watching her fondly, I don't think the word "friend" fits in his own estimation, either.

Instead of feeling threatened, I'm hopeful. Hopeful that we'll all turn into something more one day. If only I can get over my fucking problems. And Christ, no pun intended *there*.

Soon, there's a variety of food on the table, and Lina sits down with a satisfied smile and tells us to dig in. There's reheated pizza, some leftover Chinese food, a plate of cold cuts and cheese, a small container of minestrone soup, and rolls that Lina said were stale before. After a round in a frying pan with some butter and garlic, they're fucking delicious.

Lina and I aren't made of money, and while I'm creative enough to make our salaries last in certain ways, my girlfriend's creativity lies in the kitchen. She can make a feast from very little.

"Damn, these are good, sweetheart," Mark mumbles around a soup-soaked roll. "I thought I didn't have shit in my fridge. Gonna go grocery shopping tomorrow." He takes a sip from his OJ and smiles. "But you didn't have any problems, did you?"

Lina grins impishly and soaks up the praise. "It's a gift. Now, eat." She scrunches her nose. "You're lookin' a little skinny."

Mark coughs a laugh and turns his disbelieving eyes to me. "What the fuck? When did she get bossy?"

I snort and chuckle, reaching for a slice of pizza. "That's just when it comes to food. No matter how much you eat, she'll call everyone skinny. Her mom and grandmother are worse." Lina's dad may be French, but her mother's side is from Georgia. Her entire family is beyond welcoming, and the Lacroix house always smells of delicious food, regardless if it's from a French recipe or some good ol' Southern cooking.

"Mmhmm, and they want to meet you." Lina nudges Mark. "My mom is crazy curious."

That's no lie. While I've been stuck with an uptight family with too many rules and restrictions, Lina's family doesn't appear to have *any*. So long as everyone's happy and fed.

"Is that a fact?" Mark looks both intrigued and surprised. "How much do you really tell your family, Evangeline?"

"Everything," Lina answers matter-of-factly. "Well, my dad's ears are a bit more delicate—" she bats her lashes and smiles too sweetly "—but my mom and my nana know everything." She waves that off as if it's nothing. "Besides, Nana's a perv. Oh, and she's protective of Brayden, but if you just calm her ass down, you'll be in her good graces, too." She finishes with a firm nod.

Mark's mouth curves into a kind grin. "Sounds like a nice family."

Yeah, and I suppose he can relate. I've learned about Mark's parents' lifestyle as well as his brothers' rebelling their way out of said lifestyle. It's kind of funny, although not in a ha-ha way, that whereas Mark's parents would probably go well with Lina's family, his brothers would go along with mine.

With Christmas around the corner, I'm content to know I won't be spending the holidays out in my parents' fancy estate. Instead I'll be force-fed at Lina's house, and it's a pleasant feeling. In fact, it's where I've spent Christmas and many other holidays since I met my girl. The only contact I have with my folks is through the phone calls my mother makes sporadically, or the times my father's assistant contacts me to tell me on his behalf I should get a grip and return to my family and become a real man.

After some comfortable silence, the only sounds coming from our appreciative humming at the food, Mark announces it's best we catch some sleep. A lot of playing, an hour-long round of aftercare and discussion about the scene, and then freshening up in Mr. Ford's private bathroom before coming here, means it's not even the middle of the night anymore, but close to morning instead.

We have the entire weekend at Mark's place now, a time Lina and I look forward to every week, and we're eager to go to bed because we know our Master's got plans for us tomorrow up on his rooftop terrace. *Thank God he's got heaters up there.* Before that, I think he will scene with me alone, 'cause Lina has a job interview down at the wharf that she couldn't reschedule. A couple wants a tutor for their twin boys once a week, and they own a restaurant down by the bay.

As usual, we fall asleep in Mark's massive bed, Lina wedged between us and limbs tangled together under the sheets. We sleep naked, our bodies still temporarily sated from tonight's activities.

The next morning, Evangeline wakes us up too early just to kiss us goodbye. She whispers something in Mark's ear, which makes him rumble a sleepy chuckle. Then she walks over to my side of the bed, dressed and ready to go, and murmurs that she loves me and supports me, no matter what.

With a glint in her eye, she whispers, "Make our day, *mon ange*. I *know* you're ready for the leap."

Rubbing my eyes, I frown and yawn, wondering what she's talking about. But instead of clarifying, she grins and blows me a kiss.

"I'll see you for lunch," is the last thing I hear her say before I promptly fall back to sleep.

When I wake up again, my head is on a solid chest and a muscular arm is wrapped around my shoulders. My leg, I notice, is draped over Mark's thigh. *Oh, Jesus Christ.* This is what I'm supposed to rebel against. I'm not supposed to like this—want it, crave it, fucking *yearn*...

Feeling a twinge of panic, I carefully move away from his warmth. As I always do. Mark shifts and turns, his breathing even and calm, and we end up on our sides. Close, but not touching. Face-to-face, chest-to-chest, and...other parts. *Fuck.*

Willing my semi-hard dick to calm the fuck down isn't going to happen. So, I scoot down slightly, hoping to keep my morning wood away from his. Having seen Mark in action and woken up near him before, I'm willing to bet I'm not the only one who's hard. 'Cause it feels like he's always in the mood.

With my face to his collarbone instead, I hope it eliminates the risk of us, um, touching. And shit, I'm really overthinking this. But I can't help it. Around him, I tend to overanalyze everything.

There's the familiar voice in my head—my father's—and it tells me that a small scoot is too little. I should get out of bed and start my day. Or simply get away from Mark.

Yet...I stay. Close enough to feel his breaths on the top of my head. Close enough to feel his body warmth. Close enough to—*oh, shit.* Holding my breath, I lie stock-still as Mark's arm comes down over my middle. He shifts once more, and then we're definitely touching. More than his arm around me. With my head tucked under his chin and his impressive body pressed against mine, I should panic further. I should run for the fucking hills.

There are plenty of them here in San Fran.

I don't run. I'm tired of running.

I almost jump out of my skin when I hear his gruff, sleepy voice. "Why does it feel like I'm in bed with a robot?"

Maybe because I'm as rigid as one?

"Sorry," I mumble, swallowing hard. Fuck, I'm nervous. My heart is pounding too fast, and I'm painfully aware that my cock is brushing against his. Hopefully, he won't notice—oh, who am I kidding? Mark always notices. He notices everything. He knows too well I'm struggling with my attraction for him, so why I even bother to hide it—since I fail, anyway—is beyond me.

"When are you going to relax around me, Brayden?" he whispers. His hand gently rubs my back; it's a touch of comfort, because that's what he does. He's always there to comfort and support. "I can touch you during a scene, but..." But that's different. He doesn't often touch me intimately, even though his hands on me always feel scorching and sensual. "I know you want it." His soft, sleep-laced voice sends tremors down my spine.

I give a quick shake of my head in denial, except my words have run out, and despite my weak attempt at rejecting what I want, my body betrays me. All the time. The dreams I have, the fantasies running through my head...

It's wrong, it's wrong, it's wrong.

Dad's voice.

I hate him.

"Look at me, Brayden."

Forget it. No way. I can't—I...I obey.

Warily, I lift my head and peer up at him. As always, there's no judgment in his eyes. There's patience, plenty of it.

Does he know how fucking attractive he is? Does he know that, aside from Lina, he's the one I can't stop thinking about?

I bet he does.

"Such a stubborn little sub," he murmurs and cups my cheek.

It heats up in response and I try to duck my head again. He doesn't allow it. While staring at me intently, practically searing his way into my fucking soul with those deep blue eyes, he shifts a few inches closer to me. A challenge appears in his gaze, quiet determination, and...something else.

I suck in a quick breath, feeling his cock pressing against my own.

Immediately, shame floods me. I've been told too many times that this is wrong and perverse.

"You know, I could just fucking kill your father."

I stutter a breath, wondering if I have any secrets left. While I haven't told Mark about my family, it seems he already knows just by observing my behavior and being aware of my father's name.

"Wh-what?" I croak.

"It's fairly obvious that he's told you a bunch of horseshit," he replies bluntly.

If I wasn't so wound-up and ready to break, perhaps I'd laugh at his words. Instead I offer a vague shrug, not wanting to confirm anything, and I'm granted the permission to lower my head. Staring at his broad chest again, I focus on getting control of my breathing. Nothing seems to work. My mind tells me to get the hell away, yet the rest of me...

Indecision is a heartless bitch. Confliction is a goddamn cunt. Vulnerability is a fucking hag.

Lina would make this easy for me. She's been the barrier

between Mark and me, and she has the patience of a saint—kinda like Mark, I guess. I'm lucky to have her. God knows I couldn't love her more. Or maybe I could. After all, I find myself falling for that woman more every day. But right now, she's not where she's supposed to be. She's not here. Which leaves nothing between my body and Mark's. Not even underwear or the sheets. We're both using the same covers. Both touching.

Her not being here reminds me of something else, too. Whenever we spend the weekend at Mark's place, he has us servicing him in the mornings. It's extremely erotic to see Mark using Lina, and it's strangely satisfying, too. I can't even begin to explain it, but like I said, she's not here now. So, who is going to service Mark?

You're reaching.

I know, but it would be easier if I didn't have the choice. If Mark commanded me to—to...to do something, I would. I think. Yeah, because it wouldn't be my decision. It would be his. Just like last night in Mr. Ford's office.

Mark won't do that, though. I can tell. This is one thing he wants from me—of my own choosing. I have to take that first step; he won't do it. Problem is, I won't either.

You sure about that?

I bite down on my lip, a crease appearing on my forehead, and I stare at the hard planes of his naked chest. Lina's had her mouth all over it. Her hands, her thighs, her sweet pussy.

The only thing I envy is that I don't have the same closeness with him—that intimacy.

Hesitantly, before I can chicken out, I place my hand on his bicep. Other than a small twitch of his muscles, there's no reaction. Not until a minute or so later when he softly brushes his hand along my spine. Again, it's to comfort me, reassure me, and it works to an extent.

He lulls me into a relaxed state—at least to the point where my chest is no longer heaving with each shallow breath. Another few minutes later, he pauses and rests his hand on my lower back. It's casual, if not for two fingers being so close to the crack of my ass.

It's arousing and new and thrilling and scary as hell.

In the end, I succumb. My muscles unclench, and I even burrow close enough to drop my forehead to his collarbone. Dad's voice screams furiously, but Mark's protectiveness helps to keep it out. I guess he makes me feel—I don't know, accepted? Regardless, it's impossible to stay away any longer.

When he hums and breathes me in, his nose in my sleep-tangled hair, I sigh in contentment and melt. Maybe I can stay like this for only a little while—and be satisfied with that.

Bullshit.

Yeah, I know. Fucking hell.

Whatever—right now, I ignore all the voices that make me come off as a goddamn nutcase. I let myself have this. The only thing that would be more perfect is if Lina were here, too. Then again, if she were, I'd be using her as a shield again.

I realize I don't want that.

In a bold move, I nudge my foot between his and end up with my leg trapped. Arousal spikes. Desire settles like a rock in the pit of my stomach, and Mark makes his own move, hitching his leg farther up my thigh. Under the covers, my cock throbs next to his, and I accidentally—instinctively—buck my hips forward an inch or two. But it's enough for him to notice.

"Jesus Christ." He groans under his breath, causing me to stiffen. "You're killing me here, pup."

"I'm sorry," I rasp, about to panic. Overcome with too many feelings, I begin to stutter like a moron. "I j-just—I need, um—"

"It's okay." He cuts me off and cups my cheek, once again forcing me to face him, much to my mortification. "I know what you need."

Without another word, he tilts his face over mine and kisses me. Squarely on the mouth. Soft yet firm lips. Scruff. It scratches against my skin in a way that makes me shiver.

CHAPTER 4

While shock sears through me and stuns me into immobility, the parts of me that have longed for this are stronger. It's his touch—I surrender to it. Completely.

Kissing him back, I let him take control even though I participate as much as he does. A strangled noise erupts from my throat as he slides his hand down and palms my ass, then gives a slow thrust that grinds our cocks together.

He doesn't stop, either. It's merely the beginning of one of the most erotic experiences of my life. The kiss deepens, and now that I've caved, I can move on my own; I don't need his hand urging me.

That means he can use it for...fuck, anything. My cock throbs as unbidden thoughts flash through me. They trigger me, too. I become a slave—fucking desperate. I cling to him, craving more. Our tongues slide together, lips insistent and locked. Then that skilled hand of his slips between our bodies; he cups the heads of our cocks and gives a sensual tug and twist.

I groan embarrassingly loud and thrust upward, into his palm.

"That's it," he murmurs huskily. He starts to kiss my jaw, my throat, my neck—at the same time as he wraps his long fingers around us, inches away from reaching all the way, and strokes hard, smoothly, expertly. A ragged whisper, "You like this, baby?"

"Yeah—fuck. *Yesss*." I hiss when he tightens his hold. "Please..."

I didn't know it would feel this way.

I didn't know, I didn't know, I didn't know.

"Please what?" He nips at my neck. "Give me your words. Tell me what you want."

Tall order. I want too much. All of it. It's almost overwhelming. I've denied this for so long, and now that it's within reach, I have no idea where to start. The fact that he keeps stroking, rubbing against me, doesn't make it easier for me to think.

Think, goddammit; *think*. During our scenes—yeah, he's touched me. He has rolled on condoms and cock rings, and he has inserted anal plugs and used dildos. *He has prepared me.*

That's been different. He's been Master, and he's done the same with Lina. Except with her, there've also been more intimate touches—touches because it simply feels good; touches without real purpose. Kisses, hard fucking, and oral sex. None of that with me. But now—like I said, I want it all. At once.

"I want you to use me," I blurt out, panting. I kind of regret the wording, because it feels like a dark secret. Though, it's the truth— and another thing I've kept hidden in the past. Men are supposed to be strong, type Alpha-fucking-male, providers for women, and unyielding.

And here I am, dreaming of being Mark's fuck-toy.

I fantasize about him taking me relentlessly, claiming me in brutal ways.

Like always, only Lina knows my most animalistic desires. I could never hide that shit from her.

Despite her open mind, sweetest heart, and constant reminders to me that we're all different, that we all have different wants, I can't shake the feeling of being weak—a disappointment.

My body tenses up when I realize Mark has stopped. Peering at him nervously, I see that he's studying me. Hooded gaze, revealing lust, and past that is nothing but experience. He reads me too well, and it leaves me exposed.

"I'm not going to take guesses right now," he says gravely, unmasked desire in his voice. "But—" he pushes me aside and follows, covering my body with his "—one thing is fucking clear, Brayden. We *will* talk about whatever you're hiding." Slowly, he lowers his face and brushes his lips over mine. He also lets his weight press into me, probably knowing I want it—and can take it.

He can be as rough as he wants. *Just a thought.*

"But you don't want to talk right now, do you?" It's another one of his husky whispers. All I can do is shake my head and welcome his mouth. "I love seeing you like this. Surrendered, wanting, no more resistance, so *fucking* ready for me to do whatever I want."

"Mark," I whimper pathetically. *Give me something.*

I'll worry about the aftermath later.

"I've waited for this." He grinds our cocks together again. "Thought about this—countless times." His voice is addictive. "Soon, I'll have you bound and spread for me." Seduced by his fucking authority. "Both of you—you and Evangeline." I writhe and buck under him, crazed for more. "Two little subs under my care." Nuzzling the spot below my ear, he whispers his final words for the moment. "But right now I want your mouth on my cock, baby."

My mouth waters at the same time as I admit to myself that I, for some goddamn reason, like his new name for me. Term of endearment. Nickname. Whatever. *Baby.* Humiliating and arousing. It could be sweet, too, I guess.

"I want it," I hear myself moan. "I want *you.*"

Mark lifts himself off my heated body but dips down and kisses me softly. "Glad to hear it, Brayden." Rolling over, he ends up on his back next to me, and he coaxes me to come with him. "You know I want you, too."

I do. He hasn't made that a secret, ever. If he had, I wouldn't have found the guts to give in. Or maybe I would, but not yet. As it is, Mark never hides anything. He also doesn't miss anything. I've been fooling myself, thinking my thoughts are safe from him, but he knows. He knows humiliation turns me on.

It would be a different kind of humiliation than the one I've experienced in the past. Mark wouldn't bully me, push me down and leave me there, or be evil and cruel. He would use my weaknesses for him and Lina against me, taunt me, and expose me, and he would also catch me and bring me back.

Scooting down his body, I settle between his muscular thighs, again feeling my mouth watering.

"What a spectacular fuckin' sight," Mark mutters and drags a hand over his face.

Relief rushes through me, and I show it with a silly little grin I can't hide. I'm high on that relief, almost delirious, and the small grin is still in place when I lower my head and close my mouth over the head of his cock.

Fuck, yeah.

I savor his musky scent, the flavor of him, and unlike Lina, who can be a bit of a tease, I take him farther and farther until he hits the back of my throat. Our girl can deep-throat. I'm gonna need practice. All I can do for now is to finally give him the attention I'm capable of. With nothing holding me back, I hope to become the sub, *the man*, he deserves.

"Christ, that's perfect," he moans.

Peering up at him while I soak his erection with my tongue, I see tensed abs, defined pecs, and a face flashing with dark desire. When his lust-filled eyes meet mine, it's like we fuel each other. I acknowledge the urgency in his gaze by tightening my lips around his steel-hard cock, and his groaned curse makes me wanna fuck the mattress.

I suck him as hard as I can and grind my own dick against the sheets. I feel the wet spot I create on the fabric and only rub harder. My hands slide up his muscular thighs to fondle his tight sac, having watched him enough to know what he's into.

Every now and then, a spurt of pre-come coats the roof of my mouth as proof that I'm doing it right, and I savor the salty taste of him. It's been almost ten years since I was with a guy intimately, and I don't remember it being this good, this sexy, this satisfying, this *consuming*. Hell, my one and only other experience with another man ended in disaster, and it's nothing I think of fondly.

Mark bucks his hips, thankfully not treating me like I'm made of glass, and he soon fists my hair to guide me over him. "Wait," he grits out and stills me. "I want to be inside you when I come."

I whimper pitifully, nod, and lick my thoroughly-used lips. Pulling me up his body, he gives me a bruising kiss and explores my mouth with his tongue, barely letting me breathe. The realization hits me hard—that he's wanted me for a while now, and just how much he wants me. It makes me feel both desired and idiotic. Because I wish I could've been more for him from the get-go.

He rolls us over so I'm on my back. He grinds our dicks together, still kissing me hungrily, then breaks away. Breathing heavily, he mutters, "Don't move a fucking muscle." He leaves me panting and on the verge of begging for his touch, but he's only gone for a moment. When he returns, he's got a bottle of lube. "Finally all mine." He's quick to cover my body with his again, and he captures my mouth in another hard kiss.

It's night and day—Mark and Lina. One is hard, big, less pliable, and oozes power and strength. Another is soft, small, sweet, and radiates...I don't know, brightness, I think is a good word. They're both wonderful and insanely appealing to me, in different ways.

"I feel stupid for not asking." He kisses my jaw and wraps his fingers around my aching cock, giving it a slow stroke. I choke on a breath and grab on to his shoulders. "Are you ready for this, Brayden? I mean sex...with me." He nuzzles his nose to mine. "Do you want me inside you?"

"Yeah," I groan and buck my hips. Fuck, can't he see how ready I am? "I want you. *Now*."

He already knows I love it when he uses toys on me, so it can't really come as a shock that I want his cock, can it?

"Demanding." He smirks and shakes his head in amusement. "That's my job." I flush as his eyes turn dark and predatory. "And how I fucking love that job," he murmurs and sits back on his heels between my parted legs.

I lick my lips, still tasting him from before, and practice patience as Mark strokes me expertly while using his free hand to prepare my ass for him.

"Push back," he whispers. I obey; when he adds a second lubed-up finger, I push into his touch, relaxing quickly. I'm used to the dull burn, and it's one in which I find a perverted thrill. "Any discomfort?"

I quickly shake my head.

He huffs a chuckle. "I shouldn't be surprised. You love this." He adds a third finger, and I let out a long moan as my eyes flutter closed. "Just wait 'til I get to fuck you after giving you an enema." As if I needed more reasons to look like a tomato. *Jesus Christ.* I know this can be standard practice before anal sex, and I've had enemas before, mostly for hygienic reasons when Lina and I started with anal play, but I haven't had sex right after one. "You'll be even more sensitive, pup."

I'll take his word for it.

Once he deems me ready for him, he coats his cock in lube before putting the bottle to the side. Then he stuns me by engulfing my dick in his mouth. We both groan, although I always come off as so fucking greedy and desperate. I spit out a curse and place a hand on his head, though there's nothing to weave through or grasp. His dark hair can't be more than half an inch long, soft and thick. Digging my head back into the pillow, my face scrunches together as he sucks me strong as hell and massages my balls. Shudders rip through me like shattering currents, and the surprise of his actions lingers for a long time.

"Christ," I hiss.

My eyes are glued to him, and the only thing I can think is that he's still all man. Just because he's going down on another man, he's not any less masculine. There's always an air of authority around Mark, and he can play me like a fucking fiddle.

Releasing me slowly, he continues to kiss his way up my body, only pausing to get my nipples hard and tight.

"Who does your body belong to, Brayden?" he whispers and applies lubrication to my dick. "Tell me."

"You," I grit out, pushing back. He holds me tightly, making it impossible for me to move, though that doesn't mean I stop trying. "You, Mark. Fuck, just—" *Fuck me!* I let out a panted breath and remind myself once more about that fucking word: patience. *Damn.* It's not easy. "It's more than my body. Same goes for Lina," I mumble without thinking.

As he kisses my neck, I tilt my head to give him access and notice goose bumps rising across his left arm, and he falters.

"I'm sorry." I tense up, feeling like an idiot now. I should've kept my mouth shut! "I-I didn't mean to say anything. We can't help it—"

"Shhh." Mark grabs my jaw and covers my mouth with his. "Shh, baby." Lifting his head a few inches, he looks down at me with a gentle, yet serious expression. "Your feelings aren't the only ones that have changed." He dips down again and scrapes his teeth along my bottom lip. "I'm not going anywhere, all right?" I nod slightly, attempting to relax. "Just 'cause you two belong to me doesn't mean I don't belong to you, as well."

I exhale, finding comfort in those words. "Okay." I nod some more and reach up to kiss him. "Okay."

He responds by deepening the kiss, echoing a quiet "Okay," and pressing his body more fully against mine. I can feel every hard inch of him, and it sets us back on track. We focus on each other; mainly, we focus on *right now.*

With a low groan, Mark begins to push into me, and the second the head of his cock passes my tight ring of muscle, we both let out labored breaths through clenched teeth. He never ceases to kiss me or touch me. His callused hands knead my thighs, encouraging me to lock my feet around him. I do, and with a buck of my hips, I force him deeper inside me. All the way.

"Oh, fuck," I breathe out, my eyes growing large. "*Mark.*"

"Jesus," he mutters breathlessly. "You gotta calm down. I'm a little bigger than the toys I've fucked you with in the past."

You're telling me this now?

I clamp my mouth shut, wanting to scream. Again, I feel stupid. I've been up close with Mark's cock several times; I should *know* he's not a fucking piece of plastic or silicone. And I do remember how sore Lina was after our first weekend.

It doesn't take that long for the pain to ebb, though. The way he touches me and whispers obscene words in my ear heats me up like nothing else. He takes control, not that he ever lost it, and slowly starts to move, all while keeping up his other ways to satisfy me. He's a kisser, I already know, but today is the first time I get to experience it, and now I understand why Lina often gives out dreamy sighs after kissing Mark. He's a master at that, too; he's passionate about it—nothing half-assed or unemotional. He's also generous with his touches and murmurs of both affection and dirty words.

"So good," I sigh, consumed by a new kind of fire. The burn isn't as dull as it usually is, but it's not a bad thing. It makes everything more intense instead, and I move my hands up his thick biceps to feel more of him.

"Understatement." He grunts and thrusts a bit harder. I feel his long, thick cock sliding in and out of me, less resistance with each pass. "Now that I know what it's like to be inside you—" he nips at my upper lip and slips a hand between us, wrapping his fingers firmly around my dick "—I won't let you push me away." I moan as he strokes me at the same pace he's moving inside me. "I get that not everything is fixed by a fuck." A dark chuckle slips through his lips, and I shudder and reach up to claim his mouth with mine. He speaks into the messy kiss. "But I won't allow you to sink into that little hole where you're disgusted with yourself." He has an eyebrow arched when I meet his gaze. "You think I don't know how your mind works?"

I swallow thickly, not knowing what to say.

"You're mine now, Brayden." His voice is low, full of both warning and promise. "Mine and Evangeline's. And why the *fuck* would we allow our boy to hate himself?"

"Mark," I mumble, shaking my head. I avert my eyes. "It's not—"

"—that simple? I know," he finishes. "But we've got time and patience to make you understand." He kisses me again, mingling our tongues together languidly, and speeds up after having slowed down just a little. He also tightens his grip around my cock, causing me to whimper and arch into him. "Just keep one thing in mind. We want you for who you are—sure as hell not for who your family wants you to be."

I chuckle shakily and tilt my head toward his neck. "Don't ruin the mood."

"You little bastard." He huffs a quiet laugh and drives into me with force, and I'm blinded by a mixture of incredible pleasure and pain. "Better?"

"Yeah—oh, fuck." I gasp as a series of tremors run down my spine, each seemingly heading in a different direction. My balls start to tingle, my skin becomes damp with a new flush, my muscles strain, my ass tenses, and several other sensations struggle to pull me under. "More," I plead. "Fuck me harder. I *need* you."

He doesn't respond verbally, but he does pull out of me, causing me to wince, and he twirls a finger. A silent command for me to get on all fours. *Oh, hell yeah.* Scrambling into position, I push out my ass much like Rory did last night. I do it without shame, and then I drop to my elbows, ready for him.

This time there's no wait—no going slow. Gripping my hips, he pushes into me with a hard thrust. "Fuck," he growls, setting a fast pace. I cry out, the sound muffled as I bury my face in my pillow, and I take his cock the way I want it. He fucks me forcefully—plain and simple—and I'm already addicted. "So damn amazing," he groans. "My dirty little fuck-toy."

"Oh, Jesus." I gulp and bite down on the pillow. A brand-new type of arousal flares up inside me, and it's the result of his previous words. *My dirty little fuck-toy.* That line goes on repeat in my head as he hammers into me, leaving me to hang on for dear life.

"This is what you want, isn't it?" he demands, out of breath. All I can muster is a weak nod as I fight my orgasm. "You want me to use you. You want to rely on me, be dependent on me, count on me to take care of you like the little boy you are."

I squeeze my eyes shut, exposed and raw. I do want all that—when I'm his sub, and that's who I want to be right this moment. I want to curl into him, give everything away, and trust him to catch me or whatever.

It's so easy when he's Master.

I'm not saying I want it 24/7—far from it—but I do want it more than over the weekends and the few weekdays we find time.

"I'll make it happen." He suddenly stops, grabs one handful of my hair, grasps my shoulder with his other hand, and pulls me up. My back meets his chest with a muted sound, all while his cock pulses hotly inside me. He's close, I realize. "You're my little puppy, remember?" He nuzzles my neck, breathing harshly. I feel his chest's rapid movements and how he grinds deeper into my already-sore ass. "I'll keep you on a leash, baby boy; I'll make sure no one but me and Evangeline gets close to my property."

I groan and turn my head, needing more contact. "Master," I mumble weakly.

"That's right," he whispers. "Call me that whenever you want me to take control. Understood?"

"Yes, Sir—Master." I nod quickly and manage to reach his jaw for a kiss. Thankfully, he tilts his head so I get his lips. "Thank you." I exhale, more relief flooding me. "Thank you."

"My pleasure, I promise," he chuckles huskily. Humor aside, he drops a soft kiss on my shoulder and hugs me to him affectionately before pushing me down to the mattress again. "Hold on tight."

I immediately grab on to the sheets, bracing myself for more merciless fucking, and I'm not disappointed. He delivers with his entire body. The kisses are back, now along my spine. He fists my leaking cock and strokes it hard; he uses his free hand to touch me all over, evoking goose bumps and shivers, and his moans and curses only add to it all.

It's not long before I'm begging to come.

"Not yet," he grunts. "Almost. *Fuck*—almost there, baby."

Peering over my shoulder, I watch in a daze as he tips his head back, lost in excitement and concentration. Only a few seconds later, he sucks in a breath and screws his eyes shut. His thrusts become jerky and irregular, and I know he's coming. Heat surges deep inside me, and slick morphs into soaked with his release.

"Come, Brayden," he grits out.

Dropping my forehead to the pillow again, I let go of every thought that isn't centered on his cock filling my ass and his hand pumping my own cock. He keeps rocking into me, in the middle of his release, yet his hand working my dick doesn't falter. When he tugs and twists and swipes the pad of his thumb over the head of me, smearing the arousal that has leaked out, I'm a goner.

I cry out into the pillow as spurts of come begin to shoot out of my cock. With another twist, he gathers hot liquid from me and uses it as extra lube. At the same time, I feel him slowing down, gradually beginning to soften inside me.

Eventually I collapse, panting and shuddering from the aftereffects of the orgasm. As Mark gives my cock a final upstroke, he squeezes out a last little trickle of come before he slides his hand free from under me.

"So fucking good," he pants.

I nod and hum, but then I let out a noise of discomfort as he pulls out of me and drops his weight next to me. Christ, sore doesn't begin to describe it. I'm also sleepy and hungry and in desperate fucking need of a shower. But getting out of this bed seems like mission impossible. Not even the wet spot under me makes me wanna move.

"I could lie here all day." I yawn, instinctively moving toward Mark's body for comfort. Maybe that word isn't the right one; after all, I don't need comforting, but whatever. I'm too spent to think clearly. With Mark lifting his arm for me, I snuggle close and hope sleep will take me.

"Don't fall asleep." He kisses my forehead. "We're gonna take a shower now, and then we'll meet up with Evangeline for lunch."

I think I actually whine, though it could've just been in my head. "We can order in. I'm tired." Another yawn slips out and I kiss his chest before settling again. "I could use a couple hours of shut-eye."

His chest rumbles with a chuckle. "Nice try, but we're gonna have an ecstatic girl on our hands once she finds out about us, and I fear for my furniture. Remember how she jumped on this bed just because I bought a new video camera after Thanksgiving?"

I snort a laugh. "She'll probably pout and wonder why we didn't videotape ourselves this morning." Now I suddenly miss our girl like crazy, but my arms and legs feel too heavy to move.

"She loves you—wants what's best for you," he murmurs. "There's no telling how excited she'll get."

"Ugh." Fine. All right. "But I can't move." Too tired. "And where are we even gonna meet up with her?" I crack one eye open.

"She likes that place on 16th Street." Now it's Mark's turn to yawn, but he's got better self-control, 'cause he still begins to get up. "Come on, baby boy. Let's shower before we head out. We can text our girl on the way."

Well, at least we're relatively close, since Mark lives in the Haight.

CHAPTER 5

About an hour later, Mark and I get away from the cold December weather and order sodas and sandwiches before taking our seats by the large window in the bohemian-looking café. The sun is out and the sky is blue, though it's fucking frigid outside.

I shrug out of my jacket, dressed casually in jeans and a Henley, and I keep my beanie on. "I'm starving." I lean forward in my chair and immediately dig into my ham and Dijon mustard sandwich, nearly burning my tongue on the melted cheese. "Damn, this is good."

Mark runs a hand through his hair, dropping his own beanie on the table, his eyes trained on his phone. There's a smirk on his lips.

"What?" I ask, curious.

He chuckles and shakes his head, pocketing his phone. "Just Rio. He's in the neighborhood with his little brother who's picking out engagement rings for himself and his boyfriend." He unwraps his grilled cheese, amusement in his eyes. "Rio despises shopping, so he's sending me sarcastic comments about salespeople."

I snicker and return to my sandwich. "I thought Doms liked to be in charge of what their subs wear and stuff. Shopping is involved there, isn't it?"

"The internet is a fucking amazing thing," he deadpans before he grins. "Besides, look where we're at. You've met Rio and Gabriel."

True. From what I've seen, Rio—or Mr. Kelly or Master Rio as I know him—is kind of a reserved man. Then last week when Mr. Kelly's brother visited Switch, it was easy to see that Gabriel was the opposite. They share the same features—although Rio is a lot taller—with the alabaster skin, very green eyes, and close to raven-black hair, but Gabriel is certainly not dominant. One word to describe him would be flamboyant.

"So, you've got Gabriel high on life and with a million friends," Mark says, grinning, "Rio tagging along, and where are we?"

The Castro, also San Francisco's gay district.

"Mr. Kelly is straight," I state unnecessarily.

Mark shrugs. "He's done his experimenting like most of us, but yeah, he's mostly into women. Why?" He cocks his head and places an arm on the back of my chair. "You gotta relax with the labels, pup. It's not a big deal."

"I know," I mumble and look at my food. "I'm trying." I let out a soft breath and pull off my beanie. "But I'm not gay."

"Of course you're not." He smirks, not missing a beat. "You're fucking obsessed with Evangeline's pussy."

I flush and look around us, hoping no one heard him. "And you call Lina shameless," I mutter and shift in my seat.

I'm so sore, it's not even funny.

"Hey." He nudges me and leans closer. His expression is serious now, though soft and patient. "Would it be wrong if you *were* gay?"

"No," I insist honestly. My shoulders drop slightly. "It's just—" I sigh in defeat. "It's up here." I tap my temple. "How I grew up. My dad..." Fuck, am I really going into all that now? *Here?*

"Your dad, what? Tell me." It's not a demand this time. Only a request. He wants to know but won't push me.

"He caught me when I was seventeen," I admit, tensing up. "There was a guy I liked—we fooled around, had sex, no big deal, but..." I make a face and look down. We only had sex one time. He topped me. Before that, it was just kissing, touching, fooling around...

"Your father made it a big deal, and since then, he's been preaching like the devout Catholic he is," Mark finishes.

I nod; that's exactly what happened. My father, the mighty Clark Zeagler, had high hopes for me, his only child. I was gonna study politics, be great at sports, and build my own fortune.

Instead I was drawn to computers, and I only like sports for the fun of it, not to compete and bring home trophies. I was weak, according to him. Not man enough. After catching me with my old high school friend, my father looked at me with resentment and disappointment in his eyes. The lectures were cruel, and I started to shut down.

Then I left altogether; now I barely talk to my parents.

I would've cut all ties if it weren't for the concept of Catholic guilt. My mother can play that card like she invented the game. Though, while I cave on a couple of occasions and talk to her for a few minutes, I keep my distance. She's never been a part of Dad's bullying, per se, but my beliefs about her innocence evaporated when she allowed him to keep going.

"Like I said earlier—" Mark pulls me close and kisses my temple "—we'll make you understand. One day at a time. Okay?" I nod again as he cups my neck and presses our foreheads together. Even though we're in public, I like this, revel in, and want it. "You're beautiful. You know that?"

More heat creeps forward, coloring my cheeks. "Stop seducing me." I don't stand a fucking chance against this man. "You've already gotten me into your bed." I tilt my head, wanting his mouth.

"My next plan is to make you stay," he murmurs, brushing his lips over mine. "Both of you." I swallow hard and kiss him back. "I've seen your apartment. I don't like it. It's not a safe neighborhood, either."

I laugh through my nose, still kissing him lightly. "We can't all be fancy gym owners and work as bartenders only for kicks." Staying with Mark more, though? Hell yeah, I'd love that.

"Yeah, 'cause that's so fucking fancy," he drawls. "But trust me —" he lands a final kiss on my lips, a firm, warm one "—we'll revisit this topic soon. Now, eat. You're lookin' a little skinny." He mimics Lina's words from last night, making me chuckle.

Naturally, this is the moment Lina walks through the door with a beaming smile on her face and rosy cheeks from the cold.

Mark offers a lazy smirk, and I roll my eyes, though I'm smiling.

"I saw you!" she whisper-shouts and closes the distance, ripping off her knitted beret and gloves as she goes. Instead of sitting down in the empty chair, she plops down on my lap. "I saw you through the window!" Before I can even get a word in, she starts to pepper my face with kisses. Her lips are softer and poutier than Mark's, and just as addictive. "I love you, I love you, I love you. By the way, our car broke down. I had to take a cab the last bit." *That* said, she jumps over to Mark's lap to kiss him, too.

I shake my head, dazed and slightly overwhelmed. Our car... and the kisses...and if we didn't have the café's customers' attention before, we sure as hell do now.

"You're too fucking sweet, kitten." Mark's blue eyes flash with amusement, and he captures Lina's mouth in a deep kiss. I smile at them, feeling a sense of *this-is-it*, and finally get back to my neglected sandwich. "Don't worry about your car. I'll arrange for it to be picked up later."

"Mmm." Lina hums and rests her head on Mark's shoulder. "This is nice. I should go order something. Brayden, what did you get?" Leaning over, she opens her mouth, and I dutifully extend my sandwich to her. She takes a small bite, chews for a second, and her eyes light up. "Oh, yeah. *J'adore la vraie moutarde. C'est parfait.*"

"You sit tight, sweetheart." Mark lifts her off his lap. "I'll get one for you. What do you want to drink?"

"Oh, thank you. Iced tea, please. Peach!" She pops a kiss on his cheek, then sits down again and turns to me. "So—"

"Did you get the job?" I ask before she starts her inquisition.

"Yes, I did. Like *that's* interesting." She rolls her eyes. "Now, tell me *everything.*"

"I'm beginning to wonder if you're on crack," I tell her, hiding my smile.

That earns me a *look*—one I've learned Kayla is also very capable of. It's a chick thing.

"Just tell me before I *die*, Brayden." She pouts, being all dramatic.

After we're done eating and Lina has received the short version of how Mark and I spent our morning, Mark tells us that Rio is just up Castro Street and wonders if we'd like to join him for coffee. So, we bundle up and leave one café for another.

It was only a few days ago we were here the last time; when the farmer's market on Noe Street closed for the season, and I'm kinda relieved. Farmer's markets, flea markets, and antique shopping all fall under the category of Lina's favorites. I'm the one she drags with her. Or Mark, I suppose, for next season.

"I got a text from Kayla." Lina shivers from the cold and hugs my left arm. "They've landed in Mexico, and she's already scheming to make their vacation last longer, thus not going to Oregon for Christmas."

Mark, walking on my other side, squeezes my hand and we grin at nothing, not saying a word. Because we still think the whole situation, how Kayla and Mr. Ford met, is funny as hell.

Spending Christmas with your cousin, also known as your fiancé's ex-girlfriend...*priceless*.

"Oh, you two are awful." Lina notices our expressions, and I get a slap on my arm. "That Amanda woman is a bitch, and she's gonna be all claws out when Kayla and Mr. Ford get there."

"I'm sure Nicholas can handle it," Mark points out. "Hell, I'm sure Kayla can handle it, too."

"Still..." Lina sighs, ever the sweetheart. "Oh! There's Master Rio!" The subject is closed when she spots him outside a coffee shop.

He looks tired, which I suppose is the result of the shopping with his younger brother. Much like Mr. Ford, he dresses in suits, and you gotta be blind to say he's not strikingly handsome.

"You look like shit, man." Mark smirks and shakes hands with Mr. Kelly.

"Fuck you too, mate." Mr. Kelly smiles faintly and tugs up the lapels of his coat to protect him from the harsh winds. Then he nods at something across the street. "Remember the week before I flew out on my last assignment?" Mark frowns, confused, but nods nonetheless. "I had dinner with your family—met your brothers and sisters and so on."

I like that Mark sees all the kids he grew up with as siblings, even if only three of them are biological.

"Yeah? What about it?" Mark sticks his free hand down into a pocket of his jeans.

Mr. Kelly offers that ghost of a smile again, and it widens slightly when he sees our joined hands. "I know it's been a while, but I reckon I just saw your big brother—Garrett? Greg?—go into that bar across the street." At that, we all look in the direction of his earlier nod, and we spot the sign of one of the countless gay bars in the Castro.

"Are you kidding me?" Mark chuckles darkly, his eyes narrowed and trained on the bar. "I swear to Christ, if he's been acting like a douche all these years because he's hiding his sexuality, I *will* kick his fucking ass."

I don't even know what to think about that. I've heard stories about Mark's brothers from both him and Lina, and the oldest Cooper son doesn't seem like a nice guy at all. I'm glad I haven't met him.

"He's got a wife and daughter, yeah?" Mr. Kelly arches a brow.

I pinch Lina's ass 'cause she's staring. She's hypnotized—her word, actually—by Mr. Kelly's accent. She has a thing for accents, though I wouldn't say Mr. Kelly's is all that different from ours. It's just a few words and expressions he uses that sound more Australian and maybe Irish.

"Yeah." Mark sighs heavily and massages his forehead. "Ah, fuck it. Maybe there's an explanation, though I highly doubt it, but I'm not touching that one right now. Let's grab a cup of coffee." He nods at the coffeehouse we're standing in front of. "Did Gabriel find the rings?"

Mr. Kelly groans and chuckles tiredly, the old topic forgotten for now, and our day continues. We have coffee with Mr. Kelly, talk about this and that, although Lina and I are mostly content to sit back and listen, and then we part ways.

Grocery shopping is our last item on the to-do list before we go back to Mark's place to rest for a bit, make dinner together, and get ready for a scene where we'll all finally be on equal ground when it comes to intimacy.

When we kick back later that night with hot chocolates on the rooftop terrace, blankets and an open fire and everything, I don't have to pull away or tense up when Mark comes near. We bundle up and sit close, tired and sated, and share sensual kisses between the three of us.

When we go to bed, I no longer need Lina as a shield.

When we wake up in the morning, both Lina and Mark make sure I shake off the old mind-set my father's pushed onto me.

Because like Mark said, it's not gonna go away overnight. They're patient, and I want him too much to go back to being a coward.

Fueled by an urge to prove myself—to all of us—I mirror Lina's moves and we service our Master like he's our drug.

Bit by bit, I will learn to let go of my old ways of thinking, but one thing I know for sure already.

I've surrendered completely to both my Master and the man I hope to include in the relationship I have with my Lina.

I learn that surrender doesn't necessarily make you weak.

It can make you whole.

TOUCHING TRUTH

A BEHIND THE SCENES NOVELLA

PART II

GREG COOPER

I stare at the empty legal pad in front of me, unable to move and kick my ass into gear. In the solitude of my office, I hear the employees getting louder in the cubicle area as lunch rolls around. Everyone's going somewhere, either to the cafeteria on the first floor or a lunch meeting.

Lunch.

I loosen my tie.

I've been here since yesterday, so I'm not fully certain of when I last ate. I was supposed to pick up breakfast... I scratch the side of my head, thinking back. I left for a little while this morning so I could take my daughter to school. I forgot to buy food on the way back to the office.

Last time I tell my assistant I can fetch something myself.

Fetch, dog.

I wince at the memory of Angel emptying her drawer of lingerie on the floor in their playroom. With a "Fetch, boy" that packed one hell of a punch, she and Ryan had watched as I returned the lingerie to the drawer. With my teeth.

I swallow uneasily and automatically check my phone. They

had me download an app for group chats when we started seeing each other. I haven't deleted it yet, and I check it too often. Our little chat is still there.

They've forgotten me and moved on, I'm sure.

In a weak moment last week, I found myself in their bar, not really knowing why. Not that it mattered. Tory informed me Ryan and Angel were on vacation.

"Goddammit." I scrub a hand over my face, my blood sugar dropping. It's impossible to work when I'm hungry, and I need to sleep. If only I didn't have those fucking dreams. Punching the intercom, I bark out at my assistant. "Get me something from the cafeteria, Sally."

Then I slump back and release a heavy breath.

———

Ted and Seth, my brothers, subtly suggest I leave work early today. I don't have the energy to argue, so I leave the office and make my way home. Abby should be out of school, so maybe I can spend some time with her and then crash.

If I'm well-rested, I can always return to the office tonight.

When I eventually pull into our driveway, my forehead creases as I take in the sight of our front yard. There are usually a few of Abby's toys littered about. Her bike almost belongs in the middle of the path that leads up to the house, yet now there's nothing. Has her babysitter not played with her today?

Unbuckling my seat belt, I check my phone and the haunting group chat just because, and then I grab my briefcase and brave the crappy weather. A company was here last week to put up Christmas lights and a couple of decorations, and I side-eye a plastic Rudolph on the way to the door. Christmas is Abby's favorite holiday; perhaps I should've ordered more decorations...? Except, no. It's easy to spoil her, but it's not good in the long run. Balance is key.

I escape the cold and am met by the smell of Christmas in the hallway. "Hello?" I remove my coat, taking a whiff. Cinnamon, vanilla, apple, and what I can only describe as cookies tickle my nose.

"Daddy!"

There's a voice I'll never tire of. I smile tiredly and squat down as she runs out from the kitchen.

"You're early." She attacks me in a hug, and I give her a warm squeeze.

"Uncle Seth called me cranky. Can you believe that?" I kiss the top of her head and grin at her furious nod and giggle.

I catch movement in the doorway to the kitchen and immediately straighten, nodding once to Abby's babysitter. "Hello, Evangeline. How are you today?"

"Good, thank you, Mr. Cooper." She smiles politely. "You?"

"I'm well, thanks." Fucking exhausted, hanging by a thread, take your pick. Setting aside my briefcase, I remove my shoes and then grab Abby's hand. "Have you been home long?"

"Only an hour or so." Evangeline gives me space to pass her to the kitchen, and my eyebrows lift at the sight of the table. It's full of things for making... Well, whatever it is, it's the source of the Christmas scents. "We're making holiday potpourri and scented oils."

"Interesting." I pause at the table, deliberating. Crafts. That's good for a child. I nod, approving. "Any homework?" That needs to be finished before anything else.

Abby's a year ahead as a second-grader, and complete dedication is required. Discipline, variety, creativity, mental stimulation— I'll never budge on that.

"No, sir. Her teacher made the class cheer when she told them there wouldn't be any more homework until next year."

I smile faintly, eyeing the table, and then I continue to the fridge. "Fair enough."

"We're making cookies, Daddy."

I can see that. "Sounds fun, darling." My stomach tightens in hunger, the pathetic sandwich Sally got me nowhere near enough, and that was a few hours ago. "Don't forget that she needs to help with the tidying." I gesture at the counter before opening the fridge. My wife's left me a plate from dinner last night, so I put it in the microwave.

"Of course." Evangeline takes her seat at the table with Abby again, and I observe the young lady while I wait for my meal. Perhaps this one can last longer than a month or two. Abby's previous babysitters have always left much to be desired. But so far, Tess and I haven't caught Abby in front of the TV while Evangeline's with her. A movie here and there is acceptable, but cartoons won't be the substitute babysitter, not in my house.

Evangeline quickly makes space for me as the microwave dings. Food in hand, I set it on the table and smooth down my tie as I take a seat.

"What's next on the recipe, sweetie?" She points at a notepad for Abby.

Biting her lip in concentration, Abby reads from the recipe. "Two table...tablespoons? Um...lemon. Two tablespoons of lemon."

"Lemon peels." Evangeline nods with a smile. "That's what you grated earlier." She reaches for a little bowl of lemon peels and lets my daughter apply the correct amount in another bowl. It looks to be filled with apple cider and spices.

I chew slowly, savoring the taste of my wife's baked salmon and her special dill sauce. I think she may have picked a good babysitter this time. I fill my fork with mashed potatoes and peas as the oven timer goes off, and Evangeline's quick to check on the cookies.

Abby flashes her dimples in a smile to me. "I'm making Christmas presents."

"Oh, really? That's kind of you, darling." Since no one is watching, she and I exchange a funny face that's just for us. It's our *thing*, and she giggles behind her hand after uncrossing her eyes. I grin.

"Uncle Ted is getting a bottle with, um..." She grabs a slip of paper off the littered table. "Pine, cran...cranberries, and cinnamon. Aunt Jessica is getting this." She shows me a bowl of potpourri wrapped in cellophane with a red bow. I nod along appropriately, happy she's enthusiastic. "But Uncle Mark's gift smells the *best*."

I suppress a sigh at that, though my smile doesn't falter. It's not her fault she's so attached to Mark. She's a child. She doesn't know better. One day, I'm sure she'll realize my heathen brother isn't quite as good as she thinks.

"He'll love it," I tell her, gathering the last of the food on my fork.

Milk and cookies are next, though I decline the offer to taste the oatmeal treats that admittedly smell heavenly. With a pat to my stomach, I say I need to watch what I eat. Which is another new development. We have good genes, yet meeting Ryan Quinn made me incredibly self-conscious. He has a few years on me, but he's built like an athlete.

I've started going to the gym since then, though I don't go as often as I should. I don't have the time, and I suppose it doesn't matter anymore. He and Angel are not part of my life any longer.

Despite going to bed at seven that night, I sleep through the night and don't wake up until my alarm goes off at six. I'm disoriented and drag my ass into the shower where I squint due to the harsh lights, then make a face at the mirror. It puts a rock in my stomach to see the last of my bruises have faded.

I double-check, twisting my upper body to inspect my back in the mirror, and nothing.

Nothing.

No reason to wear pajamas in bed anymore. There's nothing to hide.

"Just as well," I whisper to myself. It was only a foolish indulgence. It had to end at some point. I didn't get much of the suffering, anyway. The damn Quinns care too much. Hell, they made *me* care. I shouldn't. I sure as hell shouldn't miss them.

It's been weeks...

Stepping into the shower, I do my best to wash away the self-pity. It's another day. Work calls. Abby has piano practice; if I can get away from the office, I can take her and give Evangeline the afternoon off.

Once I'm finished, I return to the bedroom where Tess is still asleep. I pick out a suit and smack some sense into myself. *New day. Work calls.* Priorities. Abby.

"What do you mean, *off the books*? Is that some sort of joke?" My lunch meeting with Ted and a client of ours turns sour right fucking there. "We won't have much of a defense if you can't provide what most companies today flaunt online for the world to see." They're quarterly reports, not the Holy Grail.

You never meet the CFO of a large corporation alone, so of course he's flanked by an advisor and two useless representatives from his own despicable legal department. If they'd been doing their jobs, we wouldn't be in this mess. I think they might be toddlers.

Ted clears his throat. "Technically, they weren't audited before the—"

"Seriously," I say irritably. "The prosecution already has two separate cases of reports where the numbers don't add up, and that's just what they've shared with shareholders." I slide my client a firm stare. "Mr. McKinney, full disclosure is of the utmost importance, and you're already facing—goddammit, pardon me." My emergency phone buzzes, so I put the napkin on the table and tell Ted to take over. "This better be important," I answer the call on my way out.

"You know it is, sir," Sally says. "I have your daughter's teacher on the line. Please hold." Fuck. I wait impatiently in the entrance of the restaurant and pinch the bridge of my nose. A beat later, she comes through. "Mr. Cooper?"

"Yes, is Abigail okay?"

Two hours later, I take the elevator back up to my office. My stoic expression feels forced, so I can only imagine what it looks like. Straightening my tie, I step out of the car and stride through the cubicle area. I check my watch. Definitely working late today.

What a fucking day.

And my poor girl... My wife couldn't get away from the hospital until later, so I drove all the way to Sausalito to pick up a feverish Abby, brought her home, waited for Tess to get there since Evangeline was unavailable, then now, back to the office. At least Ted settled things with Mr. McKinney at the meeting.

Coming to a halt next to a cubicle, I blanch at the goddamn equality symbol someone's using as a screensaver on their computer. For chrissakes, this is a law firm, not a soapbox. Since the cubicle is empty, I don't know to whom it belongs, so I shake my head and continue toward my office.

I smooth down my suit and nod at Sally, then come to a stop again. *Oh, fuck.*

"She doesn't have an appointment, sir—"

I cut Sally off with a dismissive gesture, my chest seizing painfully, and stare at Angel. *What the hell are you doing here?* She can't be here. She can't even know I work here. Rising gracefully from the small waiting area, she quirks a brow and smirks faintly at me. *Why are you so fucking beautiful?* I suck in a slow breath, willing the pain in my chest to fade. This is my domain. My scene. She sticks out like a sore thumb in her tight jeans and equally tight leather jacket which actually shows cleavage. *Lord.* It's almost freezing outside. And her heels. Blood-red and glossy, matching her lipstick and the new color of the lower ends of her hair.

She's deadly, and I'm fucking seething all of a sudden.

I can't find my words, so I give a curt nod at my door and usher her inside my office.

"Hold my calls, Sally." I close the door behind me.

Angel saunters in like she owns the place. This...this young little slip of a girl.

"How did you—"

"Google." She wipes a finger along a shelf with old cases I haven't shipped off to the archive. "I know your name and profession. Turns out there aren't many Greg Coopers who practice law —corporate law, excuse me, and...who turn up at a banquet with his lovely wife on his arm in the image search."

My stomach drops, and I slowly make my way to my desk. I sit down in my chair and try that breathing thing again. I hear it's vital.

If she were anyone else, I'd be boiling and calling for security. The fucking *audacity*... Showing up at my work. Interfering with my life. My personal life. But she's Angel, and I'm not calling for security. I'm not even seething anymore, which wasn't necessarily directed solely at her in the first place. My cowardice knows no bounds around her and Ryan. I lose my assertiveness around them.

Problem is, I adore it.

Angel approaches my desk, eyes on the handful of picture frames. One of Tess and me. A family photo including Abby. One of Ted, Seth, and me. Two others of only Abby.

When we hire someone at Cooper Law II, or someone gets promoted and is granted their own office, family pictures are highly encouraged. It shows family orientation and traditional standards.

"Your daughter takes after you. Gorgeous." Angel touches the photo, tracing the copper waves of Abby's hair, same color she inherited from me. "Same hazel eyes. What's her name?"

"Abigail." My mouth's run dry, and information I would've

avoided giving before tumbles out. When she asks Abby's age, I tell her she's almost eight. Next, Angel calls my wife pretty.

"Thanks," I answer automatically.

"You didn't make her pretty. Don't take credit."

"I didn't mean—"

"Quiet. You ruin so much when you speak."

I smash my lips together and tense up, humiliation washing over me. How on earth does she *do* it? I have at least fifteen years on her, yet she commands my mind and turns me into trash without effort.

"Do you remember when we met?" she muses, unzipping her jacket. "You were so nervous." While continuing to survey my office, she drapes her jacket along one of the two chairs in front of my desk and adjusts her snug top. "Impressive." She's found the diplomas on my wall. "Stanford, huh?"

I rub a hand over my mouth, unsure of whether to answer. It seemed like a rhetorical question. So I keep quiet.

"You said..." She taps her chin, then faces me with a wicked glint in her eye. "You said you wanted to suffer. It's what gets you off, you said. No, wait. You said it's what *arouses* you." She evidently finds my vernacular amusing.

I stare at her, wondering what her agenda is. She's caught me. I did lie to her and Ryan. Knowing the gist of BDSM from my little brother, a quick online search brought me to a community that he wasn't part of. I went there for a public event and kept to myself until I saw Ryan and Angel demonstrating choking to their friends. I was sold. I found my targets and managed to stammer out what I wanted. I lied. Although...it did turn out to be true; I know, weak defense, but nonetheless. Suffering has an indescribable effect on me. No one was more shocked than me to learn it would draw out another side of me, one I've grown to crave.

Now what? Is she going to out me? Ruin my reputation? Blackmail me?

"You're suffering right now, aren't you?" She tilts her head at me.

I don't reply. I fucking can't. My throat's closed up, and I can only watch as she inches closer and closer.

"Answer me, subbie."

I tense my jaw and manage a jerky nod, at which she sighs and fingers the armrest of my chair. She tells me to scoot back, and I obey. Then she jumps up to sit on the desk and encourages me to roll forward again.

"You're punishing yourself for something." She slips a finger under my chin and lifts it enough that I must look her in the eye. "Is it because you're cheating on your wife?"

I'm not cheating...technically. I hesitate, wanting to explain, then shake my head.

"I see." Urging me even closer, she cups my face gently, her gaze softening. Jesus, she's going to break me. "Talk to me, little boy. What hurts so much?"

"Everything." The word gusts out of me without permission, causing the levees to break. My eyes burn, and my breathing becomes choppy.

"Oh, honey. Come to me." She hugs me to her, and I bury my face against her chest. My arms sneak around her middle. I hold on for all I'm worth. "You've made quite the mess of yourself, Greg."

I'm very aware.

I don't see it changing, though.

And by God, it looks like I'll never stop crying in Angel's presence. Or Ryan's, for that matter. It mortifies me to realize I've wept like a child in front of them more than I have during my entire adulthood before I met them.

She drags her fingernails along my scalp gently. "Can you confirm you sought out pain to punish yourself for something?"

"Yes, but—"

"Silence. No buts. Master and I aren't blind. We know when you're excited and revved up. And what gets you there."

I shudder and squeeze her to me. "I'm sorry, Miss Angel."

"Not sorry enough," she replies softly. "Otherwise, you wouldn't keep doing it." She pauses. "Or is it something in the past? If it's not infidelity or anything ongoing..."

It's...Christ, so complicated.

"Greg...?" She grips my chin and forces me to look up. I blink hard, and then a twenty-something-year-old wipes away my tears. It's supposed to be the other way around. I'm a grown man. "Would you say you're a bad person?"

Her question takes me aback, and I have to think about it. And if I have to think about it, doesn't that say enough?

"I'm a good father," I croak.

She hums and drops a tender kiss between my eyebrows. "What else are you good at?"

I'll answer in a minute. Her comfort is too delectable to resist. I blanket myself in it for a brief moment, savoring each brush of her pouty lips on my skin. My eyelids, my cheeks, my nose.

My mouth.

My eyes flash open in shock. A fierce bolt of desire pierces through the fog of misery, but I can't act on it, can I? It's not the right time, and I wouldn't disrespect Ryan. Kissing—no. It hasn't ever been on the table for us.

She kisses me again, and I manage to force out Ryan's name.

"Oh, honestly." She nips at my bottom lip. I grip the desk, my self-restraint slipping. "Would I betray the love of my life? I think not."

"Then why are you—"

"Because I want to. Because I'm allowed."

"Jesus," I breathe. I'm there in a flash, carefully cupping her jaw before I kiss her back. I kiss her deeply and hungrily. Sweet mercy, I didn't know how much I've ached for this.

Angel fists my tie and lets out a breathy moan that goes straight to my cock. I taste her; in slow, passionate strokes of my tongue, I taste her sweetness. She's a drug. A dangerous, dangerous drug. Much like her husband.

I feel like a teenager. The concept of making out is strange to me. Has been, for too long.

Her mouth moves perfectly with mine. I forget to breathe until my lungs burn with the need for air. Only then do I suck in a much-needed breath. I don't even notice I've left my chair. Half leaning over her stunning little body, I devour her succulent lips and lose control.

She doesn't. "Easy there, baby boy." She gasps and moans, and then I'm pushed back into my swivel chair by a stiletto on my crotch. I wipe my mouth and toss her a heavy look before glancing down. Her footwear is nothing short of a lethal weapon, and she presses it along my erection until I groan. "Can you play nice?"

I hiss. "Yes, Miss Angel."

"Good." She fluffs her hair and collects her breath, lust evident in her rosy cheeks and emerald eyes. "As delicious as you are, I didn't come here for that."

I smile, and in another moment where I can't control myself, I lean forward and kiss the top of her hand.

It earns me a smirk, and the stiletto slips off my lap. Thank goodness.

"Back on topic." She twirls a finger. "Other than being a father, what are you good at?"

I blow out a breath and gather my thoughts. "Being a lawyer."

She makes a derisive little noise at that. "If you think about your profession on your deathbed, you haven't lived life."

Good grief. My mouth twitches in amusement. That has got to be the most adorable thing she's ever said.

"Spoken like a true millennial."

She smiles. "Maybe. Are you happy, though?"

My amusement fades, leaving me cold. "No, Ma'am."

"Who makes you happy?"

Abby, you, and Ryan. "My daughter."

206

I think she can tell there are more people I care for deeply, though I do not believe she suspects she and her husband are two of them. I'm replaceable. They're not.

"I have hatred and jealousy in me." I clearly have no verbal filter. For the love of God, I need to shut the hell up now. Enough with the sharing.

"Towards who?"

Her informal way of speaking is just a reminder of how much I truly do need to shut up and put distance between us. We're worlds apart, and she wouldn't understand. She's so carefree, casual, and brazen. If she's had any demons, she's fought them and won. Not everyone is as fortunate.

"I genuinely don't want to discuss it," I say as respectfully as I can muster.

I've gotten my emotions in check for now, so I ease away slightly and scrub at my face.

Someone has to be responsible.

Someone needs to be able to leave this office and not have lipstick on his face. I wipe my mouth again, satisfied there's no trace of red left.

"I see." She studies me intently. "You haven't asked why I came here today."

"I think we both know I don't function very well around you and Ryan," I point out. She grins lazily. "I'm certainly curious, though."

She glances back at my photos. "You came by the bar when Ryan and I were in the Rockies." Oh, of course, they're hikers or...outdoorsy. Could we be much more different? Her gaze slides back to me. "You also check our chat up to a dozen times a day—"

"How would you know that?" I ask abruptly.

Mirth flashes in her eyes. "Because every time you log in, you're listed as online."

So that's what that green dot is for. Dammit. Unfortunately, there's no way she'll believe I'd be on that app for other reasons. She had to teach me how it worked.

"Do you miss us, Greg?"

More than I can describe.

"Does it matter?" I wonder.

She shakes her head slowly. "Under these circumstances, I...no, I guess not. I came for answers, and perhaps it was a mistake, but..." For one quiet moment, I get to see her unguarded and vulnerable. She looks down and swallows hard, and it fucking tears at me. "I'm angry, for one. We inflicted pain for the worst reasons imaginable. Because you lied to us."

"That's on me."

"Even so. It ruins the memories. The trust is broken."

"I'm very sorry, Angel." Remorse fills me to the brim.

She quirks half a smile and shrugs lightly. "I feel worse for your wife." That's a slap in the face, and I watch silently while she swings her legs over the desk with ease and jumps down on the other side. "We miss you—very much." And the punches keep on coming. "Discovering you're married probably wasn't the biggest shock, but it stings to have it confirmed—and to know that you have to hide who you are." She puts on her jacket. "So...I guess that was a kiss goodbye. We'll delete our chat, okay?" Resting her palms on the desk, she faces me head on. In the meantime, I'm trying not to cower away like the weak bastard I am. "You can do better. For yourself and for the people you love."

She wouldn't understand. She wouldn't *agree*. Because she wouldn't understand.

Rounding the desk once more, she leans down and drops a featherlight kiss to my cheek. "Take care, Mr. Stanford."

Funny, it sounds like an insult coming from her.

I touch my cheek, the spot she kissed, and just stare at the door. Fortunately for me, numbness sets in, far better than crippling pain. Although, I'm sure that'll follow soon enough.

A much less attractive face appears in the doorway: my youngest brother.

I clear my throat and straighten in my seat. "What can I do for you, Seth?"

"Papers to sign." He walks in and hands me a file. "Pages one, nine, fourteen, and the last one."

I grab my pen, ready to drill some legal documents into my brain if it can erase the image of Angel walking out of my life.

"Um...Greg?"

I frown and peer over at him.

He coughs uncomfortably and averts his eyes. "You have lipstick marks on your cheek."

Son of a bitch. Shrugging out of my suit jacket, I grab a packet of tissues from my inner pocket and wipe the makeup off my stubble. "It's not what it looks like."

"It never is, is it?"

TOUCH OF TROUBLE

CHAPTER 1

KAYLA BRANDON

W hen a waiter arrives at our cabana on the beach with breakfast, I stay quiet as Daddy takes care of everything. Instead I focus on tying the two ends of my white bikini around my neck, and then get my hair up in a high, messy bun at the top of my head.

I do *not* want to get sunscreen in my hair later. It gets all sticky. After a week in the sun, my hair is more red than brown, and a few golden highlights have appeared.

This is our last day in Mexico, and Daddy's family flew home yesterday. It was fun to see them again, especially his sisters, Lissa and Sydney, who've warmed up to me since last time. At first they were wary of our fourteen-year age gap, but it's all good now.

I've tried to make Daddy extend our stay, but he's set on our flying to Oregon tomorrow. No matter how much I've bribed, whined, bitched, begged, and bargained, he stands firm. He wants us to get it out of the way so we can move on.

Silly man. Why can't we move on without seeing my family? Ugh.

Especially that damn Amanda.

"Come here and eat your breakfast, Kayla."

Scooting closer to the middle of the large, U-shaped couch that basically takes up the entire cabana, I end up next to him, and he's got everything set up on the small table in front of us.

"Do you want me to cut the crusts off your toast?"

I nod and lean my head on his shoulder. "Yes, please." It's pretty early, so I'm still tired.

I intend to make the most of our last day, though, which was why I dragged Daddy down here before eight o'clock. He didn't protest; he just changed into his black board shorts, grabbed the book he's reading, and then we headed down to the lobby, booked ourselves a cabana, and ordered breakfast.

"Something wrong, sweetheart?"

I place a hand on my tummy and pout up at him. "Maybe I'm getting sick."

"Nice try." His mouth twists into a smirk. "Does that mean you're too sick to go swimming later?"

Dammit. I scowl and look at my plate, grabbing a triangle of toast he's prepared with butter and jam. I adore swimming here, 'cause the water is so gorgeous. Crystal clear, turquoise, and the sand is almost completely white. Also, if I'm sick, we won't be able to scout for a location for our wedding next summer.

Nicholas's proposal in Venice was so beautiful that it made me cry; it was romantic, heartfelt, and made this girl's dreams come true. Maybe it was clichéd to some: a romantic dinner at a family-owned restaurant, a gondola ride under the Bridge of Sighs at sunset, and lastly a proposal back at the hotel room where he went down on one knee and asked me to marry him, asked me to be his wife, his baby girl, and his love forever...but perhaps with our less-than-ordinary lifestyle, that proposal was perfect for us. It certainly was for *me*.

My next dream is to get married on a beach, which he said he'd like to do, too. So, we decided that we're going to invite our closest friends and family down here to Mexico next summer for a few days of festivities. It'll also be around the one-year anniversary of the day we met.

"Some food might make me feel better." I backtrack and smile sweetly.

He chuckles and takes a sip from his coffee as he unfolds the newspaper he ordered to be delivered with breakfast. "Somehow I'm not surprised you'd say that." He flips a page, all while I worry the pristinely white sofa's gonna be all smudgy from the paper. "You should probably watch yourself, though. There's only so much manipulation I can take."

Oh, crap.

"I love you." I make sure to maintain my sweet smile.

He doesn't turn my way, but I do see the edges of his mouth slanting up a little. "Mmhmm. Love you too, baby girl."

I huff and cram some toast into my mouth, realizing he still won't budge.

Not only are we definitely going to Oregon tomorrow, but I'm evidently healthy as a horse.

There's just no playing Nicholas Ford.

Then again, was there ever? From the start of our relationship, I've known he's the perfect man and Daddy for me. He's a strict sweetheart; he lets me roam around and talk to people, because I love that—I'm a people person—but he doesn't take my bullshit.

There's an invisible leash, which he holds on to 24/7. Regardless of being my fiancé or my Daddy, he's in charge. The only difference, really, is that he gives me more leeway when we're Nicholas and Kayla.

Vacation spots blur the lines; I'm good at throwing out the Daddy card, because it feels so natural. At the same time, he coddles me more when we're in a foreign place, so we're even. But at home, it's more distinct. We have separate times for play, though everything remains negotiable. We prefer it flexible.

"You know," I muse a few minutes later, "if I'd had more time in Mexico, I would've done my Christmas shopping here. That would make for some fun presents, huh?"

He doesn't miss a beat. "Too bad you did your shopping back in November, then—and even before that."

My shoulders slump in defeat. "May I go swimming now, please?"

He folds his newspaper and puts it aside, then sighs and places an arm around me. "You've barely eaten anything." There's a frown in his voice. "Do you want me to order something else?"

Feeling bad, I shake my head and swipe up another triangle of toast. "No, thank you. This is really good." No lie. I just crave the water. Swimming is fun, especially when Daddy joins. "I'll eat some more. Then can I go?" I peer up at him.

He smiles and kisses my nose. "After you've let the meal settle, yes. We need to get sunscreen on you, too."

I nod, tilting my head up some more, and brush my lips over his scruffy jaw.

It's not often I see him with scruff.

"You need sunscreen, too." I softly run my fingers through his fairly short hair. In his chestnut brown mess, slightly rumpled from sleep, there're a few strands of silver, and I happen to find them incredibly sexy.

Great. Now I'm getting horny.

"Is something wrong, Daddy?" I ask, swimming circles around him. "You seem distracted."

There're pretty fish by his feet, but I don't wanna get too close. Just to look at them. Not touch. Or get bitten and die.

"Definitely not wrong." He pulls me close and makes me squeal when he dunks us underwater.

"Hey!" I splutter and laugh and push my hair back. He just grins. "That wasn't funny." But I'm laughing...

"I can see that." He chuckles.

Humming happily, I lock my feet around his hips and lean back in the ocean and disappear under the surface for just a couple seconds. Then I hoist myself up again and wipe some water off my face. "I was thinking... What kind of girl would make Rio happy?"

When Evangeline called a few days ago and told me that Brayden had finally surrendered to Mark, I'd nearly cried with joy for them. They deserve all the happiness they can find, and now I want the same for Rio. He often looks so lonely to me.

"Planning another matchmaking project?" He squeezes my bottom and pulls me closer so I can feel his semi-hard cock. Good thing there aren't people around! I'm all for public play, but this is kind of a family resort.

"I hope so." I trace the drops of water on his sun-kissed shoulders with my fingers. "I've barely even seen him play at the club." All I know is that he is *very* strict. At Switch, subs call him Master Kelly or Master Rio...and if they don't?

Yikes.

It's when only Daddy's around—or my subbie friends—that I dare to refer to Rio by his first name. At the same time, there's something gentle about him. It's tough to explain. He can be funny and carefree; other times he's quiet and withdrawn.

"Perhaps he's not ready yet." Daddy brushes some water drops away from my cheek, and I nestle my face into his palm. "He hasn't been back for that long."

True. Rio's job must've given him nightmares. I can't imagine traveling to some jungle—in hostile territory—and offering so much of myself to help others. It's beyond noble, but I'd be so scared! I'm *not* that gutsy.

Rio clearly is, and I want to see him happy.

"What kind of relationship did he have with his fiancée?" I'm curious. Rio's fiancée...I know she died in some kind of accident several years ago, that's about it. Her death was what caused Rio to uproot his life and join Doctors Without Borders.

"Vanilla."

"*Really?*" That's a surprise. I don't know Rio that well yet, but to me he's so...*Master-y.*

"Most people believe he's still mourning her..." He slowly moves us toward the shore. We're pretty far out. My feet can't even reach the ocean floor. "That's not necessarily all there is to it. They were having problems when she died." Oh, that's so sad. "About ten years ago, he went through the same thing I did when I settled for Amanda." I grimace at that, to which Daddy smiles ruefully and nips at my jaw. "Rio came back from a medical seminar in New York and said it was time for him to settle down. Before New York, he'd been raving about how single life suited him, so perhaps something happened there."

I scrunch my nose. "Didn't you ask him about it?"

"I asked; he said he didn't want to talk about it."

Ugh. Men. "You should've pushed." I playfully smack his arm. "That's what friends do."

"It was ten years ago, baby girl." He laughs quietly and nuzzles my neck. By now, we're closer to the beach, and the water would reach my chest if I let go of him. "Whatever happened back then isn't exactly breaking news today."

"Okay, okay." I sigh. "Speaking of New York, I wanna call Chelsea when we get back to the room." She's my friend from New York, and she's the one who told me I had to visit Switch if I ever came to San Francisco. Best advice ever! She's joining us in Cali soon.

"And right now, I don't want to talk at all." He reaches up to cup my breasts. It makes me giggle and squirm. "Let's get back to the cabana."

Keeping my arms and legs locked around him, he carries me out of the water, and I feel his hardening cock the entire time. It's pressing against my pussy, exciting me in the best ways.

"Do you want to play Go Fish?" I ask innocently.

He laughs a little darkly as we enter the cabana and closes the white fabric behind us. "No. That's not what I had in mind." After lowering me to one side of the big sofa, he pulls down his trunks, exposing himself to me, but he doesn't stay that way. From the other side of the sofa, he grabs a towel and wraps it around his hips. "You haven't forgotten your safeword, have you?"

My mouth forms an "o" as my cheeks heat up. I only need a safeword if we're going to play rough.

"N-no, Daddy." My voice is all shaky. Arousal rushes around in my tummy, and I get butterflies. Horny butterflies. "It's red." One of the first things I discovered with Daddy is that he likes reluctance sometimes. He wants me to fight him. Sort of like a rape fantasy, only a tad gentler and with no violent intentions.

Usually, he wants it when I've been a bad girl. He fucks me into a good little girl again, and it *always* works. But today...perhaps he wants to let off some steam? Because I haven't been bad, have I?

We do have a few trying days ahead of us, so we might need this. And I'll never back down from playtime that allows me to sink deeper into the Little I really am. It cleanses me, in a way.

"Time for your nap, sweetheart." He sits down on the edge of the sofa and reaches around me to untie my bikini top. I can see in his eyes that he's started playing. He needs a reason now—a reason to go rough. "When you wake up, I'll order lunch."

I scowl as he tosses my bikini on the table. "I'm not sleepy." I fold my arms over my chest and jut out my chin. If he wants a brat, I'll give him one! I don't exactly have to struggle to find the brat in me. She's very much alive and kicking, still mad about our going to Oregon tomorrow. "*Stop.*" I whine when he pulls down my bikini bottoms. "Daddy, I can do it myself!" I shove at him petulantly.

"Be quiet," he snaps.

I stick out my tongue at him. "You dummy."

He raises a brow, then points to the floor in front of the table. "Get over there. *Now.*"

Sulking, I make my way to the floor and give him another scowl over my shoulder.

"Bend over and hold on to your ankles." A command.

As I obey, I feel him coming up behind me. He strokes my bottom. He kneads it. He spanks it. I yelp and cringe, then whine as he rubs out the sting. He's being such a meanie!

"Stand still." His voice is gruff and quiet. "You've had this coming for days, Kayla."

I snarl. "I've done nothing wrong." My wet hair gets in my face, so I try to blow it out of the way, but it doesn't work. I give up with a huff. "I've been a good girl."

"Have you?" He *hmphs* and slides a finger down to my kitty. Wet already. I'm such a hussy. "If I remember correctly, you've been sneaky a few times." Uh-oh. "Or haven't you tried to get out of the trip to Oregon? Haven't you been a brat?"

Um. "No?" I squeak. In response, he spanks me again. "Ow! That hurts." I whimper and try to squirm away, though he holds me fast. The next thing I see is his towel being dropped to the floor. "Please, please, please, Daddy! I'll be good. I'll be good. You don't have to—" Before I can even finish the sentence, he grabs my hips and rams his cock so deep inside my pussy that it steals my breath. My mouth pops open, but no sound escapes.

"Did Daddy's cock shut you up, baby girl?"

Unable to form a coherent response, I let out a breathless wail, my nails digging into my ankles so I don't lose my grip.

For several minutes, he fucks me like that. He has me at his mercy. Doubled over. His hard cock slamming and drilling deeper. His hands holding me in place, even pulling me back on his erection with some thrusts. There's my whining—and the few moans I can't hold back—Daddy's heavy breathing, the sound of skin slapping, and the wetness I can't hide.

"Remember your safeword?" He pants, abruptly withdrawing from my pussy. I nod pitifully and sag against him as he pulls me to a stand. "Good. Lie down on the couch again."

The second my back hits the cushions, he settles between my

legs, places a hand near my head, guides his cock to my opening, and pushes forward.

"Too much!" I cry out, to which he clamps a hand over my mouth. "No, stop! Stop, Daddy!" My sounds are muffled, but he can still hear them.

I think he senses that I can handle a lot more—that my "reluctance" is too practiced—so he speeds up and goes harder. Wrapping his fingers around both my wrists, he gathers my restrained hands above my head. With his free hand, he begins to pinch my nipples, and he tells me that if I scream or become too loud, he'll bring out his belt when we get back to the hotel room.

I don't want his belt. It *really* stings!

Each slide of his big cock inside me is like feeding me Viagra for girls; I'm soaking wet, and there's nothing I can do about it. But the pinches, the rough squeezes, and the sharp nips of his teeth...they always confuse me. A part of me needs it, and even wants it, but another part doesn't. I'm swimming in indecision, which leaves me vulnerable and easier for him to dominate. It's what ultimately makes me yield.

In a final effort, I try to push him away. I shove at his shoulders and claw at his skin. He tries to kiss me, and I turn away and snarl at him.

"Feisty little baby slut, aren't you?" He hisses in my ear, sending tingles down my spine. "I think I've let you be a brat for too long, Kayla." The hand that isn't restraining my own hands slides under me and cups my butt. "Haven't I told you that I will always take care of you? Haven't I told you that I'll do what's best for you?" He lets out a gritty moan as he continues to pump into me. "Yet, for the past few days...you've questioned me, begged me, been manipulative..."

A hard squeeze to one of my butt cheeks makes me cry out. Tears well up in my eyes. He sees it, but he remains ruthless and relentless.

"Handling a little brat can be fun," he whispers, "but I want my precious sweetheart back now." With that, he takes me even harder.

Pain mingles with more pleasure as he begins to stroke my clit. Then more pain. Bites, harsh thrusts. More pleasure. He sucks on my nipples, his tongue swirling and teasing. Pain. His entire body presses down on me.

The brat in me whimpers in defeat and pulls back.

"Would I ever let anyone hurt you?"

"No..." I suck my bottom lip into my mouth. "But, Daddy—"

"No buts." He claims my mouth in a hard kiss and moans. "Trust me, Kayla. When we're in Oregon, *trust me* to take care of you and keep you happy." I flush with heat, and his reassurances finally settle in. "Work with me instead of against me. If you struggle...we both know Daddy will fuck the fight out of you."

"Oh, *God*." I gasp as a wildfire blazes through me.

His promises, his cock, his fingers on my clit—it's all too much. Too much, too much. Suddenly drowning in a big ocean of bliss and euphoria, I sink deeper and deeper into the darkness where I'm left totally free and unchained.

Tears and sweat dampen my skin. Thoughts, worries, and distractions vanish; they fade away. It's unbelievably freeing to let go. As long as my Daddy is here, everything is perfect in the world. He will take care of me. He will make all those decisions that make my head ache. In return, I will worship him.

I cling to him, my orgasm still raging inside me.

"That's it," I hear him murmur. "There's my gorgeous little baby."

His praise leaves me feeling all glowy, and it's only a few seconds later that he jerks and starts coming, coating the inside of my pussy with his release.

"Christ, Kayla..."

Still pinned down by his body, there's nothing I can do but take it. Only, now I want it with every fiber of my being.

My skin, wherever he's pinched me and manipulated my limits, is red and burning hot. It feels like each inch of redness has its own pulse, and it makes me hyperaware of Daddy's touches right now. His labored breaths against my neck, his heaving chest against mine...

I realize this wasn't about "letting off some steam." I've behaved badly, and Daddy put a stop to it before I could take it further and *really* act out. It's overwhelming, the fact that someone else knows me better than I do. I hadn't even noticed just how unsettled the upcoming trip had made me. But I feel so much better now, and not because of a fuck, but because of how he simply made my leash shorter. Sometimes it's necessary.

"Do you feel better, baby girl?" He kisses me on the forehead and slowly pulls out of me, ending up next to me instead, propped up on his elbow.

Still overwhelmed, I just nod and give him a watery little smile. Then as whimpers bubble up and my eyes won't stop welling, I glue myself to his body and begin crying. My breaths come out all choppy and fast, as if I can't let go of the emotions quickly enough.

In my head, I try to think back on our vacation here; I want to recall what I've done to make Daddy notice the problem. I know I've been restless and a bit bratty, but was that enough for him to draw the conclusion that I needed rougher play?

Evidently.

"It's all right, my little love." He soothes me, shushes me gently, kisses my hair, and strokes my back. "I've got you."

"I'm sorry..." My bottom lip quivers. "I didn't realize."

"I know." His eyes are gentle now. "But it's not your job. It's mine. Now, let's lie here for a bit. You're still trembling a little." He feels my forehead, then moves down to caress my cheek. "We'll rest, and then we'll shower before lunch. Does that sound good?"

I nod and burrow myself impossibly closer into him, sucking my thumb into my mouth. "Yes, Daddy."

CHAPTER 2

Our vacation is over too quickly, and I'm thankful for Nicholas's distracting me. On our way to LA—where we'll change flights—he asks me to go over the plans I have for the Lounge with him.

Before Nicholas bought the place next to Switch, it was a big restaurant, and the kitchen and the private lounge still haven't been dealt with. In the old dining area, however, we now have the Cave, a big space for scening.

With my tablet between us, I open up the sketchpad software and show Nicholas how the space behind the Cave will look after a couple walls have been torn down.

First, we have the Cinema—what used to be the kitchen—and this will actually open a few days after New Year's.

Switch is closed over the holidays, so Nicholas paid a construction team lots of money to work on our very own movie theater.

It will be totally dark, with black-painted walls and floors, and instead of cushy recliners, there will be four big, round beds filling the room. And of course, a massive screen on one wall that will show either porn or erotic slideshows.

Then we have the Lounge...

"This looks wonderful." Nicholas zooms in on what used to be the kitchen, or mainly, the new arched entrance that leads to it. "How many stalls in the Cave will have to be removed?"

"All of the ones on the eastern wall." Which means three stalls. A part of that wall will open up to the Lounge. "But I was thinking we could utilize the platform in the original club area a bit more. Right now, we only use it for public demos."

Nicholas nods thoughtfully. "That sounds like a good idea. There's enough space between the platform and our private booth to keep equipment, too." Exactly. Like, the furniture we have in the three stalls that we need to eliminate. "And how are we on the name? You weren't sure about calling it the Lounge?"

I shake my head and take a sip of my Sprite. "No, I don't think it will fit."

I've explained my vision already, so he knows. It's going to be a harem-like room, with billowy fabrics, pillows and mattresses on the floor, sconces with lit candles, rich colors of gold, plum, moss green, and wine red. In the middle of the room, there will be two brass poles for dancing, and between those, everything you need for wax play. Candles in various colors—with different melting points —mineral oils and other options for protecting the skin, thermometers, and holders and cups for those who prefer to play with only the wax. All of which will be set up on an altar.

"I've researched some options..." I tap my chin absently, thinking. "That kind of room is called Oda, but I'm not sure many people know that."

Nicholas hums. "It's also referred to as a chamber, no?"

"That's true." I nod and look at the screen. "The Chamber... The Harem's Chamber..."

That will actually be perfect! Because we have the Club—the original club area—the Cave, soon the Cinema; yes, the Chamber will be super perfect.

Nicholas leans close and kisses my jaw. "The *Sultan's* Chamber, baby girl." I shiver. "A place where a Dominant can drown in pleasure, be surrounded by it, and snatch up a concubine or two."

I giggle, slightly breathless. And a *lot* turned on. "Only *one* for you, *Sir*." I look up at him a little accusingly. Playfully, of course.

"Of course." He smiles and grasps my chin, tilting it for a kiss. "You're the only concubine I want." He winks at me and lets go. "But don't think I haven't noticed the way you look at Dylan sometimes." There's mischief in his eyes, and I feel my cheeks heating up. I had no idea he'd noticed! "The Chamber would be a perfect place to watch him play with Cade, wouldn't it?"

"Oh, *yes*." I grin, excited. Which reminds me, I hope Cade and Dylan's second date goes well. I already know their first was a success, and that was only a few days ago.

Nicholas tilts his head a little. "You'd tell me if you want more, right?"

"What?" My eyebrows knit together.

Now he appears guarded and careful. "More than watching."

Oh. Oh! No, no. I shake my head. "Eeek," I squeak and giggle just picturing it. "No!" I clutch my tummy, feeling all weird. "I admit that I like to watch, but—" I could never *ever* participate. I don't like to share, and I don't like to *be* shared. However, playing *near* Cade and Dylan would be *so* sexy. Especially since Cade is a Daddy Dom, too. "You're silly, Daddy." I snicker and bury my head against his bicep.

He rumbles a low, sexy laugh and kisses the top of my head. "I'm incredibly relieved, too."

That makes me look up at him. "You don't ever have to worry about that." Then I smirk a little. "You don't like Dylan much, do you?"

Okay, maybe that's taking it too far, but I know Nicholas thinks Dylan is too mischievous. Sometimes, he'll run up to me at the club, poke my boob or something, and then run off again. To which Nicholas will dole out his punishment. But now that Dylan is— hopefully—with Cade, I think Nicholas will breathe a sigh of relief.

I think it's funny. Dylan is a crack-up. He's cute, too. Silly sexy. He's a twenty-five-year-old clown.

"That boy is trouble." Nicholas grins wryly. "I sincerely hope Cade will keep him on a leash."

I shudder, a little intimidated by Cade. He is *very* nice, but he's not like my Daddy. If I didn't like Cade, I wouldn't have set him up with Dylan. That said, he's very different from Nicholas. Cade looks like a bad boy. A biker. A *hot* biker, but a biker nonetheless. With tattoos, piercings, and a leather jacket to match. He always strolls into the club in jeans, a snug T-shirt, his dark hair buzzed super short, scruff on his sharp jaw, an unlit cigarette behind his ear, and stormy blue eyes that promise indecency.

I hope Gabriella—another Little friend of mine—won't feel neglected, though. John, Gabriella's Daddy...I don't really like him. I try to give him the benefit of the doubt since he's Nicholas's friend, but I don't know. Lately I've seen John take "emergency calls" too often, and so he sometimes leaves Gabriella alone at the club. In the past, Cade looked out for her, but if Cade will be busy with Dylan...

Maybe she'll open up to me more about it, although I won't be surprised if she doesn't. We're kinda close, but she's closer with a few others. Sort of like I've grown so close to Evangeline and Brayden. I really like them, and I can't wait to see their collars when I get back home.

"What're you thinking about, baby?"

I sigh and stow away my iPad. "Brayden and Evangeline. I'm so happy for them, but I expected them to tell me about the collaring." Mark was supposed to collar them the day after Nicholas and I left for Mexico, but when I talked to Evangeline, she didn't mention anything.

"He postponed it," Nicholas answers. "I spoke to Mark yesterday. He's bringing them with him to his house in La Jolla after the holidays, and he plans to do it there instead."

"Oh! I love that idea." I smile. "I hope they get married and have a bunch of babies."

Nicholas laughs through his nose and gathers me close. "Everyone should have a fairy tale according to you, huh?"

"Of course." I nod. "Do you know what my own idea of a fairy tale would be?"

That wry smile is back. "You've told me." He taps my nose. "A kitten."

Yeah... "Being married to you *and* having a kitten," I correct him.

When we board the flight to Oregon—Portland, more precisely—I need more to distract me. We're done talking about Switch, and I'm not ready to hear more about Nicholas's other clubs in the Bay Area, because we all know I'd get a bunch of ideas for projects.

It's probably best I only have one club to focus on at a time, and there will be plenty of opportunities later for me to get creative with the other venues. I get so easily sidetracked.

So, now he distracts me with the pros of going to Oregon. He helps me focus on the people in my family whom I actually like.

It amazes me a little to know that I still have family members on my side after Amanda had called everyone to say that I had "stolen" the love of her life. She really said that.

She's such a conniving bitch. Her sister Amber, too, but Amanda was always the worst—a bully behind a sweet smile.

From the horrible night shortly after my thirteenth birthday when my parents died in a car crash, I grew up with Amanda's bullshit. She flashed that smile to Aunt Mary and Uncle Keith, and the second they looked away, she threw harsh insults at me. I didn't belong in their family, she said. I was the black sheep. Everything I did was wrong. But because my mom and dad had recently died and my aunt and uncle had graciously taken me in, I didn't have the energy to defend myself, nor did I want to cause problems.

I've learned to be completely honest since then; except, around Amanda it's too easy to fall back on bad habits. For example, at Amber's wedding...the second I found out it was my cousin whom Nicholas was dating, I remember telling him—*pleading* with him— to actually stay with her.

Can anyone really blame me, though? After all, when I was thirteen, Amanda was twenty-seven. She was an *adult*, and she acted like that. And what did it all stem from...?

Bitterness. Jealousy. Resentment. For petty reasons.

Amanda has always demanded to be in the spotlight, and she had just started her own company when we learned about the car accident. The plan was for our family to go to her "grand opening"—a party for the ad agency she'd started. Instead, it was replaced by a big funeral and mourning.

I had lost my parents. Aunt Mary had lost her sister and brother-in-law. Gramma Ida had lost her daughter and son-in-law.

Everyone forgot about Amanda's big day.

She was bitter and resentful and took it out on me every time she came to her parents' house, which was often since they lived on the same street.

Three years later, Amanda moved her business to San Francisco, and Amber went with her.

When we get in the town car that'll take us to the hotel where my family is gathered for the holidays, most of my fears have been calmed, but I'm still super nervous. My gut tightens to the point where I clutch my tummy and burrow closer to Nicholas for comfort.

"Do you ever miss Portland?" He's trying to keep me occupied with conversation, I think.

I shake my head no and hug his bicep. "No. I left as soon as I graduated from high school for a reason." For years, I thought I was a nomad. Several in my family have nicknamed me Drifter because I've moved around so much. Sure, I love to travel, but...I'm California-focused now. It turned out I was only looking for the place where I belong. "San Francisco is home."

Nicholas hums and kisses my temple, then speaks to the driver and idly plays with my fingers.

It's only a few minutes later that we arrive at the fairly large and upscale hotel, and even though we're not meeting my family until dinner, it's almost inevitable that we'll run into someone in the lobby or...in the elevator, maybe.

Having shipped our bags home from Mexico earlier, we only have one piece of luggage left, not counting our carry-ons. After thanking the driver, Nicholas shoulders his laptop bag and grabs the luggage, then places his free hand on my lower back to usher me inside the hotel. I clutch my own bag close and look around the Christmas-decorated, brightly-lit lobby, immediately spotting two of my cousins on Dad's side.

"Hello, Kayla." Michael smiles politely and gives me a friendly hug, and I exhale in relief. I hug his sister, too—Sarah—glad to have encountered allies first.

"This is Nicholas Ford, my fiancé." I smile as they shake hands; more than that, I smile at the small boost of confidence I feel. Just a few seconds later, Michael's and Sarah's spouses join in, followed by more introductions. Sarah and Michael's wife gush over my ring—or more specifically, the yellow diamond that's surrounded by smaller colorless ones—and I *really* enjoy that.

Then we part ways with the promise of seeing each other at dinner soon, and Nicholas and I check in to our suite.

"Just so you know" —I keep my voice down as we wait for our elevator— "I think we have five or six Michaels, three Marys, four Peters, two Sarahs, and three Brians in our family. Well, four now, I suppose, with Amber's husband joining the clan." I snicker. "We're not very creative with names, I guess."

"I'll try to keep up." Nicholas chuckles and ushers me into the elevator. "But I do remember meeting more than one Mary at the wedding last summer. We don't exactly have that issue in my family."

That's true. The Fords are a close-knit group, and it's small. It's really only him, his parents, his two sisters—Sydney is a couple years younger than Nicholas, and Lissa one year older—and their husbands and children.

"I liked spending time with them last week." I duck my head and grin, remembering how different this time was from the last. Nicholas's parents welcomed me into the family the first time we met, months ago, but his sisters were wary of me and protective of their brother.

All that melted away in Mexico, though. Lissa is still the mother hen as the eldest sibling, but she's also very sweet and maternal. Sydney...I snicker. Sydney is a spitfire, and we had a lot of fun together. I even found myself opening up to her about this trip over a few margaritas. *Pink* margaritas!

"Expect them to call you after the holidays." Nicholas smirks into the kiss he leaves on my forehead. "They'll want to be involved in the wedding planning."

That makes me squeal behind my hand, because I'm super excited to get married to Nicholas.

"You're too fucking adorable." His eyes dance with laughter and love as I peer up at him, and I feel my skin flushing. He touches my cheek, the mirth fading, replaced by something softer. "Don't ever change."

"Ditto, mister." I kiss his palm.

An hour and a half is all it takes for us to transform into a fancy-looking couple on their way to a nice dinner.

No one will be able to guess we've traveled all day, although I definitely feel it. Exhaustion has seeped into my bones—no bath can eliminate that—but perhaps it's a good thing. If I'm tired, maybe it'll numb the anxiety. One can only hope.

"You're so beautiful, Kayla." His eyes rake over my strapless cocktail dress with desire.

I'd usually go with a lighter color, though I found the emerald green fitting for the season. Plus, the design is similar to a baby-doll dress—my favorite kind; Nicholas's, too—only a bit more modest. But still cute, with a pretty bow and everything. Someone who is *not* cute is my fiancé. In a charcoal suit and a tie that matches my dress, he's extremely handsome and sexy.

He walks over to his laptop bag; I totally check out his tight butt, and when he returns he has a flat jewelry box in his hand—larger than one for a necklace, even. "You'll wear a new kind of collar tonight." At my surprised expression, he opens the lid to reveal several pieces of silver jewelry. At least I hope it's silver; he already spends so much money on me.

The horny butterflies are back in my tummy. "A c-collar?" But we aren't scening, are we? It's a formal family dinner!

I already have a permanent one I'm always wearing—a platinum choker only Nicholas has the key to unlock. There's also a small charm, where it says "Daddy Nicholas's Baby Girl" in *teeny*, tiny writing.

"That's right." Kneeling before me, he gathers my foot and places it on his bent knee, then proceeds to attach a silver bangle around my ankle. "I don't make empty promises, baby girl—you know that." Next is my other ankle, and I feel the cool metal with just the barest amount of pressure on my skin. Then he slides his hands up my smooth legs. Firmly. Possessing me. Owning me. "I think I need a look." He lifts my dress and starts kissing my upper thighs, all while his right hand caresses my pussy.

"Oh..." I let out a whine, wanting more. Lots more. "Mmm, Daddy." My hips buck toward him of their own volition as he presses his mouth to my cotton-clad kitty. I really don't like thongs —hardly ever wear them—but it's necessary for this dress. At least it's soft cotton.

"There you go distracting me." The tip of his tongue darts over my clit, followed by a hot breath as he exhales. The warmth sears through my underwear, causing me to squirm. He chuckles huskily and lowers the dress once more. I pout, and he ignores that. "As I was saying...I don't make empty promises." With his unwavering and intense gaze, he stands up and clasps another bangle onto my right wrist. "As always, you will be my focus, and I promise you will soon look back on this evening and wonder why you were so nervous."

A small, serene smile flits across my lips, and I close my eyes briefly. "I trust you, Daddy."

"Good girl." Lastly, he attaches the final bangle to my left wrist and finishes by kissing the tips of my fingers. "Consider the metal as an extension of me tonight." He nips at the pad of my middle finger, hard enough for a quick, sharp sting. "To remind you that I'm right there with you." *Yes.* He lulls me into a nearly comatose state with that voice—smooth, rich, warm, and with the level of command I need.

Taking a deep breath, I nod, finally ready to face my family—or rather, those who side with Amanda.

I thank Daddy profusely for making me feel better, and then we get ready to go downstairs to the hotel restaurant that my family has reserved for the evening. I slip into a pair of ballet flats that go with my dress and grab my little silver clutch—just as my phone vibrates inside. Opening it, I see that I have a text from Sydney, Nicholas's sister.

I can't help but giggle when I read it.

If Amanda gives you grief, imagine her doing so dressed like a pirate's wench.

"Anything interesting?" Nicholas asks. I grin up at him and show him the screen, to which his mouth twists into a wry little smirk. "My sister certainly has different methods than I do, doesn't she?" He shakes his head in amusement. "But by all means, little love."

Okay, wench, here we come.

CHAPTER 3

N ow I remember why I only see my family twice or so a year —Amanda-crap aside. It's because they're an overwhelming bunch of people. The restaurant is *packed* with Brandons—the most common name on my dad's side of the family—Stevens from Uncle Keith's side, and McCallisters from Mom and Aunt Mary's side.

There are also a few associates from the company Uncle Keith runs—that he once started with my dad. It's boring stuff...mergers and acquisitions.

I'm glad Uncle Keith never changed the company's name. He once said, "I started it with Henry—that'll never change." So, the company is still named HBKS Financial.

Anyway...even though there are so many of us, we work like a well-oiled machine. We have a few days here, so everyone knows there'll be plenty of time to catch up sooner or later. A handful of greetings to the people we pass and we end up at our table. My Gramma Ida is already seated, and I'm more than happy to sit down next to her. There are a couple Michaels, too, and—unfortunately—Aunt Cheryl, Uncle Keith's sister. She's an Amanda shipper.

Speak of the devil and she will appear.

I hear her cackling about something behind me; she and Amber seem to have been assigned to the table next to us.

Nicholas gives my leg an affectionate squeeze under the table, reminding me of his presence, and I offer a grateful smile in return. Then I introduce him to my grandmother, who seems enamored of him, yet protective of me. She was sick last summer, so she never made it to Amber and Brian's wedding.

"Well, now. This must've cost an arm and a leg." Gramma Ida inspects my engagement ring over the rims of her super cool, purple cat-eye glasses. Then she slides her gaze to Nicholas. "And how did you propose, young man?"

"In Venice, ma'am." Nicholas nods in thanks to the waiter who arrives with our pre-ordered drinks and appetizers. "Kayla told me she hadn't been able to visit Italy when she went to Europe this spring. After I had found the ring, I wanted to take her there."

"It was *so* romantic, Gramma." I can't keep the excitement out of my voice even if I tried. "We took a gondola ride and everything, and the food was *amazing*." I just know my grandmother will love the book of authentic Italian recipes I bought for her when we were there. "Then when we got back to the hotel, he got down on one knee and asked me to marry him."

"Good. Very good." She's satisfied, I can tell. The man taking a knee is important to her, for some reason. "And you recently moved into a new house together?" Now her full focus is on me, and she palms my cheeks. "Do you get enough food down there in California?"

I giggle and roll my eyes. "I eat plenty. Don't worry—and I love Cali."

A particularly loud round of laughter shifts my attention to the table next to us, and when I automatically look over my shoulder, I catch Amanda staring at me.

I'd love to say she looks like crap, but that would be a lie. She's still the statuesque blonde I'm used to, and she's seated between a man I've never met—her date?—and her sister.

"Hello, Drifter." Amanda's smile is brilliant, though her gaze is cold as ice. "I heard you got engaged. I'm sure it will last *forever*. Because men marry young playthings for love, yes?"

I swallow and fidget with the hem of my dress, wishing I could tear my eyes away, but I'm trapped. In an attempt to make myself smaller, my ankles brush together, making the bangles clink. *Nicholas is right next to me.* And in my periphery, I realize he's watching me. Having faith in me. Ready to help, but believing I'm not defenseless.

Emboldened, I straighten my weakened posture and shrug. "Oh, I hope our engagement won't last forever. Our marriage, on the other hand..."

"Atta girl." So, Gramma Ida is paying attention, too.

Amanda lets out a tinkling laugh, not having heard our grandmother's comment. "Well, I, for one, find your confidence *adorable*. Nick, you sure are good at making women believe in every promise you make. Perhaps you should take pity on my poor little cousin's heart."

Twisting his body so our knees are touching, Nicholas turns to Amanda's table with an expression of mild interest. "I don't recall giving you any promises, Amanda. I saved those for my fiancée." I bet no one else can see the anger simmering under his surface, but I do. However, he's still too much of a gentleman to be outright rude —at least in public. "I trust Kayla's Christmas won't be ruined by my past mistakes?" He cocks a brow.

"*Mistakes?*" Amanda loses her composure for a second, completely insulted. Her date looks confused, if not frustrated by being out of the loop. "You're calling me a—How can you—"

"I can." Nicholas cuts her off. "And that's enough." With that, he faces our table again and holds up a mini crab cake to me. "Let's focus on something better." There's joy in his eyes now.

Beaming back at him, I part my lips and let him slip the small treat into my mouth.

I hum at the deliciousness of the hors d'oeuvre, but more so at the incredible man beside me.

The day before Christmas, I'm thankful I don't see Amanda at all. While doing some extra shopping to pass time, Nicholas and I do run into Amber and her husband Brian, but she's harmless without her sister. Haughty looks are nothing compared to the vileness Amanda spews.

The rest of my day is spent lounging around our Christmassy hotel suite with Nicholas, catching up with a few cousins, avoiding looks from those who're on Amanda's side, and having dinner with Gramma Ida, who my fiancé is sure would get along great with Sydney.

He's probably right.

After making love on the soft rug in front of the open fire, we go to bed, and I'm in an awesome mood because this trip hasn't sucked at all. There's still tomorrow and the 26th, but maybe I can afford to be a little optimistic.

Waking up on Christmas morning, however...no. Just no. Doesn't matter what day it is; I'm so cranky.

"No..." I pout into my pillow and blindly bat away Daddy's hands. "Stop it. I'm *sleepy!*" I whine and try to pull the covers over my head. Emphasis on *try*.

He ignores my protests, his large hands roaming my naked body. He's naked, too, and he's currently pressing his impressive morning erection against my butt. It's just...I'm too warm and cuddly to be turned on right now. The room smells of pine, ginger, cloves, and orange—it's like inhaling Christmas, a holiday for snuggling.

"You're being awfully obstinate this morning." His warm,

rumbling morning voice tickles my neck as a hand creeps up my stomach to cup my boobs. I'd worry that he's irritated if it wasn't for the grin I hear in his tone. "Are you denying Daddy the chance to show his little girl how much he loves her?"

Against my will, my body heats up and a smile threatens to surface. "Maybe Daddy loves her so much that he'll let her sleep in?" I stiffen myself into a stick as I stretch and groan and yawn. "Mmm...let's stay here all day."

He chuckles sleepily and rolls me onto my back. "As tempting as that sounds..." His eyes follow the path of his hand trailing down my tummy. "And believe me, it's tempting." He gives my forehead a kiss. His breath is minty and fresh, I note. Has he been up already? "We have brunch downstairs in a couple hours, dinner tonight, then that gift lottery or whatever your family calls it." Next he kisses my nose. "But—" then my cheeks "—I'm sure we'll have plenty of time under the covers."

I hope so. There's nothing better than this right here.

I'm glad we've all agreed to have some alone time with our immediate family today. Those with kids want to celebrate in private as well, and...let's face it, it would be financially impossible to buy gifts for each family member. That's why we have our little game at dinner. Everyone has pitched in ten dollars, and a few women, Gramma Ida included, have been in charge of buying ten fairly lavish gifts. It's always gift baskets with themes. For instance, my parents got a basket one time, and it was full of kitchen stuff and food. Recipes, some smaller appliances, a gift card to some high-end delicacy shop, expensive chocolate, and cheese from Switzerland.

I remember giggling and blushing profusely when one of the Marys and her husband took home a basket with a bedroom theme one year. Pillowcases in Egyptian cotton are nothing to be embarrassed about, but a book about sex positions? Edible panties? Well, I was like twelve, so...

Yawning and stretching some more, I burrow closer to Daddy's warmth and drop a kiss to his sternum. My fingers draw lazy circles on his chest, feeling his light dusting of hair there and teasing his nipples.

"Merry Christmas, baby girl." His sexy murmur sends a shiver down my spine, and I hitch a leg over his hip to get even closer.

"Merry Christmas, Daddy." Tilting up my head, I beam at him and angle for some lovin'. He gives it to me right away, slowly easing into a deep, passionate, and demanding kiss. "Oh..." I breathe heavily, getting clingy and tingly.

It's Christmas morning sex with a twist. It's wonderful, it's tender lovemaking, it's *I-love-you-so-much*, and it's Daddy praising his little one for taking his cock so perfectly. As he rolls us over so I'm on top and I sink down on him, it's Daddy moaning about how tight and addictive his baby girl's pussy feels wrapped around him.

Mere minutes later, he makes me giggle uncontrollably when he flips me over again and pins my body with his. He has this playful grin as he gathers my hands above my head. We kiss sloppily, his cock still moving steadily inside me. Panted breaths mingle, and our bodies become heated and damp. I nearly arch off the bed when he reaches a spot that makes me shake and quiver.

"That's it, my little baby..." Between husky whispers and dirty words, he grinds his pelvis against my clit and sucks on my nipples, plucking at them, teasing them. "You're going to come around Daddy's cock, aren't you?"

Holding my breath, so close, I can only nod in response. I feel feverish and coiled-up, the pleasure building rapidly.

"Ahhh, *fuck*." He groans and slams his hips forward, effectively pushing me over.

I let out a breathless scream.

Daddy grabs the headboard and takes me hard through my orgasm, surrendering to his own climax when I start gasping for air.

While he jerks and releases into me, I touch him—wherever I can reach—and kiss him, tell him I love him, and inhale our combined scent.

"Jesus Christ, Kayla." Panting, he collapses on top of me, and I trace the goose bumps that appear on his muscular arms. "Kayla, Kayla, Kayla." He lifts his head slowly and kisses my jaw, then my lips. "What you do to me..." Another kiss—a firm one. "I love you more than I can say."

"I love you, too," I singsong. "And it's Christmas!" A big smile takes over my face; I'm no longer cranky, tired, or in need of snuggling. Now I wanna give Daddy his presents.

It's been super hard keeping them hidden, but I managed, and last night before bed, I put them under the small tree in the living room area.

"Can we do gifts now, please?" I give him my best puppy-dog look. "Please, please, pretty please with a cherry on top?" Had I not been trapped under him, I would've had room to clasp my hands together as if in prayer.

Daddy chuckles and moves off me. "How can I deny you?" With a touch to my cheek, he leaves the bed to put on the dark green pajama bottoms I bought him yesterday. 'Cause I told him that you *had* to wear jammies when you open Christmas presents. So, in return, Daddy had bought me a satin robe two sizes too small in light gold.

I think it's so he can see my butt.

Jumping out of bed, I rip the tag off the silky smooth robe and dash into the bathroom to go number one and get rid of Daddy's come. Then after washing up and brushing my teeth, I join him in the living room.

While I was gone, he's put on some music channel on the TV that's playing Christmas carols, and there's a room service cart near the tree—

"Oh, my God!" I run over to the tree, spotting all the little boxes that sure weren't there last night. "Wow..." Tugging on Nicholas's hand, I make him sit down next to me. "How did you manage to hide all these from me?" I may or may not have looked through our luggage. His laptop bag isn't large, which was why I missed the "collar"—the bracelets—he'd gotten for me.

"I had them FedExed before we arrived." He kisses my temple, enjoying my exuberance. I can totally tell. "They've been in the cabinet over there—" he nods at the solid oak TV stand "—since yesterday."

"Sneaky." I poke his side.

"So were you." He nods at the tree—at the three gifts that are for him. "When I woke up earlier, I thought I'd be the first one to put the presents under there." The corners of his grayish blue eyes crinkle.

I grin proudly. "I snuck out of bed after you had fallen asleep." And there was no need for me to have anything shipped. Everything fit inside my carry-on bag. My gifts for him aren't big in size.

For fun, I got him a coffee mug that says "World's Best Daddy" on it. For the gadget lover in him, I bought a portable mini sound system for his office at Switch. The salesguy said Bose or whatever it's called was *very* good. I don't know. I just scrunch my nose at that tech stuff.

Lastly, for love and possession, I got something he can wear at the club. If I'm collared, he should be, too! There's always some sub who tries to flirt with my Nicholas, so I figured a simple leather cuff with a metal plate that has the words "Kayla's Daddy" on it should at least help a little.

Admire from afar all you want, ladies, but Nicholas Ford is so mine.

Eager to get started, I thrust the box with the coffee mug into Nicholas's hands, thinking I'll go with the smallest gift first. In response, he brings down two plates with breakfast from the cart and tells me to eat my scone.

He laughs and shakes his head at the mug, then gives me a smooch and promises to use it for his morning coffee from now on. I blush and giggle at that. Then it's my turn to shake my head— totally amused—when he opens the gift with the portable speakers.

There are four of them, and he looks ten years younger as he animatedly thinks out loud about where to place them in the office at Switch. He also confirms that the salesguy was right. So...*whew.* Good purchase.

"Now that we'll have music up there, perhaps I'll order you to strip for me—maybe a lap dance?" He drops a sensual kiss to my neck. "Thank you."

"You're welcome." That came out all breathy. "Um, here." I give him the final gift and wring my hands in my lap, nervous he won't like it.

But he does. Thank goodness.

"This is wonderful, sweetheart." Putting the box aside, he smiles softly and brushes his thumb over the metal plate with "Kayla's Daddy" engraved in the silver. The black leather is only about two inches wide, and I think it will look so sexy on him. Everyone who works at Switch already wears one, only theirs are slimmer and have the Switch logo. That's sorta where I got the idea.

"I was thinking you could wear it at the club?" I don't know why I posed it as a question. "Like, um, a collar..." *To show you're mine.* The red rubber bands worn by everyone who is in a relationship aren't special; they just show unavailability. You slap it on when you enter the club—that's it. I want something more permanent and unique.

"Of course I will. Although, I don't see why I should only wear it at Switch." He attaches the cuff and nods—in satisfaction, it looks like. "Perfect. Thank you very much."

I smile in relief and nibble on my scone.

"And now I suppose it's your turn." He grins, and I bounce a little, eyeing the handful of boxes left under the tree. But then he confuses me by retrieving his phone from the coffee table a few feet away. "Let's call Rio and wish him a merry Christmas, shall we?"

"Wh...?" *What?* I frown, thinking his timing stinks.

"You owe me, Ford." Rio's grumpy voice filters through, and when Nicholas shifts closer and shows me the display, I see Rio's face, too. I guess a regular phone call isn't enough? "Oh." Rio's morning scowl is replaced by a faint smile when he sees me. "How are ya, love?"

"Um, good." I'm still confuzzled, but I manage to smile genuinely at the sight of a rumpled Rio. His nearly black hair is messy from sleep, and his bright green eyes glisten when he yawns. "How are you, Sir?"

"Bloody brilliant." He huffs a chuckle and moves around wherever he is—maybe to another room in his house. I'm not sure, but I think I recognize the rustic red of the walls in his living room. "Has Nick filled you in?"

I shake my head no-no.

"Not yet." Nicholas picks up my hand and kisses my knuckles. "All right, so perhaps I didn't call Rio to wish him a merry Christmas—"

"Cheers, mate." Rio smiles wryly.

I stifle a giggle.

Nicholas smirks and goes on. "Rio, show Kayla her present, please."

Frowning deeper, I turn to the screen again, then gasp as Rio picks up a tiny, furry ball. My hands fly to my mouth, and my eyes grow large. Oh, my God, did Nicholas—? Another gasp escapes me when the gray kitten is joined by an orange one. Like Oliver from the Disney movie!

It feels like I'm drawn closer by a magnetic force, and I snatch the phone from Nicholas.

"Rio's been watching them while we're here." He picks me up as if I weigh nothing and sits me down again, between his legs. "They're ten weeks old. Tabbies, both boys."

Rio cuts in. "And they track litter all over my house. This is why I'm a dog person."

Pure joy and excitement bubble up, and I'm torn between throwing myself at Nicholas and gluing myself to the phone; in the end, I do a combination of both. While curling up in Nicholas's lap, snaking one arm around his neck, I hold the phone tighter and closer with my free hand. I squeal and blubber about how cute they are; I thank Nicholas for making another one of my dreams come true. Twice, even! Two kittens. *Two!*

"I take it you're happy?" Nicholas smiles and tucks a piece of hair behind my ear.

"You have no idea." I sniffle, wiping away a tear, and brush a finger over the screen that still shows the kittens. Right now, Rio's angling his phone at the gray one, who is stretching on the sofa. "Look at him—so adorable." The little furball is a mix of white and silver with darker stripes.

Then the other one rolls over there and stretches, putting a small paw on top of his brother's tummy. He's creamy orange and white, spotty instead of stripey, and the colors blend together more.

"I'm a mommy now." I'm nodding, liking my words.

For humans, I'm an auntie type. Nicholas feels the same; he's said he's happy being an uncle to his sister's kids. We like children, and we also like the idea of returning them to their parents when they get fussy. But two precious little animals? Oh, I'm gonna spoil my boys so much!

"Does that make you Daddy, Nick?" Rio's face fills the screen again; so does his smirk.

Nicholas laughs through his nose. "I suppose." He gives me a squeeze. "But I'll leave the discipline to Kayla on this matter. I have my hands full with a certain baby girl."

"And she will show you how thankful she is for this." It's a promise. I pop a kiss to his chin before facing the screen once more. "Master Rio, could you please send me a few photos later?"

He inclines his head. "Of course, little one."

Unfortunately, we have to wrap up the conversation because it's time to get ready, and my baths tend to take a long time, 'cause I love them so much.

Later, as I'm getting dressed, Nicholas explains that the other gifts have a cat theme and that I can open them when we return after brunch. A brunch I don't really want anymore.

It wasn't long ago we had breakfast, darn it. But I obey and let Nicholas drag me downstairs, and later I squeal again when I open the presents to reveal cute collars, toys, treats, and a beautiful book where I can fill in important dates and memories about our kittens.

CHAPTER 4

That night after dinner, Nicholas and I sit at our table with Gramma Ida and a few others as we wait for the game to begin. We have our little paper slips with numbers, but with the amount of people gathered, I don't think we'll get a basket. Instead Nicholas and I focus on each other, his arm draped across the back of my chair, and he asks me if I've thought of names for the kittens.

Boy, have I ever!

Earlier today, Nicholas took advantage of the hotel gym, and I used that time to respond to all my Christmas texts from friends, and then I called Evangeline to volley names. She had gushed over the photos Rio sent me after breakfast, and she agreed that the orange kitten really looks like an Oliver. It may not be original, but it was my favorite Disney movie when I was little, so that's that. And with his markings, I added Spot as his middle name.

Brayden joined our conversation briefly, mostly to tease me since he and Mark are evidently also dog people. Brayden had the nerve to call the gray kitten a furry "ball of smudge."

It was all in good fun, though, and I actually found Smudge

cute as hell. But not as a first name. Evangeline and I think Jackson is a strong name for him.

"I hope it's not Mr. Cuddles." Great, now Nicholas is teasing me, too.

"It's *not*." I huff, then sniff. "If you must know, it's Oliver Spot Ford and Jackson Smudge Ford."

"Oliver and Jackson?" His mouth slants into a smile. Then a slow nod. "Well, all right then."

I grin, about to explain their names, when my phone vibrates in my clutch, and I've been waiting for Chelsea to get back to me. For some reason, I think she's avoiding me; I never got in touch with her in Mexico as planned, either. I hope it's her now.

"Excuse me..." I quickly pull out my phone, and I breathe a sigh of relief when I see that it is, in fact, my New York girlfriend. But the relief morphs into confusion when I read the text.

Sorry for not replying sooner. I've been thinking a lot about my move to SF, and I have to know something first. The Rio you've mentioned, is his last name Kelly?

"Something wrong, sweet girl?"

"Um." I purse my lips, slowly shaking my head, and I honestly have no clue. Why would Chelsea ask about Rio? Do they know each other? At a loss, I show Nicholas the text, and he frowns in response.

"We'll have to talk about that later." He nods at Aunt Mary and one of the Sarahs who are ready to start the gift exchange. Both are standing on a small dais with ten big gift baskets lined up on two tables, and as Aunt Mary addresses the crowd, Sarah holds up a glass bowl with the "lottery" numbers.

With a family including about a hundred people, it's no wonder we don't expect to bring home a basket, and we don't. So, as soon as the game is over, I lean close to Nicholas and say I'm gonna go to the little girls' room. Except, I'm pretty sure he knows I'm excusing myself to go call Chelsea.

Finding privacy in the hallway between the lobby and the elevators, I bring out my phone and click on Chelsea's name.

"I figured you were gonna call." Nice greeting.

Well, I'm not going to beat around the bush. "Do you know Rio?"

"I wouldn't go that far." She sounds nervous and uncomfortable, which is so not the Chelsea Dunn I roomed with during the three months I lived in New York a year ago.

She's sexually submissive through and through, but she's also assertive and strong. Cheeky. She's got a wicked sense of humor, and she's the one who throws caution to the wind. Never one to hesitate. Being four years older than me, she's also like a big sister to me.

"Let's just say he made an impression on me—once upon a time." She clears her throat. "He's the reason I told you to visit Switch in the first place."

That...that makes no sense. Pacing the hallway, I phrase my words and try to get all my gazillion questions in order. "Rio worked with Doctors Without Borders up until a few weeks ago. He just got home from Cambodia or something. Chelsea, he was gone for like—I don't even know, but more than a year, and that was just the last round."

"I know. I, uh, I found him on Facebook." There's sheepishness and guilt behind her admission. "He used it to keep in touch with his brother and parents while he was overseas."

I chuckle awkwardly. "Stalker warning, sweetie."

"Don't I know it." She probably just rolled her eyes at herself. "But I swear it's not as bad as it sounds. I got curious—this was maybe...three years ago? He kept popping up in my mind, so I looked up his name and found him. That's also where I saw some woman asking about Switch's opening on his wall." I nod to myself, knowing that Nicholas opened Switch a little over three years ago. "Since my current Dom at the time was taking me to San Francisco later that summer, I decided to visit Switch and see if Rio was there." But he hadn't been, of course.

"Why..." I sigh and massage my forehead. "Why haven't you told me any of this before?" I just don't get it.

"Because I know it all sounds shifty. You said it yourself, Kayla. Stalker warning? Ugh." She groans in the background. "I honestly just wanted to find him and apologize for how we met. I was such an idiot."

That sounds ominous. "How did you meet?"

She releases a heavy breath. "It was almost ten years ago—he sorta introduced me to the lifestyle."

Wait, what? "No way." I know I sound dubious, because I am. "Um, honey...ten years ago, you were sixteen. Rio was what—thirty?" Yeah, thirty. Nicholas has told me Rio turns forty in February.

"He didn't know I was sixteen," she admits. "Don't worry; nothing happened. I met him at a club—a vanilla one, and I'd been using my fake ID." Oh, Chelsea. "I flirted with him, and..." She huffs a humorless chuckle. "You know I've told you I was a wild kid." That's an understatement, but Chelsea's childhood wasn't a nice one, so I can't blame her. I *don't* blame her. "Anyway, he didn't buy into my shit—the flirting, the skimpy outfit. Girl, I was relentless. And, I think to scare me away, he told me what he usually did with brats who needed to know their place."

At that, I gotta giggle. Knowing Chelsea's turn-ons, I bet she creamed herself.

"Yeah..." She giggles, too. "I remember something snapping inside me. I swear I almost melted into a puddle in front of him." Then she pauses, and the humor is gone. "It was so wonderful to be with someone who saw through me. Back then, I pushed everyone's limits."

I feel so sad for her, because I know why she did it: to see if anyone else would abandon her. For a long time, it was her defense mechanism.

"So, what happened then?" I bite my thumbnail, worried how this will affect her move to San Francisco. "Did he find out you were only sixteen?"

"Yeah, he suspected I was underage, and he made me tell him the truth."

Made her? Uh-oh. Rio is a *very* creative Master—I'm almost afraid to ask. "How did he—um, you *know*?"

She chuckles wryly. "He called me on it—the teasing. He cornered me in the club and got all close, effectively making me blurt out the truth." Oh, I can picture that. Tall and broad-shouldered, Rio would loom over her like a tower. "He caged me in, Kayla, but instead of feeling trapped... I wouldn't call it safe, 'cause I was fucking terrified, but there was something..."

"I understand." I get quiet, knowing just the "something" she's talking about. No sensible woman would feel safe mere seconds after meeting a man that way, but...Nicholas and his friends kind of radiate it. You don't need to spend much time with them to understand how strict they are when it comes to all various codes of conduct. It's in their bones.

"I honestly don't think he remembers me, but what if he does? How's he gonna react when I move there in a few weeks?"

Ten years since they met—and it was only briefly...? "I don't think you have anything to worry about either, but you never know." I pause, thinking. "Did anything else happen afterward—after he confronted you?"

"You mean aside from the fact that I suddenly had a major crush?" Chelsea laughs, although it sounds a little empty. "No. Nothing else happened. We made introductions, and he advised me to—oh, Kayla, he said, 'You should take care of yourself, little rebel. There's only one of you.'"

"God, that's so *sweet*." I melt a little at that and pout at the floor. Rio is such a good man; he deserves...he deserves Chelsea! Oh my God, that's who I need to set him up with. Chelsea! She will be perfect for him. I think. I hope.

Imagine that reunion—when they see each other at Switch. Like...the parting of the Red Sea. They'll fall in love and get married and have a bunch of babies.

I mean, what could go wrong?

Having been too excited with my future matchmaking, I miss a few things Chelsea has said, so I swoop in and "uh-huh" and "I see" over the next couple minutes. Then we wish each other a merry Christmas before I really do need to go to the little girls' room.

It's when I'm washing my hands after going to the bathroom that I hear Amanda talking to someone outside in the hallway. Grabbing a paper towel, I dry my hands and walk closer to the exit, putting my ear to the door in hopes of hearing better.

"What do you mean, you're leaving?" She sounds totally offended.

Next it's a man who speaks up. "I didn't come here to make you look good, Amanda." Ooh, I think that's her date. "With your eyes glued to your cousin and her fiancé, I'm surprised you haven't forgotten I'm here completely."

Drama.

"You're delusional." Amanda scoffs, and it'd be perfect if she'd said that in a mirror. "You can't leave now; it's Christmas, for God's sake! Do you know how it'll look if you bail on me now?"

I shake my head, getting the heebie-jeebies. One might think she'd be the dumb blonde who gets killed first in a horror movie, but I actually believe she'd be the monster everyone's running from. She has no heart.

"Have a good Christmas, Amanda. Oh, and a piece of advice? Seek help for your narcissistic tendencies."

"Oh, snap." I giggle behind my hand.

The next thing I hear is the sound of shoes moving farther away, and then Amanda stomping her foot.

Then I hear someone approaching again, and Amanda no longer sounds angry, but smug.

"You followed me here, Nick? Keeping an eye on me?"

I back away and scowl at the door. She's out there with *Nicholas* now?

"Don't flatter yourself," he drawls. "You're not that interesting."

Double snap!

Amanda scoffs; she's good at that. "And I think you're lying. I've felt your eyes on me, you know."

Nicholas hums. "Call it a hunch. Kayla's been out here speaking to a friend on the phone" —*dammit, I knew he knew!*— "and I figured as long as you were in the restaurant, she'd be all right."

"You make it sound like I'm out to hurt her." Ugh, Amanda's doing that thing she did with her parents after bullying me— sounding all sweet and innocent. Only, at thirty-six, she just sounds pathetic. "I was merely going to powder my nose—"

"Save your shit for someone who buys it, Amanda. And evidently that doesn't include your date. He sure took off quickly, didn't he?"

See? There we go again. Rio hadn't believed Chelsea for a minute, and now Nicholas is calling out Amanda. Nothing gets past them. For all I know, Nicholas even knows I'm listening right now.

Not particularly interested in making a fool of myself, I throw away the paper towel and then unceremoniously leave the bathroom.

Nicholas simply smiles and holds out his hand for me, and Amanda shoots me a glare.

As we head back to the restaurant, I peer over my shoulder and stick out my tongue at her.

Her eyes widen, as if she can't believe how childish I'm being.

Pirate's wench.

I snicker and hug Nicholas's bicep.

"I saw that, baby girl." He doesn't look down at me; he just smirks and opens the glass doors leading to the restaurant. "And I want you to know I'm very proud of you." He huffs a laugh at my surprised look and taps my nose. "Not the part where you stuck out your tongue. But all of this—the trip, coming here and tolerating some of your family's abhorrent behavior."

Heat spreads over my cheeks at the praise. "It wasn't as bad as I feared, though. It was..." I purse my lips and sit down in my seat. "It was just a hiccup. But I still wouldn't have come here if it weren't for you."

Then I wouldn't have seen my grandmother, so I'm definitely thankful.

"A hiccup." He chuckles, taking his seat next to me, and brushes a kiss to my temple. "That's a good way of putting it."

Yup. I think so, too. Just a touch of trouble—a slice, and I gobbled that down without problems.

Sure, the occasional whisper I overhear from Amanda shippers stings a little, as do the dozen glares I've received, but Nicholas has helped me to focus on the ones who matter.

Such as my grandmother who loves the book of recipes I bought in Venice. She promises to visit us in San Francisco to cook for us, because she evidently still doesn't believe we eat enough "down there in California."

***

Two days later, we say goodbye to Oregon with the promise of returning for Christmas next year.

It gives me a year to prepare!

Our family also spends the Fourth of July together, and *no, thanks*. Once a year is plenty, as long as I can see Gramma Ida a bit more often.

I'm glad I spend most of the flight home asleep, because the moment we land in San Francisco, I'm bouncing all over the place, desperate to meet my kittens for the first time.

Nicholas knows better than to hold me back. There's a time and place for everything; this is the time and place for being the girl who acts like she's on crack.

If anything, he loves me this way. That's what his expression says as we make our way to Rio's house. Yeah, no, we're not going home first. No way, José.

"Are you gonna tell Rio about Chelsea?" I wrinkle my nose at the whole situation. Even Nicholas was at a loss yesterday when I divulged what Chelsea had told me on the phone. Oh, and my fiancé wonders if Rio's abrupt goodbye to bachelorhood ten years ago is connected to Chelsea, since it occurred around the same time.

I really don't know...

"Not yet. I want to feel him out a bit first—see if he even reacts to her name." He looks thoughtful, peering out the window on my side. "When does Chelsea move here?"

"She has a part-time job that starts February first," I answer. "But she wants to find something more stable, too." She's already found a room in an apartment she's going to share with three others, so that's cool.

"You mentioned she's a singer?"

"Not just a singer. She's like friggin' Adele." I think back on the countless nights Chelsea dragged me out to various jazz clubs in New York. "She's super good. That's the part-time job she's already found. There's a club in the Castro where she's gonna sing two nights a week."

He nods pensively. "What else is she looking for? If she has no preference, I'm sure I can find a position for her—if not at Switch, then one of my other clubs. There's always Blue Hour." That's his music club where they host open mic nights, I think.

"I'll talk to her." I'm so excited that she's moving here, really.

"Thank you—oh! We're here!" I hadn't even noticed that we've reached Rio's house, and now I'm bouncing again.

Mommy's on her way, boys.

"Nicholas!" I call from the kitchen. "Pizza's here!" I'm not sure he heard the doorbell earlier, because it gets crazy loud in our laundry room when both the washing machine and the dryer are on. That's where he is right now, after I've unpacked our luggage from Mexico and Oregon.

I'm awful when it comes to washing clothes; I tend to turn whites pink—damn red panties from my baby devil Halloween costume—but I'm good at ironing and folding, so Nicholas and I have our little arrangement.

Done mixing the salad, I open the fridge to grab our drinks... and a treat for the kittens. We've only been home for a few hours, so they're still exploring the house, which is super cute to watch, and I'm so in love with them already.

Earlier, when Nicholas and I came back downstairs after sharing a shower, they barged into the living room, stopped short, got down in a crouch, then jumped around, rubbed up against the furniture, and tried to sneak into every little nook they could find. Even Nicholas said they were adorable!

He did not, however, find it adorable when Oliver took a liking to wrestling with the remote control. Or when Jackson started knocking over our collection of bottled beach sand from the vacation spots we've visited.

It's only a small collection so far, but I think we need to find a new spot for it. The windowsill obviously doesn't work for Jackson. Thankfully, none of the small bottles broke.

"I think a gate would seal off the hallway nicely." Nicholas is muttering to himself, and I chuckle. Like a gate would stand in a cat's way! "Sweetheart, can you come here and get the kittens while I pay for the pizza?"

Oh, of course. I forgot. Jackson and Oliver are there in a flash when someone's at the door. Oliver nearly escaped before when we picked them up at Rio's. "Coming!" I deposit the drinks and tuna treat on the kitchen island, then leave the kitchen to join Nicholas in the hallway where I gather the kittens in my arms. "My little rascals."

I get a tiny paw in my face for that. *Thanks, Oliver. Mommy loves you, too.*

As the deliciousness of melted cheese, oregano, and tomato sauce invades my senses, my belly snarls, as if to say *"I want! Gimme pizza!"* so I make my way back to the kitchen. Jackson and Oliver can definitely smell the tuna on the island counter. And when I set them down on the floor so I can plate the tuna, they run around my feet—and between them so I nearly trip—and bump their heads and paws against my legs.

The second I set down the plates on the floor, they're all over that tuna.

I giggle and step back, then grin as Nicholas joins me with the pizza.

The kittens are busy, so we take our food, plates, and drinks to the living room and get comfy on the large couch. Right now, we're definitely spent from all the travels, so the only thing on the agenda is snuggling, and eating pizza and candy. And watching movies. In comfortable clothes. I'm only wearing panties and one of Nicholas's Henleys, and he's in a pair of gray sweats—the kind he usually runs in every morning—and a black T-shirt.

"God, it's good to be home." Nicholas groans in contentment and takes the first swig of his beer. "I wouldn't mind planning our next vacation already, but there's just something about coming home, isn't there?"

"Oh, definitely." I adore that I can agree now. In the past, I was always itching to get away. That was before I really felt at home somewhere. "What do you wanna watch?"

"You pick something."

So, I settle on some random movie, and we eat our pizza in easy silence before we're stuffed and relaxed in each other's arms under a blanket. By now, the first movie is over, and Nicholas finds another while I get more drinks and a bowl of candy. Though, we don't really watch the movie. Instead we're talking quietly about the past week, and also a little about next year.

"I have some free time coming up in March," he murmurs. He's all sprawled out over the couch, and I lift my head from his chest to peer up at him. "Where would you like to go next?"

I purse my lips, pondering. Meanwhile, Nicholas looks as if he's trying to memorize every detail about my face. "What?" I get self-conscious. Do I have oregano stuck between my teeth or something?

"Nothing. I'm just looking at you." He smiles faintly and brushes his knuckles over my cheek. "You're so beautiful."

"Oh." I get a bit squirmy under his gaze, because it's so intense. Almost overwhelming. "Um. Where do *you* want to go?" If I don't keep the conversation running, I'll attack. And I'm really tired and full. "Stop looking at me like that, Nicholas." I feel my cheeks heating up.

He grins and flips us over, pinning me to the couch. "Never." With a low hum, he slides his nose along my jaw. "Remind me, please. Is there really any flaw in you?"

A breathy laugh escapes me, and I poke his side. "There're tons." I start ticking them off on my fingers. "I can be messy, I can't do laundry, some say I meddle too much—"

"Not too much." He shakes his head and palms my cheek. "Never too much. I love that about you—that you want to see everyone happy." I shrug modestly and burrow closer as he settles next to me. "I'm lucky." After pulling the blanket over us again, as it had slid down before, he gathers my hand over his heart and closes his eyes. "But you're right." A teasing smile appears, but his eyes remain closed. "You can be *awfully* messy."

I don't take the bait. "I'm the lucky one," I whisper, sure of it. My gaze flits over his face: the five-o'clock shadow, the laugh lines, the sharp structure of his nose and jaw, the fullness of his firm, yet soft lips, the silver at his temples, his ruffled brown hair, his sun-kissed skin... He looks incredibly tired, but just as relaxed and content. Happy and at home.

Maybe we're both lucky.

CHAPTER 5

I t's fairly early, so people have just started to trickle in for a night at Switch, and the music isn't very loud yet.

I sit obediently on the barstool next to Daddy, but my eyes are all over the place, waiting for Mark to arrive.

He is such a greedy Master, because when the club was closed over the holidays, he kept Evangeline and Brayden *all* to himself. I get it, I get it—he didn't see them over Christmas because they were with Evangeline's family, so he wanted to spend New Year's with them. But he's got three whole *weeks* with them at his beach house in La Jolla starting in only a few days, and I wanna see my friends.

I'm glad they're coming tonight, though. It's January second, and—nose scrunch—it's S/M Night, but beggars can't be choosers. I'll just stay as far away as I can from the Sadists.

At least I saw Dylan and Cade a few days ago, which was fun. They came over to our house for dinner, and I learned that they're now in a committed Daddy/Little Boy relationship.

Matchmaking success!

They should be here soon, too—and at that, I glance around me again.

"Calm yourself, little one." Daddy gives me an impatient look. "They'll be here any minute."

I pull out the lemon-flavored lollipop from my mouth and offer my best pout in return. "I'm sorry, Daddy."

"No, you're not." He snorts and flags down Liam for another tonic water. "But you will be." With a tug on one of my pigtails, he smirks wickedly, making me squirm.

My butt is still tender from this morning when he told me Oliver and Jackson weren't allowed in the club. I was a brat; I even cussed at him, so out came the belt. Then he said that if I'm a really good girl, he might reward me by letting my kittens stay up in his office while we're here. "But it's not going to become a habit," he'd warned. "It's only when you've been good for a *long* time."

Looking down at my violet baby-doll dress, I sulk in silence and curse myself for behaving badly. I absently play with the lacy, white hem, and I wonder how I can make it up to him—

Daddy nudging me gently causes me to look up at him, and he nods at something behind me. I follow his gaze and stiffen in excitement as I see Mark walking in with Evangeline and Brayden.

As always when Mark's not tending the bar, he's in his black, well-worn leathers, boots, and a form-fitting T-shirt. Brayden's only wearing silk boxers and a pair of black slippers, and Evangeline is in her nearly see-through lingerie set with furry trim, kitty ears, and ballet flats. Standard getups for Mark's subs—always in silky black. And while I prefer pastels for myself, black is really sexy on those three.

Turning to Daddy again, I suck my bottom lip into my mouth, still ashamed because of earlier. I don't even have the guts to ask if I can greet my friends. But I'm lucky, because Daddy takes pity on me, pecks me softly, and tells me to go over there.

"Thank you so, so much!" I hop off the barstool and hug him tightly. "I love you, Daddy—"

"No running with this one." He takes my lollipop from my

hand. "I'll keep it here. Off you go." He sends me off with a kiss and a light smack to my bottom.

I swiftly make my way through the groupings of people near the bar and the closest seating area, and then I'm met with Evangeline's radiant smile as she spots me.

"Hi!" I come to a stop right in front of them and peer up at Mark's amused expression. "Permission to hug your sub, Master Cooper?"

He permits me with a dip of his chin. "Granted."

Squealing, I throw my arms around Evangeline, and she hugs me back tightly. Then I start to ramble about my Christmas, about Mexico, about Oliver and Jackson, and how I wanna know about her own holidays; I also comment on the beautiful highlights she's added to her hair, just a shade lighter than her natural chestnut brown, and—

"Take a breath, honey." Mark chuckles at me.

I inhale deeply, then exhale and smile sheepishly. "I've missed you guys." Peering over at Brayden, I wave shyly, 'cause it's different with him. Mark has him on a leash, a real one, and Brayden is the happiest when only Evangeline and Mark are close. He's quiet and soft-spoken, funny too, and at Switch, he's always in a scene.

He smiles back, a dimple denting his cheek, and then he lowers his gaze to the floor. His dark, wavy surfer boy-like hair falls forward a bit, shielding his pale green eyes.

He looks happy.

"Did Mr. Ford allow you to bring Jackson and Oliver?" Evangeline asks, hopeful.

I jut out my bottom lip. "No. I asked *nicely*—" Two firm hands clamp down on my shoulders, and I am in *so* much trouble. "Eeek." I let out a squeak as I look up to see Daddy.

His mouth is pressed thin in displeasure, though his eyes reveal mirth. "Are you lying to Master Cooper's pet, Kayla?" Soft voice, but steely and chilled. "Or was I with someone else this morning, because I seem to recall begging and whining."

Mark snickers and folds his arms across his chest. His end of Brayden's leash is looped around his hand. "You biting off a bit more than you can chew, hon?"

"Who is?" And welcome to the show, Cade Kingsley. Both he and Dylan appear behind Mark, who shifts to the side to make room. This is just great. Insert eye-roll. "Little Kayla?" He cocks a pierced brow at me. "And here I was, thinking she's always a good girl."

Daddy lets out a gruff laugh and hugs me from behind. "That's funny." Oh yeah, a real crack-up. I scowl at the ground in an attempt to hide my flushing cheeks. "Wasn't that funny, baby girl?" Dipping down, he nips at my neck while his large hands roam my upper thighs, slowly bunching up my already-short dress. "If only Cade knew just how much trouble you could be, huh?"

"Nah, I don't believe it for a second." Cade smirks in challenge.

"Well, this looks like fun..." Mark grins. "But Evangeline has a date with my new cane." I hadn't noticed it, but now I see his toy bag at his feet. "And Brayden's dying to try a new plug."

After wishing us a nice evening—and promising that Evangeline and I can catch up later—Mark steers his subs toward the Cave and the scening stalls there.

"Why don't we take this to the private booth?" Daddy suggests, and I wish my name for the booth—the Cabana—would catch on. 'Cause it really looks like a cabana! A dark and gothic one, with velvet fabrics hanging down, offering complete seclusion and an erotic atmosphere. It's big, too—eight or nine people would fit. Well, if they're as small as me. Maybe six Nicholas's? "Come on, baby girl." Before I know it, Daddy picks me up and positions me on his hip. "I think you're done running around for tonight."

I squeak and try to pull down my dress, but Daddy clearly doesn't want that. "I'm not wearing any panties," I whine. "Everyone can see my bottom."

"It's a very gorgeous little bottom." He squeezes it for emphasis, and I wince from the walloping this morning. Daddy laughs, the evil dummy.

With a *hmph*, I look over his shoulder, then giggle when Dylan crosses his light blue eyes and sticks out his tongue at me. Always the clown. Always the one who demands to see people in a good mood. Like me, he's also pretty new to San Francisco, and it took no effort at all for him to find his place in our group. He's very outgoing, a people person.

Some even think we're siblings, 'cause we share the same reddish brown hair—although his is only a few inches long and shaggy—light blue eyes, and fair skin. But that's where the similarities stop.

Like Brayden, Dylan has a swimmer's body, but that's because he actually is a swimmer—a professional one. Wide shoulders, narrow hips, and defined muscles.

Cade seems to like having all that goodness on display, because he's ordered Dylan to only wear baby blue pajama bottoms.

"Here we go." Daddy has my attention again as he pulls the velvet aside and enters the private booth. "You and Dylan can sit over there." He nudges me toward the left corner of the booth while Cade points for Dylan to take the right. "We'll be right back with drinks. And behave, Kayla." Stern look.

"Okay—but, Daddy? May I please have a new lollipop? A strawberry one?" I just love that little addition to the menu, and surprisingly, it was Mark who had thought of it.

He does the inventory—and the alcohol and snack orders—being in charge of the bars and all. I thought it was very sweet of him to think of the Littles. However, it's disturbing that he also put ginger root, lemon slices, salt, mint oil, and wasabi on the menu, all parts of chemical play.

Daddy called it genius and added Tabasco.

"We'll see if I'm in a rewarding mood later." Daddy winks, then takes off with a chuckling Cade.

That leaves Dylan and me, surrounded by solid wood, thick velvet, and leather. The small spotlights attached to the wooden posts are dimmed low, so it's not very bright.

"Are you in love with Mr. Kingsley yet?" I get comfortable in my corner and twirl a lock of hair around my finger. "If you say no like you did this weekend, I will call you a liar."

Dylan snickers and pulls up his legs, his arms wrapped around his knees. "Then maybe it's best I don't speak at all." Just a hint of a drawl. He's a Texas boy, but he grew up mostly on the East Coast. "Not everyone is looking for love, sugar." He reaches forward and tugs on a pigtail.

I scowl and smooth down my hair. "But you are. I know so." I've seen it—the way he's lusted after Cade. "Do you deny it?" I jut out my chin.

He hesitates and glances over at the opening—maybe to make sure Cade and Daddy aren't about to return yet. "It's complicated." Dylan's mouth twists into a small grimace, but he's quick to hide it. "I don't wanna pressure him, you know? He seems a little reserved."

My brows knit together as I remember Daddy telling me about Cade's former Little—who was a girl. She hadn't been truthful, so maybe that's why he is being careful.

Unfortunately, we have to stop there, because Daddy and Cade enter the booth, talking about sports or...I don't know. I hear "game" and "bet" and "you're on" before I tune out.

"One Sprite for my baby." Daddy sits down and slides my soda with crushed ice toward me, and I thank him with a big smooch. Then I climb up on his lap to snuggle. "In that mood, huh?" The left corner of his mouth quirks up.

Nodding, I bring my Sprite close and take a sip through the straw.

For a few minutes, Daddy and Cade resume talking about boring stuff, so that's the perfect time for me to study Cade with

Dylan. I don't know what he's so worried about; Cade seems aware of Dylan's every move. There's also a sense of contentment in Cade's eyes that wasn't there before.

"Time to move the table?" Cade asks a while later.

I get confuzzled, but Daddy nods, and then the two men push the glossy black table toward the draped exit. I didn't even know you could move it at all! In the end, half the table is sticking out, with the velvet drapes bunching up on the tabletop. It has left some space for us in the middle, yet it's still secluded and intimate.

"What're we gonna do, Daddy?" I wonder, playing with his tie.

"We're going to play a game." His voice has become a little huskier now, and that makes my pussy wake up. "You wanted to scene with Cade and Dylan, didn't you?"

My mouth forms an "o" and my cheeks flame red. Peeking over at Cade and Dylan, my blush intensifies at the sight of them kissing. I get all squirmy on Daddy's lap, and even more so when his hands slide up my thighs.

His words are soft and lust-filled as he shifts my pigtails forward and kisses my neck. "Cade and I have a little bet going on." A nip. I let out a shaky breath. "He's under the impression that he has better stamina than I do."

"Oh." I clutch my tummy, getting all fluttery inside. My eyes flick between Daddy and Cade, both so different, though right now they have plenty in common, too. Mainly lust. The hunger in their eyes is palpable.

Cade tugs off his T-shirt and murmurs to his baby boy. He palms Dylan's cheek, and under his predatory gaze, he has Dylan reverting to a younger version of himself right before our eyes.

It's beautiful.

They're like night and day. Cade with his tattoos and piercings, a natural tan, and a body that reveals his fifteen or so years in construction. Dylan with his lean build, not a mark in sight, and innocence and youth written across his features.

"You're going to do your best, aren't you?" Cade brushes the pad of his thumb over Dylan's bottom lip. "Give me a run for my money?"

Dylan gulps and nods. "Yes, Daddy."

At that, I quickly turn to Daddy again, needing to find out what all this is about. Boys make bets—it's such a guy thing—but I can be super competitive, so I gotta know.

"You're going to get me off." Daddy's eyes darken, and he positions me so I'm straddling him. "I'm going to hold back for as long as I can. And to keep you from wanting to help me stall—or Dylan to help Cade—there will be a prize for the Little who brings the first orgasm."

I purse my lips. "So, I'm gonna try to make you come as fast as I can?" He nods. "And if I win, you lose?" Not sure I like the sound of that...

"It's only for fun, sweet girl." His gaze softens. "If I lose, I'm going to give Cade season tickets to the 49ers."

I giggle behind my hand, then face Cade. "And if you lose, Mr. Kingsley?"

He smirks. "I'm gonna design the fetish furniture for the new area—the Chamber?—behind the Cave, for free."

"Yowza." I turn to Daddy once more. "What do Dylan and I get if we win? I mean, if I win or if he wins."

"*You*—" Daddy taps my nose "—get to bring your kittens and keep them in my office whenever we're here. For six months."

My jaw drops. Oh my God, that's exactly what I want. Well, I want it for all eternity, but I'll take six months!

Now I really want to win, dammit.

"Yeah, you'd love that, wouldn't you?" He chuckles. "But Dylan's also going to try to win."

"What will I get if I win?" Dylan asks curiously.

Cade answers. "I'll buy you that dog you wanted, *and* I'll take care of it whenever you travel for your swim meets."

Uh-oh, I'm in trouble now.

Dylan sucks in a breath, determination tightening his posture. "I'm gonna win."

The hell he is!

CHAPTER 6

I know just the way to seduce my Daddy, but it's going to take some preparation. It's not something I can jump into; it will feel fake and forced. At this point, I'm too excited to even try on my own.

Thankfully, our Daddies are good ones; they can see we need time to center ourselves and calm down. So, they suggest we simply take it easy for a bit. They coax us patiently into casual conversation about this and that. Mostly, we talk about the new year that has started and what plans we have for it.

The wedding is obviously the biggest event for Daddy and me, though the topic soon shifts to our lifestyle. Cade and Rio, according to Daddy, host the best play parties, and now that Rio is home again, there's hope a private party will take place soon. And Cade promises to plan something really special in the near future, too.

It's while Daddy and Cade are pitching ideas for theme nights at Switch for Daddy Doms and Littles that I finally reach the place in my head I love the most.

Getting all snuggly on Daddy's lap, I glance at Dylan from

under my lashes and suck in a breath when I see that he's subtly adjusting his cock. He slips a hand inside his pajama bottoms, then blushes as he catches me staring at him. *Caught you.*

Instead of bringing out his hand again, challenge flashes in his eyes, and he gives his cock a slow stroke while watching me.

Biting my lip, feeling naughty, I hesitantly part my legs a few inches and give him a peek. His jaw clenches, and his eyes darken with lust. Next, I grab Daddy's hand and slowly bring it to my pussy, which halts the conversation. Daddy and Cade nod to each other, whatever that means—maybe we've started? I'm too focused on Dylan's cock to read into it.

"Mmm..." I have to struggle to keep my eyes open when Daddy's middle finger traces my smooth slit. I'm already wet, and more of it slicks up the lips of my pussy as Dylan tugs down his PJs completely, revealing his cock.

"Daddy." He moans and hugs Cade's arm. "I'm all hard again."

"I can see that, baby." Cade wraps his fingers around Dylan's cock and kisses his temple. "You're leaking, too."

Oh. Right. Boys can also get wet, sorta. "Daddy?" I leave his lap, only to stand up in my seat and lift my dress. "Why does my kitty get wet sometimes? Is it the same for boys—because they want something?"

He coughs and clears his throat—unprepared for that, I think—and Cade mutters a bad word while Dylan just moans.

"That's right, little one." Daddy has recovered; now he positions me with my feet on each side of him, my kitty basically in his face. "It wants something inside." Leaning forward, he keeps our gaze locked as he drops a soft kiss to my clit. That one touch awakens every fiber of my being. "You know how wet you get when Daddy puts his cock inside you, yes?" I have to force air to leave my lungs, and I nod jerkily. "It's the same thing with Dylan. His cock leaks because he wants his Daddy to touch it and use it." One long digit slides down from my clit to my entrance. "Perhaps Dylan wants a soft, wet pussy to sink his cock into." Daddy fingers me slowly, all while placing sensual kisses around my clit. My knees nearly buckle. "Or maybe he wants his Daddy to fuck him." And with that, he glides his finger from my pussy back to my butt. "Right here." He circles the hole, spreading the juices from my pussy.

"In his bottom?" I get all breathy and needy and achy. "Can you put your cock in my bottom, too?"

He swallows and rests his forehead on my thigh, his breath hot and labored over my mound. "Of course, sweetheart. Is that what you want?"

"Yes, please." Excited, I jump down from the seats and wriggle in between Daddy's legs. "First, I wanna see if your cock is wet, too." I swiftly unbuckle his leather belt before unzipping his pants. I don't like the pain that belt can cause to my bottom, so *maybe* I scowl at it internally. In one fluid motion, I drop to my knees, and Daddy lifts his hips so I can pull down his pants and boxer briefs. My grin is triumphant. "I think you want something, Daddy."

I grasp his smooth, hard, and heavy cock; there's a small bead of arousal at the tip, and I lean over to lick that right up. *Mmm.* I love tasting Daddy, both hard and soft. Okay, hard is the best, but sometimes, before I go to bed at night, he lets me replace my thumb with his cock.

"*Fuck,* Kayla."

I giggle around his cock, 'cause Daddy can be so funny—cussing when he's taken off guard.

Humming and soaking him with my tongue, I take him to the back of my throat and remind myself that this is about Daddy getting off. Fast. Like a contest, and I like contests sometimes. They can be super fun.

Behind me, I feel Dylan settling on his knees, too.

Cade lets out a gritty moan. "You're not supposed to be this good, baby—oh, Jesus fucking *Christ,* Dylan."

As Daddy gets more and more into it, his breathing uneven and shallow, I release his cock with a pop and crawl up to his lap and kiss him all over. "May I have your cock in my bottom now?" I flutter my lashes—once, twice—and give him my sweetest smile. The one that melts him. "Pretty please?"

It works like a charm, and he tells me to get a condom and a packet of lube from the small compartment attached to the side of the booth. It's very convenient for the few people allowed to use our private space. What's *not* convenient is that we have to use condoms, because we don't do that elsewhere. But...safety and hygiene measures at the club and all... So, with the condom and lubrication in hand, I give it to Daddy, and he silently twirls a finger. *Turn around, baby girl,* that means.

I comply and settle on his thighs so I face Cade.

My butt clenches in anticipation; it's been weeks since Daddy took me anally, and it's been days since he used my favorite plug on me.

It's light yellow with white polka dots. Daddy had it specially ordered for me because he knows yellow is my most favorite color in the whole world.

Only Daddy's cock beats that pretty plug.

"Are you being a baby slut again?" His voice is soft, almost a taunting coo, and it sets me on fire. I shift on his lap, though he doesn't let me get too close, because he's slicking up his erection with lube. "Thinking about Daddy's cock?" I flush and duck my head as Cade's hooded eyes meet mine, an indecent smirk spreading across his lips. "I don't think good little girls are allowed to wear such pretty dresses." Before I can even pretend to protest, Daddy pulls my dress over my head, leaving me in kneesocks and my purple Mary Janes with cute bows on the straps. "You'll be naked for the rest of the evening."

I gasp at that, sort of mortified at the thought. "*Daddy!* Even outside in the club?"

"Yes." He reaches around me and pinches my nipples. They get shiny from the residue of the lubricant, not to mention hard from his teasing. Goodness, it feels so good. "I want everyone to see what a gorgeous little girl I have."

Oh, all right...I *guess* that's fine.

"Lift up." He gives my hip a light smack, and I stand up so he can position himself. But to my dismay—and then, suspicion—he circles my hole with a finger instead. As if he's going to prepare me. As if I'm not used to anal sex. As if he doesn't like to stretch me out with only his cock. As if I haven't admitted that's exactly how I like it, too!

"No! Nuh-uh." I twist my body and wrap my fingers around his cock as best as I can and guide it to my bottom. "You're not gonna distract me, Daddy. No, Siree." I won't allow him to stall.

"Clever little sweetheart you got there, Nicholas." Cade chuckles, which morphs into a hiss of pleasure when Dylan...does something. Something Cade evidently loves. I can't see around Dylan's head, so I have no idea. "Are you that hungry for Daddy's come, baby boy?" Cade weaves his fingers through Dylan's hair and gazes lustfully at him.

Closing my eyes, I slowly sink down on Daddy's cock, involuntarily tightening my muscles before I force myself to relax and push for more. His low groan against my shoulder spurs me on, as do his lips against my overheated skin. The pain as he reaches deeper and deeper gives a raw, biting edge to the excitement, intensifying everything I love instead of hurting me.

Once he's completely buried inside me, I don't pause. Need claws at me, and I lean back against Daddy to feel as much as possible. The air is thick with sex, the heavy music from outside causing the surroundings to buzz in a steady hum that only fuels my desire. Shifting my hips forward, Daddy's cock slowly slides out of me. Then I push back again, hard, and force him all the way in.

Rushing does nothing for Daddy and me, so that's the last thing I do. Instead I show him how needy I am for him. I whimper and pull at him, hugging him from behind, my arm around his neck, my head tilted so I can kiss his jaw.

"So beautiful." Daddy's hands roam the front of my naked body. His palms, warm and smooth, slide down to my knees and under them. "Put your feet up here."

I quickly pull up my knees, the angle of his cock in my butt making me wince, but as soon as my feet are planted on the seat, on either side of Daddy, a bolt of pleasure shoots through me. Squatting over him like this lets him go deeper, and it allows me more control of the movements. Control—not used to that, but I can be a greedy girl. If there's a chance to take whatever I want from my Daddy, you won't find me complaining!

"Are you watching Cade and Dylan, baby girl?"

I wasn't, but I do it now. A flash of heat surges forward, and my eyes grow heavy with lust. No longer sucking Cade off, Dylan is now bent over the table a couple feet away, and Cade is lubing up his cock, ready to take his little boy. The sight of Cade, so masculine, strong, and assertive with his bad-boy front, caressing Dylan's smooth bottom, his thumbs sliding between the cheeks...

I moan and arch my back, riding Daddy a bit faster.

When his hand covers my pussy, pushing two fingers inside and rubbing the pad of his thumb over my clit, it's sensory overload. At the same time, Dylan's whimpered pleas for more of Cade's cock—*faster, Daddy; I want more, more, more, all of you in my butt* —leave me flustered and feverish.

Cade swallows hard, his thrusts seeming rougher than intended, as if he can't help himself. He grits his teeth; his neck looks strained, and tiny beads of sweat begin to trickle down his sculpted torso.

It can't be easy for him to restrain himself when he has his Little begging for more.

"Mmm, Daddy..." I turn my head and kiss his chin. "Do you like having your cock in my bottom?"

"Jesus, Kayla." He growls through heavy breaths, then leans closer and captures my mouth in a deep kiss. "You have no idea. Maybe—maybe you should slow down a bit—*fuck.*"

"No!" I huff and move faster. "I don't wanna." Pressing his hand harder to my pussy, I ride both his cock and his fingers, all of which quickly brings me toward climax. The dull pain flares up and sharpens every feeling. I get hornier, more determined, needier, more desperate, and totally shameless in my chase.

Breathing is necessary, I remind myself as I get closer and closer.

"Daddy, my tummy tingles now." I gasp and squeeze my eyes shut. "Ohh!"

"Fuck, Dylan." Cade lets out a gritty groan. Skin slapping against skin. Panted breaths. "I can't—"

I can't, either. I can't hold back. My orgasm ricochets through me in a million directions, stealing my breath, awareness, and control. Every tiny explosion bursts toward my lower belly where a bigger sensation is set off. My toes curl; I shudder violently, and I'm only vaguely aware of Daddy coming, too—along with a string of bad words. Abandoning my pussy, he grips my hips hard, groans against my neck, and yanks me down on him a final time.

When I come to, I feel light-headed and disoriented. It's like a fog, or...or, or, like when you're dreaming, and you're all sluggish.

Oddly enough, I'm not very out of breath. Maybe that passed while I was regaining a grasp on reality.

Daddy, on the other hand, sounds like he does when he comes home after his daily five-mile runs.

"Damn..." Cade mutters that, I think. I'm not sure. "Guess I'll start working on some furniture." There's the sound of a kiss. "You were too good, sweetheart."

A tired chuckle escapes Dylan. "Does that mean Mr. Ford and I won, Daddy?"

Oh, right. The bet.

As I crack open my eyes, I catch Cade smirking at Dylan. "Don't look so smug about it. He had me beat with a few seconds. And I can still spank your ass when we get to my place." He caresses Dylan's butt and dips down to kiss the spot between his shoulder blades. "Or perhaps I'll bottle-feed you tomorrow."

I giggle sleepily, knowing that Dylan is what some refer to as a Middle. He doesn't revert to a young child like I sometimes do; he's more at home as the cheeky pre-teen he was some thirteen years ago. In other words, baby stuff isn't for him at all. Then again, that's not really my thing, either. There's a difference between being childlike and toddler-like.

Sighing in contentment, I lean back against Daddy, though a pinch of sadness seeps into me at the thought of my kittens not being allowed in the office upstairs, after all.

"I wish I'd won," I mumble wistfully, absently trailing my fingertips along Daddy's arm around my waist. "It would've been fun to decorate a corner for Jackson and Oliver. They'd love that."

Daddy hums and kisses my shoulder. "Good thing I'd already decided to let you bring them anyway, huh?"

I gasp and turn my body to face him. "You really mean that, Daddy?" He smiles and kisses my nose this time. Happiness bubbles up in me. "Pinkie swear on it?" I hold up my pinkie.

He laughs softly and hooks his pinkie with mine. "I swear, my love."

I have the best Daddy in the world!

CHAPTER 7

The monthly theme night in January takes place on the 25th, and this time it's Edgeplay Night, which can explain the good mood Mark is in. Well, he has plenty of reasons to be happy, collaring his subs being the biggest one.

They got back from La Jolla yesterday, and I was ecstatic to see the bliss on their faces. Evangeline's black velvet collar is gorgeous, and it has a tag in the shape of a kitten's paw where it says "Master Cooper's Kitten." Brayden's tag is shaped like a dog's paw instead, and it says "Master Cooper's Puppy" on it. Totally cute!

To make things even better, they've exchanged "I love you"s, and that means marriage...*um, however that would work with three people*...and lots of babies aren't that far away.

Right?

Anyway, what with it being Edgeplay Night and all, Mark is covering the early shift behind the bar, because he's in charge of two demos later. One breath-play scene with Brayden, and one scene with Evangeline where he's going to whip her with something called a single tail. *Scrunchy nose.*

A lot of space is needed for that, so Mark will do it on the platform for public scening in the Club; meanwhile, there will be several other demos in the Cave.

Right now, Daddy is supervising a branding scene in the Cave, and that's why I'm *not* there. That's icky. So, I'm enjoying a Sprite in the Club instead, and Evangeline, Brayden, Dylan, and Gabriella are with me.

The only one missing is Chelsea, who is supposed to be here any minute.

Daddy's given her a management position at The Library, another club of his, which was super nice of him. So, she flew out the day before yesterday, and we helped her get settled in the apartment she's now sharing with a few others.

"There're so many people here tonight." Brayden takes a sip from his Coke, looking a little dazed as he watches the crowded dance floor. The music *almost* drowns out his voice. "Master even told us there's some BDSM community visiting from Chicago."

Daddy's told me about that, too; they've booked the Cinema for a collaring ceremony. There're also a few who've flown in from San Diego for the demos later, lots of regulars of course, and several out-of-towners who have been on a BDSM cruise and are ending their vacation with a visit to Switch.

We're so swamped that Daddy has called in an extra man at the door, who I hope arrives soon because Ray, our regular doorman, is working too hard, and his sub can't hang that many coats without resting every now and then.

Rio, Cade, and John are filling in as dungeon monitors, supervising scenes with Daddy, along with the usual DMs that are here.

"When is your friend from New York coming?" Evangeline asks, snuggling closer to Brayden. "It was tonight, right?"

I nod, smiling widely. "She should be here any minute now. You're gonna love her." I'm sure of it. Chelsea is so funny. And gorgeous and cool and spunky.

And nervous. She's called me four times today, needing reassurance about Rio. *Understandable.* But it doesn't seem like he remembers her, because Daddy and I have both mentioned her name casually a few times.

Truth be told, I'm kinda bummed about that now—that Rio doesn't remember, I mean. I'd been looking forward to the parting of the Red Sea as they reunite.

"Is she attached?" Dylan wonders. "A friend of mine recently got out of a 24/7 relationship, and he's looking for a Little who wants something casual."

I shake my head, knowing the word "casual" doesn't fit with Chelsea. "She only has serious relationships, and she's not a Little." There's a pin or symbol for everything today—from the gay community's rainbow to, well, the cross for Christians, and we have our own as Littles. The mere thought of a Littles and Baby Pride pin on her is giggle-worthy. While she's fiercely independent and very outspoken in her everyday life, she prefers high protocol when it comes to BDSM. "When I met her—it was at a private BDSM party in New York—and I told her I was a Little, she immediately assumed it was all about AB/DL." I nearly crack up at the memory, and Dylan and Gabriella chuckle, too.

Brayden tilts his head. "What's AB...whatever you just said?"

Gabriella answers. "Adult Babies and Diaper Lovers."

Some Littles have fairly specific ages they regress to when it's playtime; I happen to have several. It's more of a spectrum than anything. I'm the youngest when I'm tired or after a chastisement, but it's still way older than baby age. I do know a few who are into that; a good friend of mine from when I lived in Texas loves wearing diapers.

"To each their own, I guess." Brayden flushes and hides his discomfort behind a shrug. "I could never wear a diaper—or use pacifiers."

Dylan smirks at Brayden. "Some put pacifiers in their mouths; you put a giant version of one up your butt. What's the difference?"

"Oh, snap!" I laugh behind my hand, my shoulders shaking.

Dylan and Gabriella high-five each other. Evangeline hides her amusement and comforts Brayden's wounded ego to turn his frown upside down.

"Could that be your friend, Kayla?" Gabriella points in the direction of the exit. "She looks like she's searching for someone."

I follow her gaze, and sure enough, it's Chelsea! Her thick and wavy dirty blond hair with highlights in different brown shades makes her stand out because it's *insanely* long. It reaches her bottom! But what makes Chelsea Dunn stand out even more will always be her eyes. I can't see them clearly right now, duh, 'cause I'm too far away, but her eyes really are unforgettable.

She has...oh, what's it called—she's explained it to me. Um, Central Heterochoma or Heterochromia or something, and it means she's got *two* colors in her eyes. Mainly, hers are silvery gray, but they blend into a deep violet shade in the center.

Excited as hell, I excuse myself and rush toward her. *Ugh.* Too many people. I duck and deftly dodge a few elbows and squeak out an apology when I almost run into Dante—a Dominant *not* to be messed with. Then I'm finally there, and I throw my arms around Chelsea.

"Hey, you!"

She laughs and gives me a squeeze. "I just saw you yesterday, pipsqueak." Her nickname for me. She once told me she could imagine calling a little sister that. "Let me get a look at'chu." Her accent always puts a smile on my face. "*Very* nice." She grins and eyes my schoolgirl outfit, complete with a pink-and-white plaid skirt, white kneesocks and shirt, and high pigtails.

Chelsea isn't much for pink, though—and definitely not pastels. Her black tube dress proves my point. It's practically see-through, extremely provocative, and sticks to her curvy body like a second skin. Even her black gladiator sandals are sexy.

"Nicholas picked that out, didn't he?" She waggles her eyebrows.

I giggle, nod, and smooth down my skirt. "Don't forget to call him Mr. Ford in the club."

"Oh, I know." She smiles crookedly and holds up her wrist. "So, can you remind me how these work?" She's referring to the rubber wristbands. "They didn't have them last time I was here, and the girl in the coat check rambled too quickly."

"Well..." The matchmaker in me doesn't like her two bands. Okay, the blue is good; it means the drink limit is in effect, but the green one means she's approachable to other Doms—not only Rio—and I explain the rules to Chelsea, adding, "Waitresses wear orange ones, DMs wear black ones; if you see someone with a yellow band, it means he or she is new to BDSM, and the red ones mean hands-off." I show her my own red rubber band. "Either because you're taken, or because you're not here to meet anyone. Oh, and we have glow-in-the-dark ones for Hide & Seek Night when we shut down the lights."

"Cool." She nods. "I picked the right bands, then." A new song comes on, a heavy, slow, and seductive one, and Chelsea looks toward the bar Mark's working. "By the way—" her gaze slides back to me "—I took your advice and became a member of Switch's online forum." That's great! An awesome way to meet more people. "Do you know a Master Dante?"

My brows furrow, and I get a bad feeling about this. "Yes," I answer slowly, then gesture to where Dante's standing in a seating area with his sub kneeling next to him. "He's the Hulk over there." A mountain of a man. Handsome, yes, but crazy intimidating. "Why?"

Chelsea replies while studying Dante appreciatively. "We spoke online, and he and his sub are looking for someone for a Shibari scene." She shrugs. "I figured, why not? We're gonna sit down and discuss limits and see what happens."

I squeak in horror and grasp Chelsea's arms. "You're gonna let Dante—friggin' *Dante*—tie you *up*?" I find Shibari and bondage in general beautiful to look at, but it's also scary. I cannot be restrained like that. I'd faint. And cry. "And what about Rio?" Now I get a bit sad, and my hands drop to my sides.

"You're supposed to reveal yourself, and then he'll fall in love with you."

Something akin to hurt flits across her face, though she schools her expression quickly. An easy smile takes over. "He doesn't even remember me, Kayla." That's because names are easier to forget than faces! "Besides, I can't afford to get hung up on that man. I sincerely doubt we're in the same place in life."

I pout.

She laughs and taps my nose. "That shit works on Nicholas, I bet." She points to herself. "Me? Not so much. Now—" she grins and throws an arm around my shoulders "—introduce me to your friends. I can find Dante later."

I'm still pouting as I start leading her to our table, and then a commotion behind me makes us stop. I can barely hear over the music, but it sounds like someone is shouting for...*Mark?*

"What the...?" Chelsea frowns.

I do too, and we see a man who enters the club with a bottle of vodka in his hand. His suit is all rumpled, hair messy, and yep, definitely shouting for Mark. He pushes people away from him as he heads toward where Chelsea and I are standing.

"Where are you, little brother?!" He's drunk, too. "Mark Cooper!"

Wondering how the hell he got past Ray at the door, I lean close to Chelsea and tell her that the man behind the bar is Mark, and I ask her to go get him quickly. "I'm gonna get help," I add before slinking into the crowd. "Excuse me, Sir. Excuse me, Ma'am." Crap, I do not want to get walloped for pushing a Dom or a Domme. "Excuse me, Sirs." And when I reach the highly intoxicated man, I pause, thinking I could go on and get Ray, or...or I can try to calm down the man on my own.

In retrospect...not my brightest decision.

"Excuse me." I tap his arm. "I work here—" Just a small lie. "Is there anything I can help you with?" I wave a hand at the exit and smile politely. "Perhaps we can take this outside where it's quiet?"

He grins creepily, causing my smile to waver, and gives me a slow once-over. "Well, well. Are you one of the whores that my little brother fucks?" While I drop my jaw, aghast and hurt, the man leans close, as if to whisper a secret. Eww, vodka breath. "I just found out he's screwing men, too." His words are all slurred, and I wince when he grips my arm. "Our parents are so *proud* of him—can you believe that?"

"Ow." I whimper as he tightens his hold on my arm. "Sir, c-can you please let go?" I tug, but he doesn't budge, and I get scared.

The man ignores me completely and laughs, going on with his story. "Mark brought his two toys to dinner with our parents; I heard that bullshit from my wife. Not only that, but my daughter's babysitter is one of his playthings. The fuckin' nerve... So, I figured..." He takes a big swig from the bottle. "I figured, since the other one is a guy, if he can fuck men and get away with it, so can I. Screw the consequences—"

"What the fuck do you think you're doing, Greg?" That growly voice comes from behind me, and I manage to turn my head to see a furious-looking Mark pushing his way through the crowd to reach us.

Hopeful, I tug some more, really wanting to get away now. The man's grip hurts a lot, and I hate being afraid.

"There you are, little brother!" The man—Greg?—cackles jovially, then pushes me aside roughly. "Probably the most beloved fuck-up in the universe! Doesn't matter what you do, does it?" I land on the floor with a hard thump and cry out in pain. "You still get worshiped!"

The pain, the loud music, the strobe lights, the ruckus, and so many people—it makes me dizzy and disoriented. I'm surrounded by legs, and then there's someone pulling me off the floor. Strong arms, a masculine scent. I'm paralyzed with fear. My eyes well up.

I don't like this, I don't like this, I don't like this!

"I've got you, little one." It's not Daddy, which only scares me more. I tremble and try to push away, but the stranger doesn't allow me. "Don't worry—your Master will be here soon."

"Daddy." I sniffle and look up, only to freeze up again when I see it's Dante.

"Did he hurt you, Kayla?" Chelsea nearly slams into me, startling me. I struggle to respond, and I fail. My head is swimming, and I'm shaking too much. "Oh, that bastard is dead!" She takes off in a rush; I tilt my head in her direction just as she flies into the man Mark is fighting—fighting with his fists!

"For fuck's sake!" Mark barks out. At someone. "Ray, hurry!"

It's literally too much for me, so I go rigid and cover my face with my hands. I hear murderous yelling over the music, accusations, familiar voices—Rio now, too?—and people are either bumping into each other to see the fight or scurrying away to make space.

"Calm down, pet." Dante's out-of-place murmur and soft hands stroking my arms do nothing to help me. "Ford is on his way—I can see him."

Daddy!

"No!" Chelsea shouts. "Let me go right fucking now! That piece'a shit hurt Kayla!"

I hear my name again, and this time—*finally, finally, finally* —it's Daddy.

He envelops me in a tight hug, and the smell of his aftershave blankets me in comfort. It's home. It's safe. I can relax here. I don't have to think; I can just let Daddy take care of things. And me.

He mutters something with a lot of bad words to Cade and Rio, but I focus solely on being in Daddy's arms.

"D-Daddy..." My bottom lip trembles, so I suck it into my mouth. My breathing is too heavy as well, and my vision is too blurry to see clearly. "I'm—I'm scared."

He picks me up, and I wrap my legs around his waist and lock my arms around his neck. "I know, sweetheart. I know." With brisk steps, he walks us out of the club area, and I think we're headed upstairs to the office. "I'm sorry I wasn't there for you." Judging by the remorse and guilt in his tone, he's beating himself up internally, and I can't allow that.

I swallow hard, 'cause it's time to fess up. "I did something stupid." I speak barely above a whisper, afraid he's gonna spank me, and my butt already hurts from landing on the floor. "I thought I could handle it. I didn't know that man was gonna be so pushy and mad."

In my periphery, I see the tension in his jaw, but he doesn't say anything. Instead he just guides me into the office and over to one of the two couches by the massive window overlooking the club downstairs.

Jackson and Oliver leave their little corner and scuttle across the light hardwood floor; Daddy picks them up for me, placing them on my lap, before he strides over to his desk for something.

"I'm *so* sorry..." I pout at my lap and stroke Jackson's soft, gray fur. "I didn't mean it, I swear."

Daddy returns and shakes his head, sitting down next to me. "Don't apologize, baby girl." He tucks a piece of hair behind my ear, then hands me a bottle of water and two painkillers. "I could just..." He grits his teeth and carefully unbuttons my snug shirt to pull it down my shoulders. "Rio told me Greg hurt you." Pain and anger flash in his eyes as his fingers ghost over the bruises forming on my bicep. "I shouldn't have left you alone."

That doesn't seem right. "I like being able to run around and have fun. This was just one thing." I grimace. "Who is Greg?"

"Mark's older brother." Out of his pocket, Daddy produces a small bottle of aloe vera cream, wryly explaining that it was supposed to be for the branding scene downstairs. An "in case" sorta thing. Now he uses it on me instead. Gently rubbing it along my arm. "Around Thanksgiving, Rio saw Greg visit a gay bar in the Castro. Mark suspects Greg is hiding his sexuality—"

"But he has a wife!" I know that much, and of course, that Mark is a proud uncle of a little girl.

"Vows don't mean everything to some people," he reminds me softly. "Regardless...Greg evidently didn't take it very well when Mark told their parents about Brayden and Evangeline. That's all I know."

I slump lower in my seat and guzzle down some water with my painkillers. "My head hurts." Tonight was supposed to be fun; Chelsea and Rio were seeing each other for the first time in years, and...oh drat, everything got shot straight to hell instead, didn't it? "Is Chelsea okay?"

He nods and tucks me close, Jackson and Oliver following by climbing on us. "Dante took over. She's fine." His eyes search mine, and I don't like the crease of anxiousness in his forehead. "You had me worried, Kayla."

"Are you mad at me?" I look up at him with my puppy-dog eyes. "I didn't mean to get in trouble, not even a touch!"

"I know." He kisses my temple and sighs. "You always mean well—I know that. But you really should've called for help."

Yeah, I should've. Stupid me. "I'm sorry."

To my surprise, Daddy lets out a small chuckle. "I recall another time where I gave you Tylenol and water, and you couldn't stop apologizing."

Oh. My cheeks heat up as I smile, also remembering. It was the night we met. "I'm really glad I came up here."

"You have no idea, sweet girl." He gently palms my cheek and presses a kiss to my nose. "You've turned my life upside down in the best ways."

And he has stabilized mine in the best ways.

CHAPTER 8

Only a few minutes pass in comfortable silence before there's a knock on the door.

I quickly gather Jackson and Oliver close before they can become fugitives.

"Reality interrupts." Daddy stands up and opens the door, revealing Mark with an ice pack to his neck. "You look like death warmed over, my friend." Daddy gestures for Mark to enter. "You all right?"

"I'm fine." Mark looks irritated, probably with his brother. I would be, too. Actually, I am! "I just came to tell you that everything's been taken care of, and..." He glances over at me apologetically. "Are you okay?"

"Yes, Sir." I nod and wave one of Jackson's little paws at him. "Wanna say hi to Jackson and Oliver?"

His mouth quirks up. "Maybe later, hon." He turns to Daddy again. "Ray thinks you're gonna fire him for letting Greg get past him. You want me to tell him anything?"

Daddy shakes his head and walks over to sit down next to me again. "He's not getting fired. I should've had two men at the door from the beginning, not waited to see if a second was needed. I knew there was going to be a big crowd tonight." He sighs and scrubs a hand down his face. "I'll be down soon, but—"

"No rush, man. We have it covered. Rio left, but Cade's called in two more DMs, and Leo has arrived now to help Ray at the door."

Daddy frowns. "Rio left?"

That makes me frown, too.

"Yeah…" Mark furrows his brows. "He muttered something about ghosts from his past." He shrugs while my eyes widen and I slap a hand over my mouth, just *knowing* Chelsea's that ghost. And I missed it! Crap, crap, crap. "Want me to call in Kevin, too?"

Oh yeah, Kevin—the club manager and Daddy's right-hand man—isn't here tonight. Can't believe I forgot that, seeing as he's pretty much always here.

Daddy waves that off. "No, it's his anniversary. The man works too much—let him have his weekend off." He pauses and gives me a fleeting look. "I have a feeling I know why Rio left. I'll call him later. And this with your brother…?" He raises a brow.

Mark's scowl is back. "Oh, trust me. I'll take care of that." He brushes a thumb over his bottom lip, wincing slightly at the cut there. "I punched him for you, too, by the way. Fuckin' scratcher." He makes a face and applies pressure to the ice pack on his neck. "The cops are taking him to the hospital for a broken jaw—silver lining, right?" He sighs. "Let me know if you wanna press charges."

Ugh. I want this past hour to go poof—like it never existed. Dragging in the police isn't gonna help me forget.

"I'd prefer to get my hands on him myself." Daddy smiles tightly. "But thank you. You should let your subs take care of you now. They're probably worried downstairs."

Mark nods, then faces me one last time. "I'm really sorry about this, Kayla."

"What?" I scrunch my nose. "Don't be silly, Master Cooper. It's not like you're to blame for your dumbass brother." I shoot Daddy a quick look of apology. "Sorry for the cussing, but I had to. It's like that."

He chuckles and touches my cheek. "That's quite all right, sweetheart."

Good.

Dumb, dummy, dumbass Greg.

Once Mark has returned downstairs again, Daddy strips me down and gives me some jammies that I keep here for late nights. Just a long T-shirt with pretty hearts on it, and he tells me to rest for a while. My precious kittens are snuggled up with me under the soft blanket, and Daddy puts on soothing music for me to listen to while I fall asleep.

"Do you know what else I remember from the night we met?" He sits down next to me on the edge of the couch, and to my confusion, he lets Jackson and Oliver down on the floor.

Shaking my head in reply, I watch as the kittens play with each other, crouching and jumping and bumping into one another and wielding their paws like swords.

"I remember the ways I wanted to cure your headache." Daddy's words certainly have my attention now! The left corner of his mouth slants up as he slowly slides a hand under the blanket. "How is your head now?"

I exhale and part my legs, his hand now caressing my inner thigh. Thank goodness for no panties. "Um." I swallow and lick my lips. "It still hurts a little." Holding up my thumb and forefinger, I show how much the painkillers haven't fixed.

He hums. "Probably best Daddy takes care of that, then." He moves farther down on the couch and bends low over my middle. The blanket is shifted aside, and then he kisses where his hands have been. "God, you smell good." He nuzzles the lips, then licks the length of my sex. "Delicious, too."

"Ohh!" My heart starts beating rapidly, almost racing. "Daddy —oh Daddy, it's not nice to tease." It's agonizing, the softness and wetness of his tongue ghosting over my needy flesh. I get goose bumps and the shivers. "Please. *More*."

He doesn't reply, but he does give me more. He kisses my pussy as if he was kissing my mouth. Passionately, thoroughly, possessing it, loving it. My headache pounds as I stiffen, but I know it's only a matter of minutes before it all fades. Daddy's skilled fingers coax more wetness out of me, his lips suck on my clit, and his tongue presses down on it, circles it, and strokes it.

The buildup is maddening.

He moans quietly and licks me harder, greedier.

I squirm and buck my hips, 'cause I can't control myself.

"That's fucking beautiful, Kayla." He watches me with lust-filled eyes as he brings me closer and closer. His right hand comes up to cup my boobs, playing them expertly and sensually.

I suck in a sharp breath and hold it, right on that edge. The pain of my headache vibrates instead of pounds, as if it's struggling to keep up. But Daddy's fingers and mouth win. As he brushes the pad of his thumb over my back entrance, I screw my eyes shut while ripples of ecstasy shoot through me, and I explode like a shaken-up soda.

I'm like a puddle of goo, barely able to breathe. I hear breathless little whimpers and realize they're coming from me, and it's not until the pleasure has subsided that I can control much of anything.

"How is your head now?" Before Daddy lets me answer, he covers my body with his and kisses me ruthlessly. I taste myself on his tongue, feel his hardness between my thighs, and sense his need in every touch. "Christ, I'll never be able to get enough of you."

"Good." I giggle, out of breath, and that's my answer for everything he said. "May I help you now? You're so hard, Daddy."

He shakes his head no and kisses me again, softly this time. "You're going to rest now." Then he composes himself and sits down next to me. "I've left your cell phone on the table here."

He taps the coffee table and caresses my cheek with his free hand. "You can come back downstairs whenever you want, but call me first. I'll come get you." He gently unties the bows that keep my pigtails together and weaves his fingers through my long hair. "I'm afraid I'll be keeping you close for a while." I understand that, but right now I'm still more focused on helping Daddy with his hard cock. "Anything you want me to tell Chelsea?"

I flush, flustered, because I can't get back to normal as quickly as he can. Hell, my breathing's not even regulated yet! Aside from his eyes being a shade darker, proof of his aroused state, he's as cool as a cucumber.

"Just...tell her I'm fine." I shake my head, gathering my thoughts. "And make sure she's okay, too. She got close earlier—I think she hit Mark's brother."

Daddy's definitely torn between worry and amusement. There might be a pinch of disapproval, as well. "I'll be having a chat with that girl. I'm proud of her for defending you, but the last thing I want to see is a sub getting hurt. You girls need to learn how to call for help." He gives me a pointed look, to which I pull the blanket up to my nose. "Speaking of Chelsea, we'll be addressing her situation with Rio soon."

Despite Daddy's light scolding, I can't help but smile super wide, and I lower the blanket again. "He remembers her, doesn't he? Doesn't he? He has to!"

"It would appear so, yes." He fights a smile as he returns my kittens to me. "What that means, I have no idea. I'll have to talk to Rio." Jackson cuddles close to my neck, and Oliver bumps his little nose to my shoulder. "He probably won't be in a good mood."

Uh-oh. "Do you think he'll be mad at me?" I do not want Master Rio to punish me.

"No. I'm responsible for you, and I've kept the truth from him, too." He dips down to kiss me on the lips. "Rest now, baby girl. We have hours until closing, so focus on feeling better. I'm only a phone call away, and you'll have plenty of time with your friends later."

A nap *does* sound good. A yawn slips out, to boot. "Okay. Love you, Daddy."

"More than words can say." He does show it well, though. I'm so lucky. "Sweet dreams."

Always. Sometimes funny dreams, too. Like...about what kind of trouble I can get into next.

THE FIRST TOUCH

A BEHIND THE SCENES OUTTAKE

A GLIMPSE

DYLAN REAVES

Showing up at a fetish club in clothes more appropriate for the gym —probably not my wisest call. I stow away my hoodie and lose my T-shirt, leaving me in the pair of black sweats I donned after practice. My sneakers are black, so hopefully they won't attract any attention.

Leaving the dressing room, I run a hand through my hair, not entirely dry after my shower, and fire off a message to Kayla.

I'm here, brat.

It's been a while. With my training schedule, I can go several weeks without setting foot inside Switch, so I guess the place is still new to me. At least, there's this thrill every time I come here.

I haven't befriended many since I moved here, mostly just Kayla and Cole. Cole's a professional swimmer like me, though he's closer to retirement. In my field, that means he's a little over thirty. You get old fast.

He should be around here somewhere, too. I look around the lobby on my way to the club area, not recognizing anyone. That's a good thing. I wouldn't want to run into Cade Kingsley. He might be a reason I don't complain about not having much time to come here.

The evening has recently started at Switch, so not very many are here yet. A handful of smaller groups of people use the dance floor to chat rather than dance, and I nod in hello when I spot Cole. He's obviously trying to score, meaning I won't get close to him. He might try to flirt with me again, and we are *not* a good match. He is too sadistic for my tastes. Instead, I veer right and order a soda at the bar.

While I wait for my Cherry Coke, my phone buzzes. I take it out of my pocket and squint in confusion at Kayla's text.

Hi. I am a sneaky ninja, and I have to get a rain check. Daddy is taking me to the movies tonight! Gots to go, he's back with my Happy Meal. Have fun! xoxoxo

This makes no sense. She specifically told me I had to be here tonight; she said she had something important to tell me. Dammit, I cut my practice short because of this!

I huff and pocket my phone again. Kayla is no ninja. She's a brat, and she's officially stood me up for a Happy Meal. One dose cheeseburger, one dose Daddy Dom.

"You look glum," the bartender tells me as he sets the glass of Cherry Coke in front of me. His name is Liam, I think. "You're Dylan, right?"

I nod and pay for my soda. "Yes, Sir. Kayla ditched me for a toy made in China." I pause. "You do still get toys with the kids meal at McDonald's, right?"

He lets out a laugh. "I may have stepped on one or two at home."

I guess it's just me, then. I'll stay until I've finished my soda, and then I can go home and catch some extra sleep. Practice at five AM most mornings means I'm usually a zombie before the evening news.

About to turn in my seat to face the dance floor, I freeze instead when none other than Mr. Kingsley walks up some ten feet away to talk to Liam. Oh God, don't move, don't make a sound. He can't see me if I don't move, right? If he can't see me, he can't notice I turn into a spaz around him.

I duck my head and turn away slightly, and while he bitches about something—too low for me to hear the actual words—I slip off my stool. There's no crowd to get lost in, so I try to be as stealthy as possible and sneak away to the seating area. Easier to blend in there. It's darker and doesn't catch your eye.

Finding one of the booths empty, I slide in and—

"Excuse me, you dropped this." A girl walks over with a polite smile and hands me my phone. "Oh, you got lucky. My screen would have cracked."

"Thank you." I'm a fucking idiot.

"Hey, aren't you Kayla's friend?" she asks.

I nod hesitantly. "Dylan."

Her smile reappears with a dimple. *Gorgeous*. "I'm Gabriella. You should join us for the subbie munch next week. She says she's been trying to introduce you to more people."

"Ah—yeah." I clear my throat. "Busy schedule, I guess. But, um...is it just for subs?" That's news to me. Kayla has mentioned the weekly munch to me, but I assumed it was for everyone—including one smoking hot Daddy Dom I tend to lose my crap around. I swear, the first time I saw him, my breathing *stuttered*. He is *that* sexy.

"Yes, only us subbie types," Gabriella responds. "It can be overwhelming when you're new to a community, and having a chance to meet up without the Doms around is nice."

I can relate to that. "I'll try to make it to the next one," I say, relaxing a bit more.

Gabriella seems like a nice girl, though we don't chat much longer. When she gets a message from her Dom, she stiffens, plasters a tight smile on her face, and excuses herself before trailing toward the lobby.

Maybe someone's getting chastised...? I wouldn't be able to muster a genuine grin for that, either. Not that I have much experience. Porn introduced me to the BDSM world, and for a couple years, fetish clips and stories were enough for me. Then I ended up in an online community and found myself wanting to try more, particularly once I figured out I didn't have to be a Little or a regular sub. I could be a *Middle*, an in-between sort of kink that clicks for me.

My real-life experience is limited to a few public scenes here at Switch, but I couldn't relax fully then. I was just an s-type. I think, for me, much of the Daddy kink appeal is reserved for an actual relationship.

It's my turn to stiffen when someone sits down across from me, and I die as I realize it's Mr. Kingsley. *No, no. This isn't happening. I can't detect a heartbeat in myself. Oh, this is bad. Have I fucked up somehow? I've barely been here, for fuck's sake!*

His mouth twists slightly in amusement. "You know, when Kayla told me you were afraid of me, I called her silly. Why would someone I've never spoken to fear me, right?"

If I just sit here and look mentally challenged, maybe he'll go away. I don't know what else to *do*. It's his fucking fault, anyway. For being so intimidating and illegally hot.

"Dylan?" He knows my name. Leaning forward, he grins faintly. "Blink."

I blink. *That asshole.* I blink again, 'cause maybe my eyes suddenly got dry from the staring.

Time to use actual words. "I'm not afraid." *Shit, it worked. Well done, me.*

"Really. That's good." He pulls out his phone and slides it my way as his screen comes to life. "Did you by any chance get a similar message from Kayla?"

I inch forward automatically and read the message.

Hi, Mr. Kingsley, this is the little love ninja. I'm so sorry, but I can't make it tonight. All I really wanted

to say was that you should speak with Dylan. He has something to say to you, but he's shy. xoxoxoxo

"Liam mentioned you've been stood up, too," he says.

I sit back again, torn between anger and embarrassment. Mostly the latter. Kayla's obviously trying to set us up, but by doing so, she's going against my wishes. Which have been for her not to meddle.

"I don't have anything to say," I tell him, ignoring my cheeks heating up. "Other than I hope Mr. Ford wallops her butt."

Hard.

Mr. Kingsley chuckles and tucks away his phone again. "Either way, I'm glad I got a moment with you. You've done a good job at avoiding me, and I just wanna know why."

Oh, goddammit. How the hell can he even know that?

"I haven't—"

His severe look cuts me off. "Don't lie to me, boy."

Crap. I snap my mouth shut and swallow nervously.

The second his stare releases me, I look away and let out a breath. Funny how I couldn't detect a heartbeat a minute ago. Now it's racing in my chest.

"Dylan," he murmurs, "I've had my eyes on you since the first time I saw you in the club months ago. Every time I decide to come up and introduce myself, you disappear. So don't tell me you haven't purposely avoided me."

He's noticed me? I can't help but perk up at that. Because *wow.* Holy fuck *wow.*

"Have I offended you?" he wonders.

Fuck, that's the last thing I want him to think. "Absolutely not, Sir," I say, nearly tripping over my words as they rush out. "You're just very—" Fuck, fuckety, fuck. "Intimidating." I try, and probably fail, to be subtle when I eye his tatted arms. His black tee is stretched across a chest that knows manual labor.

It's impossible to think he's a Daddy Dom. His appearance doesn't reveal any gentle nature. If he told me he was a Sadist or something, I would've believed him instantly. But Kayla insists he's sweet underneath his bad-boy exterior, and I did see him play once. He gave a spanking session on a sub, and witnessing the aftercare put a rock of jealousy in me. It wasn't even that intimate, but he held her for a long time afterward and praised her for being such a good girl.

I freeze up again as Mr. Kingsley decides to move closer. Leaving his side of the booth, he slides over to the corner close to where I'm sitting, and he extends his hand.

"I'm Cade. Have coffee with me, and I'll show you I'm not very intimidating once you get to know me."

Have coffee with me.

That can mean anything! Date? Unlikely. I know he's bisexual, but he doesn't know much about me. You learn a lot when you hide out and observe. So given what I do know about him, he's probably only being the concerned Top who wants me to find my way in a community he plays a pretty big role in.

After subtly wiping my hand on my thigh, I shake his and try not to freak out. "I can take your word for it, Sir. You don't have to go out with—"

"I want to." His eyes show the smile his sensual mouth doesn't. "Are you straight?"

Can he be blunter?

"No..."

For the record, he hasn't let go of my hand yet, and the freak-out is imminent.

He hums and gives me a pensive once-over. "Nicholas told me you're a Middle."

I nod, staring at my hand in his.

"Dylan, look at me."

I'd rather not, but fine. I lift my gaze, feeling like he can pick thoughts straight from my brain when he stares at me like that. How he can pull off intense and casual at once is beyond me.

The corners of his mouth twist up a little. "How about dinner instead?"

Date territory.

My pulse skyrockets some more because, let's drive me completely mad, and I manage another nod. Fuck me over, dinner with Mr. Kingsley. How is this happening?

"When?" I ask, my mouth too dry.

"Your schedule is busier than mine, little pro athlete."

How does he—never mind. Maybe Kayla told him what I do.

"I'm, um, free next weekend." I'm actually not. But for him? I damn well will be.

He flashes a brief, warm smile. "Fucking perfect. Next weekend, it is."

"What're you gonna wear?" Kayla asks.

I trap the phone between my cheek and shoulder as I zip up my pants. "The black slacks you approved and the shirt my grandmother sent. The light blue one?" I grab it from my closet and throw it on. "Don't you have a Mexican beach to run around on?" I don't want to take up too much of her time.

She makes a noise. "I'm waiting for Nicholas to get out of the shower. I'm more interested in talking about your wedding."

"Jesus Christ." It's a first date with a man I barely know, and she's got a wedding in mind? She's relentless. "What should I do with my hair?" I may or may not be too nervous to do this on my own, so it was surprisingly easy to quit pretending Kayla's on my shit list for meddling.

"Leave it," she advises. "I think he'll like it mussed up."

That's kinda my default mode. *Mussed up.* Leaving my top button unbuttoned, I check my watch and suck in a breath. He's picking me up any minute. Which I freaking told him he didn't have to do, but he insisted.

"It's gonna go great, Dylan," Kayla tells me. "I think you've been on each other's radars for some time. You just need to relax and let him see the goof you are when he's not around."

It's not easy to be goofy when you're so anxious. I may not know Cade Kingsley personally, but I know lots about him. I *like* him. Probably more than I should.

"I'll try," I promise. It's the least I can do. "I should brush my teeth again."

"That's the spirit!" she giggles and makes kissing noises.

I grin and roll my eyes, and after another minute of going back and forth, we hang up. It took a solemn vow of giving her all the details later before she could end the call.

In a record time of three minutes, I brush my teeth, put on socks and shoes, and locate my wallet—

"Dylan!" one of my roommates hollers. "Someone's at the door for you!"

"Shit," I curse. I'm not ready for this; I don't even know how I got to this point. What the fuck happened to avoiding him for the rest of my life and pining from afar like some lovesick puppy? They deserve their place in the world, too. It's not only for brave people.

Running a hand through my hair, I take a final glance in the mirror, then at the messy state of my room, before I walk out the door.

"Hot date?" Jimmy waggles his eyebrows, his ass stuck to the couch as always.

"Eat me," I reply.

Mr. Kingsley's waiting in the hallway, leaning casually against the doorframe, looking like my biggest fucking fantasy. We're dressed similarly, though his shirt is gray, and he's showcasing the ink covering his forearms.

"Hi." I smile nervously and grab my jacket. "Aren't you cold?" It's freezing out.

"My truck's warm." He doesn't move from the doorway when I approach, so I slow down. Have I forgotten anyth— "Beautiful boy." He leans down and presses a kiss to my jaw, and just like that, I know I don't stand a chance against this man. "You've kept me waiting."

I shudder and lock my knees into place before they cave. "I-I have?"

"Mm. I've wanted to play with you for a long time."

Goddamn. I guess...here's to making up for lost time? One can hope.

Mr. Kingsley takes me to his favorite steakhouse, where it's close to impossible to find anything on the menu my nutritionist would approve of. That means the food is fucking delicious.

It's a lively place with music, and we're tucked into a corner with a table full of food. I'm starving and I eat plenty of the various dishes we ordered, but it gets increasingly difficult since the volume of the music has us sitting so close. Tables are otherwise a *great* barrier to have in between us. Not with this one, though. He slipped right in next to me.

"I heard from Gabriella you were at the munch this week," he mentions, sucking barbecue sauce rib glaze off his thumb. *Yummy.* "She said she's never laughed so hard in her life."

I grin at that, 'cause meeting Gabriella has turned out to be a hoot and a half. "She's so awesome. We teamed up for charades right there in the coffee shop. People gave us the funniest looks."

Plus, Kayla got pouty and bugged when Gabriella and I won. There were maybe...ten of us in total? And everyone pitched in to give the two winners hot chocolate and cupcakes. I'm definitely making the munch a must from now on.

To be fair, I shared my hot chocolate with Kayla. It put a smile back on her face, and I tell Mr. Kingsley that.

He slants a lazy smile at me. "You're a sweet one, aren't you?"

I chew on my lip and shrug, 'cause I don't know, and I distract myself by grabbing another fried wing. They might kill me, and what a way to go. You can take a boy out of the South, but you can't take the South out of the boy, and deep-fried stuff is the *best* stuff.

"Have you ever had a Daddy Dom or Mommy Domme, Dylan?"

I shake my head no. "Only a little bit of casual play."

"Hmm."

What does *that* mean? He can be very hard to decipher, I'm learning. A bit ironic when I think of it, 'cause I know more by just watching. I know he loves to woodwork and design fetish furniture, I know he often has a cigarette stuck behind his ear even though he quit smoking a long time ago, I know he is affectionate and very giving with people he cares for, I know he has the sexiest laugh... I know my infatuation runs deep.

Because of that, he scares the crap out of me.

I side-eye him and stick a couple fries in my mouth. Another thing I'm pretty sure about where he's concerned is that he's not afraid to pursue, but I don't think he will push much. If he doesn't detect any interest, he'll back off.

Have I shown much interest? Maybe I could be better at that.

"Can—" Ugh, I clear my throat, my mouth suddenly too dry. In fact, I grab my soda and gulp down some Coke, maybe also to stall. Here we go. Deep breaths. "Can we play sometime, maybe? Only if you want."

His eyebrows give a little lift, and he sets down his burger.

He is a sadistic bastard, after all. Rather than answering me right away and putting me out of my misery, he wipes his mouth with a napkin, takes a swig of his beer, then leans back casually and rests his arm along the back of the booth.

"Come here." With his arm behind me, he nudges me closer, and my heart decides to jump up into my throat. His other hand shapes itself to my jaw, drawing a shudder from me. "When we play...is kissing all right?"

I furrow my brow, then nod hesitantly. Of course kissing is

okay. More than. I may have dreamed about it a hundred thousand times already.

"Good. Then I want a taste." That's all he says before he leans in and plants his warm lips to mine and gives me a slow, firm kiss. Oh, fucking finally. "Mm, well, that's not enough." He kisses me again, deeper this time, and I get my head out of my butt and kiss him back.

Parting my lips some more, I put a hand on his sculpted chest and get sneaky. I just wanna feel a bit, and he's not wearing an undershirt. Desire floods my senses as he swirls his tongue sensually along mine, and I slip my thumb between two buttons and come across warm skin and chest hair.

I shiver violently and accidentally exhale a low moan.

"Jesus," he whispers huskily. "You're dangerous, little boy."

I might as well give up on getting past the shudders. They set each other off, one by one. "Not as d-dangerous as you are."

"Oh, yeah?" His smile is dark and sinful, and he drops his indecent gaze to where I'm stealthily feeling him up. He lifts a brow, chuckles, then kisses me again. "Practicing patience is gonna be tough with you."

"I hope so," I admit.

He groans under his breath, and to my dismay, he backs off after one final, hard kiss. "I wanna know more about you." With a crooked smirk, he pries away my greedy fingers and kisses my knuckles. "Tell me how you found kink."

Yeah, that's literally the last thing I feel like doing. Can't we just jump in the sack?

"Don't be a slut," he murmurs with a knowing glint in his eye. The tips of my ears heat up. "Not yet, anyway. Not until I have you in my bed." About that...can't we do that now? "Fucking hell, you tempt me, Dylan."

I grin, out of breath, and I feel oddly relaxed—despite the raging lust. The relief is immense, and I wanna be playful and bratty around him. I get the feeling he's one of the Doms who enjoys that.

"I guess I can't help it around you," I confess. "You've been driving me insane for *months*, Sir."

He rumbles a quiet growl and gives my bottom lip a sharp nip. "You're testing my restraint, boy." His hand covers my cheek as he trails kisses up my jaw to my ear. "I'm already counting the minutes 'til I get to hear *Daddy* from your sweet lips, but for now...you gotta be good for me."

Oh God, I'm not even sure I can, not after he said that.

I've never been through anything like this before. The switch in my brain is automatic, because Mr. Kingsley—or Cade, as he's said I can call him—makes it stupidly easy for me to let go of everything and, for the first time in my life, really sink into my Middle self.

We discuss kinks, the people at Switch, and music, and every time I do anything remotely youthful, he rewards me with smiles of approval before I can get nervous and second-guess myself.

I gotta hand it to him, too. He's a man of his word, and his self-restraint is stronger than he gives himself credit for. The effect I have on him is clear as day, much to my excitement, and he doesn't even try to hide it. That said, he's firm. Sex is off the table tonight because he doesn't want us to rush.

The fact that he won't budge might provide an ounce of disappointment for instant gratification, but on the other hand, a man who doesn't budge? Hard to come by. I don't *want* a Dom I can manipulate or use sex with to get my way. It would give me way too much power.

That doesn't stop me from trying to persuade him, though...

On the way home from dinner, I complain about certain, uh, frustrations.

In my defense, they're very real. Never before have I enjoyed a date so much that dinner lasted four hours, and that was four hours of good food, getting to know each other, and *so much* sexual tension I could just kick the bucket already.

"You poor thing," he chuckles warmly and switches lanes. "You think you're the only one who struggles?"

"Maybe," I muse. "I'll have to take care of, um, *things* tonight —*all* by myself."

"Oh, really?" His amused expression doesn't leave the road. "You know, if we start an arrangement, that's the type of thing you'll have to ask permission to do."

Fuck, I want that. I adjust my seat belt and chew on the inside of my cheek, thinking. Debating internally. I want *him* to know I want it. An arrangement...relationship...but one thing at a time.

"Would it please you if I asked for tonight, too?" I wonder.

His smile softens a little. "It would, Dylan."

"Okay, so for tonight..." It's strangely nerve-racking. I've never asked permission before. I've only dreamed about it. "Is it all right if I—" Goodness. I have to actually say the words. Wow, I never thought that would be such a big deal, yet here I am, stuttering and getting nervous. "Okay that I, um, you know, get off?"

He grins and snatches up my hand, bringing it to his mouth to kiss my palm. "That was too adorable. But no." *Dammit!* "I think you should keep your hands out of your pants until our next date."

"Aw, *man.*" I slump back, though I'm more saddened that I'm almost home.

He laughs quietly. "Outta curiosity, how *would* the perfect evening end?"

"Hmm." I tap my chin. "Contrary to what you might believe right now, it doesn't have to be sex." I scowl playfully at his carefree laugh. "Like, duh, I like to get off, but for your information, cuddling is awesome. Kissing and cuddling and touching and being tucked in."

He grins and nods slowly. "For *your* information, I'm a big fan of that, too. I'm sure tucking you in will be fun. There's also bath time."

Ka-dunk. Like that, a ball of lust drops to my gut. "Yeah..." I have to adjust my dick at the mental image of him inspecting my body after bath time. "Sir, when can I see you again?"

"Soon, baby boy. Very soon."

LOSING HIS TOUCH

A BEHIND THE SCENES OUTTAKE

A GLIMPSE

RIO KELLY

Being a dungeon monitor at Switch is sometimes much like watching a train wreck. Pushing up the sleeves of my black button-down, I lean back against the circular bar in the middle of the floor of the Cave, and I merely wait for shit to go wrong. Eyes trained on a scening stall in which a Dom has restrained his submissive to Cade's custom-designed sex chair. The narrow chaise longue is formed like a tilde, and the sub is situated too far down in the curve for her back to arch. It leaves her neck too exposed as she leans back, hands and ankles shackled to the sides of the contraption.

Cade himself stops next to me, also on DM patrol this busy evening. "He did that intentionally, didn't he?"

"Probably." We know the Dom booked the stall for a breath play scene, and they have to be supervised. With his goal in mind, it's easy to draw the conclusion that he wants her neck bent backward to that degree.

"Jesus. Have fun with that one, Doc." He slaps me on the shoulder and continues.

Doc. It's not a regular nickname for me, but I suppose it's fitting at the minute. Scrubbing a hand over my mouth and jaw, I can certainly acknowledge that all the years I spent earning my MD have made me more, ah, *sensitive*, for lack of a better word, to Doms and Tops who put their partners in unnecessary danger because they haven't the faintest clue about human anatomy.

The Dom strokes and caresses his sub into a lulled state. She looks blissed out, yet full of anticipation. Blindfolded, restrained, flushed, nipples constricting.

Then I have to intervene. Approaching the stall, I snatch up a pair of soundproof headphones and clear my throat.

"Pardon, sir." I speak just loud enough so he can hear me above the heavy music.

The Dom tosses a scowl over his shoulder, and I raise a brow and extend the headphones to him. There's no need for the submissive to hear another Dom schooling her Owner, but I can't allow him to choke her out like that.

He grabs the headphones and puts them on his sub, after which I take another couple steps closer.

"Cutting off her air supply can cause permanent damage to her larynx." I gesture in a *may-I* way to approach his property. "It's the blood flow you want to compress." With his permission, I ghost my thumb and index finger along the sides of the sub's neck, a couple inches below her jaw. She can't feel that it's me barely touching her. By applying pressure on her carotid arteries, he'll block the oxygen to her brain, giving her the floaty carbon dioxide high she'll love. I go on, explaining how to do it in brief intervals, and—

I snap my gaze toward the opening of the dungeon, confused by the loud commotion coming from the main Club area.

"Excuse me for one moment." I leave the stall and pick up the pace when I spot Cade all but flying out of the Cave. With the loud music only getting louder, I don't see what's going on until I'm halfway across the Club.

Bloody hell.

Mark is in a fight with someone, another man, and they're not alone. Dante's holding a panicking Kayla, a sight that automatically makes my blood boil, and a young blonde then joins in on the fight.

My next curse is verbal, and I push my way through the forming crowd, jaw set and adrenaline surging.

"For fuck's sake!" Mark shouts. "Ray, hurry!"

"Get that girl away from here," I bark at Cade. I can't see who the blonde is, but she's attacking the man Mark is fighting with tight fists. Instead, Cade is busy getting ahold of the man who's clearly drunk, judging by his obnoxious yelling.

Pushing away the last obstacles, I reach the fight and quickly slip an arm around the slender blond girl, hauling her backward.

"Calm yourself, girl," I growl.

"No!" She decides to fight me instead, thrashing in my hold, so I yank her farther back and secure her with both my arms. "Let me go right fucking now! That piece'a shit hurt Kayla!"

That voice...

I shake my head, the mayhem fogging my brain. The club's strobe lights, music, and chaos aren't exactly making shit easier. This girl is getting on my fucking nerves, though. Sensing that Mark, Cade, and Ray have the situation under control now, I force the feisty sub in a slave dress up against a wall.

"Get that scum out of my goddamn club," I hear Nicholas demanding as he strides past with Kayla in his arms.

Refocusing on the blonde, I strap a forearm across her sternum while she curses and pushes back the hair from her face—*what the bloody hell.* I do a double take because it fucking can't be.

My little rebel.

"Fuck." I stumble back, shocked beyond words. It can't be, but as those three words go on a loop in my head, the puzzle pieces crash together like heavy bricks. She's the Chelsea Kayla and Nicholas have spoken of.

Before me, Chelsea—Jesus Christ, *Chelsea*—pales and widens

her eyes at me, and I glare venomously at my second glance of her slave dress. *Slave.* She's *here.* In a fucking fetish club, and God, what I told her a decade ago... What have I caused?

"Rio..."

I shake my head, refusing to accept it. I can't. By some miracle, I get my legs to work, and I escape like a fugitive. Perhaps I should be. What I did should surely be criminal.

"Is this seat taken?"

Taking a swig of my beer, I eye the young woman to my right—emphasis on young. "No."

Her dress, if you can call it that, ends high on her thighs, and the invitation in her eyes is clear as day. Too cute. Actually, she's bloody gorgeous, but way too young.

"Did you know I can read minds?"

My mouth twists up, and I lean an elbow against the bartop. "Really."

She nods. "You want to buy me a drink."

I laugh.

Taking in her appearance again, I shake my head slowly, amused and a fair bit concerned. "Why, because you can't buy one yourself?"

I push my way through the lobby and don't stop until I step outside and can suck in a deep, cold breath. The January chill fills my lungs, and I screw my eyes shut.

"Rio?"

The brick wall behind me supports me as I glance over to find Mark frowning my way.

I assume he got the drunk bastard out of here.

I'm next. "I'm not feeling well." I cough into my fist as a sudden bout of nausea turns my statement into nothing but truth. "I need to go home."

He winces at the pain on the side of his neck and lifts a brow while he checks his damaged skin. "Did something happen just now, or...?"

You could say that, though it's not related to the fight—per se. "Either I'm losing my mind or a ghost from the past has decided to come back and haunt me."

Fuck. More memories from that night in New York ten years ago flash through my mind, and I can't fucking escape them.

"Do you honestly expect me to believe you're twenty-one?"

She doesn't act well. Her confused expression is accompanied by fidgeting. "I swear it."

"Liar." I lean close, wanting her out of here. My own thoughts about her appearance are lewd enough, and I won't touch her. I know most other men in this place would. It's not safe for her. "If you want, I can get you a cab to take you home."

She chooses to see it as something that can go further. "Will you come with me?" Her hand slides up my thigh, and I eye it briefly. "I bet you're wild."

She has no idea.

"I'm sorry about bailing, mate," I force out. "I have to get out of here."

Fully aware I've left my jacket and pretty much everything but my wallet in my locker on the second floor of the club, I head down the sidewalk to flag down a cab. I can come back for my shit tomorrow. Right now, I need to be far away from Switch. And Chelsea.

Sweet little rebel...

The young girl I called out for lying to me about her age, after which I warned her with a punctuated, "You don't want to know what I usually do with brats who lie and disrespect me."

I shouldn't have told her. Holy fuck, I should not have told her.

I can't even imagine what impression I made, or how it coerced her into being in a fetish club tonight. But I just know I had something to do with it.

TOUCHING TRUTH

A BEHIND THE SCENES NOVELLA

PART III

GREG COOPER

"You were lucky," the doctor tells me.

Lucky is not the word I'd use for me. I caught a glimpse in a mirror earlier; my eyes are bloodshot, a nasty bruise is forming under my eye, my shirt is bloody, jacket torn, I've already thrown out my tie, I have a splitting headache, and my jaw is fractured. I have to hold it in place after a gruesome alignment I suffered through before. After so much prodding, I wonder idly if I should charge.

An hour or so ago, the police officer called me lucky, too. No one is pressing charges, so they left. Throwing me in a cell to sober up was out of the question since I require medical care. *Lucky* me.

If anything, I'm the picture of a man who's hit rock bottom.

"Are you even breathing, Mr. Cooper?"

"Yes," I whisper. Or I'm trying. Moving hurts. The slightest jostle sends explosions of pain through my skull, radiating down to my neck.

He eyes me, concerned. "Does your tongue feel thicker or like it's—"

"Headache."

"Ah. You'll get something for the pain shortly."

Wonderful.

"You might still need wiring," the doctor goes on. "It's important you come back to the hospital if the swelling doesn't settle or if you feel your teeth won't align." A nurse enters the room, and the doctor nods in thanks, accepting an ice pack. "Use this, please."

I wince at the cold, pressing it gently against my battered jaw.

He studies my jaw and makes sure I didn't move it when applying the ice. "Are you on any medication right now?"

"No." My voice comes out hoarse, quiet, and dull. I've been instructed to relax as much as possible without being "slack."

"Do you take anything regularly?"

Technically, no. "No." Lately, I've had panic attacks, but my wife helped me. She has a mild prescription for Xanax, work hazard of being an ICU nurse with a hectic schedule and a complete crap work environment.

"I'll be back in a little bit, Mr. Cooper. If someone's picking you up, you could contact them now."

And who would that be? Tess is out, for several reasons. I don't want to show my ugly face at home or anywhere near Abby. The sun is up, so Seth and Ted are at the office. Dizziness sways me a few inches as I scroll through my phone.

Ryan Quinn.

I swallow hard, which feels strange.

My easiest option would be to take a cab to the nearest hotel. Yet, my fingers flit across the keys in a message to Ryan.

Apologies for bothering you, Sir. I'm at St. Mary's ER (nothing serious) but would really appreciate a ride. No worries if it's too much. I can take a cab.

I press send before I can wise up. After the week I've had, I'm ready to beg for just five minutes with him. Them. Either of them. I'm beyond desperate. Exhaling shakily, my fingers tremble when the little "read" sign appears at the bottom of the message, indicating Ryan's opened the text.

My eyelids get heavier by the minute, possibly because I haven't slept much in...I don't even know. I'm approaching forty-eight hours, anyway.

The buzz of my phone has my attention, and I detest that I have to send the call to voice mail. My pulse quickens because it's Ryan, but I can't speak more than a few words. Instead, I fire off another quick message.

I'm sorry, Sir. Minor fracture in my jaw. Speaking is difficult.

His reply arrives swiftly.

When and where do I pick you up? Anything you need?

Thank you, thank you, thank you. Goddamn emotions. My eyes well up, and I text him the address, a time, as well as a request for a sweater with a hood. Knowing what the doctor has planned next, I have no desire to show my face.

I flinch as the doctor wraps my head in a bandage. Under my jaw, over the top of my head, around my face. It'll keep the jaw in place until it heals by itself. Because I got *lucky* and only sustained a minor fracture.

The pain medication is marvelous, however. It's starting to kick in, and I have a feeling I'll be dead to the world the second my head *gently* hits the pillow.

The doctor talks about everything I have to think of and count-less things I should refrain from. Ibuprofen or any other anti-inflammatory drugs; understood. Speech restriction; got it. And kinky, if I'm not mistaken.

There's a knock on the door as he finishes with the bandaging, and I return the ice pack to my face as he opens the door.

It's Ryan. In his messy morning glory. Jeans and hoodie, beanie covering his constantly disheveled hair.

"I'm here for the chipmunk," he drawls with a quirk of his lips.

I've missed his voice.

The doctor's eyes show amusement. "He's ready to go home. He needs to rest."

"Oh, I'll make sure he rests." Ryan steps in and hands me a plastic bag. "You ordered a hoodie. I took the liberty of packing a pair of sweats, too."

I nod in thanks, finding it difficult to speak for other reasons than my broken jaw. It's even difficult to look him in the eye.

He is stockier than I am, broader chest and shoulders, muscled thighs, and he has a few inches on my six feet, so I'm not surprised to discover his clothes look big on me. The sweat pants cling low on my hips, and I tighten the drawstrings so they don't come farther down. The faded gray fabric has softened with years of wear and washing. Along the leg of the pants, "USMC" is printed in dark blue.

He thinks I have no interest in getting to know them; he's wrong. For months now, I've had questions building up inside me. Everything from his days in the Marines and how he came to own a bar, to how he and Angel met and what their goals for the future are.

The doctor fills out my prescription for pain medication while I discard my button-down and put on the hoodie.

It smells of Ryan and Angel. Their apartment and fabric softener.

Drawing the hood up, I'm glad most of the bandages are hidden.

I receive another scripted speech from the doctor, and then I'm discharged and billed—or robbed blind—before I follow Ryan out of the ER. The sun is shining, which my bloodshot eyes truly love. I wince and squint at the bright light.

Ryan drives a truck. Of course he drives a truck. He's a truck kind of person. The dark green gleams in the sun. The big tires whisper of off-road adventures, the tracks filled with mud that doesn't belong in the city.

"Get in, chipmunk."

I get it, I get it. My face is a bit compressed by the bandage. Very funny.

I haul myself inside and buckle up.

"Thank you again for picking me up," I say quietly.

"No problem." He sticks the key in the ignition and drums the wheel. "Where to?"

"A hotel, please. I think there's a Marriott—"

"So you don't wanna go home." He nods once and starts the vehicle. "Then, fuck the Marriott." Looking over his shoulder, he backs out of the parking space. "Angel's with my mother today, and I'm not working. We can veg out at our place."

Thank you, thank you, thank you.

We stop on the way to get my medication, and Ryan's sadistically amused by the strict diet I'll be on for the next week or two. Heading up and down the aisles of a grocery store, he cracks jokes while my headache returns.

"I'm glad my misery amuses you," I mutter.

He ignores that. "This could be good practice for me. Here." He stops in an aisle with baby food and grabs my basket. "Plain nasty. You can't even see it's chicken and..." He reads the label closer. "Who the fuck feeds their children this shit?"

"I'd rather stick to smoothies and oatmeal."

"But the image of force-feeding you baby food is too hard to resist." He drops another few glass jars with illustrated animals and block letters in bright colors into the basket. "Maybe you can borrow one of Angel's pacifiers."

I flush uncomfortably and get rid of that mental picture.

We continue toward the produce where I can get some fruits and vegetables for smoothies. On the way, I check my phone to see if Seth and Ted have replied, but they haven't. I sent Sally a message, as well. There is no way I can see clients with a bruised face and bandaged head, so in a few days when I return to work, I'll have to stick to whatever I can do in my office.

"Am I allowed to ask about what happened to you?" Ryan asks.

I lift a shoulder, not sure why he's interested. "Ask away, but I take no responsibility if my life depresses you."

"Aw, I guess I can crash your pity party."

I shoot him a quick scowl.

He drops a bag of apples in the basket and quirks his lazy grin. "Did you deserve it?"

"I hurt innocent people, so I suppose I did."

He lifts his brows and continues perusing the fruit. "I hope you defend clients better than you defend yourself."

I know when I'm guilty or not. And on that note, shouldn't he be royally pissed with me? I'm guilty of lying to him and Angel.

After picking out a handful of bananas, he pauses to gently grip my chin. "They didn't wire you shut or nothin'?"

"No, the doctor said I was lucky."

"Indeed. You're cute when you mutter and mumble." He's having fun. He's *not* royally pissed. "Who rearranged your face?"

"My little brother."

"Ah. Brotherly love, huh?" He lets me go. "I take it you're not close."

"No, not particularly." I avert my gaze, leftover anger sparking up for a quick second. "I'm ready to get out of here."

He nods and adds a couple passion fruits to the basket. "Sounds good. Let's go home and abuse our blender."

Home.

Where are you? Mark called. I'm worried, Greg.

I frown at the message and type out a quick response to Tess.

I'm fine. I'll be home tonight.

Muting the phone, I forget it exists and follow Ryan down the hall. It gives me a slight pause when he walks past the second bedroom and continues to the one he shares with his wife. When you don't ask questions, you don't get answers, and so I've assumed it's off-limits. Then again, this isn't...playtime. I guess we're...two friends hanging out? God, that sounds wrong. I don't have friends, and socializing is reserved for work events.

"What the..." I stop short in the doorway to their bedroom. "No bed?" Well, there's a huge mattress, no doubt a California King, thick enough to reach my knees, and countless pillows, covers, and blankets—but no bed frame. There is, however, a gigantic flat screen on the wall, so that says a thing or two about their priorities.

"We keep breaking 'em."

"Jesus." I can see it, too. She's mostly submissive to Ryan, but he's mentioned she's his "primal whore" sometimes, too. That's when they, as they call it, hate-fuck and take each other apart.

Ryan flashes a wolfish smirk and sets down his breakfast on the nightstand. Which is a rustic old wooden crate. The white-painted brick walls are completely bare, aside from one that's full of black-and-white photos of him and Angel and their travels. They *are* outdoorsy. Tents, starry skies, deserts, and mountain ranges. There's a photo of Angel holding up a rifle; she's wearing a triumphant grin and standing next to a dead deer.

Angel's captured a photo of Ryan lighting up a cigarette. On the ground is a dead moose.

Good grief.

"Are you hunters?" I blurt it out, forgetting to be careful, and I flinch at the sharp pain in my jaw.

He inclines his head, eyeing the wall of photos. "My family has a cabin up north. We try to meet up a couple weeks every year. We live off the land then."

Of course they do.

I can barely manage the lands of Target.

"Come on, you need to eat and rest." Ryan yanks his shirt over his head, revealing a stocky frame, tattoos, and abs that peek out when he tenses up. "I'm rewatching *Grace & Frankie*."

"I don't know what that is." I set down my smoothie and a cup of chocolate pudding on the other crate, and then I hesitate. It's probably wise I keep my clothes on. Otherwise, I'll only embarrass myself.

"Oh, it's a motherfucking delight. Think of it as a modern *Golden Girls*."

That's...that's endearing. Stifling a smile, I sit down on the mattress and adjust three pillows to lean back on. And then I'm watching TV and eating breakfast in bed with a man who's degraded me, fucked me six ways to Sunday, cared for me, picked me up at the hospital...the list goes on. It's surreal, in several ways. I still don't belong here, yet it's the place I love more than any other. A place I can be myself.

At one point, he gets up to get me a new ice pack—or a bag of frozen peas—and my medication.

"Thank you for letting me stay here," I say quietly, finishing the chocolate pudding, "Sir."

"You're welcome, pet." He removes one of his pillows to get more comfortable, and then he extends his arm. "Come here."

Thank you, thank you, thank you.

I take a sip of water and the bag of frozen peas, then scoot closer and rest the good side of my face on his chest. He pulls the covers over us and presses a kiss to my forehead. It relaxes me. With him, I don't have to pretend. Except...I'm borrowing time and pretending I belong here.

Ryan's chest rumbles with warm chuckles whenever he finds the TV show funny. I don't pay much attention to it, more interested in the wall of photos. Glimpses into his life with Angel.

Their wedding photo twists my stomach in envy, though at the same time, I can't think of two people more deserving. Dressed in a simple summer dress, Angel smiles softly, eyes visibly misty, as Ryan bows and kisses her knuckles. She has flowers in her hair.

What would that even feel like? To love someone so deeply. To love someone who won't wave goodbye one day as she sets off for college.

"You're beautiful together."

Ryan follows my gaze and smiles. "She's my life." He pauses. "For being so young, she's taught me a shitload, too."

Is it okay to ask?

"How...how did you meet?"

"I caught her shoplifting in a buddy's convenience store down the street."

Good lord! "That's... I don't know what to say."

He laughs quietly. "Yeah, neither did I when she slammed her palm up into my chin and made a run for it."

At that, I have to see him—and know more. Supporting myself on my elbow, I flick my no doubt stunned expression between his eyes and the photos. "You're more than twice her size." Hell, *I'm* almost twice her size.

"Element of surprise." He smirks. "No one sees her little force coming—sometimes literally."

I chuckle under my breath and adjust the ice-cold bag along my jaw. "I assume you caught up to her."

"Well, yeah. Otherwise my fifteen years in the Marines would'a been a tragic waste."

He's seen battle, I'm sure of it. His muscled torso speaks of combat. A five-inch scar slashes across his left pec, and chest hair doesn't grow there. Poorly performed stitches have left dotted marks behind.

"I offered her a place to stay and a job in my bar," he murmurs, eyes on the photos. "She was a runaway. Foster kid."

"Oh." I swallow uncomfortably, worried about what she must've lived through. I can't even picture it. "How old was she?"

"Seventeen."

Really. I clear my throat, my forehead creasing. "Wouldn't it have been wiser if she worked in your friend's convenience store at that age?"

Ryan snorts softly. "That's what I get for inviting a lawyer into my bed." He grins and rolls over onto his side, his mouth ghosting a kiss to my chin. "I didn't give a flying fuck, Greg. I wanted to help her, so I did. She wasn't on the books until she turned eighteen."

"Lovely." I kill my smirk—well, I try, anyway. "What else happened when she turned eighteen?"

That earns me a laugh and a look full of dark secrets. "I'm not completely depraved, little shit."

I shrug lightly and chuckle. "Are you telling me you didn't want her until recently?"

"Ah, no. She was fucking gorgeous at seventeen, too." Exactly. "But the possibility didn't exist until..." He thinks back on something. "Must've been a few months after her eighteenth birthday. She started walking around in skimpy tops and panties. Holy fuck, she drove me bonkers."

"To seduce you," I state. Angel certainly strikes me as a person who goes after what she wants.

"Yeah... I caved there somewhere. She'd already crawled into my head. Then she crawled into bed with me one night."

The image derails my thoughts, and I have to focus. *Focus.* This is me, indulging. Borrowing time. Pretending I can get to know them. Wishing I could have more. *Be* more. It's not about sex or visualizing them together...

"What did you do?" I probably shouldn't have asked. He already told me he caved.

Ryan hums, his hand landing on my hip under the covers. "I fucked her stupid."

I shudder as heat spreads inside me. "You're a lucky man."

"I definitely am."

"She's lucky, as well."

"Mm." He shifts closer and drops a kiss to my neck. "Get some sleep, boy. Before I fuck you stupid, too."

"Christ." The desire builds up, warring with the fatigue. "I—"

"Quiet." He shakes his head and lands a final kiss on my forehead. "You'd take it, I know." Of course I would. I want him. "But it ain't right. Angel and I can't go back to the old arrangement." At that, I close my eyes in defeat, the lust dissipating like sand between my fingers. "We've grown to care for you, Greg, but we won't be part of your secret life."

Because they're better than that.

There's nothing I can say.

I wake up disoriented and in an insane amount of pain.

"Fuck." I groan and force myself to sit up, causing a bag of not-so frozen peas to fall down to my lap. The bandage is wet and my face is sticky from being smashed by plastic, but it feels like the swelling is going down. Small favors.

I blink sleepily, registering a dark bedroom. Streetlights illuminate enough for me to locate my medication on the nightstand, and I chase two pills down with a glass of water.

Ryan isn't here, but I can hear him. Angel, too. In the kitchen, perhaps.

Feeling too hot, I throw off the covers and move over to the edge of the bed where my feet hit the floorboards with a low thump.

The memories of everything that's happened over the past two, three days come rushing back, and I release a heavy breath and retrieve my phone from my pocket. Battery's about to die—hell. Several missed calls and fourteen messages. Good news travels fast.

My mother has texted a few times, worried and angry about what Mark's told her. I couldn't care less, and I scroll past those messages without responding. It's enough I have to see her and my father for holidays and family dinners here and there.

Seth and Ted pass on get-well messages and confirm covering for me at work until I'm ready to return.

You won't even tell me where you are? I can't believe you, Greg.

I'm your wife, goddammit!

Evangeline wonders if she's fired.

I'm taking Abby to my mother's for a couple days.

I touch my jaw carefully and swallow hard. It's probably best for Abby to get away for a little bit. I don't want her to see me this way. As for Tess...I have to make things up to her—stat. She deserves better, though I don't like her throwing down the wife card like that, when it pleases *her*.

The last message is from Mark.

What the fuck is going on with you?

That's the million-dollar question, isn't it?

"He's alive." Ryan gives me his signature lazy grin when I appear in their kitchen after a trip to the bathroom. The painkillers have kicked in, so I manage a polite smile in return, though I suspect it comes off too pinched.

Angel turns away from the stove and offers the frostiest look I've ever received outside the second bedroom. With a slow once-over, lingering on my face, she dismisses me and returns to cooking.

Her shoulders look stiff.

I'm sorry.

Ryan kicks out the chair across from him, and I join him at the table that seats only two. There is no room for a bigger table, and they want to raise a child here?

"Sleep well?" Ryan opens the window that faces the back alley behind the bar and lights up a cigarette.

"Yes, Sir." The hood came off in my sleep, so I tug it up again. "Those aren't good for you."

"I'm well aware." He smirks faintly and takes a drag. "I'm down from a pack to two smokes a day."

I'm glad to hear it.

"Is he staying for dinner, Daddy?" Angel asks.

"I can go." Hiding the hurt—it's my fucking fault, anyway—I make a move to stand, but Ryan gives me a pointed look that throws that out the window.

"He's staying."

I guess I'm staying.

I wish I could read Angel—past the hostility. I wish I could fix it. There's no badass little biker babe in her appearance now, the pajama shorts, bare feet, pastel blue top, and lack of makeup making her look even younger and more vulnerable.

"I've been doing some thinking." Ryan's calculating gaze slides my way, effectively putting me on the spot. "Greg and I had a nice chat earlier about how you and I met, princess. So the way I figure, it's only fair we get to know him, too."

Oh, Christ. I shift in my seat, thinking of all the reasons that's a terrible idea. They won't understand. It's better they live with their assumptions and guesses.

"What good will that do?" Angel frowns.

Ryan lifts a shoulder. "You never know. Things change when all the cards are on the table."

Not for the better.

———

Maybe Ryan's immune to awkwardness, but I'm not. He chats casually in between mouthfuls of Angel's beef stir-fry while I suffer the chilled stares of Angel and pretend to enjoy my cup of insta-oatmeal. Her resentment toward me is worse than the fact that I'm sitting on the floor right now.

When you only have two chairs, the dog takes the floor.

"I talked to Madigan and Jameson," Ryan mentions. "Next time we're in Camassia, we'll do the Primal Pursuit."

"Holy shit, that'll be hot," Angel replies. "I hope Alex joins this time."

I haven't said much, but sue me, I'm curious. I squint up at them. "Is that a hunter's version of the board game?"

Angel rolls her eyes. Fuck.

"If the prey are submissive little whores, then yeah, I guess you can say that. It's a takedown event in the woods." Ryan winks at me, causing me to flush like a pathetic boy, and then he frowns at Angel. "Roll your eyes again and we're gonna have a problem, little girl."

She lowers her gaze, sulking. "I'm sorry, Master."

I stay quiet for the remainder of the meal, after which Ryan tells me to return to the bedroom.

I hesitate in the doorway. "The guest room, Sir?"

"No, ours."

It doesn't make sense, but I obey. Angel once gave me a last kiss; perhaps this is the last play. They'll force some personal information out of me, and then they'll tell me to get the hell out of their lives.

He hasn't told me I can get on the bed, so I stay standing on the floor and hope for the best. What I don't do is spare a single glance at the wall of photos. I can't. The envy runs too deep, and I can't deny anymore that I want to be on the wall with them.

It goes against everything I deem healthy, yet...fuck, I ache for it.

"Part of this will be of your choosing, pet." Ryan enters the room and tosses a black kit of some sort on the mattress. Angel follows and rips away the covers and blankets, as well as the pillows. "We know you like extreme pain and marks by now."

I manage a small nod, nervous as hell all of a sudden.

Ryan moves closer and lifts my hoodie a few inches. "Remove your clothes."

I shrug out of the hoodie, careful not to yank off the bandages.

"How would you feel about a permanent mark?" he asks quietly. "It can be small, and you would choose the location."

Jesus Christ. I'm supposed to say no to this, there's no question about that. As I hesitantly step out of the sweat pants, I watch Ryan open the black kit and reveal some metal tool.

"This is nothing to take lightly, so it's completely up to you. We won't hold a no against you even for a second."

It's a branding iron, I realize. At least, I think so, and it would make sense because I know Angel has been branded by Ryan. She bears a small, private symbol below her left breast.

It can be something to remember them by.

Heat rises to my skin at the same time as my heart sinks. They won't go back to what we used to have, and I can't give them more. Maybe they'll keep coming to my aid when I need it, because they're genuine and full of heart. They care. But there are new lines drawn in the sand, ones they won't cross.

Not all stories have happy endings.

"Yes," I whisper, anxious as never before. I want it, though. Consequences be damned, I want something to remember them by that I can keep with me 'til the day I die.

"Are you absolutely certain?" Ryan comes to stand before me, a serious expression on his face. I nod once, firm in my decision. "All right, then. Lose the underwear and lie down in the middle. I'll set things up, and you can think of a location."

Letting out a heavy breath, I discard my boxers and end up on my back in the bed. Angel has begun to light candles around us, fairly tall ones positioned on the floor. On any other day, I can picture Ryan and Angel treating the bed like an altar for their love, a place to fuck like savages while wax melts around them.

Angel draws the blinds on the windows.

The sound of something being plugged into the wall lets me know Ryan's heat source is being prepared.

"Inside of my bicep," I decide.

Ryan's concentrating on the tools or whatever I'm supposed to call them, merely quirking a brow at my decision. Finished with the candles, Angel joins me on the bed and sits down on my right side.

"Where did you grow up, Greg?" she asks.

I look her in the eye briefly. All right, so it's started. First question's easy enough. "Berkeley."

"Did you like it there?"

"Well enough." Until I turned eleven, I'd say.

Ryan extends my arm and instructs me to face Angel the entire time. I nod in understanding, and then I see a small, bright light in my periphery, directed on my arm. A towel is slid underneath me, which catapults my thoughts into the nearest future where I'm sure I'll have blood seeping out. *God.* My stomach clenches.

"Tell me about your family," Angel says. "You have three brothers, correct?"

Most would probably find that fairly easy to answer, as well. I don't. Define family?

"Three biological," I reply quietly. "I'm only close with two of them."

"Would that be the Seth and Ted Cooper also listed on your company website?"

Was she a private investigator in her former life or something? "Yes, Ma'am. My father started the firm, then handed it over to me when he retired."

"Following in your daddy's footsteps," she notes. "Are your parents divorced?"

"No."

On my other side, Ryan cleans my arm, and the strong scent of antibacterial gel hits my nostrils. Instinct tells me to turn my head, but I keep my focus on Angel—as much as I can.

She cocks her head at me. "You mentioned three brothers who are biologically yours. That implies there are others."

And there it is. I can't elaborate and keep it short. Well, I suppose I can, but there will be countless follow-up questions.

"I grew up in a polyamorous household." The words taste like acid. "My parents lived together with two other married couples who have children of their own."

Her eyes glitter with interest. "Talk about different. How was it?"

Awful. I open my mouth to answer, only to snap it shut when I hear Ryan switching on his Bunsen burner. I tense up out of reflex, to which he strokes my arm in comfort. *It's going to hurt.* Might as well do my best to let dreadful conversation distract me. So I mutter my way through a matter-of-fact explanation about my childhood. I tell Angel—and Ryan—about Mom and Dad, one kindergarten teacher and one environmental lawyer, and their friends, Ben, Annie, Hank, and Marie. Six open-minded adults who share everything from marital beds to child rearing. They started out as friends the same age, all equally spiritual and alternative, for lack of a better word; it was one magic healer away from being a hippie community.

I'm the eldest. Ben and Annie's two daughters come next, then Hank and Marie's son, then Mark. Seth and Ted are the babies in the family, though everyone's in their thirties now. I confess that Mark and I used to be best friends, along with Victoria, the second eldest of us.

Everyone was—or is—accepted for who they are, and it never mattered if you were gay, straight, or something in between. Ben and Annie were Buddhists, Mom has always been highly spiritual, and Hank is a staunch atheist. But with love and acceptance as key ingredients, the discussions never became too heated. There was no one true way.

"That sounds so cool," Angel muses.

Ryan chuckles. "Greg wouldn't agree."

Angel raises a brow at me. "Your family essentially cultivated what the world needs more of."

"Certainly." I'm not arguing that. "I found comfort in my own odd sexuality long before I learned what society finds acceptable. But does it matter? The world isn't ready."

Ryan leans over and kisses me on the forehead. "I'm gonna start now. Keep talking when you can, all right?"

I suck in a breath and nod jerkily.

"What's odd about being bi?" Angel scrunches her nose.

"I'm not bi," I grunt. "Well...technically, I suppose, but it's more difficult for me to get attracted in the first place—*motherfucker!*" I go rigid as fiery pain shoots up my arm, and I screw my eyes shut. "Ahh!" It doesn't stop, it won't stop. Oh, *fuck.* Oh, goodness. A white-hot blade slices through my arm—at least, that's what it feels like—and Angel rushes forward to gently cup my bandaged face.

"Shhh, sweetness." She peppers my face with soft kisses. "Tell me more about your lack of attraction."

I have to lock my jaw into place so I don't crush my teeth and ruin the position the doctor had them aligned to. Oh, Jesus Christ, the pain shifts to another area, and the agony grows.

"It's nothing," I grit out, unable to open my eyes. "It's just rare—fuck." The blade leaves my skin, no doubt so Ryan can reheat it under the flame. "It's—" I let out a panted breath. "It's pretty much everything or absolutely nothing. It's overwhelming or complete indifference."

I remember the first time Ryan and Angel invited me to their home.

For a solid hour or two once I left their apartment, I was crying my eyes out in my car only because they excited me. They awoke me in a way I haven't ever experienced.

The pain returns, causing my back to arch. I let out a hoarse cry and dig the back of my head into the mattress, muscles clenching, throat and lungs burning.

"Take it for us, brave boy," Ryan murmurs. "What caused the rift between you and your brother?"

Bullying, secrecy, and— "Jesus, Ryan!" I growl. Panting, I try to breathe through the pain, but then a mindfuck joins the party when Angel engulfs my soft cock with her mouth, shucking the ability to breathe out of reach. The shock sears through me at the same pace as the blazing fire.

"I think you mean *Sir*, baby." Ryan grins—the fucking Sadist—into a quick kiss to my nose. "What's your color?"

"Charcoal," I bite out.

Angel giggles with a mouthful of cock, which just *works*. Desire flares up and pumps through my system as if it has its own heartbeat.

"Green," I amend in a groan.

It's a bit of a blur after that. Angel gets me hard and deep-throats me like she was born to suck cock, and Ryan tortures me with a blade of lava. Between bouts of pleasure and immense suffering, they drag truths out of me that I would've wished to keep to myself.

"We were bullied," I moan hoarsely. "The younger siblings more—ahhh, fuck, more so than the rest of us." So I started to intervene wherever I could. I got into trouble with those who picked on my brothers; my grades took a nose dive, my parents were disappointed in me, and I was often called into the principal's office.

I did my best to protect Mark, Seth, and Ted when I failed with the other kids in our family. They didn't matter the same amount when push came to shove, and I could only do so much.

"Please stop," I rasp. Sweat and tears burn in my eyes, the pain continues to battle against the arousal, and the heavy topic I detest with every fiber of my being doesn't belong in the erotic moment. I want it out of here.

"Where were your parents in this mess?" Ryan wonders.

"Getting high on progressive propaganda," I snap. "It wasn't the kids in school or our teachers they lectured, was it? It was me and my siblings. We were the ones who had to fight *their* war." I pant, my abs tensing up. "It doesn't fucking matter what's wrong and right. I'm not stupid. Of course I want people to accept—" A long groan escapes me as Angel's throat squeezes the head of my cock. "Doesn't matter, doesn't matter," I exhale. "I lost my friends who thought it was weird as hell I had three sets of parents, something they insisted on fucking flaunting. Getting angry didn't help. My parents kept saying we were right to live as we chose."

"But it wasn't your choice," Ryan murmurs.

I shake my head, whimpering. Fuck, let the pain end.

My eyes roll back behind closed lids, and Angel redoubles her efforts while Ryan runs another trail of fire along my bicep. I *hear* the sizzling. My balls draw up, tightening, churning and full, and I shudder violently. The tremors don't stop.

"How did you and your brother go from best friends to..." Angel's breathy voice trails off, as if she's unsure of how to phrase the last bit.

"He doesn't know I kept ignorant morons off his back." For heaven's sake, he was just a child. I have four years on him. "It was enough for him to think it wasn't very bad." So he preaches like Mom and Dad do. Love and acceptance, flowers and *fucking* rainbows.

I wanted to prove my dad wrong. Senior year, I worked day and night to get better grades. It was enough to get into a decent college, where I worked even harder. Pre-law, law school; I've been driven to the point of madness. At some point, I suppose I lost sight of the goal. All I know is...I can't ever get behind their way of thinking, and my daughter will never get ostracized for being a "freak."

It's the last part of my life I can explain to Ryan and Angel before I get punched into a time and space where I can't separate what hurts from what's about to get me off. Acting on instinct, I push my cock deeper into Angel's perfect little mouth and throw my head back. My head is swimming, my skin is crawling, and there's a strange rhythm that lulls me deeper into the haze. My breathing picks up on the rhythm to match it. Shallow, rapid puffs of air struggle to fill my lungs.

A sudden chill blankets me, raising goose bumps across my body, and I welcome Ryan's scorching trail of fire. *Give me more.* Almost there. Every sensation travels lower and lower. Murmurs float around me, and then a wave of euphoria washes over me. Time slows down as one of the most intense orgasms is drawn from my body. Yet, it's more. The release is vast on every level. Mental, emotional, physical.

"Oh God," I breathe out.

"That was...fucking beautiful." Ryan's voice. Husky, quiet, and smooth. A voice I've come to love. "Fuck, I miss him."

"He's ours, Daddy." That one, too. Whether she's spitting venom while degrading me or she's giggling in her sweet voice, I adore it.

"We'll have to wait and find out, love."

I poke carefully at the wrap around my bicep. "I wanna see it..." My tongue feels weird. I snort and smile at the sound of myself. "Did you carve 'useless mutt' there or something?"

"Carve," Ryan echoes with a chuckle and a shake of his head. "You're a silly goof when you fly off into subspace, aren't you?"

I wouldn't know, so I shrug lazily and stretch out on the bed. I'm sore everywhere, but the ache is dull and oddly comforting. There's no sharp pain. I think I know what bliss is now.

"Maybe I'm lucky," I drawl.

It certainly feels that way right now. I've got Angel snuggled up against me, asleep, and Ryan's sitting on my other side, back to the wall, and he's force-feeding me chocolate pudding because evidently I need sugar.

I can think of worse ways to spend a night.

"Isn't she mad at me anymore?" I ask quietly.

Ryan glances over at Angel and smirks a little. "Probably, but she's more determined than anything else." Before I can ask about what, he holds a spoon of chocolate pudding and whipped cream in front of my mouth. "Eat."

"Yes, Sir."

He offers a pensive look at that. "One day, I hope with all my heart it'll be Master."

What? I'm sure my expression asks the question. It's getting slightly frustrating to be foggy-brained.

"You want the whole truth?" He sets aside the pudding cup and slides down to lie beside me, elbow propped on the mattress. "We've gotten attached as fuck."

I take a deep breath through my nose and allow myself to take some pleasure from his words. They feel too damn good. "Me, too."

He smiles faintly and brushes his knuckles along my cheek. "You still feelin' floaty?"

"A little." It's fading, though.

He hums and searches my eyes for something. "Learning more about you tonight has been...enlightening. Albeit painful. You've been through a lot."

I'd rather go back to where he says he and Angel have gotten attached to me.

"Don't think too highly of me."

"We don't," he chuckles. "You're quite the fucking douchebag, but...some fall for those idiots, too."

Fall for...

"The rest is pretty easy to figure out," he goes on, pensive again. "You became your folks' opposite. Traditional, structured, *normal.* You reject what society rejects. It's all for your daughter, 'cause you don't want her to go through the same hell you did." Indeed. Some rebel against the word normal; I see it as something to achieve. "I'm gonna be honest with you, subbie. Your family should've protected you and your brothers. I agreed with you when you said it doesn't matter what's right and wrong. They drilled their philosophy into the children who already accepted it, when they should've been there on the front line to face the classmates and the unsupportive adults."

I sigh in contentment. It means so much to me to have him understand that part.

"I'm sensing a but," I murmur.

"Mm." He inclines his head. "Angel and I can't offer you normalcy. We wanna open our relationship to include you—you'd be our equal when we're not playing—but that would make us poly, wouldn't it? We'd want you there as a partner and lover, not a play-thing, and if shit works out, you'd be there one day when our family grows." He's talking about children, and it puts a noose around my neck. Simultaneously, I practically hurt with want. "That includes your daughter, Greg."

I lower my gaze quickly, for fear he'll see the sheer panic that bolts through me at those words. Good fucking grief, I could never expose Abby to this. Not in a million years.

"Look at me, pet." He lifts my chin. "Angel and I aren't your folks. We will raise our kids to be open-minded, and if they get shit for it, we'll be there for them. They won't fight our battles alone."

Nothing short of sitting next to your child in the classroom will guarantee that.

"Lemme ask you something," he says. "What makes you any better than your other family? What are *you* doing to make the world a better place for your daughter? Because...right now, you're giving her what you needed growing up. Her needs could be differ-ent, and one day she might realize she's different, and then what? She's grown up in an abnormally normal home. Maybe she'll be too afraid to open up to you. Maybe she'll fear rejection from her own parents. Or, fuck it, she could be completely *normal*, but some kid she goes to school with isn't, and she'll pick on him or her." With that statement, he sends my thoughts into a tailspin unlike anything else. "So...while I could quite fucking happily kick your folks' asses for not being there for you, you're going to extremes in the opposite direction, and there *is* such a thing as a happy goddamn medium."

———

"Think of what I said, boy."

It's still dark when the cab pulls up outside my world of *normal*.

Funny how I suddenly hate the look of it.

"$42.70, sir."

I wince at the reappearing pain in my arm and pull out my wallet. "How do you still exist with Lyft and Uber around?" I swipe my card and stifle a yawn.

"Well, there're people like you."

"Touché." Stepping out of the car, I rub a kink out of my neck and shut the door.

"Think of what I said, boy."

My house is empty—of more than people. There's no warmth, no sense of belonging, no feeling of rightness.

I used to love coming home.

A glance at the clock in the kitchen tells me it'll be another half hour before Tess is up. She's not the type of person to call off work just because she's at her mother's, so I hope to catch her then.

It's long overdue. I haven't been fair to her in years, though denial has been my form of "ignorance is bliss." I've been so firm in my beliefs... I shake my head. I still don't believe much will change, but I have to be honest and lay all my cards on the table.

Ryan thinks things change then.

"Optimistic fool," I mutter to myself. A pressure is building up in my chest, and it's impossible to shake. I'm *scared*. I've probably been scared for a long time, another thing I've been good at denying. Fear of the unknown, how unoriginal of me. With a heavy sigh, I wander through the house and trudge up the stairs.

I was instructed to wait 'til tomorrow before I could change the wrap around my new scar, but screw it, I want to see Ryan's handiwork.

"What makes you any better than your other family? What are you doing to make the world a better place for your daughter?"

Flicking on the light in the master bath, I get a minor shock at my reflection in the mirror. How on earth have Ryan and Angel been able to *look* at me? The bruise under my eye is dark, angry, and shifting in shades of black and purple. There's some swelling around it. Then the bandages around my damn head... I'm a sad fucking sight.

I carefully remove the borrowed hoodie, and my torso reveals several other bruises. Fainter, lighter, though everything stands out against my pale skin.

I hiss as I slowly peel off the bandage wrap Ryan covered my brand with.

He branded me.

More permanent than a tattoo.

"No, it can't be..." I frown, carefully lifting the soft compress. The wound is red and irritated, but clean so the design stands out.

I crumple in an instant at the sight of it and quickly cover my mouth with my hand. The second glance at the wound cracks my chest open, and part of me can't believe it. Tears spring to my eyes, blurring my vision. He fucking branded me; he gave me the same mark he's given Angel. A downward-facing triangle with the letter Q inside it. *Quinn.*

"Think of what I said, boy. And if you come back here, you've decided you want more. You've treated your wife with the respect she deserves. You've been truthful with her and yourself, and no matter how slowly, you'll be here to give a new relationship an honest chance."

I can't do this anymore, goddammit.

Redressing the wound, I pull myself together and then leave the bathroom. It's time to call Tess. I've reached my breaking point, and all I want right now is to get away from here so I can think clearly. I've lost sight of more than my goals. I've lost sight of who I am.

THE TOUCH OF A SADIST

A BEHIND THE SCENES OUTTAKE

A GLIMPSE

RYAN QUINN

"He's supposed to be with us, Daddy." Angel sniffles and buries her face in the pillow. "It hurts."

It's gonna be a rough day, I can tell.

"I know, baby." And as the pain increases, I grow more determined to take it away from her—if only for a moment. This has never been an issue with the other guys we've played with, and to be honest, it's fucked with my head. If anything, I thought Greg was the man I'd grow the least attached to.

Joke's on me.

There's something about that bastard...that I haven't felt with anyone else, other than Angel.

I shake my head, ridding the thought for now. My girl's in as much pain as I am, and I can do something about hers.

I disappear from our bedroom for a moment to wash up, and then I return with a bottle of oil and two towels.

"Whatever you're planning, I'm not in the mood," she mumbles into the pillow. "Unless it's ice cream and snuggles."

"We can do that after." I kneel on the bed after grabbing one of her vibrators. "Get on your back for me and lose the panties."

She whines.

I smack her tight little ass. "Now, Angel."

"Fiiine. What're we gonna do, *anyway*?"

"You're gonna lie there, and I'm gonna push a limit."

For being a pain-slut, there are a few acts she's terrified of in the non-pleasant way, and we're gonna change that today. It's time.

She cracks one eye open, her lashes thick with tears. "What limit?"

Crawling over to her, I slip a towel underneath her and kiss her softly. "You're gonna take my fist up your pretty little cunt."

Fear fills her eyes. "Um, *no*. Master, please don't—"

"Do you trust me?" I stroke her cheek.

She swallows. "You know I do," she whispers. "I don't like that kind of pain, though."

A faint smile tugs at the corners of my mouth. "Have you ever had it?"

Her brows knit together, and she hugs her exposed body self-consciously.

She's been my biggest addiction, almost since the day we met and she punched me. When she learned I was a Dominant, she grinned with glee and dove right in. She was reawakened by sado-masochism. She's still learning, but then, aren't we all?

"We'll go slow the first time," I promise.

She quirks a brow. "The first time?"

Oh, you'll want more, love.

Taking her mouth with mine, I kiss her deeply and make her forget ever speaking.

I wanna ruin her in the best ways. She's so small and soft in my arms, but there's more underneath. A whole world I'm still exploring after knowing her—loving her—for years.

Today I wanna see her bare her teeth at the pain.

Her fingers tease the skin under my T-shirt, and I back away long enough to yank it over my head and toss it on the floor.

I watch her watch me as I push down my sweats. The lust is

unmistakable, but she's like a skittish animal this morning. She nibbles on her bottom lip, gaze flickering.

Then we're both naked. Kissing her more, I let her hands test the waters. She touches me cautiously, as if we're new to one another. Her breath hitches while I start a trail of kisses down to her tits.

"I'm nervous," she admits.

"Good." I'll take pleasure from it.

There's no way I can do this without getting off first. She'll be too tempting once I begin. Lying down next to her, I pull her close and order her to straddle my face. Her cheeks flush scarlet, which makes me groan. *Fuck, fuck.* She can't do that. It drives me fucking bonkers.

"I want you to suck me off while I tongue-fuck you," I murmur, touching her cheek. "You'll do that for me, right?"

She nods quickly, and I save her from fumbling by flipping her over, eliciting a squeaked giggle from her. Too goddamn adorable. I grin and point to my cock—*get to sucking*—and I hike her leg over my head and curse, getting up close with her sweet pussy.

I squeeze her soft, pert ass and pull her down farther, burying my face in her cunt. She gasps and whimpers as I lick her. I eat her out, kiss her like I'd kiss her mouth. I suck on the smooth lips and swipe my tongue over her clit.

She relaxes. This is us. This is *me.* She trusts me.

A groan rumbles in my chest at the feel of her fingers trying reach around my cock. She takes it slowly at first, licking at me, sucking gently, but once I go a little rougher, she goes to town on me. I ravish her, grazing my teeth over her clit, burying my tongue inside her.

She moans and shudders.

She sucks me like a good little girl I've also turned into an outstanding whore.

"Goddamn." I grunt as I hit her throat.

She responds by sucking me deeper, gagging a little but continuing right away.

I give her ass another solid squeeze and then glide one hand up her back. I cup the back of her head, her silky hair sliding between my fingers. She gags and pulls away enough to gasp for air and tell me she's close.

That's my cue to stop, and I haul her off of me without warning. I throw her down on the mattress and straddle her upper body. Her eyes widen, but she fucking licks her lips.

"There's my whore," I mutter huskily.

She squirms like a bitch in heat, and I fuck her face until I come down her throat.

We roll around on the bed and make out like teenagers, and while I'm momentarily spent, her needs make me hungry for more. She's a sprite. Youthful, sweet.

"I need to come, Daddy," she moans.

I smirk and settle half on top of her, stroking her hip. "Actually, you need to do what I tell you." With a light smack to her thigh, I twist my body and grab the little vibrator and the oil. "Switch it on and keep it on your clit—lowest setting."

Some of her worry is back, but I pay no attention to it. I won't make it a big deal.

Staying beside her, I order her to keep her legs spread, and I kiss her senseless because I fucking need it. The low buzz of the vibrator keeps her wet and needy, and whenever I break a kiss to catch my breath, she tries to follow.

She takes two fingers in her soaked pussy without problems, and a third causes her to gasp and buck her hips.

"Don't come." I graze my teeth along her jawline. "Don't fucking come."

Peering down her flushed body, I eye the bottle of oil resting against her inner thigh. She's wet as fuck, but it'll ease her mind to slick her up more, and I'm gonna need it eventually, anyway.

I go for broke and coat her pussy, letting my fingers get slippery before I push them inside her again.

"Oh," she breathes out.

My cock grows harder along her hip. She nips at my lower lip, and I ease us into a slow, passionate kiss. I finger-fuck her just as slowly. My thumb strokes her impossibly soft folds, my pinkie teasing the spot between her pussy and asshole.

"It stings a little," she confesses, out of breath.

I brush some hair away from her forehead with my free hand and search her eyes.

Pulling out carefully, I push in again, farther than before.

She winces.

"Take it," I whisper. "Take it for me if you can't take it for yourself."

"Why would I take it for myself?" she groans in complaint. "That's stupid."

"It's anything but stupid." I kiss her hard, fucking her sensually with my three fingers, and I'm ready to add a fourth. "It can be drugging to push your own limits."

There's a million things I can say, except it's easier to show her.

I have no intention of going faster for the sake of it, though I think she'll go for this. She has it in her. After applying more oil, I get on top of her, hovering close, making sure she looks me in the eye.

"You can take it," I tell her. She whimpers as I begin to force a fourth finger inside. "Tell me when it hurts."

"It hurts," she pants, squeezing her eyes shut.

"Look at me."

She doesn't.

"Look at me, Angel," I growl. That does it; her eyes flash open again, wide and uncertain. "Before this is over, you're gonna come with my entire fist inside you." She sucks in a breath at that, my words affecting her. "When you think you can't handle anymore, gnash your teeth together and turn pain into your bitch. You're stronger than you think."

I can tell she's doing her best to relax, and I praise her for it while I resume stretching her pussy. In slow, measured thrusts, I allow her to adjust, and I let her turn the vibrator on to the next setting.

"Good girl," I whisper, looking down to where I'm fucking her. "Fuck—such an exquisite little slut." I smirk at her gasp. "You love hearing me say that, don't you?"

She gulps and nods quickly, emitting a drawn-out moan when I press my thumb down on the vibrator. "Say it again," she pleads.

"You know that's not how it works," I chuckle. "I'll tell you whatever the fuck I want, not what you wanna hear."

She arches into me, her muscles relaxing to take more of me, and I wriggle deeper. At the same time, she wraps her free hand around my cock. Good. Fucking. God.

"What do you want to tell me, Daddy?"

I grin, keeping my gaze on her pussy. Does she know I'm almost at my knuckles?

How would Greg take my fist?

"Ouch." She squirms.

"Take it," I repeat, my eyes flashing to hers. "Show me you."

She glares at me. "Go fuck yourself."

I groan and crash my mouth to hers, pushing my tongue into her mouth. She cries out and bucks into me, to which I slip deeper until the curve of my thumb gets in the way.

"Half my hand is inside you," I say, breathing heavily into the kiss. "You don't know how fucking sexy it is."

"I can take it," she pants. "Do it—more. Fist me."

She's so fucking determined right now, and few things are more beautiful. Slipping out slowly, I stroke her stretched hole softly and bunch together my fingers as much as I can. Then I slide them deeper and deeper inside, until she stiffens.

"Fuck, fuck," she snarls. I grin in admiration as she struggles with herself. "Okay—" She nods and clenches her jaw. "More."

There's a light sheen of sweat on her forehead, from exertion, from pushing her own limits. She's amazing.

I push her. She pushes herself.

Deeper.

Past the widest part of my hand.

Fuck me, she's warm—so tight, soft, slick.

Filled.

A single tear rolls down her temple.

"Such a good girl," I whisper. "I love you, baby." I kiss that tear away, tasting the salty pain she's taken for both of us. "Keep looking at me." She nods jerkily, and I shift slowly inside her, stroking parts no one has reached before. "Highest setting." I dip my chin at the vibrator. "You're gonna come so fucking hard."

There's doubt in her eyes, though she does as told. The vibrator buzzes more powerfully, and her pussy constricts, at which she flinches in pain. At the same time, she whimpers, her nipples hardening into buds.

"You're gonna come," I tell her again. "You're going to come around my hand because you can't fucking help yourself. Then Daddy's gonna reward you." She moans, getting what she asked for —what I wanted to tell her. "Do you want that? Want Daddy to push his cock deep inside and breed his little girl?"

"Oh, fuck!" she gasps and reaches for my cock. "*Please.*"

"Filthy girl," I grunt, thrusting into her hand.

She starts to convulse, her eyes falling closed and her fingers moving the vibrator in fast circles. She moans and squirms. The pain is gone. She's fucking flying, and I bat away her hand from my cock to focus better. Holy fuck, she's bared now. Begging for my cock in her, pleading for me to drench her, aching for Daddy to put a baby in her.

Right before she screams, I carefully close my hand to make a fist.

Exposed and not holding anything back, she lets the pleasure run through her, her pussy squeezing me from the inside.

I curse and shift my weight enough so I can rub my cock and slowly slip my hand out of her. The motions seem to intensify her orgasm. She lets out a breathless sob, then collapses when my hand is free.

I slick up my cock with her, push away the bottle of oil, and get in between her thighs. Oil and her sweet juices seep out of her already contracting opening, and I'll remember this image until the day I die.

I shove my cock all the way in and set a brutal pace where I fuck her into the mattress.

Angel's still flying high. "Ohhh—*hnnn*, Daddy, come..." She tosses the vibrator aside and caresses herself, cups her tits, and writhes in euphoria.

Then I'm gone, too.

My climax hits me on every level.

It leaves my mind honest and unfiltered, and I can't help but wonder... How would it be if Greg could share this with us?

COMFORTING TOUCH

CHAPTER 1

CHELSEA DUNN

It's been six days since I set foot inside Switch. Six days since some drunk asshole barged into the club—Mark Cooper's brother—and got handsy with Kayla. Six days of settling in to my apartment, focusing on my new job that Nicholas graciously offered me, and six days of dodging Kayla's calls.

Six days since I saw Rio Kelly again—for the first time in ten years.

That bastard has only gotten sexier with age. His features are as sharp as I remember them, with his black, short but unruly hair a stark contrast to his pale skin, emerald green eyes that can cast a pretty fucking vicious glare, and a voice that is both warm and cutting.

Nicholas and Kayla told me they've dropped my name around Rio a few times but without reaction. However, there was no mistaking the look he gave me almost a week ago. It was brief, including a double take followed by shock...and then the same glower he'd given me ten years ago when he caught me lying about my age.

He remembers me, though apparently not fondly.

Then again, he didn't seem very fond of me a decade ago, either.

Squaring my shoulders, I pass the lobby and enter the main club, scanning the area for Master Dante and his sub, Gretchen.

I spot them near the demo stage in the back, and as instructed, I'm wearing the same leather corset dress Gretchen is.

Fridays at Switch are, as I've learned, sometimes for public demos, and Dante's gonna use Gretchen and me for a rope bondage scene. It's crowded as fuck, and Gretchen has warned me that her Master is particularly strict when he does demos.

Or as Kayla's called him, "sooo mother*ducking* sadistic."

Cutie patootie.

Dante *is* a Sadist, but I have masochistic tendencies, so there ya go, and playing with him is mind-blowing. He knows what he's doing. As he should, considering he's a well-known rigger of Japanese rope bondage and often holds workshops and events with Gretchen around the country.

I maneuver myself through the crowd, and then I hear my name being called. Turning around, I try to see if it was Kayla or something, but no one I recognize is there. So I continue—

And walk right into a solid body.

"Oh, sh—" Not my voice.

"I'm sorry!" I say hurriedly at the two hands gripping my arms to steady me. The first thing I notice is a leather cuff with the Switch logo, which only Nicholas's closest wear. The second thing I notice is the firm muscles of a chest beneath my palms. I lift my face, my eyes growing large.

Shit, double shit, triple shit.

Rio. It's *Rio's* hands on me, and I suddenly feel all the heat he's giving off. He's so close. So close. For a quick second, I swear he brings me closer, but it doesn't last.

"Are you okay?" Rio asks impatiently.

I think I nod. I'm a little busy being mortified and flustered.

I knew it had been a pipe dream when I wished I wouldn't run into him. Of-fucking-course, I ended up doing it literally.

"I'm sorry," I repeat.

His jaw clenches. "It's fine." It's like he just now realizes he's still holding my arms, so he lets go as if he's afraid to catch something. Stepping aside, he motions for me to go on.

I flush bright red, confused and embarrassed. What have I done to get that reaction? Sure, I was a pushy little shit when we first met, but is he really holding that against me, still?

Evidently.

I duck my head and get out of his sight, trying to find the right mind-set again.

"Chelsea!"

Sigh. This time I hear Kayla's voice clearly, and I turn to see her at the bar with Nicholas and...I think his name is Brayden. Mark Cooper's sub.

I wave and force a smile, then point toward Dante and Gretchen to indicate I don't have time to talk right now. In response, Kayla sticks out her tongue at me, which earns her a harsh tug of her ponytail by Nicholas.

I grin to myself and continue through the crowd, knowing I gotta answer to Kayla soon enough. I haven't dodged her *completely*, but I've certainly ignored her questions about Rio, and the meddler that is Kayla Brandon won't stand for that shit. When we lived together back in New York, she got all up in my business the second I wasn't smiling.

Right after she left, I was relieved. For about a week. Then I started missing her like crazy, and it's nice to be in the same place as her again. She's the only family I have.

"There you are!" Gretchen beams at me as I emerge from a group of people waiting for the demo to begin. "I worried you weren't going to make it."

Yeah, well, I've noticed that Dante's little redhead worries about everything. She's called me countless times this week, only to make sure I wasn't forgetting about tonight.

Pot, meet kettle.

I know, I know. I was just as worried last week before coming here. I even woke up Kayla in the middle of the night once because I couldn't wait 'til morning to tell her how nervous I was about seeing Rio.

Turns out, I had every right to be nervous.

"Don't give yourself grays, hon. I told you I'd be here." I smirk and kiss Gretchen's freckled cheek before turning to Dante, who's focused on his rope kit on the platform. "Good evening, Sir," I say politely, stepping up on the three-foot high stage. "Anything I can help you with?"

I *need* something to do. If only to occupy my mind.

He runs a hand over his head, his buzzed, blond hair appearing blue and silver under the club's strobe lights. Every shadow cast on his face makes him look more menacing. I can see what Kayla means—why she's scared of him—but has she actually spoken to Dante? Doubtful. He might be strict and demanding, but he's also polite, genuine, and friendly.

"Hmm..." He looks out over the dance floor, pensive. I get a brief smile, and he nudges my bicep with his elbow. "You can get us water, pet. Put it on my tab. Then I want you naked. Hurry back."

"Yes, Sir." I nod dutifully and then head toward the bar. On the way, I think about whether I need to pee or not, 'cause nothing kills a scene faster than cutting the ropes because a sub forgot to use the bathroom before. But it's all good. This ain't my first rodeo.

When I reach the bar, I gotta grin at Kayla. There's nothing she can say to me now. Not when Nicholas has put a ball gag on her. The light blue ball even matches her dress. Christ.

She scowls at me before pouting at Nicholas, who lets out a laugh and takes a sip of his drink. Brayden, seated next to him, seems just as amused.

"Has she been bad, Mr. Ford?" I ask, leaning against the bar. I don't know their rules yet, so I figure it's safest to address him instead of her.

"She's interrupted Dante's scenes in the past. This is a precaution." He slides me an easy smile. "I'm also on babysitting duty—"

"I'm not a baby, Sir." Brayden gapes at Nicholas.

"Did I give you permission to speak, boy?" Nicholas cocks a brow at him, to which Brayden blushes and shrinks in his seat. "Thought not." Nicholas faces me again. "Mark's at home with a sick Evangeline, so Brayden is here to watch your scene and take notes for his Master. Worrying about Kayla's mouth is a trouble I don't need with an extra sub to look after."

"That's funny. Though, I'm sorry to hear about Evangeline." I tilt my head at Kayla and catch her wiping drool from her chin. "You're so cute, pipsqueak. Not so easy to meddle when you can't talk, huh?" I fail to withhold my mirth, although Dante's sharp whistle across the floor does the trick.

Shit, double shit, triple shit.

Kayla shoots me a smug look.

"I take it the demo's starting." Nicholas checks his watch.

I quickly order three bottles of water and put it on Dante's tab, and then I haul ass.

This night has really started off with a fucking bang, hasn't it?

Gretchen's glaring at me as I return, and Dante looks like he has a cane in mind for me later.

"I thought I told you to hurry, subbie." Dante points to the platform. "Get up there."

"I'm very sorry, Sir." I lower my gaze to the floor and obey his command, stepping up on the stage again. As always when I've disrespected a Dom, a rock settles in my stomach, and my chest tightens.

This is why I prefer not to play casually, 'cause it leaves me unsettled. I can be released so easily; whereas if I'm in a committed arrangement with contracts signed, I know my Master wants me even when I screw up.

Dante follows me onto the platform and grasps my chin, forcing me to look up at him. "You can be sorry later. Right now, I need your focus on my rope. You've followed my instructions, yes?"

"Yes, Sir." Like I've said, this ain't my first rodeo. I'm staying hydrated, no joint issues, I ate two hours ago, and I warmed up before I left my apartment.

"Good." He dips his chin at my dress. "Strip." Then he focuses on Gretchen, who asks him about the attending monitors tonight. In reply, Dante says, "Simon and Rio are wearing the DM cuffs. Now shush, love."

Blah.

"Yes, Master," Gretchen answers as the music fades.

It doesn't stop completely, but the DJ has lowered the volume so it's only a background noise.

With spotlights directed at me, it's almost impossible to see anything other than shadows and silhouettes, though that doesn't mean my traitorous eyes don't attempt to find Rio in the crowd. He would stick out in his six-foot-four-or-something glory.

I squint at the figure standing near the small DJ booth.

Stop it, you masochist.

Noticing how tense I am, I blow out a breath and try to clear my head. *You're in a scene. No need to fuck up again.* I chant those words internally as I strip down to my birthday suit. My hair brushes against my butt, which reminds me to put it in a high ponytail using the rubber band around my left wrist. As for the rubber bracelets that are a new accessory at Switch—at least, new for *me*—I hand them to Dante when he comes to inspect me.

The bright colors of the bracelets ruin the scene, he's said.

He cups my smooth pussy and quirks a brow at me. "Head in the game, pet. I want this nice and wet for a knot."

I shiver, the wheels in my head finally slowing down. Head in the game. Head in the game... "Thank you, Sir," I say just above a whisper.

Dante nods curtly and kisses my forehead then turns to the expectant observers. He speaks in a cool and collected voice about what he's gonna show them. He introduces his subs, talks about safety measures and bondage aftercare. Then he begins with Gretchen and explains the body harness he's tying and what kind of rope he uses.

I tune out the words and let his voice lull me into a relaxed state. After all, this is what I crave most in life. Serving, being restricted, and taken to new heights. People I know in the lifestyle think I only want to submit in the bedroom, but that's so far from the truth. It's just easier to cower away from love and that level of trust and stick to limited D/s relationships.

My biggest dream is to find someone I can trust enough to both hurt me and comfort me.

As it is, I can only accept pain. Not comfort. It's way too intimate and always leaves me exposed.

A gust of air ghosts along my naked torso when Dante comes to a stop in front of me. My nipples constrict, and I watch him watch me as he prepares a bundle of fifty feet of linen hemp rope for my body.

A loose tie around my neck, knots down my front, knuckles brushing over my skin, the solid rope sliding between my legs, the harness tightening with each knot, the rope nearly *vibrating* as Dante works it around my upper body... God, I love it.

This kind of hemp is smooth and heavy on my skin—and deliciously encompassing.

"Now this is a real bondage bunny." Dante chuckles warmly, adjusting one of the knots over my clit. He lingers and rubs the rope softly over my wet flesh, and I shudder violently, swaying in place. "You good, pet?"

He must've taken the swaying for something other than mmmm-give-me-more-please. "So good," I murmur dazedly, "Sir."

There's a low rumble of amusement disrupting the bubble I'm in.

Dante seems to notice my line of thought and brings me back into the scene with a few circles to my clit and smooth strokes over my breasts. And soon enough, the harness is in place.

Gretchen and I are positioned close together, back to back. Her warmth meets mine, and Dante instructs us to thread our fingers together. Then he takes more rope and incorporates new ties with our harnesses.

Every now and then, he checks our bindings. He makes sure we stay vocal, yada-yada-yada, it's important to speak up about any numbness, any pain, any pinching. I only feel like I'm floating. Heat blooms up as little burns every time he cinches the rope, causing it to tighten.

Dante's focus and voice and rope and experience send me further away from reality. He knows this about me. Bondage is the one thing that pushes me into subspace.

I get hyperaware of his every touch, his commands, and the rope. When he tells me to touch each finger to my thumb to check mobility and numbness, I obey without thinking about it. I give straight answers, no hesitation, yet I feel removed from it all. Like I'm not really there.

And it's not his face I see.

"You should take care of yourself, little rebel." He looms over me, standing so close I can taste his minty breath, inhale his rich scent, and feel his body heat. "There's only one of you."

I melt, I melt, I melt.

Fuck, that's wrong.

Rio.

"Chelsea."

My eyes flash open, and Dante smooths a thumb over the spot between my eyebrows. Was I frowning?

Being sent back to the night I met Rio shakes me to my core. I don't want my stupid crush, I don't want any flashbacks, and I wish it wasn't what he told me in that club that changed everything for me.

"I'm okay, Sir," I say confidently, though the scene is ruined for me.

I haven't been pining for Rio all these years, but he's crossed my mind every now and then as the *one who could've been* man. He triggered too much for me back in the day, making him impossible to forget. He may have been—or still is—a stranger, but he was also the first one who genuinely gave a shit about me.

He introduced me to this world, this lifestyle, even if it hadn't been his intention. He'd meant it as a threat, as a reason for me to run far, far away from him.

In that club, I'd been all over him. Flirting, giggling, swearing I wasn't underage... How stupid was I? A sixteen-year-old can't fucking pass as a twenty-one-year-old. At least *I* couldn't.

"You don't want to know what I usually do with brats who lie and disrespect me."
"Tell me."

I squeeze my eyes shut for a single second and refuse to let that memory continue. *Rope, rope, think about Dante's rope.*

When I open my eyes again, I meet Dante's calculating gaze. He studies me; my mouth firms in determination. *I'm here, I'll serve you, I can do it; I just won't get much out of it.* This time.

"We'll talk about this later, bunny," he murmurs for only me to hear. Then he takes my mouth in a hard kiss as he ties my thigh together with Gretchen's.

He leaves me breathless and my body wanting.

If only my head were in it, too.

From a spectator's view, the scene continues flawlessly, and Gretchen and I behave like the good subs we are. No one can see my headspace, anyway. They don't know the mere thought of Rio Kelly rattles me. Especially now when we're in the same state, city, and fetish club.

Remind me why I left New York, again?

Sigh.

CHAPTER 2

An hour after the scene has ended, I'm back in my corset dress, and Dante is satisfied with the aftercare. I've told him bits and pieces about why I couldn't get into the scene like I had done last time we played, which I think is why he ultimately lets me go. The Sadist even guilt-tripped me into telling him.

"How can I be a good Dom to you if I don't know what upsets you in a scene?"

Bastard.

But bastard or not, I'm quick to accept the invitation to a play party next weekend. Maybe a little fun away from Switch will help.

A friend of Dante's is hosting it, and the theme is Ancient Rome.

Now I can expect Gretchen to call me every day about my costume.

Finding a slave dress shouldn't be too hard, toots.

The music is loud and the dance floor is packed with people dancing, grinding, engaging in foreplay—oh, screw that. Literally. One Domme has her sub giving her oral, and another pair is full-on fucking.

My mouth quirks up a bit in amusement, and I walk over to the bar where I know Kayla's waiting for me. I've decided to simply take all her questions and answer as best as I can. Then we can move on with our lives.

I find her alone, though I catch the bartender keeping an eye on her. And she's too fucking cute, trying to slip the end of a straw into her gagged mouth.

"Trouble, pipsqueak?" I cram into the spot next to her, ignoring the scoff from someone behind me. "Maybe your Sprite can wait until Nicholas has taken off the gag."

She mumbles something, only to roll her eyes since I obviously can't hear what she's saying.

"Where's Brayden?"

More mumbling and some gesturing for the exit. I'm guessing Brayden's gone home already. Then she huffs and hops off her stool before she grabs my hand and begins dragging me in that direction.

"Kayla!" the bartender yells. "You're not allowed to leave my sight!"

She points upward, so I assume we're going up the stairs. Nicholas's office is there, I remember. It's where I said a quick see-ya-later to a half-asleep Kayla last week.

Speaking of her...

She tries to talk again, and she gestures wildly in order to make sense.

She doesn't.

"Ugh! Weh-weh-wahh." At last, she gives up.

I snicker. "Was that supposed to be 'never mind,' Kayla?"

She nods sullenly as we reach the landing and wipes her mouth. Next, she places a finger over it, indicating...well, that we're probably about to eavesdrop.

I narrow my eyes at her. "Who're we listening in on?"

She blinks innocently, which is total bullshit. A part of me is already annoyed 'cause I know she wouldn't be this urgent unless it was about Rio.

I hiss. "Is Nicholas in there with Rio?"

Leaving her coyness—and patience, I guess—behind, she snarls and pushes me toward the door.

Part annoyed...part fucking intrigued...it doesn't take much for me to glue half my face to the door, and Kayla follows with glee sparking up her light blues.

"...would've told you sooner," Nicholas is saying, chuckling, "had you only been answering your phone."

Kayla shoots me a superior look, as if to say I'm not the only one immature enough to dodge calls.

"I still can't believe it." Rio sounds...tired. Tired and aggravated. "It's fucking with my head." To hear him speak again is indescribable. There's no forgetting that accent. Mostly American, the nondescript kind we get on TV, but with a hint of Australian and Irish. "Nick, I...I don't want her here."

I recoil as if I've been slapped and take a couple steps back.

It *feels* like I've been slapped.

I'm not arrogant, but I'm not stupid, either. Of course he's talking about me.

Kayla appears irritated, hopefully on my behalf, but then she widens her eyes and quickly waves me forward again. She points to the door.

So I sigh and listen again, even though I'd rather go home and eat ice cream until I pass out.

"She's the reason you left the scene, isn't she?"

What? Why would—

"No," Rio growls.

"Easy, tiger," I mutter.

Nicholas laughs. "I'm sorry, my friend, but this is hilarious. And sad. We both are. You know, I went through this exact same thing with Amand—"

"She's not the bloody reason," Rio replies angrily. "I don't know what the fuck happened back then, but..." He lets out another growl, and a thump follows.

"No need to take out your anger on my furniture," Nicholas says mildly. *"I won't leave Liam watching over Kayla much longer, so unless there's something else...?"*

I arch a brow at Kayla. *You're in trouble, girl.*

She shrugs, although there's a little wince, too.

"So she's staying," Rio states flatly. *"She lives here now."*

Sorry to disappoint, asshole.

"Yes. Chelsea is staying. And you better respect her, Rio." The warning in Nicholas's voice makes me a little misty-eyed. He's looking out for me. The fondness in Kayla's eyes tells me she loves that about her fiancé. *"You're one of my closest friends, but if you refuse to tell me why her being here is so upsetting, I can't help you."*

It's clear that Rio won't talk, so I nudge Kayla back and nod at the stairs.

Time to go home.

I wake up the next morning to four texts from Kayla.

Liam ratted me out. My butt hurts, Chelsea. It hurts so much! ~Kayla

I smirk, knowing very well that she would've confessed to her eavesdropping sooner or later. She's a brat, but she would never go behind her Daddy's back without owning up to it and taking the consequences.

Btw, I found out that Rio is hosting a play party next weekend. That means you can come to the club with me in case you don't want to see him, 'cause Nicholas and I won't be at the party. ~Kayla

"Oh, fuck me," I groan, falling back against the pillows again.

When Dante had said a "friend of his in the community" was hosting the party, I hadn't thought it might be Rio.

I gotta get out of that one, and I sincerely doubt he knows Dante plans on bringing *me* as a plus-two.

My butt still hurts. I hate the belt! ~Kayla

"That's what you get, hon." I sigh and scroll down to the latest one.

Don't forget the munch on Wednesday! ~Kayla

Good thing the munch is being held like two minutes away from me. I don't have a car, and I've yet to figure out the public transportation crap. That's one of the reasons I wanted to live in the Castro—the gay district. It's close to everything I need, and I don't mind living cramped. It's the only way to live in New York anyway —unless you roll in major dough—so I'm used to it.

Putting my phone aside, I stare up at the ceiling, hearing my roommates rummaging around outside. Three roommates, all guys, all gay, all too fucking cheery in the morning.

Jase is a thirty-year-old sous chef, and I doubt he *ever* sleeps. He works, works, works. Robby develops video games and is the only one younger than me. I can always find him on the couch yelling stuff at whatever game he's playing. And Tristan is...odd. He's quiet, shy—twenty-six like me—and works at a library. But he brings home booty every damn night, and it's always a different man.

As for Jase and Robby...I'm pretty sure they're together, but they're subtle about it. Perhaps it's new—I don't know. It's cute to watch them slide each other sly smiles, though.

Dragging my ass outta bed, I survey my small room with a tired smile. I've always lived light, so I only had four boxes to unpack. And aside from food and other necessities, the only thing I've purchased was a full-length mirror. A bed, a cushy chair, and a dresser in place of a nightstand came with the room.

I grab a ratty T-shirt from the hardwood floor and inspect the faint marks on my body from last night in the mirror before I pull the top over my head. Then I sneak out of the room and freshen up in the bathroom between Jase's room and mine.

One of the first things I noticed when I moved in with these guys was that they're very casual and down-to-earth. Tristan is the only one who always walks around fully clothed, but Jase and Robby showed me that breakfast is devoured in underwear or PJs. Lounging in front of the TV also happens with fewer clothes on.

So it's not the first time I'm joining them in the kitchen in only a T-shirt and panties and they see redness streaking my thighs.

"Mornin', rope girl." Jase eyes my legs then winks and returns to the stove. "Did you do it yourself or was it someone else this time?"

He's referring to the couple occasions I've occupied my time with self-bondage.

"Nah, she was at the club last night," Robby says, blowing steam away from his coffee mug. "Didn't you see the dress she was wearing when she left?"

I grin and steal a piece of toast from his plate. "You should join me next time."

He shudders and pretends to look horrified.

Tristan adjusts his glasses. "I had a boyfriend once who was into BDSM. It's certainly an interesting lifestyle."

"I'm all for a nice spanking every now and then, but..." Robby makes a face.

"Good to know," Jase mutters under his breath, grinning at the eggs he's making.

They're so doing it.

"Anyway..." Being new in the group, I wanna make a good impression, so I change the topic to weekly tasks. "I'm off tonight. Want me to take care of the grocery shopping this week?" Everyone has wish lists on the fridge, and we leave money for our food to cover what we want. Then when someone has time, he—or she!— grabs the money and the lists and goes to the store.

"I can go with you. I'm off, too," Tristan offers. "But I thought you started that other job tonight. You said February first, didn't you?"

I nod. "I was supposed to, but the owner asked me to come on Wednesday instead." Which I'm a little bummed about. It's a small gig, singing in a bar two nights a week, but Wednesdays and Thursdays mean fewer people than Saturdays and Sundays.

Then again, it leaves my weekends free for more Switch.

"Where are you singing, again?" Jase asks.

"André's place," Robby says with a pointed look. At my confused expression, he goes on. "Babe, if you're worried about the crowd, don't be."

Jase nods and smirks. "Wednesday is *Lovers' Night*." He snickers a little. "If you sing Adele songs like you mentioned, you'll be golden. The place is always packed on Wednesdays."

Huh. Well, then! Guess I won't mope anymore about that.

CHAPTER 3

However, Wednesday arrives too quickly, and I *wish* I could be mopey. Mopey is easy. Instead, I'm nervous as fuck and not good at hiding it as I meet up with Kayla, Evangeline, Brayden, and a few others for this week's subbie munch.

I'm introduced to Gabriella and Dylan—two Littles I met too briefly last week—and Gretchen arrives with three friends shortly after I've sat down with my cappuccino.

"I can't wait to see you tonight!" Kayla exclaims, grabbing my arm to give it a shake in excitement. I'm used to it though, so I made sure I wasn't holding my coffee. "Can you come, too?" She faces Evangeline and Brayden. "Chelsea is *so* good."

"Shut it." I grin and let out a nervous breath.

"She sings like Adele," Kayla goes on, and I pinch her hand.

"I sing her songs," I correct her. "And songs by artists in that genre."

Kayla shakes her head. "Don't listen to her." It's like I'm not even here.

"I'm game if we can drag Mark out," Evangeline says with a smile. Brayden opens his mouth to say something, but she cuts him off. "Don't start, *mon ange*. You're a guy, so you wouldn't possibly understand."

"Understand what?" Kayla and Gabriella ask at the same time.

"When boys get sick." Evangeline rolls her eyes. "Mark came down with whatever bug I had. And let it be known that I had an ear infection too, whereas he only had a fever and couldn't hold anything in." I chuckle, having a feeling I know where this is going. "But it's been two days since the fever broke, and he's eating just fine, yet he acts as if he's dying."

Kayla holds up a hand. "Say no more, sweetie. When Nicholas is sick, I have to remind myself that *I'm* the Little. Because it's definitely not clear."

I nod, remembering that from my last Dom. "A papercut turns them into babies, but a chopped-off arm is something they'll 'get over.'"

"Exactly!" Evangeline cries out. "It would take nothing short of a heart attack for both Brayden and Mark to go to the hospital. But when a man-cold strikes? Jeesh."

"I'm sitting *right* here," Brayden says.

Evangeline pouts and pats his cheek. "I know."

Kayla giggles.

"I'm on your side, buddy," Dylan offers solemnly.

Brayden bumps his fist.

"Well, you're a guy," Gabriella tells Dylan.

Dylan widens his eyes. "Thank you for noticin', darlin'. I've been wondering." He smirks and rests an arm along the back of her chair. "Hopefully our Daddies will let us play together again soon."

I tilt my head, curious about Gabriella's blush. I know barely anything about her, but the engagement ring on her finger says a thing or two. And I know flirting when I see it. Dylan's definitely flirting.

I'm guessing they're poly.

"I didn't know you and Cade play with others, as well," Kayla notes curiously.

Something dims in Dylan's eyes. "Neither did I, but he's made that very clear." *Oh.* He wants more, but this Cade guy doesn't? "It's all good, though." He fakes cheeriness. "Not being exclusive means I get invited to parties like the one Master Kelly is hosting this weekend."

Oh, fuck my life. I still haven't gathered the courage to call Dante and say I don't want to be there.

Maybe because you actually do wanna go?

No, I don't. I'm not that masochistic...

Out of the corner of my eye, I see that the new topic has caught Gretchen's attention.

"What!" Kayla drops her jaw. "You're *going*? Nicholas and I were invited too, but we declined. We don't share, and apparently Rio is all about that."

Ouch. Nothing like crushing on a man you're not compatible with.

Dylan shrugs, playing it off as easy peasy. "Cade and I share. So..."

"I'm going, too," I admit, which *should* be a lie. "Dante invited me."

"It's gonna be so fun," Gretchen gushes.

"Good Lord, I need a drink. Information overload." Kayla rubs her temples before huffing a breath and facing Dylan. "Cade is working at Switch both Friday and Saturday, so who are you going with?"

"Mistress Judy and her sub." Dylan shifts in his seat, not entirely comfortable.

Kayla picks up on that and narrows her eyes. "Does Cade know?"

"I'm gonna tell him," he replies defensively. "He'll have no issue with it."

"Mmhmm." Kayla looks smug. "I'm sure." Then, outta nowhere, she turns and whacks my arm. "*You.* Why didn't you tell me you're going?"

Okay, that's it. I love my nosy little friend, but I have limits. "I think I'll have to talk to Nicholas about your fuckin' attitude." I arch a brow. "You do know I'm allowed to choose *when* I tell you things, right?"

She flushes and ducks her head. "Crap, you're right. I'm sorry. I'll back down."

"It's all right, hon." I hug her to me and kiss the side of her head. "I know you get excited and want everybody to settle down and *have a bunch of babies*."

Almost everyone cracks up at that, so I assume they've heard about Kayla's matchmaking ways, too. Even when she was single, her focus was on finding the perfect match for her friends.

I'll back down, Kayla told me earlier.

I nearly snort.

If backing down meant inviting Rio—who's here with a fucking date!—to my gig, I fear finding out what *full speed ahead* would entail.

As I wrap up another love song—a beautiful Duffy tune—I kick off my heels and attach the mic to the stand. The spotlight keeps me from seeing the faces of the people in the crowd, although I was able to spot Kayla, Nicholas, Brayden, Evangeline, and Mark earlier.

Rio, too. And the woman he's here with.

Though, unlike Kayla and the others who are occupying one of the round tables in front of the low stage, Rio and Whatsherface are standing at the end of the bar.

Feel free to leave.

After the munch earlier today, I went home and ended up bitching to Jase and Robby about Rio. They didn't deserve my ranting, but I couldn't help it. I'm frustrated, confused, hurt, and pissed. Dangerous combination for any woman.

Once I was done, Jase told me I better put on my big-girl panties and confront Rio. It's the only way to get answers as to why he treats me like I stomped on his sandcastle. So my big-girl panties are on, and I'm ready to ask what his problem with me is, but I can't say seeing him here with a date makes me wanna approach him all sweet and polite.

In fact, defiance surges forward to the point where I decide to change the last song. The house band behind me already has the sheet music because I'm supposed to sing it for Ladies' Night tomorrow, but with the lyrics in mind, I want it now. Right fucking now.

I thank my little audience and announce the final song for the evening. What with it being Lovers' Night and all, I figure some explainin' is necessary. "How about we dedicate the last song to the frogs we kissed before meeting our princes and princesses." I grin into the hot spotlight, chuckles from the people giving me a boost of confidence, and wipe sweat off the back of my neck. Turning around, I murmur the song to the drummer, guitarist, and bass player, and they nod in understanding.

As the first notes fill the bar, I swear I can hear Kayla and Evangeline laughing. Maybe they've heard the song before and know where my mind is at.

The song is upbeat and fun, and it completely annihilates the poor attempts of a guy who flirts by being pompous and dry.

"*Thanks for the offer...but I'm not going home with you.*" I bring the mic over to the rockabilly-hot guitarist. "*Trust me, mister, the attitude ain't cool.*"

He grins and sings the next words with me. "*Now who's the fool?*" Then he winks, and I blow him a kiss before returning to the front of the stage.

And my reason for picking the damn song tonight... "*Congrats on your success and all that jazz.*" I make sure to face the bar, and I fire off a playful pistol shot in Rio's direction. "*But I'm not blind, and I see you're just an ass.*"

Take that, almighty Master.

I'm in the tiny room backstage struggling to get out of my even tinier black dress when Kayla and Evangeline barge in.

"You were awesome!" Kayla hugs me tightly, and she realizes very quickly I'm in need of a shower. "Oh..." She grimaces and smiles at the same time and breaks the hug. "Gets hot with those lights on stage, huh?"

"Little bit," I chuckle. "Glad you enjoyed the gig, though."

"Girl, your voice is out of this world," Evangeline says.

I'm no good with compliments regarding my singing, so I grin and wave it off. Then I refocus on getting outta my dress, and Kayla grabs my white tank top from a chair.

"I can't wait to go home and jump into the shower." I put on the top, then get crackin' with my skinny jeans. "And I'm *starving*."

"You're not going to have a drink with us first?" Kayla gives me the puppy-dog look she pulls on Nicholas.

I snort and slip my feet into my sneakers. "Not after *someone* invited Rio here tonight." *Who. Brought. A. Damn. Date.* "Seriously, Kayla. How could you?"

I may or may not be jealous of his date, which is totally irrational.

"Pay up." Kayla makes a gimme motion at Evangeline. "Did I not tell you she was gonna blame me for Rio being here?" I frown in confusion as Kayla faces me with a smug look. "For your information, nobody *invited* him. Nicholas told him where we were going. That's it."

"That..." *doesn't make sense.* "Rio couldn't have known I was singing—that I was here."

After he told Nicholas he specifically didn't want me anywhere near him, Rio wouldn't seek me out. That's batshit crazy right there.

Kayla shrugs and pockets ten bucks from Evangeline. "Maybe he wants to talk to you. He just ordered a new beer when we left our table to come in here."

But, but, but!

I don't know what to make of this.

Evangeline hums and lifts a brow in Kayla's direction. "Then again, would he bring his slave if he wanted to talk to Chelsea?"

My stomach drops. "He has a slave?"

Considering Rio's reputation in the community, it's not that much of a surprise, but according to Kayla, he's been in a rut or something. Only playing every now and then, mostly volunteering as a DM, and never scening with a sub more than once or twice.

"I'm still working on that one." Kayla scowls into the air and bites her thumbnail. "Miranda's one of the waitresses—"

"So the bitch has a name." I gather my things and shove them into my bag.

Kayla ignores my crap and goes on. "She used to have the biggest crush on Mark—"

It's Evangeline's turn to interrupt. "Mine." She sneers, and I pull a sweater over my head. "I'd put Master's cock in a cage if it weren't for...you know, the beating he'd give me."

"I've heard you like that, though." I wink.

"Okay, you two have *got* to stop cutting me off!" Kayla huffs. "*Anyway.* Her last relationship with a Dom was a nonsexual one, so perhaps that's Rio's deal. I'll do some more digging." A firm nod.

As much as I admire her willingness to help, I'm not sure it's worth the hassle. I'm gonna be living here, so I'm still set on talking to Rio, but I can catch him when he's alone. Right now I'm only tired and itching to shower and eat my body weight in ice cream.

"Don't get yourself in trouble." I shoulder my bag and kiss her forehead. "I'm gonna head out, but you guys have fun."

"We can't convince you to stick around?" Evangeline looks concerned.

I smile and give her a brief hug. "Nah. Say hi to your men for me, but I wanna go home."

Probably sensing I can't be swayed, they let me leave, and I track down the bar's owner. He praises my performance and says, as he hands me my money, that he's looking forward to making me a regular for Wednesdays and Thursdays.

His words cause some of the tightness in my body to ease up, and maybe my private life is a little uprooted at the moment, but I'm doing pretty damn well work-wise. I gotta thank Nicholas again for my position at one of his clubs, 'cause that's definitely the paycheck that lets me live where I live.

"You'll be a local star in no time, darling." André kisses my cheeks and grabs my shoulders, a smirk on his face. "I want your two nights here in writing, because once I promote you, bitches all over the Castro will want to hire you for gigs."

I chuckle self-consciously, tongue in cheek. "Is it against policy to call my boss a drama queen?"

"Certainly!" His laughter tells otherwise. "Although, I can forgive you if you manage to bring Tristan down here sometime."

Oh, I'm *sure*. What is it with that quiet roommate of mine? Yeah, he's hot, but he's so...shy, introverted, and prim. Maybe he gives magic blow jobs or has an enchanted butt. Who knows?

Once I've said goodbye to André, I make my way down the hallway toward the back exit. The kitchen has closed for the night, so it's only me back here. I'm guessing the guys from the band are either having drinks or have already gone home.

With a push to the door, I step out into the night, and I suck in a breath as the February cold hits me.

Why didn't I bring a jacket?

An alley cat rushes past me toward one of the two Dumpsters.

"Chelsea?"

CHAPTER 4

"Jesus!" I whip to the right and squint at the mouth of the alley as the figure of a man moves closer. And my mind has already registered the owner of that voice. "What the fuck're you doin' hea'?" I didn't mean to spit it out like that, but color me fucking shocked.

It was merely a few days ago Rio told Nicholas he didn't want me here, and now... Not only did he come to my gig tonight, but he hunts me down in the alley outside the bar?

"Still the hostile New Yorker I remember," he says in a mild voice. He emerges from the darkness and comes to a stop a few feet away from me.

Too damn beautiful. Really, Rio Kelly is a *beautiful* man. All edges and contrasts, but oh, so smooth.

My heart skips a beat, and I kick myself internally for losing my shit for even a second.

I'm not sixteen anymore.

"I wasn't hostile back then," I tell him irritably. "I just wanted the D, and you didn't deliver."

His brows rise, nearly touching the edge of his black beanie.

Unlike me, he's dressed properly in a nice jacket, scarf, beanie, and gloves. "The D?"

I roll my eyes and adjust my bag. "Your dick, genius."

Now his eyes narrow. "You're lucky we're not in the club right now, little girl—"

"Don't pull that shit on me," I warn, getting heated in an instant. "Ten years ago, I had to push you for half an eternity to tell me that you cane brats who disrespect your Domly ass. But now you can whip out the Dom card ten seconds after seeing me again? I don't think so."

I don't want her here. I don't want her here. I don't want her here.

Being so close to Rio right this minute makes his words in Nicholas's office cut me even deeper. Masking the hurt with rage is easy, though.

"I see." He's displeased, to say the least. Not that I give a fuck. I haven't done anything to deserve his treatment. Or rather, avoidance. "In that case, may I ask what I have done to offend you? Because I sincerely hope you don't speak to everyone like this."

"Thank you so much for your concern." My voice drips with sarcasm. "But you don't have to worry about how I talk to my friends—or strangers. And..." I release a breath, the mist of it mingling with Rio's. "As for offending me, no, not in person." I've never been one to hold back or beat around the bush. "However, you did a fine job of it in your buddy's office last weekend."

It dawns on him quickly exactly what I'm referring to, and I can see the wheels turning. He's probably going through what I could've heard. His eyes grow wide, his lips part. But before he can even think about speaking, I get all my frustrations out into the open.

"Look, when I saw you at Switch after Mark's brother raised hell in there, I only wanted to thank you," I say. "I was in a shitty place when you and I met the first time, and you helped me set a few things straight. But with the reaction I got...?" I doubt I'll ever forget the glare Rio gave me. "Not only would I be dead if looks could kill, but you stormed out as if your ass caught fire."

"Seeing you there—in a *fetish* club, Chelsea..." He pinches the bridge of his nose.

"Yeah, I know. Last person you wanted to see in there. I got that."

His eyes flash to mine at that, his gaze intense and merciless. "What I *want* has very little to do with things. You were only a child. Bloody fuckin' hell, I was afraid you were at Switch for all the wrong reasons. I had no idea BDSM was actually for you, and considering what I told you in New York, you must admit that I didn't give you a nice introduction."

Yeah, there's no forgetting his words.

"Tell me," I'd demanded over and over. *"I wanna know what you do with those who don't respect you."* I'd pushed him too far, aggravated him enough, and in the end, he spat out a few sentences that made something inside me snap.

"I put them over my knee." He'd towered over me. *"I cane them until they cry with remorse, until they're reduced into a blubbering mess that begs to be fucked into a good little girl again, until my marks burn red."*

Most young women would've run away screaming at that, and believe me, part of me did, too. But most don't have my upbringing. And, truth be told, it wasn't mainly what he told me that made me look into BDSM. It was the air of dominance and consistency he oozed. There's structure in Rio's entire being, and sixteen-year-old me wanted that so much she couldn't even describe it.

Regardless of it being for wrong reasons or right, back then I was ready to attach myself to him like a Band-Aid simply because I could tell he was a rock.

I'd lived day-to-day, rarely knew where I'd be spending the next night, had the wrong type of friends, and was under the impression that men were meal tickets and women were holes to fuck.

Enter *this* guy. Solid, takes no bullshit, and didn't try to get into my pants. Instead he *lectured* me. He told me to take care of myself because there's only one of me.

Feeling very much like that lost little girl again, in need of so much structure and comfort, I hug myself and try to fend off the cold as well as the emotions I've suppressed for a long time.

Comfort. *Scoff.* I've never been able to trust anyone enough to find real comfort in them. The mere thought of letting my guard down that much... No way.

I'm not in the mood to go into all the things that made Rio's effect on me back then so life-altering. I could tell him a short anecdote about my aunt's strict ways that have also played their part in my life, but it seems I can't form the words. Once more, Rio leaves me vulnerable and unsettled, and revealing anything would only make it worse.

"The introduction was enough for me," I settle for. "Now, are you gonna tell me why you're here when you don't even want me in San Francisco?"

That earns me a quick look of impatience. "Again, it's not about what I want. I was shocked to see you there. But, I do admit I didn't handle things very well." To his credit, he does appear contrite. However, the damage has already been done. "I am sure there's a story behind your reasons for seeking out this lifestyle—something I may have triggered—and I have a story, too. It explains why I've acted the way I have, and perhaps we can talk—"

"Why the sudden change?" I ask abruptly.

I can't imagine sharing my story one day, especially not the part where I basically stalked his Facebook and found out about Switch that way. Heh, if only everyone knew my crush on him is the reason I sent Kayla to Switch, resulting in her meeting Nicholas.

"I spoke to Dante," he answers, and I nod and stare at my feet. "I found out you're coming to my play party this Saturday, and it made me realize that this is something I can't hide from. You're part of this community now, so I might as well get over my issues and make the best of the situation."

And what exactly are his *issues*?

What is the *situation*?

"I apologize, Chelsea," he murmurs, causing me to look up at him. "Listening in on my *private* conversation with Nick notwithstanding..." Insert a Domly brow cocked. "I'm sorry for what you heard. You didn't deserve that, and in retrospect, I would have phrased myself differently. Differently enough to change the meaning." Vague, but I guess he's not ready to divulge. "Nick and Mark said they'd be here to watch you sing tonight, and I wanted to see for myself. I also—" He pauses and frowns then mutters a curse and begins unbuttoning his jacket. "I also came to start over, I suppose. I want us to be civil. Here." He moves closer with the intention of wrapping his jacket around me.

I step back, a protest ready to be unleashed.

He doesn't let me. "Don't argue with me," he says warningly. "We may not be in the club, but I don't give a fuck."

I huff, stunned and irritated and stupidly giddy, as he eases the warm jacket over my shoulders and shifts even closer to button it. Button by button. *Sigh.*

"It's a good thing I'm used to this behavior," I quip.

He hums. "I was curious about that. You were a natural during the demo with Dante and Gretchen. I take it you're fairly experienced?"

"I dove in as soon as I was eighteen," I reply. Not for lack of trying before that, but good Doms evidently don't associate with underage subs. "It's been a life of servitude ever since." I give him a little smirk.

"Is that a fact?" He smiles back, finished with the jacket. "So, what do you say—our first and second encounters could've gone better. Should we go for a third?"

I think I'm still shocked at this turn of events, so my nod is a little slow, and I'm feeling a whole lot dazed. A few seconds later, though, I do find my words. "I'd like that," I say, clearing my throat. "And I'm sorry for acting like a bitch earlier."

"Water under the bridge." He extends a hand. "Rio Kelly."

I can't help but grin as I grasp his gloved hand in a shake. "Chelsea Dunn. I'm looking forward to your party on Saturday, Sir."

Even in the dim glow of the lamp above the door, the darkening of Rio's eyes is unmistakable. "Let's see if you say the same after the auction."

"Auction?" Heat rises to my cheeks, and I wonder if I've missed something. With the theme being Ancient Rome, I obviously figured out it's slaves versus Masters, but what else could there be?

"We're starting off with a slave auction, naturally." Amusement trickles into Rio's voice. "Didn't Dante tell you?"

I wince internally. "Gretchen sent me an email titled 'party specifics.' I should probably read that." In my defense, I was planning on reading it tomorrow.

"Probably," he deadpans. "You better pray I don't buy you as one of my house slaves. Don't think I've forgotten your gesture at me on stage tonight."

Shit, double shit, triple shit.

I called him an ass, didn't I?

"What happened to water under the bridge?"

He grins. "I choose not to include that little remark."

Wonderful.

Rio insists I wear his jacket home and that I simply bring it on Saturday.

I sleep in that jacket every night until I wake up Saturday morning.

These past few days have been a blur of work, dissecting Rio's new civility—and did he really leave the lifestyle at one point?—with Kayla and Evangeline, learning the rules for the party, purchasing my costume, having coffee with Gretchen, and listening to Kayla's gossip about some of Switch's members. Apparently Cade—excuse me, Mr. Kingsley—is furious with Dylan for attending with Mistress Judy tonight, Gabriella's Daddy Dom is being a douchenozzle for whatever reason, Miranda is under Rio's care for a punishment we know too little about, and Mark's brother is refusing to face his family by taking his wife and daughter on an impromptu vacation to Aruba.

There's some drama up in hea'.

"*Chelsea!*" Robby hollers from the living room.

"Yeah?" My mouth is full of bobby pins, so I pry open my door and repeat myself before returning to the mirror in my room.

"Jase left us food before he went out. Want some?" His voice comes closer until he's standing in my doorway with wide eyes. "What the fuck are you wearing?"

I grin and remove a bobby pin where I've measured the next leather cord to go. My too-long hair is in two low pigtails, and I'm tying the two together in the back with several thin, brown leather cords. They match my brown gladiator sandals.

Though, I assume Robby's referring to my slave dress. Sheer, flimsy fabric in a muted purple color is wrapped loosely around my body, revealing pretty much everything. Including the henna-like tattoos I had done yesterday. In intricate designs, they follow from my left calf up to my ribcage where they tease my breast before continuing up over my shoulder.

Gretchen will look the same, although her dress is greenish instead.

"This is what slaves wore in Ancient Rome," I say with a shrug. "Well, house slaves that were used for sex, anyway."

He hums and leans against the doorway. "Even the ink? Which I hope is temporary."

I chuckle. "Of course it's temporary. And you're right. The henna tattoos are more Egyptian and Asian, but it fits with our roles for the evening. Dante is the barbarian who kidnapped us from a foreign land in the East and brought us to Rome." All done with my hair, I face Robby fully and curtsy, bowing my head. "How do I look, Dominus?"

He smirks when I straighten. "Like I could be a little het for you."

I crack up.

"Anyway...*slave*, did you want food?"

"No, thank you." I smile and put on a snug black trench coat. "We're eating at the party." We might even spend the night. Dante said it was a possibility, and apparently Rio has "slave quarters" in his basement. "Don't wait up, by the way." I cross my fingers and wink at him.

"Someone's gonna get *laaaid*." He laughs and leaves me to it. "Have fun and be safe!" he calls over his shoulder.

CHAPTER 5

W e arrive at Rio's house outside the city just as a catering
van and some other truck leave.

"Of course he's hired party planners," Dante says, amused, as
he parks in the large driveway. Looks like we're one of the first ones
to arrive. Unless Rio has four cars. "You're in for a treat, Chelsea."
He smiles at me in the rearview. "Rio's play parties are something
else. Only Cade's would compete."

I eye the massive house resting on a grassy hill, his land
surrounded by a tall wrought-iron fence. What I assume opens up
to the backyard is hidden as the hill dips, and all I can see are the
tips of glowing heaters and a few trees with lanterns in them.

"Damn," I mumble, more than a little intimidated. The house is
modern, lots of windows and straight lines, and must've cost a
fortune. "He's gotta be loaded, right?"

"Like a Rockefeller." Gretchen snorts. "He bought this house
right after his fiancée died, but he's barely lived in it." Kayla's told
me about that. The fiancée died in a car accident some five years
ago. Gretchen's eyes light up. "Wait 'til you see his basement. Oh,
my God."

"He has his own dungeon there," Dante supplies, and I nod in understanding. "We've borrowed it a few times while he's been on missions with Doctors Without Borders. In fact, I think others have played there more than he has. Such a shame." He opens the door and steps out, and we follow suit.

The asphalt sparkles with frost, and I'm thankful it hasn't snowed. We were given the option to change here, but Dante said if it was possible, he wanted us to change before. The only one who needs a minute to fix his costume is Dante. He's wearing a Roman tunic but tucked it into a pair of jeans since he knew he'd be stopping for gas on the way.

"Do you girls need any reminders of the protocol?" He eases into Master mode.

"No, Sir," I reply as Gretchen says, "No, Master."

"Good." He reveals two brown leather collars and fastens them around our necks. I shiver, and not just from the cold. "What will you call me when we step inside that house?"

"Dominus," we answer.

He nods and attaches a rusty-looking chain to the rings on our collars. The authenticity only makes it more enticing. "And a Mistress?"

"Domina," we say.

"Good slaves. I have your limits for the evening right here." He pats the pocket of his jacket. "I'll give them to your new owners after the auction."

Grabbing our bags in one hand and holding the end of the chain in the other, he takes the lead up the path toward the house.

Anticipation surges through me at the thought of tonight's events. Approximately ten Tops have been invited, all of them bringing one to three bottoms. In addition, each Top has been given a certain amount of fake currency, which is to be used during the auction. Afterward, there are different tasks that will need to be completed throughout the night. Meaning, it's important they use their money wisely and invest in as many slaves as they can in order to finish the tasks well and quickly.

Dante has barely lifted his finger from the doorbell before Miranda—naked as the day she was born—opens the door, averting her eyes to the ground once she's seen who it is.

"Welcome to the *domus* of Dominus Kelly," she says softly and opens the door wider. "The guests are gathering in the atrium out back. Please allow me to show you the way."

Atrium?

Some jealousy lingers, and I can't help but sneer at Miranda as I pass her. Like Gretchen, she's a redhead and incredibly gorgeous.

"Where do we put our belongings?" Dante asks curtly. I sneak a glance at him, a little confused when I see he's practically glaring at her. "I hope you won't be in charge of them...*thief.*"

Gretchen and I exchange a brief look, and I wonder if that's Miranda's role or something. Thief? How odd.

"No, Dominus." Miranda's voice cracks, and she gestures down a hall to our left. "Everything will be stored safely behind locked doors."

Dante grunts then orders us to stay here while he follows Miranda down the hall. "You can remove your shoes, slaves," he adds over his shoulder.

"That was weird," Gretchen whispers as we obey his command. "I don't remember seeing thief as one of the parts."

Same here. Gretchen and I are foreigners, kidnapped by Dante, and our specialties lie in housework, sexual pleasure, and mending clothes and rope. Our weakness is our language barrier; we're not supposed to understand our owner's words very well. Dylan, I recall, is an injured gladiator, now being sold off as a common slave. He's been instructed not to use his right foot much. Another sub is to play the part of a former teacher who got his tongue cut off for teaching his Domina's children the wrong things, and therefore he's not allowed to speak tonight.

The list goes on.

No thief, though. Either we missed that one, or something else is going on.

The confusion grows when Dante returns. Miranda scurries toward the back of the house with tears streaking her cheeks, but no explanation is offered.

Dante grabs the leash again, and we follow Miranda past the large living room and out onto a patio. *Wow.* A huge tent covers the area, and now I see what Miranda meant by atrium. Heaters, richly colored fabrics, low sofas, cushions, and small fire pits make up the framework, and a rectangular waterhole sits in the middle. It's shallow with blossoms and candles swimming in the water. Just like I've seen in TV shows and documentaries about Ancient Rome.

It also reminds me of the Chamber—the new playroom added at Switch.

A couple subs are kneeling near the little pool while three Doms are chatting in a corner. There, two more subs are making sure their owners have drinks and snacks.

Rio is one of the Masters, and he rises from his seat as he spots Dante. The Tops are all wearing pretty much the same outfit, a Roman tunic in various colors, with or without metal ornaments. Dante's tunic is green to match Gretchen's dress, and he only has a simple rope around his midsection. Rio...oh, fuck me twice. Please. He looks primal in his dark red outfit with some kind of armor over his chest, cuffs on his wrists, a leather strap tied to his bicep, and a short-stranded flogger attached to his belt.

I'd hit that.

I stifle my grin and lower my gaze.

"Dante, my friend." Rio and Dante greet each other warmly and talk about this and that as if Gretchen and I aren't here. And it works; it changes my mind-set. I sink into my submission, the place I love the most.

"A shame Mark didn't join us tonight," Dante comments as the doorbell rings.

Miranda hurries out.

"Aye," Rio chuckles. "He's never had a problem sharing before."

Dante huffs a laugh. "That's what love does to some."

Me, included. Sharing is fun on occasion, but when I'm in a committed relationship, I have a rule that turns me into a hypocrite. Sharing my Master with a male sub is hot because we can offer the Dom different things. But sharing him with another woman would turn me into an insecure mess. I honestly don't know how Gretchen can handle it. Not only that, but she loves it. She and Dante are perfect for each other, their love and bond so strong.

"Yeah," Rio replies quietly, almost as an afterthought.

The silence that follows doesn't last long. Miranda comes back, this time with six or seven guests, and shortly after, the doorbell rings a final time. Over thirty guests fill up the patio nicely, and everyone finds a seat as Rio takes a stand in the middle.

Gretchen and I kneel on the wooden floor next to Dante.

"It's been a long time since I hosted regular play parties," Rio says, and a few Doms holler in agreement. Rio grins. "No dramas, mates. I'm getting too old to hike through jungles with too few supplies and too many rebels, anyway. I hope to make this a quarterly event, at least. Jeremy, you requested a university theme—perhaps for the next party we'll have a bunch of students and professors running around here."

It's definitely more than just the Doms exclaiming their approval this time, though the subs pipe down quickly.

University theme... Heh. Would Rio turn rooms into lecture halls? *Hot.* Maybe the dean himself would roam the halls and make sure no student was left behind.

"But let's focus on this party first, shall we?" Rio lets out a whistle, summoning Miranda. "Tell the kitchen slaves to start bringing out dinner." He faces his guests again. "In the meantime, we have an auction to attend. Every Dominus and Domina have received the list of tasks for the evening, as well as the strengths and weaknesses of our slaves. Keep that in mind when you make your bids."

Dylan is in the first group that gets called to the middle. A DM from Switch—Master Hill, I think—stands up and receives the bids, slave by slave.

Dante bids on Mistress Judy's sub, Elysia, but not high enough to win. Rio bids on her too, though it appears it's only to raise the cost and cause the final buyer to lose more money.

In the end, a Dom whose name I don't know buys her.

Dylan is next, and Rio's quick to make a decent bid. At Dylan's subtle eye-roll, it dawns on me that Rio might be bidding on him as a favor to Cade.

"Fifteen," Jeremy bids.

"Twenty." Rio smiles.

It goes on like that until Dylan is Rio's for twice that much.

I sit close enough to hear what he murmurs in Dylan's ear. "Don't roll your eyes at me ever again, slave. Yes, Cade asked me to buy you, but don't you worry. Play your cards right, and I just might arrange so you get that ass full of cock. Your Daddy only wanted a say in who gets to use you."

Umph. That begs the question...is Rio straight? Bi? Watching him fuck Dylan would be sexy.

"Understood, Dominus." Dylan ducks his head, his cheeks red.

In the next round, Gretchen is sold off to Master Hill. Mistress Judy buys two boys.

"You're up." Dante releases the chain from my collar.

I exhale and join three other subs in the middle. And like with the others before us, Master Hill takes care of introductions, which is followed by a low murmur from the bidders who compare our strengths and weaknesses on the cards they have.

A petite brunette next to me is first, and she's sold after two Doms almost argue over her.

"And here we have a beautiful little blonde," Master Hill says, motioning for me to turn around. *Little* blonde? I'm five foot six, dammit. "Long, thick hair to grab on to." He gives my leather-bound hair a tug. "Experienced with rope and pleasing a Dominus's cock. But...foreign. Doesn't understand our language very well."

"Ten," Dante offers with a smirk.

"Fifteen," another one says gruffly.

I'd rather not go with him! First, I don't know his name. Second, I've seen him use a single tail.

"Twenty," Dante outbids.

"Forty-five." *Rio*. His smooth voice silences everyone else.

My pulse quickens. He warned me, said I better pray he doesn't buy me as his house slave, but how can I not want this?

"Sold—to Dominus Kelly."

I look helplessly to Master Hill, given the role I have to play, and then to Rio, who smiles darkly and crooks a finger at me. *Come*.

Dante slides over my card of limits to Rio, and I walk around two "kitchen slaves," who I assume are waitresses from Switch or something, as they bring in trays packed with food.

"Kneel." Rio taps two fingers to the floor near where he's sitting on a low couch. I tilt my head at Dylan, and he nods at the floor where he's kneeling, too.

Mirroring his position, I kneel down and sit back on my heels, my gaze firmly glued to the ground.

"Such pretty slaves." Rio cups our faces and makes us look up. Behind me, the auction continues with the last group while Rio inspects his new wares. "I hope you'll prove to be useful, too." He sits back as he's served with wine and food, though his eyes never leave me or Dylan. "I think I want you both naked. Strip."

I make it my thing to look to Dylan for instructions since I'm not supposed to understand English. So when he stands up to remove the leather piece covering his privates, I take the hint to do the same. Rio nods at me in approval.

The wispy fabric falls from my body, but instead of cooling down, I feel hotter with Rio's predatory gaze on me.

I want him to like what he sees. I want him to see a grown

woman, not the sixteen-year-old girl he met in New York ten years ago.

"Fucking flawless," he murmurs, leaning close to slide a hand up my thigh. A shiver runs through me as he traces the designs of the henna tattoo. "Come here." With a single pull, he has me down on his lap.

I freeze momentarily. Fuck, this is new. My hands flatten against the armor across his chest, and he tugs me even closer. One hand on my right butt cheek, the other cupping my left elbow.

"No game, Chelsea," he whispers in my ear. "I need to know if this is okay, that I bought you. The correct response ends with 'Master Rio.'"

He's giving me a choice.

I nod jerkily, willing my breathing to even out. "It's more than okay, Master—" Before I can voice his name, he pinches my ass hard enough for me to gasp.

His eyes spark with something I can't decipher. "Good girl. You've pleased me."

Swoon.

Dinner passes in a haze of decadence. Wine, wandering hands, the finest meat, salads, laughter and conversation among the Tops, fine cheeses, pasta, servitude, and teasing drops of juice from berries and fruit.

Rio decides when Dylan and I eat, and every now and then, he feeds us from his hand. In return, we make sure his plate and cup stay filled.

"I believe they're sending out invitations within a week or two," Rio tells Master Hill, who was wondering about Nicholas and Kayla's plans. "Their closest will be invited down to the wedding in Mexico, and the rest to the ceremony at Switch shortly after their return." He holds out his fruit plate to me, and I'm quick to fill it with grapes, sliced pears, and plums.

"Definitely a feast to look forward to." Mistress Judy raises her glass.

They toast to Nicholas and his little one before moving on to the next topic. Entertainment. They want something tantalizing to watch while the kitchen slaves clear the dinner and make room for dessert.

"I'm happy to volunteer one of my slaves." Jeremy orders a male sub to stand up and then turns to Rio. "How about your gorgeous Chelsea?"

The exhibitionist in me gets a thrill at the prospect, but I don't even know the sub in question, and...dammit, I want Rio!

"A fine idea," Rio replies with a tight smile, "but I'm afraid I need her assistance on a surprise I have for all of you." He begins to rise. "In fact, we'll go prepare that right now. Slave," he addresses Dylan, "you stay here and talk to no one."

"Yes, Dominus."

Rio nods and gestures for me to follow him.

CHAPTER 6

Keeping my head bowed, I follow Rio into the house.

"We're going to get a cross from the basement." He stops at a door in the foyer, opening it to reveal a staircase. "Have you ever been crucified?"

I open my mouth to answer, but then I remember I'm not supposed to understand everything.

Rio looks back at me and grins.

The bastard's testing me.

"Cross, Dominus?"

He chuckles and descends the stairs. I follow and stop waiting for a reply; it's obviously not coming. Instead, I scan my surroundings, the glossy, black concrete floor, red-painted walls, heavy wooden doors leading to God knows what. One has a barred hatch in the middle with the sign "Cell" above it. Another two have the signs "Dormitory," which I think might be the slave quarters.

How friggin' big is this basement? It feels like it's as big as the house, with hallways and locked doors everywhere. Due to the faint light from sconces along the walls, I can't even see the end of some hallways.

"Since your English isn't good, I suppose I can say whatever I want," Rio muses. "For instance, I told myself earlier not to bid on you today."

What game is he playing?

I narrow my eyes at his back.

"But then you got here, and..." He sighs, slowing down. Then stops and unlocks a door. "Looking like a damn sin."

Heat pools in my gut.

Rather than opening the door, he abandons it and comes to a stop right in front of me. A few steps and he has me backed into the cold wall behind me. So close. Closer, still. Until his armored ribcage brushes against my breasts.

"It would be so easy," he rumbles in a low voice as his hands trail up my arms, "to take you right here, right now." My knees nearly buckle. "I've thought about it many times." And there goes my breath. "I've wondered what that sweet cunt of yours would taste like, how it would feel to fuck it."

"Oh my God," I whimper breathlessly. My mind swims with images of us together. Him owning me, using my body for his pleasure, controlling me...

He lifts my chin. "I assume that reaction was to my close proximity and not my *words*, slave girl. Hmm?"

I can't speak even if I wanted to. He's reduced me to a mess of need, and I'm beyond ready to beg. At this point, I'll take anything. Anything to ease the ache between my legs and snuff out my thoughts. Anything to please him, serve him, and make him want more of me.

He stares at me so intently that my body starts shaking. My vision blurs, as if I'm about to burst.

Maybe I am.

"To hell with it," he mutters, and then his mouth is on mine. A thousand emotions unleash with a snap, pummeling through me as forcefully as he kisses me. For ten years, I've fantasized about this, and nothing comes close to reality. The taste of him, feeling his power, surrendering to it.

Locking my arms around his neck, I kiss him back as hard and deep as I can. He groans and picks me up, allowing me to wrap my legs around him. *Jesus Christ, yes.* He's hard and big under the thin fabric of his costume, and if we continue this much longer, I'm gonna leave a damn spot.

"I want you on me like a leech tonight," he says, breathing heavily. In between words, he kisses, nibbles, and sucks at my flesh. "Worship, obey, and serve me. The correct answer is 'Yes, Master.'"

Not Master *Rio*? In the communities I've been involved in, it's what Doms usually make subs call them—title and name—unless there's ownership involved—*Who cares! Answer him, fool!*

"Yes, Master." I moan as he presses his cock against my pussy. "*Yesss.*"

Rio curses and stills our movements. Forehead to forehead, the only sound our panting.

"Fuck, you tempt me," he breathes out.

I search his eyes, looking for things that are probably only there in my dreams.

All I want is a chance.

I swallow my nerves and exhale shakily. "Please don't avoid me after this. Don't write me off."

He's holding back, I can tell. Maybe it has to do with me, maybe it doesn't, but there's certainly something.

His gaze softens, and he kisses the spot between my eyebrows before releasing me. "It's not about me writing *you* off. But if you wish to talk after tonight, we'll arrange something. Okay?"

"Yes..." What do I call him now? It's getting a bit confusing.

Rio notices. He smirks faintly and taps my nose. "Dominus, my foreign slave."

Pity. "Yes, Dominus."

That was only the beginning of what turns into one of the most erotic play parties I've attended. The tasks we perform turn it into a real competition with lots of fun and playfulness, but every act is laden with sex, dominance, and submission.

After the first four tasks have been completed, I've lost count of the number of orgasms I've heard and seen.

None for me and Dylan so far, though.

"One more before I present my surprise," Rio declares.

"I could use some rest." Mistress Judy laughs, having just won the last round in which the goal was to represent as many fetishes in one scene as possible. To everyone's amazement, she and her two sub boys managed to include sixteen fetishes in a single oral scene. Among them were kitten play, CBT, orgasm control, dollification, and edging.

Rio, Dylan, and I finished in second place with twelve fetishes. And Dylan got a mouthful of Rio's cock. Lucky bastard. Hopefully I can be the one to please our Dominus next time.

"Soon, dear Judy." Rio winks at her then turns to Dylan and me. The three of us huddle together, and Rio explains the next contest. "Time for you to prove your worth, Chelsea. I'm going to tie Dylan up, and I need you to assist me with the rope." As the last word leaves his mouth, the kitchen slaves exit the house with unmarked paper boxes.

They place the boxes around the waterhole and remove the lids, revealing bundles of rope that are so tangled that it looks as if it's gonna take an eternity to sort them out.

My faked confusion at the language delays us a few seconds, but my mind is already busy weeding out the serious competition from the easy. Dante is obviously going to be difficult to beat, as is Gretchen. A few others are also experienced in rope bondage, but, then again, I doubt *anyone* is used to untangling clusterfucks like this. If anything, riggers and rope enthusiasts take care of their rope.

Still, eager to please Rio, I hurry over to the water and grab one of the boxes.

I kneel down where Rio is positioning Dylan on one of the couches. Nearest to us, Elysia is only getting the three-ply jute more tangled, which happens when you don't let the rope untwist itself. Though, it doesn't take a bondage fan to figure that one out.

Spotting four knotted ends, I conclude it's two pieces of rope, and I work as quickly as I can to untangle one before I tackle the other. Each Top has a sub positioned for a hogtie; they're on their stomachs, knees bent, ankles crossing in the air, and arms resting along their sides, waiting to be tied behind their backs.

"Rio, one might wonder what beef you have with rope." Dante sends him a mock-glare that a few laugh at. "Talk about waste."

"Collateral damage," Rio chuckles, "and well worth it." He gives me a smoldering glance before he smacks Dylan's butt. "Especially when I have these two slaves to play with."

In the end, I manage to untangle the mess first, and I learn that Rio is skilled with rope, too. Which obviously leads to more fantasies about him. We win that round, though all I can think of is being restrained by him.

Then it's time for Rio's surprise I'm so curious about. The cross we carried up from the basement earlier isn't X-shaped like a St. Andrew's cross. It's...well, it's of the Christian variety, and Rio did joke about crucifixion earlier.

"Simon, I need your help," Rio tells Master Hill, and the two check the hooks the cross is fastened to on the wall of the house near the door. Next, Rio summons a scared-looking Miranda.

"What the hell is going on?" Dylan whispers to me.

I shake my head, at a loss. Fuck if I know.

"Can anyone tell me the corporal punishment for slaves in Ancient Rome?" Rio asks casually as he and Master Hill suspend Miranda on the cross.

Dante smirks. "Crucifixion."

"Indeed." Rio's own smirk is sinister.

They construct a quick harness drawn between Miranda's

biceps, chest, and shoulders, and the same between her thighs and midsection. Lastly, they shackle her wrists and ankles.

"Miranda's done something very wrong, and she's being punished for it." Rio faces his guests. "Nicholas and I are both in charge of her at the moment, and some of you know what she's done."

I catch Dante's nod, to which Gretchen and I seek each other out and frown, confused.

"For the rest of the night, she will serve as entertainment." Rio waves a hand at the note Master Hill is attaching to the cross. "Anyone who's up to torture a little thief, please feel free to step up at any time during the evening. As you will see on this list, torture includes degradation, pain—do not break her skin—mild face-slapping, humiliation, needle play, forced orgasms, and electro-play."

"Jesus," I mumble, horrified for Miranda. What the fuck could she have done to deserve a punishment so severe? They keep calling her thief, and I'm getting worried it's not a game at all.

While Master Hill sets up a bunch of toys and implements on a small table next to the cross, Rio asks what color she is, and I'm stunned to hear her say "Green." I know we all have our kinks, but Miranda doesn't appear to be a pain slut or a fan of being called nasty things. For Christ's sake, she's shaking and tearing up already.

Jealousy or not, subs stick together, dammit.

"What a treat." Jeremy rubs his hands together, looking more sadistic than Kayla could ever accuse Dante of being. "This will be fun."

Rio offers Miranda a disinterested glance. "By all means. I, personally, wouldn't touch her with a ten-foot pole if I had a choice. She should count herself lucky Nicholas and I bother with her at all."

"This is killing my mood," Dylan mutters for only me to hear.

"Mmhmm," I agree.

Dylan and I spoke too quickly.

With a vibrator attached to Miranda's pussy, her cries of pleasure put us right back in party mode. Granted, that pleasure will be short-lived; after three or four orgasms, it's gonna be hell for her, but it's enough to relax every slave at the party for now.

The Masters and Mistresses use this time to distract us thoroughly. More tasks, more sex, more laughter, more wine, more good-natured ribbing between the Tops.

I return to worshiping Rio every chance I get.

While he sits back and talks to a couple Doms and Dommes, I slide off the low sofa and make my way between his legs. I rub his calves and kiss his thighs, gaining approval when Rio shifts his costume higher and exposes himself more. *God.* He has the sexiest thighs, muscular and strong. I'm caged by him, and a shiver of pure bliss runs down my spine as I realize I want this spot so badly. I want my place to be at Rio's feet. Permanently.

It might still be only a crush, but I want to try. Already, I'm certain it'd be too damn easy to fall head over heels for him.

Pretty stupid even to try if you know he's into open relationships, huh?

Shut up.

Rio sighs contentedly as Dylan starts massaging his shoulders, Rio's armor having been taken off hours ago. And I want to elicit sounds like that from him too, so I lower my head again and kiss the inside of his thighs. His cock begins to tent the fabric of his Roman tunic, even more so when I inch close enough to smell his arousal.

My mouth waters, and I look up at him with the question written all over my face.

His jaw clenches at the same time as the corners of his mouth curve up. I feel his fingers brushing down my cheek, chin, and throat. His eyes follow every movement those long digits make. Then he reveals his cock and retrieves a condom, rolling it on with one hand.

I knew this would happen; it's a play party, and safety comes first. Dylan got the same treatment, of course. Still, I can't help but feel a small pang of disappointment. I would've loved to taste him without the damn rubber.

"I'm not so sure," I hear him murmur. He offers a subtle nod to me, and I lower my head to take him in. *Finally.* I close my eyes and lavish him with my tongue, gentle grazes with my teeth, and eager sucks. He groans quietly and caresses my cheek. "Chelsea?"

I flick my gaze to his as I swipe my tongue along the underside of his hard cock.

"Fuck." His lips part with a labored breath before he schools his features again. "Domina Judy thinks you're avoiding her question as part of your character's inability to understand the language."

I frown and slow down, sliding Mistress Judy a glance. She asked me a question?

Guess I've been too busy focusing on Rio.

Oops?

"That's what I thought." He catches my attention again, and unless I've got my wires crossed, he's incredibly pleased. But I'm clueless as to why. "Keep sucking, my little slave."

All my focus is on him, and I obey immediately. I lose myself in the moment, getting drunk on the pleasure I give him. Every time he tenses and curses and breathes faster and loses his composure, my insides turn liquid with warmth and satisfaction.

After a while though, I can sense a change in his mood. I look up at him to see a pensive expression, and then he gently halts Dylan's hands on his shoulders. Right after, Rio stills my movements as well, and I ease away to see what's wrong.

I think it's Dylan. He looks a little lost.

Rio speaks to him, too quietly for me to hear, and a minute later, he gets up and talks privately to Master Hill. Moving up on the sofa again, I touch Dylan's arm to get his attention.

"Are you okay?" I whisper.

He shrugs. Almost dejectedly. "Guess so." He averts his eyes.

Hmm. I know he's like Kayla; they both regress or whatever they call it. Not only do they act younger with their Daddy Doms, but they *feel* younger. Though, I think I remember Kayla telling me Dylan doesn't revert as much as she does. He's a...Middle? And Kayla's a Little. Or something like that.

Regardless, it makes me wary of how to approach Dylan. I don't know what he needs—not if he's in that mind-set right now.

"Do you miss your Daddy?" I decide to go with comfort and understanding; I can't go wrong with that, right? I weave my fingers through his hair and scoot closer.

He closes his eyes and tilts his face so I palm his cheek. "I shouldn't," he mumbles. "He's not mine."

Damn Cade! I don't even know the man, but whatever they're going through, they should fix things before Dylan's heart gets broken. *Easier said than done.* Ain't that the truth. With a wistful sigh, I hug Dylan close to me and peer over at Rio, who's walked over to Miranda with Master Hill.

"I think I found out what happened to the Miranda girl, by the way." Dylan speaks under his breath and discreetly wipes his cheeks. *Poor kid.* Who...is most likely my own age. *Whatevs.* "I heard it from those two over there." He nods at two male subs across the patio. "Apparently Miranda stole money from the register at Switch last week. Like, a hundred bucks or something, and Liam caught her and handed her over to Mr. Ford and Master Kelly."

Shit, double shit, triple shit.

My spine stiffens. Given my past, Rio's reaction to Miranda's crime suddenly makes all the difference. I need to know his take on things and whether or not he's acting appalled by Miranda as part of her punishment or if it runs deeper.

"I presume Miranda's sorry since she's still here," I murmur.

"I don't know." Dylan doesn't appear to care about it. "Makes sense they're calling her a thief now, though."

Yeah...

"Isn't this where you should be all, 'Oh my God, she stole? What a bitch!'" He fails at sounding like a girl.

I give him a wry look and point to my shoulder. "Isn't this where you cry on me and call out for your Daddy?"

"Ouch." He both grins and winces. "You don't play nice."

Never said I did, although I'm a whole lot nicer now than when I was a teenager. We all have our pasts, and mine happens to be dirtier than most. I refuse to be ashamed of it, but that doesn't mean I'm proud of it, either. It just is. And if Rio has issues with that...

"We all make mistakes, and we don't know Miranda's story," I settle for saying.

Doesn't mean I like that she's Rio's slave, but whatever.

Dylan nods quickly, his eyes trained on something—someone—behind me, and I turn to see Rio heading our way again.

"You know that Cade is working tonight, right?" Rio asks Dylan.

"Yes, Dominus." Dylan stares at his lap. "I don't wanna leave—it's just..."

He doesn't feel like playing, I suppose.

"I get it." Rio shows a ghost of a smile and extends his hand. "Come on, then. I think I know what to do with you. Chelsea, you're coming, too."

CHAPTER 7

W e follow Rio into the house and up the stairs, down a
hallway that doesn't look anything like the basement.
Dark wood doors, light green walls, carpeted floor, and countless
pictures of family, friends, beautiful landscapes, and patients. I
assume some of them are patients, anyway. One looks like it was
taken in a jungle, and Rio is surrounded by children. Another
photo is of a little boy who bumps his fist with Rio's. The boy is
holding a lollipop and is positively beaming. Rio looks just
as happy.

He's not only a Dom. Or a doctor. He's changed lives. He has
amazing friends. He's part of a loving family, which I should know
considering how much I've stalked him on Facebook over the years.

Groan. How can I ever admit that? It'll be so damn embarrassing.

I smile to myself when I see a photo of Rio, Nicholas, Mark,
and Cade, all wearing different sports jerseys but the same drunken
grins.

"Here we go." Rio opens a door that leads to a room I can only
describe as a *man cave.*

"Holy crap," Dylan whispers in awe.

Rio chuckles and leans against the doorway as Dylan enters and eye-fucks the arcade games, the entertainment center, the gigantic, cushy chairs, the bar, the speakers set up here and there. *Christ on a fucking cracker.* On the table in front of the chairs there are no fewer than seven remote controls. On the walls, there are shelves upon shelves with DVDs, video games, and CDs. Cabinets filled with collectibles, comic books—friggin' *comic* books? Heh. Who knew Rio was a nerd.

It kinda makes me like him even more. Combined with the photos in the hallway...*girly sigh.*

Rio pulls me close, causing me to squeak then giggle, and I peer up at his face. God, his smile is gorgeous.

"Do you think you can spend a few hours here, Dylan?" Rio murmurs, though he never looks away from me. He's warm, so I snuggle closer. Dylan's *"Hell yes"* makes Rio grin. "Good. Go nuts. Chelsea and I will be down the hall if you need anything. But... knock first."

I swallow a needy noise that would no doubt sound like *"Hnnngh."* Not very flattering.

"Come on, little rebel." Rio gives my chin a sharp nip. Then he releases me and slaps my butt. "We're going to my bedroom."

Yes, please, and thank you.

I shoot Dylan a smirk over my shoulder, but he's preoccupied with the remote controls.

Two doors down is Rio's bedroom, and I shiver just walking inside. Like the hallway, it's decorated in warm colors, and there are more photographs of family members and friends. I recognize his brother in one of them; they look so much alike that it's scary. From Facebook, I know his name is Gabriel.

As my gaze lands on the large four-poster bed, butterflies kick in and I get nervous. This doesn't feel like a part of the play party downstairs, but I'm probably wrong. I gotta be careful and not let my crush do the talking.

"So this is where the magic happens, huh?" I don't know why I had to fill the silence. Firstly, I haven't gotten permission to open my mouth, and, secondly, I don't want his reply to my question. I chuckle awkwardly and shake my head. "I'm sorry, Dominus."

"Master Rio," he corrects quietly from behind me. No more Roman games, then? I shudder, feeling a hand trail up my spine. His warm breath along my shoulder. Then a featherlight kiss. "I'm giving you one out, Chelsea. Otherwise you're mine for the next few hours, and we won't be leaving this room."

"No out." I bite my lip to keep a gasp bottled up inside. "I want this, Sir."

"Perfect. Undress me."

I turn and grasp the hem of his costume, swiftly getting it over his head. Well, sorta swiftly. I may not be all that short, but Rio's a skyscraper.

This is only fair, too. I've been naked the entire evening. It's about time I get to see every inch of Rio Kelly. And hot fucking *damn*, what a sight. The fabric falls to the floor, leaving him in absolutely nothing else, and I...gawk. I gawk at his imperfectly perfect body. Black hair mixing with a hint of silver, flawless skin marred by a few scars and birthmarks, strength from a healthy lifestyle mingling with the fact that his life's been filled with danger, too. The years he's spent in third-world countries whisper of stories on his body.

"You're not favoring your left leg," I note softly. I close in and touch him reverently, curious about the scar that runs along his upper thigh. When I reach his hip, I catch sight of his hand. Another scar. From a burn? Looks like it. "What did you do here?"

He opens his hand and shows the faint line across his palm. "Somalia. We were pulling crates of supplies up a cliff." He chuckles wryly under his breath. "Rope burns."

"No gloves?" Silly Dom.

"No time." His humor is gone now, and I see something

haunting in his eyes. The green dims, perhaps an unpleasant memory taking over. "My one and only run-in with actual pirates."

"What the fuck?" My eyes grow wide.

He inclines his head. "Big money in medical supplies. We made it out of there alive, though." He taps my nose. "And we can save the rest for another time." Next, he points down. "Should my clothes be on the floor?"

Shit, double shit, triple shit. "I'm sorry, Master Rio." I'm an idiot. This isn't some romantic let's-get-to-know-each-other rendezvous. It's a scene. Playtime. Nothing lovey-dovey. "Where would you like them?" I pick up the clothes and keep my gaze lowered.

"On the chair over there, please." He lifts a hand in the direction of the corner nearest the large window wall overlooking the street. I hadn't even noticed it until now, and it makes me hesitate. Which Rio evidently sees. "We can see out, but nobody can see in."

Phew. I'm all for a little exhibitionism, but I like being prepared.

Once I've hung his costume over the chair, Rio tells me to clear the bed then lie down on my stomach and wait for his return.

"Oh—" He pauses in the doorway. "Arms and legs spread."

Then it's just me.

I release a shaky breath and get crackin', removing the bedspread. The dark blue blanket follows, revealing pristine, white sheets and fluffy pillows. I push them up against the headboard, then get on the bed and into position. Facedown, arms and legs spread.

I hope I don't get fake henna on his sheets.

My temporary tattoo is still perfect, but who knows what Rio has planned. He could have me sweating buckets and ruining the ink in no time.

"Fuck, you're beautiful, Chelsea."

Just like that, the temperature goes up a hundred degrees. I hear his feet pad closer on the hardwood floor, and then feel the bed dip with his weight, and, finally, he covers my body with his.

My bones turn liquid.

His large hands roam my back and sides as he kisses my shoulders and neck. I love his weight on me, pressing me into the mattress. Caged by his warmth, by his sexy body, all I can do is take whatever he gives.

"We're going to have a few rules." He shifts my hair to the side and nips at my neck. "You're familiar with speech restrictions, yes?"

"Yes, Sir." I let out a moan as one of his hands slides underneath me and cups my pussy. I try to push up my ass, but he responds by pressing his cock harder against me. It's nestled so perfectly between my butt cheeks, but I want more. I want him inside. Now, now, now.

"Excellent. Only three words are acceptable—not counting your safewords." He eases away, and I hear him rustling with something. A bag? "The words are 'yes,' 'Master,' and 'please.' Understood?"

"Yes, Master." A thousand times yes. Then a buzzing sound has my attention, and soon I feel a vibrator being positioned to my clit. *Fuck!* I suck in a breath, almost cursing out loud. But damn, he put that on high. The vibrations ignite me and make me wanna squirm like crazy.

"Good girl." After that, he's quiet for a while as he ties me to the bed. Silk ties for my ankles and wrists. Lastly, a blindfold. "Lie still. Just. Like. That. Bloody gorgeous."

I bite down hard on my lip. Behind the blindfold, I screw my eyes shut tightly, and I grab on to the ties that restrain me. The buzzing is just so fucking powerful, and after a whole evening of merciless teasing, I could come in a few seconds.

Rio gets behind me once more and this time encourages me to lift my ass off the mattress. Other than a brief sound of crinkling foil, there's no warning. He inches forward, and then he pushes his cock deep inside me in one smooth stroke.

Oh my God. I mouth the words in a silent scream, the pleasure exploding behind my closed lids like its own little orgasm.

"Christ," he grits out.

I stifle cries, sure I've never felt this contained. Bound by him, fucked by him, surrounded and covered by him. *Him*...the man I've crushed on since I was basically a kid.

"*Master*," I whimper.

"Fucking finally." Rio shudders on top of me and splays a hand between me and the bed. "God, I've waited..." *Waited?* Forcing himself deeper into my pussy, he stretches me and grinds me harder against the vibrator. All of it, what he's doing, is enough to turn my brain into mush. "Incredible." With a kiss to my neck, he begins to move in slow but firm thrusts. "You're allowed to come as many times as you want, but—" He pauses to catch his breath. "But I'm not sure you'll be able to in a little bit." That last word is followed by his teeth sinking into my neck and his free hand fisting my hair. He tugs me back harshly, causing me to arch and tighten my grip on the ties.

Pain sears through me, and I can't help but cry out. It's the weirdest thing, loving pain and getting a sense of euphoria from it. It's exactly what happens; tears well up in my eyes, and while my mind wants to fight it, my body craves it. My pulse skyrockets, my heart drums rapidly, and my breathing becomes shallow.

"Please," I moan, writhing beneath him. "Please!"

He mutters a curse and rises to kneel behind me. He pulls me with him too, and my wrists ache from the straining ties and my need to support myself on the mattress. Just thinking about the possibility of wearing marks tomorrow has me quivering.

"I want to test you, pet." He grunts and fucks me harder. "I've been told you like pain. Which..." A dark chuckle escapes him. "Fuck, the things I wanna do."

"Yesss," I hiss. Every thrust he gives me, I try to push back just as much. He turns me into this greedy little slut. *"Please,* Master."

Another curse, and he stops. For several seconds, all I hear is our labored breathing and the toy.

"I need to see you." He reaches over me and quickly unties my restraints, then removes the blindfold. Like a rag doll, I'm tossed around so I'm on my back, and then I have him slamming inside me again.

The shock of the sudden movements makes me forget the rules, and I let out a hoarse wail. "Jesus fuck!"

For some reason, Rio grins. "And now I have an excuse to hurt you even more."

Oh, my fucking *God.*

"Don't worry." With a grip on my jaw, he gives me a hard kiss, then brushes the pad of his thumb over my lip and smirks down at me. "Just this once, I'm going to allow you to enjoy a punishment."

I'm by no means a brat—usually—but I find myself triggered by that smirky smirk. So I mirror it in a teasing way and bite his thumb.

He hisses and yanks it away, only to laugh and kiss me again. "My beautiful little whore," he murmurs. "You're gonna regret that."

I gulp as he backs away and twirls a finger.

"Get on all fours again."

I obey and face forward, even though I'm dying to find out what he's looking for in his toy bag. The vibrator is switched off, and he replaces it with a tiny one that comes with an actual clip. *Oh, motherfucker.* It hurts like a son of a bitch when he attaches it to my clit, but the pain mingles with the relief of pleasure.

What follows next is a session of torture and mind-blowing ecstasy. I lose track of time as he spanks me, fucks me, flogs me, and twists a plug inside my ass.

I'm a sobbing mess who has lost count of the orgasms, as well.

Wearing his marks tomorrow isn't only a possibility anymore, but a certainty.

"Color?" he asks for the umpteenth time, panting.

"Gr-green," I mumble, feeling as if I'm spacing out a bit. "So green, Master." Every inch of me is burning. My skin is alive, pulsing and aching.

When he removes the plug, I wonder which implement is next, and I get my answer when he brushes the flat wooden surface of a paddle along my back.

"Your ass is such a lovely shade of red right now." He hums. "A little bit of purple here, too."

Without warning, the paddle comes down with a resounding smack on my left butt cheek. I let out a powerless wail, only to scream and clutch the sheets impossibly tighter when he rams two fingers inside my pussy. Combined with the buzzing vibrator on my clit, I'm pushed toward another orgasm.

I can't breathe. I can't fucking breathe. I'm locked in a cage of pain and pleasure, both immobilizing me.

He strikes again and again, all while the climax crashes down on me. Then he drops the paddle somewhere on the floor before gripping my hips and slamming his cock into me.

The edges of my vision get blurry, and I see my limit approaching fast. Flipping me over a final time, he fucks me into the bed and grabs my throat in a light choke hold. His breathing is as harsh as his thrusts. I feel hot puffs of air and kissable lips against my cheek.

"I think that's it," he groans hoarsely. "Color, baby?"

I scream out in pain as he locks my legs around his hips and draws his blunt fingernails along the back of my thigh. After all that paddling and flogging, I can't anymore.

"Yellow," I choke out.

He nods and removes the vibrator on my clit. "Good girl. I'm proud of you." Blood surges to my clit, exactly like it does to nipples after being clamped, and I'm thrown into a last orgasm. "God, Chelsea... You feel so damn amazing."

I can't see, I can barely hear, and I can't control any part of my body. Rio dominates me completely.

"Goddamn—I'm gonna come." He kisses away the tears that have evidently fallen down my face, and throughout the after-shocks of my orgasm, all I register are out-of-place murmurs about what a perfect girl I am.

Another kind of warmth seeps into me. His praise settles like a blanket, and I cling to him like a needy baby.

He called me that. He called me baby.

I don't wanna find him perfect already. I'll only be setting myself up for heartbreak. But what else am I supposed to feel? He's given me the perfect mixture of pain and affection. He hurts me physically then wraps me up in...comfort.

Oh, fuck.

I tense up momentarily before exhaustion wins. There's simply no fight left in me. I can't struggle against Rio. Not him. Even if this is my only time with him, I gotta let myself take whatever I can get. And I hope—God, I hope. I hope for more.

CHAPTER 8

I wake up in the middle of the night, disoriented and tired as hell. Someone called my name, right?

Dante.

I blink drowsily. Only the small lamp on Rio's nightstand is lit, just enough for me to see Dante sitting on the edge of the bed and Rio standing in the doorway.

In a heartbeat, a flood of memories comes rushing back. The party...who won? Is Rio disappointed we never returned downstairs? Where's Dylan now? What time is it, exactly? Why the fuck is every part of me throbbing? Oh, that's right. Rio...the pain, the amazing sex, the comfort...

Afterward, he'd carried me to his bathroom and drawn me a relaxing bath. He'd dried me, rubbed aloe into my skin, massaged me, kissed me, held me...until I fell asleep in his arms.

It really happened.

"You can be the big spoon another time," he'd chuckled sleepily when I had tried to face him.

Another time. Let's hope.

Back to the present, I blink again and peer up at Dante's tired grin. Looks like he's enjoyed the party.

"Is it time to go?" I whisper hoarsely, clearing my throat. The thought of getting dressed and going home ranks somewhere near swimming with sharks and cuddling spiders.

"Well, Gretchen and I are." Dante smiles and touches my cheek. "You look very comfortable here. It's up to you. Rio tells me he'd like you to stay the night."

I look over to Rio, warm and fuzzy that he wants me to stay, and he nods. "If you want."

If I want? Are ya kiddin'?

"I want." I manage a cheeky grin and turn to Dante again.

He chuckles. "I'm glad your playtime was that good. I still feel responsible for you, though. If you don't mind, I'd like to come get you in the morning. Where you and Rio go from there is up to you, of course."

Sounds reasonable.

"Bring your sub, and we can have breakfast here tomorrow," Rio suggests.

Dante agrees, and after setting a time, he goes downstairs again. Rio follows, letting me know that he just has to show Miranda to the slave quarters in the basement first.

I shake my head to myself, thinking it's sort of disturbing. Again, my kink might not be Miranda's and vice versa, but jeesh. I'm looking forward to the entire story, and I need Rio's take on it, too. Otherwise I know I won't be able to move on, no matter how much I'm hoping for it.

When Rio returns, he strips off his boxer briefs and gets under the covers. He pulls me close and tucks my head under his chin as if we do this every night. As if this is normal.

"You're stiff as a stick." He kisses the top of my head and lets his lips linger. "Relax, Chelsea."

I'm trying, but this is weird. Scening is one thing, but spending the night like this? At the very least, shouldn't I be shown to the slave quarters, as well? What makes me so damn different? Especially with our past and his reaction to my moving here—*stop*.

I blow out a breath.

Tomorrow. Or soon. I'll ask my questions then. Not tonight. Not right now. I'll savor this.

Except for one thing. "Miranda," I blurt out. "Is she forgiven? For whatever she's done." I add that last part in a rush. After all, Dylan and I are probably not supposed to know that she apparently stole money from Switch.

Rio doesn't seem affected by my question at all. "That's what punishments are for. Once you've been punished, you're forgiven."

I need to see his face for this, so I lift my head to search his eyes. "Do you really mean it?" *I need you to mean it.*

"*Yes*. Now, shush." He silences me with a hard kiss, and I'm torn. Never in my life have I considered myself insecure. I've worked hard to get to where I am, even though I'm not exactly a huge success. But I manage fine, and I will never be ashamed of my past. Still, closing the subject so fast has me wondering if he really does mean what he says. Then again, he has no reason to lie.

Ugh. Overthinking is a bitch.

"Let me look at you." Rio slides his hands underneath my armpits and hoists me up with a grunt, positioning me so I'm straddling his hips. "There we go." He grins faintly in the dim light, his eyes raking over my naked body. "Hell." At his whispered curse, I peer down to see what's causing that look of reverence in those green peepers of his. "You grew up, little rebel."

I watch as he traces a finger along the henna tattoos then derails to brush his thumb over a thin welt on my hip.

"Seeing my marks on you..." His jaw clenches. I feel his cock thickening between us. Heat pools in my stomach, and my brain struggles against the cobwebs of exhaustion. "Perfect," he murmurs, his eyes searching mine. "I'd like your thoughts on our scene before we sleep." His voice remains low and warm, but I can tell he doesn't have another round of sex at the forefront of his mind. *Shame.* "The level of pain—do you want more or less?"

"Not more." I smooth a hand down his chest, feeling the sparse hair under my palm. "Tonight was incredible, right up until I reached my limit."

He nods pensively, his gaze never leaving mine. "Good. I wouldn't be able to inflict any more, regardless. It was my limit, as well."

To hear we're perfectly matched in at least this department is a heady feeling, but it will probably only fuel the heartbreak if we don't want the same kind of relationship.

I'm no stranger to sub frenzy; it happens too often. A sub desperate to find that special connection, and as soon as someone comes along and ticks off several boxes, it's easy to delude yourself and think you're in love and want it forever. I've been through it before, but this feels different.

I'm experienced enough to not rush into things because once that frenzy settles, you're back to where you started. The crazy attraction and the lovely butterflies evaporate—unless it's real. Unless you're cautious. Unless you take time to build a steady foundation. Unless your limits match.

With Rio, though... I sigh internally, tracing mindless patterns on his torso with my fingertips. My crush on him is consuming and alive, but my head is still in the game. I won't fold and give into him unless we find out we're really good for each other. Because this time around, I *am* looking for the real thing.

I want to find someone I won't hold at arm's length.

Of course I want it to be Rio Kelly. I ache for it.

"I'm still a little dazed about all this," he says out of nowhere. "Having you in my bed..." The corners of his mouth twist up a little. "It was too farfetched to think we'd end up here."

I can see how he'd feel that way. Being thirty years old and stumbling on to a sixteen-year-old little shit wouldn't make anyone consider a future together with whips and chains.

Time has changed things, though.

"Will you treat me like a plague again?" That's really all I need to know before this night is over.

"God no, baby." He sits up and hugs me tightly, dropping a soft kiss on the spot behind my ear. "I can't apologize enough for my reaction to your moving here. I was shocked, angry, and confused—and I have some shit I still have to work through." Grasping my chin, he makes me face him. "But I won't avoid you."

I can't describe how relieved I am. Locking my arms around his neck, I squeeze him back and close my eyes against the emotion threatening to surface.

"You changed your mind fast." I guess I'm still worried about that—if only a little. He's explained that seeing me at Switch and then Dante telling him I was coming to the party made Rio realize that I'm part of this community now. He said he needed to accept that and make the most of things, but is that all? And is he reluctant about it?

Feels like he can't be *too* reluctant, considering how quickly he bought me at tonight's slave auction. Not to mention where we are right now.

"It was more about caving." He brushes his lips along my shoulder. "I'll tell you all about it one day. But now I think we need sleep."

That totally gives me reason to voice one more curiosity. "Here or in the slave quarters? I mean, it's where Miranda is..."

What makes me different? is what I'm really asking.

"Too cute." He rumbles a sleepy chuckle and lies down again. He brings me with him and kisses the top of my head, his arms snaking around me to keep me on top of him. *As if I'd leave voluntarily.*

Rio doesn't offer any other response.

The next morning, disappointment settles over me for a brief moment when I wake up alone in bed. But then I see a note on Rio's pillow.

Good morning, little rebel. I'm out on my morning run, but I will be back soon. I hope to find you waiting for me in the bathtub.

I smile giddily and squeal into the pillow. I'm so silly, but I don't care. I want this with Rio, and that means I gotta suck it up and find the courage to be up-front about everything. My intentions and wishes, my past, and even my, um, innocent Facebook-stalker tendencies.

Maybe he'll take a chance on me, and that note doesn't do anything to deflate my hope.

Jumping outta the bed, I practically skip into the ensuite bathroom. As I wait for the tub to fill up, I survey my naked body in the mirror. A shiver runs down my spine, my fingers brushing along some of the bruises and welts Rio left behind.

Faint shades of blue, red, and purple decorate my skin, along with the fading henna. I almost wanna take a picture of his marks on me, but I'll settle for the dull throb and ache they've left behind, plus the wish for more some day.

That's not to say I always want to get beaten—far, far from it. My nature lies in servitude and worship, but every now and then, there's nothing like the fiery pain of physical sadism.

Wanting to please Rio as much as he's pleased me, I leave the bathroom, walk through his bedroom, and tiptoe out in the hallway. I can hear voices from downstairs, possibly Dante and Gretchen. Maybe even Dylan? And Miranda? I can't be sure, but if I could just sneak downstairs and maybe get Rio some coffee, perhaps some fruit—anything; the paper?—to show I'd love to go the extra mile for him, I'd feel better.

I close the door behind me again and scan the bedroom, my eyes lighting up in triumph when I spot my bag in the chair by the window. Dante must've brought it for me before he took off last night.

Inside, I find a pair of jeans and a T-shirt once I've taken out the jacket Rio let me borrow—screw underwear. I'll be naked in the tub soon enough.

When I'm dressed, I walk down the stairs slowly, not wanting to get caught. *Oh, shit.* Didn't even make it three steps! Stopping short, I watch as two guys walk briskly toward the front door carrying furniture that was used at the play party.

So maybe it's not Dante and Gretchen who are here already. It could be whatever company Rio hired to turn his patio into a Roman villa.

"What are you doing?"

I suck in a breath and whip around, only to see a sleepy Dylan rubbing his eyes and yawning.

"Um, hi." I don't really *know* what I'm doing, so I don't answer. With people milling about and Rio returning any minute, I might as well wait with my extra mile. "Did you just wake up?" He's dressed, but it looks like he threw the clothes on seconds ago. His hair is sticking out in every direction.

He nods and hikes a bag up his shoulder. "Master Dante's driving me to Gabriella's place."

Gabriella, huh? I raise a brow at him. I don't know him very well, but after having my hands all over his body—and vice versa—during the contests last night, I think it's okay to be curious.

"Shouldn't it be Cade's house?" I ask carefully.

Anguish flashes in his eyes, and he tries to cover it up with a tight smile as he descends a couple steps. "I'm done with that. He can't expect me to ask permission for every little thing when he doesn't want more than a casual arrangement. I don't function that way."

My face falls, and I feel sad for him. "Have you told him you want more, sweetie?"

He nods again, this time a quick jerk as if he's uncomfortable.

"I'm sorry, but I'd rather not talk about it." He offers a weak smile and passes me with a kiss to my forehead. "I'll go check if Dante's here yet."

Blowing out a breath, I wait until he's outta sight. Then I slump down and sit on the landing, thinking of ways to help Dylan. But I don't know him enough yet. I'll call him later and offer support—

My thought flies out the window when I hear Rio's voice. *Back already?* "It doesn't matter," he chuckles darkly, and I peer down to see him heading toward the living room. He's on the phone. His back is facing me, and from up here, he looks slighter. "You're clearly more forgiving than I am." Definitely not dressed in workout clothes. Instead he's wearing black dress pants and a light blue button-down. His black hair is slicked back, which...huh. Didn't figure Rio as one for having his hair styled all prim and proper. "I would've fired her immediately. She stole—simple as that."

I freeze at those words.

"If you say so," he says dryly. "But I can't believe Nicholas isn't pressing charges. What she did is unforgivable."

Oh, my God.

My stomach drops and rolls with nausea. Hurrying back to the bedroom, I only have one word on a loop in my head, along with the crushing blow of rejection. *Run.*

I've done it before, though it's usually my own fault. Whenever a guy's gotten too close, I've reacted by fleeing.

Even worse was when I was younger. Then I'd deliberately push anyone away from the get-go. That way, there was never any risk of getting close at all.

I shut off the water in the bathroom and then grab my duffel and zip it up. There's no way I want to face Rio now—God, that lying mother*fucker*—so I do my best to sneak downstairs without being seen.

He said he'd forgiven Miranda after the punishment. He fucking told me.

Humiliation burns hotly in my eyes as I stumble in an attempt to put on my shoes in my escape. I manage at last, and I yank the front door open just as another couple movers pass me with furniture.

Dylan's waiting down the driveway by Rio's mailbox, so I join him there, praying to God Dante can pass up breakfast.

"You okay?" Dylan tilts his head at me, concern creasing his forehead.

I nod curtly. "Yeah. No." I shake my head. Fuck, I'm stupid. Fucking sub frenzy. I wasn't careful enough with Rio. I didn't guard my heart enough. Or even at all. I wanted it too much. Still goddamn do. "Ugh." I shudder against the cold and blow out a breath. "I'll be fine."

Dylan's eyes soften, and he takes a step closer to squeeze my arm gently. "You can talk to me, you know."

At that, I let out a shaky laugh. *The irony.* "That goes both ways." I look to him pointedly.

He smiles sheepishly. "Fine. I'll talk if you will."

It *would* be nice to ramble a bit, maybe host a pity party that isn't only about me. And Kayla would get too upset. She would involve Nicholas and try to figure things out before I'm ready for it. Besides, what is there to figure out?

Once a thief, always a thief, huh?

"Is Gabriella expecting you?" I ask, my throat closing up.

He hesitates then shakes his head no. "I just don't wanna spend the day alone, and she's my best friend."

"Okay." A particularly harsh wind blows past, and I clutch my stomach, beyond nauseated and embarrassed. I can't get Rio's voice outta my head—his words, what he said. It wasn't the rich warmth I've gotten used to so fast. His tone was clear and crisp. "Wanna come to my place?" I look up at Dylan. "I have ice cream and bourbon. We can bitch and moan about the Domly fuckers who say one thing and mean another."

Dylan's mouth tightens grimly. "I'm really lookin' forward to hearing what happened. I mean, you were happy like a minute ago."

I don't reply, merely waiting for his answer.

He sighs. "All right, darlin'. Count me in. You better have real ice cream—not the nonfat shit you girls seem to love so much."

Oh, please. "Häagen-Dazs." One of the few things I don't skimp on. "Now we just gotta convince Dante to drive us home without breakfast." Dylan appears confused at that, so I elaborate. "He and Gretchen are coming to pick us up, and Rio invited them for breakfast, too."

"Oh." Dylan frowns. "I didn't know that."

But for once in my fucking lifetime, I get lucky. When Dante and Gretchen show up a couple minutes later, he takes one look at my face and demands to know what's wrong. *Guess my poker face has run off.*

"Please just take me home," I ask beseechingly. I glance over my shoulder, fearing that Rio will walk out, but so far, nothing. "I'll explain everything, but I-I can't stick around."

Dante gives me a serious look. "If Rio hurt you, I need to know. There could be a misunderstanding or at least an explanation. He's a good Master, Chelsea. And I know he wouldn't let you leave upset."

I have no doubt about that. "It's personal," I reply. "I heard him say something about me—" The pain of rejection flares up once more, fiercer and ruthless. "Fuck. I'm sorry, Sir." I cover my mouth for fear I'll throw up.

"Christ—come here, sweetheart." Dante hugs me to him, and Gretchen moves close to offer comfort, as well. Fucking comfort. Am I that weak? "We'll get to the bottom of this, but if you feel like you can't do it right this minute, I'll take you home."

Thank you, thank you, thank you.

CHAPTER 9

Several hours later, Dylan knows everything. Every little thing.

It hadn't been my intention to spill the beans about my friggin' past, but the little fucker drew it out of me. And maybe, just maybe, the bourbon-splashed ice cream helped coax the words out of me, too.

Occupying either end of my bed, our pajama-clad legs tangled together in the middle, Dylan and I form a friendship that is as easy as breathing. Perhaps it's easier to open up to a stranger and go from there, as opposed to opening up to someone who already knows so much about you. Additionally, it's nice to get a new perspective on things. A submissive guy's perspective, to boot.

I hadn't been able to speak this freely with Dante, who spent the entire ride from Rio's place asking me what had happened. In the end, I blurted out the latest events—that I had heard Rio downstairs on the phone, talking to whoever-the-fuck, about stealing being unforgivable.

To give Dante a clearer picture, I also told him my childhood was rough. I wasn't always honest and law-abiding. I did what I did to survive, and I left things at that, and Dante grew silent and pensive.

With Dylan, the rest came out in a jumbled mess. My past, how I met Rio, losing my brother, getting into BDSM, meeting Kayla...all of it. Even the Facebook-stalking part.

It's liberating to get it all out, especially with someone who seems genuinely interested and concerned.

In return, Dylan gets quiet for a bit before he scoops up another spoonful of ice cream and tells me he can't imagine Rio holding my past against me. "He doesn't seem like that kind of person," he adds and sits up to lean back against the wall.

"I didn't think so, either." I sigh and take a swig from the bottle of bourbon. *Damn.* Fire slides down my throat. "I know what I heard, though." The smooth numbness that takes over is my number one reason for loving bourbon. The aftertaste is exquisite, too. "I am so fucking stupid."

Really. Only a fool would let herself go so completely the way I did. Ten years of nothing—a crush lingering from a single encounter—and then I allowed him to take so much from me in one night. What was I thinking?

Scooting close, Dylan ends up next to me, and he bumps his shoulder to mine. "Hey, none of that crap. If you're just gonna sit here and berate yourself, I'll go out and flirt with your hot room-mates instead."

I snort at that. "Oh sweetie, we both know that's not what you wanna do." Dylan doesn't respond, so I set the ice cream and bourbon aside and then place my cheek on his shoulder. "Your turn. Tell me about you and Cade. And Gabriella."

"Nothing much to tell," he mumbles, the side of his face resting at the top of my head. "Since I moved to San Francisco, I've wanted Cade. I watched him scene a few times before Kayla set me up with him. He's...he's fucking amazing. But he only wants a casual arrangement. He's honest about it too, so I can't really be mad at him." He shrugs dejectedly. "Maybe I need a break. I could always visit my grandparents in Texas for a few months."

"What—*no*. No, Dylan." I lift my head to face him. "Don't do that."

He offers a small smile and tugs on a strand of my hair. "I have to get over him, Chelsea."

"What about Gabriella?" I'm ready to grasp at straws, but I really don't want Dylan to move. "Kayla mentioned something about Gabriella having problems with her Daddy Dom. She'll need you, you know."

"Fucking John," he mutters, releasing a breath in frustration. "I'm waiting for her to dump that asshole." At my look of question, he goes on. "They got engaged two years ago, so one might think they're serious. Well, she is—was, whatever. But he stopped giving a fuck a long time ago. Work is more important." Dylan's clearly pissed. "More often than not, John left her with Cade and me."

"The three of you have played together?" I ask curiously.

He flushes and nods. "Some, yeah."

I purse my lips, studying him. It's obvious Dylan doesn't mind scening with both of them. Hell, I bet he loves it. And seeing it from Cade's perspective, I can imagine feeling...hmm, not threatened, but cautious?

"Do you have feelings for Gabriella?" I ask softly.

He lowers his gaze. "I don't know," he whispers. "I didn't even consider it before. I've denied it to Kayla, but..." He sighs heavily. "I'm so fucking in love with that bastard." I assume he's talking about Cade now. "But when he started pulling away from me—well, he didn't really pull away, but he got more, um..." He thinks for a beat, phrasing himself. "He realized I wanted more, so he focused on playtime instead. Before, he'd text and call every now and then; he showed interest in my career, came to the pool a couple times when I practiced—stuff like that. Then all of a sudden, it was all about Switch. He said he preferred it if we only played there. But, anyway—I got off track. Gabriella and I grew closer, and I guess I started wondering if there was more there. I'm not sure, though."

Gotcha. "How long have you and Cade been together?"

He rolls his eyes for some reason. "That's the thing. Not long. I mean, I fell hard and fast, so I knew I wanted him before we even got to the first date. But it's barely been two months since Kayla set us up—" Before he can finish the sentence, Dylan's phone vibrates against my hardwood floor. "It's probably Cade." He rolls his eyes again.

Reading his text, he frowns at first, only to widen his eyes the next second.

"Um." He shows me the screen.

Hello, Dylan. If you're still with Chelsea, please have her call me. I'm incredibly disappointed that my subs left without a word this morning. I've spoken with Dante, and I'm expecting apologies from both of you. —Rio

"What the hell?" I bristle. "He's got some fuckin' *nerve...*"

"I screwed up, though." Dylan grimaces. "I really shouldn't have left like that. Master Kelly was incredibly nice to me yesterday."

Biting my thumbnail, refusing to admit anything, I reach over to my nightstand where I put my phone earlier—after having made sure a hundred times I'd shut it off. Now I'm wondering if perhaps that was a stupid idea. Then again, seriously? Who the fuck does he think he is, telling me I shouldn't have left without a word?

He shouldn't have lied to me. *He* should get off his high horse and smell the shit. Not everyone is born with a silver spoon in their mouth. I grew up with an abusive alcoholic for a mother, a dead-beat father, no money, and I lost my brother to drugs.

I won't apologize for how I survived, whether I sold my body, stole food, or pickpocketed.

As I switch on my phone again, I square my shoulders and let my internal guard slam right back up where it's supposed to be.

Text after text, all from Rio.

My run took longer than I thought, but not long enough for you to bail. Is something wrong, Chelsea?

That must've been before he talked to Dante, and the next text confirms it. There's a sense of urgency to it, as well.

I spoke to Dante. Pick up the phone when I call you.

But...hmm. My brows furrow at the first message. His run sure as fuck didn't take long, did it? He was showered and dressed when I heard him on the phone, which doesn't explain his request to find me in the bathtub.

I'm serious, Chelsea. Answer the fucking phone. It's all a misunderstanding.

I swallow hard, wishing it could be a misunderstanding, but unless he's got a split personality, the fact remains. He said he'd forgiven Miranda for stealing, and the next morning, his tune had changed.

Given how I treated you when you arrived in San Francisco, I understand why you ran off before I could explain myself, but my patience is wearing thin. Get back to me immediately.

"Shit, double shit, triple shit." Unease tightens itself like a fist around my heart, and I begin to doubt my initial reaction. I heard what I heard, but when I think about it, it doesn't add up to what I've learned about Rio. Same goes for what those closest to him say. Everyone seems to agree that he's a great Master and a good man. A man of his word. Fair. Reliable.

Just then, a new message pops up. A lengthy one.

It was my brother you heard. It's taken me all goddamn day to puzzle everything together, and I didn't want to do this through a fucking text message. But since you refuse to call me, there you go. I hired

my brother's company for the party. He was at the house while I was out. We argued over the phone. It was his end of the conversation you heard. It wasn't me, Chelsea. Now I'll stop bothering you. Thank you for yesterday.

I slap a hand over my mouth and run toward the bathroom, nausea winning at last.

The. Bourbon. Wants. Out.

"Chelsea!" Dylan calls after me.

I don't answer, too busy losing the contents of my stomach into the toilet. *Oh God, oh God, oh God.* The relief of finding out it was Rio's brother was short-lived and has already been replaced by anger directed at myself and shame. *Oh God, oh God, oh God.* It was his brother. Gabriel. Gabriel Kelly. Holy fucking hell, I'm stupid. I should know better. I do know better! Having checked Rio's Facebook so many times over the past decade, I'm no stranger to Gabriel. I know how similar they look. Practically twins, not counting the few inches Rio has on his younger brother. *Oh God, oh God, oh God.*

Outside the bathroom, I hear Jase and Robby asking Dylan what's wrong.

"*I-I don't know,*" Dylan answers helplessly. "*She was reading messages from a Dom—uh...*"

"*We know about her lifestyle,*" Jase says wryly.

I'd chuckle if another round of nausea hadn't made me puke again. Tears roll down my cheeks, and my lungs burn with my need for air.

I'm so sorry, Rio.

The girl I once was, the one who pushed everyone away, screams at me. Tells me my hasty exit was justified, and I agree to some extent; I thought it was Rio. I *saw* Rio. Well, his back. And the words cut deep. *Fucking Gabriel.*

Combined with our rocky start, yeah, my departure was a bit justified. But the level-headed person I usually am these days would've stayed behind to confront the bastard. Yet, I ran like the child I was years ago.

Rio apologized several times for running hot and cold—or rather, cold then hot as fuck—and now I hope I can get a chance to do the same.

Time to call Kayla.

CHAPTER 10

The following Friday, there are two public demos at Switch. It means the music won't be as loud as it usually is, and if the guests are focused on the demo, it might mean fewer eyes on me.

At the play party last weekend, Rio wanted me to worship him. Cling to him. Make everything about him.

Tonight I will offer to do it publicly.

I've been a nervous mess about it all week, but the brief contact Rio and I had through Kayla on Sunday evening was enough for me to go on. Like a middle schooler passing notes in class, I called Kayla and asked if she could speak to him on my behalf.

"Ask him if he can allow me to apologize," I'd said.

I would've called him myself, but I was afraid I'd lose my shit and not make any sense of what I was saying.

"He said yes!" Kayla had responded with a squeal.

I'd released a breath and nervously requested, *"Ask him to be at Switch on Friday."*

At that, Rio had texted me.

I'll be there.

Locking myself into a stall in the small dressing room next to the lobby, I remove my coat and shoes, revealing a sheer, black slave dress that hides absolutely nothing. I touch up my makeup and pull back my hair into a high, messy bun. Lastly, I attach a two-inch wide leather collar around my neck, careful not to put too much pressure on the bandage taped over my new—very real—tattoo.

For a second, the volume of the music from inside the club rises, and I hear the door to the dressing room closing again. "Chelsea? You in here?" Kayla's voice.

"I'm here." I muster a shaky smile at the mirror. "Just a sec." Okay. Deep breaths. I'm ready.

Stowing away everything in my bag, I open the door and face a beaming Kayla. To match that bright smile, she's wearing a yellow baby-doll dress with enough lace to fill up a lingerie store.

"Eeeep!" She squeals behind her hands. "So hot! Master Rio's gonna come in his pants!"

I laugh nervously and roll my eyes.

Next, she widens her eyes and shakes her head. "Still can't believe you got a tattoo, though."

It's not like that. The tat isn't related to Rio—yet. If my dreams come true, it will be for him in the future. But for now, it's just my slave registry number, and I'm listed as ownerless in the database. I've been meaning to have it inked since I registered four years ago, but something always held me back. It wasn't significant enough.

"He hasn't claimed me, pipsqueak," I remind her.

"Oh, please! Since he got here like an hour ago, he's looked at the door a hundred thousand bajillion times." She scoffs while I get all warm and fuzzy. "He will claim your butt—soon. He gots to. Anyway," she says, waving a hand, "let me take your bag. Master Cooper will deliver you. Daddy said that was best, cuz the high-protocol stuff isn't his kink like it's Mark's."

"Okay." I nod and let out another breath. Have I ever been this anxious? Christ. "Who has the leash?"

"Master Cooper has it now." She takes my bag and moves for the door. "You ready, gawjuss?"

Her attempts to speak with a New York accent never fail to make me grin.

"I love you, Kayla," I chuckle.

"I love you, toooo!" She tackles me in a hug.

The heavy bass of the industrial metal playing inside Switch thunders through my soul as I pause right outside the entrance. Lowering my gaze respectfully, I stop in front of Master Cooper and hold out the key to my collar for him.

I don't *have* to ask permission about anything when it comes to Master Cooper, but it's been a long time since I could fully sink into submission, and I do it eagerly now. Completely. Names fade away, replaced by titles.

"Permission to speak, Sir?" I request.

In my periphery, Kayla disappears upstairs—presumably to leave my bag in Mr. Ford's office—with Evangeline. Which leaves me with Master Cooper and Brayden, who's standing slightly behind his Dom.

"Granted." He takes a step closer to accept the key.

"Thank you for doing this for me. It means a lot." Understatement.

"You're very welcome, Chelsea." His voice carries the same kind of warmth Master Rio's does. "Are you ready to be presented to Rio?"

"Yes, Sir." I lift my chin enough for him to attach the leash to the ring at the front of my collar. Even as I keep my eyes downcast as much as possible, I see the edges of Master Cooper's mouth turn up in approval.

"Beautiful." He gives the leash an experimental tug, causing a surge of adrenaline to rush through me. "Look at me." I obey, and he gives me a smile. "I won't tell you anything that's not my place to divulge, but I don't see any harm in helping a subbie in need." His eyes crinkle at the corners. "Rio knows you're submissive through and through now—he knows you belong in the lifestyle. But he's been resigned for a long time, believing he wouldn't find that one girl who can find a balance between sub and slave." He pauses, making sure he has my attention. Boy, does he! "Nick told me about your new tattoo, so I have no doubt you and Rio are on the same level. Do me a solid and show him the ink quickly, okay? That oughta stop his stubbornness."

"Understood, Sir. Thank you." I tamp down the urge to run into the club and show Master Rio the tattoo right this second. God, I want this.

Master Cooper nods with a dip of his chin, and then motions Brayden forward. "Come here, pup." He cups the back of his sub's neck. "When we go in there, I want you to walk behind Chelsea. Remember we've worked on posture?"

"Yes, Master."

"Good boy. Study Chelsea." Master Cooper unlocks Brayden's own leash, maybe so he can walk behind me. "Observe how she walks and stands."

"Yes, Master."

I make a conscious effort to make sure my posture is perfect, but after eight years in the scene, it's one of those things that comes naturally.

"Pssst!" Only Kayla would make herself known with a not-so-subtle *pssst*. I grin at the floor, spying her out of the corner of my eye. She points toward the club entrance, and I nod discreetly. After that, she and Evangeline run off again.

Deep breaths.

My longing grows as I watch Master Cooper lean in for a brief but passionate kiss that makes Brayden relax into him. *I want that.* I'm gonna do my best to get it too, with one Rio Kelly.

Breaking away from Brayden, Master Cooper composes himself and gives me a quick *here-we-go* nod. Then he takes the lead, and we join the other dozen or so people who are trickling into the club. I don't know when the first demo is supposed to start, though I'm guessing soon. The music is still loud, but a crowd has formed near the center stage.

I spot Master Rio standing to the side with Mr. Ford, Kayla, Evangeline, Mr. Kingsley, and Gabriella. Before we reach them, Master Dante and Gretchen show up, too.

Where's Dylan?

It's easy to see the casual conversation flowing between a few of them. Mr. Ford is sipping on his drink, Mr. Kingsley on his beer, and Master Dante passes a bottled water to Gretchen, who kneels next to her Dom. There're chuckles, bouncing from Kayla and a beaming smile from Gabriella as Mr. Kingsley gives them lollipops, but Master Rio...he's not part of the relaxed atmosphere. Right before I lower my gaze, I catch him checking his watch.

I can practically sense when they've seen us. The conversation comes to a halt, strangers around us lowering their voices, too.

"Gentlemen," Master Cooper greets, a grin in his voice.

"Well, well," Master Dante says slowly. "What've you got here, my friend?"

"She's *not* for you!" Kayla blurts out. "S-Sir. Oh, crap."

I bite my lip to keep from laughing. Evangeline and Gabriella giggle—even Master Dante lets out a snort of amusement—but Mr. Ford isn't amused one bit. He grabs Kayla by her arm and excuses himself to go deal with his brat.

"But, but, but, *Daddy!*"

Daring a quick peek at the men, I see Mr. Kingsley smirking, though it fades fast. Wistfulness and pain flit across his features before he schools his expression, all of which makes me really worry about Dylan. Where *is* he? We've texted a bit this week, but he's been busy with practice, and I've had so much work. I'll have to call him later.

"Never a dull moment around that little girl." Master Cooper laughs, turning to Master Dante. "To answer your question, Chelsea is under my care until someone claims her. She does have a

Dom in mind though, so I'm not sure you'll be able to scene with her anytime soon."

"Shame." Master Dante would be more believable if he didn't sound so pleased I've found someone. For being so strict and sadistic, he sure is a romantic.

I've been lucky to have played with him and Gretchen.

"Maybe her new Master can share her?" Gretchen speaks up hopefully from the floor.

My gut clenches. I've thought about this for days now. If Master Rio gives me a shot, I'll...I'll try to accept it. If he's poly—or even if he "only" wants to share during scenes—I'll do my damnedest to give it a chance.

"I sincerely doubt he will." Master Rio's voice shakes me up with its rich timbre, and yearning for his statement to be true brings me forward.

It's as good time as any, so I brush my hand against Master Cooper's lower back, to which he faces me. He cups my cheek and studies me intently, looking for something, then ends his observing with a warm smile. With a peck to my forehead, he nods firmly and hands me the end of the leash.

My stomach does somersaults as I walk up to Master Rio and kneel before him. I dip low, my forehead nearly touching the floor, and I present the leash for him in my open palms.

Please, please, please give me a chance.

The low murmur of the crowd near us tells me I have an audience, and I don't care. It's about the Dom before me, nobody else.

After a few erratic heartbeats, Master Rio squats down in front of me and ghosts his knuckles across my cheek. It heats up under his touch. Then he lifts my chin, and I swallow hard at the intensity of his gaze.

He has to see the vulnerability and want in mine.

Please, please, please give me a chance.

He curses under his breath and leans close, skimming his nose along my jaw. "You're fucking dangerous, little rebel."

I shudder violently.

Rising, he takes the leash and tells me to stand.

I obey without hesitation, and I overhear Master Cooper mentioning something about my posture to Brayden again. Guess the guy's in training, huh? *Head in the game.* Right. I refocus on Master Rio and follow him dutifully toward the Cave. It's where all the scening stalls are, but it's also the direction of the Cinema and the Chamber, and I hope he's not going to the latter.

Kayla told me tomorrow is Master Rio's birthday, so obviously I want to celebrate it. So there's nothing Middle Eastern or harem-like about the Chamber tonight. Instead, Kayla and I turned it into a birthday bash for Master Rio earlier this morning. The décor is still there, but so are countless balloons and garlands.

Much to Kayla's dismay, I went with black and gold for a theme.

"You know, pink and yellow is funner," she'd argued.

Imagine Master Rio's face.

He's not aiming for the Chamber, though. Thankfully. He makes a turn around the circular bar in the middle and guides me into one of the bigger stalls.

Oh, fuck yes. A large spider web created out of thick rope is constructed on a solid, wooden frame.

CHAPTER 11

"Let's make this private." Master Rio lets the curtain fall, and then he spins to face me fully. "Christ, Chelsea." He backs me up against the web of hemp and steals my breath in a bone-crushing hug. "A simple apology would've sufficed."

I'm too stunned to speak, but I've barely begun apologizing. And showing him. Showing him that we should give us a try.

"Permission to speak, Sir?" Happy tears well up in my eyes, and I return the hug as tightly as I can.

"Speak," he murmurs, kissing my neck. "*Fuck.* That was the most beautiful thing I've ever seen." He palms my cheeks and claims my mouth with his. "Seeing you by my feet—indescribable."

Desire stronger than I've ever felt swirls around me, leaving me dazed and needy as fuck. "I'm sorry for running out—"

"You're forgiven." He breaks the kiss and lets out a low chuckle. His dark green eyes track his thumb brushing over my bottom lip. Then his gaze lifts to mine, and he shakes his head slowly. "I'm a fair man, Chelsea. You went from overhearing me telling Nick I didn't want you here...to being fucked into my mattress and wearing my bruises—in what, a week?" I flush at his words, completely breathless. *And wetter than a river.* "I understand your reaction. There wasn't enough time for you to build a trust in me, and you believed I was the one who said those things about Miranda."

The rope digs into my back deliciously, almost as much as the relief pierces through me.

"I saw you," I say with a small nod. "I wouldn't have fled like that if I hadn't seen you. Well, I thought it was you. Master Dante even told me it might've been a misunderstanding, but I was so sure..."

Master Rio inclines his head and smiles faintly. "Gabe and I look that much alike, huh?"

I make a face. Everyone's smarter in retrospect, and I'm no different. "I was on the stairs, and I saw him in the living room, facing the patio. I noticed he looked smaller than you, but I chalked it up to me being upstairs. And his voice—it wasn't really yours. Or his hairstyle. Ugh." I look away and bite my lip. "I'm sorry."

"It's okay, sweetheart." He rests his forehead against mine and grips my hips firmly. "So, did you have a plan for tonight, or can I take advantage of the evening since I have you alone now?"

As badly as I want to say *"Whatever you wish,"* I do have an agenda.

"I want this, Sir," I admit, searching his eyes. "I think we can be great together."

Surprise is the first thing I see. But he quickly becomes guarded —or maybe wary. "You're talking about more than a D/s arrangement where we play together every now and then."

Hell, yes. "Yes, Sir."

In a matter of seconds, he ages ten years in resignation and forfeit.

He's really given up, like Master Cooper said.

"Full disclosure," I say, ready to lay it all out there. "Ready to hear my story? You might wanna sit down." The last part was only half a joke.

He doesn't, though. He just stares at me.

Very well.

"My parents were shit." I go with bluntness, and I sure as fuck don't plan to draw this out. "Deadbeat dad, alcoholic mom. My older brother and I were close until he started hanging out with the wrong people. He died of a drug overdose when I was twelve. He was sixteen."

"Chelsea..." He palms my cheek, concern evident on his face.

I shake my head. I like my life to the point where my past is merely experience, not a sob story. "It's okay," I tell him. "Anyway, I had an aunt who took me in when I couldn't be around my folks. Strict as fuck, and I didn't know I missed her until she was gone."

He lifts a brow.

"Cancer when I was fourteen," I explain. "When I messed up, she disciplined me. Sometimes with a ruler, sometimes with a time-out—like I was some kindergartener. I hated it of course, and I'm hardly an advocate for that kind of punishment on children today, but... It wasn't the punishment. It was how swiftly the bad was over. I fucked up, I got the ruler, she forgave me, hugged me, and that was that." I take a breath and stare at my feet. "I never had to fear that she'd leave me. She doled out her chastisement and enforced a shitload of rules, but she cared. She had my best interests at heart, and I miss that structure." I lift my gaze again and meet Master Rio's expression of understanding. "She was my rock until she passed. After that, I lost it. I quit on life. I drank, did drugs, pushed away the few who tried to help me, fucked to pay rent" —I ignore the way his jaw clenches— "stole to buy food and clothes..." I trail off with a pointed look.

He scrubs his hands down his face. "I haven't figured out how so many can know about Miranda, but no wonder you reacted the way you did." He sighs and lets his hands fall again. "You were just a child," he says quietly. "I wish I could've made things better for you."

He doesn't get it.

"You did, though." I poke his chest. "I'd been on the streets on and off for two years when you cornered me in that nightclub, Rio. Master, Sir, whatever-the-fuck." I wave a hand and pretend I don't see his mouth twist into a little smirk. "I don't care how outta line you might think you were when you told me about caning brats who don't obey you. *I don't care.*" I grit my teeth, so fucking frustrated. "You gotta understand what it did to me. You were just a meal ticket; I wanted a cab ride or food or a place to stay, and I was willing to spread my legs for it. Hell," I scoff as I think back, "you were hot as fuck. Spreading my legs would've been a bonus. But you didn't react the way *all* other guys had done before you." I release a breath and try to calm down. "You were rock solid. You couldn't be budged. You told me to take care of myself because there's only one of me." His eyes soften, and it causes the fight to drain out of me. "I remember every minute of that little encounter," I whisper. "Maybe it wasn't very significant for you, but it fucking changed me. It woke me up."

Rio pulls me close again and hugs me tightly. He takes a breath, and I can sense him wanting to say something, but I'm not done. I gotta get this out so I can move on.

"Yes, what you said was the first I'd ever heard about BDSM," I mutter against his chest. "But that's not why I looked into it. It wasn't what you said. It was you—because of how you acted. Who you are." I tilt up my chin to look him in the eye. "I made every mistake in the book when I first got into the scene, but I knew I was on the right track. At first, it was just about structure. I wanted someone to rely on." But that was the kid in me who'd grown up in a shitty environment. Every child needs stability. "Then I learned more. I evolved and tried different things. I met new people and got lucky with a Dom who was willing to mentor me."

I smooth out the frown creasing his brow.

"This isn't some phase for me, Sir," I murmur. "Casual arrangements don't satisfy me, either. My vanilla life, dreams, and goals aren't going anywhere, but when I submit, I do it fully—body, mind, soul. Even in my everyday life, I'd feel better with rules to follow and having a Master to please."

The glimpse I got when I first met Rio a decade ago—of what my future could hold—has changed drastically with each thing I've learned. But the nature of it has remained, and after coming to California, I want it so much it hurts. Scening with him, hearing his friends speak about him, seeing his home, and the tidbits I've picked up over the years through Facebook have all contributed to a fairly clear picture of what kind of man Rio is.

"I never stood a bloody chance against you." Rio closes his eyes and presses his lips to my forehead, lingering. "I knew it ten years ago; I know it now."

"That's...cryptic." I tug on his silvery gray tie, though I stay in his hold. I love being so close to him. Close enough to smell his aftershave, feel the softness of his black button-down, and hear the gentle rasp of his five-o'clock shadow against my skin whenever he kisses me.

"I suppose it's my turn to be honest." He nuzzles my hairline and brushes his fingers along my collar. "Trust me when I say you're not the only one who recalls every minute—" He pauses and backs away, brows knit together. "What's this?" A finger ghosts over the bandage covering my ink.

Oh, right. So much for not delaying that reveal, as Master Cooper had requested.

Oops.

"It's my SLRN," I answer honestly.

At that, his eyebrows shoot up. "SLRN, as in...?"

I nod him along. He knows the answer, and he's silly for hesitating.

The hesitation in his eyes fades, thankfully, and it dawns on him. Hopefully he now understands that I'm goddamn serious when I say I know what I'm doing.

"You have a slave registry number?" He still phrased it as a question, of course. *Domly types, man.* And because he might've grown cynical over the years, the doubt comes next. He narrows his eyes. "It's new."

"The tattoo, yes." I don't miss a beat. "But I registered four years ago. You can check the database if you want."

"*Jesus.*" He backs away and runs a hand through his hair, his slightly widened eyes finding me quickly. *Yes, that's right. I know what I want, mister.*

I place my hands on my hips. "When are you gonna stop looking for obstacles and reasons why we shouldn't—" I haven't even finished the sentence before he closes the distance between us, cups my cheeks, and leans down to kiss me. Hard.

I let out a muffled *umph* sound, and it takes a couple seconds for my brain to catch up. But once I do, I throw my arms around his neck and return the kiss with all the passion I can. I moan as he strokes my tongue with his, his fingers digging into my hips possessively.

At the feel of his cock pressing against my lower abdomen, my knees get weak, and a dull throb of lust drops to the center of my body. Wetness dampens my pussy, and I instinctively wrap my legs around him and clench my thighs.

He groans into my mouth and bunches up my dress. "Fuck, baby. Hold on to the rope."

My breathing hitches. I comply. I release his broad shoulders and bring my hands high above my head, getting a good grip on the webbed rope behind me. Then I watch Rio retrieve his wallet from the inner pocket of his suit. *God yes, please. Fuck me.* He finds a condom, tosses his wallet on the chair in the corner, and inches away just enough to unbuckle his belt, then unzip his pants.

I take the hint and loosen my legs around him, though I try to pull him close the second he's pushed his pants and boxer briefs down his hips. His clothes pool around his knees, already forgotten.

My mouth waters at the sight of his long fingers rolling the rubber onto his thick erection.

"I won't return you to Mark," he tells me, slipping a hand

between my thighs. All I can muster is a whimper as he traces my
wet slit. He slides two soaked fingers up to my clit, then down again
until he circles my hole and slams them inside.

"Fuck!" My head falls back against the rope. My body fucking
trembles, and he's barely even begun. "Oh, God..."

"'Oh, Master,'" he corrects. His teeth gnash together when he
replaces his fingers with his cock, and I cry out in pleasure at the
intrusion. He lets out a panted breath and stills. "I won't be able to
fight this anymore." Don't ask me why he posed it as a threat. "I'll
take it all."

"*Good.*" I squirm and whimper, wanting more. "Please, Sir."

He grinds deeper and grabs my jaw. "You don't get it," he grits
out. "I've always been an all-or-nothing kind of man, and I've
settled for nothing for a *long* time. If we do this..." He screws his
eyes shut, his lips ghosting over mine. "My feelings for you terrify
me, Chelsea." I swallow a gasp as he opens his eyes again, and the
emotion swimming there is overwhelming. I've never seen him both
so exposed and so predatory. "I'll want you in my house several
days a week as soon as your training begins." Now we're talking.
Fuck, at last. And...he finally starts to move inside me. "There'll be
contracts and protocols." Yes, yes, yes. "I'll never be completely
vanilla. When I take you out for dinner, every decision is still mine.
What you wear, what you eat. And my idea of romance is antici-
pating your needs, knowing your wishes, and choosing when to give
it to you." Holy hell, his words seduce me as much as his body does.
"You don't know how much power you have over me already, little
rebel—*fuck*. Or how many of my own rules I've broken." He groans
and shoves his cock deep. I mewl and meet every thrust. "But I
don't have to worry about you trying to take charge, do I?" He
finally understands.

"Sweet Jesus—Master," I pant, flushed with arousal. "Of
course you don't. My... My..." God, it's getting too difficult to
speak. "My philosophy is—*ungh*—" I gasp as his pelvis rubs against
my clit, and I can't help but close my eyes. "The sub's needs are as

important as...as the Master's, but the Master's desires trump the sub's."

"Perfect." He kisses me hungrily and moves faster, harder. "Consider yourself my sub-in-training, beautiful." Those words trigger an explosion of happiness and euphoria to wash over me. "I'll own every part of you. You'll be my property. *Only* mine."

A needy whine slips through my lips as my orgasm threatens to set off, and my arms ache from holding myself up. "May I please come, Master?" A bead of sweat trickles down between my breasts, and my breathing goes from labored to barely there.

"No." He grunts and cups my ass roughly, then slides one hand up my front and pushes down the sheer material of my slave dress. "I can't wait to mark these." Dipping down, he palms one of my tits and sucks the nipple into his mouth. I groan in response, feeling his teeth graze teasingly against my sensitive flesh. "Out of this world," he moans. "Imagine how they'll look with my come on them."

I can't fucking take it. I'm right on the brink.

"Whatever you want." I suck in a shaky breath. My lungs burn, needing more air. "Oh fuck—*please*, Master!" My pussy tightens around his slicked-up cock as he rams forward.

No luck. He tortures me for half an eternity, alternating between quick, shallow thrusts and deep, I-can-soon-feel-you-in-my-throat ones. And what was once an ache in my arms and wrists from holding the rope so tightly is now a fiery throb that pulses and spreads down my neck and back.

When my fingers slip and I nearly lose my grip, I hiss at the rope burn and grit my teeth together. I will *not* fail him, goddammit. But it's clear that two yoga classes a week will soon be three.

"Good girl," he murmurs, outta breath. His eyes are warm with...approval? "You're not one to complain, are you?"

"I wanna be the best I can be for you. Even if my arms die." I manage an impish grin, though it's cut off when he strokes my clit.

Oh God, oh fuck. My entire being seizes up, and I scream internally in protest at my climax surging forward. Any second, any second—

"Come." Rio—*my owner*—buries himself to the hilt and groans against my neck, and the last thing I'm aware of is his cock pulsing deep inside my pussy.

The ecstasy tumbling through me numbs out any pain. I lose my senses and awareness. Spots appear behind my closed eyelids, and I hold my breath for as long as I can, wanting the bliss to go on forever.

I don't know for how long I space out. Sound by sound, feeling by feeling, I slowly regain consciousness. The delicious soreness between my thighs makes itself known. My arms aching when they're lowered. The music in the background. Screams of pleasure and pain around us.

When I come to enough, I notice we're not even by the spider web anymore. Master's seated in the leather chair, and he's cradling me close to his body. Black shirt and dress pants back in place, but his suit jacket is around me instead.

"My beautiful little rebel," he whispers against my temple.

I sigh blissfully and cuddle closer, pressing my nose into the crook of his neck. Never before have I felt this safe.

"Thank you for giving me a shot, Master." I nuzzle his jaw and press a soft kiss there.

I feel him shaking his head. "Thank *you* for being brave when I wasn't. We wouldn't be sitting here right now if it weren't for your determination and faith in us. I've grown cynical enough over the years that I sometimes don't see a good thing even if it smacks me upside the head. Especially when it's a bright, gorgeous young woman who has her entire life ahead of her."

I smirk drowsily at the image of me smacking him *anywhere*—eeep!—and lift my head from his shoulder to look him in the eye. "I've lived enough to know I wanna do the rest of my living with a collar around my neck." I kiss him on the lips. *Kissing his smile.* "And I've experienced enough instability and loneliness to know I wanna achieve the rest of my goals while serving at my Master's feet." Then, to make it playful, I chuff him lightly on the chin and say, "We'll find our balance, champ."

He gives me an incredulous look before barking out a laugh and squeezing me tightly.

CHAPTER 12

The outside world reminds us of its presence when Evangeline carefully peeks in and says, "Mr. Ford asked me to let you know it's almost time."

Oh!

I'd almost forgotten the birthday party Kayla and I planned for Rio.

"We'll be there in five," I answer. "Thanks, hon."

She grins and disappears again.

Master lifts a brow, the corners of his mouth tugging upward. "I believe it's up to me where we'll be in five minutes."

I lean forward and kiss his nose, just 'cause. "You can start bossing me around the second we get there, but you can't say no to this. You're the guest of honor, after all." With that, I hop off his lap, wince slightly at the soreness, and straighten my dress. "You wouldn't wanna miss your own birthday party, would you? I made the cake myself." And I'm damn proud of it!

"My birth—" He closes his mouth, and his initial confusion is wiped away with a soft smile. "You amaze me."

It's my goal to keep doing that—and to keep that smile on his face.

"Come on, Master. Your friends are waiting." I hold out a hand for him.

True to his nature, Master gives me his first instruction right before we enter the Chamber.

"If I tap my thigh, it means I want you to kneel next to me. We'll work on poses later. You're free to speak, but keep in mind you have to ask me before you make any plans with your girlfriends."

Easy enough. Though, the one I'm most anxious to talk to isn't a *girl*friend. At this point, I'm really fucking worried about Dylan, and his face is the first one I seek out the moment we enter the dimly lit Chamber. But he's nowhere to be found. Mr. Ford, Mr. Kingsley, Master Hill, Master Cooper, Mistress Judy, Master Dante, their subs...Gabriella—I'll have to ask her.

Seated with Mistress Judy's sub, Gabriella looks as happy as Mr. Kingsley does across the room—as in, not at-fucking-all.

"Happy early birthday, Master Rio!" Kayla cries out, bouncing in her seat. It's followed by a wince, so I'm guessing Mr. Ford didn't go easy on her butt earlier. "Daddy, can I go hug him?"

Before friends swarm Master to congratulate him, I ask if I can go over to Gabriella and talk to her about Dylan. Master nods and tells me to hurry back.

I leave his side the second before Kayla and Evangeline run up to hug him.

I smile to myself, happier than ever. It's an amazing and close-knit community I've joined.

Making my way over to Gabriella, who's now alone, I sit down next to her on a couch and peer out over the room and the people around us. I catch Master glancing around, taking in the balloons, the banner attached between the two brass poles in the middle of the floor, the garlands, the small bar that has replaced the wax play station, and I see the smile he directs at the floor before he shakes his head dazedly.

Pleasure fills me.

"Hey." I nudge Gabriella's shoulder with mine. "I know you and I haven't talked much, but are you okay?"

She sends a polite smile my way and tucks a piece of her chin-length hair behind her ear. The shiny, dark hair looks like it's been straightened, not a strand out of place. *"Perfect little girl"* comes to mind with her baby pink dress, light makeup, and huge rock on her ring finger. But for some reason, I think her green eyes should be filled with mischief. The faint freckles on her cheeks and nose should be displayed proudly—not hidden under foundation—to show she just might be the hottest mix between Italian and Irish.

I wanna muss up her hair and remove the invisible corset that has her sitting stiff as a stick.

"I'm fine, thank you." She flashes her pearly whites. "My Daddy wanted to be here to celebrate Master Kelly, but he was held back at the office."

Uh-huh. According to Dylan, that's a common occurrence.

"All right, sweets." I drape an arm around her shoulders and lean in a little closer. "We're still strangers, so I get the polite nonsense. But whenever you wanna cut the shit and talk about your Daddy Dom, or, you know, maybe Dylan and Mr. Kingsley, I'm here for you. Deal?" I stick out my hand for her.

Her eyes widen comically, her gaze flicking between my face and my hand. Then she composes herself, but not before I see a glimpse of hesitation and curiosity.

When she averts her eyes, I follow to where she's looking, and what a surprise, Mr. Kingsley's watching us with a small frown.

"Deal." Gabriella shakes my hand quickly and exhales shakily.

Maybe she will, maybe she won't. She's back to her schooled self, so she might be humoring the sub she only recently met.

"I didn't mean to get pushy," I feel the need to add. "I came over to ask about Dylan, but I saw you lookin' sad, so..."

Another smile, this one more forced. *Pained.* "It's okay, Chelsea. Thank you for your concern." Man, she's formal. "As for Dylan..." There's that pain again. "He left for Texas this morning." That leaves me queasy in an instant. "He told me you two hung out after Master Kelly's party. He likes you." This time her smile is a bit more genuine.

"You can't have too many friends," I respond. "I like him, too." Looking down at my lap, I frown and wonder if Kayla has his email or something. *Wait.* I've friended him on Switch's web forum. I'll try there.

In the extremely short time I've known Dylan, I've already started feeling protective of him in a kid-brother sorta way. He's this cheeky yet vulnerable sweetheart, and a part of me wants to go over to Mr. Kingsley and give him a piece of my mind. But I don't know enough about their situation, and it's none of my business to interfere.

That's Kayla's domain.

"He didn't tell me when he's coming back, but he will," she says, nodding firmly. "He has to. He's got the Nationals this summer, the short-course World Championship in December, and then the tryouts for the Olympics next year. He wouldn't go without his personal trainer for long."

Huh. So when Kayla told me Dylan's a professional swimmer, she really fucking meant it. I mean, the Olympics? Christ on a cracker.

"If you talk to him, tell him to PM me on Switch's site?" I ask, noticing both Mr. Kingsley and Master walking over.

"Of course—" Gabriella nods and purses her lips as the two Doms reach us.

Master taps two fingers on his thigh, at which my heart rate spikes and I quickly remember his instruction. Sliding off the couch, I kneel next to him and direct my gaze downward.

He strokes a hand over my hair.

Shiver.

"Everything okay here, princess?" Mr. Kingsley asks Gabriella.

"Yes, Sir," she answers demurely. "Master Kelly, my Daddy sends his congrats."

"I'm sure he did, little one." There's a wry smirk in Master's voice. "You're here—that's what matters. Isn't that right, mate?"

I smile to myself.

"Hell, yeah." Mr. Kingsley's whiskey voice fills with a gruffness, and unless I'm reading too much into it, he's not happy with Gabriella's Daddy Dom. "Now, how about we get these girls some cake?"

Rio brings me home with him after Switch, and for the second time in as many nights I've spent at his house, I wake up in his bed alone, the moonlight shining through the wall-sized window.

After rubbing the sleep out of my eyes, I see Rio standing by said window, hands in the pockets of his sweats. He's more of a silhouette than a person. His body is shadowed by the night, from his head and broad shoulders, past his narrow hips and muscular thighs, down to his bare feet. His hair sticks out a bit more than usual, either from sleep or from running a hand through it too many times.

Reaching for the black dress shirt he wore earlier, I slip it on and leave the bed. The hardwood creaks quietly under my feet, but other than a small tilt of his head, Rio doesn't move. He knows I'm awake now, though.

"Can't sleep, Master?" I ask softly.

He hums as I slide my palms down his back and around his middle.

"Just a few things on my mind." He covers my hands with his and brings them up to kiss my knuckles. I rest my forehead between his shoulder blades. "I was trying to remember the last time I felt this way—happy, excited...nervous." I feel his smile against my knuckles with another brush of his lips. "I suppose last time should've been when my fiancée was alive, but it's not. Far from it."

That's sad.

"Did you leave BDSM for her?" Because I know his fiancée was vanilla, according to Kayla. And though Nicholas's suspicion of *me* being the reason Rio left the scene has wreaked havoc in my thoughts for days now, I can't wrap my head around that. It makes no sense.

"No." With a gentle tug on my hand, he silently tells me to face him. I kiss his back then sneak under his arm and peer up with a smile. "I left because of my reaction to meeting you."

That wipes the smile off my face.

I swallow, suddenly nervous as fuck. "What do you mean?"

He sighs and clasps his hands around me, resting them above my butt. "Like I started telling you before I...well, before I attacked you at the club—"

I can't help but chuckle, and I smack his chest playfully.

His eyes show both mirth and challenge. "*That*," he murmurs and nips at my fingers, "will get you punished when you begin your training."

"Which starts tomorrow, Sir," I point out, not deterred. "But okay. You were saying."

He inclines his head, his hands returning to their previous position behind me. "You're not the only one who remembers every minute of when we first met." He parts his lips to continue then changes his mind. "Come here." Guiding me over to the cushy chair in the corner near his closet, he sits down and draws me onto his lap. "I got into BDSM when I was nineteen, so I considered myself experienced at thirty." *When we met.* "I learned new things frequently, sure, but nothing surprised me anymore. I knew—I *thought* I knew exactly what I wanted. I played often, went to events, and had a few steady—very obedient—partners I scened with. Doctor by day, Master by night."

Inching closer, I rest my cheek on his shoulder and give him a squeeze.

He kisses the side of my head. "Then I went to New York for a seminar, and a few of us went out one night. And there you were." He grows silent for a beat, absently fiddling with the buttons on his shirt I'm wearing. "Back home, I had a sub waiting for me. She never questioned a thing I said. Did everything I ordered. Pleased me. Never bothered me. We played together here and there—alone or with others." Ah. The sharing. "She was the perfect slave, exactly what I was used to—what I thought I wanted."

Thought he wanted...

"Look at me." He lifts my chin, his gaze penetrating. "You have unforgettable eyes, Chelsea. In every sense of the word. Did you know that?"

I roll them and ignore the blush rising to my cheeks. "Yeah, I know they're weird." My brother had normal eyes—an intense gray color. I have Central Heterochromia, and in my case it means a dark violet color around the pupil that merges with the gray.

Rio shakes his head slowly and palms my cheek. "Not weird. Unique and exquisite. They kind of sucked the air out of my lungs when I first saw you." He kisses me chastely, and there's no ignoring the heat in my face now. "Even at sixteen, you looked like a goddamn sin." The man has a way with words. "That's what shook me, too." The light dims from his eyes, and his mouth thins. "You said I reacted differently than the other motherfuckers you hit on, but I didn't." His hand falls from my face. "I wanted you. You have no *idea* how close I was to bringing you to my hotel and screwing the daylights out of you."

I choke on nothing and sit up straight; however, that gives Rio the wrong idea, and more resignation shadows his features. He thinks I'm grossed out by him.

"You didn't," I say unnecessarily.

"I wanted to," he repeats. His leans back and grasps the ends of the armrests with both hands. Distancing himself from me. "Even after you confessed your real age. Even though I could clearly see what you needed was stability and—Jesus fucking Christ." He releases a breath and pinches the bridge of his nose. "What you needed was a home, a damn meal, and people who cared for you."

Now I'm annoyed, so I straddle him to face him fully, and I fold my arms across my chest. "You could see all that, huh?" I respond dryly. "You've got skills."

"Give me a break." He cocks a brow. "You were sixteen and dressed like a prostitute. You were stick-thin, under the influence, and your friends looked like addicts. It didn't take a genius to figure out you came from a broken home."

I stare at him a bit longer, his words sinking in, punching me in the gut, and then I look away grudgingly. I guess it *was* fairly obvious.

He gets up close again, a glare fixed in place. "And I still thought with my dick." His jaw tenses. "I still wanted to take you away from all that and make you my personal property."

Wait... My eyes narrow. "Hold up. Either you wanted a quick fuck, or you wanted to make me your sub—slave, whatever. Make up your mind 'cause there's a fucking difference." Especially since he'd been in the BDSM community for close to a decade when we met. He would've known, back then, that owning a sub isn't all about blow jobs whenever you want or having your meals served with a snap of your fingers. It's about nurturing and...so many other things.

Rio shrugs with one shoulder and leans back once more. "It really doesn't matter, Chelsea. I *did* want to take care of you as well, but I also wanted my cock shoved up your cunt."

I bristle at his crudeness, which I know he's laying on thick solely to come off as the disgusting bastard *he* seems to believe he is...or was.

I've got one hell of an argument bubbling up, but just like that, the urge to dispute him drains outta me. Once again, he's fighting us.

Is this how it's gonna be?

I don't know how much more I can take, nor do I think I deserve it.

"Okay." I stare at him flatly. "Will that be all? Am I being released before I can start? I'd like to know."

A frown knits his brows together. "What—" And he gets it, what I'm wondering. "God no, sweetheart." He's quick to close the distance between us and press our foreheads together. I'm still irritated, but I can't deny feeling relieved, too. "If it's up to me, you're not going *anywhere*. I only wanted to tell you this. I don't want you to think I'm all that noble—"

I cut him off, shaking my head minutely. "I don't care about what you thought. What matters is what you didn't do. You *didn't* bring me to your hotel—for a quick fuck or not. If people had to be held accountable for their thoughts, we'd all be in prison. Everyone thinks some fucked-up shit at some point."

His mouth twists into a small, rueful smile. "You may be right. But for me, it was fucked-up enough to leave my lifestyle behind. Everything about you rattled me. I've never felt less in control of myself. What I believed I wanted didn't do it for me anymore, and the image I had of the man I was changed."

I tilt my head, curious. "You keep saying that—that you thought you knew what you wanted. Are you saying you *don't* want a perfect sub?"

I'm hardly perfect, but I love high protocol and feel more at home when I can be who I am, which is completely submissive.

"I'm saying that my definition of *perfect sub* changed." His hands return to the armrests, though he stays a little closer now. "After I came home from New York, I tried to get back to normal. But the partners I'd once enjoyed annoyed me, and I realized they were never people for me. They were playthings without opinions and views. It got old. To each their own, of course, but I wanted less of a doormat and more of...more of the defiance and strength I saw in those eyes of yours that night." Hmm. Sure, I was defiant at sixteen, but— "Defiance might be the wrong word," he murmurs, frowning to himself. "Opinionated." Much better. "You might be submissive, baby, but that doesn't mean you're weak. You're a strong young woman who isn't afraid to speak up. You go after what you want."

Yes. You.

More than ever.

He sees me, all of me, I'm sure of it now.

I haven't questioned that, though. It's more about whether or not he sees himself.

"All right." I look down between us. "So...instead of leaving the scene, why didn't you just go after the new kind of sub you wanted?"

"Because—" he lets out a hollow chuckle "—I couldn't stop seeing your face. I built up this girl who didn't exist, and she looked like you." He sighs and twirls a strand of my hair around his finger. "It got to the point where I was sick of myself, and I ended up walking away. I went for the cookie-cutter, all-American dream. Got a vanilla girlfriend, poured myself into work, and kept my old friends at arm's length."

Well, I definitely get it now. My beautiful Master is a jaded mess because he's been punishing himself for over ten years for something he never did.

What if everyone punished themselves for the times they've *wanted* to do something wrong? Like lying. Like cheating. Like stealing. Like fucking killing. It all boils down to what you do, how you act, not what you sometimes wish. God, I wish I could strangle ninety percent of our country's politicians, but that doesn't mean I'm gonna do it. I want a roll in the sack with half of Hollywood, but if they paraded into my bedroom, I'd suddenly have standards. It'd be cool to rob a bank, get away with it, and live the rest of my life in Mexico.

Fleeting thoughts and urges that are taboo don't make a person bad, and sometimes we have fantasies that come to life in our heads. We covet them, but we draw the line at imagination.

"You're a wonderful man, Master." I kiss his lips and move my arms around his shoulders. "And the girl you cooked up in your head who happened to have my face just might be real. Gimme a shot and we'll see. Okay?"

Rio hugs me back—hard—and holds us still for several minutes.

It hits me that maybe I'm not the only one who's been looking for comfort. Having grown so cynical over the years, Master's shut out any potentials. He's kept everyone at a distance, effectively alienating himself from whatever he's wanted in his life.

CHAPTER 13

I press the fancy fob to lock Rio's Lexus, and with Jase holding one of the boxes and me the other, we walk up the driveway toward my Master's house. Part time, I guess it's my home now, too. Not that I've moved a lot of stuff here, but I've been ordered to spend at least three nights a week here.

Definitely not complaining.

After Nicholas offered me a new position last week in his... *what should I call it—club empire?*...Rio's house is now also where I'll have a small study.

A month into my training as Rio's sub, he felt inspired to go back to work. He didn't want a full-time gig at a hospital though, so he decided to volunteer at a free clinic. Dr. Kelly is one sexy mofo.

It was my job as a hostess at Nicholas's club The Library and Rio's hours at the clinic that prompted my Dom to call in a few favors. *"With you working nights and my working days, I don't see you enough,"* he'd told me before dialing Nicholas's number.

As of yesterday, I'm one of Nicholas's assistants. 'Cause apparently the man has several.

He's opening two clubs in the Bay Area this year, so all meetings concerning his new projects go through me now. Which is daunting as fuck, because I've never been a PA before. Nor do I have the amount of faith in me Nicholas evidently has. But damned if I'll screw up, hence buying and borrowing a bunch of material for me to read up on.

I love the challenge, though. It's exciting, and that's certainly a new feeling for me when it comes to work.

"You forgot to mention your new man owns a mansion," Jase drawls, scanning the large façade.

I chuckle nervously as I dig for the spare keys Rio's given me. Truth is, it's a bit intimidating. He keeps telling me to feel at home, but that's gonna be a while. A part of me is still waiting for the other shoe to drop. Or for Rio to start fighting us again.

That said, he hasn't done anything lately to feed that fear. Quite the opposite. I have my own room next to Rio's—although he wants me in his bed whenever I spend the night—I have access to a fucking Lexus, I have keys and a damn credit card in his name, and I practically run his household.

As part of my training, I take care of groceries, laundry, sending the cars to be washed, and I deal with the cleaning service that comes once a week. I also run by the clinic with lunch for him if I have time, and on the days I'm here, I make sure dinner's ready by the time he comes home. And when he does arrive, he finds me kneeling naked in the foyer.

It's never been this intense for me before, but I love the workload. I love all the tasks and responsibilities. Just the other night, Jase and Robby saw me writing in my sub journal, and that's why Jase is here now. He wants to meet the man who's ordered me to reflect on every scene and write out my thoughts on all the changes in a notebook that I present to him at the end of each week.

My roommates are sweet as hell. They've sorta taken on the roles of big brothers, something I've missed since I lost my own brother years ago. But Jase, Robby, and Tristan have nothing to worry about.

"We're a bit early," I say, opening the door. I quickly shut off the alarm system and then close the door after Jase. "Rio won't be home for another hour."

When I told Rio about my roommates, he was quick to invite them over for dinner. Tristan's working though, so it's just Jase and Robby. Robby will get here later.

"Where do you want this?" Jase nods at the box in his arms.

So I lead the way down a hallway. We pass Rio's study before we reach the smaller one that is mine now.

Fifteen minutes later, I'm pouring Jase a glass of red and I've just put the lasagna I prepared this morning into the oven. *Jase's recipe.* He'd smirked and nodded in approval after inspecting it.

"The guys have appointed me the interrogator," he tells me.

I raise a brow and sit down at the kitchen island with my own glass.

He stares right back, serious. "This guy, Chelsea. We wanna know he's good for you. You've only been with him for two months, and now you're practically his live-in maid." I open my mouth to argue, but he shuts me up with a simple look. "I know you get off on serving, babe. That's not the issue. We'd like to know if there's more. Does he take care of you? Does he want more than a servant? Does he have your best interests at heart?"

I let out a breath, torn between gratitude for their concerns and annoyance because Rio's intentions couldn't be clearer to me. But Jase and the others don't see Rio—how he is with me at Switch, at home, and how well he balances the strict orders with the gentlemanly sweeping me off my feet.

It's partially my fault, because maybe I've only told my roommates of the things Rio demands of me.

"He's incredibly caring," I start off by saying. "My job—he didn't take that lightly. While he was dismayed by how little we saw each other the first couple of weeks, he didn't want me to take just any job. He was getting ready to help me when Nicholas—"

"Your friend Kayla's fiancé, right?"

"Exactly." I nod. "He suggested the PA gig before Rio could get more involved." And I think I'm gonna really enjoy my new job. "Hmm, what else can I say to ease your mind..." I grin and tap my chin, all while Jase waits expectantly. Damn, he was serious. Okay. "Look." I reach over to put my hand on his. "I'm extremely thankful for you guys, but you don't gotta worry. My entire relationship with Rio is about him slowly but surely taking over almost every aspect of my life. To any outsider, that will look weird."

"That's why we're worried," he reasons. "We just want to make sure it's what you want."

"It is." I sit up straighter and smile. "I mean, there are things about my vanill—everyday life that won't change, but a lot of things will."

He tilts his head. "What kinds of things won't change?"

Oh, that's an easy one. "I'll never be a housewife, for one," I chuckle. "I don't feel the need to contribute financially, but I *want* to. I also need to have that small part of me remain independent." And Rio wouldn't change that. He's already told me he ultimately wants to provide for me, but he also encourages me to have my own life. "I still have the same dreams most people have, settling down, getting married..." *Having a child.* But it's too soon to voice that dream, and frankly, the topic makes me nervous to bring up.

My Master isn't a damn flight risk, so maybe I'm not being fair, but I can't help it, dammit. Baby steps.

Jase gives me a knowing look. "Uh-huh. And what about his brother? Have you guys talked about his reaction to that other sub— what she did? Have you told Rio about the Facebook thing? Have you opened up to him about the fact that involving others in your relationship makes you uncomfortable?"

I chew on my thumbnail.

Honestly, the Facebook issue isn't even an issue anymore. The more I get to know Rio, the more certain I become he'd only get a good laugh from hearing about my stalking. But the rest Jase mentioned? *Ugh*.

"Talk to him, rope girl," he tells me gently. "I get that this is new, but those are some fairly major concerns. You're halfway in love with the man already; you don't want to set yourself up for heartbreak."

I sorta wanna stab his hand with a fork.

Robby shows up some twenty minutes before Rio's due, and Jase and I are putting together a salad and setting the kitchen table.

I'd go with the dining room, but I figured this was more relaxed.

"How did the pitch go?" Jase asks Robby, and I see how they nearly lean in to kiss but catch themselves and back off.

I shake my head.

"The chick had some interesting ideas, but I dunno." Robby shrugs and scratches his nose. "Nothing original about a game where you hunt werewolves. I doubt it's a project they'll continue with, much less hire me to develop."

Leaning my hip against the counter, I face them both and ask, "Video games—good times—but when are you two gonna stop sneaking around?" I sure as hell have their attention now. "You do a piss-poor job of it, too. Both Tristan and I know you guys are together."

A flush creeps forward on Robby's cheeks, and he runs a hand through his hair and looks away.

Jase coughs and tries to focus on the salad a bit too intently.

I snort and roll my eyes then take four plates over to the table.

"I thought we were being subtle," Robby whispers to Jase.

"You weren't," I say frankly. "Apparently you can't whisper very well, either." I blow him a kiss.

At that point, I see Rio's Jeep rolling up the driveway, and I swear I get butterflies.

Hell, I might be more than halfway in love with him. Because unlike what my roommates are aware of so far, it's *so* much more than D/s between Rio and me. For a Dom with sadistic tendencies, he's incredibly sweet and romantic.

Walking out into the foyer, I straighten my pencil skirt and snug button-down, then open the door for him just as he reaches for it.

His eyes roam my body from head to toe, then up again, a smile lighting up his handsome face.

"My little walking felon." He drops his briefcase inside the door and pulls me close. "If this is how you'll dress when working for Nick, I think we'll have to play out a few librarian and schoolgirl fantasies." I shiver and grin as he engulfs me in a hard squeeze, his five-o'clock shadow rasping tantalizingly along my neck. "God, I missed you today, love."

There it is.

"Me too, Master." I sigh contentedly and drop a kiss where he's loosened his tie. "Let me take your jacket."

He hums and straightens, watching me as I remove his suit jacket. "You're singing tomorrow night too, yes?"

I nod and hang up his jacket in the closet. "Yes, Sir. Master Cooper will be there with Brayden and Evangeline, too. Date night and all."

He grins as he rolls up the sleeves of his gray button-down. "Good place for it. I'll be there, of course." Thing is, it has turned into an "of course" too because he hasn't missed a single gig. He'll be there tonight, as well. "I'm having dinner with Gabe and his fiancé before, so we'll drive over to the bar afterward."

"Oh. Okay." I really don't wanna see his brother, and I don't want Rio to see how badly I just want the floor to swallow me whole right now, so I take a step toward the kitchen and say, "I should check on the lasagn—"

"Not so fast." Ugh. Firm, unyielding voice. "Get back here."

My shoulders slump, and I obey.

"What?" I ask dully.

"Don't think for a second I've forgotten what my brother said about Miranda—by default, you too." He grips my chin and forces me to look him in the eye. "My priority is not only you, but also standing up for what I believe in, and I would never hold your past against you." Despite the firm tone, his eyes remain fairly gentle. "With your permission, I'd like to explain everything to Gabe. Then give him a chance to apologize to you. He's a smart guy, but he can be ignorant at times."

I swallow my emotions, touched by his gesture. I mean, this is Rio's own brother. They're family. Yet, he stands up for me.

"Thank you, Master," I whisper. "You can tell him."

He smiles in approval and gives me a soft kiss. "Thank *you* for offering him a second chance. I don't take it lightly."

Okay, I love him, dammit.

And after only one dinner, my roommates appear to love him, too.

CHAPTER 14

After my gig the following night, I stop at Mark's table and chat with him and his partners for a bit. Oh, I'm totally stalling, but can anyone blame me? Rio's at the bar, looking irritated, and his brother and fiancé aren't here. Which means Gabe hasn't changed his mind.

"Well, I didn't mean to interrupt your date," I start telling Mark, but he shakes his head.

"Nonsense, honey. Any chance Evangeline gets for some girl talk works for me." He winks at his girl, who ducks her head.

"Amen to that." Brayden chuckles and takes a sip from his beer. "Earlier she tried to gossip about Gabriella with me."

I lift a brow at that, incredibly curious.

"But this is huge!" Evangeline argues. "She dumped John!"

Hot fuck.

"No shit?" I take a step closer to their table.

"Mmhmm." She nods with a gleeful grin. "After what he did to her on Valentine's a few weeks ago, she's finally had it."

"What did he do?" And why haven't I heard anything about this? I was walking on air after Rio surprised me on Valentine's

Day. He cooked for me and then finished off with dessert and an intense bondage session in his dungeon. He used a new jute rope he'd purchased solely for the purple color it was dyed in that he said matched my eyes. But news about Gabriella would've cracked the daze. I'm pretty sure.

"He forgot their date." Evangeline shakes her head. "Poor girl. She even arrived at the restaurant, but he never showed."

"Bastard," I mutter. "I'm glad she dumped his sorry ass."

"Know what else?" Evangeline smirks, tongue in cheek. "Instead of throwing the ring at him like chicks do in the movies, she sold it and kept the money."

"My kinda girl!" Damn, I'm proud of her.

Midnod, Evangeline's grin fades, and she stills.

Then there are suddenly two hands clamping down on my shoulders. I squeak.

"I think I've let you stall enough now." Rio's husky voice tickles my neck, raising goose bumps in its wake. "Mark, I'll see you and your lovely subs this weekend?"

Mark raises his beer. "Wouldn't miss it."

"What happens this week—" That's all I get out before Rio stuns me by throwing me over his shoulder.

"Gah!" I shriek, to which Mark and Brayden laugh. Fuck, so do other guests sitting near us.

Rio chuckles and swats my ass. "We have a date in the dungeon, my love. See you guys later."

Mmmmmy love. Yes, please.

The bastard carries me out into the cold like that, though it only lasts a minute. Then he reaches his car, and he sits me down on the passenger's side.

"I could've walked, you know," I quip.

"Really?" He closes my door and walks around the vehicle to get in. "You seemed to have problems joining me at the bar, so I wasn't sure."

I sulk at that, remembering the fact that Gabriel never showed.

"You were incredible as usual this evening." Rio leans over and kisses my temple before starting the engine. "I know you've said you don't want anything beyond singing in bars, but you should at least record some of it."

His praise has buttered me up enough, but there's no forgetting the Gabriel issue.

"Your brother didn't come," I mention quietly.

Rio sighs and gives my thigh a squeeze. "No, he didn't. He's set on being stubborn."

"Well, I've always dreamed of being hated by my boyfriend's family, so yay me," I mutter sarcastically.

To my annoyance, Rio lets out a laugh in amusement. "That's a bit of an exaggeration, isn't it? My parents adore you, and my brother has no issues with you whatsoever. I'm afraid your *dream* will go unfulfilled."

Oh, please. Okay, I admit that his parents are wicked cool and seem to like me. Not that I've met them; they live in Australia, but Rio's introduced us over Skype. But the part where Gabriel has no issues with me is total bullshit.

I give Rio a sugary sweet smile. "On Facebook you only have one brother listed, so unless you have another sibling hidden somewhere, you, dear Master, are full of it."

"I'll let the attitude slide since I haven't explained how tonight went yet," he answers, stopping at a red light. He grabs my hand and kisses the top of it. "We forget that Gabe wasn't actually referring to you that morning when he and I argued. After I explained everything to him tonight, he said your situation was completely different. You did what you did in order to survive; you were a child without a family." He lets go of my hand to drive again once the light turns green. "In other words, he's as understanding as I am about your childhood, but he still believes what Miranda did was unforgivable."

Ummm. All right, while I'm practically giddy to be accepted by everyone in Rio's family, I'm a little irritated with Gabriel's reasoning. Because after having spoken to Miranda, I only feel sorry for her. I admit, I reached out to her at the club because I wanted to know how her arrangement with Rio and Nicholas had worked. The latter is obviously monogamous and would never go behind Kayla's back, but he and Rio were both in charge of Miranda during the punishment. Sue me for wanting to know if my Master fucked her.

I had a jealous moment, okay?

I tried to not let that show, though. I asked her if she was okay and how everything had worked. Thankfully, it had been a nonsexual thing. She'd been his house slave for a few days, and then the punishment had ended at the play party. And once I'd relaxed, to which she'd grinned and totally seen through me, we sorta became friends. She opened up about the theft, how ashamed she was, and I learned she'd acted out of desperation.

Miranda's sister is a flighty runaway who recently bailed on her kids.

Unless Miranda wants to alert CPS, she has no choice but to take care of her young nieces herself. She's told Nicholas and Rio the truth, but she refuses help from them, stating she wants to do it on her own and that she's too embarrassed after what she did.

How the fuck can Gabriel think that's unforgivable?

I shake my head and look out the window.

Whatever—all I can hope is that Miranda accepts help soon. Regardless if it's my offer to babysit, Nicholas's offer to give her more hours at the club, or Rio's offer to help her with rent.

"Your brother's kind of a jerk," I mumble.

"In this matter? Most definitely. We've butted heads countless times over the years. I love the guy, but he's spoiled as hell."

I huff and turn to Rio. "You grew up equally privileged with the same parents, and you're not a douchebag."

The corners of his mouth turn up. "Different tastes, different pursuits." He shrugs, and then smirks. "I'm glad you don't think I'm a douchebag, though."

"Only when you deny me orgasms," I tease.

His eyes grow devious. "But I get off on hearing you beg, baby."

And beg I do. Shamelessly.

"By the way, when did you find me on Facebook?" he asks.

Shit, double shit, triple shit.

"Uhhh..."

"I hardly ever use it," he goes on.

"I, um, just found it one day." About eight years ago. Jeesh. Is it getting hot in here? I squirm in my seat. "I was curious."

Side-eyeing me, he grabs my jaw and brushes a thumb over my cheek. "Now I'm the one who's curious. About this little blush of yours."

Kill me now.

"Is my beautiful little property hiding something from me?"

Why oh, *why* is lying a hard limit of his?

"Maybe," I groan in embarrassment. Slumping back in my seat, I fold my arms across my chest and screw my eyes shut. After that, the words come tumbling out in a rush. "Maybe I searched your name like eight years ago, maybe you popped up, maybe I checked in from time to time, maybe a little more when you were overseas. But I was worried! You actually got malaria when you were in Ethiopia! Do you understand how much that freaked me out? I almost messaged you."

Stunned silence is what I get in return.

I'll take that laugh I was hoping for *aaaany* second now.

Please?

As I open my eyes and chance a glance in his direction, a knot of nervousness forms in my stomach. His expression is too blank, and I can't get a read on him. He definitely doesn't look mad, but he doesn't appear thrilled, either.

"I'm sorry." I bite my lip. "I should've told you sooner, but I was mortified."

Eventually, Rio lets out a breath and shakes his head. At the same time, his hand finds mine again, and he holds it tightly. "Don't apologize." He clears his throat. "Christ, don't apologize. I'm just... shocked, I think. And I can't help but wonder where we'd be if you'd contacted me back then as opposed to now."

"My guess is you weren't done being grumpy and cynical then." I try to make light of it.

It works, and Rio chuckles quietly. "I fear you might be right, but I also know I never stood a chance against you." He kisses my hand. "Regardless, the man I am today is eternally grateful for you. And hearing this—that you worried about me—makes my admiration grow tenfold. You continue to amaze me, Chelsea."

My cheeks hurt from smiling so wide, and I gotta blink past the tears welling up in my eyes. It feels like he just took away the weight of the world from my shoulders.

CHAPTER 15

An hour later, we're home and I've showered and pulled back my hair—as instructed—in a neat bun. Heading down the stairs to the basement, I walk naked toward Master's dungeon where he told me he's setting up for our scene.

Instrumental goth metal and the sconces on the blood-red walls of the corridor lead the way for me.

When I reach the doorway, I see that the equipment has been cleared from one of the black-painted walls inside the dungeon, and the spotlights in the low ceiling have been directed to the emptied area.

Master is a fucking vision. His hair is disheveled and damp from his own shower, and he's only wearing a pair of well-worn jeans. He notices me while he's working the settings on his camera, and all he has to do is snap his fingers and point to the floor where I'm standing.

I fall to my knees and lower my gaze, my hands clasping behind my back.

Every Dom has his own set of rules, and I love learning Rio's ways. He's incredibly strict and demands perfection, a bar set high enough for me to always have a goal. There's always a challenge.

My biggest goal is to wear his permanent collar, but I know that can take time. It's a commitment as highly regarded as marriage in my opinion, and Master feels the same.

For now, I cherish his training collar, which he brings over soon enough.

He speaks in a low voice as he smooths the leather around my neck. "Remember what we agreed to do when we got our test results back?"

Anticipation and excitement roll through me. "Yes, Master. We're going to have a TPE weekend." Total power exchange is something I'd love every once in a while, and the prospect of experiencing that this weekend with Master makes me wet just thinking about it.

"What else was I going to do?" He sticks a small key into the collar to lock it into place.

I shiver. "Review my sub journal entries."

He hums. "Very good. We'll begin first thing tomorrow morning, but I thought we could ease into it a little tonight. That way, you'll be more comfortable when Mark and his subs join us for dinner and playtime on Saturday."

I swallow, remembering one of his rules when we discussed TPE. I'm not allowed to speak unless there's a direct question, and that suits me perfectly fine, except...I sorta have a question right now.

"Permission t-to speak, Master?" Motherfuck, am I not too old for stammering?

"Granted."

Here goes. "How intimately will we play with Master Cooper?"

I thought for sure they didn't share, but maybe I'm wrong. Either way, I need to mentally prepare myself before I attempt to witness Master with someone else.

"Look at me, little rebel."

I sigh internally and obey, definitely not expecting to see him smirking.

"Come on." He holds out a hand, and I take it, confused and curious. "This is why I wanted to start tonight. You've mentioned future play parties in your journal, and I noticed something."

He leads me over to the cleared spot and tells me to face the wall. Then he disappears, only to return with his rope bag.

"*No matter who we play with, I will focus on You, Master—hopefully to the point where I forget others are even there.*"

I recognize those words, and it takes me a second before I realize he's quoting me from my journal.

My spine stiffens as I feel his palms rubbing down my arms firmly. He kisses the back of my head, then retrieves a bundle of the purple jute rope he bought for Valentine's.

"Remember the position I asked you to practice?" he murmurs, and I nod obediently. The reverse prayer is nothing for newbies, and many have sustained injuries while trying.

"Yes, Master." I make sure my voice carries conviction. My Owner needs it. One night, we were browsing bondage art together online, and we both found the reverse prayer incredibly beautiful. I know I can do it.

Grabbing me by my biceps, he rubs and massages my arms, and I roll back my shoulders as much as possible. Then I cup my own elbows behind my back so he can get started.

"Perfect." He starts with a chest harness, the rope constricting me in the best ways. Around my shoulders, between my breasts, under, over, around once more. "*In the end, it's always about Your pleasure.*" Great, he's quoting me again. "*I will do everything in my power to please You, including acts I don't enjoy. At the very least, I have to try when You include others.*"

That makes me slightly uneasy, but his skilled hands work me too well. The rope keeps most of my attention.

"Ready for the hands?" He drops another kiss to my hair.

I relax and close my eyes. Rather than answering him verbally, I twist my lower arms so my palms are able to meet behind my back. My wrists and shoulders protest a little, but nothing painful.

Master begins to tie my hands together immediately. "Numbness?"

"No, Owner."

He smiles into the kiss he gives my shoulder. "Perfect slave."

The praise and the rope take me beyond space and time. My mind floats away. The dull ache intensifies and morphs into pain, but the pleasure overrides it so far.

"Chelsea, can you repeat what you told me the first night I offered you my training collar?"

I bite down on my lip, processing his request. "As you wish. I said I'll obey you like a submissive obeys her Master. I'll consider myself property like an object to its Owner. And I'll worship you like the religious worship their God."

"Fuck." The word leaves him in a whisper, and he presses his nose to my neck. His arousal against my ass certainly doesn't escape my notice. "That's right, my love." He nips at my shoulder as he finishes the last knot. "How's the pain?"

While his warmth fades and I hear his feet moving away, I flex my fingers and roll my shoulders. It causes a flush of discomfort to bloom inside me, and perspiration beads along my hairline and chest.

"Seven, Master. No, six."

I hear his acknowledgment from across the room, followed by the quiet but distinctive sound of the camera.

"Bloody gorgeous." He joins me again, this time at my front. "Kneel for me."

I get down on my knees as gracefully as I can, noting he didn't bring the camera. My guess is it's on its tripod, which is pretty much confirmed when another flash goes off a few seconds later.

"I want to cover these walls with photos of us." He peers down at me and strokes my cheek. "I want everyone to see my most precious belonging." *Jesus.* "I want to show you off." He smiles faintly and unzips his jeans. "But, sweet pet, contrary to what you seem to believe...and unlike other gods...I just want one worshiper. I want it all, Chelsea—with you and only you."

A gust of air leaves my lungs in a whoosh. The relief radiates from me. Next, my vision blurs, the pain gets more bearable, and my mouth waters.

Without a word, he cups the back of my head and brings me forward. As if I need coaxing. As if I won't swallow his cock greedily, willingly, for the rest of my fucking life.

I close my lips around his thick erection and take him as deep as I can—for the first time without latex in the way. His fresh, salty flavor hits my taste buds, and I can't help but moan around him. *God, finally.* I suck him hard, wetly, and hungrily.

Every time the pain grows fiercer beneath the tight rope, I try to block it out and redouble my efforts to focus on Master.

The camera captures the bound submissive who kneels with her hands in prayer behind her back, pleasing her Owner, who has his head tilted back in pleasure.

A drop of sweat trickles down his chest as he fucks my mouth. Curses and quiet groans slip through his parted lips.

He wants me and only me.

This day can't get any better.

"Any numbness?" His hooded eyes meet mine, his cheeks flushed with desire. I shake my head no in response and suck him harder. My jaw aches, the pain in my arms causes tears to roll down my face, but none of it matters. "So fucking exquisite." He strokes a thumb across my hollowed cheeks. "Swallow every drop I give you." His head lolls back again, and I watch his Adam's apple bob. He grunts, curses, then shudders and rocks deep into my mouth.

Streams of come pulse out of his cock and slide down my throat.

When he's done, he backs away to catch his breath, and I try to catch mine, too.

"Master," I pant. "My fingers..." They're starting to go numb, and he'll punish me if I don't tell him right away.

"Of course, sweetheart." Master scrubs his hands down his face then tucks himself away and zips up his jeans. *Pity.* "Pain scale?"

"Eight." I make a face.

He nods and grabs his emergency shears from his bag.

"But the rope, Sir," I protest. Rope gets cut all the time, but this bundle was special, dammit.

"Shush. I bought more than one, and even if I hadn't..." He snorts quietly and stands behind me, carefully beginning to cut up the rope. "There we go. Readjust for me slowly, okay?"

I know that, and I let him lower my arms inch by inch. In the meantime, a sense of euphoria washes over me. It always does. It's the releasing of the pain and the feeling of my chest not being squeezed together anymore.

I whimper and lean back against Master.

He hums and rubs my arms and neck, eventually squatting down behind me to capture me in his embrace. The floaty sensation is back. I get needy. Horny. His flavor lingers on my tongue, which isn't helping.

Then I feel his kisses.

His hands cupping my breasts. Massaging, stroking, pinching, teasing.

"Do you need your Owner, little rebel?"

I'm stuck in a heavenly daze. "Yes, Master. Always. Only you." My head rolls back to his shoulder, and I barely react when he picks me up off the floor and carries me over to...oh, joy. His gynecologist table.

I flush with both lust and embarrassment. I'm very comfortable with my body, and I have no qualms when it comes to desire. But *this* friggin' table...it can't leave me more exposed. It's not built for kink, so I guess that's why it brings an extra sense of taboo.

Master doesn't say anything about his plans, and I'm content not to know.

"You've been worried about the sharing, huh?"

He wants to talk about that now? *Now?*

"Answer me." He pinches the inside of my thigh.

I yelp and jump. "Yes, Master." *Head in the game.*

He grunts and uses Velcro to strap me into place. "I suppose that's partially my fault. You subs talk, and I can only imagine what you've heard about me from the other girls." After getting supplies from a cabinet, he blindfolds me and sits down on a chair between my thighs. "Never assume anything, though. Always come to me with your concerns."

I hiss in pain when he attaches clothespins to the lips of my pussy. *Motherfucking God.* Then he rips off bits of tape and fastens the pins to my inner thighs, effectively keeping my pussy completely open for him.

"Such a beautiful cunt." He strokes the length of it with a finger. "Now, where was I?" *Man, I have no clue.* "That's right. Sharing. I've always been fine with it, but it's been because of the lack of intimate feelings. I've never been in possession of someone I felt territorial about, Chelsea."

"Oh, my God." I gasp as he lowers his mouth to lick me. But an equal amount of bliss is from his words. The combination makes my head swim. I wanna squirm and hold on to him, but I can't move an inch.

"No talking." The bastard grins against my wet flesh, then takes my clit into his mouth and sucks on it. The Velcro straps strain at my jolt. "Fuck, you taste good. Know what else is new for me? Falling head over heels in love."

A breath catches in my throat.

I thought the day couldn't get any better...

"Master, permission to—"

"No."

Goddammit! I wanna tell you I love you, too!

I'm about to burst. He says something like that, and then the magic with his tongue—fuck me running, I need to say it back! But he doesn't let me. Instead he keeps driving me bonkers. He owns my pussy with his sensual mouth, fucks me with his fingers, and murmurs wicked promises about the future.

I sob with the need to come, but he denies me.

I tremble and mouth silent pleas, but he ignores them.

Then he stands up, and I hear the rustling of his jeans. Only a beat later, he rams his hips forward and hits deep.

I scream.

He stretches me as perfectly as he plays me.

Every thrust hurts when he rubs against the clothespins, but the pleasure of his cock is ever present, too. Slowing down, he keeps his strokes deep, but he lingers more and leans closer.

I feel his mouth kissing a trail up my throat to my mouth.

"I love you so much," he whispers, removing my blindfold. To prevent myself from responding, I gotta bite down on my lip. He smiles and wipes some stray hairs away from my forehead. "I'll spend the rest of my days striving to be the best Master for you."

Oh, Jesus. I choke up, and the next thing he has to wipe off my cheeks is tears. When the hell did I turn into such an emotional mess? This isn't me. Tears from pain—granted, they happen—but from being overwhelmed? No.

Master pulls out then pushes forward again, and he reaches between us to massage my clit. "Anything you want to say?" His eyes flash with amusement.

I nod quickly. *Please, please, please.*

"All right," he chuckles. "You may speak."

"I love you, too." I whimper and try to buck my hips to get closer. "I love you, Master."

His amusement is quickly replaced by hunger, and he kisses me aggressively and deeply. "Come for me, love." He gets me there with a few more strokes to my clit, and I moan out my orgasm while he chases his own climax.

CHAPTER 16

Saturday evening, I'm practically floating down the stairs after
putting on the lingerie I've been ordered to wear. Master
tends to want me in dark purple, but today he picked out a push-up
bra and thong in silvery satin.

The table in the dining room has been set, the dinner is ready
to be carried out of the kitchen, the wine is breathing, and we're
only waiting for Master Cooper to arrive with Evangeline and
Brayden.

As instructed, I kneel in the foyer and wait for Master's
inspection.

He takes his sweet-ass time doing whatever he's doing and
wherever he is, so I quickly gather my hair into two low pigtails. He
didn't specify about my hair, but he doesn't want it getting caught
in anything if we're going down to the dungeon after dinner.

Eventually, I hear him coming up from the basement, and I
divert my gaze to the floor right before he appears.

I feel his eyes on me, but he says nothing. My posture's perfect,
I'm sure of it. Bowed head, straight spine, hands behind my head,
chest pushed out, and knees aligned with my shoulders.

His bare feet come into view, and I see he's wearing the jeans he wears in the dungeon. Then his hand reaches out to stroke my cheek, and he lifts my chin enough for me to see a simple black T-shirt hugging his torso. *Unf.*

"Master Cooper will be here in ten minutes with a kitten and a puppy," he murmurs. "So I thought I'd turn you into a pet tonight, too. And you're already my bondage bunny."

I smile in reaction, understanding his choice of lingerie for me tonight now. Or the color, rather.

"A bunny needs ears." So he slides a pair of gray bunny ears on my head. "And a tail." *Gulp.* Squatting down next to me, he keeps one hand on my stomach while the other moves down my back. "Bend over."

I obey, and I spot a bottle of lube next to him. He drizzles some liquid onto a stainless steel butt plug that has a fuzzy ball attached to it.

Then he pushes my thong aside. On the front, two fingers tease my slit, causing me to shudder. On the back, the blunt, slicked-up plug circles my ass.

"Breathe out for me." He drops a featherlight kiss to my shoulder, and I relax my muscles and exhale. But it quickly transitions into a long moan as Master slowly pushes the plug into my ass and simultaneously eases his fingers deep inside my pussy. "Good pet."

I suck in quick breaths, the burn and his touches turning me on beyond words. My body craves him like a drug. I clench around his long fingers, but he's gone too soon, and he tells me to stand.

Easier said than done when my knees wanna cave, but I manage.

"Bunnies don't exactly wear leashes," he says as he puts my thong back into place. Next, he moves in front of me and retrieves a bundle of rope from his back pocket. It looks like cotton rope. White. "Let's get you into a harness, shall we? Arms out."

Arms out.

He works swiftly, always looking so fucking sexy when he's in the zone.

"Perfect." He pulls the rope tighter around my breasts, loops it over my shoulders, and down my chest again. "Will you be a good little bunny whore for me tonight?"

Good God. Seems he's dead set on ruining my underwear.

"Of course, Owner. If it pleases you."

"Oh, it will please me greatly." His eyes flash with indecency. "I want you by my feet unless I tell you otherwise. All your focus on me. The only exception is when our guests arrive. Evangeline has requested to speak with you in private, and I told her it was okay."

Understood.

"Anything you'd like to say before we begin?" he asks.

"No, Master. Other than...thank you. I appreciate everything you do for me." I've told him he doesn't have to buy me new lingerie and more stuff for the dungeon, but he seems to enjoy it.

He smiles and kisses me on the forehead. "That goes both ways, my love."

The sound of a truck rolling up the driveway ends the subject, and my Owner adjusts my collar before taking a step back so I can play hostess.

Passing Master, I wriggle my butt and bunny tail playfully at him, to which he chuckles. Then he disappears to stow away the lube, and I grab the door handle and listen silently as Master Cooper reminds his subs outside of the protocol. I hear two "Yes, Master" in acknowledgment before there're two firm knocks on the door.

I open it widely and stand to the side with my eyes on the floor. Greeting Master Cooper would feel natural, but I'm not allowed to talk, and I don't want Master to gag me. Or, if I consider his wicked creativity, stick a bunch of carrots in my mouth. Trust—he'd do it.

Instead, I offer a small curtsy and let my Owner do the talking.

He returns just as our guests have entered. "Good to see you, Mark."

"Ditto, my friend. Ditto." Master Cooper shakes his hand firmly. "Thanks for having us."

"Anytime. Chelsea, take their coats," Master directs. I comply and start with Master Cooper, who hands me his parka with a little smirk. "There are a couple cold ones waiting for us in the living room while the girls get their talking out of the way." Then I get to Evangeline and Brayden, and they both squeeze my hand in silent thanks.

"Sounds perfect to me," Master Cooper replies. "Brayden, you're with me."

After hanging their coats in the closet, it's just Evangeline and me, so I grin and link my arm with hers, guiding her to the kitchen. As always, she's dressed as her Dom's kitten. Black, see-through lingerie with furry trim. Cute kitty ears, tail, and collar, too.

"You look hot," she whispers, smirking. "Are you allowed to talk, by the way?"

"Right now, I am." I smile and open the fridge to take out the salad. Might as well get some work done while we talk. "So, what's up?"

Her smirk is gone, replaced with obvious nervousness. "I need to tell you something." She keeps whispering, even though there's no way the men can hear us from the living room. "I thought about pretending to be sick, but Master would see straight through me."

Must be serious. I leave the salad on the counter to give her all my attention. "Something wrong?" I touch her arm.

She fidgets with her furry, black tail and hesitates for a beat. "I...I think I'm pregnant." *Oh, my God!* "Actually, I know I am." She huffs. "Seven tests can't all be wrong."

"Evangeline!" I whisper. Next, I throw my arms around her and squeeze her tight. "That's—*wow*. Congratulations!" I'm so happy for her!

She sniffles and chuckles at the same time. "Thanks. I'm just... This isn't how we planned it."

I break the hug but keep one hand on her shoulder. "What do you mean? Aren't you excited?"

"I am." Her response is both soft and full of conviction. "It's incredible. After taking the tests and throwing up and sobbing my eyes out, I may or may not have jumped on the bed for ten minutes. Of course, that made me puke some more." She flushes and facepalms at my grin. "*Anyway*. We talked about this, and the plan was...you know, later."

"Later," I repeat.

She nods and makes a face. "Yeah. I mean, we want this. We want a big family, but since there are two men..." She raises her brow pointedly.

And boy, do I get it. From what I've seen and heard, they might as well be married for how committed they are, and I sincerely doubt they care whether it's Brayden or Master Cooper who knocks her up. But when it comes to medical records and blood typing, it's probably a good idea to know who the father is. Which takes planning from the get-go when talking contraceptives.

"So..." I try not to let the amusement bubble over, but I can't help it. A snort escapes me, and I lean down to pat her flat stomach. "Hey, peanut! Who's your daddy? Huh? Who's your daddy?"

"What the f—you suck, Chelsea!" Evangeline squeaks and bats away my hand, at which I crack up for real. "I can't believe you!" Her tear-filled glare and embarrassment only last for like two seconds, though. Soon enough, a chuckle slips out that morphs into laughs. "Oh, my *God*..." She groans through a giggle.

Down to chuckles myself, I wipe my cheeks and beam at my friend. "Seriously, Evangeline. I'm really happy for you guys. I'd ask you all kinds of questions at the dinner table, but I'm pretty sure Master will have me kneeling at his feet. Mouth shut." I smile ruefully, zip my mouth, and throw away the key. "I'll definitely listen in to the rest of you, though."

She scrunches her nose at that. "You seem to be under the impression I'm telling Master and Brayden before dinner."

"Duh." I narrow my eyes. "When else were you gonna do it?"

"Umm...." She bites her lip. "I was thinking tomorrow morning when we get home."

"That's funny." Only, I'm not laughing. "I know you well enough to know you're a smart chick. This is just overwhelming for you and obviously causing you not to think clearly. So, lemme help." I place my hands on my hips. "What does RACK stand for?"

She frowns, confused. "Risk-Aware Consensual Kink."

"Mmhmm." I raise a brow and fold my arms across my chest. "And how aware of risks can your Dom be if he doesn't know you're carrying a baby?"

"Oh, shit." She pales.

I feel for her. I do. But there's no way I'm going down to Master's dungeon with her, knowing she's pregnant. Knowing that her men *don't* know. It wouldn't be safe.

"I'm horrible." Her bottom lip trembles and she looks down. "Oh my God, I'm *horrible*—"

"Hey." I cut her off gently but firmly, placing a hand on her shoulder for comfort. "None'a that shit. Chin up, buttercup." I nudge hers up. "You're amazing, Evangeline. You're smart and loving. You're also human. You're overwhelmed and nervous. You forgot. Simple as that."

She wipes away her tears and hiccups. "An emotional mess is what I am."

Sounds like me the past couple of weeks. "See? Another reason you're not thinking clearly," I say, lightening the mood. "You're too busy crying."

She snorts at that but offers me a small smile. "Thanks, Chelsea. Really." Then she sighs, her shoulders drooping. "Guess I should tell them, huh?"

"No time like the present." I smirk, and then cup my hands around my mouth and holler out. "Master Cooper! Brayden!"

"*Jesus,*" Evangeline hisses, shoots me a quick scowl, and then she's busy straightening her hair, wiping her cheeks some more, and adjusting her clothes.

Her men appear in the doorway seconds later, and Master's right behind.

I point to Evangeline. "She's got news."

Not wanting to crowd the lovely trio, I walk over to Master in the doorway while Brayden and Master Cooper stalk over to Evangeline, lookin' confused and worried.

"What's up, kitten?" Master Cooper asks, concerned.

That's the last I hear from them. They stand close and speak in hushed tones.

"Something wrong?" Master asks quietly.

I shake my head no and hug his middle. "Everything's perfect, Owner." I smile at Evangeline and her two men. "She's pregnant."

That oughta make their playtime interesting the coming months. I've been in the lifestyle long enough to know BDSM can be perfectly safe for a pregnant woman, as long as they stay away from...well, most of Evangeline's favorite activities. Pain, predicament bondage, being squished between the men she loves...but I have a feeling it'll be hella worth it.

"Well, I'll be damned." Master holds me a little tighter, and I watch as both Brayden and Master Cooper move in to hug their girl. There are tears, beaming smiles, two proud daddies-to-be, kisses, and more murmurs between them. "I take it this is...good news?"

"Of course." I grin and tilt up my face to look him in the eye. "Look how happy they are."

He stares at me intently, seeming to debate something internally. "Yes, but...but what I mean is...do you think it's good news only for *them*, or...in general?"

My brows knit together, and I stare at him confused before it slowly dawns on me. Had I not understood, I know he'd be more direct, 'cause my Master has no issues being straightforward. But I *do* get it, and I'm pretty damn sure he's basically wondering if I want kids.

"Personally—" Master clears his throat, appearing uncharacteristically nervous. "I've barely dared to dream of what Mark and Brayden are feeling right now."

Holy shit. My heart jumps up in my throat.

I peer up at him and refuse to cry. "I mean it's good news in the sense that I'm happy for them and hope you'll do more than dream about it one day."

The look he gives me is one of wonder and amazement, as if he almost can't believe it.

"Just when I thought I couldn't possibly get any happier." He palms my cheeks and kisses me on the forehead. Then a kiss to my nose. My chin. My cheeks, and traitorous emotions threaten to surface. "Christ, I love you."

He draws me impossibly closer, and I smile widely as he finally captures my mouth with his. Standing on my toes, I kiss him back with everything I am and bask in the warmth he provides.

Like I said earlier. Everything is perfect. In Master, I have found everything I've ever wanted and never had. Someone to submit to completely, all-consuming love, someone I can grow and share dreams with. Someone who gives me both pain and comfort.

So fucking perfect.

TOUCHING TRUTH

A BEHIND THE SCENES NOVELLA

PART IV

GREG COOPER

"Daddy, look!" Abby points excitedly down the beach where two flamingoes land gracefully in the shallow water. "They're so pretty."

"Not as pretty as you." I smile and sit down in the sand with a juice box for her, knees pulled up a bit so I can rest my forearms on them.

She blushes and flashes me a simpering smile before returning to chasing waves. Or perhaps they're chasing her. Peals of laughter fill the air whenever a wave splashes water on her sun-kissed body.

"That was a *big* one!" She grins and runs over to plop down next to me. "How come the sand is so white here?"

"You know, I haven't the slightest idea. We can look it up when we get back to the hotel." I dig out a small bottle of sun block from the pocket of my cargo shorts and pour a generous amount into my hand. "You don't want to try out the pool?"

After ten days in tropical Aruba, she's barely glanced at the massive pool at the hotel. She absolutely loves the beach and its white sand and turquoise waters.

"Nuh-uh." She turns her back to me so I can apply some more lotion. "Where's Mom?"

"Resting a bit." Our hotel is a five-minute golf-cart drive inland, so we've rented a cabana for our lazy days on the beach. Blinding sun, heat, and salt water make us grownups sleepy here and there. "I remember when you used to take naps with me on the couch at home."

"But I'm a big girl now, Daddy," she states, almost scolding me. "Napping is for babies."

I smirk, making sure to get her neck, too. "There, all done."

"Thank you," she sings. She adjusts the straps of her purple bathing suit. "I'm thirsty. Can I—"

"Ah, sorry. Almost forgot." I brush some sand off the juice box I brought her and hand it over. "Should be cold, still."

"Yummm. Thank you." The tip of her tongue pokes out when she concentrates on punching a hole in the little circle of foil with her straw. Too adorable. "Are you all better now from the accident so we can swim in the deeper water?"

"I am, darling. I thought I could take you snorkeling tomorrow. How's that?" It's been a couple days since I removed the bandages around my head, and the bruise under my eye has mostly faded. I have to keep Ryan's mark hidden from the sun, so I dress it or leave a T-shirt on. Based on the story Tess gave Abby, the concealed wound on the inside of my bicep is related to the "accident."

My jaw is certainly still sore, but not enough to keep me away from more physical activities. I'm doing a decent job stalling and postponing the inevitable, and for some very unknown reason, I'd like to try some outdoorsy things—to see if I have what it takes.

"Yeah, can we snorkel *all* day?" Abby asks, and then she makes her funny face. Eyes crossed, brows furrowed hard, head cocked, and mouth pinched like she's bit into a lemon.

I chuckle and mimic her, earning myself a loud giggle from her. "We can snorkel until Daddy gets tired."

"Okay, don't get tired," she replies frankly. "I want to send a picture of a turtle to Evie."

Hmm, I'm unfamiliar with that name, and I thought I knew all her friends. "Is that a friend from school?"

"Silly!" she laughs. "She watched me *after* school!"

Ah. Evangeline. I do recall Abby struggled to pronounce her name. "Right, of course." I manage a stiff smile.

"Mom says she is together with Uncle Mark," she goes on happily. "She gots two boyfriends now also. But, Daddy? Why won't she watch me anymore?"

Because I had her fired.

I didn't personally speak to Evangeline; I was busy freaking out over the failure of my personal life. Tess took care of that call.

"Let me ask you something else first." I do my utmost to sound upbeat, probably failing miserably. "What do you think about someone having two boyfriends or girlfriends?"

She squints in the sun and scrunches her nose. "I dunno. Nana has two boyfriends and a Pop-Pop. I don't want that. So gross!"

I feel oddly stricken by her words, and my face falls slightly before I snap out of it, because I agree with her. *Oh, you lousy liar.* Well, I *used* to believe the very same. Polyamory isn't normal yet, therefore not accepted.

"Why—" I clear my throat as my stomach knots uncomfortably. "Why would it be gross?"

"Because boys are *yucky*."

I stare at her blankly, only to let out a breathy laugh of sheer relief. Good Christ, I should be smarter than that. It's not the number of boyfriends she's bothered with; it's the fact that it's boys. The truth of the matter is, polyamory is normal to her. She's been around my parents' strange family structure since birth.

Mark has joined the same ranks now. I'm hardly surprised by that. If anything he's done has surprised me, it was when he married Alexa. Although she was as open about her kinky life-style as my little brother is, her passion for BDSM was skin-deep.

Naturally submissive, no doubt, but not into the high protocol like Mark. I'm fairly untrained where that terminology is concerned, but I do believe that means he's very strict and demanding. Which means my daughter's former babysitter is a submissive, and what of her boyfriend? Brayden, was it? Perhaps another sub.

I tug on my ear, scratching it, and think of the miles-long list of epic screw-ups I need to tend to.

Tess is waiting on the top of that list.

"I'm so full," Abby complains.

And visibly exhausted, I note. The hotel we're staying at is a golf and spa resort. There are only a handful other children present in the restaurant on the terrace by the pool, and I don't think the other guests are too keen on having a seven-year-old getting fussy during their dinner. Scooting out my chair a bit, I pat my lap, and Abby bounces right over to me. If she's declining dessert, she is ready to pass out.

She blinks sleepily and settles in for a cuddle.

"She is such a daddy's girl." Tess smiles indulgently and takes a sip of her wine.

I wink at her, knowing very well our daughter has a special bond with Tess that I'll most likely never experience. Thick as thieves, best friends, that's what they are.

"You look like you're feeling better," she comments.

I nod slowly. "I'm getting there."

"Does that mean you can face your own firing squad soon? Your family keeps calling me, you know."

I wave a hand, dismissive, and reach for my beer. "Ignore them."

"That might work for you."

It does, indeed. Over the years, Tess has become my middleman. I don't attend all family functions; she does. If she's available, she's there.

"Greg..." Tess leans forward a little and smiles knowingly, softly. "The other week, you all but pleaded with me to go away with you. You needed time to think, and you wanted to talk. And now...time is sort of running out, honey. We're going home in four days. There's no room for ignoring any longer."

Goddammit. She's been far too patient with me.

Alerting a waiter, I press a kiss to Abby's head and smile ruefully at Tess. "Why is the truth so hard?"

She shrugs lightly and finishes her wine. "Because it kills?"

Good grief. "Only you can reference a philosopher to me and get away with it."

"If the truth shall kill them, let them die."

Tess blows me a quick kiss, and I chuckle. In many ways, she's much the same as when we met in college. Quietly accepting, never one to make a fuss. She has a great inner peace one can only admire. She certainly fit in when we ended up taking the same course in philosophy—for me, a part of political science. For her, an interest. We argued endlessly, long enough for me to forget everyone at home. She became my reprieve.

After requesting to have the check added to our room, we make our way through the gardens toward our apartment complex.

"Drinks on the balcony?" she suggests.

I nod, knowing I'll need a drink or two. "I'll put Abby to bed."

Ten minutes later, we meet up on the balcony where Tess has dug out the bottle of Amaretto we bought the other day. A candle flickers on the low table in front of the love seat, and the expansive view of the golf course reveals nothing but darkness at this hour.

I sit down with a sigh and breathe in the scents of the ocean, after-sun lotions—that somehow insist on being coconut-flavored— and freshly cut grass.

"Thank you." I accept a glass of the amber liquid and let my eyes adjust to the dark. "I'm...I'm not sure where to begin."

She takes a sip, then rests her head on my shoulder. "Whatever it is, I hope it leads to you coming out of hiding. It's time the rest of the world sees the real you, Greg."

My brow furrows, and I look at the drink, swirling it slowly. The knot in my stomach has returned with a vengeance, because I know the truth will kill. Namely, our marriage. Our illusions and our façade.

"I've met someone." *Two someones.* Two beautiful someones I can't forget or move on from. Two beloved Sadists who are my complete opposites and would turn my world upside down more than they already have if I let go of everything I know.

Tess lets out a soft, ragged breath but doesn't move from her position. "I know," she whispers. "It's been months since you started pulling away from me."

I blink past the sudden sting in my eyes and take a long swig from the bittersweet liqueur. "I'm sorry," I cough. *I'm fucking sorry, my dear.* "I thought—I thought I could get past it."

"God, Greg. You think everything is an itch you can scratch away." Releasing another breath, Tess straightens and sets her drink on the table. Then she stands up. "If the truths are spilling out—at long last—here's one of mine. I smoke on occasion, so now I'm going to get the pack I keep hidden in my makeup case."

I frown deeply, too anxious to reprimand her for putting herself at risk, but that doesn't mean I won't bring it up later. *Later.* I feel too awful now. People with educated guesses and fair assumptions can call me a cheater all day, and it won't hurt as much as my betraying the one vow Tess and I made to each other when we married. *To always be truthful.* We knew what we were getting ourselves into. Two different souls aiming for a box that never fit us. But normal is *easy.* Or, it's supposed to be.

In more ways than one, I have cheated. Just not in the conventional way most believe. When I told my brother *it's not what it looks like*, I wasn't lying.

Tess returns, lighting up a cigarette on the way, and takes a drag from it before leaning against the balcony railing.

"So what's wrong with this person you've met?" she wonders, facing the night. "They must be different for you to think it would pass as a phase."

She knows me well. Knows my need for *normal* well. "Emphasis on they," I admit. "It's a married couple."

She lets out a wry chuckle. "The irony. Or maybe it's karma. Your family will be mind-blown."

It's none of their fucking business. I only care about making things right with Tess at this point. She's been my shield for almost twenty years while I've been her safe port. Her background isn't alternative as much as it's abusive. With me, she found a place to heal—with a man who wouldn't take advantage or carry a secret agenda. We've been amazing companions, up until I met Ryan and Angel and I stopped sharing the truth with the one person I promised to always give it to.

"You love them, don't you? This couple you've met." Tess studies me with an open, curious expression. "I don't see you walking away from everything you've built with me otherwise."

I hesitate, then nod once and finish my drink. Jesus, I think I actually do love Ryan and Angel. How else can it physically hurt to be away from them?

"Abby still comes first, Tess," I tell her quietly. "I'm not walking away from anything she's not okay with."

"Oh, Greg." She sighs heavily and stubs out her cigarette. "Under normal circumstances, no child is okay with their parents divorcing. She'll be far from alone, though. Half the children in her class have two homes." She sits down next to me again and refills our glasses. "You've rebelled against this long enough, honey. Perhaps you're not polyamorous by nature, but here you are. You're falling for two people. So maybe it's time to realize you've been fighting the wrong war."

"What do you mean?"

She quirks a weary smile. "You've been so set on fighting everything your parents do and say by doing the opposite. *Nothing* good
comes of it." Clearly. Look where I am. "They *hurt* you by not
being there for you, but that doesn't mean their nature is wrong. It
just means they went about it the wrong way. You can correct that.
You can learn from their mistakes and create a healthy environment for our girl—all while getting what you want."

That's much like what Ryan told me.

I squint down at my drink, ever so reluctant to admit I'm
wrong. Dead wrong, in this case. I've been so angry and resentful
that I've pushed away people rather than speak my mind.

"What about you?" I side-eye her, concerned. Abby's not my
only priority. I won't leave Tess behind, either. "Have you been...I
don't know, seeing anyone?" It's unlikely, given her history, but...

"My biggest offense was keeping my smoking from you." She
snorts into her drink. "I haven't changed. I'm the happiest when
I'm alone."

A concept difficult for me to grasp. Regardless of how difficult
it is for me to form an attachment—much less feel an attraction—it's
ultimately something I crave. Closeness, companionship, love, and
passion. I've been lucky to share the two former with Tess, but I
want the rest, as well.

She's different. For a long time, I couldn't quite believe it. I was
certain her own nature was caused by the abuse she suffered at the
hands of her father from an early age, and I may have been a
complete asshole when I pushed Tess to seek counseling for it.
Well, my disbelief focused on the part where she claimed she didn't
want anyone to share her life with on an intimate level.

A few years after Abby was born, I know Tess met a man at the
hospital where she works, but it didn't go beyond a date or two.
There's never any panic or anxiety triggered, just a sense of unhap-
piness and resignation.

"I think it still worries me," I confess.

She's not surprised. "That's because you confuse alone for lone-

512

liness. I'm far from lonely. I have amazing friends, a family I love, a job that's slowly killing me in a hectic but good way, and plenty of time for my hobbies." She pauses. "I'll miss the familiarity of having you at home, but you and I..." Indeed. We were never in love. We needed each other for different reasons. "It hurts you haven't been honest with me, though."

"I know." I swallow hard, filled with regret. "Would you...be willing to let me make amends? I want—I want what we used to have." My life has never come as close to perfection as it did about ten years ago. We were on the exact same page, wanted to start a family, and most of all, we were best friends. She knows all there is to know about me. And the other way around. I want us to find a way back to that.

Tess shakes her head, amused. "I can't wait for people to learn you're not the arrogant patriarch you've had them believe. *Quite the opposite.*" Way to point out I'm actually the uncertain one in our marriage. "We'll get there, Greg." She pats my arm and settles against me, to which I automatically drape an arm around her shoulders.

I kiss her temple too, the rock in my stomach becoming smaller. At the same time, I get nervous like never before. So much is about to change.

"I love you," I whisper against her skin.

"I love you, too." She tilts her head up to face me. "Tell me about this married couple?"

"Oh God," I mutter. "I'm going to need more alcohol for this." I take a gulp and swallow against the sweet bitterness. "Believe it or not, but they're into the same nonsense Mark is."

Tess chuckles. "BDSM?" I nod in answer, and she grins. "Hmm. You've hidden your body quite a bit these past several months. Are you into that *nonsense*, too? Painful nonsense that gives you reason to hide something, maybe?"

I make a face. "I'll plead the Fifth."

"You're not on trial, honey. You know it's okay to enjoy it."

"Mm, it's just going to be a bitch to admit to certain people." Mark comes to mind. That level of resentment is a hard pill to swallow, but I have to remind myself that he didn't know. His treatment toward me stems from my behavior; he doesn't know what sparked it.

It twists my stomach to acknowledge I miss him.

"Technically, you don't have to tell him you're kinky, do you?" Tess wrinkles her nose.

"Most definitely not." I shudder at the thought. "But I have a feeling he'll figure it out once he learns of Ryan and Angel." In our family, it's a certainty. Gossip arrives more promptly than the mail. "I do have to face him sooner or later."

"True." Tess gazes at me, her light brown eyes twinkling. "Ryan and Angel, huh?"

"Ah. Yes." I clear my throat. Perhaps we should change the topic. "I'm feeling highly uncomfortable discussing this with *my wife*, so how about we—"

"Discuss it further? I agree."

"Good grief," I sigh. "You are a stubborn woman, dear."

"Hey." She palms my cheek gently, and her gaze softens. "Who's been telling you to be yourself around more than just me for the past twenty years?"

I turn my head and kiss the inside of her hand. "You."

Christ, I feel even worse now. Downright spoiled. For as much shit as I've thrown in my own path, Tess has been there to support me. I've had no right to dispute the fact that I'm a lucky man.

"I think that entitles me to choose the topic," she concludes, "so go on, I'd like to know more about Ryan and Angel."

Wonderful.

"Abby!" Tess calls from upstairs. "Sweetie, come help me unpack!"

I'm in the kitchen with Abby, and I frown at how she literally sticks her fingers in her ears and goes back to reading her comic book at the table.

Clearing my throat loudly, I sure get her attention.

"That's very rude, young lady." I point toward the stairs. "Go help your mother."

"But—*ohh*," she whines. "I wanna finish my—" At my stern look, she shuts her mouth and sulks her way up the stairs.

It leaves me alone, and I tug at my tie for the hundredth time this hour and grab the phone. Coming home last night had me in high spirits because of how Tess and I wrapped up our vacation. Decisions were made, plans were set in motion, and I feel like I've gotten my best friend back. On the other hand, now I'm *home*, and I have to find the courage to call Ryan and Angel.

I'm not getting divorced.

Ryan once mentioned they had new terms. Now, so do I. A lot is at stake.

I would like at least a semblance of privacy, so I bring the phone to the enclosed terrace beyond the living room. Our backyard is a mess, neglected during the winter. A backyard is something I want in my life. A house, not an apartment above a bar. A house with a backyard in a good school district.

"Here goes everything," I mutter and dial Ryan's cell.

It's past six, so he and Angel should have finished their shifts.

"Ryan here, who's this?"

I nearly drop the phone like an imbecile. "Ah—shit. Hello? It's me. Greg."

There's a pause before the rich timbre of his voice fills the receiver again. "I don't recognize the number."

Right. Of course he doesn't. "This is my home phone number."

"Oh, yeah? Hm. So what's up?"

He's not going to give me an inch before I've made a gesture. I understand that.

Another moment of truth. My face warms up. "I, uh, I was calling to ask if you and Angel want to have dinner with me."

This second pause causes my throat to close up. Have I missed my chance? He told me to take my time and think things through, and the next time I showed up, it would be because I wanted more. Despite that I've missed them like crazy, it's only been a couple weeks. I hope that's not too long to—

"Like a date?" A trickle of mirth in Ryan's tone eases some of the nerves.

"Yes, a date."

"Well, hell. Count us in, boy."

I rub my mouth, hiding a smile of relief. "I'll make reservations."

The following weekend, I find myself in the city driving toward the Wharf. I'm here often enough for business dinners and lunches, but this time it's different. There's a romantic little place with a great view where I plan on pleading my case to Ryan and Angel.

I run a hand through my hair and check the rearview. The bruises have faded, and Aruba even grazed my Irish body with a slight tan that isn't lobster red. *Small miracles.* I won't be ordering a nice steak to sink my teeth into, but my jaw can handle salmon and softer meats.

The valet takes care of my car, and I straighten my tie and head inside the restaurant. I received a text earlier from Ryan; he told me they'd be a few minutes late because they missed their transit.

They don't like to drive in the city, he said.

"Cooper, party of three," I tell the hostess. "My companions will be here soon."

"Of course, sir. Follow me, please."

As requested, there's a table farther in the back for us. The windows give us a great view of the marina. With the low ceiling and intimate lighting, I hope I've picked the right place for a first—official—date.

The rich aromas of seafood and herbs invade my senses, and I accept a drink menu with a polite nod. Time to show I've learned at least a little by paying attention.

"Would you like to order something while you wait?" the hostess asks.

"I would, yes. Thank you." I open the menu, and she tells me she'll send a waitress right over.

It gives me a moment to shrug out of my suit jacket and smooth down my tie once or twice too many. Sue me, I'm a nervous wreck.

Once the waitress arrives, I order a stout for Ryan and red wine for Angel and myself. It's one I've seen her drink more than once, so it better be because she likes it.

"Yup, right over there," I hear Ryan say. Fuck, they're here. I look up as the hostess leads Ryan and Angel, two more menus in her hand. How the hell can they be so *fucking* beautiful?

I manage a careful smile. "Hello, you two." More relief fills me at the sight of Angel's soft grin, and I leave my seat to help her with her coat. Then I have to swallow past a river of desire. Her platinum waves linger down her tempting cleavage, and she's wearing a stunning satiny dress, the green color matching her gorgeous eyes. It's the first time I've seen either of them wearing anything remotely formal.

They do it well. So goddamn well.

She hasn't said a word. Instead, she chooses a wider grin that makes a dimple appear, and she taps her cheek for me.

I dip down and brush a kiss to her soft skin. "Thank you for coming, beautiful girl."

"There was no question," she whispers back.

I smile and slide my gaze to Ryan, and holy hell, I'm screwed. He hangs his jacket on his chair and smirks lazily, looking hotter than sin in tailored dress pants, a white button-down, and a charcoal vest that goes with the pants. Who knew the rough-around-the-edges bad boy owned a three-piece?

"We're not complete heathens." He tugs me close and cups my neck, letting our foreheads touch. "It's good to see you, pet."

"You too, Sir," I manage.

A neatly trimmed beard completes his look and turns my sadistic bartender into a dapper rogue with a devilish smile.

With an affectionate squeeze to my neck, he lets me go, and we take our seats around the round table.

Angel comments on my tan, and I have just enough time to explain I took my family on vacation before our drinks arrive. Then we order our food, and I admit I fret a little when Angel goes with a linguini sans the seafood. I doubt the pasta with only the sauce will taste good, even though she orders a couple side dishes.

"Do you not like seafood?" I do my best to keep my worry to myself. I could've sworn I've heard her mentioning that she loves shrimp.

The Quinns share a smile, and Ryan lifts her hand to kiss her knuckles.

"Not much seafood for me for a while." Angel's eyes dance with joy. "I'm pregnant."

"Oh—" My own eyes smart, but I blink past it quickly and grin, happy for them. "That was—damn, that was fast." I squeeze Ryan's hand on the table and lean over to Angel, kissing her cheek. "Congratulations."

"Thank you." Angel blushes, a rare sight. But oh, so lovely.

"We can go someplace else," I offer.

"Hell, no. I'm starving," she says. "I ordered plenty."

All right. I eye her untouched wine. "So much for me impressing you by knowing what drink you like."

She laughs then winks. "It's the thought that counts."

"Luckily for me, I like wine, too." Ryan steals Angel's wine, setting the glass next to his beer. After taking a sip of both, he leans back casually and steeples his fingers across his stomach. Under the table, he stretches out his legs and locks my left foot between them. "How was your vacation?"

"Much needed," I answer. "I opened up to my wife about everything, and..." I clear my throat and shift in my seat. "I have to open up to you, too. About my marriage, I mean. It's not...conventional, in that sense."

At Ryan's patient expression and "Go on," I follow Tess's advice and start at the beginning. With her permission, I tell Ryan and Angel about my wife's background with abuse and what she looked for in a place to call home. Safety, comfort, platonic love to keep her warm. And how it fit me too, since I was so adamant about normalcy and how hard I strived to adopt traditional values.

"Wait, so you're saying you weren't unfaithful?" Angel wonders.

"I'm saying we don't have those boundaries," I murmur. "We're married—she's my best friend—but we're not together." I pause. "I did betray her. We vowed to be open and honest with one another, and I've failed since the day I met you two. But, no, being intimate with you didn't cross any lines."

"Then why didn't you say so?" Her face falls. "I called you a cheater."

"I've been called worse." I lift a shoulder in a shrug. "When you let people assume, it leads to fewer follow-up questions, and it's a pretty fair assumption."

Ryan observes me but doesn't have any questions. It hits me that he rarely does in the beginning. He's much more content to sit back and gather information until the image is clearer. In the meantime, he'll merely listen and be patient.

"The thing is," I continue nervously, "I've made the decision to stay married to her—for the time being. What she and I share has nothing to do with everything I want with you. She's been my biggest supporter and companion for almost twenty years, and together we've created a good home for our daughter."

Ryan's calculating gaze is becoming unnerving, and Angel is suddenly unreadable, as well.

"I would like to keep a sliver of that with her," I admit. "That said...I—" Good fucking hell, this is harder to divulge than I thought. Never have I felt so damn vulnerable. "I want to belong to you." I avert my gaze, finding it to be too much. "I want to share my primary home with you. I want Abby to know you." At last, Ryan thaws a bit. "I won't hide anything. Given my daughter's age, I do want to keep her from unnecessary instability, and if a child can have two homes, so can an adult. Tess and I both feel it would be an easier transition for Abby if I, say, can come and go as I wish—come over for dinner a couple times a week and maybe even spend the night every now and then. But my real home would be with you." As soon as those words leave me, I feel the need to backtrack. "If this dating thing goes well, I mean. I have no clue about your thoughts or expectations."

Ryan's mouth twitches. "You're adorable when you ramble, subbie."

I gather enough guts to send the bastard a quick glare.

What if they saw me in court? They wouldn't know it's me. There's certainly no indecisiveness or fumbling there.

He grins and leans forward. "As long as we're honest with each other and no one is kept a secret, we're flexible. Angel and I are married, so it'd be unfair of us to ask that you let everything go before we've even established a relationship." He finds my hand on the table and weaves our fingers together. "Make no fucking mistake, though. We're not open."

"Not even a little," Angel supplies with a quirk of her lips. "It'll be you, Ryan, and me. No one else."

"That's a nonissue," I promise, wondering if I can relax now. It's bizarre how much I want this—and that I'm positive I'm more than halfway in love with both of them, yet I haven't kissed Ryan. Nor have I fucked Angel or ever been their equal.

"Furthermore," Angel goes on, "D/s is a natural component in our everyday life. You and I submit to Ryan, you submit to me, but love comes first. We will have clear boundaries for playtime, and no more denying aftercare or running away. You'll come to me or

Ryan with your problems, like any partner. He and I will do the same."

She's in her Domme mode, which is as arousing as it's cute and scary.

"Understood, Ma'am." I halt the conversation there as our food arrives.

Ryan takes the reins once the waitress has left and our table is full of food.

"How is your wife dealing with this?" He breaks off a piece of bread and drags it through his lobster sauce. "Would it be possible to meet her some day?"

"She's probably handling it better than I am." Because isn't that how it always is for us? "She's mentioned having you over for dinner, so I don't think that's a problem."

"That would be nice." Angel smiles. "What about this are you struggling with now?"

"The fact that she'd like my younger brother to come to the same dinner," I say wryly. "She likes it when everyone gets along."

"Good woman," Ryan murmurs. "Nothin' bad about reconciling."

I furrow my brow, side-eyeing him as I cut into my salmon. "I'd dread it if you two got along."

He chuckles. "He a part of a community?"

I incline my head. "A close friend of his runs a fetish club called Switch. Mark works the bar there."

"Well, hey. We've been there a couple times." Ryan winks at Angel, who flushes at some decadent memory, no doubt. "We'll have to go again."

"It would have to be without me." For which I'm goddamn grateful. Coming clean to Mark and perhaps opening a dialogue that's less venomous is one thing. Going to the same BDSM venue is another ball game entirely. "I'm sure I've been banned for life." At Angel's confused expression, I explain that's where I fought with Mark. And hurt people in my intoxicated path.

Good grief, those were some dark days.

Ryan hums around a mouthful of food. "As your Owner, I reckon it's my job to see if that can be fixed."

Owner.

The restaurant suddenly feels a lot warmer.

"Can I break in our new pet when we get upstairs?" Angel asks from the back seat. "Pretty please with a cherry on top?"

I'm the new pet. What *breaking in* entails, I'm not sure my balls want to know.

"Nope. Daddy comes first, princess." Ryan smirks at his pun and gives my thigh a squeeze. He's testing my self-control. Or my driving skills, perhaps. "I have plans for you."

I'm unsure of whether that "you" was plural. I can only hope, though I'm counting my blessings here. Our first date went well, and Ryan didn't put up *much* of a fight when I insisted on paying for dinner. That bodes well for the future, I think.

Hitting the corner by their building, I wait for the lights to turn green before taking a left.

"The space next to my truck should be empty," Ryan says.

I nod in acknowledgment and turn into the narrow alley between two buildings, and I park my car next to his behemoth.

"Angel, you can head upstairs, lose the clothes, and get in bed," Ryan orders.

Since he doesn't make a move, I don't either. My hands remain on the wheel.

"'Kay." Angel leans between our seats and busses our cheeks before stepping out of the car and disappearing.

The little light above us flicks off after a few seconds in silence.

"Is something wrong, Sir?" I haven't fucked up already, have I?

"No..." He faces me slowly, a lone streetlamp outside giving his eyes a dark glint. "Just a new rule for you. You don't strike me as a one who's into Daddy Doms, so that's a title reserved for Angel. From now on, you may call me Master or Owner. The latter's only for you."

Jesus.

The heat rises again, and I swallow past the dryness in my throat. "Yes—Owner."

"Perfect." He leans over the console and traces his thumb over my jaw. "You're mine now. You understand that, right?"

"Hell," I exhale, shivering violently. "Yes, Owner."

He smiles faintly, and finally, after weeks and months of longing for it, I feel his lips brushing against mine. "Good," he whispers. "You can let go of the damn wheel." He flashes a brief grin and applies more pressure to the next kiss. My hands fall limply to my lap, and I follow his lead. For every kiss he gives me, I return one with a bit more need lacing it. "You need something from me, baby?"

"You." I can't help myself. "You, Master."

"You got me." He cups my cheek and deepens the kiss. It grows hungry and dizzying, and tasting him for the first time creates powerful sensations that shoot through me, each one aiming for my cock.

I groan under my breath as he swipes his tongue sensually into my mouth. My hands end up at the nape of his neck where I find purchase in his hair.

"*Fuck*," he says in a low growl that rocks me. "We better get upstairs before I take you right here." He palms my erection firmly, and I moan and buck into his touch. "I've missed this beautiful cock."

"Please," I grunt.

"Please what?"

"Anything, Owner."

He takes another hard kiss. "Everything, then. Let's go."

OUT OF TOUCH

A BEHIND THE SCENES OUTTAKE

A GLIMPSE

MARK COOPER

The best part of demos at Switch is that no one cares about refilling their drinks. I lean back against the lit-up wall of bottles and snatch my soda from the counter, idly wondering if my entire shift is going to be a long break.

I've sent Evangeline to watch the fire-cupping scene in the Chamber. Brayden is catching another demo in the Cave, and Rio and Dante are demonstrating predicament bondage on the platform here in the Club. With three public scenes taking place, the guests are busy with anything but drinking.

My brows knit together, and I'm a little surprised to see Brayden weaving through the crowd so soon. The demo in the Cave can't be over yet.

He's flushed and fidgety as he slips behind the bar and walks over to me.

"Something wrong, pup?" I ask. "I told you to take notes."

He widens his eyes at me. "Master, I don't think it's for me."

I stifle my amusement. Anal fisting is not for the faint of heart; it'll look intimidating to most people. But I think he'll enjoy it, eventually.

"I do the thinking for you." I point across the dance floor toward the Cave. "Get back in there."

He chews on the inside of his cheek and shifts from foot to foot. "Will you do that to me, Master?"

I stare him down and wait. My lovely boy is not a disobedient one. Right now, I know his mind is scattered, though. It was one of the reasons I wanted him to watch the scene tonight—as a distraction. It's only been a couple weeks since we learned our girl is pregnant, and Brayden is fighting against some leftover notions about men being in control of the situation so the woman can relax.

"Don't make me repeat myself, sub."

He lowers his gaze and lets out a breath, his shoulders sagging. "Apologies, Master. I didn't mean to ignore what you said. I'm very sorry. I'll return to the demonstration now."

"See that you do." I watch him leave with his proverbial tail between his legs.

Too fucking precious. He'll let go soon enough. His surrender hangs in the air every day in our dynamic, and every time he goes over that crest and reminds himself I'm in charge, I get to witness the sweetest goddamn fall back into complete submission.

It's rare these days. He's been submissive through and through with me, but I suppose Evangeline's pregnancy threw him off a bit only because we didn't plan to start trying for a baby until next year.

"Cute subbie," a man comments, watching where Brayden's disappearing into the crowd. "He looks good in a collar."

"He does." I set down my soda and approach. "What can I get you?"

"Corona, cheers. Hold the lime."

He's not wearing a blue rubber band, so I assume he's not playing. Opening a fridge, I grab a Corona and remove the cap. "You thinking about collaring someone?" Otherwise, it's not the first topic that comes to mind where my Brayden is concerned.

"I've been on the fence for years. My wife wears one when we play in public, but I don't know... Branding might be more my thing. Recently got my mark on my boy—that felt good."

I chuckle and set the beer in front of him. "My little masochist is reading up on that. Maybe in the future." The man's already slapped a twenty to the bartop, so I ring him up and return the change. "You new at Switch?"

"New member, but I've been here a couple times before." He extends a hand, and I give it a firm shake. "Ryan Quinn."

"Mark Cooper."

"I figured." A lazy smirk appears, and he eyes Rio and Dante's scene over his shoulder before glancing back at me. "You and your brother look alike."

At that, my brows shoot up. "Which brother would that be?"

The man in front of me reminds me more of Cade than one of the clients my brothers would deal with at their firm. Hardly lawyer material, either. That leaves one, though we're not biologically related, so we don't look—

"Greg," Ryan replies. The unlikeliest answer of them all. I'm sure it shows on my face, too. "He told me he raised hell here a while back."

"You can say that." I fold my arms and straighten, suspicious. "How do you know each other?"

"Intimately?" He smirks, and I...yeah, no. This isn't funny. "I promised I'd let him explain. I just wanted to check the place out, and..." He eyes his watch. "I have an appointment with a Nicholas Ford in five minutes about lifting Greg's ban."

"Good luck with that," I answer automatically. "You know he has a wife, yeah?" I can't fucking believe this. Literally. It's too much. Then, there's no forgetting that Rio saw my brother enter a gay bar last winter.

"Tess." Ryan inclines his head. "I respect your concern, and I'm sorry to keep you in the dark. If you hate it half as much as I do..." No need to finish the sentence. "I hope we'll get to know each other, Mark. Apparently, we have a lot in common."

I wouldn't fucking know, would I?

"You're serious," I state. "You're *dating* Greg?"

"My wife and I both are," he confirms. "He'll have to tell you the rest."

"Be easier if the asshole picked up the phone," I respond irritably. "Our family's been trying to get in touch with him for weeks." Aside from Ted and Seth. They don't have much to say, only that they see Greg at work most days.

That gives Ryan pause, and then he lets out a dark chuckle. "The little shit neglected to mention that. Fair enough. I'll make sure he calls you."

I say nothing else, 'cause I see Nicholas approaching.

"He's the man you're after," I tell Ryan before finding an escape in a guest who wants to order a drink.

I gotta fucking process this. And get some goddamn answers.

As soon as I have a free minute again, I pull out my phone and text my brother.

Who the hell is Ryan Quinn? Or maybe I should ask, who the hell are you?

———

No response from Greg twenty-seven minutes later when Nicholas returns—without Ryan.

Nick sighs and sits down on a stool. "Judging by your impatient look, I'm guessing you know who I met."

"Barely." I pour him his usual tonic water. "Did he really ask to get rid of my brother's ban?"

He nods once, features grim. "He gave a pretty convincing speech in Greg's defense, too."

I shake my head and run a hand through my hair, utterly and completely mindfucked. Stunned. At a loss. Not only is my brother seeing a man, but he's possibly in the lifestyle, as well? Fuck me over, I don't know how to deal with this.

At the same time, how common is it for closet cases and bigots to preach so loudly and then live completely different lives on the down low? It's goddamn sad, and it pisses me the hell off.

I shake my head again, because evidently it's all I can do. "I don't know what to say."

"Frankly, neither do I, so that's why I told Mr. Quinn I'm leaving it up to you," Nicholas tells me. "The way things are now, Greg cannot come here. I believe in second chances, but if he hurt Kayla again, I don't know what I'd do. He needs to be vetted properly before I even consider giving him a probation run."

And I get to do the vetting? How gracious of him. Not that it matters. If Greg won't answer the phone, I can't do much— Goddammit. My phone buzzes in my pocket, and I retrieve it to see his name on the display. He's replied.

I'm sorry. I didn't know Ryan was going there tonight. I just spoke to him. If you would like to meet up, I'm ready to talk.

My forehead creases, and I read the message over and over.

I'm not sure I've ever heard or seen him utter the words "I'm sorry."

What a clusterfuck.

"Where do you think you're going?" I mutter sleepily.

"To make you breakfast?" Evangeline laughs softly.

I huff and pull her under the covers with me. Brayden left for work about an hour ago; I was awake long enough to receive a good-morning blow job. Now I could go back for seconds. Then get some more sleep.

"That can wait." I nuzzle her neck, my hand automatically seeking out her stomach. It's almost impossible to think it'll grow and be round with our family's first child soon. "How are you feeling?"

"Better now. I've already had my morning sickness extravaganza."

I blink drowsily and force my eyes open, concerned. "You know you can wake me up for that, sweetheart."

She smiles and touches my scruffy cheek. "A morning grumpy Master is *grumpy*."

Cheeky little minx. "I'd hold your hair up better than a scrunchie."

She giggles and cuddles closer. "Of course you would. You need to eat if you're going to make it to Sausalito in time for your much-anticipated reunion, though. Let me fix you some breakfast."

Despite the reminder of seeing Greg today, I can only smile and pepper her beautiful face with kisses. She knows how to make me feel ten feet tall. And since I'm insatiable for my subs, one thing leads to another. Breakfast can be many things, and she catches on when I roll on top of her and capture a nipple between my teeth.

"I think..." I hum into a wet kiss as I taste her breasts. "My kitten's sweet pussy will be my breakfast."

She shivers.

Pulling up in front of my brother's house a little after ten, I frown when I see Tess and Abby in the front yard. For some reason, I expected to speak to Greg alone. For fuck's sake, we're talking about him suddenly having a relationship with two people, neither of whom is his wife.

I kill the engine and step out, sliding on my shades. Spring is in the air, something that should brighten the day. I'm always stoked to see my niece, but right now it's difficult to hide my sour mood. I've told Brayden and Evangeline the little I know, and now I'm rethinking Evangeline's offer to accompany me out here.

"Uncle Mark!" Abby's hazel eyes light up.

I muster a grin and open the gate to their yard. "Hey, pumpkin." She flies into me, and I pick her up and give her a tight squeeze. "How's my favorite niece?"

"Awesome! How's my favorite uncle?" she replies cheekily. "Mom and I are waking leaves."

I laugh and kiss her nose, then let her jump down again. "I think you mean raking."

"That's what I said." She returns to her hot pink, plastic leaf rake, and I walk over to Tess.

We exchange a weary smile, though hers is notably brighter. Does she know what's going on?

"Hey, hon." I kiss her cheek. "How're you?"

"All good. You? You look tired."

I point to my face. "This is my I-don't-know-what-the-fuck-is-going-on expression."

She laughs. "Well, you'll find answers in the backyard. Greg's dealing with his nervousness by cleaning the pool about two months early."

I scratch my eyebrow and nod once. As far as I knew, my big brother didn't *do* nervous, but it seems there's a lot I don't know about him.

"Mommy, is this when I hafta stay here with you?" Abby asks.

I smirk faintly and head up to the porch.

"Yes, so Daddy and Uncle Mark can talk," Tess replies.

Once inside the house, I slip off my shoes and carry them past the hallway and through the living room. Nothing's changed. It's as picturesque as ever. It doesn't look like anyone's moving or separating. Abby's in her usual happy mood. Tess clearly knows whatever it is I don't.

I come to a stop at the door. Greg's taken a break from the pool and is sitting in a lawn chair just outside the glass-enclosed terrace. Dressed in a pair of jeans and a hoodie, he's not a stark contrast next to me anymore. No longer opposites.

I'm met with a wall of heat as I open the door, making the definition of a sunroom abundantly obvious, and I cross the floor in a few quick strides. Greg looks up when I step outside, and I notice the worn-out expression on his face. The mindfuck continues. This isn't the brother I know.

"Hey, stranger." My shoes hit the ground, and I step into them.

"Hello, Mark." He clears his throat and moves to another chair, leaving the one he vacated for me. "How are you?"

"I don't know yet." I frown and take a seat.

The rest of the lawn furniture leans against the side of the house next to a big pile of leaves. So while I'm wondering what the fuck this alien host next to me has done to my brother, they're enjoying a day of spring cleaning? Fuckin' A.

"You know Mom and Dad are worried, right?"

He rubs his forehead and slumps back a bit. "I can't bother with them at the moment. I've told Tess she can tell them I'm doing well—"

"She's not your messenger."

He's not wearing any shades, so I see the look of annoyance he sends me.

I lean back as well, not leaving until I know what's going on.

"Are you getting divorced?" I ask.

"Ah, no." He clears his throat once more, a typical trait of his for when he's uncomfortable. However, I haven't *seen* him uncomfortable in a long goddamn time. "Not in the near future, anyway. I... I don't know where to begin, but I suppose I can start by saying Tess and I don't have a conventional marriage."

Really. Because that's kinda been the very description of Greg for years and years. Conventional. Conservative. Since he started pre-law or thereabouts.

"I want to apologize for how I behaved at Switch," he says quietly, choosing a new direction. "I was...drunk and jealous. Tess came home from dinner one night and told me about you and Evangeline, and I just... I didn't take it well."

If I stare at him a bit longer, will all puzzle pieces finally come together? I stare and fucking stare, and I don't recognize the man who was once a boy I called my best friend.

"I'm listening." That's all I can say. There's gotta be a truckload of things he needs to get off his chest, and it's gonna take a while before each statement doesn't raise at least a dozen questions.

I don't know what pulls harder at me, the anger or the crippling grief. Keeping my glare directed at the ground, I lean forward with my forearms on my legs and listen to Greg until the words bleed together and make my skull throb.

"I carried the resentment with me through high school and college. I just wanted to be whatever you guys weren't, and I wanted to do it *better*. Then when Abby was born, I couldn't bear the thought of her going through what I did in school."

I crack my knuckles, needing something to do. Throughout my upbringing and—fuck, until now, I've believed the shit we took growing up was nothing. Sure, it fucking hurt. There was often some little prick who laughed at the Coopers for having a weird-ass family. But it stopped, and... Well, it didn't, apparently. Greg just took over. He dealt with the bullies and took the heat himself.

And he didn't fucking say anything—holy shit, my blood is boiling. Scrubbing a hand over my jaw, I gnash my teeth together and force my ass to sit tight and listen to the rest. God knows, I wanna do anything but.

"I don't care on my own behalf, Mark. I go out with Ryan and Angel, and I don't even look at others and how they react. But then I see Abby, and I think of the venom our classmates hurled at me— at us—and it's too much. I could take it—somewhat—but I can't put my daughter through that."

So he's not the cold, distant father who works too much. He cares to the point where he makes incredibly *stupid* decisions in hopes of protecting Abby. And if he'd only told me, he wouldn't have been alone; maybe it wouldn't have led to these extremes because he can't protect her from everything.

I would have defended him, though. If this is really what happened, our parents should have done a better job at fighting alongside him.

I pipe up once, wondering why he didn't tell our folks it was worse than he let on.

"I did," he replies with a one-shouldered shrug. "I was the one who got the lecture about what's right and wrong. They didn't do crap about the teachers and students."

That hurts, in a betrayal kind of way. It seems obvious to me our parents should've contacted the school.

I side-eye Greg as he speaks, and I can't see it. His image doesn't change that easily. I'll have to experience it, and it's not that I don't trust him—I believe him—but it's a huge fucking change.

Taking in his revelation about his and Tess's marriage—hell, even when he tells me about Ryan and a girl named Angel—is nothing compared to the news about Mom and Dad. Two people I love and admire for their acceptance of diversity and openness. To learn they weren't there when they should have been... It's gonna take time to process.

Anger flares up again. Anger toward Greg, because he kept this from me. Childhoods end, and I stopped being the kid he wanted to protect at some point. Instead, he continued down his own path and drove a bigger wedge between us every time we saw each other. I didn't fucking know.

"I can't help but feel cheated," I admit. "I get that it must've hurt like a son of a bitch to hear me defend the way our folks live. I get the resentment. But you knew I didn't have the whole picture, Greg."

"I know." He nods and looks down, fidgeting with his clasped hands. *Fidgeting*—my lawyer brother. "I've carried a lot of hatred in me, and, justified or not, it hasn't done me any good. I understand it's a big possibility you hear me out and then walk out."

Like I'd fucking do that. I've always loved Greg. I just haven't liked him.

Now... "Christ." I release a heavy breath and pinch the bridge of my nose. It's like learning you've been kicking someone you didn't know was already lying down. I haven't hesitated even once to give him grief during family dinners. He starts his conservative bullshit about gay people remaining discreet and polyamory being wrong—I've jumped right in to throw a punch. Actually, I still would. But he hasn't been fighting what he says he's been fighting. He doesn't find any of that wrong; he's just terrified that anything considered remotely different will pose a threat to Abby and children in general.

He isn't much different from Mom and Dad there, with these new developments in mind. He'd rather shield and change the victim than attack the problem. And I tell him as much, to which he sighs and admits I'm not the only one who's pointed that out lately.

"Ryan," he goes on. "He's been knocking some sense into me about finding happy mediums. He was infuriated because my beliefs didn't make any difference in the grand scheme of things. Or, as he phrased it, I'm not doing my part in making the world a better place for my daughter."

Maybe Ryan's a good man, then. 'Cause I won't have Greg spouting shit about people who don't fit into the cookie-cutter mold of normal. My Brayden is proof of how many scars that leaves behind.

"One thing I won't apologize for," he adds in a firm tone, "nor have I changed my mind about it, is how much we put on our children and expect of society right off the bat. Of course I want everyone to be able to live without judgment from others, but let's be realistic. We're not an accepting society as a whole. Mom and Dad didn't even prepare us."

It's easier to concede on that point. I can't imagine sending off my son or daughter to school without introducing them to the fact that our family situation is considered unusual. However, it was a completely different story when Greg, our siblings, and I started school almost thirty years ago. Society as a whole, as he put it, has become more accepting since then. But no matter what, there'll be no apologetic behavior for being uncommon. Over my dead body.

"Preaching to the choir on that one, Greg. Just quit trying to jam a square peg into a round hole." I drag my tired gaze away from him as the sun disappears behind clouds, and I lean forward again, thinking. Mind fucking spinning. "How open have you been to Ted and Seth?" I'm asking since they're closer. They see each other every day at work.

"Not at all. I'm sure they'll be shocked when I tell them."

And how's that gonna work? Now I know why Greg's been fighting us and our way of life, but he's not alone. Our younger brothers share the view Greg no longer supports.

"That's their right." He shrugs in response. "You have to realize they were so young when our parents moved in with the others that it's all Ted and Seth knew. They were completely blindsided in school when classmates called them weird." He pauses. "I won't try to convert anyone or object to their personal beliefs, but they won't make any fuss in the office. What I do off the clock is none of their damn business."

"What about finding a fucking solution?" I frown. "I can't sit back and accept what is without trying to get our folks to understand. Times change. Maybe they'll get it now."

He inclines his head. "I'm not ruling it out, but right now, it's not my priority. There are still consequences to one's behavior, and my childhood won't be altered because they suddenly understand better. I want to focus on working on the relationships I personally damaged."

Speaking of consequences, eh? I suppose that's fair.

"Does that mean I can dole out punishment as consequences for your shitty behavior?" I figure it can't hurt to ease up on the heavy.

He lifts a brow, not missing a beat. "Does that mean we can work things out?"

That chance was always there. He's my brother.

"I guess I can put you on probation." I use Nicholas's word. "You'll be on probation at Switch too, if you choose to return with your new partners."

"Good grief," he mutters. "That will never be my choice, but Ryan does like to make me suffer."

I turn away for a beat and smile to myself.

Who the fuck would've suspected this? My patriarchal big brother, a kinky, polyamorous *masochist.*

"So how long have you been sneaking out to get your kinky rocks off?"

He coughs and shoots me a glare. "You were always the crass one, little brother."

Yeah, yeah, heard that before.

He sighs. "It's actually new. I sought out punishment for how I felt—for how I acted toward people."

That ends my fun, and I scowl. "Are you fucking serious? Do you know how dangerous that is?"

"Spare me the Master lecture, Mark. I've already had that conversation with two Sadists. I'm good."

Ah, karma can be stunning. Two Sadists. Priceless.

I don't think he's complaining, though. He looks happier.

It must be serious, too. Ryan did mention branding his boy.

Jesus. *Branding his boy.* This is Greg we're talking about—yeah, definitely looking forward to processing all this.

"I would like to apologize to Evangeline," he mentions. "Abby was devastated when we let Evangeline go. It was stupid of me. If she's interested in coming back, let her know she's more than welcome."

"I appreciate that." With things looking up, it's easier to focus on the future. "We're having a baby." That one being the biggest part of my future right now.

Greg looks at me in surprise. "Oh...wow. Damn, you work fast, too. Congratulations, little brother."

"Thanks," I chuckle. "Work fast, *too?*"

"Yes, Ryan and Angel. They're expecting their first, as well. They didn't try very long."

Interesting. Up until Rio spotted Greg in the Castro, I considered us night and day. Now...? Mother of Christ, we have a *lot* in common all of a sudden.

I'm ready to work it out, though. Greg and I were very close at one point. It'd be nice to have my older brother back in my life. We've been out of touch for too long.

TOUCHING INK

CHAPTER 1

CADE KINGSLEY

"Morning, Daddy."

I smile into the pillow, feeling his curious fingers wandering along my spine. "Good morning, baby boy." Knowing he has work soon and then his weekly Skype call with his parents, I pull him into my arms to get a good dose to hold me until I see him tonight. "Mmm, fuck work today. I wanna stay right here."

He laughs softly. "You make me wanna be little aaall the time. No adulting—blegh."

That makes me happy.

"I know of another boy who never wanted to grow up," I murmur. "Are you my little Peter Pan?"

He nods and smiles widely. "That's me! Forever and ever."

I tickle him, ignoring the warning bells. Forever and ever, forever and ever. Fuck, are we going too fast? It's only been a month. I don't want anyone to get hurt.

Something rouses me from sleep, and I blink and stare up at the ceiling.

"Goddammit," I sigh tiredly.

Dreaming of Dylan has become the norm the past three months, and it never fails to weigh me down. I scrub my hands up and down my face. My chest feels tight. I fucking hate missing him.

With the dream fresh in my mind, it's impossible for my thoughts to stray from him. Memories attack me—all the mornings we shared, taking him for ice cream, dates, playing with him at the club... The mornings here at my place were always a favorite.

"Daddy?"

"Yeah?"

"You know how you give me a morning surprise every day? Down there, I mean."

"Mmhmm. I love that."

He snickers. "Me too, 'specially when the surprise comes."

Sensing there's something he wants to bring up, I put the paper on the nightstand and turn to give him my full attention. "You can tell me anything." I touch his stomach lightly, the covers riding low.

He gets shy and inches toward me. "Could I do that to you sometime?"

Damn. Just the thought is enough to get me hard. I cup the back of his neck and kiss him gently. "You wanna put your hard little cock inside Daddy?" I graze my teeth along his bottom lip and sneak a hand between us to feel him. He gasps and nods jerkily. "Of course you can." I stroke him unhurriedly and—

"Motherfucker," I groan, throwing a pillow over my head. Hard as a rock and depressed—what a lovely combination.

Did we have to be so damn perfect together?

I drag myself up and scowl at the alarm clock.

I've only slept an hour.

I eye my erection, only to look away and glare at nothing.

I remember that first time he fucked me—too vividly. Too excited to contain himself, he'd lost control fast. "I can't stop it,

Daddy, I can't stop it," he'd whimpered. He took me purely on instinct, rocking and thrusting, telling me his surprise was coming... Afterward, I was too revved up, and a minute of his sweet mouth suckling my cock later, I'd blown my own load.

Glancing at the clock again, I slump down on the mattress for some more staring at the ceiling.

I did the right thing.

One day, I hope I'll be able to sleep through the night. It fucks with my mood—a lot. And it doesn't matter what I dream. Sometimes, it's nights like this one, full of fucking and sweating and dirty words and missing his innocence. Sometimes, I relive the moment I told him we should slow things down. Sometimes, I have nightmares about him being with others...

He was opposed to having an open relationship in the beginning. There's no forgetting that. There's also no forgetting how quickly he changed his mind when we invited Gabriella to play. And, in a way, it's strange to me even now that I didn't react badly to that, given what happened with my last Little. Additionally, the thought of him playing with anyone else I can think of puts a rock in my gut. Not that it stopped him. He had fun elsewhere anyway.

Fuck him. I clench my jaw and screw my eyes shut.

I did the right thing.

Three *months*, and the pain hasn't faded. I sleep restlessly, images rolling past like a flickering movie.

"I'm not closing any doors, Dylan," I murmur. "I'm only saying we shouldn't rush into this. It's heady, yeah? There's a lot of new feelings, things to adjust to..."

He nods minutely, eyes on the ground.

Have I fucked this up?

I'm trapped in that useless state of sleep where I *know* I'm asleep, where I *know* I'm dreaming, yet I can't change anything. I can only watch everything unfold—again. Repeatedly.

"You're very new, little pan." I walk over to hug him to me. "Remember I told you my last relationship didn't end well?" Understatement, really. That girl managed to screw me over good. Being all vulnerable and sweet... A fucking act, that's what it had been. Only out to use me, and then I wasn't enough. "I'm human, sweetheart. I still have a lot to learn, too. By taking this slowly and focusing on building a good D/s foundation for us, I think it'll be easier—"

"Wait." He looks up at me, hurt. "You mean we're not dating anymore? It's just Daddy/Little Boy?"

I sigh, unsure of how to phrase this. Too much shit is rushing through my head, one part screaming no, the other a bit more level-headed and cautious.

I roll over, stuck thinking about where our miscommunication began.

I was the one who asked him out. One dinner quickly became two, and then he ended up in my bed for play. The lines had been blurry from the start, and though we never labeled anything, I guess we were dating. We were. Nothing else would describe it, now when I look back on everything we did. The texts we sent each other, the dinners we went to, the nights we spent fucking and talking until the sun rose...

Despite all that, maybe given who we are as kinksters and where we met, I thought of him as my Little, not my boyfriend. We had both expressed interest in a Daddy/Little Boy relationship, and somewhere down that road, it morphed into more.

I wasn't ready for the "more" part.

"I don't want you to see it as taking a step back," I reply. "More

like...refocusing. It hasn't been very long, and you're..." I can't say it, for fear he gets even more hurt. I see it, though. He's very attached, he soaks up every word I say, he practically lives at my place now. And I like it a bit too much. "I don't wanna stop you from exploring."

Being new, that's what he should do. If he doesn't, who's to say he won't wake up one day and realize this ain't enough, and then I'm fucked all over again. It's crushing. I'm already anxious about it. He loves being with Gabriella, though I've truly enjoyed that too, but who's next? A Daddy Dom? A Top I don't know? A Mommy Domme?

I don't wanna be replaced.

Dylan nods pensively, and he takes a step back and clears his throat. "Maybe you're right. It's only been a few weeks."

I wake for the tenth time that night and lie unmoving on my side. A car drives past down on the street. The digits on my clock flash 2:49 AM. All I see in my head is Dylan, his expression when he backed off a bit and nodded.

I did the right thing.

I did the right thing, dammit.

No, fucking no.

I groan.

The knocking returns.

"Jesus, where's the fucking fire?" My feet hit the floorboards with a thump, and I reach for a pair of sweats as I get out of bed. Whoever's pounding on my door at... I squint at the alarm clock. 3:27 *AM.*

Someone has a death wish. As if I need *more* reasons to be kept from sleep.

Tightening the drawstrings, I cross the open space that makes up my home. Down the spiral staircase that creaks just a bit too much to be considered safe. Into the garage where I have my workshop—my life—and I nearly knock over a stack of cherry wood strips leaning precariously against my workbench.

There's another handful of rapid knocks, and I'm officially pissed.

Given that I don't live in the safest neighborhood in San Francisco, I grab the bat next to the door before I open it.

My brows shoot up.

"Sorry to wake you," Mark mutters. He's exhausted. So am I, for obvious reasons, but I'm not the one carrying a girl who doesn't belong to me. Unless Evangeline, my buddy's pregnant submissive, has gotten her leg inked while I was gone.

"Am I dreaming?" I frown and set down the bat.

He rolls his eyes. "If only. May I...?"

I guess my manners aren't awake yet. "Yeah, sorry." I back up and let him in, then close and lock the door.

I've been on the East Coast the past two—almost three—months, so I suppose I have a lot of catching up to do.

Mark Cooper, one of my closest friends, is either at home with Evangeline and Brayden, making plans for the family they're starting, or he's bartending at Switch, the fetish club and local community we're part of. Never before has he brought over girls in the middle of the night.

"Mind explaining?" I roll my lip ring absently and eye the girl. A sub? Passed out drunk? I can't see much, other than white cotton panties and a matching top.

Inked ivy slithers up her toned thigh.

I rub my eyes and yawn.

"I know you just got back into town, but we've had it." He carefully situates the girl on my bench, and she falls forward to his chest. Dark, messy, chin-length hair shadows her face. Arms slack. "Nicholas and Rio are worried sick—hell, so am I." That would be the other two who make up our closest group of buddies. Well, the toppy types, anyway. "We understand; she's been through a lot, but the way she's changed...?" Mark shakes his head and strokes the girl's back. In the meantime, my confusion is morphing into frustration. "The wardrobe change was nothing. The tattoos raised a few brows, but then she started drinking—"

"*Who?*" I widen my arms. "Sorry, buddy, I'm tired as fuck. You're gonna have to walk me through this slowly. I don't know who that is."

That makes him scowl. "Are you serious?"

I shoot him a glare in return, 'cause it's not the fucking time for jokes.

He looks dazed for a moment; then he sighs and tucks the girl's hair behind her ear. My brows knit together, and I cock my head.

"It's Gabriella, for chrissake."

"What?" My gut flips, my jaw momentarily dropping. *No goddamn way.* I walk closer without realizing it, and holy fuck, it's actually Gabriella. No longer the dolled-up baby girl with frilly dresses and impeccable makeup.

"You missed a lot while you were out playing woodworker, Cade."

Playing woodworker? Prick. He didn't seem to have an issue with my business when he had me design his entire bedroom. He seems to enjoy the fetish furniture I created for Switch, too.

Besides, Mark knows very well I needed to get away after all that shit with Dylan.

"So fill me in, asshole," I reply. "Unless it's about Nick and Kayla's wedding. I already got my invitation in the mail." Closing the last distance, I murmur, "Let me," and take over for Mark.

My brain refuses to catch up. Even as I gently cup Gabriella's cheeks and gaze down at her face, I don't wanna believe it's her. It makes me fucking queasy.

Her closed eyes are smudgy with eyeliner and mascara.

"Christ, princess."

Mark's words from before echo in my head. How she's

changed. The ink. *Drinking?* Good God, the girl I knew disliked alcohol. It made her scrunch her nose.

"We think she rebelled," Mark says quietly.

"*That* doesn't surprise me." I press a kiss to her forehead and let her lean against my shoulder. Damn, she's out for the count. "John turned her into something she never was in the first place." Sugary sweet, with barely a will of her own.

Her ex used to be my buddy, too. Then he started neglecting his girl, and I noticed he was micromanaging her—when he actually spent time with her. It sent her on an emotional roller coaster, losing the stability he was supposed to provide. I couldn't fucking stand it. To any kind of partner, that's terrible. To a Little who regresses, it's downright traumatizing.

Last time I spoke to her was over the phone. She'd just dumped him—at last—and I told her how proud I was. It was a weight off my shoulders after months of wishing I could steal her away and keep her from harm myself.

This still worries me, though. It seems to be about more than breaking free and starting fresh as an independent person.

Mark goes on. "She's been playing a lot—with Sadists. She approached Dante."

I wince. "Did he scene with her?" Gabriella's never shown interest in receiving pain.

"Tonight, actually." Mark runs a hand over his head, tired. "She dropped afterward and refused aftercare. Dante was understandably pissed, but she left the club before we could intervene. Then she came back a few hours later, plastered."

I curse and turn back to Gabriella.

What are you doing to yourself, little girl?

She makes a drowsy sound in her sleep. My heart jumps, and I brace myself for her waking up. Instead, she mumbles something I can't understand and goes under again.

I want her to open her gorgeous green peepers and flash me a dimpled grin like so many times before. John may have changed her temporarily, but I've seen glimpses of the wonderful brat she really is.

"That was our limit," Mark says. "She's allowed to play with whomever she wants, but she can't show up drunk. She can't disobey the rules, interrupt scenes, throw tantrums, and ignore what Doms demand of her after she's already agreed."

Of course she can't. I'm surprised they haven't banned her. We've booted people for less.

"I hope you'll talk to her. You know her best," he finishes.

It goes without saying that I'll talk to her, but I'm afraid I don't know her as well as everyone might think. She was already with John when he introduced her to our local community, and I didn't really get to know her properly until I noticed he was taking more and more work calls.

"I'll do what I can." My hand comes up to feel her forehead. "Thanks for bringing her over." Now that she's here, I'm not sure I'll let her go anytime soon.

With John out of the picture, I won't have to hide that I'm protective of her.

"We had a feeling you wouldn't mind," Mark murmurs. "Any word from Dylan?"

I draw in a deep breath through my nose and shake my head. "Last I heard, he was training for Nationals. I reckon he's started fresh in Texas."

That had been a punch in the gut. First finding out he left, then being ignored like a plague. After calling him relentlessly, texting, calling again, leaving an embarrassing number of messages, and even checking Switch's online forum, I've given up.

He posted a status update on his Switch page that he was happy down in Texas and training was going well. Nick's and Rio's subs congratulated him and said they missed him, before Dylan, for some reason, deleted the update. He hasn't been active much since then, so maybe he's found a new community. Or he's focusing on his career.

"Perhaps Gabriella talks to him," Mark offers.

It's a possibility, considering how close they were before Dylan left. I'll ask her, even though I'm not sure I can stomach the answer. Seeing more proof he's willfully avoiding me ain't exactly pleasant.

"You get some rest, man." Mark squeezes my shoulder and walks toward the door. "You working tomorrow?"

"No, I'm not on until next weekend." To be honest, I'm not itching for it like I used to. Being a dungeon monitor for the past three years has been fulfilling and fun, and all that sorta runs down the drain when you feel like roadkill.

To make matters worse, my friends are all sickeningly happy and in love. I've caught bits and pieces online. There's Nick and Kayla's wedding in Mexico later this summer. Rio and Chelsea's collaring ceremony is coming up, too. And who could forget Mark, Evangeline, and Brayden having a baby.

"Well, we miss you around the club, buddy. Come down for a drink, at least."

"We'll see," I say.

He gives me a two-finger wave and then leaves.

I return my focus to Gabriella.

"Let's get you to bed, princess." I lift her up and position her on my hip so I have one hand free. I flip off lights as I head back upstairs, and other than another mumbled sound from Gabriella, she remains oblivious.

She's gonna feel wonderful tomorrow. If worshiping the toilet won't get her there, my reprimanding her for not taking care of herself will.

CHAPTER 2

There's no more sleep for me that night. Having no clue how much alcohol Gabriella's had, I worry too much to relax. I sit in my pop's old rocking chair while she sleeps restlessly in my bed.

I didn't see it before, but the print on her top speaks volumes about her rebelling. "Daddy, close the door" is written across her chest, and the filthy implication of wanting Daddy to close the door so they can do unspeakable things—that no little girl should know about—is the opposite of what John turned her into.

If he still visits Switch, it'll be virtually impossible to hold back from rearranging his face.

Around five, I can tell it's time to move this party to the bathroom. Gabriella lets out pitiful moans and clutches her stomach. Standing up, I carefully gather her in my arms, and then I carry her to the bathroom near the stairs.

"No..." Her forehead creases as the nausea builds up, and she rouses slowly.

Lowering her to the floor, I grab a towel and pat it over her damp forehead. "Gabriella. Can you wake up for me?"

She groans. Her eyes are still closed, but she seems more aware.

As if knowing what's about to happen and where she is, she hugs the toilet and rests her cheek on the seat.

A minute or two later, she starts throwing up.

For the next couple of hours, I rotate between the kitchen to get Gabriella water, the bathroom where she whines and tells me to go away, and my computer so I can tell her friends—who are worried and checking in—that she'll live.

Earlier, when she first noticed I was with her and that she was at my place, her expression was fucking priceless. It's been a while since we saw each other, so her eyes had widened adorably; she'd stuttered my name and then cried for me to get the hell out.

"I don't think I have anything left..." She slumps against the toilet and flushes for the umpteenth time.

"Drink more." I stand next to her and extend a glass of water. "I'll get some toast ready for you."

"No," she moans. "No food. Go on without me. Leave me behind."

I chuckle. "Glad to see your humor is waking up, but that's not how this works."

We may be friends on equal ground, but our relationship is heavily influenced by our lifestyle, and we're close enough that I can enforce some rules. It's common, not to mention an easy dynamic to slip into when it feels so natural.

Same goes for Nick's little Kayla. She obeys her Daddy yet takes directions from those Nick trusts. In Gabriella's case, that means she'll suck it up and let me take care of her until she's on her feet. She'll listen to me, she'll do as I say, even though we're not together.

"Are you going to be a pain in my ass, mister?" She scowls up at me.

I smile at the *mister*, a nickname that stuck even after she learned my name.

"I can guarantee the answer is yes if you don't watch your language."

She huffs then pouts. "You have a potty mouth."

I point to myself. "Daddies can curse. Are we clear?"

"That's so—" She wisely shuts her trap at my look of warning.

"Here." I almost forgot. Retrieving two painkillers from the pocket of my sweats, I hand them to her with the water. "Hopefully, you won't upchuck these."

She whines. "I'm mortified."

"Don't be silly." I squat down next to her and feel her forehead. "Go on, drink up."

She obeys, visibly weak and exhausted. "I'm tired."

Join the club.

"We'll take a nap soon, how's that?" I gently push back her hair, reminding me of something. She's been sick, and she's covered in makeup and hair products from yesterday. "I'll fix you something to eat, and you can take a shower. Then we'll cuddle it up in front of the TV."

She hums and closes her eyes as I scratch her scalp. "That sounds amazing, except for the food."

I grin.

I've changed the sheets and prepared a light breakfast for us when Gabriella emerges from the bathroom. Wrapped in a towel, her hair clinging in short spikes that just barely touch her shoulders, she forms a silent "o" as she takes in my place for the first time.

Wide-open space, low ceilings, two pillars in the middle, kitchen nook, and windows by the bed. Living alone, I don't have to worry about privacy. I bought the house for the garage that I turned into my workshop, and then I saw the massive loft and figured I might as well make it my home.

"So this is how Cade Kingsley lives," she murmurs. "I love it."

I smile and bring two plates of food to the bed. Then I walk over to the dresser the flat screen sits on and open a couple drawers to find her something to wear.

"Come here." I pull out an old college tee and a pair of boxer shorts that Dylan must've left behind. Being a professional swimmer, his hips are narrower than mine. They'd never fit me, and they can't belong to someone else. He's the only one who's been here. "Will these work? I think they're Dylan's."

She nods, and with one hand grasping the towel, she accepts the clothes. "Do you miss him?"

I hesitate to answer. I'm angry, hurt, bitter, and tired. And yeah, I fucking miss him.

"Every day."

"Me, too." She smiles sadly then tiptoes back to the bathroom to change.

I sigh and slump down on the bed, feeling eighty-seven as opposed to thirty-seven.

It feels nice having Gabriella here, though.

Losing Dylan this past February made me step back from kink. Months of working in various fetish clubs on the East Coast and being surrounded by kinksters couldn't bring me out of my funk. I delivered and customized new furniture, then kept to myself.

Maybe my break can come to an end eventually. I just have to figure out a way to ease back into it without taking advantage. Gabriella's obviously in a bad place herself, so the last thing I want to do is suck the last of her positive vibe.

Gabriella returns, swimming in my T-shirt, and she hops up on the bed and gets under the covers.

"I hope you don't mind I stole a toothbrush from under the sink," she says. "I can replace it."

I shake my head and scratch my eyebrow, brushing over the

barbell there. "I should've given it to you before I turned you into a thief." I flash her a look to show I'm kidding, and she rewards me with a beautiful little giggle.

Drawn to that sound, I join her under the covers and pull her close. It's amazing how heartwarming Littles can be, regardless if it's their laughter, silly faces, or merely their presence. I hug her hard, letting go of the final worries from last night. Determined. She won't be alone in this, and I'll get to the bottom of everything that's made her sad and act out.

I can do that and remain a friend, someone she can always turn to.

"You're squishing me!"

"I *know*." I blow a raspberry on her cheek, to which she laughs and tries to shove me away. If only I weren't twice her size. "So cute." I kiss her on the forehead before backing off. "Time to get some food in your tummy."

She scrunches her nose and combs her damp hair with her fingers. "I'm really not hungry."

"You need to eat." I give her a plate with a few triangles of toast and a glass of ginger ale. "If you want more, you can snatch from my plate." My breakfast is far more appealing, with eggs, bacon, and a blueberry muffin.

I happen to know she loves the latter.

"Will it cost me anything?" Her green eyes spark with mischief, trained on the muffin. "I'm afraid I don't have any money, mister..." My gaze averts to my arm as she trails two fingers over the ink that covers the skin. "Maybe we can work something out?"

I stare at her. It's a new side to her I have to adjust to. One I've known has lurked underneath the pastels and the glitter, yet it takes me off guard. Between her and Dylan, he was the flirty tease while she was the angel.

Now she owns a tank top that instructs Daddy to close the door.

"Filthy little girl," I mutter under my breath and reach for the remote control. "Eat."

I dig into my scrambled eggs and turn on the news.

Gabriella nibbles on a piece of toast and rests her head on my shoulder, and it's quiet for a while. I can't say I'm paying attention to the news. My mind is racing, focused on the near future. I let everything go when I took off, and now I gotta get my shit together.

Dylan is gone. I've done everything in my power to reach him that doesn't involve getting on a plane to Texas. And considering he's the one who fucked up, I'm done.

We have a lot of things unresolved, which I hope we can work out one day, though that's up to him now. It's time I move on. It'll be the single life for me, and I think it'll be good.

Work, friends, Switch, Gabriella. That's it.

Technically, she is a friend. She's included in that bunch. I don't know why I separated her.

"Are you feeling better?" I offer her the blueberry muffin, and she accepts it with a sweet smile.

"A little." She picks bits from it and puts them in her mouth. "Do you know what the Horny Hangover syndrome is?"

"*Jesus*." I shake my head and ignore the thrill that shoots through me. The girl needs to learn a fucking lesson, and it doesn't involve sex.

"I'm just saying." She grins impishly. "I can count your piercings with my tongue while you use me as a bed warmer."

And I'm no longer hungry. My gut twists, and I set down my plate before I level her with a serious look. I barely know where to start. She wasn't fucking joking. She's casual about it. The offer is there. I frown and begin to speak, only to change my mind about the wording. I can't shake her or yell; it won't work. I can't threaten her, either.

If you say something like that about yourself again...

"Gabriella. Why... Why the fuck would you say that?"

Already, she gets defensive. Guard up, inching away, casual

expression forced. "There's nothing wrong with sex." She scowls. "You're hung up on Dylan, I'm never having a relationship again, but that doesn't mean sex stops being awesome."

"Why won't you have a relationship again?"

"Because they su-uck," she sings.

At twenty-four, she's too young to believe that.

"Not with the right person." Even in my jaded, fucked-up state, I know the facts. "I'm very sorry you got burned, princess, but don't let one asshole—"

"I don't want to talk about it," she interrupts. "I made bad choices, and now I'm over it."

Christ, she has it wrong. She did nothing but love John. She went above and beyond to please him, and he took a shit all over her. It wasn't her bad choice to be stood up when they had agreed on a playtime. It wasn't her bad choice to be mindfucked when she was at her most vulnerable.

"You're not over it," I murmur. "If you were, you wouldn't be acting out the way you have. Playing with Dante...? For fuck's sake, Gabriella. I know you well enough. Pain's the last thing you want when you're vulnerable."

"I'm not a Little anymore," she replies, and it's the stupidest thing I've heard all year. "I can't take care of myself or make the right decisions when I let go and regress, so now I'm having fun exploring masochism."

For what reasons, I wanna ask. I'd never stand in the way of anyone exploring curiosities and fetishes, but I gotta know her reasons. She wouldn't be the first person—primarily sub—who uses pain to punish themselves for something that's happened to them.

As for not being a Little anymore? I call bullshit. I've seen her happy. Her relationship with John wasn't always bad, and when she relaxes and allows her Little self to come out and play, she soars. It's her nature.

"What is it about pain you enjoy?" I ask.

I have sadistic tendencies myself, but they don't stray far from sensual sadism. I dole out pain that heightens the sub's pleasure, leaving the more hard-core pain to Dante and Rio and their subs, who get off on actual suffering.

Gabriella shrugs and flicks her gaze to the TV. "It makes me hot."

She's lying to me, which is fucking disappointing.

"Besides, you don't know me that well," she adds. "We've never even played. Not really."

I narrow my eyes at her. No, she and I have never played, but she has played with Dylan—twice—while I was there to film and watch. Other than the two being gorgeous together, I distinctly remember her reacting badly to Dylan trying my flogger on her. So how's that for enjoying pain?

I wanna shake her, not to mention chastise her for lying and worrying me.

Forcing her to be straight with me won't work, though. I'll earn her trust. In the meantime, I'll keep an eye on her at the club, and she can kiss public play with Sadists good-bye.

Looks like I'll be going back to Switch sooner than next weekend.

CHAPTER 3

Two days later, I show up at Switch again. I saw Gabriella and Kayla talking on the message boards online, and they have plans to meet up here tonight.

The doorman greets me and says it's nice to have me back, and then his girl hands me a black T-shirt. Confused, I hold it up and see "Dungeon Monitor" printed in white on the back. These gotta be new. Before, the DMs only wore special cuffs.

I'm not scheduled to work, but this might help. If Gabriella shows up, I'll have more authority, so I duck into the men's room in the lobby and change. Then I leave my belongings in my locker upstairs before I enter the main club area on the first floor.

A demo has recently ended on the platform past the bar, so the crowd is slowly scattering to continue their evening with play and socializing. Metal pours out of the speakers.

Mark is behind the bar in the Club, and given the number of people swarming, it'll be a while before he has a break. I continue toward the Cave, the area that used to be a restaurant next door. The ceiling is lower here, providing a more intimate atmosphere, and the walls are lined with scening stalls and contraptions.

"Kingsley!"

I nod at Liam, who's manning the bar in the middle of the floor.

"What's up?" I rest my forearms on the bartop and glance around the stalls to make sure everyone's playing by the rules. If I wear the shirt, I better make myself useful.

"You've been on hiatus." Liam sets a soda in front of me, and I cock a brow. "For the girl running up behind you."

I look over my shoulder and see Kayla heading my way. That little chick makes me grin. Too fucking adorable.

"You're back!" Excitement brimming over, she jumps just as I turn to her, and she's lucky I catch her. "We've missed you—oh, you've let your hair grow out a bit. I like it. When you did the buzzy thing, you looked meaner."

"I remember you were afraid of me in the beginning." I chuckle and give her a hard squeeze. "Where's your Daddy?" Nicholas is never usually far away from her.

"Upstairs, working." She makes a face. "He says he's gonna ground me, can you believe that?"

I can, actually. Kayla's a brat.

"What did you do this time?" I smirk and let her down, and she smooths out her baby-doll dress then curtsies as a thank-you for the soda.

"I didn't do anything," she insists. She takes a big gulp from her Sprite before wiping her mouth with her arm. "Daddy was irritated at the kittens. Jackson and Oliver were playing innocently by his feet, and he did this!" She makes a choking motion with her hands. "Like he wanted to strangle my babies? Oh, I was so *mad*."

I laugh. "He wouldn't ground you for being bugged by cats."

"Well, no." She squints and looks away. "Maybe I put glitter in his shoes."

There it is.

"I had to defend Oliver and Jackson!"

I fold my arms over my chest, grinning. "From a gesture?"

She scowls up at me. "Ugh, you don't get it. I should've known. All Tops are on Daddy's side."

"Just how many have you told?" Christ, the girl cracks me up.

"All of them." She slumps her shoulders. "So it looks like I'm grounded tomorrow, which means I'll miss the munch. Totally sucks donkey—"

"I wouldn't finish that sentence if I were you," I drawl. Nicholas and I are close since we're the only Daddy Doms in our group of friends. We have each other's backs, and I know for a fact Kayla's not allowed to use foul language.

She bites her lip. "I'll change the topic instead. How long are you going to let Dylan mope around in Texas?"

Can't say I'm a fan of the topic change, but her question raises one of my own. "How do you know he's moping?"

"He and Chelsea talk sometimes."

That's interesting. And it pisses me off, 'cause then Dylan's also avoiding Gabriella.

Before she left the other day, I asked if she'd spoken to him, and I got a no in response. She's upset by it, too. They haven't argued as far as I know, so what the fuck is Dylan up to? He can talk to Chelsea, Rio's sub, whom he got to know a *week* before he bailed, but not Gabriella, his best friend.

"Then he can drag his moping ass to the nearest phone and call me," I say. "Unlike him, I'll answer."

It wasn't my intention to air my personal issues, and I already regret it. Kayla sees it as a challenge and dives into matchmaking, something she's known for. In fact, she's the one who set me and Dylan up last winter. She firmly believes we're meant to be and speaks about life like it's a fairy tale.

I gotta cut her off, and I tell her it's time for me to work.

"You know I make the schedules, right?" She cocks her head and sips her soda. "You're not on tonight. Just...sayin'."

I let out a laugh and kiss her on the forehead. "Good to know. Go have fun with your friends."

Giving one of the other DMs a break, I fill in at nine.

No sign of Gabriella yet.

Rio's covering the Club area along with the Chamber—another playroom—and Simon's doing the Cinema, where he basically watches couples fuck to porn. That leaves me with the Cave and all its scening stalls.

Walking to one, I peer inside before letting the curtain drop again.

A little early in the evening to walk in on a gang bang, but all right. In the next stall, a Domme is torturing her sub with a fucking feather, making me shudder. I'm disgustingly ticklish, and I would rather get whipped than tickled.

Poking my head into the third stall, I clear my throat pointedly, albeit quietly, when I see a Dom and his property engaging in breath play.

He looks up, no doubt irritated. I get it, but we have fucking rules.

"All breath play acts gotta be supervised," I tell him. "I'll leave the curtains open. One more strike and you're out."

He nods in understanding, and I move on.

Half an hour later, I meet up with Rio in the wide entrance between the Cave and the Club.

"Busy night," he notes. "Good to have you back. You've been missed."

"I appreciate it." I lean against the doorway and scan the row of booths next to the dance floor. Everyone's on a fucking spree, it seems. People are talking over the loud music, drinking...and fucking. Personally, I enjoy at least a semblance of privacy. "Congrats on the collaring," I say. "I saw Chelsea's announcement online. When's the big day?"

He smiles. "We're doing a small ceremony in the Chamber the

weekend after we come home from Mexico. I hope you'll be there, mate."

"Yeah, for sure." I nod, tilting my head at the exit. Where the hell is she? I suppress a sigh and refocus on Rio. "Speaking of that sub of yours, I hear she talks to Dylan." I rub the back of my neck, feeling like a pathetic schmuck for going there, but I won't stand for him hurting Gabriella. She needs her friend. "You don't happen to know how he's doing, do you?"

Rio frowns. "Can't say I do. I don't believe they talk often." He pauses. "I spoke to him once—briefly. He called to apologize for running out after my play party without telling me."

There's a reminder I don't need. Rio's actually the last one Dylan played with, and it's getting to be too much for me.

The bitterness is probably etched across my features, and I let out a hollow laugh and rub a hand over my jaw. *Fuck you, Dylan.* I'm done, which I've said before. Goddammit. Now I mean it. I'll be here for Gabriella instead. Only her.

Yeah, good luck with that.

"If there's anything I can do, Cade..." Rio's forehead creases in concern, and I'm ready to wave it off, pretend to be dismissive, except that's when Chelsea shows up and kneels next to her Master.

She's a girl of grace and submissive devotion, though I've heard she's also rough around the edges and has a dark past.

"Didn't I order you to stay at the bar, rebel?" Rio asks and threads his fingers through her long hair. "Speak."

"Apologies, Owner." She keeps her gaze lowered. "Permission requested to go to the bathroom?"

My brows rise, though I make no mention. Their kink is their kink. Several high-protocol subs need permission for basic things. They're obviously on the right path if they're happy, so more power to them.

"Chelsea!" Kayla skips over with a wide smile on her face, and although I find her approach much more to my taste, respect for everyone comes first. So I give her a look that says *zip it*. She has to go through Chelsea's Master if she wants to talk to her friend. "Oh, right." She widens her eyes and offers Rio a sheepish expression. "I'm sorry, Sir."

His mouth twitches. "No troubles, love. You can accompany Chelsea to the bathroom if you want to chat." He addresses Chelsea next. "You have five minutes, then you return to the bar."

"Yes, Owner." Chelsea rises from her position, and just as she's about to turn toward the exit where the bathrooms are, she slides me a look I can only describe as bitchy. It's brief and dismissive—chin jutted, one brow cocked, a quick once-over.

I frown, confused, and have no intention of asking what's up. I don't know her very well yet. In fact, I'm not sure we've spoken more than once or twice, and it was in the company of others.

Rio evidently notices her look too, and he speaks up without hesitation. "Oi, hold on, pet. What was that?"

"What do you mean, Master?" Chelsea stops and wrings her hands.

Meanwhile, Kayla's curious, albeit impatient, to talk to her friend.

"You know very well." Rio's expression chills, and he folds his arms over his chest. I'd be amused if I wasn't genuinely baffled. "You're already on thin fucking ice for stalling. Think about that before you lie."

She swallows hard and averts her gaze to the floor. "I'm sorry, Owner. I would never lie to you. My focus should be on you, and I made a mistake by thinking about my personal opinion of Mr. Kingsley."

Oh, *really?* I fold my arms over my chest, too. This oughta be good, and it doesn't take a genius to figure out it's related to Dylan.

Rio's mouth thins. His displeasure is clear enough for Kayla to shrink back and excuse herself to find Nicholas.

"Cade and I have been close mates for years, Chelsea," Rio says grimly. "I trust him. You haven't had the opportunity to get to know him yet, so I wonder what that opinion is based on."

Chelsea flushes then steps to the side to let a group of guests pass. The entry between the Cave and the Club is getting crowded.

"He hurt my friend, Master." Her confidence has already faltered, and after what she just said, I'm enjoying her fumbling. "I don't question your loyalty or reasoning; I only know what I know. Dylan left because he was heartbrok—"

That's it.

"All right, I've heard enough." I clench my jaw and rub a hand over it, going from mildly irritated to pissed in a second. Fuck this shit. "Enjoy your evening." With a curt nod, I begin to leave them, and I shake my head when Rio starts speaking up. Fuck that, too.

I need a minute to cool off—

"Actually," I laugh bitterly and get in Chelsea's face, which so wasn't the plan. Jesus Christ, what am I doing? For what useless reason? "Since you're Rio's sub, I'm gonna say this as politely as I can." I tighten my fists, and I hear it; I hear my mind yelling at me to take a step back and go calm myself down. Yet, I can't. I rant heatedly to a young girl I don't even know. About personal affairs I detest airing like gossip. "I had less than two months with Dylan, and I did the responsible thing when I noticed how quickly he got attached. He was new in the scene, I got burned by my last Little, and I didn't wanna repeat—"

"Cade," Rio interrupts, "you don't owe her an explanation."

"It's fine," I bite out, turning back to Chelsea. She's struggling to hold on to her tough-girl front. "Dylan lied to my face and said slowing down was okay. Then I found out it wasn't, but he kept giving me bullshit lies. I was bending over backward to make that kid happy. He got to play with Gabriella, his best friend, who he's now ignoring for no reason at all, and I gave him the goddamn puppy he wanted." I finally inch back a bit, and Chelsea's staring at the floor. I haven't even told her the worst part yet. "It wasn't enough, though. He got it into his head that I didn't want him, despite what I said, so he decided on a fucking whim to go to Rio's play party with someone else. 'Cause, hey, he was practically single, right?"

I remember working here that night of Rio's party, and at the last second, I called him for help. It'd been some Roman theme for the event, complete with games and a slave auction. Rio agreed to buy Dylan, because I could at least stand having them play together.

"I didn't know." The music almost drowns out Chelsea's voice.

"Of course you didn't." Emotionally exhausted, I rub a hand over my face. "*Fuck.*"

I should've kept my mouth shut. Venting when angry skews things, and I fear I've made Dylan sound worse than he is. Everything I told Chelsea is true; however, there are circumstances, previous agreements between Dylan and me, and of course, shit I've done wrong, too. It's easy to blame him for everything when it feels like your chest is about to cave in, but when I'm clearheaded and not so damn broody, there's more to the story.

"Cade!"

I groan under my breath and throw an irritated look over my shoulder. I'm not short at six two, nor am I scrawny after seventeen years in construction and woodworking, but Dante stands out everywhere. He moves his imposing form through the crowded Cave and stops next to us.

"I don't care if you come as a monitor or a friend, but control Gabriella," he says impatiently. "If she wants to scene with me and Gretchen, she follows my fucking rules." He flicks Rio a glance. "Sometimes I miss Chelsea."

Rio smiles tightly, the previous moment between Chelsea and me not off his mind yet. "I'm not even sorry, mate."

"Gabriella's *here?*" I ask incredulously. Funny how quickly the argument I had five minutes ago is gone for *me*. Worry shoots up my spine, and I curse myself for not paying more attention. "Lead the way."

Dante nods curtly and heads toward the Chamber, one of the areas I haven't checked much tonight. Go fucking figure.

"Explain shit to your girl, please," I tell Rio before taking off after Dante. I stew in my own stupidity at having opened my goddamn mouth, and now that the damage is done, Chelsea should know the things I omitted in my rant. Rio knows most of it, thankfully. He can take over.

"I know you guys are close, Cade," Dante says, shaking his head, "but she can't act the way she wants to."

"Don't worry, I'm banning her ass." I have the authority, and I won't hesitate just 'cause we're friends. That's not how we operate. "Why the fuck would you play with her again, man?"

She refused aftercare last time, the night Mark brought her over, so I don't understand why she would approach Dante and his sub again—or why the hell he would agree.

"She puts on a good show." Dante seems bitter about that. Can't blame him. "I bought her remorseful act and thought a scene could smooth things over." He side-eyes me as we walk past the last scening stalls in the Cave. "She was gonna play with someone I don't trust, otherwise."

I nod with a dip of my chin, respecting his line of thought. He'd rather have Gabriella play with him. I'd do the same.

We enter the Chamber, a hazily lit area with sheer fabrics, low couches, and an altar-like setup for pole dancing and wax play in the middle of the room. The Middle Eastern-themed space is a popular feature at Switch, and it takes me a beat to find Gabriella in the throng of kinksters engaging in orgies and sensation play.

Gretchen, Dante's sub, is kneeling next to a couch in the corner, her leash fastened to the wall. And there's Gabriella next to her, looking sufficiently pissed, cuffed to Gretchen.

"Good thinking." Now she won't be able to escape.

As we get closer, I see her clearer, and I can't fucking believe there are more changes in her to digest. She's gotten pink streaks in her dark hair, and unless I missed it last time, there's more than ivy creeping up her leg. Jesus Christ, I saw her two days ago.

It's time she learns I won't tolerate this anymore. She can't play me, nor does our friendship give her a free pass. Daddy Doms are generally known to be kind in comparison, gentler in nature, and she's about to find out what kind of Daddy Dom I can be when the situation calls for it.

When she spots me, she slants me a lazy smile and a little wave.

Dante steps forward and turns the key in her locked cuff. "Have fun with Mr. Kingsley."

"He's a sweetheart," Gabriella says.

We'll see if you say that soon, princess.

Dante eases off, and before Gabriella can stand up, I'm there to grab a fistful of her hair and yank her head back. She gasps, eyes growing wide, and stares up at me in shock.

"Apologize to Master Dante and his sub for *fucking* up their night."

"What!" she splutters. "But I didn't do anything!"

"Apologize," I growl.

She obeys when I tighten my grip on her hair.

"Owww—damn it, I'm sorry!" she cries out.

I shake my head and grab her arm, hauling her off the floor, and I face Dante. "You'll be getting a better apology as soon as she's actually sorry."

"Don't worry about it, my friend." Dante steps aside so I can get Gabriella out of here. "She's in good hands, and there's plenty of time for Gretchen and me to play."

Nah, respect is big for me, and Gabriella will own up to it and make things right. End of. But until then, we're out of here.

CHAPTER 4

"Let me go, Cade!" she snarls.

I side-eye her, failing to reply. Now that I'm close enough, I see princesses from children's movies have joined the ivy along her thigh. Four pieces are still covered in plastic wrap, but she's unveiled two. Hiding behind leaves or sitting on narrow branches, pastel-colored dresses and sweet smiles have been replaced with slutty lingerie and dirty smirks.

Never thought I'd see Snow White in a corset that pushes her tits together.

Never thought I'd see Tinker Bell wielding a whip.

"You have no right to boss me around," she grits out over the music.

I nod to Nicholas and Kayla, both of whom are watching from the bar in the Club. Nick, in obvious concern and with a frown on his face, and Kayla, biting her lip in worry.

"Are you even listening to me?" Gabriella snaps. "You're not allowed to touch me!"

"Actually, I am," I argue mildly. "You signed a form when you became a member here that says any DM has the right to remove you from harm's way." *Or escort you off the premises if you violate the rules.*

She scoffs as we reach the lobby. "And that's what you're doing? *Please.* I didn't need any damn saving. I was having fun until Dante decided I was too rough for him."

Too rough, right. "That's cute." Walking her over to the girl at coat check, I ask to borrow a set of handcuffs.

"Cade!" Gabriella tries to pull herself free over and over, and she hits my arm when I knock her wrist to the nearest wall and slap one of the cuffs on her. "Oh my God, stop it!"

Ray at the door chuckles. "Let this be a lesson, people," he tells the half a dozen people watching. "Our dungeon monitors mean business."

In-fucking-deed. She's no match for me, and it doesn't take much to attach the other cuff to the hooks meant for subs who come here as pets. Bratty kittens and puppies have been attached to this wall while their Owners go to the bathroom ever since Nicholas opened Switch.

"Now I know you'll be here when I get back." I leave a seething Gabriella alone and jog up to the second floor to get my shit. I don't make a habit of bringing an extra helmet, so I'll have to break a couple laws tonight.

Returning downstairs, I put on my jacket and tell Ray's sub to issue an alert for Gabriella.

"She's banned?" the girl asks sadly. She taps a few keys on the computer and pulls up a form. "Violations, Sir?"

"Repeatedly ignoring the terms of use." I uncuff Gabriella and grab her hand as I give back the cuffs. "Willfully disrespecting superiors... Did I forget anything?" I raise a brow to Gabriella. She's glaring at the floor. "Oh—interrupting scenes."

"Yikes." The girl types it all down. "Um, I need a photo."

I grip the back of Gabriella's neck and position her in line with the webcam attached on top of the computer. "Smile, princess."

She flushes in anger. "Fuck you."

"Duration, Sir?" the girl wonders.

"Six months, but—"

"That's unfair!" Gabriella exclaims. "Six *months?*"

I shoot her a glare, getting heated. She doesn't wanna deal with me then, that's for fucking sure.

"Six months," I grit out, sliding my gaze back to the girl, "but she can visit if she's accompanied by a DM. Actually, make that me. She's allowed to be here if she arrives with me. I'll be responsible for her."

"Understood." The girl nods. "That's it. Gabriella's now banned." She offers Gabriella an apologetic look, which isn't necessary. The girl hasn't done anything wrong.

"Thanks, hon." I rap my fingers along the counter and hand Gabriella my helmet. "Let's get your clothes, and then we're leaving."

"Can you upsize that shit?" I pull out my wallet.

The cashier nods. "Of course, sir."

I pay for my meal and stand aside while I wait for the food. Gabriella stays outside and looks appropriately fuming about the detour. It makes me grin to watch her struggle with the helmet. Now that I've simmered down, it's just fun seeing her pissy.

Eventually, she stomps inside and joins me. "You could've done your Mickey D run after you dropped me off." She huffs.

She thinks I'm taking her home to *her* place.

"I was in the mood for fries." I shrug.

"Gross." Folding her arms over her chest, she scowls at the world like the teenager she was a few years ago. "Your bike's uncomfortable, by the way."

No need to get nasty. My bike's just fine.

"You know what else would be uncomfortable?" I drawl. "If I

flipped up your skirt and turned your ass red in front of these strangers."

"You wouldn't."

I would, and I think she knows it. I'm shameless. She's not, judging by how she inches away from me and zips up her sad excuse for a jacket. Looks like something a doll would wear. Same size, anyway.

We're back on the road soon enough, and she holds my food trapped between us while I head toward the outskirts of the city. The engine rumbles as I speed up, at which Gabriella fists my jacket harder.

Moments later, I hear her yelling over the roar.

"You missed the exit, dumbass!"

I don't answer, continuing straight ahead. A plan's forming in my head, and she'll regret all the venom she's been spitting my way soon.

By the time we reach the edge of the subdivision where I have my shop, I can practically taste Gabriella's seething.

She's first off the bike, and she tears off the helmet with a snarl. "What the hell, Cade!"

"There's been a *lot* of yelling my name tonight." I dismount my precious Harley. "None of the good kind, either—*Hey!*" My arm shoots out just when she was about to throw my helmet on the ground. "Fucking *watch* it."

She knows she almost went too damn far there. She's in a shitty place—I get it—but I have limits.

She swallows and looks away from me, holding the helmet and my food securely now. "I wanna go home." Sounding more tired than angry, she gives me a wide berth to open the garage and push my bike inside.

"That's too bad. You'll be staying with me for a while." I gesture for her to enter so I can shut the garage again.

She gives me an exasperated look, almost pleading, and sets my helmet down on my workbench. "You can't *make* me do that."

"You're right, I can't." Up the spiral staircase, I think of Mark and the others who have basically babysat her while I was on the East Coast. I think of her subbie friends who are worried. "I believe you'll stay anyway."

Furthermore, I think of everything she could've done if she's seriously trying to get hurt. Whether she wants to punish herself for some unknown reason or if she simply doesn't give a shit anymore, Switch is the wrong place for her to do that. Sure, the Sadists and the more hard-core Tops can make her suffer. They can give her hell.

They'll also insist on aftercare and making sure she's all right. We vet our guests properly at Switch, and regardless of how unsafe certain kinksters choose to play at home or at private parties, no one will stand for anyone being harmed at the club.

So coming around there to be a menace... My gut says it's a fucked-up cry for help.

"Why would I do that?" Gabriella extends the bag of food to me, and I set it down on the kitchen counter.

"Because you don't wanna end up losing your friends for good." I toss my jacket on the table and run a hand over my hair. Short as it is, it stands in every direction after the ride home with no helmet. "That's where you're heading, princess."

I sit down at the table and kick out a chair for her to join me. Then I dig around the McDonald's bag for my burger, large fries, and my shake. Strawberry ain't my flavor, though I know someone who loves it. Someone who was adamant about not being hungry. I've heard that before.

"Everyone's worried about you." I unwrap my burger and take a big bite, and I watch her mulling over what I tell her. "What John did to you, hon...? He wouldn't look pretty if I got my hands on him. But you gotta stop pushing away those who've done nothing wrong."

"I'm not pushing them away," she says defensively, albeit

weakly. She's a smart girl. She can't talk herself outta this one using the logic she's lived by the past three months.

I give it to her bluntly. "By behaving like an obnoxious little bitch, you kind of are."

That works, and she turns away as her cheeks burn.

Fingers crossed she doesn't have the energy to fight anymore. The help is right in front of her. Me, her friends—she's not alone.

"Excuse me." She stands up abruptly and heads for the bathroom, the only place she can find privacy.

With an internal sigh, I set down my burger and hesitate. Every part of me wants to follow her and offer comfort. But another thought creeps in, and I eye my laptop over by the bed.

You should fucking be here, Dylan.

A minute later, I have booted up my laptop, and I'm shoving fries into my mouth as I struggle to form an email to Dylan.

Dylan,

Get your head out of your ass and call Gabriella. I don't even care about you and me anymore, but—

Nope. I erase that. I do care—way too much for my liking—and I won't lie.

When I hear sniffling coming from the bathroom, the words come quickly. Short, to the point, because I have more important things to deal with.

Dylan,
Call Gabriella. She needs you.
Cade

"Are you feeling better?" I give her a squeeze and press a kiss to the top of her head.

"A little," she croaks. She snuggles closer. "I'm so tired."

I have a feeling she's not saying that because it's late.

Getting her out of the bathroom earlier took surprisingly little effort. Falling into my arms, she'd let me carry her to bed, where I spent the next hour consoling her. I can only hope she's letting go of that tough-girl attitude. It's not her.

"Tell me what's going through your mind," I murmur.

She exhales shakily and shivers. "Your place is cold."

I smile into her hair and draw the covers up higher. "I like it cold. Quit stalling."

"Bossy." She sniffles, though her tone is lighter. "I don't know what to say. He betrayed me. At first, I blamed myself, and I know I told you I was the one making bad choices—it's hard to explain. I get so mad when I think about all the times I accepted everything he did." She sounds frustrated. "I was in denial for months before I finally walked out, and I guess I'm angry with myself for not facing reality sooner. He always made promises about next weekend and how we'd do something together, and every damn time, I fell for it. One canceled dinner turned into a promise of us going to look at houses the next week, and I'd get my hopes up."

I brush the last of her tears away from her cheeks, practicing patience before I speak up. I want her to get it all out.

"He toyed with me...or he just didn't care," she mumbles. "When he proposed, he told me I was his everything. We put each other first and talked more. Then, all of a sudden, it was 'Daddy has to work so he can pay for your pretty dresses,' and I felt awful. He insisted I wear the damn things, yet the blame was on me?" She gets worked up again. "He was big on guilt. That was the worst, how he made me feel like it was my fault he was away so much."

I remember that too well. She would be quick to defend John when we questioned his bullshit. We said he was neglecting her; she claimed he was working hard to take care of her, and that she wasn't easy to be with.

"It's pointless to dwell on the past." She rubs at her eyes and blows out a breath. "I left when I left, and I know he took advantage of me now. He knew so well how vulnerable I am when I, you know, get more little."

I nod slowly, having seen enough with my own eyes. Gabriella regresses and lets go of her adult side, allowing her to sink deeply into the mind-set of the young girl who lives inside her. It's part of who she is, a part I've been lucky to experience several times.

John had no right to make decisions and fuck with her head when she was that exposed.

"At the same time..." Gabriella falters. "I mean, I don't miss him. Just the thought of him makes me want to vomit. But I miss who I could be... I hate it, Cade. I don't want to be a Little anymore." She glances up at me, her eyelashes thick with tears, and she looks so small. "How can I trust anyone not to try to change me again?"

"You'll get there, I promise." I stroke her cheek and tuck some hair behind her ear. "It'll take time, but I have no doubt you'll learn to trust again."

She pouts and rests her head on my chest again. "So now I have to suffer these damn headaches. It's hard finding a balance, you know? I was his Little for so long. I could do whatever felt natural—whenever I wanted. Now I don't know how to keep a lid on it. I just end up angry and upset most of the time."

It's impossible for me to relate. I am who I am every hour of the day, three hundred and sixty-five days of the year. I don't have to hide anything. Littles do.

"Do you trust me?" I wonder.

She furrows her brow and tilts her face up. "Duh."

I snort a quiet chuckle and tap her nose. "Brat." I know that's what she is. Hidden and suppressed by John, but I know a playful imp is in there, wanting to jump out with a big, goofy grin. "You can always do what feels natural around me. Whenever and wherever. You know I would take care of you."

She lowers her gaze and bites her lip. "I don't know... Wouldn't that be weird?"

"Why would it be weird?"

"You and Dylan." She shrugs a little. "I feel safe with you, but

I'd probably worry about being in the way, and...like, you're hung up on him, and you'd wish I were him—"

"Don't ever think that, princess." I press my lips to the crease between her brows. "I'm not sure what exactly it is we're discussing right now. If it's you regressing with me, I wouldn't have offered if I didn't care about you—if I didn't *want* to be there for you."

I'm unsure of how to broach the rest, mainly because I don't know where her mind is at. Is it about sex? Or would it be strange for her because she and Dylan are—or were?—such close friends?

"I'm not a non-sexual Little. What if I cross a line?" She cringes. "Ugh, it's weird talking about it."

I let out a low laugh and hug her to me. "You're too fucking adorable, Gabriella." Easing away, I grip her chin to make sure she looks me in the eye. "I'm very aware of you not being a non-sexual Little." I pause, hoping I get this out right. "Would I be down to fuck you first thing tomorrow morning? I highly doubt it, but it has nothing to do with desire. You're a gorgeous girl, one I've been attracted to since day one."

Fuck me if she doesn't blush.

"And yeah, I'm hung up on Dylan, as you put it," I go on. "I won't deny that, but keep in mind, we had an open arrangement." She of all people should know that. Thinking back on the two occasions they scened together at Switch... In-fucking-describable. "I wouldn't have enjoyed seeing you and him together if there was no desire."

She bobs her head slowly, eyes fixed on my wife-beater. "I think I understand."

That's good, but I'm not done. "So here's what I'm thinking. No one would be more honored than me if you felt comfortable enough to lean on me, whether you regress or not. And the rest, we'll take it as it comes. You focus on relaxing and feeling better. It wasn't long ago you ended a relationship you thought was going to last forever."

With the past three months in mind, where Gabriella rebelled, lived destructively, and buried her pain, I can't see her thinking about sex anytime soon. She may have been able to lie to herself for a while, and I sure as hell haven't forgotten she offered up herself on a platter to me a couple days ago, though that was before tonight. Before she stopped pretending.

I'm hopeful that's over now. It appears to be.

"Can I think about this?" she asks softly.

"Of course." There's no rush. "Take all the time you need. But you're staying here for now, yeah?"

"Um, sure... I can do that, but...why?"

That's an easy one. "For one, I've felt protective of you since John began neglecting you, and I'd feel better having you here until I know you're okay. For two, you need some structure back in your life." That comes with a raised brow from me when she peers up.

"That, uh..." She twists her lips. "That sounds like there will be rules."

My chest rumbles with a laugh. "You can bet your sweet little ass there will be rules."

I'll be starting fresh with her. I have a shitload of questions about her thought process, her recent history at Switch and how she's played, her physical health as well as mental, and whatever else I'll think of.

Gabriella buries her face against my chest. "Thank you for giving a crap, Cade. I don't want to feel like this anymore."

"We'll get through it together, princess."

CHAPTER 5

Over the next couple of days, Gabriella keeps to herself a lot. She borrows my truck to get some clothes and personal belongings from her place, and then she retreats to be alone on my roof.

There's nothing up there, and it wasn't designed to be some swanky roof terrace or anything. But Gabriella brings up a plant, an old rug, and a beanbag, sitting there for hours on end with a book or her journal.

I have orders to catch up on, so I'm stuck in the garage most of the time. Unlike when I'm alone, though, I push up the door so Gabriella can hear the radio playing. Every now and then, I hear her hollering her opinions on my *shitty* taste in music.

It makes me grin.

Kids these days don't appreciate the oldies.

As I ease fine sandpaper over a carved piece of oak—which, when ready, will be a whipping post for a fetish club in Sacramento —I hit up Mark and Rio to give them an update. One earbud in my ear, the other one dangling inside my T-shirt, I tell them I'll be at Switch as scheduled this weekend, and I'll be bringing Gabriella.

Nicholas has told them she's banned from being there alone, so Mark's the first one to offer to keep an eye on her if I get busy. And Rio says he's more than happy to help me instill some respect in Gabriella again.

"She scared the bloody hell out of me once when she asked a Top to choke her out," he tells me. "If she'd been mine, I would've strung her up and beaten her senseless."

I chuckle. "I'm glad I wasn't there. I'm too young to have a heart attack."

I appreciate my buddies. They all want what's best for Gabriella, and they've been frustrated to stand on the sidelines and watch helplessly. She's her own person, and their hands are tied unless she violates the rules.

"Well, I'm glad she has you now, mate," Rio says. "Have you spoken to the others?"

I nod even though he can't see me. "Just got off the phone with Mark. I'll call Nick later."

"All right, that's good." He pauses. "Have you and Gabriella discussed her previous scenes? The ones I supervised... I kept waiting for her to safeword."

We've covered some of it. Last night at dinner, I learned she's only sought out Tops for impact play and pain. I brought up going through a physical so she could get tested, something we encourage regularly, but she said it wasn't necessary. She did that twice after leaving John, and she hasn't been with anyone sexually since then, which I'll admit surprised me. And maybe pleased me.

"We haven't talked about specific scenes, but she's told me her reasoning." Brushing my hand along the smooth surface of my work, I inspect it critically and closely before deeming it ready for the finish. "She spoke to masochists who raved about being punched into subspace—quite fucking literally—and she wanted that, too. In my day, we smoked pot to numb pain."

I shouldn't joke about it, but it's all I can do. After listening to her saying she's been feeling weak, and seeking out pain could—

aside from numb her—prove she's strong, I lay awake all night and cursed my sorry ass for leaving San Francisco.

One of the first nights I wasn't haunted by dreams of Dylan.

I should've known Gabriella would need a place to land after her breakup.

"Poor girl," Rio sighs. "Here's to hoping she'll get better now."

"Agreed." I straighten up and take a swig from my lukewarm coffee. "How's your own girl? I hope you weren't too rough on her."

He chuckles wryly. "Well, orgasm denial tends to work. I gave her a few weeks."

"Ouch," I laugh and wince.

His humor fades. "She will apologize to you, Cade. I explained what I know, and she feels bad. She knows there are two sides to every story."

If not three.

An apology isn't necessary; I'd rather put that evening behind me, but I get where he's coming from. "Count on the same from Gabriella. She'll be making rounds at Switch soon."

That lightens the tension, and we leave the topic to discuss what he and I are best at. Play parties. I haven't hosted in ages because I've moved, and there's no room to have a bunch of people over unless I fix up the backyard, which is now a haven for weeds to grow wild. The last owner ran an auto shop and used half the area in the back as a parking lot for the vehicles they were working on. A wooden fence surrounds the property, saving the neighbors from seeing how bad it looks out there.

May has brought some nice weather, though, so maybe I can work something out in a couple months.

"What're you in the mood for?" I spread out the takeout menus on the kitchen table and grab the phone.

Gabriella hums and lifts a pamphlet from a Greek place. "I

need to learn how to cook. I only know some basics. Except for lasagna. My lasagna is the *best*. That and my last name are the only Italian left of me." She giggles.

I lean back against the counter. "I'll have to bribe you into making it for me some time." I'm useless in the kitchen unless a diet consisting of cereal, grilled cheese, and scrambled eggs is sufficient. Last time I checked, it wasn't.

I'm good with takeout, though. I even order salad sometimes. Well...on the side.

"No need to bribe. I'll pick up the ingredients soon." She holds up a menu from a restaurant that does stellar Thai. "What say you?"

"Sounds good." I grab the menu from her, only to pause with my gaze trained on her body. And I reckon I might be in trouble at some point soon.

She was pretty in the dresses John wanted her to wear. She was sinfully slutty in the threads she chose to rebel in. This, on the other hand, hits the perfect spot for me. Dressed for comfort in barely there jersey shorts and a top saying "Define Good Girl" that lets me know she's not wearing a bra... Yeah, I approve.

I like the bed head she's rocking, too. Without any fucking products in it.

Less makeup.

Damn.

I wave my fork at where Gabriella's journal lies next to her plate. "You gonna tell me what you've been scribbling in that book of yours the past two days?"

Maybe I'm a little curious.

She smirks around a spoonful of soup. "It's nothing fun, I can tell you that."

"I don't care." I've already guessed it's nothing pleasant, 'cause she's looked troubled when I've seen her writing in it. "Thing is, Gabriella, we know each other without really..." I chuckle. "Without actually knowing each other. I know where you live, what your primary fetishes are, what makes you laugh, what soda you prefer at Switch... I know what you do for a living—"

"I quit."

"Huh?"

She bites her lip, lifting one shoulder in a shrug. "I worked in retail because John liked my schedule."

Fucking hell. It pains me how much her life changed—and will change again—all because of that asshole. She wanted to please him and be there as much as possible, and so he played her like a fiddle. He had no fucking right.

I blow out a breath and shake my head. "Motherless bastard."

She offers a small smile. "I'm focusing on moving forward."

I nod, and I won't rant about what I would do with John if I ever see him. I've done that enough. Instead, I get back on track. "All right, then. I don't know what you do for a living. I also don't know a whole lot about your hobbies, taste in music—other than the fact that you have no respect for oldies whatsoever."

She bursts out a laugh, a cute fucking sound that makes me grin. Then she falls silent, and we sorta just watch each other.

I'm glad she's here. My home is different, warmer, when she's around. I focus on work easier, and I've only checked my email once today. Still no response from Dylan, but the bitterness hasn't spiked as it usually does. No extra tightening of the vise grip on my chest.

"You're right." She sets down the spoon. "I want to know more about you, too."

Leaning back, I wipe my mouth with a napkin. "Well, I already know me, so I'm more interested in you—and your journal. We'll start there."

She laughs. "I already told you it's nothing fun." As if she's reminded of what her journal is about, she sobers and touches the book gingerly. "Mostly, I've been writing down goals and stuff. I hope it will help me to stay focused? I don't know. And the rest..." She stalls, uncomfortable. "You said it, Cade. I acted like an obnoxious bitch, and I want to apologize to everyone I disrespected, so I made a list of things I remember doing that make me cringe."

First instinct is to take what I said back and smooth things over. I don't do that, though. I admire her for facing this head on, and it makes me believe in her.

"I'm proud of you, princess." I reach across the table and squeeze her hand. "That's a great attitude, and I'll be here every step of the way."

She smiles and ducks her head.

"Whiny fuckin' morons," I mutter and flip the channel. Arm behind my head, pillows propped up, I try to find a news channel that's worth watching.

I showered while Gabriella was on the phone with friends earlier, and now she's taking a bath. She'll probably be out soon. I heard the shower running a minute ago.

Tonight, I'm getting rid of some modesty. I've raised the thermostat a bit so Miss Icicle won't complain—too much—about the alleged cold. So no more sleeping in sweats and beaters to be polite and shit. She should be lucky I've kept my boxer briefs on.

The door to the bathroom opens, and Gabriella emerges in another one of my tees. She's taken a liking to those, not that I mind. She's beyond beautiful.

"Hi." She runs over to the bed, quick to get under the covers. Meanwhile, I'm lying on top of them, and she spots some piercings and ink she hasn't seen before. "Oh wow, mister."

I smile softly at the return of the nickname.

"Did that hurt?" She points to the barbell in my left nipple.

"Not in comparison." I lower the volume on the TV.

"To...?"

I smirk.

Her gaze darts south to my crotch, and then she's blushing furiously. "Really?" she squeaks out.

I chuckle at how a fucking adorable she is. I make no mention of it, but I'm guessing the call with Kayla and whomever else went well—and that she feels more relaxed. The changes in her behavior are subtle, although easily picked up on. She carries herself just a tad more innocent, speaks a bit softer, and doesn't guard her expressions as much.

It's humbling as fuck, albeit frustrating. She'll be trouble for me sooner rather than later at this rate. Good thing I have self-discipline and know how to turn a shower cold.

"I had no idea." Her gaze travels up to my rib cage and my chest again. "I feel like I should've known?" She gives me an uncertain look.

Dylan. There's no need to tiptoe around the subject.

"I left the piercing out mostly," I explain. "Taking his ass is a bit different from fucking a sweet pussy. The barbell scared him, so it's not weird he didn't mention it."

"Such a potty mouth," she mumbles, squinty-eyed.

"Mmhmm, but we've been over that." It's time I get under the covers, too. "Daddies can curse all they want."

"No!" she protests as my ink disappears from sight. "I want to know about your tattoos. Please? You have so many!"

I'll share the stories one day. Scenery from sights I've traveled to, a few quotes, an oak to represent my love for woodworking, song lyrics, a Harley, and some fillers—it all bleeds together along my arm and rib cage.

"Tell you what." Twisting my upper body, I reach for my clock so I can set the alarm. "When you're ready to discuss your new body art, I can tell you about mine."

I was surprised when she told me she doesn't want to talk about that yet. It's ivy and princesses in slutty outfits. There has to be some significance or background story I don't know.

Gabriella sticks out her tongue at me. "Fine."

My ears fill with the sound of her heartwarming giggles as I stick out my tongue right back at her.

"Time for you to get some sleep." I kill the light and shut off the TV, and she slides on over to me. "I won't work late tomorrow, so I thought we could be at Switch early."

"Okay."

I yawn, waiting for her to get comfortable. Her cold feet glide up my legs, and I wrap my arms around her and kiss her on the forehead. With one hand on her hip, I'm beginning to have a difficult time not feeling more of her. It'd be easy to cup her delectable ass and—*goddammit*.

"You're a tempting little thing," I murmur.

She chuckles breathily. "You're one to talk, mister."

Well, hell. I hope she'll be ready for me to crash and burn soon, then.

"Mister?" Gabriella knocks on the door.

I open it for her and let the steam out from my shower, then return to the sink. "What's up, buttercup?" I grab a towel and wrap it around my hips and wipe the fog off the mirror.

She looks away from my ass, eyes wide, which I find funny.

"Um." She fumbles. "I don't know what to wear. I'm nervous. What if they don't want to hear my apologies? I was so bad."

"Hey." I abandon the plan to shave and pull her close, tilting up her chin. "First of all, there won't be much apologizing tonight. Second of all, when you're in a bad place, you tend to do bad things. That doesn't make *you* bad. You made mistakes. You hear me?"

"Yes, Sir." She nods, her eyes remaining full of uncertainty. It's all right. She'll find out for herself tonight. "Why won't there be much apologizing? I wrote letters to, like, eight people."

I didn't know that. That's sweet of her. "It's Hide & Seek night." Which means most of the club will be blanketed in darkness and smoke. "You can leave the letters if you want, but no one's expecting you to do anything but enjoy yourself with your friends." I press a kiss to her nose. "As for your clothes, I'll be more than happy to pick those out for you. Come on."

Grabbing her hand, I lead her to my closet where her clothes take up half the space now. Her fetish wear hangs in the back, and picking out a pair of black briefs—or hot pants or whatever women call them—is the easy part. Then I sift through her tops.

"We're taking my truck, so you can change here," I tell her.

"Okay."

I pause at a little thing that looks to fit my thigh. A white top with a black pacifier illustrated across the chest. Perfect. Handing it to her, I move on to grab a pair of jeans for myself, a black tee, the leather cuff with Switch's logo—which gets me thinking. Gabriella's off-limits to everyone else.

I open a drawer where I have my insignificant collection of accessories. A couple watches, some cuff links, and several rubber wristbands I've accidentally taken with me home from the club. Wearing a red one means no Top is allowed to approach you for play, so I extend one of those to her.

"You stay by me tonight, understood?"

She nods. "Yes, mister." She's changed into her shorts already, yet she's waiting with the top. Maybe seeing her toned legs and the perfect shape of her tight little bubble ass is what makes me take it further.

"If you can change into shorts with me here, you can do the top, too. No need to be shy."

"Oh," she mouths. "Um, okay."

In fact, I wanna enjoy the moment, so I usher her out of the closet and sit down on the foot of the bed.

She stops in front of the TV, twisting the top in her hands. "Oh, you mean with you...w-watching?"

"Is that a problem?"

She shakes her head, visibly nervous, and then she sets the top on the dresser behind her. She fidgets for a beat before releasing a breath and removing her sweater. When she reaches for the top again, I shake my head.

"Little girls can't wear bras. Take it off."

That earns me a blush, and she unclasps the white cotton and lets it fall to the floor.

Fuck me.

I reckon I just crashed and burned.

"Don't hide from me," I say quietly before she can shield herself. "Come here."

She shuffles closer until she's standing between my legs.

"You're staring, mister," she whispers uncomfortably. "I've gained a few pounds—"

"Shut the fuck up," I whisper back. Unable to keep my hands to myself, I place them along her sides and slowly slide them up her front. Mother of Christ, she's perfect. A perfect mix of soft and toned.

The ivy that travels up her thigh ends in a swirl of stardust above her hip. It's beautiful work. She put thought into the design.

Her nipples constrict before I get there, and I love watching her skin break out in goose bumps and shivers.

I lift my gaze to her face as my hands tease the undersides of her full tits.

"You're gorgeous, princess." I stroke her a bit higher, my fingers brushing over her hard nipples. She swallows audibly. "Do you like it when I touch you?"

She jerks a quick nod. "Yes, Sir. It tingles."

"It does, huh? Where?"

"Here." She puts a hand on her lower stomach.

"Are they good tingles?"

"Oh, yes." She widens her eyes. "But it makes me think dirty things."

Fuck.

"I see." My attention returns to her tits, and I cup them fully, my mouth watering. Anticipation is good, but fuck if I don't wanna skip work and begin exploring Gabriella's body. "It's a good thing I like filthy little girls with dirty thoughts."

She shudders as I drop my hands and finger the hem of her minuscule shorts. Her gaze follows, and her mouth forms a silent "o."

"You're hard, mister."

I give my junk a squeeze through the towel to relieve some pressure. "Of course I am. It's thinking dirty things, too."

Patience.

Right.

I check the clock next to the TV and see we gotta go soon.

"We'll have to continue this later." Rising from the bed, I put my hands on her hips and dip down to nip at her jaw. "I'm done pretending I don't wanna fuck you silly."

"Oh my God," she whimpers.

CHAPTER 6

With desire, my natural role as a Daddy Dom rears its demanding head, and by the time we arrive at Switch, I'm strung tight and aching to get back in business. My three months away from kink, all while being surrounded by it, have come to an end at fucking last, and Gabriella's about to take the brunt of my depravity.

There's no line at this hour, and only a handful of people are in the lobby to hear a beeping sound when Gabriella scans her membership tag.

I smirk at my banned girl, who looks away in embarrassment.

A male sub is on coat check duty, so I explain to him she's allowed in the club if I'm here. Eventually, he nods and sees it in the notes, too.

"Of course, Sir." He hands us two glow-in-the-dark wristbands for the event. "Enjoy your evening."

"Thanks. I'm gonna need a DM shirt, too," I tell him.

"Right away, Sir." He gets me one, and then I usher Gabriella up the stairs to my locker.

The door to Nicholas's office is open, so I know he's here already. Which makes sense; Kayla loves Hide & Seek night.

"You can put your jacket in here." I open my locker for Gabriella and remove one black tee for another. "You ready for me to put you to work?" Given that we're here early, they're in the middle of preparing for tonight. Foam blocks big enough to hide in —and behind—will fill the Club area of Switch. We'll help set up.

"I was born ready," she replies cheekily.

I grin, finding her too cute for words. Especially now when she's shucked eighty percent of her makeup and whatever she put in her hair. Her hair is naturally messy, giving her a short do that says freshly fucked. The pink streaks... I've grown to like them. Shows she's a wonderful little brat.

It's a popular event for Daddy Doms and their Littles, and by ten o'clock, the place is buzzing.

"Come on, Daddy! It's about to start!" Kayla drags Nicholas along—or tries. "Oh, I *swear*. Someone should give your butt a whooping for being so slow!"

Annnd that ends her fun.

I'm on break, so I chug my water by the bar and enjoy the show. Gabriella's giggling next to me. Nick ain't as amused.

"I kidded," Kayla says quickly, seeing her Daddy's flat expression. He shrugs out of his suit jacket and removes his belt. Said belt remains in his grip. Mark takes the jacket and stows it under the bar.

Gabriella steps closer to me and wraps her hands around my bicep. "She's in *so* much trouble." She laughs, peeking at her friends, while using me as a shield. "Eeep! Mr. Ford looks mad."

Christ, she tempts me. She doesn't have to do much to drive me nuts, does she? A smile, a giggle, a squeal behind her hand—I'm fucked.

There's no clear signal of the event starting, but everyone knows. The light is dimmed until it's difficult to see, smoke machines release billows of thick mist, the music changes into slow, seductive Goth with a heavy beat, and tiny spotlights in the floor show the line between playground and off-fucking-limits. Basically, it leaves the bar and the seating areas in the Club, as well as the scening stalls in the Cave for spectators and the few who aren't joining.

We hear Nicholas more than see him. "*Run*, Kayla." He doesn't sound happy.

"Oh, crap." Kayla takes off, along with dozens of other subs and bottoms.

The event starting means the end of my break, and with low visibility, more DMs are on duty. My eyes adjust around the time most Tops decide their partners have had plenty of time to find a hiding spot, and then all we gotta do is watch and listen.

Occasionally, subs argue over who reached a hiding spot first, though they usually get along and share.

"Thank you, honey. I appreciate it," I hear Mark say. "Are you feeling better?"

Tilting my head, I catch Gabriella's nod, and I see Mark holding a letter in his hand. I kiss the top of her head, silently letting her know I'm here. My respect for her continues to grow.

"Mr. Kingsley's helping me lots."

"That's good." There's a grin in Mark's voice. "I'll read this later on my break, okay?"

"Of course, or whenever—no rush, Sir. Thank you for being there for me."

"Anytime, subbie."

I exchange a nod with my buddy and pull Gabriella in front of me, her back to my chest.

"Proud of you," I murmur in her ear. Inhaling her scent, I can't help but linger and taste her skin. She squirms and leans her head back against my collarbone as I find my way underneath her top and touch her stomach, up her rib cage. "Looks like I can't keep my hands off you, princess."

Seeing her lips part when she gasps, the desire to kiss her senseless hits me with a force I couldn't have anticipated.

Countless times in the past, I've had semisexual play and little to no urge to kiss. It's intimate for me, nothing I can fake and play off as mere fun, yet with Gabriella, I wanna get under her skin and fucking consume her. It fucks with my head, 'cause it's only happened once before. Dylan.

It's too soon to go down that road again.

If only I knew how to slow it down.

"Do rounds with me." I give her neck a sharp nip and then grab her hand.

Adjusting my cock, I lead Gabriella deeper into the smoky darkness.

Seven or eight large foam blocks are spread out across the dance floor. They come up to my chest, and the designs vary, some circular with the option of squeezing oneself inside a swirl-shaped maze, others square and designed like a playhouse up to five bottoms can hide in. But the subs know they're stuck once they get tracked down if they enter the blocks, so Gabriella and I are surrounded by bottoms who mostly just run between the blocks while their Tops search for them.

However, once a Dom has chased down his sub, the blocks are suddenly more desirable. We pass a boxlike block as a Mommy is pushing her sub inside to claim her prize.

I run a hand over my head, antsy, picking up on the primal feel in the atmosphere. Glow-in-the-dark wristbands dart back and forth, screams join the music, and the subs' fear of getting caught—combined with the anticipation—is thick in the air.

Gabriella's on the other side of the spectrum. Creeping closer to me, she grasps my arm tightly and glances around nervously.

I groan under my breath.

What would it be like to chase her?

"Fuck." The music drowns out my defeat, and then I'm pressing Gabriella up against a block. With her back to me, I can't see her shock, but I feel it in the way she stiffens.

"Spread your legs," I growl.

Placing her hands on top of the block, she looks every part of someone who's about to get frisked.

My hands roam her body, and I lower my head to nuzzle her neck. She trembles, arching into me. I lick the soft skin below her ear and cup her tits roughly, pushing them together.

I slip a hand underneath her tight shorts, and in one fluid motion while she lets out a cry, I slide a finger along the slit of her pussy. It drives me crazy, feeling her soft, baby smooth, warm, and slick.

I finger her deeper, firmly, and force two digits inside her. Out again, sliding through her juices, up to her clit, then down once more.

This time, I hear her gasped moan, and it sets me on fire.

"*Daddy.*"

I freeze.

So does she, and she seems to realize what she called me.

"Oh fuck, I'm sorry!" She spins around, the embarrassment rolling off her in waves, and covers her mouth. "I'm sorry, I'm sorry, you haven't given me permission to call you that, please don't be mad, I'm sorry—"

Not interested in hearing another word, I grab her jaw and take possession of her mouth, kissing her deeply and brutally. She has no clue what that word does to me. Hell, right now, I'm not sure *I* understand. I can't fucking explain the wildfire surging through me, turning me into a goddamn savage.

I invade her mouth with my tongue, slowly coaxing her out of her shock. For me, it's an opportunity to take advantage, and I walk her backward to the nearest wall. Unlike the foam blocks, it doesn't budge when I slam her up against it.

My lungs burn for air, and I draw a ragged breath as I grind my cock against her pussy. For someone who prefers a bit of privacy, I wouldn't mind tearing off her skimpy shorts right now to fuck her where we stand.

"Say it again," I bite out.

She shakes and quivers in my arms, uncertain but turned on by my assault. She's wrapped her legs around me, her hands are gripping my shoulders tightly, and desire clouds her gorgeous eyes.

"I don't want y-you to feel pressured," she stammers. "Please forgive me if I crossed a line—" Her eyes well up. "I've never b-been able to control myself around you and—oh God, I'm so sorry."

I press my forehead to hers, breathing heavily, and give a slow thrust of my hips. It shuts her up.

"Say. It. Again."

She regresses right before my eyes. She's been on a steady path these past couple of days, testing the waters and allowing herself—bit by bit—to let that little girl out again. And now, the last line of defense was just ripped away from her.

Say it, princess.

Her vulnerability shines through, and she sucks her bottom lip into her mouth. *Fuck.* Mine to suck on. I eye-fuck her and touch her on instinct. Her top is pulled up to expose her tits, and I cup one in my hand, pinching her nipple hard.

She cries out and falls forward, burying her face in the crook of my neck. "I can't help it," she says tearfully. "I've tried to fight it, I swear."

"Please say it, Gabriella," I grit out.

She whimpers, surrendering. "Daddy?"

There it is.

I shudder and close my eyes. If I thought I was screwed earlier, it has nothing on having my chest cracked wide open at the sound of this sweet little girl calling me Daddy. A sweet little girl I've felt the need to protect for months. Something is unleashed inside me, and shit I didn't even know I was holding back rushes forward.

I don't need to stay on the sidelines as a *friend*. I want to make sure she never gets hurt again. I want it to be me.

I kiss her again, this time unhurried. Not knowing the future or how deeply this runs makes me uncertain, too. Bordering on anxious. I guess I've been burned one time too many, and I gotta know—gotta be in control. No more *we'll see what happens and play it by ear*.

Gabriella kisses me back passionately, clinging to me, arms locked around my neck.

"I just—" she gasps as I squeeze her ass. "I mean, please try... Don't hurt me?"

I shake my head and touch her cheek. "I won't allow it."

I'll be the first to admit I'm a shitty DM tonight.

The night drags on forever. I'm like an impatient kid, for chrissake. But as soon as we get back to my place, there's no stopping me. Her giggles are all I hear when I toss her onto the bed and pounce.

"Why are you taking off my clothes?" she laughs. "I can do that myself!"

"I'm not sure you can." I grin darkly and throw her top on the floor. That leaves her shorts, and I yank them off her in one go. "We're gonna continue where we left off before we went to the club." After pulling my T-shirt over my head, I lower myself across Gabriella's beautiful body. "I wanna touch you everywhere, princess."

She shivers as my chest brushes against hers. "E-Even my no-no places?"

I groan at the innocence in her voice. "Especially your no-no places." Peering down between us, I skim a hand up to her right breast and cup it firmly, teasing it with slow strokes of my fingers. "You said you liked the tingles, yeah?"

She nods and searches my eyes anxiously. "Is it okay to like that, Daddy?"

Jesus Christ. It'll never get old to hear that.

"It's always okay."

Gabriella exhales and squirms. "Is that when you get hard down there?"

"All of you makes me hard." I sit back on my heels between her legs and unbutton the fly of my jeans. "You wanna see what Daddy looks like?"

"Yes, please." She's a perfect mix of shy and eager, sitting up to be closer and teeth sinking into her bottom lip. "It's weird in my head. I used to feel bad for my dirty thoughts because, um, I wasn't allowed to talk about them."

The itch to kick John's sorry ass grows more persistent. Daddy Doms are all different; we have our own rules, but stifling someone's nature? Fucking disgusting.

"I wanna hear all your thoughts. No exceptions."

She smiles timidly, diverting her gaze to my crotch. "I have many thoughts." She cautiously extends a hand to my upper thigh, and I rise to push down my jeans. "*Oh*. You're not w-wearing any —holy crap."

With my jeans down and no boxers to drop, I grip my cock and stroke it slowly. I brush the pad of my thumb across the piercing and watch Gabriella's breathing grow more rapid. Her chest falls and rises, and her nipples tighten into little buds I wanna suck on.

"How will that fit?" she whispers, seemingly to herself.

I smirk.

"You won't put that in any of my no-no places, right?" She stares up at me with wide eyes.

"Of course I will." I push her back against the mattress again and follow, kicking off my jeans as I nuzzle her jaw. "I plan on putting it everywhere." Grabbing her hand, I guide it to my cock and grunt as her little fingers wrap around it as far as they can. "That's it."

"My mouth is watering."

"Fuck," I whisper. "Sounds like you're having dirty thoughts about sucking on Daddy's cock."

She nods, again watching for my reaction, as if she's still unsure such thoughts are okay. I'll be patient. I have all the time in the world for her to get comfortable enough to unleash her inner slut with me.

"That's perfect," I murmur when she fingers the piercing carefully. "Just as perfect as your slutty thoughts."

She sucks in a breath and tries to clench her thighs together.

"I've, um..." She swallows. "I've fantasized about you like this, even before, you know, when..." When she was with that douchebag?

"Oh, yeah?" I close my eyes and press my lips to her temple. Her hand on me is getting goddamn distracting. She scratches me lightly, traces the veins with her fingers, and sends shivers down my spine. "What, uh, what did you think about?" I grunt, thrusting into her hand in reflex. She does a little twist with her hand and spreads pre-come down my shaft, only to go farther and cup my balls. "Fuck."

Her eyes stay trained on my cock. She's fucking amazing, her touch soft yet confident with experience, her eyes betraying both lust and curiosity. She's exploring me. Her expression is unguarded, allowing me to see the innocence, too.

"I thought about you touching me under the table at Switch." Her cheeks turn pink. "Like, when others were around."

I see we have some exhibitionist fantasies to explore.

"I wasn't allowed to touch myself often," she confesses. "But I found a loophole." There's mischief as well as shame in her eyes. "I, um... I can't. It's too embarrassing."

"Tell me." I remove her hand from me and inch closer to her pussy. With a firm grip on my cock, I slip between her warm, soft pussy lips and elicit a breathy moan from her.

She covers her face with her hands. "I used my stuffie."

That confession sets me off. The fire ignites in a fucking heartbeat, and images of her using a stuffed animal to touch her pussy rush through me as quickly as thoughts do of making her do it again with me watching.

"That's dirty of you, princess." My voice is all whiskey, full of lust and filth. "Did you slip your stuffie underneath your panties and rub him against your wet clit?"

"Yes," she whimpers. Shame has her captive for a moment, and in an attempt to get away from me, she squirms and tries to close her legs. "Ugh, I can't believe I told you that."

Her struggle only turns me on. We've discussed safewords, limits, and birth control. I see her take that pill every damn morning. I trust her. We covered protection on the way home when she admitted to having breeding fantasies; another thing that had turned her red with embarrassment. And I've been sporting an erection since then. So what the fuck am I waiting for?

I curse under my breath as she keeps struggling.

"What's your safeword?" I speak through clenched teeth, dragging the head of my cock closer to her tight opening.

"Red?" She frowns in confusion, then resumes pushing at my chest. "I'm sorry, I just need a minute. I feel bad."

No. There will be no hiding from me.

"Remember your safeword." That's all I say before I push my hips forward and bury myself inside her pussy.

Gabriella chokes on a sharp gasp, and her eyes flying open is the last thing I see before my own eyes close. The pleasure pummels through me, her sweet pussy stretched to the point where it squeezes the hell out of my cock. The sensitive spot where I'm pierced brushes against her, even more so each time her inner muscles constrict.

"Jesus fuck," I groan.

"D-Daddy, it h-hurts," she cries.

"It'll pass," I promise hoarsely. "This is what that little story of yours did to me." Pulling out, I pause briefly to grab her jaw and get something through her skull. "This is it, Gabriella. Your giggles and dirty confessions will get you fucked. I'm nothing like your previous partners." I kiss her cheek and taste the salt of a stray tear. "You'll be my good girl as well as my filthy little baby whore."

She sucks in another breath. Though the pain in her expression lingers, her eyes fill with raw need.

As I push inside her again, I dip down to whisper in her ear. "Daddy will take his little girl whenever he wants. Just as he'll spoil her, care for her, give her baths, and explore play with her."

"Oh, God," she breathes out.

"You will never have to be embarrassed about anything around me," I murmur. "If I could get inside your head and read every thought, I would."

She shifts below me, this time to spread her legs farther apart. She trembles and swallows audibly, and when I set a steady pace to fuck her into the mattress, she grips my biceps and digs her fingernails into my skin. No longer pushing me away.

There's only one more thing to say. "I won't stop unless the pain is bad and you safeword. That goes for everything. You will always be honest with me, and I'll always listen."

She sniffles. "The pain isn't too bad anymore, Daddy."

I know. I can feel her pussy soaking me, and I've observed her enough in the past to know what will excite her. I've seen the scenes of rough sex she enjoys watching. I know the fetishes she's scared of but is secretly mesmerized by because she can't look away.

"We'll have fun together, won't we?"

"*Lots* of fun." She mewls and locks her arms around my neck, and I grind deeper to rub against her clit, too. "Oh, *yesss*."

I give her a wolfish smirk. "And if I wanna fuck you with a stuffie, I will."

"Oh," she whines. "You had to bring—*ungh*—that up?"

I chuckle, outta breath, and pull out from her. "Get on all fours, baby. Daddy wants to taste your sweet cunt before he fills it with come."

She squeaks and mumbles red-faced about my filthy mouth, all while obeying and wiggling her ass at me.

I smack it, the sound ringing out along with her yelp.

"What a perfect ass," I murmur. I stroke it from her thighs and up, my thumbs spreading her soft, round cheeks to expose another place I wanna fuck soon. I tap it gently with a finger. "You know what goes in here?"

"Daddy's cock once I'm dead and can't feel him splitting me in half?"

I laugh and lean close, giving the spot a soft kiss before moving down to her glistening pussy. "Necro play—never tried that, but there's time, I guess."

That's not what she had in mind, and she makes it clear I know that, though she's easily shut up.

With one long, firm, slow lick from her clit to her opening, I have her moaning and whimpering and burying her face in the pillow.

"Fuck, you taste good." The tip of my tongue snakes around her clit before I suck it into my mouth. "It'll be a while before I let you come, princess."

CHAPTER 7

That's the night guilt sets in.

 I wake up four times after dreaming of Dylan. Reliving the sweetest and the worst moments with him, I doubt every decision I've made. He *wasn't* fucking okay with slowing down. I've been trying to convince myself I did the right thing based on what he told me, not on what was actually true.

This isn't a new revelation, but I've been finding my defense behind the fact that he lied about it being all right.

He was just protecting himself.

I curse internally and carefully leave the bed without waking up Gabriella.

Dylan's the gray areas, and I've only looked at the black and white ones. I've seen what he's done. I haven't given as much thought about the causes.

It's frustrating the ever-loving fuck outta me. Okay, even if I understand his reasoning—which I'm not entirely sure I do—it doesn't mean he didn't run me the hell over.

Walking over to the sink, I fill a glass with water and rub at my chest. The guilt is new, and the beautiful girl in my bed is no doubt the reason. After everything John put her through, she deserves a Daddy who won't wake up in the middle of the night because he's a bitter motherfucker about his ex.

I drain the glass in a few gulps. Then I grab my phone and put on a pair of sweats before taking a seat at the kitchen table. I scroll down text after text, all unanswered.

We need to talk about this, Dylan.

Call me.

You can't end things like this. Call.

If you won't pick up the phone, I can't fix things.

Do you have any fucking idea what this is doing to me?

I gotta know how you're doing. Let me know what I did wrong. You said you were okay with everything. Why did you go to that party with Judy and her sub?

There's nothing pleasant about reading the texts, though they do lessen the guilt marginally. I've fucking tried to reach out to him. And the little "read" sign at the bottom only pisses me off. He's seen them. He ignores them.

No, fuck it. There's nothing else I can do—or even should do, maybe. I gotta stop dwelling. Gabriella deserves my full attention, and I want to give it to her.

Putting away my phone, I get back under the covers and hold Gabriella to me.

The next morning sets the tone for our first two weeks in a D/s relationship. She wakes me up with her singsong voice saying "Daddy," and then she takes my cock in her mouth. She hums, licks it like a lollipop, sucks, plays with the piercing, and drives me crazy until I come in hot streams down her throat.

My work suffers—and no fucks given—when we spend most of

the day in bed. The less-than-stellar night I had fades bit by bit, and she finally reveals the story behind her tattoos. I vow to myself never to let her doubt herself like John did.

"He made me feel dirty in a bad way. Like it was wrong to want certain things." She makes invisible circles on my chest, lost in her thoughts. "I've always been drawn to the taboo, and I couldn't really shut off my fantasies. So when I got out of that relationship, I wanted to wear it on my body." She looks up at me, chagrined and shy. "I never told you this, but when you first called me princess, I hated it. I thought you only saw me as this meek doll who smiled pretty and never spoke out of turn."

I shake my head and touch her cheek. "I knew there was a playful brat hidden underneath the frilly shit."

She nods. "I discovered that. So I started liking the nickname more and more. I don't know if you remember, but like six months ago, I stuck my tongue out at you and crossed my eyes, and you hugged me and called me a delightful little princess." I smile at the memory. "It made me wonder if you called me that for reasons other than the pretty dresses."

I tell her I've always been attracted to playfulness, so yeah, the few times she's let her bratty side shine through, I've seen her as my version of a princess. Carefree, all smiles, a naughty glint in her eye that she doesn't reveal to everyone. The outfits have been a part of it, I admit, but she's a shitload more than what John made her out to be.

"I guess I came to the conclusion that I wanna be a wicked princess." She grins impishly. "Hence the princess tats. I'm not comfortable in lace or satin, but I still like being a sweet girl. One who happens to also want it twisted and filthy behind closed doors."

Sounds fucking perfect to me. As long as she's true to herself, I'll encourage her.

"*But*...you know. Old habits die hard." She clears her throat and keeps her gaze fixed on my chest rather than facing me. "I was dead set on being loud about everything I had to hide, but in the end, that kind of fizzled. I got the ink. I was just too chicken to explain it."

"Until now," I point out quietly. "Healing takes time. You weren't ready to let anyone know why you chose those tattoos until now, and there's nothing wrong with that." I pause as I slide a hand up her thigh that's hooked over my hips. Her skin is so smooth and soft, and the shadowed ink gives the sweet girl a sexy edge. "Any significance to the ivy?"

She purses her lips, hiding a grin, then shakes her head. "I wanted a drastic change and thought this one was cool?"

No idea why she phrased it as a question.

"It's sexy as fuck," I tell her.

***

Our exploration continues, and most of all, I bask in seeing Gabriella relax fully with me so she can jump between Little and her adult side as she pleases. She's surprisingly old-fashioned, and though her attempts at cooking have been, ah...*interesting*...so far, she's adamant about learning. She admits she likes the idea of a fifties' household, with the exception that she wants to work.

One night, I'm chewing on her too-al-dente pasta—while stifling my laughter—and she pushes her plate away with a scowl. Then she says, "Maybe I should just stick to drawing. Ugh, no, I won't quit!"

Already forgetting the food, I wanna know what she meant about that—the drawing.

It's the first time she shows me a sketchbook, in which she's drawn people from Switch, patterns, random objects, and mainly, tattoo designs.

"This is fucking incredible, Gabriella."

"I've applied for an apprenticeship at the place where I got my work done," she confesses shyly.

My baby girl wants to be a tattoo artist?

I end up taking her on the kitchen table, sending spaghetti flying everywhere.

It's two weeks of bliss, two weeks of cautiously hoping we're on the road to better. Both careful and wary where feelings are concerned, we focus on getting to know each other, establishing boundaries, and exploring one another.

It's been nearly four months since we ended our last relationships, yet it's fresh in my mind since my feelings for Dylan refuse to vanish. Not rushing seems like the best option, though there's that niggling, annoying voice at the back of my head that says not rushing didn't work out so great last time.

I guess my issue is that I've never been very good at separating play and reality, mainly 'cause play is real to me. I don't care about Gabriella at only a certain level—a D/s level, or whatever. I just fucking care, end of.

I had the same problem with Dylan, and then I'd chosen to slow things down to protect him—and myself—from getting hurt.

What's a fucker to do, hope for the best?

Doubt is a fickle bitch.

———

One fine evening, we find ourselves arguing—also a first—on the way to Switch.

"It's nonnegotiable," I say firmly.

"It can't be!" She scowls and fastens her seat belt, then sits back with a huff and stares out the window. "I'm not taking your money."

What part of nonnegotiable doesn't she understand?

I won't cave on this.

Some Daddy Doms coddle their Littles when they're upset; I'm not far behind. I worry easily and need to make sure she's okay, but I'm also the man who will teach my subs to fight their own battles. I believe in learning by doing, and that means I won't be there to protect her from every mistake. I won't shield her like some do. I won't stop her from trying something new, even though I'll have a feeling she won't like it. It's important we experience life, the good and the bad. I will, however, catch her when she falls.

Tonight, she is going to make one of those mistakes, and I told her I'll agree to it on one condition: she'll accept a weekly allowance from me. It's not that fucking hard. She wants to try caning? Fine. She won't like it, but she needs to find out on her own. And the allowance ain't a goddamn handout for food and bills. It's for fun. She's a Little, and I want her to be able to indulge in hobbies that come with her personality, whether it's to buy a new toy—adult or otherwise—go see a movie with friends, or find new fetish wear.

I enjoy the latter more than she does, anyway.

"Your silence bothers me." She gives me a pout. "I don't understand why I can't use my own money."

"You won't do it." I shrug, getting onto the freeway. "Just two days ago when we booked our tickets to Mexico, you told me money would be tight for a while. Is it so damn weird I wanna make sure you can still have fun?"

To this day, it makes me grin in pride at the memory of her admitting she didn't throw the engagement ring at John or, hell, into the ocean. She sold it and kept the money. He's a loaded bastard, so I can only imagine she walked away with quite a bit. That said, her apprenticeship—at which she got accepted yesterday —won't pay the bills. She's on a budget.

The first things people stop buying when the going gets tough? Shit they want, not shit they need. For her, that would be stuffies, pacifiers with funny graphics, sex toys, and ice cream at the weekly subbie meet-up.

"I'm having fun with *you*," she argues. "I don't need—"

"It's not about what you need, princess." I grab her hand and kiss it. "It's about me wanting to see that adorable fucking look on your face when you pick out a new blankie."

She slumps back in her seat. "I can't be scowly when you say that stuff."

"Good, so I win." I send her a wink.

She sticks out her tongue at me. "Excuse me for feeling bad about using your hard-earned money."

"Hey." I grab her arm. "What did you just do?"

She groans. "Come on! You found it *delightful* before!"

It takes a huge amount of effort to hide my amusement. "Know what's spectacular about being Daddy? I make the rules. Now, lose the skirt. You're entering the club in panties."

If she's really unlucky, I won't find a parking space right outside Switch.

Gabriella doesn't say anything, though her mortification is written all over her as she removes her skirt and fruitlessly tries to tug down her top.

"Come here." After switching lanes, I hold up my arm so she can slide across the seat and let me grope her a bit. "Gimme a kiss." She dutifully kisses my cheek, and I ignore her pout. It's just cute. "For the record, that money's not very hard-earned. I inherited my pop's business ten years ago and sold it to my uncle."

"Semantics," she mumbles, though she's already surrendered. "Ugh, everyone will see my butt, Daddy."

"I know." I smile. "They'll see what a lucky bastard I am for being allowed to play with it, too."

I wanna say the *only* bastard.

"Oh," she whines, "isn't it enough that you're going to cane it?"

"That's funny," I chuckle, distinctly remembering she's the one who wants to try caning. "Although, technically, it won't be me."

"What?" She frowns up at me.

I shrug, turning the wheel for our exit. "Caning's not my kink, so I'm not very good at it. I called Mark for you, though. He'll be happy to show you."

Mark knows as well as I do that it won't be her thing.

"I thought you were gonna do it." Gabriella clutches her stomach and looks disappointed. "Now I'm thousand times more nervous, and I don't want his hands on me that way."

"Oh, baby, it won't be anything sexual." Fuck no. That's a mistake I won't make twice. I need to be secure in a relationship before considering sharing play partners again. "He'll try a cane on your ass and thighs, that's it. I'll be there the whole time." I kiss the top of her hand. "Only I get to do the fun stuff."

"Whew." She relaxes a bit, though not fully. "I'm still nervous."

Well, she should be.

Gabriella calls red after ten minutes of being caned by Mark.

Picking her up, I carry her to a corner booth in the Club. My buddy follows with his two subs and an aftercare kit. Rio and Nicholas are doing a demo on the platform across the dance floor, so there's no music to compete with when we talk.

"How are you feeling, honey?" Mark asks, concerned.

Gabriella cries silently and wipes her cheeks. "It hurts." She shifts on my lap, wincing in pain, and faces Evangeline. "I don't understand how you like it so much. Felt like punishment to me."

I weave my fingers through her hair and stroke her back. In the aftercare kit, I find a small packet of aloe, so I empty it into my palm and tell her to scoot out a little. That way, I can access the backside of her thigh. I rub the lotion over the thin welts while Evangeline explains the endorphin rushes pain gives her.

Evangeline's quick to pout at her Master. "I miss it."

Mark smirks and pats his girl's little baby belly. "Soon, kitten."

Brayden joins in, kissing Evangeline's cheek. "Once our son is born, Master can string you up and beat you until... Well, I'll probably cry before you do."

I shake my head, amused.

Gabriella perks up and sniffles. "You're having a boy?"

Oh, right. I should've picked up on that news.

Evangeline nods, her smile rueful. "Have mercy on me, we're having a future bossy Dom or a sub who gets off on ass play and humiliation."

Brayden flushes and ducks his head while Mark bellows a laugh.

"Or he could turn into a complete momma's boy." I wink at Evangeline.

She smiles widely and crosses her fingers.

Mark gets a waitress's attention, and we order drinks since we're not going anywhere until we know Gabriella's all right. A beer for me, a Fanta for my girl.

"So who's excited about Mexico?" Evangeline asks, eyes lighting up. "It's going to be so fun. Will you two possibly be sharing a room?"

She might as well have asked if we're together.

"We sure will." It wasn't that long ago I dreaded the trip. Now things are looking up.

"Aww, I knew it!" Evangeline looks triumphant.

"Have you seen Kayla's dress?" Gabriella smiles and wipes the last of her tears. "It's so gorgeous."

Evangeline nods eagerly. "It really is."

Mark, Brayden, and I are less interested in dresses—unless they're on the floor—so we make plans for activities instead. With our closest all going, it'd be a damn shame if we didn't get together at least one night to play.

Then there's the non-kink fun. Brayden and I end up betting on who'll be fastest on jet skis, and Mark and I decide we gotta do poker night when we're there, too.

It's not until I hear Gabriella say, "I don't like that name," that I divert my attention to the girls.

"Why?" Evangeline wonders. "I've heard great things about her from Kayla."

"Who?" I ask.

"Sydney—Mr. Ford's sister," she replies. "She'll be at the wedding, of course."

Gabriella shakes her head quickly. "Oh, it's nothing personal. I am sure his sister is lovely. It's just...a while ago, John mentioned he was interested in adding a third to our relationship."

Mark and I both scoff, probably thinking the same thing.

"How would taking care of two Littles work if he failed with one?" Brayden asks the obvious question.

Gabriella shrugs and takes a sip of her Fanta. "I dunno. He even went as far as meeting a girl—named Sydney." That explains that, but this is news to me. "He wanted us to be sisters, you know?"

Common enough, especially in the poly scene. Dylan and Gabriella scened as play siblings the times I filmed them, the titles of brother and sister having the same significance as Daddy. A fellow Daddy Dom friend of mine from the East Coast has an established House, complete with a sadistic Mommy—who happens to be his wife—and their three subs, two play sisters and a brother. But they have their shit together. My buddy and his wife can take care of their kink family. John sure as fuck didn't.

Mark drains the last of his beer. "Let's hope for his sake he doesn't show his face here again, but I think Nicholas mentioned he's moved out of state."

That would be a blessing for John's face.

Mexico returns as the hot topic, and Gabriella shifts on my lap, her head on my shoulder, while the rest of us discuss other things we can do. It's a small but luxurious resort, half of which Nicholas has booked for the wedding.

"Tired?" I stroke Gabriella's hair, noticing her eyes are closed and she's sucking on her thumb. "Let me know if you wanna take a nap in Mr. Ford's office."

She shakes her head and burrows closer. "Wanna stay here with you."

"Okay, princess." That warms my heart. I give her a hard squeeze that makes her grin.

Mark and I shoot the shit for a while longer, occasionally pausing when acquaintances pass by our table to say hey. Dante's one of them, and he thanks Gabriella for the letter she gave him, and she blinks sleepily and blushes as he accepts her apology.

"I'll get back to my scene," he says. "Just my luck to end up with a second plaything who's a Domme in disguise. There's no way this is gonna work out."

I laugh, having been there.

"Fuck you," Mark tells me, which makes me crack up harder. "Not a single word!"

"I haven't said anything, *boy!*"

"Something you wanna share with the class?" Dante drawls.

Down to chuckles, I jerk my chin at Mark. "Fifteen years ago, I picked that guy up in a bar he had no business at." He was only nineteen or twenty at the time and greener within BDSM than me. "He thought he was going to run the show because he'd had some training from a Dom."

"Oh my God." Evangeline looks fucking giddy. "*You* two?"

Brayden stares at his Master, shocked. "You submitted?"

I snort. "I wouldn't go that far." We'd wrestled for it. Which, in its own way, was sexy as hell.

"I was an awful bottom." Mark shucks his front and admits it's funny. "I bailed before he woke up, and the next time we ran into each other was a few years later at a play party."

"And we kissed and made up." I smirk and tip my empty beer bottle at him.

"Jackass." He smiles and flips me the bird.

"Yeah, I don't foresee my situation having the same outcome," Dante replies wryly and flags down a waitress for us. "Enjoy your night, guys. I'm gonna...yeah..." He sighs and walks away.

Considering that man is drowning in play partners, it's difficult to feel sorry for him.

Liam's manning the main bar tonight, and he comes over with more drinks on his break, saving a waitress the trip. Scooting farther into the booth, I make room for him, and he launches straight into manly moping about sports, much to Evangeline's disappointment. I have a feeling she was planning on pressing further about Mark and me.

So, sports it is.

I'm a huge football fan; anything else can suck my dick. Liam, on the other hand, loves it all. And talks about it all.

"You watch cricket?" Mark chuckles and lifts his brows.

"Damn, straight." Liam takes a sip of his water, then turns to me. "Sorry to hear about Dylan, by the way. I saw the press conference last week."

"What?" I'm not the only one who's suddenly interested. Gabriella sits up straighter too, and the others look confused.

Liam goes on. "Yeah, he was injured real bad. Not only won't he make it to Nationals in August, but they're being hush-hush about his career—whether he'll be back at all or not."

"Oh, no." Evangeline covers her mouth.

My heart starts hammering against my rib cage while my blood runs cold. It's funny in a fucking-kill-me kinda way how all the shit that went down between him and me becomes insignificant. The worry explodes inside me, and I gotta know how he's doing.

"Daddy?" Gabriella faces me with eyes full of unshed tears. "We have to do something."

CHAPTER 8

Two weeks, that's all I got. Two weeks of feeling better, two weeks with Gabriella.

I stow my carry-on in the overhead luggage compartment, then sit down in the middle seat and yank my hoodie over my head. Gabriella's right next to me, gazing out the window, yet she might as well be miles away.

The vulnerability rolls off her, as does her never-ending attempt to slam back up her internal defenses. I told her all morning—last night, too—that nothing changes between us. And I guess I can't blame her for not believing me; I've been open about my feelings for Dylan, so she's protecting herself by shutting off.

The guilt is eating me up. She wouldn't have that need to protect herself if I was over Dylan.

Going to Texas to see him was never really optional for either of us. We care about the fucker, and we know too much about him to sit back and let him handle this on his own. So we're stuck in our situation.

Liam sent me the link to the press conference before we left

Switch last night, and I reckon it's playing on a loop in Gabriella's head like it's doing in mine. We can't unsee that—or ignore it.

At the press conference, Dylan let his spokesperson do most of the talking. He appeared lost and withdrawn, not to mention in pain. His faded blue eyes were blank and shadowed, his coppery hair a matted mess. He mumbled about hoping to return to work but made no promises. Then the team doc took over to debrief the press about Dylan's injuries, which he sustained in a car accident almost *three fucking weeks* ago. A fellow swimmer, who'd driven the car on their way to the pool, broke both arms but would make a full recovery eventually.

The same can't be said for Dylan. Ligaments torn, crushed kneecap, and a concussion have likely put an end to his career as a professional swimmer. I did a quick internet search and know he's undergone surgery twice.

"He looked depressed, didn't he?" Gabriella murmurs. "God, why didn't he call us?"

I blow out a heavy breath, having asked myself that question a hundred times in the past twelve hours. He hasn't reached out to anyone, not even Chelsea.

Three *weeks* since the accident. Not a word. I had no clue. He's been in pain while I've been...fuck. And there's some more guilt.

"Do you think he's alone?" she asks.

"I don't know, princess." I hope not. He can't be completely alone; he's been living with his grandparents. No idea about friends, though.

The plane taxis out onto the runway, and I grasp Gabriella's hand, weaving our fingers together.

"You know I need you, right?" I gotta get this out before shit gets worse.

"What do you mean?" She swallows and stares at our hands.

I lean on the armrest, speaking so only she can hear. "I won't beat around the bush or talk in circles, Gabriella. I know you're afraid to get left behind. You think I want Dylan more than I want you, which—" I let out a hollow chuckle, my gut twisting. "It's ridiculous. That's not how I function. There is no him and me anymore, and even if there was..."

She peers up at me, her expression closed off. "Yes? Even if there was, Cade?"

I shake my head. "I care about his well-being. Despite everything he pulled on me, he's a good kid—a sweetheart. But it's you I feel slipping through my fingers right now, and it fucking hurts."

Her face falls. "I'm sorry. I'm terrified of—ugh." Her bottom lip trembles, and she takes a deep breath. "You're the last person I want to hurt." She hugs my bicep and rests her cheek on my shoulder. "You're right. I'm scared of losing you."

"It won't happen as long as you don't shut me out, baby." I kiss the top of her head, lingering. "I need you by my side for this."

She nods and hugs my arm tighter. "I promise, Daddy."

That's one weight on my shoulders easing off slightly, though it's far from gone.

"Let me guess. No answer." I jimmy with the AC, stuck in traffic, and Gabriella ends the umpteenth call to Dylan's cell. "We'll be at the house soon enough." According to the GPS, anyway.

Thank fuck I never threw away Dylan's address. Of course, when he taped the address of his grandparents on my fridge, it was just a place he sent postcards, letters, and photos of San Francisco. Now he lives there, and he's done avoiding us.

"Do you think it'll be hard getting him to come home with us?" Gabriella asks.

I side-eye her, frowning. "We're doing what, now?" All of a sudden, I'm not sure we're on the same page. "Hon, I wanna make sure he's doing okay. That's it. I don't think he'll go anywhere with me unless it involves a gag and duct tape."

"Well, what's wrong with that?" She squints at the beaming

sun. "I don't trust anybody but you to get through to him. You know how stubborn he is."

As flattered as I am, her plan is a bit...out there.

"You were willing to help me," she points out. "Like, platonically. You wanted me to stay with you so you could help me. Wouldn't you do the same for Dylan?"

I make a face, wondering how goddamn bizarre that would be. In a house without privacy, I'd have my current baby girl and the guy who basically dumped me...? Then with the guilt and the uncertainty in the air—no, thanks.

"Let's keep thinking, princess."

Texas is hot as balls.

We make it out to suburbia in the afternoon. Sweat is trickling down my back, and a persistent Little is certain that only we can take care of Dylan. There's lists, even. She rattles them off over and over as her reasons for why we should leave Texas with him next to us.

"He loves everyone at Switch! We're his family!"

If that were true, he's not showing it very well.

"He gets vulnerable like I do, and you're a Daddy Dom. He needs someone with experience."

There are plenty of Daddy Doms right here if he's looking for one of those.

I ignore the stab in my chest at that notion.

"He's going to need support when he tries to figure out what to do now."

He walked away from the support in San Francisco.

"This is it." I park outside a one-story ranch house with a white picket fence and a perfectly manicured lawn. "I hope someone's home." There's no car in the driveway, so if no one's here, we'll have to come back later.

With my stomach in knots, I haven't eaten anything today. My nerves are shot, and I don't have a fucking clue of what to say. Still, I leave the car without thinking twice. 'Cause if I don't get this over with quickly, I'll change my mind and get my ass on the next flight back to California.

"I'm so nervous." Gabriella darts after me and clutches my hand tightly. "I gots to find my warrior face for this crap. Like, pretend he didn't crush me when he decided I wasn't his friend anymore."

I don't know whether to laugh or to comfort her.

Fucking feelings. Fucking...giving a rat's ass.

Part of me wants Gabriella to be right. It'd be nice to drag Dylan home with us so I could simultaneously beat his ass and take care of it. *Him.* Christ. Ground him, get it through his thick skull how much he's hurt his friends, make him *see...* All while ensuring he won't take the same road as Gabriella did after John.

I can't deny Dylan has the same tendencies to self-destruct when everything goes to piss.

Steeling myself, I give the door a knock and then take a step back. I wipe sweat off my forehead and remove my shades.

"Sticky." Gabriella tries to blow cool air into her top. "Don't throw up, don't throw up, don't throw up..." Her mumbled chant fades away as the door is opened, and we see Dylan on crutches and balancing on one leg.

I swallow whatever shit bubbles up—emotions or vomit, whatever—and Dylan's eyes grow wide. Fuck, fuck. I didn't prepare myself for this, that much is clear now. My grip on Gabriella's hand tightens, and she sniffles and whispers his name.

"What, um—" Dylan's voice falters. Before he averts his gaze, I see those blues well up. He focuses intently on the door and leaning against a crutch. "Y'all shouldn't have come," he croaks. "I g-gotta rest—"

Dylan stumbles, and Gabriella and I act out of instinct and

rush forward to grip his elbows. The familiar scent of his aftershave invades my senses, making it even more difficult to speak.

My girl's crying silently and failing to hide it, I can't form a fucking word, and Dylan's clearly not in a good place. This is gonna rock.

"Let's get you inside." Gabriella wipes her cheek on her shoulder. "Where are your grandparents?"

"Florida," he mumbles. "Their fussing got too much." He grunts, reluctant to let us help him. "I want to be alone, please."

"No," I manage to say.

We guide him into the living room, a space filled with family photos, books, and several of Dylan's trophies. He's fairly close with his parents too, but he chose to live with his grandparents when he wanted to focus on swimming. Coming from an army family, his folks move around too often for him, so it worked out with him staying in Texas. Until part-time studies and curiosity toward BDSM brought him to San Francisco.

Dressed in only a tee and sweats that cling to his narrow hips, it's easy to see he's lost weight, which bothers me a shitload. If his grandmother and grandfather ain't around, I doubt he's taking care of himself the way he should.

"Do you have a cast?" Gabriella steps aside while I lower Dylan to the couch. It's already set up as his temporary bed, complete with magazines strewn about, his GameBoy on the table, water, snacks, and—fuck. An old shirt of mine that he used to wear or snuggle with when he didn't spend the night at my place.

He offers a small nod and taps twice on his right knee.

"I'm guessing you're supposed to keep it elevated." I grab a couple pillows and tuck them under his leg. With nothing else to do, I retreat and sit down in a chair, having no idea what to say.

I reach for Gabriella, wanting her close to me, though my eyes don't stray from Dylan. Surveying the damage, I soak up every visible inch, from cuts and bruises that are fading from his accident, to the definition of tight muscles after hard training. Despite his sharp jaw and taut form, he comes off as younger than his twenty-six years. It's his light eyes and dimpled smile, although I haven't seen the latter in months.

Gabriella sits down on the armrest, and instead of fidgeting or wringing her hands, she plays with the hair at the back of my neck. She won't look away from Dylan, either.

He, on the other hand, looks anywhere but at us. Lying flat on his back, he stares at the ceiling, his Adam's apple bobbing with a swallow.

"So, are you two, um, a thing now?"

Gabriella and I exchange a quick glance.

I clear my throat. "Yeah, we're..." The hell do I say? Calling it a plain D/s relationship feels like downplaying the possibilities, except those are the exact terms I gave Dylan.

No matter what I tell him, I'll sound like a fucking idiot. There's nothing wrong with me and Gabriella being together, so why does it feel like I've been cheating on him?

Gabriella's eyes flash with mirth at my fumbling. "It's new, and we're not sure what to call it yet."

Dylan nods. "Congrats." When his chin quivers and his eyes well up once more, I'm ready to rush forward again. In the end, he covers his face and turns toward the back of the couch, and I'm outta the chair before I even know it. "I don't know why you came, but I'd really appreciate it if you'd leave."

"Not gonna happen." I drag him up enough to leave room for me. He puts up a good fight, not that I budge. Sitting down in the corner, I hug his upper body to me just as he loses his struggle and cries.

That sets Gabriella in motion too, and she kneels in front of us.

"Talk to us," I whisper. "You're a fucking mess, little pan."

He keeps his hands over his face, though he's stopped fighting me. He lets me hold him and sway him a bit. "I can't do this," he whimpers. "You can't be here."

"We're not going anywhere," Gabriella says vehemently, stroking his hair. "You've been such a douch—"

"*Gabriella.*"

"He has to know!" she argues. "If we don't get to the bottom of everything, we can't work stuffs out."

"You think I don't know what I've done?" Dylan struggles to sit up, and he glares through his tears. "Trust me, Gabby, I know exactly what I've ruined."

Gabriella bites her lip. "Why wouldn't you return our calls?"

I'm itching to jump in, but maybe this is one of those times I should let them do this their way. They function similarly and have always spoken the same language.

Dylan swings his legs off the couch and winces when his right foot hits the floor. "I don't want to talk about it, okay?"

"You have to." Gabriella stands up and folds her arms over her chest. "Didn't our friendship mean anything to you?"

"Don't you freaking dare," he growls. "You have no clue just how much it meant—"

"So tell me!" she snaps. "I deserve an explanation, Dylan! I don't even know what I did wrong. We didn't fight. One day, you were just gone!" Her face crumples at that, and I can't keep my mouth shut anymore.

"She's right, Dylan. If there's even a small part of you that wants to work this out with Gabriella, you gotta be honest and explain why you shut her out."

He shakes his head and looks away. "Doesn't matter. You'll only hate me if you knew, anyway."

"I'm not sure it can get any worse, Dylan," I drawl. The bitterness is seeping out again, at a shitty time where we should be focusing on his physical recovery.

"I'm sorry," he croaks. "I know I messed up." He covers his face again and leans forward on his knees. "I didn't mean to, I swear—it just hurt, Cade."

There's only so much suffering I can take before I fold. Shifting closer, I put my arm around him, and Gabriella kneels by his feet again, placing her hands on his legs.

"I'm sorry I hurt you, too," I murmur. "I'm not innocent in this."

Dylan had to suffer for how my previous relationship ended. I did a decent job of denying my feelings, and when I noticed he was getting attached so quickly... I didn't trust him. So I created new limits as a shield. That's on me. I wasn't honest, either. I hid like a fucking coward, pretending the limits stating that we should focus on the D/s aspects were for his—or our—protection. When in reality, I was just jaded and fearing he'd do what my past ex had done.

It's frustrating, knowing what I want, *having* it, only to set it up for failure.

"It took me a long time to see I was wrong there." I rub his back as he wipes at his cheeks with his arm. "You didn't seem to have any issue slowing down, so I figured I'd done the right thing."

He shakes his head. "What did you expect me to do? The man I was in love with was more interested in my kinks than my hobbies." Having it confirmed he was in love with me is a punch in the gut. I only suspected he was headed that way. "I didn't wanna look like an idiot, Cade. I did that enough as it was."

Jesus. All the miscommunication and confusion are giving me one hell of a headache, and I can't help but doubt myself as a Dom. Dylan—and Gabriella, for that matter—ain't the only one with insecurities.

It's different here, too. With Gabriella and Dylan, the connection has run deeper. I may be an experienced Dom and down for a lot, but some things are new for me, as well.

Safe to say, my whirlwind relationship with Dylan wasn't healthy for either of us. We agreed on casual, when all we needed was complete honesty and more boundaries. I reckon we invited Gabriella to play with us too quickly, as well. I'll chalk it up as two of the hottest evenings I've experienced, at the same time as it added to the doubt of not being enough. What a shitstorm.

"I miss you, Dylan." Gabriella takes his hand and holds it in both of hers, pleading silently. "You were my best friend and my brother. Then you left."

"I'm sorry for not being there for you." Dylan screws his eyes shut. "I was so ashamed."

I release a breath, sick and tired of everything that's gone unsaid.

"Why were you ashamed?" she asks.

He doesn't wanna talk about it. Easy to tell. It's possible he's less eager to discuss it with me around, too. Given that he looks to be in pain from his leg, I take the cue to give them some privacy.

"Where are your painkillers?" I rise from the couch. "I assume the doctor's given you something."

He wipes his nose. "Kitchen, next to the microwave. Thank you."

I incline my head and escape the room.

CHAPTER 9

Once in the kitchen, I slump back against a counter and scrub my hands over my face. It's been a while since I was this mentally exhausted and wrung out.

It's painful seeing Dylan again, even more so now that we've witnessed the state he's in. Remorseful, embarrassed, lonely... That will take a toll on any person who gives a shit.

Four pill bottles sit by the microwave, all with Dylan's name on them. And as if it wasn't bad enough already, I check the meds to find one antidepressant—fairly mild dosage, but nonetheless—and one for anxiety. I'm guessing that one's related to the accident. Dylan's troubles come out in nightmares, and he gets worked up pretty bad.

The dates on the bottles tell me he's been taking the antidepressant for three months.

"Goddammit, Dylan," I sigh and massage my forehead.

I can't go so far as to say Gabriella's right and we need to bring him home. Maybe I'm in denial—I wouldn't be surprised anymore. Staying like this is outta the question, though. Outside of our lifestyle, he's a bossy little fucker. Assertive. Stubborn. He doesn't take orders from anyone, and he's able to push away those who wanna be there for him.

I can only imagine the effort it took to send his grandparents on a damn vacation shortly after his accident. It says a lot about what he's capable of.

On my way back to the living room, I pause and take cover in the hallway when I hear Dylan and Gabriella speaking quietly. She's still on the floor, there for him while he cries into his hands.

I'm beyond fucking sick of seeing people I care about crying.

"*Listen* to me, Dylan," Gabriella pleads softly. "We can fix this together, I know it. Cade took me in, you know. I was behaving so badly, and he stepped in. I don't know what I would've done without his intervention, and I'm sure he will do the same for you."

I pinch my bottom lip, rolling my piercing, and process the princess's words. She seems to think so highly of me, and I can only hope I deserve it.

Dylan sniffles and shakes his head, his hands falling to his lap. "I'm happy for you two—I really am—but I can't be around that, Gabby. It's better I stay here so y'all can focus on yourselves. I bet you're great together, and you can be there for him like I couldn't."

That makes me frown, not to mention wonder what the fresh hell he's referring to. Up until the end when everything went wrong, he was an amazing partner. We were fucking amazing together. We clicked so well, and he's a genuinely good person. Whether he was working toward his next goal in a swimming pool, or he was trying to make a difference in our community, he gave a hundred and ten percent.

His cheerful mood meant the world to me. He was as easygoing at four in the morning on the way to practice as he was at midnight after staying late at the animal rescue center where he volunteered.

"What on earth are you talking about?" Gabriella looks as confused as I am. "He adores you. If you think those feelings have gone away, you're such a dummy."

My mouth twists up.

"Can't you see what's going on here?" She creeps closer and whispers something in his ear.

Dylan's brow knits together before he reels back at whatever he heard her say. "You're crazy," he whisper-shouts. "Don't do that, Gabby. Don't think like that. It's exactly why I felt bad and left—well, one of the reasons."

Jesus, are they gonna clue me in, or...?

Gabriella gasps. "Wait, you left because of what? You mean—I mean, did you think about..."

"*Yes.* Okay?" Whatever Dylan let slip, he regrets it. Jaw set, tense shoulders. "I couldn't face either of you."

Something dawns on Gabriella, and her expression softens. "That's why you wouldn't talk to me. Because you had—"

"Keep your voice down," Dylan hisses, all while looking ten shades of embarrassed. He won't look her in the eye anymore. "I'm sorry. I couldn't help it. I'm a big fraud."

Figuring I've eavesdropped long enough, I make my presence known and hand Dylan two of the pill bottles from the kitchen. I'm unsure of the contents of the fourth bottle, so I brought it in case he needs it.

"Thank you, Sir," he mumbles. He reaches for his water bottle on the table and takes two pills. "I'm about to be the worst company when I fall asleep, so maybe it's time to wrap this up?"

Gabriella snorts.

"That's funny." I pat his thigh as I sit down next to him, then drape an arm along the back of the couch. "Where's your demon puppy?"

I gave him a rescue pup in January, and as a small mutt, it was a rambunctious hellion. I'm not sure I wanna know what he's like now that he's grown significantly. Dylan appropriately named him Devil.

"Doggy daycare," he replies quietly. "I can't walk him now, so a lady picks him up every mornin'."

I nod slowly, my gaze traveling across the shelf with his trophies. Swimming was really everything he ever wanted to do.

"You know what we gotta do, Daddy," Gabriella says frankly. "Kid can't stay here."

I huff while Dylan scowls.

"*Kid?* I'm older than you, pink streak." He flicks her hair.

"Sooo missing the point," she retorts. She leaves the floor and crawls up into my lap where she juts her chin at Dylan. "I'll be super mad if you don't come home with us."

"Gabriella," I say tiredly.

"What?" Her turn to scowl.

Dylan smiles sadly, his eyes empty. "I'm staying here. It would be too weird for Cade, and I've put y'all through enough hell."

I narrow my eyes at that, 'cause he shouldn't fucking stay if it's for *our* sake.

"Hold up. Level with me, Dylan. Tell me why you're staying in Texas. The truth."

He shifts, visibly flustered and uncomfortable. "I don't know what you want from me. I don't have my place in San Francisco anymore, and—"

"Oh, God." Gabriella rolls her eyes. "Daddy, how many nights have I spent at my place since you and I started our thingy?"

A handful at the most, but that's beside the point. He's dodging the question.

"I didn't ask why you won't come back," I tell him. "I'm asking why you're staying."

Gabriella pipes in. "Yeah, and like, we won't pressure you to come home if you *want* to stay here. But if you wanna fix things, you know, and start over where you belong, I will make the mister kidnap you."

Fuck, she's cute. And I can't really argue with her logic. If he wants to be in San Fran, he should be there. It's simple. As for *making* Daddy do *anything...?*

"You want a shot at rephrasing that, princess?" I raise a brow at her.

"Well..." She squirms on my lap, cheeks coloring a little. "I'll ask you nicely to kidnap him?"

"I guess that's better," I chuckle wryly. Then I face Dylan again. "But she's right. Life's too short for regrets. If you wanna be in San Francisco, we can work shit out."

He chews on his lip and fidgets with the corner of his pillowcase.

I assume one of the pills he took was to fall asleep, 'cause he yawns and rubs his eyes.

"I don't deserve it," he whispers.

Gabriella opens her mouth, and this time, I intervene.

"That ain't up to you, Dylan," I murmur. "You fucked up when you went behind my back to go to that party, but I understand everything else. I know what it's like to put yourself out there and be shot down. You tried to protect yourself, I get it. I didn't make it easy for you by switching gears when we were doing well."

I pause, remembering Rio filling me on the events of the party, and it does matter that Dylan eventually bowed out. Halfway through the evening, he was feeling awful and he retreated.

I also know Dylan didn't intentionally set out to play with someone. He arrived with a Domme and her sub from Switch because he wanted to go, not because he wanted to have sex.

"I was sure you were about to break up with me," Dylan mumbles. "I wanted to pretend I didn't care."

That didn't go so well.

With Dylan's yawns overlapping, I tell him Gabriella and I will give him some space so he can rest, and he's quick to say we don't have to leave. So the plan changes, going from looking up a hotel to ordering pizza and chilling on the porch.

Gabriella and I sit on an old swing and share a meat lover's pizza while Dylan gets his sleep, and my girl's mouth is running a mile a minute. She talks about fate, how maybe this is how everything was supposed to happen, and that she's confident Dylan will come home with us.

I envy her high spirits as much as I adore watching her be happy. I'm guessing it's my jaded self holding me back from hoping.

"Do you know something I don't, princess? You seem awfully cheery, and he hasn't said yes."

She takes a bite of her pizza slice and swings her legs back and forth. "He's gonna say yes, I know it." She accepts a napkin from me. "And maybe I know something you don't."

Color me not shocked. "Yeah, I saw you whispering to each other earlier."

"Oh." She grins and flushes. "I wanna tell you, I swear, but I think it's best he tells you himself. I'm so silly! I should've seen this coming sooner, really. Not about him, 'pacifically—specifically!— but this, us, how we're, um, *special*."

I can't help but laugh at her adorable rambling.

"I'm not sure I even know what you're talking about, but it's a sight to see. Go on." I wipe some crumbs from the corner of her mouth. "I reckon having Dylan in your life does you good."

It's a big change from her worrying this morning.

"It will for you too, Daddy." She leans over and kisses my arm. "Once we let go of all the hurt, everyone will go bananas with happiness."

I won't rain on her parade, so I settle for stealing a kiss.

I can only describe the rest of the evening as awkward. Dylan wakes up, we return to the living room, and he talks to Gabriella without much issue. In fact, they have moments where it's like nothing has changed, with the exception that it's a bit more subdued. The tension comes from him and me.

I don't know how the fuck to act around him, and he's good at avoiding eye contact.

Something prevents him from admitting he wants to return to California. Chances are it's our situation, but he stammers his way through a suggestion: he'll visit for a few days next week when his grandparents are back from Florida.

"If that's okay?" Dylan flicks me an uncertain glance.

"Of course." I nod with a dip of my chin. Jolts of undeniable relief catch me off guard, and it's growing increasingly difficult to stay in denial. There're so many thoughts I don't even dare to entertain. "What about the wedding? You RSVP'd yes."

He grimaces. "I completely forgot about that. But I'm sure they've already taken my name off the list."

I grunt. "You're sure about a lot of things, huh? If I were you, I'd talk to Kayla and Nick."

"I can't wait for *that*." Gabriella smirks. "I wanna be there when you tell Kayla you won't make it." I chuckle as Dylan cringes. "But I'm glad you're coming home," she adds with a smile. "We'll find you a good physical therapist for your rehab thingy."

I shake my head in amusement. She's relentless, that one.

"I don't need one every day. I'll be fine until I get back here," Dylan says.

"She thinks you're staying for good, kid," I tell him.

Gabriella rolls her eyes. "Well, duh."

"Oh." He shifts uncomfortably.

When the princess gets ready for another grand speech about his homecoming, I zip her mouth shut with a pointed look. Enough is enough. It's been a long day, and I don't think he'll open up more anytime soon. That said, I have every intention of cornering him when I see him next week. There's certainly something he's hiding.

633

Gabriella and I spend the night in a guest room, and I buy our tickets home before bed. Then when we wake up, she picks out a pair of shorts that end right below her ass, with the sole purpose of showing Dylan her new ink.

"He needs to see what he missed." She shrugs. "I don't put random people on my body."

"Random people?" I button up my jeans.

"Yeah, I didn't put the first letter of his name on my leg for no reason."

Huh?

I cock my head. "Baby, I've licked every inch of that sweet body. I've never seen any letters."

"*Unf.*" She shivers and clears her throat. I smirk at her flustered expression. "They're hidden." She places her foot on the bed and brushes her hand over her exposed thigh. "Right here. 'D' for Dylan." I step toward her, and fuck if I can't see it now. The vines of the ivy form a cursive letter, and Cinderella sits on top of it with a flogger in her hand. "My parents and little brother." She points out another three letters around her calf. "And...'C' for Cade."

Fuck.

She gets shy as I touch the soft skin of her upper thigh. Meanwhile, as I'm skimming my fingers over the fancy "C" that a slutty cartoon princess is leaning against, I clench my jaw to keep a lid on the intense urge to claim. Like a fucking caveman, I feel nothing but possessiveness.

"Those last months with John," she murmurs, "I don't know what I would've done without you and Dylan. You were, and always will be, my bright spots."

Gripping her thigh harder, I cup the back of her neck and kiss her. I kiss her hard and lower her to the bed where I cover her body with mine.

"Draw me something when we get home." I nip at her neck as I slip a hand underneath her shorts. "I'll make it permanent."

"Oh," she breathes out. Her head falls back when I find her

slick and warm, and I finger her slowly, slow enough to make her squirm and grow frustrated. "Please, Daddy. I need it."

"What do you need?"

"*You.*" She pushes up my T-shirt to reveal my abs, then begins undoing my jeans. "I want my Daddy between my legs."

I groan and grind my cock against her, more than happy to oblige.

We're not leaving our room for a while. Not until I've expressed everything I can't find the words for.

———

Dylan's still asleep on the couch downstairs when Gabriella and I descend the stairs half an hour later.

"Can I wake him up, please?"

I nod. "No funny business. He might be in pain, so be nice."

"Yes, Sir." She skips into the living room while I leave our bags in the hallway.

There's no rush; we have a couple hours until we gotta go, but I'm hoping to take Gabriella and Dylan out for breakfast. The boy needs to get out of the house.

Looking around me, I expect to see Devil, the golden retriever mutt that lovingly licked my face and crushed my nuts last night. If he's not here, I'll assume Dylan's already been up to see the dog off for daycare.

"Daddy!" Gabriella calls, and I pick up on the distress in her tone. "Can you bring Dylan's medication?"

I head out to the kitchen and bring all the bottles, 'cause it's stupid he has them out there when he can barely get around.

Dylan's trying to sit up when I enter the living room, and I hurry forward to help him.

"Easy there, sweetheart. Lemme help you." I get a glass of water for him and pull him up gently so he can take his meds. "Where does it hurt?"

"Everywhere." He blinks sleepily and swallows the pills, and Gabriella fusses by fluffing his pillows and rubbing his neck. "I forgot to take the pill earlier when Darleen came for Dev. Fuck," he groans and touches his casted knee. "I'm so over this crap. It fucking radiates pain."

I press my lips together. He's not mine. Right here, right now, he's not even a sub. I can't order him to see a doctor, nor can I take charge and make sure he heals as fast as humanly possible. I hate this shit. I hate sitting by all helpless and doing fuck-all.

"Tell me what to do." I push my fingers through his bed head and scratch his scalp. It comes naturally for me, and I'm glad he doesn't stop me.

"I'll be fine. I cramp up for a bit." He sucks in a breath and squeezes his eyes shut, the pain worsening for a second. "The meds kick in pretty quick. It was way worse last week." The twinge passes, causing him to collapse against the back of the couch, and his next groan is quiet and more of pleasure. "That feels nice." Whether it's from the scratching, the rubbing, or the painkiller setting in, I have no idea.

"You have to come home soon, like tomorrow." Gabriella frets, hating seeing him this way as much as I do. "We can't take care of you when you're a gazillion miles away."

Dylan cracks one eye open and musters a small grin for her. "I've really missed you, Gabby. You seem happy."

I smile faintly and let my hand fall.

"I am." Gabriella hugs him hard. "I'll be even happier when you come home."

"Wait, what's that?" Dylan's spotted the ink along her thigh.

"Heh. Funny story," she says.

―――――

It takes some effort and my *serious-business* tone to get Dylan to leave the house. We head to the nearest diner, and he sulks in the back of the car, occasionally glaring at his crutches, but I catch him looking wistful, too.

He grew quiet after Gabriella told him about her tattoos, and I've got my fingers crossed that he'll realize he's not so damn replaceable. Especially to that girl. And me.

I'm having a hard time wrapping my head around the ink, too—or rather, the significance. To learn I've made an impact that great kinda fucks with ya in the best ways.

We arrive at the diner, and Dylan lets me help him out of the car after I tell him to shut the fuck up. I've lost my patience for pride. Even my own. So much has happened because of pretending, omitting, and denying. The littlest things can blow up and create mayhem, and I'm over it.

Needing help is all right. Needing reassurance sometimes is okay, too.

Breakfast is a quiet affair, other than Gabriella trying to lighten the tension with plans for us when Dylan comes. She deserves a medal for not giving up, and she even manages to get Dylan to set a date for his arrival.

"Thursday, okay?" He sets down his fork and sits back, frustrated and in a pissy mood.

I eye them and finish the last of my scrambled eggs. "Princess, could you give me a minute alone with Dylan?"

"Sure thing. Later, grouchy pants." She pats Dylan's head and excuses herself from the table to check out the old-fashioned jukebox by the door.

I wipe my mouth with a napkin and clear my throat. "We gotta do something about this, kid. If you're upset with me, don't take it out on her."

"I'm not upset with you," he mutters. "I'm in pain, and I sort of just want to crawl into a hole and—"

"Don't." I shake my head. "Don't finish that sentence." I lean forward, resting my forearms on the table. "Be real with me, Dylan. Tell me what's going on inside that head of yours."

He swallows and stares at his plate. "It's hard seeing you again. Both of you. I want...shit." His bottom lip trembles, and he covers his mouth while taking a deep breath.

Hating the distance between us, I hook his good foot with mine under the table.

"Hey." I make him look me in the eye. "I'm here, Dylan. Whatever happened before only hurt because I care. And I still do. I'm willing to work it out. Are you?"

He sniffles and takes another breath. "What's the point? And don't get me wrong, Cade. I valued your friendship so much, but being around you...? Right now, it's just a reminder of what I lost."

I don't know what to say to that. I can relate, since I feel the same exact fucking thing, but I have no answer.

"If it makes you feel any better, I know what it's like," I murmur. "You got attached fast, but so did I. It won't disappear overnight."

"Really?" He seems dubious. "You mean you still, um..."

"Of fucking course I do." I loathe how little he thinks of himself. "Those feelings haven't even faded. So the way I'm thinking, we can either tiptoe around each other like idiots and pretend everything's gravy, or we can be straight for once, admit our situation sucks, and try to move forward as friends." I catch the face he makes, and I laugh quietly. "Trust me, that word tastes like acid to me, too."

He tests a smile and looks away.

Gabriella was right all along, dammit. He needs to get his ass back to San Francisco so we can make sure he gets better. It has to be us. I don't trust anyone else to get it done. More than that, I *want* it to be us.

"For the record, you don't belong in Texas," I tell him. "Now, finish your breakfast. Don't think I can't see you've lost weight."

"Yes, Sir." The eye contact remains a struggle for him, but at least the smile is still there.

Progress, right?

CHAPTER 10

"**H**e's late, Daddy. He's late!" Gabriella paces the open space between the bed and the kitchen table and keeps checking the time. "Ugh, we should've picked him up at the airport."

Agreed, but I had to let Dylan win one fight. He won't be winning any others while he's here. With that in mind, I relented after twenty minutes of bitching, him stating he didn't want to be coddled and treated like a disabled person because of a pair of crutches, and me stating he was full of shit.

I've had a few days to process everything now, and the past doesn't matter anymore 'cause it doesn't change that I wanna be there for Dylan. That's what it boils down to. Despite the bitterness, despite the hurt, despite the tension. I care more than I can describe, and that means I have several fights to win to ensure he returns to San Francisco—if not indefinitely, then at least on an extended vacation. Or whatever term to use for a month or five.

I check my watch, and yeah, he should be here by now.

Food's ready, Gabriella's planned a movie night, and the sleeping arrangements have been taken care of—kind of. She turned my bed into a fort this morning, and I reckon they will fall asleep there after the movies. It's a California King, so I know I'll fit too, though I might bring out a spare mattress. We'll see how I feel. Either way, it's not a big issue.

"I hear a car!" Gabriella rushes toward the kitchen window to peer down the street. "It's him!"

I inhale deeply, nervous, and follow her downstairs.

My girl's excited. "I can't wait to see everyone's faces when he shows up at Switch this weekend."

Ah, yes. She wants it to be a surprise. No one knows he's back.

Gabriella swings the door open as Dylan's getting out of the cab. I pick up the pace to pay the driver and then help the stubborn boy, whom Gabriella's hugging the hell out of.

"I'll get that." I shoulder his bag and hand him his crutches. "Good to see you, kid." Understatement.

Mother of Christ, I miss him. *God.* I miss him. The thought voices itself unbidden, and the guilt trails after. I miss him too much.

He smiles anxiously. "You, too. I almost backed out."

"I'm not surprised."

"I would've kicked your butt so hard," Gabriella huffs. "Come on, let's get our awesome evening started! I made lasagna."

She races ahead to hold the door for us, and I walk beside Dylan.

"I thought she sucked at cooking," he mumbles.

"She's...learning." I chuckle. "Her lasagna's stellar, though."

On the way to the stairs, I side-eye him for signs of...well, anything. The cast isn't very thick, but thick enough so his jeans won't fit, hence the switch to wearing sweats twenty-four seven. A beanie covers most of his messy hair. I think the shadows under his eyes have faded slightly. The cuts and scrapes from the accident are gone, thankfully. Leaving only a small scar above his left eyebrow.

When we reach the stairs, I cup his elbow so I can help him up the narrow steps.

"Can't wait to get rid of the crutches." He grunts, climbing another step.

"Know when that'll be?" I ask.

"They're fitting me for a brace next week." He takes a break halfway up. "I'll have one crutch after that until I don't need it anymore."

By the time we reach the landing, he's winded. I guide him over to the foot of the bed—or fort—so he can sit down. I drop his bag on the floor.

He looks up at the blankets thrown across and over the four posts of the frame and smiles tiredly. On the inside of Gabriella's creation, string lights circle each post to make it, using her words, supercozy.

"Movie night, huh?" He looks over at where Gabriella's bringing the lasagna outta the oven. "Did she pick all the movies?"

"You bet." I smirk.

I remember the feeling of having Gabriella, for all intents and purposes, move in with me so I could look after her. I remember it felt good. And this is no different. Having Dylan nearby feels right, and I won't shy away from using my Dom card to get my way.

"I'm glad you came," I murmur.

"Really?" He pulls off his beanie and fidgets with it on his lap.

"Really."

"Me, too," he admits so quietly I almost miss it. "I always liked your place."

"I remember." We've had some good times here. Unforgettable times. "Are you hungry, or do you wanna rest?"

He snorts. "I wanna be spoon-fed while I doze off."

I grin, unable to take my eyes off him. "That can be arranged, so watch what you say."

"Oh—" He flushes and laughs, the sound strained by memories taking him back. I see it. We shared too much. I've fed him before, as a playful punishment.

"Dinner's ready!" Gabriella sings.

I hold out my hand. "Come on, cripple."

That earns me a scowl, though he takes my hand and uses me to pull himself off the bed.

Gabriella and Dylan sit down across from each other, and I take my seat at the head of the table. The princess is wearing a permanent smile, one she's been sporting all week because of today, and Dylan's eye-fucking the lasagna, the garlic bread, and the rabbit food.

My gut's tied in knots, and it's a strange feeling, 'cause it's not entirely unpleasant. There's hope. Hope that this is a good thing, that it'll lead to something better.

"Dig in, kids." I help myself to a full plate and let them do the talking while I observe and probably overthink. Thinking less about the past, my mind has begun spinning with focus on the future instead.

I don't know what any of this means or how long this unfamiliar but decent feeling will last. I guess that's how it is when you have a lot to lose—or when your body is a time bomb waiting to go off. I feel it in my bones that I'll either explode or implode soon.

"This is so good." Dylan speaks with his mouth full of food. "The upside of not having a career in sports anymore is I can eat whatever I want."

His joke falls flat, and Gabriella launches into ideas of what he can do and still stay in the same field. Coaching? Become an expert commentator?

Dylan shrugs, reluctant to talk about it. "There's no money in coaching, and there're people far better suited for commentating. I dunno. I'll figure it out eventually, I guess."

"There's no rush," I tell him. "Focus on your recovery and rest."

He nods and picks at his food. "Let's talk about you guys instead." He lifts his gaze to Gabriella. "How's the tattooing busi-ness? By the way, I'm waiting for you to say that's a joke."

"Ha. Why? I love it. I mean, not that I've ever done a tattoo. It'll be a while." She adds some more salad to her plate. "Yesterday I was stuck doing inventory all day. And I'm studying techniques a lot."

I point to her nightstand across the room. "You can see the pile of portfolios there. They're her bedtime stories these days."

Dylan laughs quietly. "I don't know, I wouldn't go near you if you're holding a tattoo gun."

Gabriella's jaw drops. "What! *Why?* I'll be a good tattoo artist. Right, Daddy? Tell him!"

"You'd probably ink a dick on my forehead or somethin'." Dylan crosses his eyes when she sticks out her tongue at him.

I chuckle, enjoying watching their banter.

Gabriella juts her chin. "Daddy's letting me design a tattoo for him, so *there.*"

Dylan wags his fork at her. "But he's not letting you hold the machine, is he?"

That makes her smash her lips together and glare.

I laugh under my breath and shovel some lasagna into my mouth.

Please let this be a good thing. Please let this be a good thing.

I don't want any more great times ripped away from me, or us.

After dinner, Dylan's pain catches up to him. He retreats to the fort for some rest and for his meds to kick in. In the meantime, I help Gabriella clear the table.

With the last of the leftovers wrapped and tucked into the fridge, I come up behind the princess as she does the dishes, and I give her a squeeze.

"Thank you for a delicious dinner, baby." I kiss her neck, my hands traveling from her hips up to her breasts. "Do you know how happy it makes me to see you smiling?"

She tilts her head up and gives me one of those smiles. "You're making my tummy tingle again."

"Fantastic." I dip down and claim her mouth, and I slip a hand under her pajama shorts to cup her pretty little pussy. "The evening's looking good so far, isn't it?"

"Mmhmm." She shivers, dropping a plate back into the water. "I've got my amazing Daddy *and* my annoying brother back in my life."

It's not the first time she's referred to Dylan as a brother, and before everything went straight to hell, he often joked about Gabriella being the best little sister he never wanted—

Oh, hell.

No, no, no, is that what she wants?

"Dirty little slut," I whisper into the kiss. "I know what you're thinking." And it's impossible to *unthink* it.

Anxiety mingles with lust, and I slam two fingers deep inside her pussy, torn between wanting to jump into the unknown that terrifies me and...shit, I don't know, talk it all out? Find out what she wants?

"You want it, too," she gasps.

Confirmation right there. She's got play for the three of us in mind. What I don't know is how far that goes. Or how I feel about it.

Fucking hell, man, you want it.

"Why do you want it?" I let out a low growl against her neck, finger-fucking her faster. "Tell Daddy everything."

"Because—" She stifles a moan by biting down on her lip. Her eyes close. "Oh my God—because it's us. Us three, never anyone else. When I think about it, it all makes sense."

I swallow a groan and withdraw my fingers from her.

"Cade," she whispers, turning around in my arms. "I *know*." Her eyes are filled with more than lust. "I know, and it's *okay*. I know you're struggling with your feelings. I know they run deep —maybe even deeper than you think. I know you want what's best for us, and I know you always put us first." She raises her hands to my neck. "When I first met you, I was friggin' scared.

The tats, the piercings, that indecent look in your eyes—heck, your whole body. Then you turned out to be the sweetest man I've had the honor of knowing. You're the first one to help out and offer whatever you can. You shoulder so much responsibility."

I close my eyes and press my forehead to hers.

"It doesn't have to be difficult." She keeps her voice soft and quiet. "I'm indescribably happy with you, but I can't shake that feeling of unsettlement, and I think you feel the same. We don't wanna hurt or betray anyone. So it keeps us from going all out."

Her words flow through me, solidifying things that've been shaky for months. Confusion and uncertainty morph into yearning for something concrete. Blurry images become clear, and whatever I couldn't put my finger on before, I now can.

"We deserve a break," she murmurs. "We owe it to ourselves at least to try, and we shouldn't feel guilty about it."

I think she's saving me from that implosion.

"Try..." *Spell it out for me, princess.*

"To become something—the three of us. I want it, Cade. I have all these feelings, too."

I almost fucking break at those words. Instead, I cup her face and kiss her as if I'm kissing her for the first time. As if I'm seeing her for the first time, ironically, while having my eyes closed. And, in a way, it is a first. A first with a new perspective and a better grasp of what I'm feeling.

"I want to be your little girl forever," she mumbles against my lips. "I want to let it all go because I trust you."

"Jesus," I whisper hoarsely. "I have no words, Gabriella." I'm screwed where this girl is concerned. Falling, falling, falling...like a motherfucker. My heart pounds furiously. "I need to make sure I got this right. You feel more for Dylan?"

She falters, as if hesitant, then nods once. "It's been in the back of my mind. I did my best not to think about it for a long time. I've been too afraid. I'm sorry, Cade. I should've told you this sooner."

I can't fault her for that. I get it, and it's painfully over-whelming to sort through.

Perhaps I should've seen it. They have amazing chemistry.

"I've reached my limit, thinking about everything that's happened," I admit. "I go back and forth with blame and self-pity, and it's been killing me not to be able to work this out." I blow out a breath and scrub a hand over my face. "I wanna let go too, princess. I wanna quit restricting myself and set up the boundaries I need."

It sounds crazy when I hear it, what I just said. But there's a difference. I put up restrictions when I was with Dylan. I caved for damn fear.

"So what're those boundaries?" she wonders.

"No goddamn uncertainty." The words escape me in a gust; it feels good to finally have it out there. "A relationship where those involved are fucking stuck with me. No getting out. No sharing outside those parameters. I wanna be enough—the only Top."

Gabriella giggles, her expression tender. "Mister, we're not *stuck* with you. We adore you."

We.

She can't speak for Dylan, but right now, I only need to know how she feels.

"I adore you, too." I cup her cheeks and kiss her softly. "I'm with you, princess. You can let go."

"Yeah?"

I nod and kiss her again. "We'll try." Although, the most impor-tant thing right this minute is that I can let go of the damn guilt. She doesn't hold anything against me, and I can be open with her. Like she said, she knows.

"And you and I are solid?"

"You won't get rid of me." I pick her up, wrapping her legs around me, and shift some hair from her beautiful eyes. "More solid than diamond. Let go of everything."

She beams at me and peppers my face with kisses. "We'll make him stay."

I chuckle, dazed, feeling tons lighter. How the hell does she do it? I gotta blink past the burn in my eyes.

"One thing, though." I sit her down on the counter and level her with a serious look. What I'm about to say is bizarre because it hasn't been an option, and I haven't processed it. "Before you speed ahead and try to get into his pants, I want to feel him out. He's been through a lot, and we don't wanna add to that. He needs comfort and stability more than sex."

She nods, sobering. "I understand. Important stuffs."

"Good." I press my lips to her forehead. "What you can do, however, is convince him to get his butt to Mexico with us."

That oughta keep her distracted while I focus on getting more involved in Dylan's healing process. He needs to be able to trust me again.

"I can do that." She giggles behind her hand.

"If he doesn't wake up soon," Gabriella whispers, "the gummy worms will be all gone."

"For some reason," I whisper back, "I think he'll live."

"But, oh," she whines. Sitting up in the middle of the bed, she pouts at Dylan, then looks pleadingly at me. I shake my head in response. *Patience, princess.* He needs his rest. "I can't show him cool pics of Mexico if he's sleeping."

I laugh silently and place an arm under my head as an extra pillow. "Good thing he's staying a while."

She gives me the sad eyes, and when that doesn't work, she makes a show of pushing out her chest as she reaches over me to place the bowl of gummy worms on my nightstand. I'm not sure how she thinks using sex is going to sway me, though. She knows better, I hope.

"Watch your movie," I murmur.

She picked a stellar horror movie but wanted to see a rom-com first, so I've just been lying here, surrounded by blankets and string lights, waiting for the damn movie to end, all while doing some classic Cade overthinking. There've been countless doors opened now, and I wanna consider all possibilities.

Gabriella admits defeat and gets snuggly, her head on my chest. Her hand sneaks underneath my sweats to casually rest on top of my cock, and I grin and shake my head at her. Relentless.

As if that's not enough, she slowly moves her foot to Dylan's side.

"Gabriella," I warn.

"*Fiiine.*"

More interested in her than the movie, I turn toward her and hike her leg over my hip. Her fine ass gets a squeeze through her panties, and then I get her to remove her pajama shirt, leaving a skimpy top. Much better with all that skin on display.

"Delectable baby girl," I whisper in her hair. I've grown addicted to her curvy little body, a stark contrast to the sculpted form of Dylan that I'm equally drawn to.

Tucking her head under my chin, I glance over at him, breathing easier now that I can allow myself to relax. Having never bothered to define anything sexually in the past, I guess, on some level, I've still considered myself monogamous. Now it makes more sense. For some people, there's more than one.

Gabriella giggles at something happening on the screen, and a beat later, Dylan's eyes flutter open. He blinks drowsily, unaware he's being watched, then stretches and yawns.

The kid makes me ache.

He gains his bearings and eyes the blankets creating a ceiling, and when Gabriella laughs again, he tilts his head our way, and our eyes meet. Immediately, he looks caught—though, it should be me—and he lowers his gaze.

"Did you sleep well?" I murmur.

"Yes, Sir." There's time for one nod before Gabriella turns to him and says it's about time he woke up.

"I had a thousand gummy worms while you slept," she adds. "Daddy bought that licorice you like, and there's chips and salsa. Want some? I can go get it!" She's off before Dylan can even answer.

He grins, half lazy and half shy. "She's different."

"She is." She's a happy little sprite with me, but she comes to life on another level with Dylan around, and that's okay. More than okay. There's obviously more than one for her, too. "That's because of you. She's happier when we're both by her side."

He bites his lip and sits up, his hair pointing in every direction. "The tattoos she's gotten," he says quietly. "It's hard to understand why she would add my name."

"I know the feeling." I smile faintly.

"You're just too humble for your own good." He rubs his eyes, a smirk tugging at his lips. "You always were."

I huff. "Are you talking to yourself?"

"No. It's completely different with me," he insists. "I have a good reason to think I don't deserve a tribute on her body."

I sigh and sit up, too. "We're gonna talk about all that tomorrow. There're some things you need to understand. For now, humor Gabriella and pretend you wanna watch the rest of this god-fucking-awful chick flick with her. Or us. I'm really loving it."

He laughs at my deadpan expression and agrees, although I don't miss the flicker of nervousness at the mention of our talk tomorrow.

"I need to go to the bathroom first."

"I'll help you." I leave the bed as he gets ready to protest, which I'm happy to shut down. "It wasn't a question, little pan."

He sighs heavily, all dramatic like. Removing the pillows that keep his leg elevated, I offer him a hand and carefully get him on his feet.

"I thought you were only supposed to boss around Littles," he mutters.

"Pretty much what I'm doing." I pick up his bag from the floor. "Do you have PJs in here, or do you wanna borrow a T-shirt?"

He half sits on the foot of the bed and opens his bag. "I mean Littles you're in charge of."

Pretty much what I'm doing.

Honesty, right? Baby steps. Easing into it. "Dylan, if you didn't object, I'd be in charge of you, too. You know how to worry me— and probably make me go prematurely gray."

He's surprised by that, and he falters with the bag. "Wh-what?"

Gabriella's almost done in the kitchen, so I keep it short.

Cupping his jaw, I kiss his forehead briefly. "Gabriella's not the only one who missed you, kid."

I treat them equally from that moment on. Knowing how reluctant Dylan's been to open up, me acting as a Daddy to both of them will give him time to adjust and think about things. Hopefully, it'll jog his memories of what we used to have when everything was great. Hopefully, he'll want it again.

He's red-faced most of the evening, though he never complains, and he seems to like being included. Even when I tell them to pipe down or when I chastise them for eating too much candy.

"You'll get stomachaches," I warn.

"My tummy's fine," Gabriella sings. Next, she pats Dylan's stomach. "He's a bit *hard*, though." She gigglesnorts at her pun as she gets up on her knees. "Daddy, you lie in the middle instead. Scary movie time means you're our stuffie."

Damn. When they hit the candy like there was no tomorrow, I grabbed leftovers, and now the lasagna's making it difficult to budge an inch. But I comply, and the princess rolls over me as I scoot toward the middle.

"All right. Come on, cuddle monsters." I place two pillows behind me so I can see the flat screen even when Gabriella rests her head on my chest. Dylan hesitates, for which I can't blame him. I don't pressure him into doing anything he's not comfortable with, so I push play on the movie and give his hand a squeeze. "That includes you unless it's too much for you, Dyl—Gabriella, I swear to Christ, it's a nipple ring, not a chew toy."

Both she and Dylan burst out in laughter, and after replaying the ridiculousness of what I just said, I can't help but chuckle. But seriously, the girl flicks and nibbles on that barbell a tad too much.

"I'm sorry," she wheezes behind her hand, laughing so hard she's almost in tears. "It fascinates me!"

Dylan snickers. "Chew toy—too funny."

"Okay, okay, simmer down, you two. The movie's started." I smile and pinch Gabriella's ass.

She yelps and yanks the covers higher up, and Dylan settles a few inches closer than earlier.

After that, it's ninety minutes of exorcism and general terror for Littles.

CHAPTER 11

It's nearing lunch when Dylan half hops down the stairs without his crutches the next day. I notice his T-shirt, the one the American team wore at the World Championship last year where he won his first silver. It was before he and I got together, so it was as an acquaintance I headed over to Nick and Kayla's with Mark to watch Dylan on TV.

I turn off the lathe and wipe dust off my hands. "Morning, sleepyhead. Where are your crutches?"

"I couldn't bring them if I was holding the railing." He makes the last jump off the final step and lets me guide him over to my workbench. It's been cleared, so I help him up to sit on it. "You're covered in sawdust."

"Hot, right?" I smirk and lift my T-shirt to wipe sweat off my forehead. "Did you sleep well? You gotta be hungry. I can order us something."

"I already did." He directs his smile to my shop rather than at me, and I remember he liked spending time down here while I worked. "I ordered a bunch for us from that bagel place." That's sweet of him. The garage door's open, country rock is spilling out from the speakers, and the sky's blue. Here's to hoping for a good day, now with the best bagels in the Bay Area. "When did Gabby leave?"

I check the clock on the wall where I have all my chisels, gouges, and other hand tools. "About an hour ago. She's learning how to disassemble a tattoo gun and change needles today. She was excited." By excited, I mean she bounced out of here earlier.

"It's weird picturing her in that field." He laughs softly and scratches his bed head. "So what're you workin' on?"

"Knobs," I reply dumbly. It's the short answer. They're knobs. Hundreds of lathed knobs. People have used beds of nails for meditation and whatnot for ages; now a fetish club in Baltimore is introducing a highly uncomfortable mat with wooden knobs in various sizes to get fucked on top of. I'm the lucky, lucky designer of said contraption. "Your accent's changed a bit. It's more Southern."

"Grandma mentioned that." He squints at the opening of the garage, the sun beaming outside. "So, um, you said you wanted to talk?"

I chuckle and return to the lathe. "Itching to get it over with?" I get a sheepish look from him at that. "First things first, I was wondering if it's all right if I give your doctors a call later, especially the team doctor."

His forehead creases. "Why?"

"Because I spoke to Liam earlier this week, and I did some research." I can't speak when the lathe is on, so I throw the dozens of knobs I've done so far into a paper bag and bring them to the workbench. I can do the sanding there. "I know you're not ready to think about your future yet—career-wise—but that doesn't mean I can't do it for you. So depending on what your docs say, maybe you can stay in sports."

He scoots to the side as I pick out a sheet of sandpaper. "Um, I appreciate it, but my knee's fucked indefinitely unless I do a total knee replacement, and even then, I'll end up too far behind to catch up. I have more screws and junk than tissue under here." He knocks his cast lightly. "Best-case scenario, I'll be a half-ass swimmer who never makes the national team again, and my sponsors won't renew any contracts when I can't even qualify for major meets."

Actually, hearing he can be a half-ass swimmer is enough to give me hope.

"What would you say is key in swimming? To compete at your level, I mean." I rip off a piece of fine sandpaper and begin checking the knobs for any uneven surfaces. "Technique's gotta be important."

"What? Well, of course it is."

I nod. "And in the off-season, you do open-water swimming as part of your strength training, yeah?"

He shoots me a brief, exasperated look. "What's your point, Cade?"

I set down the paper and face him fully. "A triathlete's biggest issue is generally swimming 'cause they don't put in enough hours on technique, and they tend to come from backgrounds of running and cycling."

"Tri..." His brain catches up, and he frowns. "Are you suggesting I compete in triathlon?"

"That's exactly what I'm suggesting." Actually, Liam put it in my head, and I spent all morning reading up on it, 'cause once again, big football fan here. I don't know much about other sports. "I reckon your background as a swimmer will give you a serious edge in the water. None of those fuckers would make the national team, either."

He opens then shuts his mouth, only to open it again. The crease is back in his forehead. "That's three sports where you don't want a mangled knee."

I make a speed-forward motion with my finger. "Think further. You mentioned knee replacement and said it'd set you back because the recovery's too long—for *swimming*. Swimmers peak in their early twenties. Triathletes? Add ten years to that."

That shuts him up, his mind spinning, and I take a step closer, my hands on his legs.

"You're a fighter, Dylan." I lift his chin when he looks down. "But you need something to fight *for*. Without it, you drift. So I'm saying you have options. In a few years, you could be bringing home that Ironman Triathlon Cup or whatever it's called."

His mouth twitches. "Ironman World Championship."

"That's the one. Talk about a cool fucking comeback." I step back to return to work. "A call to your docs might give you the motivation to try. Your life's not over."

Dylan grows quiet, staring out at the street while pinching his lips, a telltale sign of his that lets me know he's miles away in his head.

I believe in him, and America loves a comeback. If he goes public with it, I'll bet my life sponsors will be all over him to share his journey. More than that, the light in his eyes can come back. I miss it something fierce.

A delivery guy shows up shortly after with our food, and I take care of it so the boy who's lost in thought can get some grub in his snarling stomach.

———

The next few hours fly by quickly. Dylan remains fairly quiet, only occasionally commenting on what I do, be it sanding the little knobs, lathing new ones, or airbrushing them black. I'll do the top coat another day 'cause I wanna wrap up as soon as possible so I can enjoy the rest of my Friday away from work.

"Anything special you wanna do tonight?" I go over to my cleanup station in the corner to wash my hands. "We have Switch tomorrow, so maybe there's a restaurant or a bar."

"I'm kind of limited." He adjusts his leg and checks his phone. "Gabby keeps sending me photos of Mexico."

Limited, my ass. "She's on a mission." Wiping my hands on a

towel, I move closer and make him face me. "Do you really not wanna go with us?"

"Of course I do," he mumbles. "I just don't wanna be in the way. I'd be no fun to have around. Last time I checked, a new couple isn't interested in babysitting someone who can't walk."

I sigh. "Then check again." Besides, his condition will have improved in a few weeks.

I'll leave that mission to Gabriella, though. My agenda is about making him extend his stay here. "Do you miss the lifestyle?"

The question makes him uncomfortable, but he answers nonetheless. "Yes." It's quiet and cautious. Enough to go on.

"So stay." I cup his cheek when he tries to hide from me. I'm so over that. "You have absolutely nothing to lose. You can try it out and let us be here for you. Reconnect with your friends, find a PT here for your rehab, bring your pup home, go see your dogs at the rescue center..."

Dylan swallows hard, and I see a million questions he's too afraid to ask. His gaze flicks between me and empty space.

"We don't have to do anything you're not ready for," I murmur. "First and foremost, I—we—wanna help you get better. If you stay here as a friend we care about, or if you're comfortable enough to let me take over is up to you. Being a Daddy is nothing I can switch on and off, but I'd do my best to rein it in if it's too much."

He exhales shakily. "You really want me around?"

"Fuck, yes." I can't stress that enough.

"But—" He swallows again and blinks back the glassiness. "I don't understand. You'd be toppy with me, too?"

His wording causes me to breathe out a laugh. "Aren't I always a toppy bastard?"

"You know what I mean," he whispers.

I do, and I nod. "If you'll let me."

He trembles for a beat and pinches his lips. "Is Gabby okay with that?"

More than. Jesus, she's ready to jump his bones. Then again, I'd be a fucking liar if I said I wasn't on the same page. But I don't wanna overwhelm him. I know too little about the months we spent away from each other, and I'm extra careful due to the fact that he's on medication, mainly the antidepressant. During rough times, the smallest changes can put a man through the wringer. I've been there.

"She's very much on board." I give him his iced tea when I see him reaching for it. "I'd treat you equally, kinda like I did last night. Same rules would apply to both of you, and I'd be in charge of your recovery."

Another reason I want to call his doctors. I need to get my facts straight so I know what he can and can't handle.

Dylan offers a wobbly little smile. "I don't have the strength to say no, so y'all better be sure this is what you want."

My chest fills with relief, and I bet it shows on my face. "Thank fuck." Running a hand over my head, I get antsy to seal the deal somehow. I know what I want; I wanna kiss the ever-loving hell out of him, but I don't know if that's too soon.

I open my trap to ask before I assume, though that flies out the window when he flinches in pain and begins rubbing the spot above his cast.

"I'll get your painkillers," I tell him.

That night, my intention is to take Dylan and Gabriella out to dinner and sort of celebrate. Emphasis on intention, 'cause the result doesn't come near celebratory.

Dylan's leg kept him from getting any rest earlier, plus he almost fell in the shower after declining help, so he's tired and cranky. Gabriella's happy but spent after a day running ragged at the tattoo shop. Which leaves me in a 49ers steakhouse with two Littles who would rather cuddle in bed than discuss some fun plans for us now that he's sticking around.

I shake my head in amusement and eat my burger. Gabriella's sitting next to Dylan, and she leans over to hug his arm several times and say she's thrilled about him staying, but then she's back to struggling to stay awake.

"I have over ten years on both of you, and you're the ones yawning like it's three in the morning." Leaning back, I sip my beer and wait for their excuses.

Okay, Dylan's got a solid one. His pain has been brutal today.

"What can I say?" Gabriella pouts and shrugs. "My soul is *ancient.*"

"Or lazy." Dylan snickers and pokes her side.

"Not true!" She scowls.

"Is, too."

"It's *not.*" Gabriella lets out a cute growl. "I have CrossFit on Tuesday at six in the morning. Wanna come? I mean, you're not *lazy,* right?"

He rolls his eyes. "No, but I *will* be in *Texas* then, genius."

That makes me frown, and I set down my burger. "What? But you're staying."

"Oh, um, yeah." He shifts in his seat. "I have to make it to my doctor's appointment for the leg brace fitting, though. And I have to speak to my grandparents about watching Devil, take care of some things, pack... Renew my prescriptions."

That makes sense, though I don't like the idea of being away from him now. Everything he mentions is shit I wanna take over for him.

"I understand, but you're bringing the pup." I know how much he loves Devil.

"Actually, I was thinking..." He hesitates, glancing between Gabriella and me. "If you want, I could go back, get everythin' taken care of, and then fly from there straight to Cabo and make it to the wedding."

"Yes!" Gabriella fist-pumps the air, and her outburst mirrors what goes on inside me. There's no stopping the grin. "Yes, yes, yes!"

Maybe I can draw some celebration outta them anyway. "Don't you dare change your mind now."

He smiles, seemingly surprised and unable to grasp that we want him with us. "I won't, Sir."

"Good boy."

"Here, let me." I can't sit by and watch him struggle anymore. Removing the covers, I carefully rub his thigh above the cast. His skin is itching underneath the plaster, but he says the cramping is far worse. His painkiller hasn't kicked in yet, and massaging the tissue helps.

My touch deepens, and I rub his thigh slowly, firmly through his pajama bottoms until I see his abs unclench. He groans through a whimper, his head landing on the pillow, and he throws an arm over his face.

"Daddy!" Gabriella calls from the bath. "PJs, please! My fingers are pruny!"

"In a minute, baby," I call back. "Almost done here." Watching Dylan's chest, I see his breathing evening out. The muscles in his thigh aren't as tense anymore, either. "Feeling better, kiddo?"

He nods minutely. "A little. Thank you."

"Let me know if you need more, okay?" I head to the closet to grab a pair of panties and a top for Gabriella.

Once in the bathroom, I help her out of the bath and wrap a towel around her.

"My beautiful girl. Let me see those fingers."

She grins up at me and flashes fingers that have been in the water a long time.

I kiss them.

"Don't forget to brush your teeth." It's my turn to shower, so I drop my clothes in the hamper and get in. "Have you picked out a movie to fall asleep to?"

My showers take about five minutes, unless there's someone in here with me, so by the time she's brushed her teeth, put on her nightwear, and told me Dylan and I can pick a movie because she wants to draw on his cast, I'm done.

I step out as she skips away to find a Sharpie, and I hear her telling Dylan he can go in now. Running a towel over my head, I put on deodorant and then leave the towel around my shoulders while I brush my own teeth.

A blurry image of Dylan appears in the fogged-up mirror, and he stutters to a halt, clanking his crutches against the doorframe.

"Sorry, I'll g-go later."

"Get in here, sweetheart." With the toothbrush in my mouth, it's easier to hide my amusement, and I fasten the towel around my hips instead. "How's your leg?"

"Better." He flushes, stammers, and gestures at his toothbrush by the sink. "I-I was just gonna..."

He makes it fucking impossible to stay a gentleman. Not that I ever was one.

He approaches cautiously, his hand trembling as he applies toothpaste.

I make him nervous.

I also catch him staring when I bend over to spit and rinse my mouth.

Once I'm finished, I straighten and give his shoulder a squeeze. "Don't take too long. I want my two favorite people in bed with me."

I leave the bathroom and throw the towel over a chair as I go, and Gabriella greets me in bed with a sweet smile, her hand clutching a case of markers. The blankets are still hanging over the bed and off the sides, so I get in from the end and crawl over my girl, pushing her down on the mattress.

"Hi." She beams, a dimple appearing. "You're all naked."

"Am I?" I look down between us. "Shit, you're right." I smirk and give her a smooch. "I think maybe you're wearing too much."

She shakes her head at that. "Nuh-uh. Boys can't see my boobs."

"They can if Daddy wants them to." I slip a hand up her stomach, revealing her soft skin. "Lucky for you, there's only one boy who gets all the access he wants."

She squirms and makes a sound of complaint. "Oh, Daddy, the tingles come back all the time when you say stuffs like that."

"You poor thing," I mock. Getting off her, I tell her to lose the top, and I get comfortable on my side of the bed. Since she brought her duvet here, my place is nice and chilly again, excellent for regular covers and heavy cuddling. I draw a sheet over my lower body as Dylan stumbles back from the bathroom.

"See, princess? Dylan's not wearing a shirt, either."

"He's a boy!" She hides herself by lying on her stomach. "Ugh, let's get the drawing started, Dylan." Scooting down to the foot of the bed, she opens her pencil case. "Cast here, please."

Dylan's looking anywhere but at us, and it's time to put a stop to his shyness. He used to be so flirty and outgoing.

"Keep your legs in this direction, Gabriella." I pat the empty spot between Dylan and me. "I wanna show Dylan something."

"Um, okay." She obeys and squirms around like a little worm until her head is at the level of Dylan's casted knee and her feet are...well, she's short, so they're nowhere near the pillows, but almost.

It doesn't take many seconds for her to get lost in her drawing on Dylan's cast, and she barely reacts when I tell her to spread her legs. Like the little girl she is, her ankles are crossed in the air, and I nudge her knees apart.

"Gabriella takes a bath every night," I tell Dylan, keeping my voice low. "Now that you're finally coming back to San Francisco, you'll have chores."

"Okay...?" He bites his lip, struggling with where to look.

juices from her pussy glisten around her tightest opening. "You have to check her inside there, too. You can use fingers or a toy. She hasn't taken my cock yet."

"Daddy," Gabriella mewls, lifting her ass from the mattress. "Pretty please? I need something."

Soon, baby.

"Better yet, tasting her. She becomes a needy slut when you put your tongue in her." My thumb covers her little hole, and I push it past the tight muscles as I encourage Dylan to finger her pussy a bit faster.

"Ohhh," she moans. Her forehead lands on the mattress, and she begins to move with each thrust. "Please, please, please?"

"C-Can I, please? I mean," Dylan stammers. "Taste her —may I?"

"Of course, sweetheart." I withdraw from Gabriella and order her to stand up in the middle of the bed. Perfect height for his mouth. "If she tastes like body wash when you eat her out, you know she's rushed through her shower or bath too quickly."

"Yes, Sir." He tries to be subtle about hiding his erection by bunching up the covers. Meanwhile, Gabriella moves closer to him, one foot on each side of him, until he's right there. "She smells so sweet." He moves his hands up her legs, then behind them to cup her bottom.

"Go on." I thread my fingers through his hair and urge him forward. The last distance is closed, and he groans as he closes his mouth over her pussy.

Fuck me.

The same kind of inferno I experienced when I first watched them together months ago builds up inside me again. I watch his tongue delve between her folds, and he licks her greedily, sensually, fucking perfectly.

She cries out and grabs on to my shoulder for support.

Needing to get in on the action before I burst, I urge Dylan to lie flat on his back. Gabriella follows so she can lower herself over his face, and I make sure not to touch Dylan's injured leg when I get behind her.

Their sounds fuck me up. He moans uncontrollably, instinct taking over, and pulls her down harder on him. I know those moans. I've missed them. I've felt them around my cock, I've heard them while I've fucked him.

I stroke my cock roughly for a beat, enjoying watching them. As a voyeur, I've never been so satisfied. Seeing them together... There are no words.

Dylan senses me and focuses on her clit so I can open up her pussy for my cock. Gripping her hips tightly, I fill her in one push that elicits a breathless wail from her.

I clench my jaw, momentarily lost in the sensations of her inner muscles milking me.

"Daddy, I'm already close," she moans. "It's tingling everywhere."

"I wonder why." I grit my teeth, my hands traveling up her curvy sides to where I meet Dylan's hands over her tits. I pull out slowly as I pinch her nipples. "Could it be 'cause you're getting fucked by Daddy and having your clit—" I slam in again "—sucked by your brother?"

She loses her breath, and Dylan's hips jerk. His muffled groan is strained, and if I didn't hear his need right there, I feel it when he grasps my fingers on top of Gabriella's breasts with all he's worth.

"You can come whenever you want, princess." I lower my head and suck on that soft spot along her neck. Dylan and I focus all our attention on her. I fuck her deeper, he drinks from her hungrily, we pinch and stroke her tits, and we're rewarded for it. She falls apart with a sob, her body going rigid. The sexiest sounds slip out, and she clenches down on my cock.

Knowing the moment's almost over, Dylan lifts his head and redoubles his efforts. I grow still inside her, and I feel Dylan covering every inch he can reach. I haul in a jagged breath and shudder when the tip of his tongue snakes around the base of me.

"Too much, too much, too much..." Gabriella comes down from her high, chanting deliriously under her breath about being too sensitive. She gasps and squirms away from our touches, eventually collapsing onto the mattress. "Oh my God, oh my God." She shivers and curls into a little ball, quick to pull the duvet up to her chin. "I'm out of commission now." Letting out a mewled *ungh* sound, a violent shiver runs through her, and she draws the duvet up higher.

I chuckle huskily, careful when I ease off Dylan's body. Gabriella's got the pout going on when I reveal her flushed face from under the covers, and it's clear she's done for the evening. She looks sufficiently spent and overwhelmed. I dip down and kiss her on the forehead.

"Get some sleep. I'll take care of Dylan."

"But again tomorrow so I can watch, please." She sucks her thumb into her mouth.

I nod and tuck her in. "Sweet dreams, baby."

She exhales the last of her exhaustion and closes her eyes.

I smile at the precious sight of her and then refocus on Dylan. The desire clouding his eyes has been joined by uncertainty, and he's pulled up his covers, too. I lie down next to him, strung tight with need for him, but I'll take it as slowly as he wants.

"We don't have to do anything," he murmurs nervously. "I understand."

I don't think you do.

CHAPTER 12

"You know how to say stop." That's all the warning I manage to give him. I skim my hand up his chest as I shift closer, and then I'm cupping his neck, leaning over him, and covering his mouth with mine.

The raw cravings for him build up until he whimpers, and every emotion gets unleashed. His fingers make their way into my hair, and I push my tongue into his mouth. It's new and familiar at once. I kiss him hard, pouring all my hunger into each touch. I taste him, I taste my sweet girl, and it's not fucking enough.

"I missed you." I palm his cheek, my lips never leaving his. "Christ, I missed you, Dylan."

"So much. I missed you." He groans and tries to pull me closer. "*Cade...* Please, I—"

Being mindful of his leg is becoming second nature, so I move over him with ease and let my hands wander freely, greedily. He pushes away the covers between us as we make out, and I carefully inch down his bottoms. His body is just so fucking... My mouth waters. *Out of this world.* With our cocks lined up, I deepen our kiss and stroke as much of us as I can.

He can never disappear from me again. I won't allow it.

"Tell me what you want right now." I spread the leaking fluids around the heads of us and thrust against him. "Anything you want."

Dylan moans. "I wanna suck you. I think about it all the time. Oh, God."

I hiss a curse, my balls feeling heavier and tighter. "You wanna play our special game?"

His eyes widen, and he nods furiously. "Yeah. Please, Sir—"

I shake my head, grabbing his jaw as I graze my teeth along his lip. "You know who I am, little pan. It's not really Sir, is it?"

He gulps. The insecurities come back with a vengeance. "A-Are you sure?"

I couldn't be surer. "I miss it a fuckload, but I'd respect if you're not—"

"If you miss it half as much as I do..." He releases a breath and kisses me. "I loved being your boy," he whispers. "And calling you Daddy."

I smile against his lips and stroke his cheek. "The best baby boy ever."

"Really?" The light finally returns to his eyes, and he hugs me tight, so rightly. "Best Daddy ever."

I moan gruffly, pushing my cock alongside his so he can feel what Daddy wants to do. "Are you ready to play our game?"

He nods, and he's quick to scoot down the mattress once I've slid off him. "We give each other secret kisses, right? The dirty kind we don't tell others about?"

"That's right." I sit back on my heels and stroke myself. His fingers tremble, and he touches his cock apprehensively, waiting for my command. "God, you're fucking beautiful, Dylan." My free hand ghosts down his abs.

He shivers then grunts when fisting his cock. "I wanna do secret kisses *now*."

Fuck.

"Eager?"

"Yeah," he breathes out.

Loving drawing it out for him, teasing him, I dip low and kiss him one more time. Then I leave a trail of unhurried kisses all over his chest on my way to his perfect cock.

He lets out a short, frustrated whine and jerks his dick impatiently.

When I reach him, I nuzzle the base where he's mostly smooth, warm, and smells of fresh man. I lie down on my side so we can sixty-nine each other, twisting my hips so he doesn't have to move much. Cupping his firm butt, I bury my face against him, breathing him in over and over. His anxious whimpers only make me wanna torture him with anticipation more.

"Fuck." I thread my fingers into his hair at the back of his head as he leans in and laps at my cock. Long, wet licks to trace the vein in the middle, ending with a quick suck at the tip. "You like secret kisses, don't you?"

"They're the best." He grips the root of my shaft and suckles at the slit, memories of him using me as a pacifier rushing back to me. "You smell like..." His cock throbs in my hand, and he whispers the last part while blushing. "Daddy and little sister."

Said little sister makes a couple sleepy sounds behind me.

Unable to wait any longer, I suck Dylan into my mouth. I savor the taste that I've missed as much as his noises. His mouth engulfs me too, and he's a natural cocksucker, insatiable and instinctive.

He moans around me, often flicking the tip of his tongue over my piercing. What he can't fit when I hit the back of his mouth, he creates a tight ring around with his fingers.

"When's the surprise coming?" He hums and sucks me harder, soaking me in his warm mouth. "I want a big surprise."

I chuckle huskily and thrust deeper, hitting the roof of his mouth. Judging from his sounds and the pre-come seeping out from his cock, he got a bit of a surprise right there.

"It won't be much longer, I promise." I suck his smooth balls into my mouth one at a time, stroking his wet cock persistently. The noises of slick come and saliva being rubbed along a hard dick that's about to burst are making my muscles clench. The impending orgasm pools lower and lower, and I stop trying to prolong the moment.

The second he tenses up and gasps, I take him down my throat and swallow around the sensitive head. I both hear and feel him choking on me, and it takes all my strength to keep at it. The sensations are too fucking amazing. I stop breathing, my eyes closing, and lose myself in the pleasure.

Several shots of come flood my mouth. I deserve a fucking medal for not losing my shit, but then it's finally my turn. With his salty, delicious flavor on my tongue, I lose control of everything.

"Daddy's surprise is coming, baby boy," I grit out.

I plant my forehead on his thigh, and with a firm grip on his hair, I rock deep and let go. I become unglued by his slutty sucking, tasting him, feeling him everywhere—Jesus fucking Christ, it's all of him. Only he and Gabriella have this effect on me, and it fucks me up in the best ways possible.

It's a panting Dylan I find when I manage to drag myself back to where a pillow has my name on it. I melt into the mattress and exhale a laugh at the sight of him licking his fingers.

He grins bashfully and turns to press his face against my arm.

"Uh-uh, you're done hiding that gorgeous face from me," I murmur.

He's so unbelievably adorable when he's in his Little mind-set. Acting a few years older than Gabriella, he's more of a cheeky preteen than a child, but he has his moments, usually when he's at his most vulnerable or he's tired, when a shy little boy appears. Shy and fucking filthy.

I cup his cheek and brush my thumb over the smooth skin. His faded blue eyes search mine, his smile curious and soft. I return the smile and kiss him tenderly. I'm surer than ever that Gabriella's right. It's supposed to be the three of us.

"I'm really sorry." He rests his forehead on my chest. His hand, too. "About everything before, I mean. I'm so sorry. I never wanted to hurt you."

I hug him to me and press my lips to his hair. "I know you didn't. And I'm very sorry, too." Thinking back on it now, it's almost surreal. Depending on my mood and how much I've missed him, I've gone from being a bitter old bastard and blaming him for all of it to understanding why he lashed out—and everything in between. "We made mistakes."

He sighs and rolls over, his head on my arm instead, and stares up at the string lights in the corner. "I hosted awesome pity parties for myself for weeks. Then I told my grandpa some of it, and you know what his first question was?"

I shake my head.

"He wondered what happened to easing into things." Dylan sends me a brief, rueful smile. "Technically, I knew we weren't together long, but it didn't *hit* me until then. I felt so stupid. Like, what, I was waiting for grand love gestures?" He rolls his eyes, and I notice they're glistening. "It was just so powerful, those feelings— being with you—that I guess it seemed more than that."

It did, didn't it? It seemed more than that. All the fucking fears, anxiety, and tensions running high, the depression of being away from him... You don't suffer that much unless the feelings involved are enough to bring you to your knees.

I wrap my arms around him, breathing deeply.

I wonder how falling in love with him flew right past me.

"If I could go back in time," I say quietly, "I would've provided more security for you. We never should've started an arrangement that was open; it only left shit more unstable."

He thinks about it, pinching his lips.

"When I offered to help Gabriella, I almost made the same mistake." I'm relieved I didn't let that go too far. I could've ended up ruining that, as well. "We discussed rules and limits but no actual boundaries for whatever we entered. I pulled the same bit on her: let's see what happens, let's not rush."

Thankfully, it happened to be what suited her—both of us—at that time. She was processing her own failed relationship, and I couldn't get past mine. But Gabriella is Gabriella. A girl I've always been fond of, not to mention inexplicably drawn to. In the beginning, it was masked as a need to keep her safe. Now it's clear it's something else entirely.

"Then we learned about your accident," I continue, "and she shut down in an instant, afraid of being cast aside. I'd had it with the charades, so we talked things out pretty quickly, but it could've gone the same way you and I did."

"I'm glad it didn't," he whispers. "You need her in your life."

"I think you do, too." I touch the side of his head and tilt it my way. "You light up when you're around each other."

He bites his lip.

Not saying anything for a while, he shifts close again and wraps his arm around my middle, holding me tightly. I give him a long squeeze too, and he lifts his head to kiss me.

I hum in contentment, the relief continuing to course through me. That discomfort of feeling unsettled eases, and I let my hands wander his sexy body to get a bigger fill. As if he's a drug, touching him and keeping him near bring me comfort.

"If I could go back in time..." He pauses to catch his breath, and I brush my thumb over his thoroughly kissed lips. "I would've been more honest. I shouldn't have lied and pretended it was okay to go from dating to just D/s, and I hope you can forgive me for that. I also hope you can forgive me for going to that party without your permission. It never sat right with me anyway. I was miserable there."

"There's nothing left to forgive, Dylan."

CHAPTER 13

"Breakfast's ready, ya lazy runts." I leave the kitchen and grin at the mess they've made of the bed. Almost naked and surrounded by the blankets they've yanked down from the epic fort days, Gabriella's on her stomach, humming happily while she draws on Dylan's cast. He, in turn, is watching cartoons and absently caressing her thigh.

"We should eat in bed," Gabriella says.

"You think so, huh?" I give her cute ass a smack. "Then we'd be cleaning up your crumbs all day." With a grip on her ankles, I pull her down to the foot of the bed, causing her to squeal, and turn her over onto her back. "You're the messiest, most perfect little girl I could ever dream of. Did I mention messy?"

Her squeals and laughter ring out louder as I dip down and blow raspberries on her stomach.

"Oh my gosh, *stop* it!" she gasps.

"Never," I chuckle, doing it again. Then I hook two fingers below her panties and reveal her pretty little cunt and do it there, too.

A breathy, moaned shriek leaves her.

"Daddy! Ohhh..."

I hum, giving her clit a wet, openmouthed kiss. "Mmm, delicious," I rumble. "Sometimes, Daddy can't help himself." After readjusting her panties, I give her a hand and help her off the bed. She reaches for her pajama top and puts it on. "Go sit down."

"Mm'kay." Skipping has become her normal. I love it.

Next is Dylan, and I join him at his side of the bed so I can assist him to the table. Someone's excited under his boxers.

I guide him to his feet—or foot, as it is—and once he's standing, I peer down at his underwear and raise a brow at him.

"You're hard, baby boy."

He sucks in a breath and nods.

"Why's that?" I grasp his cock firmly, his skin warm and smooth in my hand.

"*Unf*—" He shudders. "It m-made me hot to see you kiss her down there."

I stroke him teasingly and lean in, nuzzling his jaw. He smells of sleep, soap, and sex, and it gets my own cock thickening. "Down where?" I whisper in his ear. "Tell me the truth."

He groans softly, his forehead falling to my collarbone, and he reflexively thrusts into my hand. "Her pussy, Daddy. Okay? You kissed her pussy."

I smile against his neck and drop a kiss there. "Good boy. Let's eat."

When breakfast is over and everyone's gotten ready for the day, we head out. It's Saturday, meaning allowance day, and Gabriella wants to hit up Build-A-Bear for a new stuffie.

Dylan doesn't put up the same fight as she did about accepting some money for fun stuff, mainly 'cause we went over this the first time we got together. With an eye-roll and a timid grin, he thanks me and says he would like to buy something for the club tonight.

We arrive at the mall, and Gabriella runs into the store to find the toy she looked up online earlier. Dylan and I aim for a bench and wait right outside, and I take the opportunity to see if there's a theme or any special event at Switch.

"You might wanna log in and let your friends know you're alive, kiddo," I tell Dylan. Scrolling down the wall of mutual friends, Kayla and Chelsea are two of those who have recently left him messages. "Rio's sub has defended you well." I smile wryly.

He winces and leans his head on my shoulder. "I told her everything when I was still delusional and thought I'd done nothin' wrong."

I chuckle and kiss the top of his head. "Either way, you've got a good friend in her. Let her know you're okay."

He nods. "I'll see her tonight, I think?"

"Doubtful." I show him the screen on my phone so he can see the theme for tonight. Appropriate for us that it's Little Time, not so much for a pain-slut slash slave slash 24/7 submissive.

"That looks *fun*." Dylan smiles widely and grabs my phone. Fucking adorable. He scans the description, the special items on the menu, and the demo listing. "Yeah, no, Chelsea and Master Rio won't be there."

Probably not. Rio's very fond of the Littles in his group of friends, but a whole club of them is a bit too much for him.

Lifting my gaze, I check in on Gabriella, and she's having fun perusing the shelves in the store. She's on the phone too, I'm guessing with Kayla. They like shopping for toys together.

"I'll call her before Switch." Dylan returns my phone, and I pocket it. "Did you see the bar menu? They'll be serving gummy bears with every soda. *And* there's gonna be a chocolate fountain. I remember the last event, there was mostly stuff for *little* Littles, but I can get behind a chocolate fountain, *no* problem."

I laugh, finding his excitement too cute for words. Nick's been hosting more themed nights for Bigs and Littles since he met Kayla, and I'm guessing she's the biggest inspiration when picking activities and so on.

"There's a suggestion box in the lobby, you know." I nudge his shoulder. "Or you can talk to Nicholas. I'm sure he'll be happy to put together something for the boys, too. Or Middles in general."

He grins and looks away. "Mr. Ford says I rile up Kayla."

"Well, you *do.*" I snort a chuckle and throw an arm around his shoulders. "You're a brat, and Nick's the one who has to deal with Kayla's reactions to your bratting." In the corner of my eye, I see Gabriella walking up to the register to pay for her stuffie. *Good Lord.* I clear my throat. "Actually, I take that back. You're the perfect older brother who infuriates the girls with hair pulling, pranks, and general mischief. With that in mind, please lie to your sister and say her new pony is pretty."

Dylan follows my gaze and cracks up.

It *is* funny, but I'm proud of her.

Gabriella's finding herself after John's hell, and she's experimenting to see what fits her. Clothes, hair, style, toys, hobbies—all of it. No longer interested in the classic little-girl items, her wish list at home is packed with alternative options. By alternative, some would say weird as fuck. Like her new purple pony, decked out in a leather jacket, tiara, sparkly tutu, and what look like fake rollerblades.

She doesn't give two shits about matching. She's grabbed the accessories she finds the coolest, and it shows she's a mix of badass and sweetheart. Same with her clothes, where she's often blending cool with cute.

Wicked princess. That's what she told me she wants to be, and she is.

I watch her politely decline a bag for the stuffie, and she automatically gives a small curtsy when she's paid.

Jesus Christ, I love her.

I love her.

Exiting the store, her eyes light up, and she walks quickly

toward us. Her smile becomes smaller, as if she's nervous about our reactions. She knows her choices are a little out there by comparison. I'm just stoked she doesn't care about following. She's creating her own path.

"Look what I got." She sits down next to me and holds up the pony. "What do you think?"

I grin faintly and reach out to touch the shiny, cotton-stuffed rollerblades. "It's perfect for you, princess."

Dylan bobs his head, this time pinching his lips for other reasons than being lost in thought. "Pretty. Very, uh, *unique*."

I do the sighing in my head.

There's no way Gabriella buys that, but it's evidently my lucky day and I'm spared any Little drama.

"All right, Dylan's next. PJs for Switch, yeah?" I stand up and hand him his crutches. "Anything else you wanna get, Gabriella?"

She shakes her head. "No, Sir. The rest goes into my piggy bank." Next, she stands up on her toes to whisper in Dylan's ear. "We gots to save for Daddy's birthday, don't forget."

I pretend I didn't hear that and direct my smile at the nearest shop window instead.

"Duh, like I'll forget that," Dylan whispers back.

After scanning my membership tag at Switch, I help Dylan set up a new account. He's just offered his driver's license when Gabriella scans hers and the blip goes off.

Dylan thinks it's hilarious that she's the latest kinky criminal, and I, personally, think it's hilarious that he's being a brat. Maybe I'll get to punish him tonight. There's something I've been meaning to try, and I need a disobedient sub for that.

"Daddy, Dylan's being a meanie." Gabriella scowls.

"And you're a rat." Dylan shakes his head.

I suppress my amusement and hand Gabriella her bag so she

can go change. Dylan arrived in PJ bottoms and can simply remove his tee. The princess couldn't exactly get here in her pink, very see-through camisole, a matching thong, and her bunny slippers.

She takes off to the changing room, and I lean a shoulder against the wall, hands in the pockets of my jeans.

"What did I tell you about being nice, little pan?" I ask.

"Sorry." Dylan chews on his lip, struggling to kill his mischievous grin. "It's just funny to tease her. She gets so mad."

This is where I'm stuck. I get off on their playful rivalry—hell, so do they—so it's near impossible for me to prevent it, or even try. There's no will for it.

"It's your ass that gets it." I shrug.

By the time Gabriella comes back, Dylan's a member of Switch again, a handful of kinksters have welcomed him back and expressed their well-wishes for a speedy recovery, and he's managed to mention the chocolate fountain twice.

Two Doms openly eye-fuck my girl as she shuffles close to me, not that I can blame them. She's sin personified.

"Gorgeous, baby."

"Christ, Gabriella," Dylan mumbles.

She blushes and grabs my hand.

"Come on, you two." I have a booth in mind. Dylan's pain hasn't been too brutal today, which is a relief, though he's been on his feet most of the day, and I can tell he's tired.

Nicholas has been shopping. Half the dance floor in the Club is now a playground, complete with tunnels to squirm through, a couple portable sex swings on stands, rocking horses with dildos, mattresses and pillows for wrestling and pillow fights, and a station for body painting.

What's been left of the dance floor is covered in balloons, and Littles hop around and dance among the strobe lights in various states of undress.

How the hell are the Doms gonna be able to control their Littles here?

"Oh. My. Gosh!" Gabriella stiffens and covers her mouth, eyes wide and taking in her surroundings.

She's not the only one excited. More people pour into the club, and several squeals ring out. There's the usual music playing, though not nearly as loud.

Dylan smiles. "Where's the chocolate fountain?"

I let out a laugh and point toward the bar. "Right there." Mark's behind it, and he's not alone. He's got Brayden working with him tonight. Either Evangeline is at home, or she's around here somewhere.

"Daddy, can I play?" Gabriella begins tugging on my hand. "Please, pretty please? I'll be so good."

I spot Kayla by the body painting and nod in that direction. "If you stay by Kayla, you can go. I gotta be able to see you at all times, though."

"Yes, Sir, thank you, thank you." She hops up and gives me a peck on the cheek, and then she's gone. "Kayla!"

So much for her revealing Dylan as a big surprise.

"Looks like it's just you and me, beautiful boy." I usher him to an empty booth where he can put his leg up and get comfortable. "What do you want to drink?" I slide in after him and nod at a waitress.

"Cherry Coke, please." He shrugs out of his T-shirt while I set aside his crutches. "Can I have some marshmallows from the fountain, too?"

"Yeah, of course." There're a few subs running fruits and candy through the drizzling chocolate right now, so I'll make sure he'll get the chance to do that when he's rested. The waitress comes over, and I order a beer for myself, Dylan's Cherry Coke and sweets, and Gabriella's Fanta.

It's not long after that I see Nicholas heading over. He stops the waitress on the way, says something to which she nods, and then he joins us with a warm smile.

"This is a pleasant surprise. Good to have you home again,

Dylan."

"Thank you, Sir." Strobe lights briefly hit his face before moving on, revealing a ghost of a blush on his cheeks. "I'm lucky they wanted me back."

"We're lucky, too." I stroke his leg under the table.

"Less happy to hear about your accident." Nick's forehead creases, and he eyes Dylan's leg that's propped up on the seat. "You'll make a full recovery, I hope?"

Dylan phrases his words for a beat before answering. "Kind of," he says slowly. "With some career changes, it'll be good. I'm motivated."

His hands find mine, and I bring it to my mouth for a kiss.

"That's good. You know we're here for you." Nick adjusts his tie and turns to me. "What do you guys think of my last event?"

"Last?" My brow furrows. "You've created heaven on earth for these brats. If you rip it away, I'm gonna have to think you're a bit of a Sadist, buddy."

He chuckles and runs a hand through his hair. "No, this one's staying. It's only the last one I plan. I don't have the time anymore, so Kayla's starting a committee and taking over this part."

That makes sense. Nick owns five or six clubs in the Bay Area, this one being his baby. It's his only fetish club, and he has his main office here. Despite that he has people managing the clubs for him, I reckon he's drowning in work anyway.

Nick nods at Dylan. "You should join the event planning, little one. If Kayla's in charge by herself, it'll be like this every night." He smirks while I chuckle. "I told her she'd have to include Doms and subs who're into kinks that scare her, too. That was a fun day."

Oh, I bet.

The waitress returns with our drinks as well as a bowl of Twizzlers that gets Dylan excited. Then as he's munching on marshmallows and licorice, he nervously asks Nicholas if it's all right if he still attends the wedding.

My buddy shrugs, removing garnish from his vodka. "As far as

I'm concerned, nothing's changed. You've been on the guest list since you RSVP'd. I assume you'll be staying with your Daddy and sister?"

"Yes, Sir," Dylan replies.

"Then there's no problem." Nick smiles.

"Eeeep! *Dylan!*" That would be Kayla, who's spotted Dylan now. With Gabriella in tow, she runs over to our table. The bratty sweetheart has glitter all over her face, and her fingertips are covered in paint. "Gabriella *just* told me you were here!"

My princess twirls a pink streak in her hair with a sheepish expression. "I forgot—I got so excited by the body paint."

Kayla tosses her a frustrated look. "When people you love come home, you *tell* your friends!"

"Easy there, baby girl." Nicholas's eyes show the mirth his tone doesn't.

"Well, I told you now," Gabriella says. "Daddy, can I go back to the playground? I picked out a cool butterfly to paint on my cheek."

"You can wait for Kayla," I reply.

"But, *why*? I'll be right over there." She points.

I shrug, draping an arm along the back of the booth. "You're still banned, hon. Doesn't leave a lot of wiggle room for complaints. Either you go with your friend, or you don't go at all."

I don't believe for a second she'll do anything wrong, but consequences are consequences. She'll take them.

"I'm almost finished here," Kayla promises. "I just gots to get past these domly types who are blocking me from hugging Dylan."

Nicholas and I exchange a smile, and we offer Kayla mild looks of confusion.

"I don't see how we're in the way, Kayla," I say.

"Me either." Nick shakes his head. "If you want to hug your friend, there's a clear path right here." He pats the table.

That flusters Kayla, and she tugs on her tiny dress. Barely covering her butt as it is, she knows she'll flash the club if she gets on the table.

Dylan snickers and hugs his bowl to him.

"That's so cruel," Kayla huffs. "Aren't they mean, Gabriella?"

"The meanest of them all," she sings. *Keep it up, girl.* "Sometimes, I wanna spank them and say, 'Bad Daddy!'"

The girls fucking lose it, bending over in laughter and wheezing out "Bad Daddy!" over and over.

"If that's not inspiring, I don't know what is," Nicholas drawls.

Yeah, couldn't agree more. I guess it won't be Dylan who gets it tonight. That's okay, I can try public plug fucking on him another time.

"They're in trouble, aren't they?" Dylan's practically vibrating in his seat. "Can I watch?"

"Everyone can watch. Excuse me, I'll be right back." Nicholas leaves the table.

I *think* he and I are on the same page, 'cause the girls made it so easy for us, so I take it from there.

"Are you done laughing?" I ask them.

Gabriella's all attitude tonight, and she holds up a finger, silently saying almost.

She's putting me on hold...

Swiftly leaving the booth, I stun her to silence when I grab her neck and roughly push her facedown onto the table. I tighten my grasp on her delicate neck and speak in her ear.

"Are you done now?"

She gulps and nods jerkily.

"Good." I straighten and move my beer out of the way. "Both of you, drop your panties and bend over the table."

The laughter has stopped, and so have a few fellow club goers in view of our table. Watching punishments is always popular.

Nicholas returns with a black marker, and he gets down on one knee to write on Kayla's ass.

"I've been a bad girl. Spank me, please!" is written across her cheeks.

I laugh, and it's my turn with the marker. The girls aren't happy campers anymore, squirming and apologizing for all they're worth.

"Hold still, Gabriella," I reprimand. She whimpers in defeat and stays still so I can write, "Spank the bad baby slut."

Satisfied, Nick and I appreciate our work for a moment before we sit down to return to our conversation. We pretend the girls aren't even there, only acknowledging the Tops and bottoms who come over to ask if they really can spank our Littles.

"Have at it, gentlemen." Nicholas inclines his head. "They don't have the highest thresholds for pain, but make it count."

"You're not for real."

"Why, what's so strange about it?" Nick furrows his brow.

Dylan and I glance at each other, and he shrugs, so maybe it's just me?

I shake my head and lean back a bit. "I wouldn't care if I was the groom, but as your buddy, I feel like you're robbing your friends of the sheer joy that comes with bachelor parties."

I almost miss Nick's chuckled response because Gabriella and Kayla are crying so loudly, though I manage to get the gist. I get it, a joint party before the wedding would give us kinky strippers in the form of our partners, but I don't know. It's *tradition*.

Simon thanks us for letting him warm up by spanking the girls, and then he guides his sub into the Cave. Dante's next, and he doesn't go easy on either of them.

Gabriella screams out her anguish, so I tilt to the side to get a good look at her ass. It's only beginning to turn purple, and she bruises easily.

"I'm s-sorry," she sobs.

The tabletop fogs up with every choked breath where they have their mouths, and drops of saliva and tears spot the surface.

ping and rolls the rubber down his cock. "You're not so concerned about her pain now, are you?"

Dylan purses his lips, thinking. "I'll care a lot when I'm done, I swear."

I laugh as I help Gabriella climb over me.

The tears haven't stopped streaming down by the time she carefully squats over Dylan's cock and takes him inside, her back to his chest. She flinches when he grabs two fistfuls of her ass to guide her up and down on his cock, and she screws her eyes closed.

It's a sexy goddamn sight, and it's to the sounds of Nicholas belting his girl and the peals of laughter ringing out from kinksters having fun that I watch my two Littles fuck.

I'm not the only one watching, but the others fade away. The second Dylan reaches for me, I'm there to cup his cheek and kiss him. Wanting pleasure to win over the pain, I find my way between Gabriella's thighs and stroke her little clit. Her cries become breathier, and she asks if she can turn around.

That works great for me, actually. In the new position, her ass will rub against Dylan's thighs even more. She regrets asking the second time Dylan thrusts into her sweet pussy and grinds to get deeper.

"Ow, ow, ow—it hurts, Dylan!"

"No," he groans. "It feels so fucking good. Please don't make me stop, Daddy."

"You don't have to stop."

I don't *ever* want to stop this.

"Come here, both of you." I go from kissing Dylan to kissing Gabriella, and they inch closer to each other. I hear how her breathing changes, I taste the remnants of her tears, and then it's the three of us kissing. It's wet, sloppy, and fucking fantastic.

Behind me, Nicholas rolls on a condom and slams his cock inside Kayla, who screams in both pleasure and pain. The sound, the tension, all of it, flows between us and drives me batshit. I rub

Gabriella's clit in tight circles, spurring her on to want more. It shows whenever she takes Dylan deeper and tries to move faster.

"Close," he gasps.

"Fill her." I graze my teeth along his jaw, my fingers working Gabriella's clit harder. "Come, sweetheart."

He loses control and thrusts upward once, twice, three more times before a long moan leaves him.

Gabriella follows moments later when I pinch her soaked clit and slip a finger inside her ass.

There's no release for me, yet it's strangely satisfying to see them collapse against one another. It also means I get to be greedy and selfish when we get home, and I plan on making the night last.

CHAPTER 14

Unfortunately, Dylan's trip here doesn't last. Despite that it's a temporary break, it leaves a rock in my stomach. He and I sit at the kitchen table; the sun's about to rise, and Gabriella's asleep.

"You look so broody." Dylan tries to keep things light.

"I don't like it." I stare down into my coffee mug, my mind going to everything that can go wrong. "It'd be easier if it was only three or four days. This is three weeks we're talking about."

It's the season for swim meets and tryouts, and he's following each event on his phone, often ending up withdrawing. Now he's going back to Texas, where I won't be able to pick him up when he's down.

I can't even imagine going from having everything figured out to being pushed back to square one. Not about something as big as one's career, which has been his dream for fifteen years. And even though he fights to stay motivated most of the time, there are going to be moments everything crashes down around him. I've seen it firsthand, in glimpses. He hasn't opened up fully yet. He'll save that for when he's alone.

"A lot is happening right now," he says quietly. "I think...maybe it'll be good? You and Gabriella can take this time to process everything."

That right there. He retreats so we can make sure we know what we want.

We already know. "We're done thinking. You belong here with us." I won't have him leaving today believing he's only a plaything we invite to our relationship. "This isn't temporary, Dylan."

I fucking *see* that he doesn't dare hope it's true.

Shifting in his seat, he keeps his gaze on the table, and he fidgets with his ticket. "I'm not in a good place," he whispers. "I'm tired. I get angry a lot. No one wants that." It's not the first time he's hinted at being a burden. "Isn't it better I return when I feel like a person again? Then you can know what you're getting yourselves into."

I shake my head, though I don't reply verbally. Mere words won't shake his belief, so I'll have to show him.

"I want to show you somethin'." He pushes his chair out a bit and rolls up the sweat pants to reveal his cast. "I want this more than anything."

He shows me what Gabriella has drawn, images I haven't looked at very closely until now. I lean closer to see beautiful illustrations of the *little things*. The sun shining on three animated characters, the guy in the middle tall and smiling at the other two. The girl is holding a stuffie, and the boy is laughing, holding an ice cream cone. The design is innocent and childlike, though unmistakably professional and flawless. Gabriella has created a tattoo sleeve in anime. A background image of the Golden Gate Bridge stands out between the three of us along with a Santa's bag that is brimming. A flogger hangs over the edge, a teddy bear sits at the top, I see a set of cuffs, a blindfold, and a hula-hoop.

She hasn't strayed from the Japanese style of anime, and that includes several signs I don't understand.

"What does it say here?" I ask, ghosting a finger across a banner.

The entire cast is filled. A swimmer in the ocean, three puzzle pieces connected, illustrated candy, more Japanese signs, balloons shaped like bloated stars, a bicycle, a pair of running shoes…

"I asked her," he murmurs. "It translates roughly to 'Daddy's boy, naughty and nice.'"

Someone's studying Japanese styles at the tattoo shop, I'm guessing. She has an eye for it.

"It's beautiful." I tap the puzzle pieces before sitting back in my chair again.

He nods, studying the artwork. "I want this so much, Cade. And I don't want to ruin it before it even has a chance to begin."

His mind is set. Stubborn kid. Again, I'll show him otherwise. He won't ruin anything.

"Here's the thing, Dylan," I tell him. "I make the decisions in this household, and I think you'll be away from us too long. Mexico's three weeks away, so I'll give you ten days. Then you'll be here with Devil. It'll give you plenty of time to wrap things up in Texas and have your belongings shipped."

He didn't see that coming, and he gets flustered and ready to protest.

"It's not a suggestion." I stand up and ruffle his hair on my way to the fridge. "Your recovery comes first, but Gabriella and I will be here every step of the way. Good times and bad. You will be home in ten days, end of discussion."

Taken aback, he has no response.

With Dylan back in Texas and Gabriella pulling long hours at the tattoo shop, I'm left alone to work and make plans for the future. I'm more driven than ever to turn my place into a home for all of us, and it's time to make some changes around the house.

In three days, I have my entire backyard torn up, and I call my uncle to help me out with things I can't do on my own or purchase ready-made. My uncle disapproves of the latter, saying *ready-made* as if it tastes like poison.

I chuckle. I can't blame him, but I want this done quickly. Dylan and Gabriella should have their own space for when they want privacy. Since I can't build them their own rooms, playhouses for the backyard will do. That's the ready-made part. Two little cottages will be delivered and assembled while we're in Mexico. They're not big, only 170 square feet each, though I reckon my Littles will be able to fill them with what they want.

I'll build a shelving system for Gabriella so she can put all her research and sketchbooks someplace. She comes home with new books every day.

Dylan works out a lot, so I'll have a chin-up bar installed, along with a built-in space for his kettlebells and whatnot.

"Pastels. One gray, one purple..." My uncle's muttering to himself, scanning my order for the two sheds. Or he's studying the image of the aforementioned sheds. They do look like mini cottages. They'll sit nicely in the corner of the backyard. "Freakin' porches, all idyllic-looking. Son, are you having kids, or is this a kinky thing? Don't tell me I'm building a jungle gym."

I laugh and put my pen behind my ear. "No, that's not why I called you." I ignore the kinky remark. He and my aunt are swingers, so they're close enough to our lifestyle to know I'm a Daddy Dom. He likes to make digs. "I want a deck right here." I gesture to where we're standing behind the house. "And stairs from there." I point up to my bedroom window. "To reach the backyard now, we gotta go down the front and through my workshop. If we build stairs, we'll have better access."

"All right." He starts taking notes on what needs to be done. "Elevated deck?"

I nod. "And I want windows and a patio door installed on the first floor." The house wasn't built to be a home, but as the area gentrified, I was able to get it rezoned. It was first and foremost an auto shop, so the big garage door on this side has to go. By the time it's done, I wanna be able to look out the window from my workshop and see Dylan and Gabriella in the yard.

I see it clearly, what I want, and I'm not letting go of that image this time.

"Big plans," my uncle notes. "It'll look good. Anything else?"

Yeah. A hot tub or a pool. Trees and bushes along the wooden fence. A lawn for future play parties. A hammock for me. A grill and a seating area. Better access to the roof than a simple ladder, since the princess has claimed the spot as hers. A doghouse for Devil. But, one thing at a time.

"It's a good start." I slap him on the back. "Beer?"

"Let me help you." I leave the shop and walk out to the driveway where Gabriella's hauling grocery bags out of my truck. "I thought we were going grocery shopping tomorrow."

"No." She grunts as she sets a case of my favorite beer on the ground. "I gots a bone to pick with you, mister."

"That so?" I drop a kiss at the top of her head before taking over. She's dyed her hair again, and these days it only makes me smile. Even if it's green. Or as she calls it, teal.

"Yeah, a big bone." She huffs and closes the door. "Remember what you told me the other day after your uncle left?"

Sure. I suggested it's time she consider giving up her apartment —or the one she's sharing with four others. Gabriella got misty-eyed and proceeded to show me—more than once—what she thought of the idea. Before we crashed, I had to change the sheets.

"About the apartment?" I grab what I can, and we head for the stairs.

"Yes, Sir. And it got me thinking." She rushes up ahead of me with her backpack and one of the grocery bags. "If we're really going to be living together, I will put my foot down about money. You have to let us pitch in with what we can."

This shit again.

"I talked to Dylan earlier," she goes on, "and we decided that I will pay for food and he will cover half the bills. I'll do more once I get paid—"

"That's ridiculous—"

"It's been decided, Daddy!" she snarls. Oh, boy. The princess is feisty today. "This is a fight you can't win. You're doing so much for us. We're helping." Next, she mocks me by using an adorably gruff voice. "End of discussion."

My mouth twitches, and I leave the groceries on the kitchen table. She and I are having dinner with Rio and Chelsea tonight, and I think I'll ask him for some pro tips on how to intimidate a snarling Little.

"We can talk about this later," I say. "I'll get the rest of the groceries. You get ready for dinner."

She juts her chin and saunters toward the bathroom. "Like I said, end of discussion."

I can't help but grin.

We arrive at Rio and Chelsea's in Sausalito around eight, and it bothers me I haven't heard from Dylan yet. I work from home, so I can take calls pretty much whenever, which is why I told him to call me when he had time—at least once a day. It's been more than that; he usually calls first thing in the morning and then sometime in the afternoon. Except for today.

Gabriella's spoken to him, though. I guess that's something.

Four days to go, and then he'll have been away for ten days. I can't wait to see him again.

Leaving the truck, I type out a quick text to him.

Thinking of you, sweetheart. Call me when you can.

I pocket my phone and ring the doorbell, Gabriella twirling her hair nervously.

"Master Rio is scary," she whispers.

I smirk lazily. "Scarier than me?"

"Well, no. You can do stuff. But he has a torture dungeon, and what if you want to borrow it sometime?"

I nod slowly. "True. That could happen."

She snaps her mouth shut, having not expected me to say that, and then Chelsea opens the door.

It's supposed to be a casual dinner, so I'm not sure why she's quick to lower her gaze and kneel on the floor. That kind of behavior causes Gabriella to regress a bit.

"Hi, Miss Chelsea," she says shyly.

I jerk my chin at Rio. "What's up, buddy?"

He stands in the foyer, hands in the pockets of his slacks. "My pet has something to say before we eat, if that's all right."

"Sure." I let Gabriella enter before me, and I pull off my hoodie.

"Mr. Kingsley, I owe you an apology." Chelsea keeps looking down, and she picks anxiously at the hem of her skirt. "I'm so happy to be talking to Dylan again, and he—and Master—explained everything to me. I shouldn't have made a judgment on your character. It wasn't my place, and I'm very sorry."

I exchange a look with Rio and raise a brow, to which he inclines his head.

Taking a step forward, I gently grasp Chelsea's chin and make her look me in the eye. "Water under the bridge, sub. Dylan's lucky to have friends that loyal."

She smiles carefully, her silvery violet eyes filling with relief. "Thank you, Sir."

I smile back and help her to her feet, and it ends the formality of the night. We're here for pizza on the patio and to discuss our gift to Nick and Kayla, not watch our lovely s-types stare at the floor.

Those s-types of ours get bossy when it comes to gifts, though. They shoot down every idea Rio and I have.

"We can't do that, Master!" Chelsea exclaims.

Gabriella giggles behind her hand, and I wink at her.

"Why not?" Rio frowns and grabs another slice. "When you and I get married, I'd be thrilled if my mates gave us a pillory. I don't have one yet."

That makes Chelsea flush.

"Hold on." I lick grease off my fingers and retrieve my phone. "I *feel* like that can be arranged, so I'm taking notes."

"See? Cade's a good friend," Rio says.

Chelsea groans while the princess laughs.

"What're Mark and his two giving the newlyweds?" I wonder.

Chelsea answers. "They've arranged for Mr. Ford and Kayla to have a vacation at Master Cooper's house in La Jolla. It'll be so cool. They've set up activities for them, couple's massages, wine tasting, catered breakfast every morning, dinner on the beach, and a brand-new collection of sex toys for them to have fun with."

So that's why Evangeline emailed me. She asked if I work with leather too, which I do, and so she wondered if I could make a suede flogger. The soft material makes more sense now that it'll belong to Kayla and not Evangeline.

"They travel a lot," Gabriella mentions. "Should we pitch in and give them a trip?"

That topic leads to a BDSM cruise, and the girls say they would love to go on that as well. In the end, we make loose plans to go on a cruise next year, and we still have no idea what to give Kayla and Nick.

We've finished our food, the girls have crawled up into our laps, the beer is cold, and other than that lingering concern for Dylan, it's a fucking great evening. Speaking of him...

"Dylan suggested separate gifts," I say. "One for Kayla and one for Nicholas."

"That *would* be easier," Rio notes. "I assume most guests will give them typical couple gifts, but they're still two people."

That gets the ball rolling, and two beers later, we have a list of things to put together into two gift baskets for our friends. And, in my humble opinion, what Rio and I came up with for Nick beats what the girls picked for Kayla.

"Another beer, mate?" Rio asks.

"Sounds good." I nod and lift Gabriella off me. "I'm just gonna take a leak."

I follow Rio inside and steer right toward the guest bath. I've closed the door behind me, about to unzip my pants, when my phone rings, and I get a call from Dylan that cuts the night short.

"What's wrong?" Worry spikes as I hear him sniffling.

"I-I don't feel so good," he croaks.

Early the next morning, I pull up outside Nicholas and Kayla's house.

"Princess. We're here." I unbuckle her seat belt and round the car to help her out. She blinks sleepily and rubs her eyes. "Want me to carry you?"

She nods and sucks her bottom lip into her mouth. She's been on the verge of tears since last night but has kept it together so far, probably because I'm going to handle it.

I shoulder her backpack and pick her up, positioning her on my hip.

Nick opens the door before I can knock. Clad in sweats, an expression of concern, and his hair disheveled from sleep, he lets us in before the two cats can escape.

"Thanks again for letting her stay here," I say.

"Of course, of course." He takes a step back as I get Gabriella on her feet. "How are you feeling, little one?"

"I miss my brother," she mumbles. "He's being such a dummy. I *told* him not to go to Texas."

The corners of my mouth twist up, and Nick smiles.

"Good thing your Daddy's bringing him home then, huh?" He accepts Gabriella's backpack. "I've set up a guest room for you, and I thought I'd take you girls to the zoo later."

"Won't that be fun, baby?" I comb back her wild hair with my fingers. She smiles, more genuinely this time, and nods. "I appreciate this, buddy," I tell Nicholas. Understatement, really. "More than I can say." Gabriella's a grown woman, but thanks to him, she can stay in her preferred mind-set while I go get Dylan. "If there's anything you need, call me right away."

"It's no problem at all," he assures me, giving the princess a wink. "Kayla's been itching to have a sleepover." His gaze returns to me with an easy smirk. "If they're occupying the guest room with ice cream and movies, maybe I can get the downstairs TV for myself and watch a game."

I laugh quietly, completely with him on that one. When football season starts, it'll be good for my two to have their own space, 'cause I won't be so generous with the remote.

"Okay, I'm gonna go so I don't miss my flight." I cup Gabriella's cheeks and give her a kiss. "Be a good girl for Mr. Ford, yeah?"

"I will, Daddy," she promises. "Text me lots with updates, and don't forget emojis."

I chuckle and kiss those soft lips again. "I'll include a bunch."

CHAPTER 15

Stressed out and exhausted, I arrive back in Texas and the suburb where Dylan's expecting me. Even his grandmother is. I spoke to her briefly last night. I'm relieved Dylan reached out, considering his recent past of not wanting to be a burden. Then when he was too upset to talk, Rose took over.

All his sponsors have dropped him.

Dylan knew it was coming, but it hit him hard, and no one can blame him. Retiring from his dream career was bad enough. Now he's been forced to accept calls and terminations of contracts, each one having clauses for this particular event, if he sustained injuries or otherwise that threatened his performance.

Of course, he feels like he's been kicked to the curb.

I park the rental outside their house, my chest tightening at the sight of Dylan waiting for me on the porch. He looks small and lost, barely holding it together. The smile he gives me as I head toward him is wobbly and pained.

Last night, he told me I didn't have to come. That's not why he called. He only wanted to hear my voice. Thank fuck I didn't listen to him.

"Hi." His eyes shine, which he tries to blink away.

"Hey, little pan." I sit down next to him and hug him tightly, and he shudders. The levees break.

He hugs me back and cries silently. I stroke him along his spine, kiss the side of his head, and I *don't* tell him it's okay. Things are far from okay, and the boy needs to grieve.

"I don't wanna stay here." He whimpers and covers his face with his hands.

"That's good, 'cause I'm bringing you home." I smooth back his messy hair and press my lips to his temple. "I'll make reservations for a hotel downtown. We'll go out and have a nice meal, and then we're going home first thing in the morning. We can arrange for Devil to come home after we've been in Mexico." That was the original plan, anyway. "How's that?"

He nods and wipes at his cheeks. "I'm so fucking sick of it. I feel worthless."

It's gutting, seeing him this way. "That's bullshit. We're putting you to work as soon as we get home."

I haven't suffered a fraction of the pain he's in, but I know him. He needs to feel useful and accomplish something to get well. I know, 'cause I'm exactly the same.

He's gotten rid of one of the crutches. His knee is in a brace, and he's walking with a customized shoe that lessens the impact of every step, much like a walking cast. We can ease him into a new routine of work and more rehab.

"I'll always need help in the workshop," I murmur. "You can take over local deliveries for me. Save me from hiring companies I don't trust, anyway. Nick needs more DMs, too. Then when you feel better, we can revisit the triathlon idea."

It's not a time to encourage him to let go and say Daddy's got this. He needs to recover as a man first. A young, beautiful man with the attitude of a warrior. It's in there somewhere.

"It seems so farfetched. Me, as a triathlete?" He snorts quietly and wipes away another set of tears. "I don't know."

"Is it a field that would work for you?" I wonder.

He shrugs with one shoulder. "I mean, it's a cool sport. I'm sure it'd be lots of fun—challenging as fuck—but I don't see myself being very good at it."

"Well, I see it." I smile faintly and kiss his knuckles.

Dylan sniffles, his head hitting my shoulder. "How?"

"Because I know you." I rub his neck soothingly, resting my cheek at the top of his head. "I've seen you work. I believe in you."

He shivers and lets me comfort him for a while. I catch movement behind the curtains in the living room window, so I'm guessing Rose is giving us a moment. She's a nice lady, one I've spoken to a few times, though I've never met her.

"Cade?" Dylan murmurs nervously. "I don't know the exact parameters of our relationship, but I'm-I'm in love with you."

I swallow hard, and then I'm the one blinking back emotions. Kissing him deeply, I get my shit together and take immense pleasure at having another few bricks set in place to solidify our future. The relief is indescribable.

"I'm in love with you too, Dylan." I kiss his cheeks, the tip of his nose, and his eyelids. And his face breaks out in a timid, hopeful smile. "I've loved you for longer than I've known."

"Really?" He licks his lips, eyes searching mine. "And Gabby? I mean, is it okay I like her, too?" I nod, about to answer, when he goes on. "It's been eating me up alive, because I loved you so much when I left, but-but I was feeling differently about her, too."

I can tell it's been on his mind for a long time. It all comes out in an adorable verbal vomit, but I don't care about the past anymore. I've dwelled too much on it.

"You have absolutely no reason to feel bad, baby boy." I give him a solid squeeze, too relieved for words. "I love you both with all that I am, and those parameters you mentioned say you're stuck with me now. On every level. It's us three."

That's one load off his chest, and he slumps against me with a soft smile.

"I love that you're mine again," I whisper in his hair. "This time, we're not letting go."

"Never."

Dylan and I check in to a hotel in the city that evening, and our plan is to go home the following day. That is, until Gabriella sends me a photo with the caption, "I hope this makes you smile, Daddy. I miss you both!"

It's a sketch. I asked her to draw me a tattoo design, and that's exactly what she's done. Much like her own slutty princesses, she's followed that theme and drawn Peter Pan, arms crossed, wearing low-riding PJ bottoms and a cocky smirk, his signature hat tilted. He hovers above the dark silhouette of a princess crown, and "Let them never grow up" is written in a faint cloud of what I assume is pixie dust.

The princess is fucking amazing.

I grin. How she can capture both the badass and the playful is beyond me.

I think Dylan can see the wheels spinning in my head and where my mind is at, because he limps over to the bed and unzips his bag. Then he pulls out his cast.

"You saved it?" I pocket my phone again.

He nods, pensive. "What she drew on it—I'm getting it inked on my leg. I've already had a stencil drawn up. A friend of mine from the team, his brother is a tattoo artist."

"Wow, really? That will be sexy as hell." I join him and eye the sawed-up cast. "Which leg?"

"I was thinking my bad one at first." He sits down on the bed and sets the cast next to him. "But...well, if I'm going to become this cool triathlete..." I smile at that, proud of him and his will to fight. "My knee can be good enough. I can go far, but it will never be perfect. I'll probably always wear a supportive sleeve, and I'll want the ink to show."

"Makes sense." I sit down next to him, giving his good knee a squeeze. "It'll be better, anyway. You know chicks dig scars."

He laughs and head-butts my shoulder. "As long as you and Gabby dig them, I'm good."

Better than good.

"So here's the thing," he says, clearing his throat. "I wasn't gonna do this until next week, but if we pay extra, maybe my buddy's brother can reschedule and fit us in tomorrow?"

I scratch my eyebrow, thinking it through. It would be a cool surprise for Gabriella, who's already gotten inked for us, and I'm sure she wouldn't mind extending her sleepover with Kayla. Additionally, it'll be nice spending some quality time with my boy before we head home. I think we need it.

"You call your friend, I'll change our flights," I say.

"Morning, Daddy."

I smile into the pillow, feeling his curious fingers wandering along my spine. "Good morning, baby boy."

I tense up, fully prepared for it to have been a dream. Until I feel his fingers again, wandering up and down my back. *It's real.* I roll over and bury my face against his neck, where he smells of sleep and boy.

"Morning, little pan," I whisper in my morning voice.

"You just said that." He laughs softly. "I got you coffee, by the way. I had a big hot chocolate."

"Of course you did." I hum in contentment, feeling him up because I can. "Thank you for the coffee. That's sweet of you." A glance at the clock tells me we have an hour before we need to get ready. My morning wood pokes him in his stomach, so I reckon he knows how I wanna spend that time.

I have time for a few sips of my coffee, too.

"I miss your surprises," he confesses and presses his face into his pillow. "I've practically become a virgin again."

That makes me laugh into my mug, and I return it to the night-stand and then roll half on top of him. "It's been a week, you poor, deprived thing." My lips trace the definition of his shoulder blade. "Should Daddy reintroduce you to everything?" I won't say no to sexy-as-hell role-play with my boy.

"Yes, please." There's excitement in his muffled voice. "I know nothing about grown-up fun at all."

Fair enough.

Reaching behind me, I grab my wallet and retrieve a single-use packet of lube for later. When I ask if he wants me to remove my piercing for now, he admits he's been fantasizing about it. So that's a no. The boy wants to get fucked and have his prostate rubbed by my apadravya.

I don't wanna come off as an impatient teenager with stamina issues, so I ease us into our little morning game. Lying on our sides, close enough for me to feel his body heat under the covers, I ask if he's nervous about today. Not only is it his first tattoo, but it's a big project that will take hours.

"It will be worth it." He tucks his hands underneath his cheek and blinks sleepily. "I thought the chocolate was going to give me a sugar coma, but I could nap."

I smile and push back his hair gently, loving seeing him this way. With tough times ahead as he gets better and better, it's nice knowing there will be moments where he's serene, too.

"I love you, Daddy," he yawns.

"I love you, too—forever and ever." I inch closer and give his cheek a lingering kiss. "You always smell so good." I nuzzle his jawline, drawing out a lazy snicker from him. "It makes me wanna taste."

"You're too funny," he laughs. "You can't taste me."

I reach his neck, his skin soft and warm, and the kiss I drop there is more sensual. "Looks like I can." I suck lightly on his flesh, to which he inhales sharply.

"Wh-what're you doing?" His gaze flicks with heat and nervousness as I push down the covers to expose his upper body.

"I'm admiring my boy. I can do that, can't I?" I trail a hand over his chest, feeling slight tremors coming from him. "Getting a tattoo is a very grown-up thing to do, so I think it's time I teach you a bit about other grown-up stuff. To do that, I need to see you."

"I'm right here." He grins curiously.

"All of you," I reply pointedly. "These are in the way." I yank back the covers from him completely, revealing he's hard, naked, and covering his crotch poorly with both hands. "You're not allowed to hide from me, you know that."

Even his chest tints darker. "But it's...you know. I can't help it. It happens sometimes."

"What happens sometimes?" I stroke his thigh, focused on his hidden cock. Jesus, I want to swallow him whole.

"I get hard down there," he whispers and throws an arm over his face. It lets me see a bit more of his erection, and I close the distance to lie right next to him. "Something's poking me."

I smirk to myself. "It happens sometimes."

"Is that—" He lifts his head to look, though he can't see much. My cock is trapped against his hip.

"Show me, sweetheart. Remove your hand."

He obeys reluctantly and tilts his head back to look away.

"So beautiful." I wrap my fingers around his perfect cock. He jumps and stammers, wondering why I'm touching him down there. "I told you, it's what big boys can do," I reply. "In secret. We don't tell anyone about it. Does it feel good?" I stroke him teasingly, swiping a finger over the wet slit.

He licks his lips, unsure of what to answer. "I think so. It's wrong, isn't it?"

I shake my head. "Never with me. You can do anything you want with Daddy. In fact..." I lie back and fold an arm under my head. "Come here. I'll show you how to make it feel really good." He follows obediently, only to freeze when I uncover myself. "See? I'm hard, too."

He swallows, transfixed.

"Touch it," I encourage.

That earns me a frightened look, and he's driving me to the brink of *fucking* insanity with that innocence. My cock throbs against my lower abdomen, my balls already tight and full.

"Do you love your Daddy?" I grip his chin and brush my thumb over his cheek.

He nods timidly. "Forever and ever."

"And you want me to be happy?" Another nod from him, and I give my cock a pointed look. "Then touch me. It will make me happy."

Dylan takes a breath and extends his hand as if he's afraid he'll get bitten. The first ghosting contact causes me to shiver. He touches me tentatively, and I clench my jaw. At this rate, I'll become a two-pump chump.

"You don't have to be so careful." I rub his neck soothingly, and he grasps me a little firmer. "That's better. Now you move your hand up and down slowly."

He follows commands easier, and soon enough he's stroking me just the way I love it. He seems mesmerized by the fluid that seeps out every time he tightens his hold.

"You know what would make Daddy even happier?" I murmur.

"What?" he rasps. Clearing his throat, he turns so he's on his stomach. The muscles of his tight ass clench, letting me know he's pressing his own cock against the mattress.

"If you kissed it." I don't let go of his neck, so he can't move away. "Give it a kiss. I think you'll like it." With me guiding him closer, he lets out a trembling breath that I feel along my cock. A second later, it's his lips I feel. "Fuck," I whisper. "That's a good boy. Keep kissing it."

Over and over, he brushes his lips over the wet tip. I keep my mouth firmly shut to stifle a groan when his tongue darts out across his bottom lip.

"It tastes salty." Another little lick.

"That feels amazing, Dylan. Such a good boy." My fingers disappear into his hair so I can control his movements better. "Now you can suck on it. If you do that long enough, you'll get a grown-up surprise."

"I like surprises," he admits. He stalls for a beat, unsure, but eventually closes his mouth around the head of my aching cock. "Like this?"

I nod quickly and breathe in deeply through my nose. It would be too easy to lose control here.

"So good," I exhale. "You can take more." I push him down another inch or two, taking it as slowly as I possibly can. "Perfect, perfect."

That's encouragement for him. He wants to please me, so he takes a big breath and redoubles his efforts.

"That's it," I moan. "You're making me very happy, sweetheart. Fucking beautiful. You look so good sucking on Daddy."

He whimpers, leaving a trail of saliva trickling down my shaft, and I gotta stop. *Christ.* I withdraw from him and tell him to lie down in the middle of the bed 'cause I wanna show him something.

"Hang on." I halt him, spotting a dark patch on the sheets where he's been. "Do you see this? You have to tell me when you get this wet, little pan."

"Why?" He sits on his butt, legs spread, showing me every inch I wanna get lost in. "I don't know why it leaks like that."

"It's because you like playing secret games." I crawl over him, pushing him down flat against the mattress. "And we don't waste come."

His breathing grows rapid in an instant, and I have his undivided attention. The anticipation is thick between us, and he gives me another one of his sexy, needy sounds as I lower my face to take his cock into my mouth.

"Fuck!" He fists the sheets, and I hum and suck hungrily, up and down, tightening my lips, stroking him, faster, wanting his hot spurts to flood my mouth—but I stop. "Nooo!" He pants, expression wild. "Why did you stop? Please don't stop!"

"I'll give you something better, I promise." I sit back, my hand moving absently over my cock. "I need you on your stomach. Be careful with your leg."

I slick up my erection with lube while I wait.

I have no words for how sexy he is. On his stomach, legs spread, he's mine for the taking.

"Do-do you also like sucking, Daddy?" he asks over his shoulder.

"I love it." I crawl over him once more and kiss his shoulder. "I love tasting my little boy's come right before I fuck him." I drop more kisses along his shoulder blades as I slip between his firm ass cheeks with coated fingers.

"Oh, my *God,*" he moans. "I'm losing my mind."

Maybe he's dropped the act of not knowing what's gonna happen because he needs this as much as I do. Maybe it's because he can barely control his breathing, much less talk. It doesn't matter, and I wouldn't be able to keep up the charade, anyway. My body's tense and ready to go off, my senses zeroing in on one thing and one thing only. To fuck him until he's begging me to stop.

Dylan's sounds are constant, and he moves with my fingers as I prepare him. When I force two fingers in, he meets my push. When I pull out, he grinds his cock against the mattress. Filthy boy is gonna leave a wet spot for the cleaning crew.

"Fuck me," he begs.

Wiping the excess lube on the sheet, I press my cock against his glistening opening. In return, he tries to relax and push back. It's enough for the pierced head to breach the first ring, and then I don't have patience to treat him like a beginner. With a firm, unhurried thrust of my hips, I bury myself inside his tight ass.

Dylan chokes on a breath. "It burns, Daddy."

I grit my teeth, assaulted by the ecstasy. "Give it a minute." But I can't give it a damn second. I pull out, only to drive forward again, and I set a steady pace to fuck him into the mattress. "Move with me."

He groans and lifts his ass, allowing me to push deeper. All the way, until he gasps and goes rigid. *That's it.* His moans turn pleading. He gives me all the access I want, and I fuck him harder. My balls hit his soft skin every time I ram in, and he lets me know in his own sexy way when I hit that sweet spot.

"More," he whimpers into the pillow. "Fuck me harder."

It mutes his sounds too much, so I push in all the way and reach up to yank the pillow from him. "What have I said about hiding, Dylan?" I withdraw from him and sit back. "Turn around. I wanna see your face."

He scrambles into position quickly, turning into a boy slut the way I love. Legs spread, he pulls me closer, and I laugh into a messy kiss. A second later, I'm balls deep again.

We both lose it. Touching morphs into grabbing and clawing, I slam my cock in and out, our kisses are as choppy as our breathing, and a steady string of come pulses from his cock, pooling across his defined abs.

"There." He screws his eyes shut, holding my face close to his, and takes a shallow breath. "Oh fuck, right there."

I stroke his slick cock and swivel my hips, making sure the barbell teases his prostate.

"It's not scary anymore," he groans. "The piercing's not scary, Daddy. It feels so good—*unngh*—I'm c-close."

A low growl emanates from my chest, and I tense up when he clenches down on me. Heat travels through me, causing my body to flush and the orgasm to rush forward.

"Will you make a big mess for Daddy?"

He jerks a nod and holds on to me, his body moving erratically with my thrusts. He's gone. Ropes of come splash across his stomach and chest, and the sight almost sets me off. The smell of sex is heavy around us, and I forget everything that isn't him and me.

The moment Dylan's muscles unclench and he starts panting after holding his breath throughout his climax, I succumb to my own release.

"Sensitive," he gasps.

I push in hard, my chest sliding up along his messy one, and my forehead lands on his shoulder. A bead of sweat trickles down my neck, ripping a shudder through me.

"Daddy, I—*ahhh*."

"Not yet, baby boy." I groan as the pleasure explodes within. "*Fuck*," I growl. "Not yet, not yet."

"Daddy, please." He squirms underneath me, only making it better for me. I pull out and push in, rocking as deep as I can, and I start coming. "Oh shit, I can feel—fuck, too much."

I know the exact feeling he's battling. When it's too much and not enough at the same time. I torture him with it, fucking him while I'm coming, fucking my come into him, and he cries out and trembles, one second trying to get away, the next second pulling me close.

The intensity fades slowly, leaving me boneless and sated. I reluctantly get off him and collapse on the empty spot next to his spent form. A perfect fucking mess. He drapes an arm and a leg over me, and we're quiet while we regain our breath.

"That was..."

I chuckle, still out of breath. "Yeah."

"Holy shit." He shivers violently. "I wanna laugh and cry." He lifts his face, his eyes shining and his smile wide. "We need to do that lots, Daddy."

"As much as we want." I cup his cheek and kiss his sweet lips. "My perfect little boy."

I kinda wish we had another few hours, but unfortunately, we don't.

The smiles last longer. Dylan's sporting a shit-eating grin when we enter the tattoo shop, and it's difficult keeping my hands to myself. I'm glad we stayed an extra night; we did need it, and I make a mental note to plan something for Dylan and Gabriella, too. They'll benefit from having some alone time as much as he and I did, and they'll grow even closer.

Having a needle leaving a sharp trail of piercing fire along my calf wipes the smile off my face eventually, though nothing can steal my good mood. Ink is permanent and finally as solid as the three of us are, and I'm a lucky motherfucker to wear the princess's work.

It's only because of the simple design of Dylan's tattoo that it's even possible for him to get it done in one day. Anime is straight lines with minimal shading and not many details. Even so, it's still half a sleeve to cover his knee and a few inches above and below, so he's stuck in a chair for nine hours that day.

My ink is done in three and a half. After which, I sit by Dylan's side and make sure his blood sugar doesn't get low. The skilled tattoo artist calls him loco and laughs.

"What's your longest session?" Dylan asks him, wincing when the artist hits a sensitive spot below the knee.

I silently hand the boy his milk shake, and he takes a long suck from it.

"Fourteen hours," the man replies. "Never again. Fucking hell, this li'l chica was doin' a big cover-up, and she wouldn't stop shakin'."

The buzz from the machine is constant, both mildly irritating after so many hours yet oddly lulling.

Every part of me wants to remove the wrap on my calf so I can take a picture and send it to Gabriella, but I hold back. I wanna see the look on her face when I show her. The guy who did mine complimented the beautiful artwork, and of course, I was proud like nothing else.

After hours and hours, Dylan's nearly done, and I quietly mention that I'll go pay.

As I reach the front desk, Dylan's tattoo artist hollers to the girl by the register. "Kid gets half off, Ally!" He turns to Dylan, continuing his work. "My little brother told me about your accident. Keep fightin', yeah?"

Dylan smiles, humbled, and nods. "Yes, sir."

The following afternoon, it's a cranky Dylan I guide through the airport back in California. He can't put much pressure on his knee, his other knee is itching and sore, and he's stiff after we ended up in seats with no extra legroom.

He's home, though. We have two bags of his personal belongings, the rest to be shipped, and he's not going anywhere without us for a long fucking time. Now we'll focus on physical therapy, settling into our home, and look forward to our upcoming vacation.

"Don't scratch it again, kid," I tell him. "I'm serious."

He scowls at the ground as we near the exit. "I wanna remove the wrap."

He can do that when we get home. I'm in khaki shorts, so I only wore my wrap for a few hours yesterday. His session was a hell of a lot longer and more intense, plus the fresh ink would be rubbing against his sweats. No need to make the healing process difficult, so I reapplied a wrap around his leg this morning.

"If you don't let it heal properly, you won't be able to swim in Mexico," I say. "I don't think you wanna sit on the beach while the rest of us get in the ocean because you didn't let the scabs fall off on their own."

That makes him pout, though it doesn't last long. The minute we step outside and he spots Gabriella, he lights up.

So does she. Leaving the truck, she rushes over to hug us.

"You're home!"

Yeah, at fucking last. Everything is the way it's supposed to be.

I collapse on the bed after my shower, more tired than I can say. Happier than I can say, too.

Dylan's in a daze. When we came back, he asked why the backyard was torn up, and Gabriella's been chatting him up about my plans for the space ever since.

Standing by the window that overlooks the backyard, he sends me a smile and mouths that he loves me.

I do the same, and I hope he sees now we're serious about this. It's no longer the house I live in but the home we're creating together.

Having exhausted the topic of the backyard plans, Gabriella moves on to tell us about her sleepover. I wanna know everything, but Dylan needs to get off his feet.

"Princess, why don't you help him in the shower?" I suggest. "I can order us some food."

"Okay. Come, Dylan." She takes his hand. "Let's clean you up. You smell like airplane and boy."

I chuckle, watching them retreat into the bathroom, hand in hand.

"Your hair is green, sis," I hear Dylan say.

"It's teal, dammit!" Her voice echoes in the bathroom. "It's gonna be purple for the wedding—what is that?"

I smirk to myself, having a feeling I know what she's seeing for the first time.

It's quiet for a moment. Some soft rustling. The crutch clanks against the floor, and then Gabriella's saying "oh my God" over and over.

"It's from the cast," she murmurs thickly.

A beat later, they're kissing and whispering to each other.

I sigh contentedly and shut my eyes, wondering how the fuck I got so lucky.

When the shower starts running, it doesn't take long before Gabriella reemerges from the bathroom, and she's perfectly flushed and giddy-looking. Jumping up on the bed, she becomes my cuddle monster and reveals she's falling in love with Dylan.

"That's wonderful, princess." I smile and tuck a piece of hair behind her ear.

"He said he's falling for me, too," she whispers.

"How could he not?" I dip down and brush my lips to hers. "One day very soon, he'll love you as much as I do."

Her breath catches, and she blinks slowly, twice. "You—you love me?"

"So very much. I never stood a chance against either of you."

She grins shakily, her eyes brimming. "I love you, too. I get butterflies."

"Oh, yeah?" I slip a leg in between hers and stroke her tummy under her top. "I'll do my best to keep those butterflies safe."

"I trust you." The serene look in her eyes—so fucking gorgeous. "I can't believe Dylan did all that ink in one session."

"He wanted to surprise you," I murmur. "So did I." At her curious expression, I bend my knee so she can see the back of my leg.

"Daddy!" She flies outta my embrace, eyes wide, and gets up close and personal with the ink. She touches it gingerly, the area still irritated. "It's my sketch!"

"Of course it is," I chuckle. "Come here. I wanna see you."

She giggles as I pick her up and position her on my hips, her delectable ass wriggling over my semi.

"I'm the luckiest Daddy in the world." The sappy moment is

ruined by my stomach that growls in hunger, and it makes the princess laugh and laugh. "I guess I should order our dinner, huh?"

"I think that's what your tummy wants," she sings. She leans down and gives me a loud smooch. "I'm the luckiest girl in the world, so *there*."

Let's keep it that way.

EPILOGUE

"**D**ylan, get back here!" I yell from the terrace.

He groans and half jogs, half limps. "It's been half an hour since breakfast. That's what you said."

Mark chuckles and sips his coffee. Brayden's halfway down the beach already, along with Gabriella and Chelsea.

"That's not it. Put some on." Not leaving my chair, I toss him the bottle of sun block for his leg. "And be careful in the sand, will ya? It's too soon for you to be fucking running." The kid can give me heart palpitations.

When walking on a steady surface, he does all right without the crutch, but in the sand, it puts too much pressure on his bad knee even with the brace. Fuck if I'm having him getting worse on vacation.

"There." He shows his sun block-smothered tattoo. "Can I swim now, please?"

"Give Daddy a kiss first."

He grins and kisses me before he's off.

That leaves me, Mark, and Evangeline to enjoy the shade of my bungalow's terrace. With a perfect view of our private beach, we drink coffee—juice for the pregnant girl—and eat pastries, all lazy-like. It's vacation.

"I think I'll go down to the pool." Evangeline gives Mark a kiss on the cheek and rises. "Anything I can get you first, Master?"

"No, enjoy yourself, kitten. Stay where I can see you." He smiles and watches her as she trails down the stone path to the pool. "Rio should be back from his run soon, shouldn't he?"

I check my watch. "Yeah—and speak of the devil." The man appears between two bungalows, drenched in sweat. "It's eighty-six degrees, man."

"Piss off, mate." He wheezes a breath and sits down in a chair, quick to reach for a water bottle. "Unlike some, I can't sit around and do nothing and look this good."

It helps doing manual labor all day long. I'm not doing fuck-all like Mark. Which is ironic. He owns a chain of fitness centers that a team of employees runs for him, and as far as I know, he never uses them.

"So we have a week here," Mark says. "Shall we discuss some fun ways to terrorize our subs?"

I grin over the rim of my coffee mug. "You bet. Although, I promised Gabriella I wouldn't be a *meany* until tomorrow. Wedding day is off-limits."

Today's a short day. Kayla and Nicholas are having brunch with their families, and our girls will join in a few hours for hair and makeup.

"How benevolent of you." Rio's eyes flash with mirth.

I smirk. "That's what I'm saying."

"Are you guys going to sightsee any?" Mark asks. "Evangeline's looking forward to being lazy by the pool, but Brayden wants to head out."

"We're just gonna chill," I reply. It's been a rough year. I want my two close, and we've decided that we wanna take it easy and spoil one another rotten with good food, sex, and beach fun. "We have everything we need right here."

"Chelsea and I will leave the area a bit." Rio kicks off his shoes and runs a hand through his sweat-dampened hair. "There are some hiking trails she wants to take on, and I have plans for our last day here."

I smile, having a good guess of what he's planning. Chelsea will sport an engagement ring at their collaring ceremony when we get home, I think.

Mark whacks Rio with a rolled-up newspaper. "Don't look so nervous. You know she'll say yes."

"Jesus. Am I that transparent?" Rio rolls his eyes, seemingly at himself, and snorts. "Bloody hell. I blame it on that girl."

"Usually easier that way," I laugh.

Mark jerks a thumb my way. "Isn't he a bit too cheerful these days?"

I flip him off while Rio grins.

"I'd say we all are," he answers. "So let's get cracking on that terrorizing before we get sappier?"

That's probably best.

Leaning against the doorway to the bathroom, I watch in silence as Dylan and Gabriella get ready in front of the two mirrors. He helps to zip up her light purple summer dress, and she assists him in a futile attempt to tame his hair.

They haven't spotted me, so it's one of those moments I get to see how they are together when they're alone. Sweet, open, equal, and without the playful bickering they draw from each other around me.

"Do you think this will be us one day?" Gabriella asks softly. "I mean, I know we can't get married, but...I don't know."

Dylan hums and stands behind her, helping her with a necklace. "I don't care about a piece of paper. We can have a ceremony if we want anyway."

I smile and put my hands down into the pockets of my dress pants.

"We could do our wedding bands in ink." Gabriella giggles and spins around, glancing up at Dylan while she adjusts his vest. They're fucking stunning, dressed up pretty, wearing those smiles for one another.

Dylan kisses her nose and folds up the sleeves of his button-down. "As long as I get to spend my life with you and Cade, I'm kinda game for anything."

Time to make my presence known. I clear my throat and walk closer, and they look up, smiles widening.

"Damn, Daddy," Dylan mumbles. "You look—yeah."

"Yeah?" I cup his cheek and kiss him. "So do you. Both of you —gorgeous."

"I love these." Gabriella fidgets with one of my suspenders. "Smoking hot, badass Daddy."

I laugh softly and ruffle her hair. It's already messy—dark purple and shiny. But evidently, that still makes her huff and check the mirror.

"Are we ready to get sand in our shoes?" I ask.

They nod, and we leave the bungalow together. The sun is setting, painting the sky in beautiful colors, and most of the sixty-something guests have already arrived at the beach. Before we reach our friends, I only have one thing to say to Dylan and Gabriella.

"Inked wedding bands sounds perfect to me."

Their sun-kissed cheeks gain a bit more color, and they grin at the ground, perhaps a little embarrassed to have been caught.

I greet my buddies and compliment the girls' dresses, and it doesn't take many minutes before it's time to sit down.

"I'll be right back." I guide Dylan and Gabriella to our seats and then head up the aisle with Rio and Mark where Nicholas stands with the officiant.

He told us early on he couldn't pick a best man, which isn't strange. We're a fortunate group of guys to be that close. Even so, tonight's about him and Kayla—and immediate family. We won't get much time to be ourselves with him at the reception; speeches will be vanilla and sweet, as opposed to kinky and hilarious. That's why we've made plans to meet up before we go home so we can congratulate the newlyweds our way.

"Congratulations, mate." Rio steps up and hugs him. "Enjoy your lovely bride and join us in a couple days when you're ready for some play."

Nicholas chuckles and nods, adjusting his tie. "Wouldn't miss it."

Mark's next, and they exchange well-wishes and thanks as well before it's my turn.

"I'm happy for you, man. Kayla will make a great little Ford." I give him a firm hug. "Congratulations."

"Thank you, my friend." He gives my shoulder a squeeze. "I'm happy for you, as well. You three are good for each other."

"I appreciate it, Nick. No arguments from me." I smile and take a step back. "Go marry your girl."

I return down the aisle and find my way to Dylan and Gabriella.

"It's about to start!" she whispers excitedly.

Soft violins begin playing as the sun touches the horizon, and my girl crawls up into my lap. I place an arm around Dylan's shoulders, and we all turn to see Kayla and her grandmother, who's giving her away.

The devotion and love in Nick's and Kayla's eyes kinda say it all for us. The Little in Kayla bubbles to the surface as she reaches her husband-to-be, and she hops up and gives him a quick kiss. He chuckles and touches her cheek, murmuring something we can't hear.

"It'll be us one day," I promise quietly. "If not in ink on paper, then in ink where it matters."

Dylan places a kiss on my jaw and grabs my hand, and Gabriella sighs contentedly, watching our friends with a big smile on her face.

SYMBOLIC TOUCHES

A BEHIND THE SCENES FUTURE TAKE

A GLIMPSE

KAYLA FORD

Gross. It's been so long since I wore jeans. Black, skinny, with very little *give*. Nothing yellow or pink or soft. I push back my hair into a simple ponytail—no cute bows. A snug white button-down. I scrunch my nose at my reflection in the mirror by our bed. But my shoes—dammit, a girl needs *some* comfort and a boost of Little confidence—so I grunt my way into a pair of baby yellow Chucks with purple stars on them.

Okay, I'm ready to lay down the law.

Nicholas is already at the club, so after kissing my kittens bye-bye, I leave our house and get in my shiny purple Mini Cooper. It's *fierce*. Just like I will be today.

Butterflies wreak havoc in my tummy, though Chelsea has given me pointers on how to distract myself from them. By pinching my thigh really hard, I can take that pain and let it fuel my anger and determination.

Sweet, little Kayla Ford... It's common for people—mostly Dominants—to think little of Littles. We're only into Disney and coloring books and sucking on pacifiers all day. I shake my head. I'm superlucky to have found a community where there's none of that. At least, not around me. If I noticed it, those *people* would be hearing from me.

I won't be so sweet tonight.

"What can I get—what the fuck?" Mr. Cooper is not the first one to be surprised by my outfit.

"Hi." I smile nervously.

I think he understands after a couple seconds. His expression grows gentle, and he pours me a Sprite with lots of crushed ice.

"It kills me that it's come to this, subbie—that you can't relax and be who you are." He hands me my soda and rests his forearms on the bar. "You don't have to speak to him. You know that, right?"

I know. I take a big gulp, the fizz of the bubbles tickling my nose. "Nicholas has told me everything, and I believe in second chances, too. It's just... I would like to make your brother understand what his behavior caused that night."

He dips his head in a nod. "You have every right. Do you want any help?"

I shake my head. "No, thank you." Nicholas has already offered. Maybe a gazillion times.

The girls know about my plans, so I wave at them when I spot them by the booths. Gabriella, Evangeline, and Chelsea told me they'd be ready to assist if needed, too. But dammit, I can do this on my own.

The only time I accepted help was when I wanted to reach out to Mr. Quinn—Mark's brother's Master. He is a stranger to me, and my nerves got the best of me. Nicholas contacted him first, and then I spoke to Ryan myself. For a whole two minutes, where he thankfully understood my side of things, too. Then he was the one who kindly pointed out *my side of things* should come from me, not anyone else. And that's when I came up with my plan.

"How are you and your brother dealing with things now?" I ask Mark. "Is everything okay between you?"

"We're...getting there," he replies pensively. "Did Nicholas tell you about our parents?"

"Yes, Sir." I do see where Greg is coming from. I understand the hows triggered by the whys. Then the slope was too slippery, and he made lots of mistakes even though he had good intentions—for the most part.

Mr. Cooper nods once. "Greg and I had dinner with them shortly after Mexico, and I think we found some common ground there. Took us a while to make our folks see where they went wrong and the ramifications of it."

That must've stung for the brothers. Hopefully, it's all worked out—or it will. I'm glad they have each other.

"They're here." Mark's looking over at the entrance, and I follow his gaze to see his brother. Greg looks a lot different from last time. Jeans and a black T-shirt have replaced his suit, and he walks a few steps behind a slightly larger man, who I assume is Ryan Quinn. A gorgeous woman my age is with them. *Angel Quinn.* Is she a Little? Because she looks the part in a lacy baby-doll dress, even though it's black. Her platinum blond hair flows down in loose, thick waves, the tips matching her hot pink lipstick and knee socks.

Ryan hands over what I think might be a toy bag to Greg. Then he speaks in Greg's ear before stealing a kiss, to which Greg bows his head.

"Yup, still weird seeing him that way," Mr. Cooper says with a smile.

I'm more thinking...this Ryan and Angel must've seen—and possibly unlocked—very good parts of Greg in order to open their marriage to include him. I'm ready to forgive and forget—once I've talked to him.

Ryan and I agreed we'd meet up in the Cave, so when they start making their way across the Club, I thank Mark for the soda and get off my stool.

"You sure you wanna do this alone, honey?" he asks, concerned.

"Yes, Sir, though I suspect the doorway will get crowded." I say that with a pointed look and a wry smile, because I know my husband. He will be there, as I'm sure the girls will.

"Good idea," he notes. "It's a nice spot."

I chuckle, and then I zigzag across the dance floor, careful not to bump into dancing foreplayers and, um, fornicators.

Liam is working the round bar in the Cave, and I take a seat there. It looks like Ryan is letting his wife pick a stall for a scene. She picks the stockade with an expression of glee. I've been told she's a switch, meaning I have no idea if the excitement comes from being a Top or a bottom. But then Ryan tells her to "be a good little whore for Daddy and get naked," so I'm *guessing* she's gonna bottom.

It's while Greg helps Angel into place that Ryan spots me, and he lifts a brow, a curious expression on his face. The butterflies are back. I nod in confirmation. *Yes, I'm Kayla.*

He walks over, looking awfully kind despite the sharp features, intense eyes, and ink. "Hey, Kayla. Good to finally meet you. I'm Ryan." He extends his hand.

I swallow my nervousness and shake his hand. "Nice to meet you too, Sir." The last part slips out from habit. "Thank you for letting me speak to Greg today."

He quirks a faint smirk and half leans against the bar. "He's the one who will be thanking you. I spoke to your husband yesterday, and he voiced some concerns about what you wanna bring up."

I should've known. Nicholas will do everything in his power to make sure I'm not walking into a minefield.

"Will there be a problem, you think?" I wonder.

"None at all." He shakes his head. "They're valid points— maybe ones a Top doesn't always consider. He needs to hear them." I'm glad. And relieved. Ryan turns toward their stall and whistles sharply—without even sticking two fingers in his mouth!—and Greg looks our way. Ryan jerks his head in a get-over-here nod. "I'll give you two some privacy," he tells me, "but don't hesitate to come over. Angel's particularly passionate about Greg getting it through his skull what damage he can do in a place like this."

I manage an anxious smile.

Greg, as he walks over, looks anxious, too. Stiff in his posture, eyes flashing with apprehension.

Ryan claps Greg on the shoulders. "Save your apology for afterward so you know what you're apologizing for, boy."

"Yes, Owner." Greg waits 'til Ryan is gone, then takes the seat next to mine. "Thank you for meeting with me. May I call you Kayla?"

Well, yes. No matter how detached I'm trying to remain right now, subbies still use each other's first names at Switch. The lines just blur sometimes with new Tops, as well as Tops I'm close to. The first name slips out on occasion.

"Yes." I nod and take a breath. "Given what happened last January and that this is your first official time at Switch, I've taken it upon myself to explain some things to you." In my periphery, I see both Nicholas and Mark in the wide doorway to the dungeon. *Sneaky Doms!* "Nicholas, your brother, Rio, and Cade go way, way back. I have so much respect for what they've done here, creating this community—and most importantly, keeping it a place where we can let go and be ourselves." I pause, struggling not to fidget. "A good environment is crucial for many of us who aren't merely here for the physical play. You see, when I step foot inside Switch, I relinquish more than control. I give up all adult notions and leave everything to my Daddy Dom. I regress mentally and let my Little run free, because that's one of the reasons he opened Switch—so we would feel safe enough to do that."

Greg swallows and nods with a dip of his chin, and it takes him a moment before he can face me again. When he does, the remorse is more than evident.

"This applies to very many s-types, whether we're Littles, slaves, or any other type of submissive," I say. "Now, when you barged in here drunk off your butt and hostile—" He flinches, and it's getting more and more difficult for me to stay so strict. It's not who I am. *Crappity crap.* I take a sip of my soda, my mouth dry. "I recovered quickly." I want him to know that. "But the fact remains, I was in a completely defenseless position mentally, and I don't get out of that headspace with a snap of my fingers. It's a landing that requires time and a practiced touch unless I want to crash. So you getting pushy and grabbing my arm was literally the least amount of damage you inflicted. It's what happens up here." I tap my temple. "Someone who regresses further or has been in a TPE relationship for an extended period of time can be utterly traumatized if a stranger violates their boundaries."

I want to wrap this up, because it's starting to hurt me. I don't for a second think Greg is a bad person after learning all the circumstances, and I hope he understands better now.

"I trust you read the rules now that you're a member," I tell him, and he nods. "It clearly states you do not approach a couple in a scene, you do not touch anyone without consent, and now you know why. It can be dangerous, even if it appears to be safe or harmless. So...yeah, now I'm done."

He clears his throat. "I—I understand. More so now than before. I've...started to discover just how big of a part the mind has in D/s, and for what it's worth, I'm truly sorry for hurting you, Kayla. I was ignorant and took my anger out on the least deserving." He takes a breath and looks away, then faces me again. "Would you be interested in giving me a second chance one day?"

Feeling better already, I slump a little in my seat. How some Doms stay so rigid is *nuts.* It's not comfy at all. "The second chance is already yours, Greg. I'm looking forward to getting to know you now that you won't be, um, you know, a dummy."

He lets out a laugh, both relieved and surprised, and I manage a small grin.

"Let's put the bad behind us, please?" I stick out my hand, ready to symbolize a new beginning. "I'm Kayla Ford. I'm trouble, but Daddy says it's okay. Until it's not."

Greg smiles carefully and shakes my hand. "Greg Cooper. I'm sure your Daddy likes the trouble."

I widen my eyes. "Um, not when I'm the one violating boundaries around here." I hold up two fingers. "The first time doesn't really count because Master Dante wasn't in a scene, but I was still rude. The other time, though...*yikes*. I interrupted when I thought he was hitting too hard on his sub, and Daddy got *so* furious." Rightfully so. Now I cover my eyes when I see too much pain. "He even threatened to put me on probation."

Nicholas was *not* happy with me.

Greg winces and lifts his brows. "Ryan's good at punishment, as well. Now I know what it's like to sleep on the floor."

Ouch. That would make me cry for sure. "Nothing hurts more than disappointing your Dom, does it?"

He glances over at Ryan and Angel. He is turning his wife's butt bright red, and she's *cursing* at him. Wow, she must be gutsy.

Ryan seems to find it funny.

"It's gutting," Greg murmurs in confirmation. I think he loves his Owners. It looks like it, anyway. "I have a lot to learn."

"You've come to the right place." Remembering something, I squirm in my seat and retrieve a folded slip of paper from my back pocket. "Everyone who identifies as submissive to some degree—so this includes Angel—is very welcome to join the weekly subbie munches. We discuss events, demos, and talk smack about our D-types. Oh, and when it gets too girly for the guys, they sometimes go someplace to shoot pool and probably talk smack about *us*."

He chuckles and accepts the information, pocketing it. "I appreciate that, and I'll do my best to show up. I may not have the biggest interest in gossiping—" he winks "—but I'm certainly up for discussing this lifestyle. My eyes are more open now, as is my mind."

"Good, I'm glad." I smile. "I should probably go fill Nicholas in, and your Master looks like he's waiting for you."

"Indeed, he wouldn't be him if he didn't want to give me some suffering, too."

And Greg likes that suffering. Easy to tell. Sliding off the stool, I wish him a good time and then walk toward the Cave's opening where Nicholas is waiting. Mark must've returned to work.

My mouth stretches into a big smile of relief, and I go right up to Nicholas and hug his middle super, duper hard.

"It worked, Daddy."

"I know, baby girl." He squeezes me tightly and presses a lingering kiss to the top of my head. "I may have had Liam eavesdropping on your conversation." *Sneaky, sneaky Doms!* "He just told me what you said. I'm so very proud of you, Kayla." His praise fills me with warmth, and I lift my head to grin up at him. He smiles back and kisses my nose. "You deserve a reward." *Yesssss, they're the best.* He glances at his watch. "That little ice cream shop you like so much closes in twenty minutes. We can make it. What do you say?"

I drop my jaw and stiffen in excitement. "I would *love* that."

"It's a date." He gathers my hands and kisses my knuckles. "And tomorrow we'll pick out a new dress for you."

I fist-pump the air.

TOUCHED BY THE EVER AFTER

A BEHIND THE SCENES FUTURE TAKE

A GLIMPSE

RIO KELLY

"I appreciate you offering to do the demo." Nicholas sits back against his desk. "Kayla saw it and legitimately screamed, then asked why I didn't love her anymore."

I chuckle as I picture it. "She thought it was for her?" I unpack the vacuum bag and hold it up, the glossy black latex reminding me more of a garment bag than a way to torture a lovely sub. "Poor girl." This is definitely up Chelsea's alley, however. Mine, as well. "Is everything set up downstairs?" I pocket the extra mouthpiece to demonstrate later.

"Yes. The bench, correct?"

I incline my head and put Nicholas's new purchase into my toy bag. Then we make our way downstairs to the club where Chelsea is waiting by the bar.

"I miss Mark." Nicholas sighs, and with a narrow-eyed look at my smirk, he excuses himself to deal with the new bartender.

Thankfully, we'll get Mark back in a few weeks. With Evangeline going into labor any day now, he wouldn't be of much use here, anyway.

I reach my little sub and lightly caress her neck to get her attention. Since I collared her this past summer, I haven't quite been able to stop touching the inch-wide, platinum choker. It fills me with possessiveness and pride every time I lay eyes on her.

"Owner." She smiles softly and bows her head a little.

"My slave." I drop a kiss at her temple and examine her—work habit. In the past couple days, she's had my mind spinning, though I could be reading into things too much. Around her, my radar for changes and concerns is ultrasensitive. "How do you feel?"

Her smile turns curious. "Good, Master."

Fair enough. I can shake it off for now, since our play won't be too physically straining. "We have a demo in the Cave." I help her off the stool. "Gather your hair in a low ponytail."

She quickly removes a rubber tie from her wrist. "Yes, Master."

She follows me across the crowded dance floor and past the bar in the dungeon. Some ten people who are interested in watching are already waiting outside the stall with the spanking bench. It's one of Cade's contraptions, so nothing has been half-assed. A lower, padded level is waiting for her to kneel on, accompanied by both Velcro straps and shackles.

"You can lose the clothes, love." I eye her sheer slave dress, then address the viewers. "Questions saved for when the scene is over, please—that includes aftercare. This will be a regular scene for my property, so no interruptions." I nod in thanks as one of the staff walks up to prepare the upper-body vacuum bag for me. "One thing I'll say right now is that for those of you who are thinking about exploring vacuum bags—or beds—keep your level of activity in mind. If you plan for more strenuous play, I'd suggest a hole for breathing rather than the common tube." I show them the silicone mouthpiece that will keep her lips stretched around it, the design not much unlike the one scuba divers use. "Additionally, it's a perfect opportunity for breath play." Because the breathing hole is wide enough to fit a cock.

This is the first time Chelsea hears of my plans for tonight, and

I watch her stand in her graceful position, taking a deep breath and closing her eyes while she reminds herself she can trust me. It's an exquisite surrender to witness.

I stow away the spare mouthpiece, as the vacuum bag comes equipped with one that's attached securely. "Are you ready?"

"Yes, Owner." The words leave her in a whisper, more visible on her lips than anything.

"My beautiful bunny." I grasp her chin and dip down for a deep kiss. This next bit will be fun for me. When I took her to Sydney and asked her to marry me last fall, she got *giggly drunk* on champagne and said it would be "superfun" to see my expression if she managed to steal the control device to her wireless bullet. No need to steal anything, though. I'll happily hand it over tonight. "You once said you wanted to be in charge of this one." I retrieve the toy from my pocket and place it in her hand.

She blinks, then pops her mouth open.

I chuckle. "Don't get any ideas, little rebel. It'll be your safe-word tonight. Switch it on if you reach red. I'm keeping the egg." It'll vibrate in my pocket if it gets to be too much. "Understood?"

She purses her lips and sends me a rueful little smirk. "Understood, Owner."

I laugh under my breath and grab the vacuum bag, carefully slipping it over her upper body. "Wrap your lips around the mouthpiece," I instruct, guiding it to her mouth. It leaves a wider breathing hole than the common rubber tubes, and who doesn't enjoy seeing their sub with their mouth open widely enough to insert a cock? "Don't fuck up." I stroke her latex-covered cheek. "You wouldn't want to lose your only chance to get air."

She shudders violently, and I bend down to my toy bag, pausing at the roll of bondage tape. Then I shake my head. Duct tape will hurt more to rip off. Duct tape, it is.

"Burial pose with your arms, sub."

She rustles underneath the soft latex to comply, crossing her arms over her chest, and I start sealing the edges of the vacuum bag along her waistline. With that done, I usher her closer to the bench.

I help her kneel on the first step, where I strap her into place with the Velcro. Bent over the bench, ass out, secured, and legs fairly spread, she looks like sin. And she's all mine. I take a few seconds to appreciate my property, then refocus and accept the vacuum that will suck all the air out of the bag.

She stiffens when I plug it into the valve but relaxes soon enough.

I caress the soft skin of her sweet ass and watch the last of the air disappear from the vacuum bag. The latex plasters itself to Chelsea's slender form like a second skin, restricting her completely, all while giving the viewers and me the stunning sight of her body shape. The contours of every little curve beg to be touched.

"Test the vibrator, please," I tell her, and I feel the vibrating signal in my pocket. "Good girl."

I stare at her, my mind slowing down. Now that I have her where I want, restrained and exposed to me, I want to enjoy her. Ignoring the people outside the open stall, I circle Chelsea and let my eyes drink her in. I trail my fingers along her spine, up between her shoulder blades, and follow the dip of her neck. Over her head, down her forehead. She's an object. Immobile and here solely to serve me. No eyes, no nose, no arms...only a collection of holes.

I squat down in front of her and finger the edges of the mouth-piece. "Such a beautiful toy to fuck." Slipping a finger inside her mouth, I smile faintly when she automatically tries to close her lips, but the piece of silicone is in the way. Her second choice follows, and she swirls her tongue around my finger. "Whore," I murmur. "Your Master might take that as an invitation." In fact, I do. I stand up and unbuckle my belt, arousal surging to my gut. "Remember the toy can't breathe through its nose now."

Pushing her limits brings the same high every time. I don't get greedy. A tiny nudge is enough to satisfy me for weeks, and I savor each opportunity. Removing my belt altogether, I get my trousers and underwear down my hips. I fist my semihard cock and ease it past the mouthpiece. Once she knows what's happening, I inch out again to let her take a deep breath. Then I push in once more and let out a sigh as she immediately coats me in saliva.

"That's it. Get me hard." I stroke her head, the smooth latex giving me ideas for future fetish outfits for her. "Bloody hell, pet—" I chuckle huskily as her teeth graze my cock carefully. Making up for what she can't do with her lips at the moment. "Fuck." I withdraw from her mouth and stroke myself, then tuck my cock back into my pants. She's ready to be used, and I'm more than ready to use her.

After locating another vibrating little egg, I get down on one knee between her spread legs and drop a wet kiss along the slit of her pussy. That makes her jump and gasp, the sound just barely reaching me over the music. I hum in pleasure and indulge greedily. Deep, long kisses and firm licks. *That's my girl.* I feel and see her muscles working, one shiver setting off another. Her attempts at squirming only fuel me to drive her mad.

As I switch on the little vibrator, I suck her clit between my teeth and flick the tip of my tongue over it. Drops of her juices form at her opening, and inserting the egg takes no effort. It slips right in while Chelsea lets out a choked moan.

"Clench down, little rebel," I order. "If it slips out, I'll have no choice but to assume you don't want to come."

I rub my mouth to hide my grin and reach into my toy bag for my most recent purchase, a cat-o'-nine-tails Chelsea's quickly come to hate. The long leather lashes sting enough as they are, but the knotted ends take the pain to a new level.

I'm not sure what I love the most, her sharp gasps and cries when she receives the pain, the marks the strands leave behind, or the mindfuck she goes through because, in the end, the pain that makes her beg me to stop will eventually get her off.

I give her no warning. After pushing up the sleeves of my

button-down, I pull back the whip and flick it forward to let the leather knots scatter across her ass. Chelsea shrieks and goes rigid, and I continue while the initial pain has her paralyzed. Over and over, I paint her fading tan with red blotches and dotted welts.

Her screams have morphed into breathless sobs by the time I'm done—with this implement. *She* is far from finished. With the jagged hurt in place to send fire through her, I retrieve my heavy suede flogger.

The change in the atmosphere is instant. The first strike of the flogger gives her a sudden shock, and then... A drawn-out moan escapes her, and I feel the same sense of pleasure coursing through me. In a figure eight motion of my wrist, I make the strands rain down in quick succession, creating a rhythm that never fails to sweep her away.

Hell, it has a similar effect on me. Everything else disappears. My senses sharpen, Top space setting in, emotions flowing like a steady current between us. It's an indescribable feeling.

Although she can't move her upper body or her legs, she writhes as best she can. She swivels her hips and pushes out her perfect ass more and more for every mark I give her. I reach my limit when her bottom and the backs of her thighs glow pink and red.

I can't trust her to safeword if she's in subspace regardless, so I discard the flogger and find a condom. "Test the vibrator twice, Chelsea," I command as I slick up my cock with coconut oil. My trousers are hanging off my hips, but I feel two signals after a couple seconds. "Quality fuck toy, aren't you?" Coming up behind her, I wipe off the residue of the oil by giving her pussy a hard squeeze that makes her moan through a gasp. She's a sodden mess. "A sweet, cock-hungry cunt, too."

I grip the base of my erection and rub the melting oil over her ass, then slowly but surely apply more pressure. *Relax for me, love.* I groan under my breath as I sink deeper and deeper into her tight little ass.

A shudder rips down my spine. Pressing downward, I feel the vibrations from the egg inside her pussy. I pull out slowly, then push in deep and hard. All her anal-slut training is paying off. I fuck her in long strokes and get inspired when I see her trying to arch her back. The vacuum bag won't let her get far, but something will.

I get my leather belt, fist both ends, and loop it around her neck. Next time I push my hips forward, I yank her back and hiss at the pleasure exploding inside me. Chelsea chokes and clamps down, all her muscles taut, her back creating a beautiful curve.

It sets the masochist off, and I lose it. I growl a curse and fuck her through her climax. *Bloody hell.* Another groan leaves me when I see her gushing between her lovely thighs. My chest expands with a deep breath, and the intoxicating scent of her G-spot orgasm makes my mouth water.

"Messy fuck," I grunt. Releasing the belt, I grab her hips tightly and slam in harder, deeper, faster. Her muscles continue to constrict around me, no doubt sensitive and itching to get away from the buzzing toy that's still inside her. Unfortunately for her, I love the sensations too much. My head tips back as my own orgasm approaches. My thrusts grow rockier and irregular, shudders raising goose bumps across my arms and back.

Moments later, the release crashes down on me, and I shove my cock deep inside once more before I slump forward, my damp forehead hitting the dip between her shoulder blades.

"Fucking..." I pant.

This might be the only downside to playing at Switch. After I'm finished, I just want to be at home in our bed and have Chelsea cuddled up next to me. I blink tiredly and swallow dryly, forcing myself to function. Removing her vibrator comes first.

With a tilt of my head, gratitude fills me. Someone's closed the curtain to our stall, probably one of the DMs, so we can have a moment alone. That makes it marginally better.

I pull out and make quick work of ridding the condom and

zipping up my trousers. I'll put on the belt later. Twisting the valve to the vacuum bag, it's like watching a lung slowly fill with air. No longer clinging to her like second skin, the latex is more loose-fitting.

Once I've unstrapped her legs, I dig out a soft hand towel from my bag and swipe it up the insides of Chelsea's thighs. She squirms and whimpers in response.

"You please me very much, pet." I drop a kiss to her reddened ass before straightening. "This might hurt a bit." I help her stand on two shaky legs and pinch the corner of the tape. She knows it's coming, and she braces herself. Then I tear it off all around her in one fluid motion, and Chelsea lets out a weak sob and stiffens further. "All done, baby. It's gone." I drop the sticky tape on the floor and roll up the vacuum bag, inch by inch exposing flushed skin.

She's shaking, panting, weeping silently, and shivering as I let the latex fall to the ground. With barely any strength left in her, she merely collapses in my arms, and I carry her over to a comfortable chair in the corner.

"I've got you." I hold her to me, positioning her sideways across my lap, and press a kiss in her hair. It's damp with sweat, and I can imagine the rush of cold shocking her system after being locked in an airless plastic bag with very little give. "You did so well, my love." I stroke her back soothingly, spotting the gooseflesh on her shoulder. "Want a blanket?"

She shakes her head and burrows in closer. "S'nice," she croaks. "God—I feel all weird."

"How so?" I push back some hair that's escaped her ponytail. "Walk me through it."

She sniffles, another tremor rocking her. "It hurts to move, but I feel itchy and squirmy. I want to cry and laugh, and I'm exhausted and full of energy at the same time."

I smile softly and lift her chin, needing a quick kiss. "Messes with your head a little, doesn't it?" Realizing she's still clutching the remote control for the temporary safeword device in her hand, I gently pry her fingers open and take it from her.

"A *lot*, Master." She giggles through a fresh round of tears. Then she lowers her gaze, her vulnerability shining brightly. "It was suffocating even though I could breathe. I *hated* it. But then... God, I came so hard."

I chuckle quietly and give her a tight hug. "How I adore getting inside your beautiful head, Chelsea. You're a delight, you know that?"

Her cheeks turn a pretty shade of pink, and she buries her face against my neck, eliciting another warm chuckle from me.

Knowing her past issues with letting her guard down only makes the moment that much sweeter. She lets me comfort her and relaxes more and more with each passing minute.

"You smell delicious," I murmur, dropping a kiss to her shoulder. "Sex and latex." So much sex. A bit of coconut from the lube and a hint of the perfume she bought in Rome. Mouthwatering.

When she tilts her head up, I capture her mouth in a passionate, unhurried kiss and let my hands roam her body. And despite the intimacy, it's peaceful and soothing rather than arousing. At the moment, anyway.

"I guess...we have people to face, Owner?"

I hum and cup one of her breasts, loving the weight of it in my hand. "In a minute. It's my duty to make sure every inch of you is okay first."

Her soft laughter makes me grin.

The serenity is still there when I wake up the next morning to the smells of coffee, blueberry pancakes, and strawberries.

"Good morning, Master."

I manage to mutter something unintelligible and haul her close to me for a round of snuggles. My shift at the free clinic doesn't start until ten, and one sleepy glance at the clock tells me we have two hours 'til then.

"Mmm..." I slide a hand down her ass and crack a tired smirk at her noise of complaint. Someone is sore this morning. "You spoil me, slave."

"I love spoiling you." There's a smile in her voice that wraps me in warmth, but there's something else, too.

So I force my eyes to open, and I'm quick to frown. Something is *wrong*. "How are you feeling?" I brush a hand to her forehead; she doesn't feel feverish. The concerns from yesterday are back with a vengeance, though.

"I don't know," she replies thoughtfully. *"Weird.* Sensitive. Like, my skin."

"Hm." Propping myself up on an elbow, I lift away the covers and inspect her body. As always when we're home, she's dressed in a skimpy thong and her collar. Nothing else. If she felt cold, she would've told me. "Have you dropped from the scene last night?"

She shakes her head. "I don't think I will." Amusement makes her silvery violet eyes spark up. "You're in your doctor mode."

Possibly. I pinch her nipple.

She gasps—more than she normally would. *"Ouch."* Interesting. "I bring you breakfast in bed, and you pinch me? Nice."

"Hush. That twist probably went straight to your little cunt." I stroke her breasts, down her stomach. She squirms, ticklish and more sensitive than usual. "Are you eating as you should? How's your appetite?"

"I'm not getting sick, my handsome worrier. I don't think."

I raise a brow. "Do I really need to repeat myself?"

Properly chastised, she corrects herself. "I'm sorry, Master. My appetite is pretty normal—except for struggling a little with my diet."

What the fuck? Chelsea and I both enjoy the outdoors and strive to lead healthy lives; I've never had the need to adjust her diet or suggest other options. She knows moderation and values proper, home-cooked meals with healthy ingredients much, much higher than anything store-bought and processed. Wolfing down pizza and greasy goodness is reserved for those rare days we just say *fuck it* and land on the couch in front of Netflix. Or if we have plans with mates.

"Since when are you on a diet?" I do my best not to scowl, but this is news to me. I don't handle surprises very well.

Chelsea widens her eyes. "Since I gained two pounds last month."

My mouth twitches, and I hope it's not wishful thinking anymore. I *hope*. Fucking hell, I hope with all my heart. "Nonsense." I can't even pretend to sound stern at this point. "So why are you struggling with this silly diet?"

"Because carbs are delicious," she laughs.

"Carbohydrates are *good* for you." Lord, I won't allow her to go on any stupid *trend* diets that are more ridiculous than... Actually, nothing is more ridiculous. "There is such a thing as choosing the right carbs. You will not go without. That's an order." I tap her nose. "Now, when was your last period?"

That snaps her mouth shut, and I can practically sense the wheels turning.

We haven't been actively trying for a baby yet, but we've been careless about her birth control in an "if it happens, it happens" sort of way. If I'm not mistaken, she even forgot to bring her pills to Sydney.

"Do you think..." she whispers, a hand going to her stomach.

I feel my gaze going gentler, the doctor mode—as she so eloquently put it—slipping away. "Only one way to find out." I stroke her cheek and dip down to kiss her. "I may have prepared for an event such as this one. You'll find a few tests in my study. Bottom drawer of my desk."

It's a visibly anxious Chelsea who returns to our bedroom a few minutes later. I'm keeping a lid on my own nervousness by cramming half a blueberry pancake into my mouth. Leaving the bed, I yank on a pair of sweat pants and walk her over to our bathroom where I open the cabinet under the two sinks.

"You're not staying, are you—"

"I most certainly am." I find a cup for her to pee in and hand it to her. "I don't understand why you'd be modest. You're not a stranger to bathroom control." A particular favorite of mine when I want to push her. Giving her a beating while she needs to go to the bathroom, then forcing her to orgasm right before she goes...? A delicious sight, when humiliation and shame dance with relief and ecstasy.

"That's entirely different." She huffs and sits down on the toilet. "You don't give me a choice then."

My mouth twists up. I don't give her a choice now, either.

Once she's finished, I extend my hand expectantly, and she sighs heavily and hands over the cup. Tearing the foil around the pregnancy test, I retrieve the stick and count the seconds as it absorbs the sample.

My stomach tightens with nerves and hope.

"How do you feel, love?" I side-eye her while she turns off the water and dries her hands.

She releases a shaky breath and offers a small smile. "Anxious as hell." She pauses. "And maybe a bit miffed that you would notice before me."

I chuckle at that, and then I pull her close to kiss her forehead. "Good luck marrying a doctor."

"I think I'll live." She hugs my midsection tightly and rests the side of her head along my sternum. Like me, she's no doubt watching the test. "Is it too soon, Rio?"

"A little—might need a few more seconds."

She grins up at me. "I mean to have a baby."

Ah. I kiss her nose. "I sincerely hope you don't think so. Otherwise, it hasn't been very wise to go unprotected." I lift a brow pointedly.

"I'm asking *you*, bastard." She narrows her eyes at me. "Can't you recognize a woman being overwhelmed and needing reassurance?"

Of course I can. That's why I'm ignoring it. "Did you just call me a bastard?"

She notices her slip and widens her eyes. "Shit, double shit—I'm sorry, Owner."

"No, no, I understand. You're having one of your rare brat moments." I hide my amusement, knowing this is working far better than reassurance she doesn't actually need. What she needs is a distraction, nothing else. "It's a good thing there are ways to deal with such behaviors. My little imp."

She pouts up at me. "You're cruel."

I laugh. Then I figure it's time. Clearing my throat, I push down the sudden burst of anxiousness and reach for the test.

The result is right there, and I'm filled with so much love and protectiveness that it nearly floors me. It's a head rush. My mouth goes dry, and no words come out.

"Rio..." she whispers, eyes glistening.

I dip down and kiss her deeply, acting on instinct when I pick her up and carry her back to our bed. Never did I believe I'd ever have this. Before meeting Chelsea, I knew contentment and resignation. My home was a much, much colder space. And now...now I'm starting a family with the love of my life.

"I love you, Master."

"I love you more." Hovering over her on the mattress, I press a lingering kiss to her forehead and let my hand roam down to her toned stomach. I am who I am, so my mind is already racing ahead to the next seven or so months. "Bloody hell, now I understand why Mark and Brayden have been so overprotective."

Chelsea lets out a teary laugh and slides a hand down to my ass. "Don't go completely vanilla on me."

Not a chance.

I smile and shake my head. "Not that there's anything remotely vanilla about locking you up in a padded cell until you go into labor, but..." I chuckle at her horrified squeak. "Get the clover clamps you hate so much. We have a lot to celebrate, little rebel."

TOUCHING TRUTH

A BEHIND THE SCENES NOVELLA

PART V

"Do you really think you can convince them?" Mark asks.

Christ, I hope so. "If I present my case well enough—"

"Seriously, Greg. Drop the lawyer brain for one minute." He stops in the middle of the stairwell and peers back at me. "They love you. There's no need to act like you're on trial."

I throw him a quick glare, and he continues up the stairs toward his rooftop terrace.

"Are you going to tell me why you wanted me to come over?" I ask impatiently.

"Your current issue, actually." He pushes the door open, and we step out to a million-dollar view of the city. "It's now partly mine, too."

I'd enjoy the view more if it weren't so damn frigid out.

"How so?" I take in my surroundings, hoping Mark will utilize his terrace in a better way than this. They've built a deck, complete with a seating area under an arbor with thick vines and string lights. There's also a fire pit and a couple supply chests with potted plants on top. But that's not even half the terrace. The rest is bare.

"I'm gonna level with you, Greg." Mark puts on a beanie before folding his arms over his chest. "I've met Ryan and Angel on numerous occasions now, and I seriously doubt you can convince them to go for a house in the suburbs. Sausalito, least of all. They're not fancy people, and they love the city too much."

I scowl. "We can't raise a family in a two-bedroom apartment above a goddamn bar, Mark."

There is no question; sexually and D/s-wise, I am a submissive masochist through and through, but outside of the bedroom and our dynamic, I'm still a man very protective and family-oriented. There is a degree of control I will never surrender, and I've been hoping for a relocation if our relationship allowed it. Now I've been humbled beyond belief because Ryan and Angel want everything with me. *Everything*. A family, sharing a home, the making of major decisions. *That* sort of everything. And it's kicked up my need to give us a better place for that. Abby is already a part of this, and soon, there will be two—yes, *two*—little boys with us. We're expecting twins. I won't apologize for seeing the urgency, though I must wonder why no one else does. Have people lost their fucking minds?

My brother gives me a dry look. "There are *alternatives*, dumbass."

"Such as?" I respond irritably.

He twists his upper body and nods at the vast space behind him. "Evangeline wants to turn the rest into a garden. In other words, she—*we*—wanna make it kid-friendly."

"Yes, and...?" Good for them. Their firstborn will be here any day now.

"We can't," he replies. "Thing is, we technically share this roof with the lady across from us, but she's like ninety years old. In the time I've lived in this building, she's never been up here."

I wave a hand, dismissive. "Everything can be settled with money in these matters, even if it would lower the value of her condo."

"She moved into a home last weekend." He quirks a wry smile.

"What're the odds the new owners have no interest in being up here?"

Probably not good.

"You could always contact the new owners and try—"

"You're missing the point, big brother." He chuckles and rubs the back of his neck. "The condo hits the market soon. Plenty of good private schools in the area. It's in the city. Close to Ryan's bar..." He jerks a thumb over his shoulder. "And if we end up sharing this area with people who wants something similar, this could be a backyard by next summer."

Oh.

"Well, hell."

"It's a four-bedroom apartment, Greg."

I nod, thinking, or trying to—in fact, my mind is spinning a bit too quickly. Christ. "The prospect of this makes me strangely anxious and hopeful."

It's just very fucking new. The image is entirely different from the one I've had previously. A house in the suburbs is virtually all I've ever seen as an option. Yet, this...this could actually work. Ryan and Angel certainly would prefer a place in the city, and it would be closer to work for me, too. Then good schools, as Mark mentioned. A place for the kids to run around... I look over at the edges of the terrace, satisfied. The brick wall is at least at chest-level for me.

"Good, me too." Mark grins faintly. "So you'll talk to Ryan and Angel?"

I'll do more than that. I'll present my case like the good lawyer I am.

The following week, I ask Ryan and Angel to meet me outside of Mark's building when they get off work. I adjust my tie and check my phone, these days living with the constant reminder that more children will join us soon. Evangeline went into labor last night, and I'm waiting for updates from Mark.

Angel is next.

Moments later, Ryan's truck pulls up along the curb, and I walk over to help Angel out of the monstrous vehicle.

"Ugh." She kicks a leg out. That's progress. Now the rest of her body needs to follow. "I had this vision of running up to you and jumping into your arms. Then I remembered I'm carrying two twenty-pounders."

I chuckle, always sure I can't possibly love her more, always finding out I'm wrong.

Ryan snorts a chuckle. "Twenty-pounders might be overkill, love."

Either way, if the boys are anything like Ryan, Angel will be in severe pain when they want to come out. "Come here, sweetheart." I place my hands under her arms and lift her out. "There we go." I lift her chin and dip down for a soft kiss. "I missed you today."

"Mmm, missed you too." She smiles curiously. "So what're we doing here?"

"Right." I clear my throat and produce a set of keys. "I would like to show you something."

Ryan joins us on the sidewalk, and I need some confidence, so I grab his hand and weave our fingers together.

We take the elevator to the fourth and top floor. As we exit the elevator, Angel guesses we're here to see Mark, though she's visibly confused since she knows they're at the hospital.

"Actually, we're going this way." Across the hallway is the only other apartment on the floor, and I use the key I sweet-talked myself into getting from little Mrs. Goldman. To be fair, I had Mark's assistance. Thanks to him, we can see the condo before anyone else.

The place is spotless and completely empty, leaving burgundy walls I'd like to change and nice, old hardwood floors.

You can see where picture frames have hung on the walls.

"Oh, wow." Angel enters the living room and waddles over to the windows. We'd have a lovely view.

Ryan looks...less excited. Goddammit. Of course, I expected him to understand what's going on the second we walked in, but I had hopes he'd hear me out.

"How many bedrooms?" he asks quietly.

"Four." I become even more worried when he releases my hand. "There's more." I lose my nerve in a way I'd never do in a courtroom, and I lay down my arguments in a ramble while Angel continues from room to room. "We'd be sharing a rooftop terrace with my brother. Barbecue area, garden, you name it. It would be nice for the children."

"Greg—"

"No, please hear me out. Your apartment has become a fresh start for me, and I won't lie. I like the place very much, but you must admit it's too small. If we share the bedroom, that leaves only one room for *three* children, even if Abby might only be there for weekends here and there—"

"*Greg.*" He gives me a stare that silences me swiftly. "I'm fully aware we have to move."

"Then...then what's the problem?" I ask, at a loss. "Mark reasoned with me, and I understand you want to stay in the city. To be perfectly honest, it has great appeal to me these days, as well. So this place should be perfect. It's even close to the bar."

He hasn't left the hallway. Could he not at the very least give it a shot and *see* the place?

His mouth twists. "If you don't see the issue here, you gotta be the very definition of privilege, baby."

My forehead creases. "If this is about money—"

"Of course it is!" he groans through an exasperated chuckle. "I'd be lucky if I could get a mortgage to cover half this place."

Sounds fairly accurate. Being a bartender might not sound fancy, but it's a bar and an apartment he owns in an extremely expensive neighborhood. That said, yes, this area is part of the kill zone. Realtors go above and beyond to make sales here. Or commission, rather.

"I could be ready to sign the papers in five minutes." I straighten and fold my arms over my chest for this part. It's imperative he understand. "I'm all for egalitarian relationship standards, but Ryan, we're equals even when you're my Owner. What we do in and out of our bedroom has nothing to do with our say in the relationship." I pause, and he cocks a brow at me, listening. That's all I can ask. "What I'm saying is, if I covered the condo—or most of it; I truly don't care which—it wouldn't make us any less equal. Good grief, you give Angel an allowance as part of your dynamic, yet she decides as much as you do. So if you meant every word when you told me you want us to share everything, then...what's mine is yours, too. You're not the only one who gets to share what you bring to the table." Which is an awful lot, in my opinion.

What he's already given me can't be measured in money, and that's the truth.

"Well, aren't you a stubborn little shit," he mutters. "All right, come on." He drapes an arm around my shoulders. "I can't argue logic, so let's check out the joint and see what happens."

I smile in relief.

His own smile is indulgent as I show him the kitchen and explain the little things I see in our future. It's big enough for a table that seats six, there's even a walk-in pantry, something I know Angel will appreciate, good work surfaces, the kitchen island doesn't make it feel crowded, we could replace the old fridge and freezer, and—

"I love you." Ryan leans against the doorway, hands in his pockets. "You're adorable when you get excited."

I chuckle self-consciously. This level of excitement is new to me. "I love you, too."

He nods toward the next room. "Should we tell our girl we have a new home?"

"But you haven't even seen—"

"Hey. Not that your anal retentiveness ain't cute, but I don't need to see the rest." He grabs my hand as my thoughts take a nose dive at a certain word. Cannot be helped. Good grief, I'm going back to adolescence. Ryan gives my jaw a sharp nip. "Get your mind outta the gutter, boy."

And of course, he just *knows*. "You're essentially asking me to make my mind homeless."

He barks out a laugh.

THE WINNING TOUCH

THE TOUCH SERIES EPILOGUE

EPILOGUE

Dylan Reaves

5:*17 AM*
Breathe in...
Breathe out.

"The other side, please," the volunteer requests.

I turn so she can apply the temporary tattoos on my left arm, too.

The buzz around me makes it impossible to think this is a hotel parking lot on a normal day. Now, the tent-covered lot is the check-in area for triathletes from around the world. *Breathe in... Breathe out.* I check the time and rub my neck. Dozens of messages from family and friends fill my inbox, though that'll have to wait. I gotta keep my head in the game. Instead, I recheck the weather reports and see if there are any alerts about the sea currents.

The woman peels off the paper on my biceps, revealing my race number. "All done."

169.

It's my first Ironman World Championship. I'm getting those digits inked somewhere after this.

One year of therapy and Cade and Gabriella beating sense into me, then three years of hard training. I've shed blood, sweat, tears, and given up once or twice.

Breathe in...

Breathe out.

Leaving the busiest area, I make my way over to T1 to double-check my gear. The first Transition area is close to the pier, and because I'm blessed beyond words to have Cade and Gabby in my life, they insisted on buying VIP packages that give them pier access. For me, it means I can see them before the race starts, and I fucking need it.

They're waiting for me right where the pier begins, and I push down my fears and hug them over the wooden railing.

"You've got this." Gabriella squeezes me tightly. "I'm so proud of you."

"Thanks, sis." It's basically all I can say. I'm too goddamn anxious. You can feel it in the air: it's battle day. All week has been crazy—a media circus with events, interviews, and meeting fans I barely knew I had. An eye-opener.

"Come here, little pan." Cade engulfs me in a warm hug, knowing I've struggled recently. "We're celebrating you tonight no matter what, and then tomorrow..." He lifts my chin, and I nod. I can't fucking wait. "You itching to let it all go?"

"So much." I smile weakly.

Being a professional athlete and keeping the schedule I do right before major events leaves little to no room for, well, being little. Just these past four months, Cade and I have come to Hawaii at least ten times so I could get used to the terrain and the climate. Not once have I come here as his little boy. It's the opposite mind-set of what I need when I race. But tomorrow, fucking finally, we're out of here. I have some interviews after breakfast, and then Cade, Gabby, and I are flying to one of the smaller islands for a week alone. Private beach, our own safe haven, *lots* of play.

That said...today matters more than I can say. This is my comeback. I qualified and earned myself good sponsors. Now I show the world what I'm made of.

Kayla Ford

6:03 AM

"Daddy!" I scream.

Stepping into my new, sparkly yellow running shoes, I try and fail big time not to mess up tying them. I'm so freaking nervous I could die, I think. Okay, okay, I've got this. I know how to tie my own shoes, damn it all.

There.

"Jesus, where's the fire? What's wrong?" Daddy joins me in the hallway of our bungalow, and I tap my wrist impatiently. Goodness, I might puke. Nicholas gives me a *look*, which then turns into a little chuckle, and I hope it's one of understanding. I've been a wreck about this day all month! "We're on time, little one. I promise, we won't miss it."

"I'm gonna die." I stare panicked at my reflection in the mirror and smooth down my pigtails. "My stomach's in knots." Next, I lean closer and inspect the war paint on my face. I give the mirror a cool, mean look. *Rawr.* A temporary tattoo of number 169 covers my left cheek.

It's Dylan's race number.

The toppy types have chosen to wear simple white tees with his number on the back, but we subs...we know this is a day to go all out. Yes, it is.

"Everything will be fine." Daddy kisses the top of my head on his way to grab his shoes. "I spoke to Mark and Ryan. We're having breakfast with them later."

Okay. I don't care. I just care about the biggest sportsing war in the world today! Right here in Hawaii. Oh, here come the nerves again. Or more of them. I clutch my stomach, and if I'm this much of a mess, I can't imagine what Dylan's going through.

"Daddy, I'm dying," I say frankly. "I cannot think about breakfast, 'kay?"

He laughs softly. "Fair enough. Can you think about having your cute little bottom filled?"

"Wh...what...?" I gape at him. This is not the time for sexy stuff!

He inclines his head and brings something out of the pockets of his cargo shorts. "Lift your skirt for me." Oh my God, it's a butt plug and a small bottle of lube. "Since you're so nervous, I thought this could provide a decent distraction."

"Maybe I'm not nervous anymore?" I give him a hopeful look.

"Nice try. Bend over for Daddy."

Dylan Reaves

6:35 AM

After adjusting the swim cap, I bend down to make sure the Velcro strap around my ankle is secure. It's got my race chip attached to it, and it'd be a fucking shame if I lost the one piece that times the biggest event of my year.

The water's filling up with the first starting group. I'm one of them, so I walk down the steps and pull at the drawstrings of my Speedos. Goggles ready. Almost no surf today—that's a relief. Walking farther out, I join the other professionals, painfully aware that I'm surrounded by at least a dozen men who are predicted to win.

I hope to be the winner one day. My debut Ironman is unlikely to get me far; my only goal is to finish among the top ten in the first leg of the race and to make a name for myself in triathlon. Swimming, though... Here's where I have my edge.

I'm good on my bike, too. Then the running? Well, fuck me running. I still need to work there. On a great day, my time is decent, even for someone on a professional level. But on most days, I rage.

This isn't a hundred-meter race I can do over and over in a pool. It's a hundred-and-forty hellish miles through rough waters, lava lands, and hillsides. It's blazing sun and sometimes headwinds that will make a grown man cry.

Breathe in...

I allow myself a few seconds and disappear under the surface where everything is quieter and peaceful.

"Kill out there, Dylan." Daddy's murmur from earlier runs through my mind as a reminder. *"You may be my cheeky baby boy at home, but never forget you're a strong young man and a force to be reckoned with. Today is your day."*

Breathe out.

I resurface, determined to give my all.

I can't let my fear of failure hold me back. When you have a lot to lose, you have everything to fight for. I choose to fight.

———

Chelsea Kelly

6:45 AM

The shot of an actual cannon signals the start of the championship, and I hold my breath automatically. It's impossible to see where Dylan is, mostly because Rio and I are farther out on the water, but partly because all that's visible are countless heads wearing colorful swim caps.

"It goes boom, Mommy!" Hunter jumps and claps.

I laugh softly and gather him in my arms. "It did, didn't it? Uncle Dylan's out there somewhere."

"Yeah." He pokes my painted cheek, only to touch his own, maybe reminding himself of his own wickedly cool "grown-up tat." He's gonna scrub it off before the day is over at this rate.

Rio returns from below the deck, and we find a good spot on the starboard side of the big yacht to eat our breakfast, enjoy the race, and watch the sunrise. Our little nook gives us a semblance of privacy on the otherwise fully occupied boat. Tourists flood the area, and we were lucky to get tickets.

"I can't hear what they're saying." I cock my head at the announcer who sits God knows where. Whatever their expert commentators are saying just sounds like garbled nonsense out here.

"There's supposed to be a live stream on the website." Rio pulls out his phone, and I take the opportunity to stir some creamer into his coffee. He calls it his vacation treat. For myself...a decaf iced tea will have to suffice. "There we go—well, hell. Look at that, love."

I lean closer and grin when I see Dylan's name illustrated on the screen. He's in fourth or fifth place. That's so fucking awesome. I couldn't be prouder.

"You can jump on over to me, son." Rio snatches up Hunter and growls playfully against his chubby cheek. Our son finds that hilarious. "Time to give your beautiful little mum a break, isn't it? I think so."

I smile at their sweet exchange before refocusing on Dylan. Finding an online radio station that covers the Ironman only takes a quick search, and then we finally have a feed we can listen to.

"*...and we know the most common mistake a rookie makes is to overexert themselves in the beginning.*"

"*True enough, but this is Reaves's edge. I wouldn't count him out just because he—a former Olympic swimmer!—takes the lead sooner than we anticipated.*"

"He's in the lead!" I whisper-shout.

"Yay!" Hunter cheers. "Unka Dylan winning, Daddy."

Rio laughs then takes a sip of his coffee. "We certainly hope he will, buddy."

Taking a bite of my muffin, I stand up and smooth down my simple wraparound dress. When I was pregnant with Hunter, I quickly learned to appreciate clothes that, um, expand. "Excuse me for a moment. I need a bathroom," I say. "Sir, can I get you anything?" I much prefer to call him Master and Owner, but in public and around our boy, Sir is far less conspicuous.

"I do." The gorgeous green eyes he's passed on to Hunter flash with amusement, and he gestures at my seat. "You can wait. I like having something lovely to look at while I eat."

Shit, double shit, triple shit.

"Whatever pleases you." I offer a tight smile in return and sit down again.

Freaking Sadists. Can't live with them, can't live without them.

Dylan Reaves

7:18 AM

Fuck me. Best part of being in second place is you can follow in the lead's slipstream. Now that I'm first, I have only myself to rely on, and today—of fucking course—I get caught in the swell of the waves. Gritting my teeth, I give a hard kick underwater and slice right through a wave before I resurface and switch to butterfly. It gives me the advantage of staying completely horizontal. Through a wave, catch air in lower water, through a wave, catch air...

I push myself to the limits, my body fluid and burning. As soon as the current calms the water, I return to freestyle, and I'm confident for the first time since my feet touched the ocean. This is my sport. My discipline.

Picking up the pace, I do a quick sighting to make sure I'm staying on course, and relief fills me when I see I'm nearing the finish. *Don't look behind you, don't lose time by looking behind you, swim faster, use the currents, alter the strokes, rest your legs for the next discipline, more arms.* I clench my jaw and give everything, knowing my arms can rest when I get on the bike.

Let it burn.

At the last stretch, I keep Cade at the forefront of my mind. Since I committed to starting a career in triathlon, he's become my biggest and best source for support, tough love when I need it, structure, and guidance. I'd be crippled with grief without Gabby's love and support; it's just that Cade goes another few extra miles, and he's gotten so invested in my progress. He's more than a Daddy Dom. He's a best friend, a ruthless coach, and a rock-solid constant.

He inspires me to fight harder and go beyond what I thought possible.

Almost there.

I register the sounds of cheering. The seafloor is closer. Another few feet and I can start running. I quit breathing, doing the final yards as quickly as I possibly can, and then I'm touching the ground.

"First out of the water—Dylan Reaves!" blares out on the PA system. I quickly spy 48:52 on the time board.

Fuck yes, one of my best.

Sprinting up the steps, my eyes seek out the crowd on the pier —or rather, Gabby and Cade. My goggles and swim cap get torn off, landing where-the-hell-ever.

"Kayla's in place, Dylan! Kayla's in place! Love you!" Okay, Gabby's voice carries, but I can't see her. Either of them. Too many people. I appreciate the message though, and I push forward.

Step by step, all through T1. It can't take more than one minute. A volunteer jogs up alongside me and extends a bottle of water. I accept it, and a protein bar is next. Nothing like inhaling granola while taking a cold shower to rid the saltwater. I'm in and out in seconds, and, um, long enough to relieve myself. Jesus Christ, it's dizzying, and people keep screaming. Running over to the bike racks, I pull on my short-sleeved black trisuit. Shoes already strapped to the bike pedals. Helmet and shades resting on the aero-bars. Faster, faster. While putting on the helmet, I grab my bike and jog toward the mount area, and then I'm gone.

Nicholas Ford

7:41 AM

"Are we on the right side, Daddy? Are we on the right side? We can't let him get a penalty!"

"He won't get a penalty, baby girl. We're exactly where we're supposed to be." The sun is already hotter than hell, and I slide on my shades as I check the time. According to Cade's last message, Dylan recently left the pit on his bike, so he should pass us soon. "Are you ready?"

"Super, duper ready," Kayla swears.

Cade's next message arrives.

At least seven minutes on the gap. I'm gonna go puke and get to our next stop.

"Jesus, the boy is good," I mutter to myself. I'm incredibly glad to be here to share the day with Dylan, and I'm pleased all of our closest ones could be here, as well. We couldn't ask for a better community for our little family of kink. "Dylan managed to create a seven-minute margin."

"Oh, wow! Isn't that awesome?" Kayla squints up at me.

I nod and wink, then turn her pretty little head toward the street. "Very much so."

As the crowd along the sealed-off street grows louder, my adorable little wife leans over the fence, taking her job seriously. Two peanut butter cups are in her hand, and she extends her arm as soon as we spot Dylan coming around the bend.

I smile widely, proud of him.

"Oh, he's coming in fast, Daddy," Kayla says nervously. "Dylan, I'm here!"

"It'll be okay, baby." I let out a sharp whistle. "You've got this, Dylan!"

"Seven minutes, seven minutes!" Kayla shouts.

Hunched over the extra set of bars on his bike, he gives a firm nod, reaches out, and passes us in a blur. My pulse kicks up a few notches, and I chuckle to myself, having not anticipated the thrill of the race to hit me this much.

"He took the peanut butter cups!" Kayla spins on me with a victorious grin. "Oh." She scrunches her nose at the sight of her chocolate-covered hand. "Melty. I hope he won't mind."

"I doubt he will," I laugh quietly. "They're probably already in his stomach." They better be. He'll need all the fat and protein he can get this early in the day. Fast carbohydrates will fuel him later on. "Are you ready to get breakfast?"

She giggles and licks her hand. "I already started."

Dylan Reaves

9:23 AM

The Hawaiian lava fields can suck my dick.

Both sides of the open road—all black, all barren, all *hot*. The heat is liquid along the asphalt, and I know I won't stay in the lead much longer. This is where I start to lose my speed. My thighs burn more than I can handle, and I *ache* fucking everywhere.

Passing another aid station, I ignore the cups of water a few volunteers run along the road to offer. I will *not* stop for any of that today. Precious seconds can't be wasted. The bottle attached to the bars keeps me hydrated and tops me off with some energy, though I wouldn't mind if it magically turned into vodka at this point. Or a tranquilizer.

"One day, you're going to win that race, big brother."

I approach another hill and stand up to gain some speed again. Gabby's pillow talk about my career in between cuddles and dirty touches fuels me. She and Daddy make this possible for me. I can't compete without them. Or, I can, but...it holds less meaning. Significantly less in the way that it wouldn't be worth it at all.

The Ironman is a humbling race. You're forced to face yourself, and no matter how much this hurts, I would only get angry with myself if I complained now. How lucky am I? I have everyone I love with me, except for my grandparents who don't have the health to travel this far. Instead, they are following everything on TV. But everyone else is here, including my mom and dad. They made plans over a year ago to have their vacations here just because I'm competing.

I don't wanna let any of them down.

With a glance behind me, I glare when I see the first athlete trying to catch up to me.

Fuck you, I'm not ready. I *need* to create more distance and stay in the lead all throughout the first half of the bicycle route. Otherwise, running will be a bigger fall in the ranks than I can accept.

Mark Cooper

11:03 AM

"I think we have a Domme in the making." I speak under my breath for only Evangeline to hear, and I gotta say, it's funny as fuck to see my twelve-year-old niece turn Ryan into a whipped yes-sayer.

Evangeline laughs quietly and reaches across the picnic table to grab another waffle. Our breakfast has morphed into brunch, and the plate of waffles is right next to a plate of sweet and spicy sliders. "With all due respect—"

"Funny how that's never followed by anything respectful, kitten."

She snorts in amusement. "You're hardly better, *Sir*. You guard that baby monitor as if someone's going to run up to our table and steal it."

It could happen. We're right on the beach. Plenty of joggers around. And without the monitor, I won't know if our kids are up to no good in our bungalow. Who knows, today could be the day our boy decides to discover the internet. For now, both little runts are asleep—thank fuck. Brayden and I were up all night.

"What're you two mumbling about?" Ryan cocks a brow behind his Ray-Bans.

"You being wrapped around a certain pinkie." I smirk at Abby, who giggles around a mouthful of toast.

"The girl doesn't eat enough!" Ryan argues.

I frown, and I admit Abby *is* a little on the skinny side. "Finish your food, pumpkin."

"Oh, shush. We've been eating all morning." She waves me off, and my eyebrows shoot up. Did I just get shushed? By a preteen? "*Finally!*" She glances toward the restaurant farther down the beach, where we can see Greg coming closer with more food. "Dad, when are we gonna go see Dylan?"

Greg checks his watch. "We're leaving in about...half an hour."

At the same time, Brayden reemerges from our place with our daughter. I assume it's feeding time.

"Everything good, pup?" I make room so he can sit down next to me, which he does after handing Olivia over to Evangeline.

"Yes, Sir. Ready to go see Dylan." He smiles and puts on his sunglasses. "Did we decide who's staying behind with the kids?"

I incline my head. "Evangeline and Angel." They'll be there for when Dylan crosses the finish line, though. We've acquired babysitting through the hotel starting this afternoon.

Ryan takes a sip of his coffee. "Angel can't go anyway." Yeah, poor girl. Her second pregnancy is evidently putting her through the wringer more than the first did, and she had *twins* then. Ryan jokes about it, saying—since my brother is the father this time—it's Greg's payback for Angel's sadistic treatment.

Greg is torn between amusement and worry. "I should go check in on her—"

Ryan won't have it. "You did that twenty minutes ago, sweetheart. Sit your ass down and relax."

I smile.

Meanwhile, Abby pretends to gag. "I'm never having kids. You people never *sleep*. When I grow up, I'm gonna be like them." She points down the beach where Nicholas and Kayla are getting back in the water.

"We'll see if you say that in fifteen years." I wink at her.

"Twenty-five, maybe," Greg mutters.

Ryan grabs Abby's hands and kisses her knuckles. "You crumb snatchers are a beautiful blessing."

I can only agree with that. But...yeah, it's awesome to have family who will babysit whenever. For this vacation, the Quinns opted to leave their boys with Ryan's mother.

"You're up, Master of the Household." Evangeline smiles cheekily at me and holds up Olivia. "Someone needs to be burped."

"Is that so?" I nod and accept my baby girl. "Does Daddy need to burp you, Olivia?"

She coos and grabs my nose, so that's gotta be a yes.

Dylan Reaves

12:06 PM

I don't know what burns hotter, the sun, my anger, or my leg. Either way, it's a triathlon trifecta of hell. Realistically, I know I've exceeded everyone's expectations so far, even my own. I'm in second place—some smug Frenchman passed me a while ago—and this from a Texas boy who may have created some hype but definitely wasn't considered a threat. I'm still not, but despite my accomplishments, I'm pissed. *And I need to piss.*

T2 is approaching, so I start preparing. By a stroke of luck, I'm granted tailwinds on the way down a slope, and it gives me the opportunity to stretch out my bad leg. It's been cramping on and off the past hour. Chafing is a real goddamn problem when I run, so next is the emergency kit under my saddle. Using my teeth, I rip off a square piece and unzip my suit.

When I scored my slot to compete in the World Championship, I made the monumental mistake of using a suit—this one—for the first time. And the nipple chafing during my run almost made me cry. Once Gabby had fussed over me, she laughed so hard. Now I'm better prepared. Once I'm taped up, I zip up again. Then I just focus on stretching my leg, hydrating, and shoving an energy bar down my throat.

The viewing stands along the road, when I get that far, are filled to maximum capacity with cheering spectators. It adds a thrill that courses through my veins, though I can't afford to pay any attention to them. I know, though, that the Coopers and the Quinns are in place, as are my parents, and I'm pretty sure I hear Mom shouting my name.

Cade...

There's a hitch in my breath as I rush up to the racks and dismount my bike. I see him and, fuck, I wish I could hurl myself at him. While I throw off my helmet and locate my gear bag, I have these visions of him carrying me, all romantic, to the nearest port-a-john. Then he'd massage my leg and feed me ice chips.

Instead, I'm quickly changing to my running shoes, donning new shades, and putting on my leg brace. It's a thirty-second rest that doesn't provide any rest whatsoever.

Now I have a marathon to run.

Cade Kingsley

1:14 PM

"Five hot dogs, thanks." I retrieve my wallet so I can pay, and the princess stands next to me, barely able to see over the high counter, and prattles what she wants on her two. One of which I know she won't eat, but she's stubborn. "Basically, you want everything on," I chuckle.

She grins sheepishly. "Yes, please."

I kiss her on the forehead, noting she needs to apply more sunscreen. "Go find us a table, baby, and put some lotion on."

"Okay," she sings and skips off.

Five minutes later, I join her at a pastel green-painted picnic table under a yellow umbrella. The vendors that share the serving area fill the air with rich, smoky scents that make my stomach growl and tighten in hunger. This is our first meal where we have enough time to sit down for at least twenty minutes, and fuck me if I had any idea being a spectator would take it outta me this much. Driving from viewing site to viewing site, hoping to get a glimpse of him, and keeping up with what the commentators are saying, *plus* checking in with Dylan's grandparents at home has left me...well, fucking exhausted. And nauseated, prouder than words can describe, and nervous as all *shit*.

Dylan's mother, who knows we're a triad that's into BDSM, had a twinkle in her eye earlier when she made a comment about Dylan's father and me acting the same—like it's our boy's first day of school. Dylan clearly got his bratty streak from her.

"Um." Gabriella lifts one of her hot dogs to face-level and eyes it like it's her Everest. "Daddy...?"

"Yeah?" I grin and take a bite of my own. *Fuck, this is food.* The flavors of the spicy sausage and freshly baked bun mix with the relish, cheese, mustard, and other fixings. I love being on vacation.

"I didn't know they were going to be this big," she explains.

I check my watch and decide to mess with her. "Well, you have half an hour to finish both. If you don't, maybe I'll feel inclined to leave you at the hotel while the rest of us go out to celebrate tonight."

She drops her jaw and looks positively outraged. "Daddy, what—*no!*"

"Princess, what—*yes*," I mimic.

Dylan Reaves

1:47 *PM*

I need to pee, I need to pee, I need to pee.

"Motherfucker," I pant.

I run past an aid station, sorely tempted to pause at one of the port-a-johns. But no. Time waster. Even more tempting is to stop at the side of the road, but a technicality in the rules makes it possible for a ref to disqualify anyone who does it. It's not a judgment call I want hanging over me.

I can hold it. I fucking better. I'm not ready to be one of those pros who just...goes. In the ocean, sure, not an issue, but on the bike? Or while running? No, thanks.

An Australian guy runs past me, much to my fury, and he doesn't seem to have the same qualms I do. He relieves himself on the go. Then, he's aiming for a podium spot, and right this second, the silver is his. That weighs heavier than decorum.

My margin is gone. My leg is killing me, and I can't go any faster. At least four athletes are close behind me, one of whom I know has a background in running that's as impressive as mine in swimming.

I throw a quick look behind me and curse. Make that seven runners behind me.

Is it even possible for me to make top ten?

Gabriella Bellandi

3:02 *PM*

"Can they change the fucking topic?" Daddy snaps irritably. "We get it—it's a close race. Give me an update instead."

I exchange an *uh-oh, Daddy's mad* look with Kayla.

Both he and Mr. Ford stand behind us, arms folded, shoulders squared, matching white tees and tanned skin, equally matching frowns, and they're sharing a set of earbuds so they can listen to the radio. Daddy says that's better than the PA system that only announces tidbits here and there. Like, when someone crosses the finish line, and a man booms out, "You. Are. An. Ironman!"

Clutching the waist-high fence that seals off the finish area, I squint at the scoreboard and bite my nails. I have over a million butterflies in my stomach, and they want *out*.

We have a gold medalist. And a silver and bronze medalist.

"He's in eighth place." Mr. Ford is looking at his phone when I peer over my shoulder.

"That's freaking *awesome!*" Kayla cheers.

I can only nod, too nervous. I can get very competitive for myself, but this is Dylan. One of the two loves of my life. He gets competitive to the point where he might injure himself and care less about his leg. That's my biggest worry, that he will limp across the finish line and be in pain.

"Kayla! Gabriella!"

My head whips around, and I flatten my hand at my forehead to shield my eyes from the sun. There! In the six-row view stands on the other side. Evangeline, Angel, Brayden—well, all of their peoples. Kayla and I wave and grin.

"It's too goddamn close to tell," Mr. Ford mutters. "Here. It's a cluster of almost a dozen athletes." He speaks to Daddy, though I make sure to listen. "He's right in the middle of that."

"Oh, God." I'm hit by another million butterflies.

Kayla feels it, too. "Daddy, I have something to get off my chest." She pauses, and Mr. Ford lifts a brow. "I think...and I'm being honest now, I swear. And I think I—Gabriella, too—should be spared from a year's worth of punishments after today, because this *feels* like a punishment."

Oh, I nod. I'm nodding quite furiously. "I agree. I don't think I've ever been this nervous in my whole *life*."

Daddy's mouth twists in wry amusement. "Cute."

"Actually, this is interesting," Mr. Ford muses. "By that logic—given that Cade and I are nervous as well and certainly not enjoying it—we're being punished in advance, too." Oh, crap. Here comes *Daddy Logic*. "And since we haven't done anything wrong, does this mean you will be good girls for a year?"

We stare up at the sexy bastards. Flat looks. Because, *seriously*.

We'll have to solve this mess later though, 'cause the crowds surrounding us start roaring. My heart jumps up into my throat, and I turn back to stare at the finish line. Palm trees, Ironman banners, and sponsor flags wave in the air. The excitement goes through the proverbial roof, and—*oh my God!* I think I screamed that. And I don't care. My eyes widen, my pulse skyrockets.

"Holy fuck," I hear Daddy exclaim.

"Dylan! Dylan!" It's fucking him! Tears fill my eyes as the overwhelmingly loud noise from the spectators blurs into the background. "Dylan, I love you!" Almost, almost, almost, he's almost there. Fourth place! He finally crosses the finish line in *fourth place*, and then I'm pulled away, the motion giving me a somersault. "Gah!"

"You. Are. An. Ironman!"

"You. Are. An. Ironman!"

I realize it's Daddy. He holds me close and quickly ushers me toward the area where family members can have some space to greet their athletes. We flash our cards to the security to get access, and then we step onto the humongous red mat as several runners make it to the goal farther away.

"Dylan!" Daddy hollers.

"Eeep!" I jump in place as Dylan spots us and jogs over, a panting and sweating *mess*. "You did it! You *did* it!"

"I did it," he pants. "Fuck me. I can't—" Yeah, no, he can barely breathe. Daddy hauls him in for a tight hug; I fly into them both, to which Dylan whimpers, and it looks like he's both laughing and crying. "Please don't—oh God, I gotta pee so fucking bad."

I crack up *hard* and slap my thigh.

Daddy grins widely and wipes at his eyes. It makes me even more teary-eyed in the process. "Okay, let's get you to a bathroom, baby boy." He supports some of Dylan's weight, and we walk toward a row of bathrooms. "Fourth motherfucking place. I have no words."

Duh, me either. I'm just a ball of emotions right now.

Dylan Reaves

7:00 PM

"Nooo..." I mumble into my pillow. Actually...Daddy's pillow. It smells like his cologne. "I can't have slept long."

I must've fallen asleep when Gabby massaged my leg earlier.

"A couple hours," Daddy murmurs. I hum in pleasure as he weaves his fingers through my hair. "We have dinner reservations in fifteen minutes, and there are a lot of people who are excited to see our champion."

My mouth stretches into an involuntary grin.

I did it.

By some miracle, I managed to use the pain and gain more speed. I passed one...then two...three... A handful of fellow athletes. *Fourth place.* To be fair, we were all grouped together in a ten-second gap. But still. I could not have asked for more.

I had to face some press right after, and one journalist predicted I'm gonna be a big name and someone everyone will keep an eye on now.

"How are you feeling?" Daddy wonders.

"When I lie completely still, everything is perfect."

He chuckles warmly at that. "My sweet little pan." Leaning over me, he presses a kiss between my shoulder blades. "You need to get some food in you, though. We're not going far. It's just down the beach—the place with the barbecue you liked?"

Oh... As if on cue, my stomach rumbles. I only ate some snacks, energy bars, and inhaled a truckload of water before. God yes, I need to eat. I just have to figure out how to *move*.

Rio Kelly

7:21 PM

"So beautiful." I smile and tuck a piece of hair behind Chelsea's ear. "Tired?"

She grins sleepily and leans against me. "Yeah, but in that lazy it's-been-such-a-good-day kind of way. What about you?"

"Sounds about right, what you said." I take a swig of my beer and hug her to me. The beach restaurant could have been mistaken for a traditional luau, and the sound of the ocean behind us is lulling as hell. Combined with the rich scents of the barbecue and every other dish that fills the long table at which we're seated, as well as having been in the sun all day, and my mind is sort of sluggish. Perfect state of being for Hawaii, I'd say.

As I kiss the top of Chelsea's head, I spot Cade, Dylan, and little Gabriella coming down the boardwalk lined with tiki torches.

"Dylan's here, my love." I speak quietly, and she straightens so I can stand up. "Oi!" I let out a whistle to get everyone's attention and raise my beer. "Let's get off our asses and toast to a fan-fucking-tastic performance by Dylan today."

"You were so good today!" Chelsea calls.

Heads start turning, private conversations get wrapped up, and once they see the young man of the hour has made it, they're quick to bring him into the fold.

Cade smirks and guides a visibly humbled and embarrassed Dylan to the head of the table.

"To our family's own little Ironman." I smile and dip my chin at the boy, and he grins tiredly. I can't imagine how sore he must be. Eight hours, fourteen minutes, and twenty-nine seconds—that was his bloody *amazing* time today.

"Hear, hear!" Ryan tips his bottle at Dylan. "Seriously fucking impressed, kid."

Nick goes next. "We couldn't be happier to share this with you. Well done today, Dylan."

Several toasts and enough praise to turn him red follow before Cade cuts us off with a comment on our *sadisting*. Ryan, Mark, and I share a smirk as the resident Sadists, and little Kayla musters the courage to shoot us a cute scowl.

I feign a lethal stare, the type I usually reserve for newbie Doms at Switch when they put their partners at risk.

Kayla squeaks and hides behind Nick.

"You are so cruel, Owner," Chelsea laughs softly behind her hand.

I chuckle, and we take our seats again. "That's a fine compliment." I grip her chin and take a kiss before reaching for a bowl of Hawaiian rolls. It's time to eat our body weight in what Hawaii has to offer.

"Hey, Rio," Mark says, seated farther down the table. "What would you say about a triathlon play party?"

"Well, now." I'd say I'm more than a little intrigued. "Three painful disciplines for a certain amount of time... So many possibilities."

"I'm RSVP-ing a hell yeah for me and my two," Cade says and raises his beer bottle.

Gabriella scrunches her nose. "Can I suggest lollipop-tasting, bubble baths, and laser tag?"

Ryan and I bark out a laugh while the s-types are quick to agree with Gabriella.

Greg purses his lips in thought. "Technically, that would be the opposite of what a maso wants, so..."

"Mission accomplished for *you*," Angel says with a smirk. "A marathon of pink bath bombs with glitter."

Greg makes a face. "That sounds awful."

"Let's just leave the planning to us," Ryan drawls. "Trust, we know how to make you suffer."

The Tops have a drink at that.

"I *think* I've suffered enough," Dylan states.

I laugh under my breath, and I notice how no one argues his point. Even Sadists have limits.

Give it a day or two, though.

Dylan Reaves

11:13 PM

I rub my eyes and yawn, letting Cade guide me back to our bungalow. Gabby's awfully energetic, rambling adorably about all the activities we're going to do when we get to Kauai.

In the meantime, Cade has to personally assist me with the brushing of teeth and taking off of clothes. I'm a zombie. A happy, full, tired, lucky, achy zombie.

At least I can sleep in a little tomorrow before our breakfast with my parents.

"Okay, time for bed." Cade smacks me lightly on the butt, and I stumble out of the bathroom. He can take care of the light. I can barely take care of myself right now. "I'll be right out." The door closes again.

Gabriella is sitting on the bed in just panties, and she's channel surfing so quickly I don't think she actually knows what she's zapping past.

"Um, you're breaking the rule on no underwear when you sleep," I point out.

"I'm not sleeping yet," she retorts.

I shrug and get rid of my boxers, and then I crawl over her on my way to the middle, effectively flattening her to the mattress.

"Dylan!" she complains.

"Hi." I dip down and wrap my lips around a nipple, 'cause it was calling to me.

She lets out a breathless laugh and gets squirmy. "I was watching TV."

"I don't care." It was only supposed to be some boob kissing, but now I kind of want more. She is so gorgeous and soft and pretty and perfect. "You're fair game." I hook two fingers into her panties and yank them off. My mouth waters at the sight. Maybe a few pussy kisses, too. *Then* I can sleep.

Kneeling between her sexy thighs, I lean down and kiss her private place. I ignore her gasp, and maybe I get a bit greedy. She tastes so good. I go back for more and lick her slit, tasting her natural sweetness and the coconut of her after-sun lotion.

"You have the smoothest, most delicious pussy, little sis." I rub her clit lightly and go lower, sucking at the spot her wetness comes from. *Oh, fuck.* This wasn't supposed to happen. Now I'm getting all hard. Hard and sleepy is *not* an awesome combo. I get cranky and rougher because I lose my patience, and I also forget stuff. Like *asking* her if I can fuck her.

I mean, we have our rules; I know what's okay for me to do, but I still have manners.

Well, not at the moment, evidently. After a few more tasty licks, I crawl higher up and waste no time pushing my cock inside her.

"Ah, shit," I groan.

"Dylan, wait," she whimpers as I stretch her.

"Shhh." I kiss her fervently and start fucking her in long, deep strokes. She gets wetter and wetter, and her moans become muffled when she presses her mouth to my neck. Her hands roam my back, fingernails scraping lightly. "Fuck—I love you," I whisper, out of breath. "You feel so perfect."

"I love you, too," she gasps. "Oh, God—give me more..."

The mattress dips behind me, letting me know Cade's finally here. I moan as he strokes my butt and drops a kiss to my spine. Next, I feel his long, thick cock pressing against my ass.

"Push in all the way, baby boy," he murmurs. "Fill her pretty little cunt and stay there."

"But I wanna fuck her—"

A firm touch on my back kills the rest of my sentence. He grabs a fistful of my hair and yanks me back hard enough for fire to tear through my skull, and I choke on the sharp stings.

"I don't think you heard me." His low growl rumbles between us, and my brain powers down. "Daddy's here now, Dylan, and you fucking obey him. Is that clear?"

My eyes well up. It's like a flip of a switch. He's no longer Cade. I don't have to be in control anymore; the race is over. I can let go.

"Yes, Daddy," I croak.

Oh, goddamn. The relief floods me, my vision gets even blurrier, and my throat closes up.

I can let go.

"There's my baby," he whispers, his warm hands stroking my sides. "You'll be good for me, won't you?"

I nod obediently, mentally sinking lower and lower. I'm his. He'll take control again, like we both need. He keeps touching me sensually, soothingly, while I surrender parts of my will and submit to the man I love. Pushing in slowly, burying myself inside Gabby, I take pleasure from what Daddy lets me have, and I find peace in just waiting for his next command.

"Good boy." His touch ignites me, rubbing seductive patterns across my bottom. There's the sound of a bottle opening. Then cold. I hiss and shudder. "Princess, give your brother a kiss for being so good."

I hadn't realized my eyes had closed. At the soft brush of Gabby's lips against mine, I open my eyes and see the tenderness in hers. And the sense of knowing. Knowing I've needed this for so fucking long. I wasn't made to be in control.

I smile and kiss her back.

I'm amazed by the power a touch can have. Gabby can draw out my playfulness with one little nip, Daddy can make me admit defeat with a firm hand on my body, and that's just the physical touches. It would take me forever and a day to fully grasp the mental and emotional bondage they both have me in.

I don't need to grasp it, but I'll take that forever and a day with them, please.

MORE FROM CARA DEE

Cara freely admits she's addicted to revisiting the men and women who yammer in her head, and that's why you can often spy her characters making appearances in other books of hers. If you enjoyed *Touch: The Complete Series,* you might like the following.

Forbidden Gem
Power Play
Auctioned

Check out Cara Dee's entire collection at www.caradeewrites.com, and don't forget to sign up for her newsletter so you don't miss any new releases, updates on book signings, giveaways, and much more.

ABOUT CARA

I'm often stoically silent or, if the topic interests me, a chronic rambler. In other words, I can discuss writing forever and ever. Fiction, in particular. The love story—while a huge draw and constantly present—is secondary for me, because there's so much more to writing romance fiction than just making two (or more) people fall in love and have hot sex. There's a world to build, characters to develop, interests to create, and a topic or two to research thoroughly. Every book is a challenge for me, an opportunity to learn something new, and a puzzle to piece together. I want my characters to come to life, and the only way I know to do that is to give them substance—passions, history, goals, quirks, and strong opinions—and to let them evolve. Additionally, I want my men and women to be relatable. That means allowing room for everyday problems and, for lack of a better word, flaws. My characters will never be perfect.

Wait...this was supposed to be about me, not my writing.

I'm a writey person who loves to write. Always wanderlusting, twitterpating, kinking, and geeking. There's time for hockey and cupcakes, too. But mostly, I just love to write.

~Cara.

CPSIA information can be obtained
at www.ICGtesting.com
Printed in the USA
LVOW13s0242120818
586683LV00029B/901/P